Mariana Zapata is a *New York Times*, *USA Today*, and a multiple No. 1 Amazon bestselling author. She is a five-time Goodreads Choice Awards nominee in the Romance category. Her novels have been published in thirteen languages.

Mariana lives in a small town in Colorado with her husband and beloved Great Dane, Kaiser. She loves reading, anime, and dogs. When she isn't writing, you can usually find her picking on her loved ones.

Website: **www.marianazapata.com**
Facebook: **/marianazapatawrites**
Instagram: **@marianazapata**
TikTok: **@marianazapataauthor**
X: **@marianazapata_**

By Mariana Zapata

Under Locke
Kulti
Lingus
Rhythm, Chord & Malykhin
The Wall of Winnipeg and Me
Wait for It
Dear Aaron
From Lukov with Love
Luna and the Lie
The Best Thing
Hands Down
All Rhodes Lead Here
When Gracie Met the Grump
The Things We Water

THE THINGS WE WATER

Mariana Zapata

Copyright © 2025 Mariana Zapata

The right of Mariana Zapata to be identified as the Author of
the Work has been asserted by her in accordance with the
Copyright, Designs and Patents Act 1988.

First published in 2025 by Mariana Zapata

First published in the UK in this paperback edition in 2025 by Headline Eternal
An imprint of Headline Publishing Group Limited

1

Apart from any use permitted under UK copyright law, this publication may
only be reproduced, stored, or transmitted, in any form, or by any means,
with prior permission in writing of the publishers or, in the case of reprographic
production, in accordance with the terms of licences issued by the Copyright
Licensing Agency.

All characters in this publication are fictitious
and any resemblance to real persons, living or dead,
is purely coincidental.

Cataloguing in Publication Data is available from the British Library

Paperback ISBN 978 1 0354 3266 0

Book Cover Design by Sarah Hansen, Okay Creations
Editing by Hot Tree Editing

Typeset in 10.75/12.85pt Minion Pro by Six Red Marbles UK, Thetford, Norfolk

Printed and bound in Great Britain by Clays Ltd, Elcograf S.p.A.

Headline's policy is to use papers that are natural, renewable and recyclable
products and made from wood grown in well-managed forests and other
controlled sources. The logging and manufacturing processes are expected
to conform to the environmental regulations of the country of origin.

Headline Publishing Group Limited
An Hachette UK Company
Carmelite House
50 Victoria Embankment
London EC4Y 0DZ

The authorised representative in the EEA is Hachette Ireland,
8 Castlecourt Centre, Dublin 15, D15 XTP3, Ireland (email: info@hbgi.ie)

www.headlineeternal.com
www.headline.co.uk
www.hachette.co.uk

To my love, my heart, my soul,
My bestest best friend,
Kai
You will always be the best love story I'll ever be a part of

Though most of the statements regarding The Night of the Meteor vary depending on geographical location, two claims remain undisputed: it happened on a night with a full moon, and the world was never the same again.

Chapter One

I wasn't surprised they didn't know what to say. What had just come out of my mouth sounded like something I'd hallucinated— or an excerpt from a fantasy novel.

But this was no fairy tale. No legend. Not even a bestselling novel being adapted into a movie.

It was reality.

My reality.

So, I wasn't exactly surprised either when my two best friends leaned forward, mouths slightly open, and said almost simultaneously, "Explain that again." The only part they differed on was that Sienna called me "Nina" at the end of her sentence, and Matti didn't.

I *almost* made fun of them for being that kind of married couple now. It was one thing to finish each other's sentences, but for them to choose almost all the same words and have nearly identical expressions? It made me want to bear hug them and tease them at the same time.

But we didn't have time for that. I could make fun of them later.

First, I needed them to understand. Needed them to help me. Help *us*.

The truth was, I couldn't blame my friends for struggling to comprehend what I'd just told them. *I* had a hard time accepting everything that had happened over the last month, and I'd watched it go down with my own two eyes. I had *lived* it. None of us were strangers to unbelievable things, but this pushed the limit.

Dipping my chin like I hadn't looked at the body sleeping in my arms at least ten thousand times in the past couple of years—a huge chunk of those peeks having taken place over the last few weeks—I focused down on Duncan for the ten-thousandth and one time. I smiled despite the uncertainty and near panic I'd been living on the verge of lately. Because he always cheered me up. Honestly, it was impossible not to be happy when the cutest thing I'd ever seen in my life snored in a way that reminded me of how my dad used to nap in his recliner after dinner.

In Duncan's case, it was a lot of work being adorable; it was a full-time job.

And maybe it was better just to show them why I was here instead of explaining with words one more time.

This whole situation was half miracle and half *Teen Wolf*, *Lord of the Rings,* and *Ancient Aliens* combined, after all. It depended on how you looked at it and what you believed. But that wasn't important either. They needed to see the big picture first.

In our case, I guess you could say the puppy-sized picture.

Peeling back the blanket I had him wrapped in—to hide Duncan, not because he was cold—I angled my arms so Matti and Sienna could get a better look at the ball of black fur that had turned my life upside down—not once, but twice now. I wasn't mad about it. Overwhelmed and more scared than I wished, but not angry.

Unlike some people I knew, I didn't believe that Fate was working behind the scenes, smoking a cigarette and planning people's lives out before they were even born. For one, that was too much work with eight billion people on the planet. I didn't have a second reason because I thought the first one was enough.

But sometimes things happened that made absolutely no sense in the moment but eventually turned out to be blessings. Maybe you cried before you saw the good in them, but that was hindsight.

I figured there were plenty of things in the world that weren't easily explained, but it didn't make them any less real.

Like countless beings in existence at that moment.

Like every person in this room, if you wanted to be specific, and especially like the small body tucked up against me, which was why I was here.

Without the blanket covering the majority of him, Duncan's black coat gave the initial impression that he was a short-haired black dog, and his long ears gave the idea he had some kind of hound in him, but as I tugged the blanket away inch by inch, the poofy tail that could have belonged on a fox peeked out.

And so did the star of this whole shit show.

The moment would have called for spirit fingers if our situation wasn't so dire.

"He has a flame on the tip of his tail now," I told them like they couldn't see it with their own eyes.

It was one of the two things on Duncan's body that were a dead giveaway that he was no baby basset or bloodhound or even any kind of household pet—not that he'd ever been, but it hadn't been so noticeable before. You had to have an excellent nose or be sensitive to magic to mistake him for anything else.

Six weeks ago, Duncan's tail had solely been fluffy, and his eyes had been a bright brown. We had *known* he wasn't what he looked to be—Matti and Sienna could smell it, and I could sense it—but now it was blatantly obvious, and they hadn't even seen his eyeballs yet. In the span of a single night, he had gone from a believable black puppy with a mixture of breeds and a hint of magic in him to something else. Something undeniable.

Unfortunately, from the shocked glint in Matti's dark brown eyes and the way Sienna's mouth was hanging open even wider than it had after my crappy explanation, it confirmed that any hopes I'd had of Duncan being normal-ish were long gone.

Because normal-ish was the most I could ask for.

I had crossed every finger and toe on my body in hopes they were going to tell me he was a werewolf. Any kind of mythological wolf creature would have been perfect. Even a Cerberus would have been great; there were a lot of tales about them out there. But a werewolf would have been my first choice, if I'd had one. Wolves were some of the most highly revered creatures throughout history.

Sometimes even my brain struggled to understand what kind of universe we lived in that Duncan being one would have made life so much easier.

I couldn't even begin to imagine explaining *that* to someone who didn't know the truth about the beings that roamed the planet in plain sight. People could barely tolerate others exactly like them. You tell them that magic crashed into Earth thousands of years ago and that all the mythology and folklore that had been written about was based on *reality*, and that would send almost anyone into a fit.

There were countless movies and stories—fiction and nonfiction, if you counted history books with mythology in them—about humans that could shapeshift. There were stories about wolf shapeshifters that dated back to Babylonian times. I was pretty sure cultures on every continent had tales of them. I could remember sitting through a class on Aztec history and having to keep a straight face while the professor went on about the symbolism regarding the Aztec believing that some of their warriors were nahuales, shapeshifters.

I'd gone through a phase as a teenager where I'd read every werewolf romance I could find, and *I* knew the truth. What normal people weren't aware of was that there wasn't just one type. Off the top of my head, I could name several types of werewolves. There were the Amarok, a line of massive wolves whose ancestors inspired the Inuit stories. An iron wolf, from those found in Baltic tales. Someone had told me once that there was a rumor even Fenrir, from Norse mythology, had a sacred line still in existence. Most of the ones I'd known and grown up with had been descended from the Mexican wolves who traced their ancestry back to Mesoamerican myths.

It was easy now to look back and think all those ancient civilizations had nothing better to do than use their active imaginations to explain things like droughts and terrible storms as the work of beings with good and terrible gifts, but some people knew the truth.

They hadn't been making things up.

The fact was, in a world of mythological legends that weren't exactly fiction, being a person who could turn back and forth between a man and a wolf—it was their choice after all, and their size depended on their heritage—was a well-accepted concept by those aware of the magic that had permeated the world and its beings a very long time ago. The magical.

And if anyone knew what *wasn't* as easily accepted, it was me.

"Nina," Matti exhaled my name. He sounded like he was having trouble remembering how to breathe. His eyes were wider than I had ever seen, and we'd gotten into trouble together plenty of times as kids, so I'd seen them big. "How *the fuck* does he have a flame on his tail, and how the hell didn't that blanket catch on fire?"

I snorted at his deranged tone. Wasn't that the freaking question? "I was kind of hoping you two might know," I answered him with a tiny shrug so I didn't wake my donut up. "And the flame is magical. It only burns things when he's scared or mad. Neat, huh?"

I knew Matti was transfixed when he didn't respond; he always had something to say. Part of me was convinced he might not have even heard me. It was one thing to come across a man walking along the street, radiating magic that he carried in his cells and looking to the world like just a normal, tall guy when you knew in your gut—or through your nose—that he wasn't.

But *this* was different. And I had known it to some degree from the moment that Duncan had come into my life. Now? I definitely had a better understanding of how unique he was.

So different that someone would try to hurt me to kidnap a puppy with red eyes and a blue flame on his tail.

Not once but *twice*.

But I was going to save telling these two about those incidents a little while longer. We had other things to get through first. I didn't need Matti or Sienna distracted when there was nothing anyone could do about the past.

With the arm I wasn't using to support his sleepy body against mine, I pinched the blue flame to show them. They gasped like kids on Christmas. I'd expected to get burned by it, too, the first time. That hadn't happened, fortunately, or else doing anything with him would have been impossible.

"It doesn't hurt?" Sienna asked in a voice I was pretty sure I'd only heard her use on the day she'd met Matti. Like she was in awe.

Me too, Sienna, I thought. There were magical beings—races that could trace their lineages back to ancient lore, who could look and act like normal people when they wanted to—and there were *magical beings that looked like puppies.* Specifically, a really, really cute puppy with big, innocent eyes and a sleek, soft coat.

"No." I pinched the flame again to show her.

Her wide, pale green eyes moved from me to Duncan and back. This was as close as she got to being speechless, which said a lot because she wasn't the quiet type either. It was part of the reason why we had become friends as teenagers and managed to stay such good friends for so long. We had never struggled to talk to each other.

Until now.

But I guess I could take responsibility for that. I had kind of blindsided them by showing up like this. There wasn't much I kept from them, but I'd hidden this until now since they'd been in Europe for most of the time since all this had gone down. I hadn't wanted to spoil their vacation.

"I don't understand," she whispered eventually, still stunned.

I bit the inside of my cheek, taking in her black hair and a shade of skin that was almost milky, no matter how much sun she got. She was the first person to say she wasn't classically beautiful, but she was the cutest. Her round face and pink cheeks hid the fact she had super sharp teeth sometimes and an ultra-protective personality all the time. An hour ago, she'd opened the door wearing a fitted red blouse and black pants with her hair tied up in an elegant bun, and now, she'd swapped that outfit out for a sweater and pajama pants I would've bet my money she'd taken out of her husband's drawer. This was the version of her I knew the best, but I loved Sophisticated Sienna as much as I loved Sweatpants Sienna.

And she loved me even though 95 percent of my wardrobe

consisted of T-shirts I'd picked up in towns Duncan and I had visited, paired up with jeans or jean shorts. My three nice blouses were hand-me-downs from Sienna herself. She and Matti both thought it was "so cute" I had four pairs of shoes total: hiking boots, beige sneakers that matched with everything—and if they didn't, too bad—Crocs, and one pair of sandals.

Then I looked at Matti, who I had known over a whole decade longer than I had her, since we had become neighbors at three years old. I took in the brown hair that used to be so long he'd had it in a ponytail for a while, but now he had a "real job," as he called it, and had to keep it professionally short. His skin was on the medium spectrum of tan, and those features that I'd seen grow from a toddler to a thirty-two-year-old had gotten sharper with high cheekbones and a defined jaw. Plus, he'd gained around two hundred pounds over that period. And gained a mustache at some point since I'd last seen him; one I wanted to give him crap about, but he somehow managed to pull it off. He might be into clothes now, but he hadn't lost the twinkle in his eye: the dead giveaway a mischievous little asshole still lived in his body.

They were such a beautiful couple. Such great friends. The best people I knew, other than my parents.

And you would never, ever know at first glance that they both came from old magic that allowed them to turn into something straight out of a folktale—a wolf, or a werewolf, as some chose to refer to themselves. And by werewolves, I meant the "real" kind: giant wolves, not some hybrid bipedal monster like in most movies.

To "normal" people, people born without magic—the word almost everyone threw around as an explanation to what gave certain folks the ability to become something out of a tale—Matti and Sienna didn't look any different, other than the fact they were both considered taller than average in most cultures. But to those with sensitive noses or feelings—me included—who had been born with a magic-heavy bloodline, you could just tell there was something else in them. Some people liked to say they were "blessed" when they referred to their ancestries.

Like being different and having to lie about it your entire life was easy.

It wasn't. Secrets were a burden no matter their size. For some people, it might be *easier*, but it was never *easy*.

"It doesn't burn anything when he's calm," I went on about Duncan's tail. "He caught a few things on fire at first, but we haven't had an incident in almost two weeks." I thought I could still smell burnt hair if I tried hard enough. It brought back memories of the time when Matti and I had tried to start a bonfire when we were eleven because our families hadn't wanted to take us camping. We had gotten into so much trouble, especially when our parents had seen our eyebrows. Matti's right one had never grown back in the same.

"When you said you had something you wanted to show us, I thought you'd gotten a tattoo or bought a new trailer, Nina," Sienna admitted while staring at Duncan's flame.

It wasn't that I *wished* that were the case, but it would have made life a hell of a lot less complicated than it'd been lately.

Less dangerous too.

My sore neck silently agreed as I snorted, getting more comfortable on the couch we were sitting on in their living room. Unlike the small, rural town where I'd met them both, they now lived in Chicago. In an apartment. On the tenth floor.

They were the least werewolfy werewolves I'd ever met, I swear. But that was one of the many reasons how and why they had ended up together—their own small pack of two, though Duncan and I were honorary members by default.

I pressed the little button that held his collar together and watched them both take deep inhales.

There was no recognition on either of their faces, but there was even more surprise on them. I clicked the snap back on. No way was I leaving it off.

"How?" Sienna leaned forward a little more. "You woke up, and he was . . ." She waved her hand up and down.

"I don't know how," I told them honestly with another shrug. "We went to bed, and the next morning, he was on my chest, his head right there, looking at me. His eyes were red, and then he started wagging, and I thought his butt was on fire." I had tried to put it out with water, sand, and dirt, but nothing happened. It had been pure luck that we'd been at a mostly empty RV park, and that I hadn't started yelling like I had the time he'd carried a rat into our travel trailer. "It hasn't gone away. His flame changed when he got scared right after it appeared, and it got even brighter." *That* was when he'd lit things on fire. I'd tested it out with my fingers first.

RIP to my favorite hoodie and some of my hair.

And then there'd been the times he'd experienced a different kind of fear, but I'd share that tidbit with them later. We had to focus on the big stuff before we could get there.

"I had really hoped he had a little wolf DNA in him to explain all of this, but you're both looking at him like he's an alien, so that's not it, huh?" I kept going, still hung up on that dream.

They stared at me.

Matti and Sienna should have known about Duncan, of course. We had just figured that Duncan had been too young to express any of the noticeable traits that came with their kind of mythological being. They had both been five years old when they had gone from normal children to being able to turn into a puppy. On the other hand, my own nature . . . magic, whatever you wanted to call it . . . hadn't made an appearance until I'd been a teenager. But that was like comparing steak to chicken breast. They were both proteins, but not really the same at all.

In the end though, that was exactly what had happened. Duncan's true nature *had* revealed itself, at least in the form of his tail and eyes, right after his *second* birthday. Days later to be exact. Except his changes weren't of the werewolf-kind. But to be fair, my friends' lives, like mine, had started with us as normal, human babies.

My donut's had not.

"Yeah, yeah, *I know you said he wasn't,* but I still hoped," I grumbled. I was an optimist, and they knew it. I still held out hope that my favorite boyband would get back together, and the

McRib would come back. "I thought maybe we were all wrong and he was some kind of werewolf hybrid."

The snicker that came out of Matti's nose... "A werewolf hybrid?" He made a smug face.

He didn't need to make it sound like I was dumb. "You thought Santa was real until we were thirteen," I reminded him. "Maybe you aren't the best person to make fun of me for dreaming. Weirder crap has happened."

He gave me a look as Sienna snickered. She knew that story already, about me having to lie to him for two years after I'd found out the truth about ol' Saint Nick. "I'm not, but... have you been watching *Underworld* again?" he scoffed.

"Maybe, but only because I was looking for clues."

To be fair, I had already known the folklore in the movie was all off and there was no way anyone who had worked on the movie was one of their kind because they'd gotten it so wrong, but I had been desperate, couldn't sleep, and the storylines were entertaining. I regretted nothing.

And peeking down at the still-napping puppy on my lap reminded me of exactly why that was the case. I couldn't believe he'd slept through our trip up to Matti and Sienna's apartment. I couldn't believe he was *still* asleep now. He loved them. There was no reason he should have been *so* exhausted, but my gut said something was there. Something that had nothing to do with him being sick.

He was stressed, and I blamed myself.

"I don't know what to do," I told them, my childhood best friend and teenaged-Nina's best friend. "I've done so much research, and I still don't know what he is. But now, I can't hide him anymore, during the day or at night. It's too obvious he's different." Which was why I was in this predicament of panic and helplessness. Why I was considering doing what I was considering doing.

Why I was here.

The expressions on both their faces said exactly what they thought about me not telling them about this change in him until now, and I was positive they were going to give me shit over it later, which was fair enough. But you had to put out the fire before you figured out what started it.

Just like I could read their faces, they could do the same to mine. Plus, they could smell my feelings. I could count on one hand the number of things I'd ever been able to hide from them before this. The fact I'd made it this long was only because I hadn't seen them in person or talked to them on the phone since they'd gone on their trip.

Now that they were back, I needed advice. We needed help. I had to be realistic about our situation. Duncan and I couldn't keep going the way we'd been going before, that was a fact.

I knew in my heart that our time traveling around in my RV, just the two of us, while I worked remotely, was over.

I had spent the last couple of weeks thinking and thinking, then thinking a little more, trying to figure out what our options were and why 99 percent of them couldn't work. What it all came down to was this final act of desperation. The only idea I could come up with that might work long-term.

Life hadn't been the same since I had found my furry donut, and now it was changing again. And I could either ride this new reality out with him because he had attached himself to my life and my heart like a cherished barnacle that gave me the kind of love that I'd become addicted to or . . . I could do something that I would never be able to live with.

There wasn't even a choice to be made. The only thing I wanted to do was make sure they couldn't think of something I hadn't been able to first. Just in case.

"I don't know what I'm supposed to do, but I have to figure something out," I told them, trying to stay neutral. "He's gained four pounds since his tail happened. He was eight pounds up until then. I can hide him in a blanket right *now*, but barely. What about in a month at the rate he's going? In six months? How big is he going to get? What else is going to change about him?" My voice got higher and higher with each sentence, and I had to clear my throat by the end.

There were too many variables, and Duncan wasn't the only

one stressed out. I hadn't even gotten to the part about his telepathy. "He can't live out in the world anymore unless he pulls a Pinocchio and turns into a real boy." That was the best way to explain what Matti and Sienna, and every other nahual, or shapeshifter, like them could do: go back and forth between their fairy-tale body and their human one.

It was such a weird concept if you thought about it. To be human one second and something so totally different in the next, still fully aware of yourself—or so I'd been told. It was kind of a miracle, depending on how you looked at it.

And a curse, sometimes, in some ways, for some. For people who weren't likable werewolves. Or nine-tailed foxes revered in so many different mythologies. Or *unicorns*—everyone loved a unicorn. Or dozens of other beings like that, that were cute or honored or respected.

But there was a reason why civilization after civilization had equally worshipped and feared certain entities, as my mom used to tell me. There was the good, the bad, and the tales of beings who struck sheer terror into so many hearts, their stories continued being told throughout the centuries. I knew a lot about the latter.

"And he might not ever be able to, I don't know," I kept going, laying it all out there in a ramble. "The problem is that I don't have a safe place for him to be himself if he stays like this. He can't live his whole life not ever being able to go outside. And what if he needs more people around him than just me?"

Some people and beings were fine being solitary, but so many weren't. There was a reason why werewolves, ogres, and centaurs raised their children in communities: for safety *and* for family ties. You had to learn to be a functioning magical being in a modern world from someone or *someones*. Kids were a handful under the best conditions, and add a magical chromosome with the potential of scaring the crap out of the majority of humanity?

Honestly, it was incredible the cat hadn't been let out of the bag after so long.

Magical beings had managed to remain a secret.

I had thought about moving back where I'd grown up, a small town in the middle of nowhere in New Mexico that had been rich with magical beings when I'd been young. It had mostly been the wolfy kind, but there had been some ogre families too, plus a couple of others who I had never known, *for sure*, the truth about; they'd been so secretive.

Or *maybe* they hadn't known what they were either. I'd never thought about that possibility before.

But things had changed over the last decade, and the town wasn't what it had once been. The population had dwindled as businesses closed, and the elderly, who had held the community together, passed on, leaving the younger population to move away. Matti's parents were gone. My parents weren't there either. Sienna's had moved after we'd graduated, and they lived in Wyoming now. There was no one left that was worth putting up with the heat for. Going there would only bring more attention to us at this point.

"Letting him out to pee and play has already given me a few grays," I told them.

I was scared now every time we left my trailer. The entire way up to their apartment had me sweating bullets. What if I slipped on a recently mopped floor and he fell out of the blanket? What if I moved my hand too much and someone happened to see his tail? What if his collar broke and popped off? I'd lost a lot of sleep worrying about all those scenarios.

"You already had gray hairs before," the smart-ass I knew and loved replied, his brown eyes flicking down to the mystery in my arms as I touched the "collar" that I'd gotten for Duncan last week. It was basically a bracelet with a clasp so I could put it on and remove it easily, if I needed to. "Is that obsidian like on your bracelet? Is that why we can't smell him anymore?" He rubbed his nose. "I didn't notice I couldn't sense anything other than his shampoo and his breath until now."

At least my savings had been well spent. If Matti couldn't sense him, no one else should be able to either.

"Yeah," I answered. After the two incidents, it just made the most sense to hide as much as I could about Dunky. Looking back on it, it's what I should have done from the beginning, butttt... I couldn't turn back time and make wiser decisions: like paying for overnight shipping. Fire obsidian wasn't cheap or easy to find, unless you ordered it. "Better to be safe than sorry." Even though that was kind of a lie. We hadn't been safe, and we had been sorry because of it.

But since I couldn't rewind time, and my regrets wouldn't do a single thing, all I could do was *do better*. Duncan needed me, and I wouldn't let him down. Not again.

All three of us glanced at the legs that stretched out from beneath the blanket. There was a small paw with shiny black fur, dark paw pads, and short black nails.

And then a flame, a little bigger than the kind you could find on a lighter, on the tip of a fluffy black tail slipped out from the blanket too.

Sienna sucked in a breath like she was surprised all over again.

Matti made a grunting sound in his throat that honestly sounded foreboding, and I wondered if he'd already come up with the same solution as I had.

His eyes slid in my direction.

My favorite woman on the planet, beside my mom, blew out a breath before scrubbing her cheeks with her long, slender fingers, oblivious to her husband side-eyeing me. "Honestly, Nina, I got nothing." She shook her head. "I thought you could build a cabin out in the woods, but that's not safe unless you bought a thousand acres. The chances of being caught would be too high, and that doesn't solve the issue that Duncan might need a pack. We talked about that."

We had. I remembered that discussion right after I'd found him. That conversation had been a lot like this one, except now I had an idea of what I was doing and what I was willing to do for him.

When we first met, I would've *probably* done anything for him.

Now, there was zero doubt in my mind I would, and I'd do it with a smile on my face.

"Every option I think of has a dozen reasons why it wouldn't work. You can't hide what he looks like. You're in danger every time you travel. What if you break down and have to pull over? What if someone looks in the window of your truck or trailer and sees him when you're not around?" Sienna went on, her round face scrunching up.

That was *exactly* what had gone through my head too. Nothing worked. At least not long-term.

Matti cleared his throat. "I have an idea."

We blinked at each other.

My oldest friend might be a different gender, a different species of magical being, and his own complete person, but so many times throughout our friendship, I'd thought there was something that tied us together. Maybe we'd been twins in a different lifetime. Maybe just siblings. I didn't know, but there was something that had bonded us together.

And with just that look, I knew we were on the same page.

"You know what I'm going to say," he warned.

I nodded. "I'm pretty sure I do, but go for it."

The next words out of his mouth were exactly what I'd expected them to be. "You need to go to the ranch."

I smiled, and it wasn't a happy smile exactly, but it wasn't a bad one either. Two weeks ago, there was no way that would have been my reaction to his solution. To what it meant. Much less what it required. At this point though, I'd already convinced myself of all the reasons why the ranch was the only choice Duncan and I had.

It wasn't ideal, it wasn't necessarily what I would've chosen if I had a few million dollars to buy a thousand acres of land, but . . . I was at peace with it. Life had thrown enough wrenches at me, and I had dodged, ducked, dipped, and dived them all, time after time.

Maybe it was time to start throwing some wrenches back at it.

This was my choice. My future. Our lives.

I'd had a decent idea of what I might be signing up for when I had kept Duncan instead of finding someone else to care for him. No one knew better than I did the kind of sacrifices you might have to make to care for a child with secrets even they didn't know they carried. It wasn't just the least I could do, paying the favor I'd been given forward; I liked to think it was my destiny. If I had one.

"I had a feeling you were going to say that," I admitted and earned myself a satisfied, almost smug nod from him. There was a certain amount of pride you could have when you knew someone almost as well as you knew yourself. That was almost thirty years of friendship for you.

"Wait," Sienna cut in with a wave of her hand. "Whose ranch? What ranch are we talking about?"

I raised my eyebrow at Matti in surprise, and he winced. "It's where I lived with Henri for a few years after my mom passed away," he explained vaguely.

It was the mention of Henri that had me glancing up at the ceiling.

Sienna picked up real quick on his word choice. "You've never *really* talked to me about that time in your life, Matti," she said slowly, squinting a little. "And I've never brought it up because it was a painful time for you, but now I think I've missed something important."

"Not *important*," he emphasized that word, "but I don't like talking about it because of Mom." There was a beat of silence after he brought her up. He rarely ever did, and that went for both his parents. Matti cleared his throat. "I had to move hundreds of miles away to live with my cousin, who I barely knew back then"—I was pretty sure he still barely knew him, but I kept that thought to myself—"and had to deal with this new life I didn't want," Matti explained, seriously. "I wasn't supposed to talk about the ranch while I lived there or after I left it."

That got me a side-look from him.

There were a lot of things Matti hadn't been able to talk about that all revolved around one side of his family. Some of them he had kept to himself, and other things had slipped through. The ranch being one of them.

I drew my fingers across my lips and tossed them over my shoulder. I'd never told a soul and never would. I hadn't even shared its knowledge with Sienna, and she knew the intensity level of my monthly period cramps. Plus, it wasn't like he'd shared any information that valuable with me anyway—at least I didn't think so.

"You knew?" Sienna asked me, and I nodded.

"Just a little bit, and he did it on the phone a couple months after he got there. We've never talked about it again since," I clarified, knowing she wouldn't be upset about it but still not wanting to risk it. There had never been any weird feelings between us where Matti was concerned. Even if I hadn't always talked about him like he was my best friend, she had always been able to sense with her nose that there was zero sexual attraction between us. It was the same with Matti and my friendship with Sienna. I loved them both differently and equally, and that love was reflected back in the same way.

My favorite people were married. Mated. I got to see them both at the same time. It was a win–win.

Fortunately, Sienna's reaction didn't let me down. She made an understanding but squinty expression. "Okay, so why would living at 'the ranch' work?" Sienna snapped her fingers. "Wait! He owns a lot of land in Colorado that we've never been invited to but that he inherited from someone." She snapped again. "Is that the ranch? That's where you lived back then?"

He nodded.

"Ahh. You haven't brought it up much, and the couple times I've seen Henri, he's . . . *oh*." It dawned on her. "I see. It's a secret. Is there that much acreage there? Is that why we're talking about it? If Henri doesn't want us to visit, why would he let Nina move there?"

There was that mention of Henri again. I was well aware that Sienna had met him a few times and that she thought he'd been standoffish and "a little cold." That had been one of the few mentions of Matti's older cousin I'd heard in years.

My oldest friend sat up and angled his attention to focus on his wife. "There's enough acreage that there's been a village of magical beings who have lived there for hundreds of years, and no one bothers them. Henri inherited it from his dad's side, which is my dad's side. Except my dad gave up his rights to the ranch when he moved away permanently, and I did the same when I left too. I had to sign legal paperwork. Now it's all Henri's. He doesn't live there by himself," he said all matter-of-fact, like it was a suburban subdivision with a billboard off the highway.

From the look of her face, I wasn't the only one who thought he'd framed that explanation loosely. "Aren't those 'magical communities' cults? Like communes?"

Everyone who had any kind of mythical ancestry in them had heard of the kind of communities that were whispered about in small circles. The places where magical beings lived in homesteads of sorts, out in tracts of land where most normal people had no interest in living or visiting—at least that's how those places had been explained to me. Places where privacy was affordable, or had been at some point.

It was a place for beings who wanted to live near others similar to them, so that they didn't have to pretend to be something else. The closest to that I'd ever found had been where I'd grown up, and even then, there had been a certain level of hiding because it hadn't been a strictly magical place. There hadn't been walls or security, just people who knew how to keep their mouths closed and were really good at pretending.

"It's not like that. It's . . . a village, and some people work for it, and some who live there work outside of it. But everyone there is magical, and they're all expected to participate in running it and maintaining it."

"Still sounds like a commune," she argued, shooting me a look like she was expecting me to agree with her.

And I mean, it kind of did with just the small amount of information he'd shared just now.

"It's not," Matti assured her. "It's as self-reliant as they can manage. It's also supposed to be a secret. How people keep their favorite vacation destinations to themselves so that everyone doesn't start going there and ruin it."

"If it's so great, what's wrong with it then? Why did you leave?" A thought occurred to her. "Why didn't your mom and dad live there to begin with?"

"My dad said it was too much responsibility. He left as soon as he was old enough." Matti's throat bobbed. "There's nothing wrong with it, but it never felt like home when I lived there, and I like the city. There's a small town close by, and there are a lot of people like us who live in it, but . . ." He shrugged. "The residents like their privacy and don't want strangers constantly trying to move in and mess up their balance."

"So they aren't friendly," Sienna muttered, casting me another look.

"Friendly-ish."

I laughed. "You're blowing this so bad I think you might be talking me out of it, and it was my idea to start with."

"I swear . . ." Matti groaned but collected himself. "The point is: it's secluded, and Nina and Duncan would be surrounded by people who are more likely to understand them than anywhere else would. It's as safe as you can get because everyone's objective is to live in peace, in secret. It's on a big piece of land." Matti paused and blew out a breath. "You can run until you get tired and still be well within the perimeter. It would give Duncan space to stretch his legs and grow up. I wouldn't have been happy anywhere back then, but it was good for me while I was there."

I'd kind of blocked that period of time out in my memories: when he'd left after his mom had passed away. His cousin, Henri, had picked him up one day while I'd been in class, and he'd been gone—his room cleaned out, the house basically abandoned—by the time I'd gotten home. It had been IMs that kept us in touch afterward, where he'd vaguely explained that his cousin had taken guardianship of him, and he was going to live in Colorado from then on.

It had been devastating. First his dad in a terrible car accident, then his mom, and finally him. Each loss had been sudden and unexpected.

I'd only heard from Matti once a month after that and never details about where exactly he was, no matter how much I asked. There had only been that one conversation where he'd revealed more than he should have. And in the years afterward, Matti had been real cagey about talking about that time. I'd never brought it up. If he'd wanted to talk about it, he could have.

He hadn't.

"The majority of the residents have Amarok or iron wolf in them."

Nina perked up at the mention of her iron-wolf ancestry. There weren't many of them left after all. Matti himself was a blend of Amarok, on his dad's side, and Mexican wolf, on his mom's. Like my parents were.

Matti kept going. "You know werewolves love kids, it doesn't matter what kind they are."

We both knew that from experience. But he didn't need to sell me on it. I had already sold myself on the community. The *ranch*.

My chest, though, still felt tight at the idea. I hadn't lived around people like us in years, not since I'd moved out of my parents' house when they'd finally retired. Of all the places I'd ever been, my childhood home had been a safe haven back then, and I knew exactly how lucky I was to have been raised around the people I'd grown up with.

Now, I knew that some beings sent others screaming at just the scent of them. At the potential they carried in their bodies. I touched the bracelet around my wrist on purpose.

Being different was hard. I didn't care what anyone said.

Sienna snapped her fingers again and pointed at Matti. "It's not a bad idea, baby."

"I never have bad ideas" was his reply.

Her eyes slid to mine, and we both scrunched up our faces. "Yeah, okay," I muttered before snickering. She leaned over, and we high-fived. We looked at each other, cackled, and then high-fived again.

I loved her.

He ignored us. "Something Henri mentioned the last time we saw each other made me think there are sasquatches that live there—"

That got me. "Did you say sasquatch?"

Matti nodded, like referring to the big, hairy mythical creatures was no big deal.

Which I guess it wasn't since he was a big, hairy creature that belonged in folktales too.

Then he said the one thing that would have won me over more than anything. "You know how wolves are toward people we consider to be members of our pack."

I did know firsthand. I'd been raised by them. Adopted by two of the best ones. I used to stay up at night and wish and wish and wish that I was like them too, even though no one had ever made me feel bad about being different. My parents used to try and sell me on how lucky I was to be special—like I even knew what that meant. I missed them so much, but thinking about them reminded me of my duty.

And that was to do what they had done: do the best I could for a child that might not be biologically mine but was in every other sense. In every way that mattered.

That meant moving to a place with a strong wolf presence. *They* didn't mind me and the way I smelled. Neither did ogres. But werewolves were as overprotective, possessive, and family oriented as books and movies made them out to be, especially around children and family members. Most screenwriters had gotten that part right.

There were worse things in the world than a group of people who all took it upon themselves to raise every child in their proximity as their own.

"You haven't brought up the 'but,'" I pointed out to Matti. "Tell her."

Sienna's face lit up. "There's a 'but'? What is it? Do you have to shave your head to live there? Animal sacrifice? Are they polygamous? Because I can't see you having sister wives."

My eyes strayed to Matti's. He smiled, and then I smiled.

"I was getting to it." He was being so ominous I was grateful to already be aware of what was going to come out of his mouth. He met his mate's gaze. "She would have to join the pack. They won't let her live there without a commitment to them. It's how they've kept it a secret for so long, and part of the reason why they don't have beings constantly trying to move there."

She scrunched up her face again. "What kind of commitment are we talking about here? It can't be that bad if you still see Henri every once in a while. They aren't keeping him hostage there, are they?"

"You think someone could keep Henri hostage?" Matti scoffed.

If he was anything like how I remembered, that was going to be a negative. My memories of him had been stored in some part of my brain that I had locked up. Most of them had been neutral, some positive, some very positive, and then there were the parts that hurt. The ones I'd clung to until I had been old enough to process them and understand why Matti's cousin had done what he'd done.

She snickered and shrugged her agreement. "So, what's the catch?"

Matti side-eyed me again like he was testing to make sure I was prepared for his answer.

I smirked at him, because *I knew*. The tuna-sized catch had kept me up at night wondering if I could go through with it. Testing the boundaries of how much I loved Duncan. How much I would be willing to do for him.

And if me agreeing to do this didn't tell the universe that I adored my boy, I wasn't sure what else could.

Matti had a gleeful little glint in his eyes as he dropped the explanation that would've driven a less desperate person away from moving to a secret ranch. "Nina's going to have to get married."

Chapter Two

"Do we need to go over the plan again?"

With my hands around the steering wheel, I glanced over my shoulder to find Sienna and Duncan cuddled up in the back seat of my truck. Sienna was holding a red toy I'd never seen before that he was gnawing away at. The cutest part was that they both looked like there was nowhere else they would rather be. A few hours ago, it had been Matti in the back with Duncan sprawled across his chest, both of them snoring away. Sienna had recorded a video of them, giggling under her breath while she did.

It made me so happy. Duncan loved the attention. Loved the love. And my friends loved him right back. There was that saying about how it takes a village to raise a child, and it had clicked, on a different level, how much sense that made.

Which was why I had told my friends that same night we went to them that I wanted to take him to the ranch. The fact that they didn't argue and tell me that I should move closer and raise him with them around said everything. It wouldn't work, and it wasn't safe. So it hadn't exactly been a surprise when Sienna had bumped my shoulder, and Matti had said, "I already texted Henri."

And that was how the four of us had ended up in my truck, pulling my travel trailer across state lines two days later. We drove and drove—Matti and I swapping every couple hours—eating up mile after mile between Chicago and wherever we were going in Colorado. Matti had entered a latitude and longitude address in the navigation. If this community was as quiet and secluded as he'd made it seem, why would it have a real address?

Surprisingly, it made me feel a hell of a lot better that the people who lived there would go to these kinds of extremes.

I didn't know how they made it work, but I figured that was something I'd find out when we got there in . . . fifteen minutes, according to the app. I hadn't let myself get nervous. Either they let us stay or they didn't. I either found someone who wanted a family enough to marry a stranger . . . someone like me . . . or I didn't.

It wouldn't be the first or last time someone did it to live there, Matti had reminded me.

If there was anywhere in the world where it would be normal to marry a practical stranger, it'd be at his cousin's ranch.

But as the tree lines along the road got thicker and the evergreens got taller and wider, the scent of magic filled the cabin with so much potency, despite the fact the air-conditioning was blasting, I had started to wonder what exactly we were driving to. Matti had warned us the magic here was strong, but I'd thought he'd been exaggerating. This was the same person who had held his hands three feet apart to describe a spider he'd found in one of the men's bathrooms at a gas station. It took most of my concentration to focus on driving and not pull over and stick my head out the window.

If Matti noticed how hard I was gripping the steering wheel, he didn't call me out on it.

"Nina?" The sound of my friend's voice brought my attention forward, away from the magic outside. He was sitting in the front passenger seat, and he had been since our last stop when we'd switched drivers so he could eat a hot dog—a hot dog that I'd just about begged him and Sienna not to buy.

Just looking at it had made me feel like I was going to end up with an upset stomach.

I relaxed my grip around the steering wheel. "No, we don't need to go over the plan again. I got it." We had gone over it twice already, but I got that this might be our only chance. "When we get there, you're going to do all the talking. I'm going to leave my bracelet on until they ask me to take it off, and we're going to do the same with Duncan's collar."

It wasn't *that* complicated. Just . . . important. Our acceptance hinged on so many things that were outside of my control that it made me itchy.

It was either going to work or it wasn't.

I squeezed the steering wheel again. "You haven't been back here since you moved away?" I asked him, realizing I wasn't sure he'd ever mentioned returning to the place where he'd lived for a few years.

"Not since I left at eighteen. There wasn't anything here for me, other than Henri," he answered. "Most kids who grow up on the ranch eventually leave. Some come back, but the majority don't. At least that was the case back then. You grow up here, want to see the world, and then you come back, or you don't."

"And you didn't." Like his dad.

"Fuck no."

Sienna and I both laughed.

"I know you don't know the comforts of food delivery and next-day shipping, but it's everything it's cracked up to be," he explained. "First time Henri took me to Denver, my brain almost exploded."

"Next-day shipping," I groaned with a laugh. "Spoiled." Where we'd grown up, the nearest fast-food chain had been thirty minutes away. Our town had had two gas stations. It had been that kind of small.

"Yeah, yeah, but that's why I think you'll do just fine out here," he noted, like I had another option.

As long as they don't hate me on the spot, I thought but didn't say out loud.

Matti reached back behind the console, and I could only imagine he was petting Duncan. Or feeling up Sienna. "It's going to be fine."

He sounded like he believed it.

"If things don't work out, we'll come up with another plan.

Find another community. I can only take a few days off right now because I have a meeting I can't miss, but in two weeks, we can try something else. I heard a rumor a while back that there's a place in Alaska . . ."

That struck a long-forgotten bell in my head. Before I could ponder it too much, I leaned forward. Something moved in the distance, darting across the road. It sure as hell hadn't looked like a deer.

Blinking a couple of times, I watched the same spot, knowing I hadn't imagined seeing things. Something else crossed the road. It was smaller. Fluffier.

"Matti . . ." I trailed off.

He stopped talking about Alaska. "Yeah?"

"I swear I just saw a centaur baby."

He leaned toward the passenger window, his attention on the side mirror.

"No, through the windshield." Letting off the gas, I slowed us down just as something even fluffier, white, and on four legs ran by. I pointed. "I'm pretty sure a centaur baby and two little wolves just ran by." I pulled the truck and RV over to the side of the road and put it into park. The road hadn't been busy since we'd turned on it off the county highway. There had been nonstop signs about it being a dead end, about there not being national forest access, but . . .

Matti was already unbuckling his seat belt.

"They probably shouldn't be running around in the middle of the day, huh?" I asked as I started to unbuckle my seat belt too.

He shook his head, hand going to the door. "No, they shouldn't."

Turning, I looked at Duncan who was still on top of Sienna, his long ears grazing her lap. His attention was sharp. I'd been so relieved when he'd finally woken up at their apartment, bright-eyed and acting like himself, minus his Sleeping Beauty reenactment. "Si, will you stay with him while I help Matti find the kids?"

She wrapped her arms around her little buddy, her light green eyes widening. "The baby is safe with me, but we'll get out and sit by the tree line. I've seen too many videos of people getting hit by other cars when they're parked on the shoulder. I'll hide him with my jacket and his blankie."

I blew a kiss at Duncan and Sienna as I reached for the door. "Be right back then."

But I froze the second I got out of the truck.

Wow, I thought, filling my lungs with the fresh air and the magic entwined in it. That was . . . *wow*. It felt like goose bumps but inside my body. Like smelling your favorite scent in the world but better.

Matti was already waiting though. He took a long inhale, swiveling his head from one side to the other before tipping it to the left. He was trying to find the kids, not absorbing our surroundings like I was. Did it not affect him the same way? His sense of smell was about a hundred times better than mine . . .

"They went that way." He pointed. "How young did they look?"

We crossed the well-maintained road and came to a stop at a chest-high predator fence that Matti somehow climbed over effortlessly despite wearing spotless sneakers that didn't look very comfortable and pants I called khaki, and he argued were toffee, whatever that color was. 'No Trespassing' signs were posted along the fence, and another sign claimed there was video surveillance. Too dang bad. I stood there and looked up and down the length of the fence before holding out my arms toward Matti on the opposite side. He grabbed them and took most of my weight as I used the fencing as a wobbly staircase to the top, and then he slowed down my fall as I jumped off.

"The centaur looked like a boy, maybe? He might have been about the size of a baby deer? I think he might have only had two legs, but it happened so fast, I'm not sure. The wolves . . . one was bigger than Duncan, and the other one was bigger than that one, I think." Real descriptive, I knew, but it had happened so fast. I hadn't expected to see any magical babies running around this soon.

He frowned but nodded, his nostrils flaring wide. "Badass kids."

"Right? Who goes exploring away from home in the middle of the day?" I slid him a look that he returned with his own and a smirk. We had, so many times. Almost every weekend until he'd moved away, probably. "They looked too young to be on their own—" I stopped myself and snickered. "I sound like an adult and a hypocrite, but you were bigger than them when we went on adventures without telling our parents where we were going."

Matti's chuckle was one of the most familiar sounds in the world to me. "They could have found us if they wanted, and snakes were the only dangerous thing around us back then. There's a hell of a lot more things out here that can hurt these kids." He glanced at me. "There are fences that surround the areas close to where everyone lives. They shouldn't be this far out."

Way to backtrack.

But total safety wasn't guaranteed anywhere. I wasn't going to worry about it. "Matti, the magic here is so . . ." I took another big whiff of the air. It was hard to describe what it smelled like, much less how it felt.

Matti had more than once tried to explain how scent signatures came across to him, and it had been like someone trying to explain advanced physics when I was struggling with middle school science. "It's rich. It smells really good." The hairs on my arms agreed. Every part of me, really. It was clean and wonderful and . . . it shot a shiver down my spine.

"Some of the elders used to claim that a part of the meteor landed around here."

I glanced at him, surprised, and yet not.

He kept going. "There are parts of the property that look and feel like nothing else. You'll see." He pointed to the right, and we moved in that direction.

Just in this section of forest, sensing the invisible weight surrounding us . . . I understood what he was saying. Duncan and I had stayed in South Dakota a while back, and at the time, that place had felt special. But the magic there hadn't been anything like here.

I took another lungful of it, a jitter running through my body afterward.

"I like it," I told him quietly, peeking up at the looming branches overhead before he nudged me to the right with his shoulder. I wasn't sure what to think about the little smile he gave me when he did it. This must have been what every character in every sci-fi movie, discovering a new planet, must have felt like—awe, wariness, and maybe more than a little hope.

We sped up, and I tried my best to listen for voices, but it was almost impossible with the birds in the trees singing the songs of their people as loud as possible. We had just crossed a narrow creek when Matti palmed my shoulder and pointed again.

Straight ahead of us were two furry pups and what might have been a centaur baby . . . or whatever the goat versions of them were called. The name was escaping me at the moment. But that didn't matter, because the three small beings were in a half-circle, and towering over them was a creature that looked like . . . well, like a . . . swamp thing?

The kids were cowering though, and I didn't need my friend's nose to know they were scared.

I met Matti's eyes, and he frowned just as the green thing growled, "Too far from home, children. Too small to be away from your protectors, eh?" The thing's lips peeled back into a smile straight out of a dentist's nightmare, revealing sharp, dark teeth that definitely needed a cleaning. Probably braces.

"You're . . . you're on our land," the centaur/goat replied in a voice that was just as childish as I'd imagined. It wobbled and went to a whisper, back and forth, high and low, with every word. He wasn't a baby-baby like my donut, but I didn't think he was a tween yet either.

"Your land?" the swamp creature answered with a laugh that made me real uncomfortable. I wasn't *scared*, but I didn't want to touch it. I didn't want to be near it. It was humanoid shaped, easily six feet tall, and even had what I would call hair—hair that was very long, hadn't seen a brush or shampoo in a few years, resembled seaweed or slimy grass, and was plastered to its cheeks and body. Its textured skin was various shades of green.

Was it wearing a long skirt?

I'd studied mythology over the years, but I couldn't recall a single green-skinned being off the top of my head.

The smallest of the pups—the white one—lunged at the swamp thing's reply, baring its teeth, growling, the hair along its spine standing straight up. It was bigger than Duncan, who was still travel-sized, but my God, the puppy didn't give a crap that it was squaring off with something about a hundred times bigger. The brave little wolf was freaking nuts.

The swamp-looking thing, though, wasn't impressed from the way it leaned down and snarled right back at it, the sound ferocious.

The mini psycho *didn't give a crap*. It lunged again, baring more teeth with every ounce of spirit in its body and more. It was so mad and cute at the same time.

I wanted to give it a hug and congratulate it. It wasn't easy being brave. Standing up for yourself and others didn't come naturally to most people, myself included. My neck was still sore because of it too.

"I'm gonna eat you first!" the green creature snarled.

I looked at Matti who raised his eyebrows, and I did the same right back just as the green-colored bully growled so loud I was surprised leaves didn't fall off the branches they were clinging to. The sheer volume of it made me flinch. Even Matti reached up and covered his sensitive ears with a scowl.

That was settled then.

My best friend pointed at himself, then at me; the question silent but hanging there. But what was Matti going to do? Fight the thing in front of the kids? He might be one of the most easygoing people in the world most of the time, but under that trimmed mustache and those khaki pants, lived a predator. And like most werewolves I'd ever known, there were a handful of things that could make him tap into that other part of his personality that he usually kept stashed away. In that moment though, he was dressed to go boating, not to get into an altercation with a forest monster.

I didn't like to hurt people, but I didn't like bullies even more. And nobody messed with children. Over my dead body would that go down.

Only feeling a little resigned, but mostly irritated at this jerk, I held up my finger between us, silently volunteering for the job of intervening to help, earning me a smile of surprise.

Matti was bigger and stronger than me, there was no denying that. I was strong enough to hold a growing puppy in one arm for a decent amount of time, and I could usually carry all my grocery bags from my truck to my trailer without breaking a sweat as long as it wasn't a long distance, but I was nothing like my werewolf friends. At five foot six, I was slightly taller than average. My strength was normal, I didn't have sharp teeth, and I kept my fingernails pretty short because I *hated* when they got so long I accidentally bent one.

But . . . sometimes you didn't have to use a sharp weapon or your physical strength to win. And I could say that, other than the two incidents with the people who had tried to take Duncan, I'd been able to get out of almost every unfortunate situation I had ever been in without resorting to other options. Like Hercules had his strength and mermaids had their beautiful but deadly songs, I had resources too.

Because, if this had been Duncan, I would hope someone would protect him from something dangerous.

And that's what I told myself as I started walking toward the little group, calling out, "Hi, hello!" even though I was pretty sure I was close enough now that they could hear me crunching over branches and leaves despite the sounds of wildlife around us.

The green swamp thing's attention snapped over to my direction, and it bared its teeth again. Two of the poor kids yelped; the little centaur/goat thing jumping between the two smaller pups, while the crazy white one growled for its life, snapping its teeth from behind the goat being. Kind of rude, but I guess

I understood I was another stranger in a place I shouldn't be, and they were already scared.

"It's okay. I'm not going to hurt you, kids," I said calmly as I approached the group slowly. It would have been nice if there was more space between the children and the swamp person. I smiled at the green being, trying to come off as friendly. "I'm Nina, and you are . . .?"

"None of your fucking business, idiot!"

All right then.

I pressed my lips together when what I really wanted to do was sigh. Some people could be so disappointing and predictable.

The green thing bellowed, "They're mine!"

Just like that, I couldn't help myself. I smiled again. "I hate to tell you that you might be in for a surprise if you take a DNA test. None of them look like you."

Behind me, Matti snickered, and that just made me smile bigger—he was the worst influence, and there was a reason we couldn't stand by each other around holiday dinner at Sienna's parents—even as the swamp-looking thing's facial expression morphed enough to actually look pretty pissed. "I will gorge on your organs and sip the marrow from your bones, human trash!"

Ouch. That was almost scary and hurtful. *Almost*.

I wasn't the one threatening to eat babies and calling people idiots out loud.

It wasn't done either. "When I'm done, I will use the children's bones to pick your meat from my teeth!"

Matti burst out laughing. I couldn't take him anywhere.

But I had to focus. "What I was trying to tell you is that I liked your creativity with that first line, but I'm pretty sure I've heard the second one before. Are you going to tell me what your name is before you try and pick my flesh from your teeth or . . .?" I shrugged.

The green creature went still, its "What?" at a lower volume, like it was confused all of a sudden.

I bet it didn't get laughed at that often. Or maybe it did and that's why it was so mean. That was something to think about.

"Never mind," I called out before lifting my hand and waving toward myself. "Come on, kids. I'm taking you home, and I cross my heart, I won't hurt you or let anything hurt you. Promise."

From one blink to another, the slightly bigger wolf pup shimmered for a second, and in the next, in its place was a child. A boy. A boy dressed in shorts and a T-shirt, and I thought, not for the first time, how incredible it was that magic worked that way. It wasn't like in the movies where beings turned up naked going from a fur body into a skin one, or where they ripped through every item of clothing they had on when they turned into their other nature. Magic wasn't so wasteful. Even seeing all this with my own eyes was hard to comprehend.

Whatever was on their person was there, and then it wasn't when they changed. Once, Matti had held a hammer just to see what would happen, but that hadn't survived the transition, and it ended up falling to the ground. Glasses, cell phones, keys, all made it . . . as long as they were in pockets.

Watching beings go from one form to another never got old; it was even cuter when they were young.

"We don't know you!" the little boy shouted, and the ferocious white wolf snapped its jaws at the green thing, then at me.

Someone had lost control of the situation, and I wasn't sure it knew it yet.

I lifted my hand toward them in greeting, palm out. "That's fair. I'm Nina. My friend back there has a cousin that's a member of your pack—"

"Henri!" Matti offered, sounding closer. Like Henry but fancy with an i. After a great-grandfather, if I remembered correctly.

"No one is going anywhere," the green thing claimed, rearing up to its full height, anger again visible in its sturdy shoulders and boxy frame.

Some part of me realized I should've been frightened. This green swampy-looking monster might be able to rip me apart if it had the chance. It had nails so long, they'd classify as talons. It was creepy-looking too, no offense to it. It wasn't like it chose to be born a being that wasn't going to win any beauty contests with its mildewy skin and snarly-looking hair. Butttttt... it would have to touch me first, and it didn't know it yet, but that wasn't going to work out in its favor.

I kept inching closer, stopping when I was about twenty feet away from the kids, close enough to see that the creature resembled a decaying green woman with wild hair, and the kids were even smaller than they'd seemed from a distance. They *were* young. Way too young to be out here by themselves. No parent would have let a child at their ages out and about without supervision.

They were going to be in so much trouble when they got home.

Was someone already looking for them?

I could worry about that later. For now, I had a big mythical being with an anger problem and a taste for young magical meat to deal with. To each their own and all, but what a jerk. If it was going to eat someone, it might as well pick on somebody who could at least fight for their life.

I shrugged at it one more time. "They're going to come with me, and you're going away, hopefully somewhere far from here. And that's if you're lucky and their pack doesn't hunt you down first, and if you don't piss me off between now and then." I crouched and held my arm out to the kids before meeting the green creature's dark eyes. It had no irises or white in them, just a nearly black pupil-looking eyeball.

The kids, though, didn't react to my gesture.

The thing laughed, and in a move so fast that my eyes missed it, it reached down and swiped the white pup by the back of its neck—it cried even as it snapped its teeth some more—and the swamp monster held it up. "You think I would have anything to fear from—" it started to threaten.

I hope this works.

I pulled my bracelet off and dropped it. I couldn't send a message if it was touching me in any way. By some miracle, though the wind had been nearly dead up until that point, a breeze picked up through the trees, carrying my scent upwind now that it wasn't hidden by my obsidian beads.

Sending *me* straight to the green thing's nose. The real me. All of me.

And I said, in the calmest voice I could, "You're about to piss me off. Put that puppy down before we start playing a game of tag that you're not going to like."

It was obvious the second my scent reached it.

It worked exactly the way I'd hoped it would. The way it had before when dealing with beings with noses who could sense magic, which was almost all of them. There were very few who had survived this long without evolution gifting them a biological warning system. It was mostly only people like me, I thought, who didn't have those kind of life-saving gifts.

I'd come across people who liked the way I smelled from the get-go. Some beings, like werewolves, were almost always a sure thing, but I'd met a hell of a lot more who started off hesitant, and just as many who were repelled. I didn't blame them, but I'd been banking on the latter just now, hoping it would be enough without having to touch anybody.

The swamp thing's body stiffened. The look in its eyes changed to a very, very uncomfortable one dang near instantly. Its mouth parted, its teeth disappeared as it quit snarling, and it took a step back reflexively. I would have bet money that it didn't even know it had done that—backed away, that was.

Some people smelled like sugar and spice and everything nice. Some of the time it was part of their magic, part of the way they lured things to them. Every once in a while, they just smelled good because they were good. That was how my friends with good noses had explained it to me. You could smell lies, anger, jealousy, and love, among a whole lot of other emotions that made up a person.

Me? I was good in my heart and in my actions. I liked to believe everyone who knew me thought the same.

But I was well aware that to a lot of beings, I smelled like sugar, spice, and sometimes everything not nice.

And in that moment, in this forest that felt like it was dusted in good drugs and some of the most impressive trees I'd ever been around, the green thing did what I had tried to avoid as much as possible since the truth about one of my parents made its appearance in me: the swamp thing sensed the magic that made me as different as its made it.

And I wasn't sure what exactly I expected from the children who had never met me before, but what happened next wouldn't have been it in a million years.

The white wolf turned its head and bit the swamp thing's wrist so hard the creature cried out and dropped it. The instant the puppy fell, the centaur/goat child picked it up in his arms, and they, along with the boy, were out of there. They *ran*. Straight for me.

Not away.

To me like their lives depended on it.

The boy—who had been the bigger pup before—kept going, but the centaur/goat child, with the white puppy in its arms, skid to a stop behind me. Hiding. Shivering. Terrified.

There was no way the boys were even ten years old. That just made me mad all over again.

"I would leave now," I warned the green being as I bent at the waist to pick up my bracelet and put it back on.

When I stood up, the swamp creature was rigid. Its dark eyes seemed wider than they'd been a minute ago. It was breathing faster too. I could've sworn I heard a faint squeaky sound come from it.

"Now," Matti demanded from behind, sounding even closer, stern like I didn't think I'd ever heard before from my easygoing friend.

The creature that had to belong to a folklore I wasn't familiar with took a step back, then another, and with a long look in our direction, it took off as Matti came up beside me, the wolf boy in his arms.

My best friend grinned the same grin he'd had his entire life—mischievous, likable, and friendly. Just with a mustache he'd let me tug at during one of our stops after I'd accused him of gluing it on his face, it was so thick. "You made it fart." He sounded so proud.

I shrugged and smiled a little, and he smiled even wider.

"You smell like Henri," the child he was carrying blurted out, leaning into Matti's neck, taking a big ol' whiff.

"He's my cousin," Matti explained, tilting his head to let the boy get up in there and check him out. It was the way of their world.

There must have been enough of a familiar olfactory connection that he understood they were related. Honey-gold eyes slid over, and the boy lifted his finger to point at my wrist, done checking Matti out and verifying his story. "What's that?"

I tapped my bracelet. "This?" He'd never seen one before?

"Yeah," the child answered, his eyes widening, his nostrils flaring. He had dark hair and skin just about as peachy brown as mine. "You smelled like . . ."

I didn't mean to tense, but I couldn't help it. *Ugly. Death. Bad.* They were all words I'd heard before more often than I'd wished if I had the choice . . . but only around certain beings.

". . . yummy," the goat child sighed from my other side, sounding . . . *did he sound dreamy?*

He'd moved closer without me noticing.

"Yummy," the boy in Matti's arms agreed in a voice that was definitely sweeter than anything I could have expected.

I blinked at the same time Matti gave me an I-told-you-so face.

The little werewolf boy made sense. I knew wolves liked me. The centaur/goat boy . . . that was new. Huh. "Really?" I didn't like how hesitant that came out of my mouth, but it'd be a lie if I said I hadn't been expecting him to devastate me.

The goat child leaned closer, pressing his nose to my hip without a second thought. "Mm-hmm," he whispered.

All right then.

"I think you smell like moonshine," the boy in Matti's arms claimed.

Freaking Matti snorted, and I had to press my lips together for a second. I squinted one eye. "I think you mean moonlight?" I offered.

The boy shrugged.

I smiled at him, ignoring Matti's even louder snort, while the white puppy, who had been silent up until that point, decided to growl.

I barely managed not to smile at it too. It looked like an animatronic stuffed animal. Like a Samoyed and a polar bear had a baby, all white and soft, apart from the growling and snapping teeth. Up close, the puppy wasn't as small as I'd thought. "You were really brave, mini wolf. You should be proud of yourself," I told it, hoping it would understand I was on its side.

My words didn't do anything. The pup growled again, and the goat child sighed. "Stop, Agnes."

Its name was *Agnes*? I wanted to hug it. Give it a little smooch. I might lose a knuckle, but it might be worth it.

Agnes didn't stop, but that was okay. I still wanted to hug her. I bet it'd be like holding a cloud.

Matti shifted the child in his arms, who under normal circumstances would have been past the age of being carried around. "Ready to head back and take them home?"

The sooner we got there and got an answer to my situation, the better, right? "Let's do it," I agreed.

Chapter Three

The centaur child kept peeking at me as we walked. He was so gangly, it was adorable, and with his splash of freckles, huge brown eyes, and eyelashes so long they looked like extensions? I wanted to give him a hug too.

"Are you okay?" I asked him after the fifth time I caught him.

On the ground, trotting next to him, Agnes the crazy puppy followed. She had tried to bite Matti when he'd offered to take her. She was on her own now.

"Can I hold your hand?" the little boy asked shyly.

That made me miss Duncan, and it had been less than an hour since I'd left him with Sienna.

I held my hand out, and his slipped into mine. It was warm and sweaty, and it made me like him even more. "What's your name?"

"Shiloh," the centaur/goat child answered. "What's your name?"

I had already given it to him, but he'd had other things to worry about. "Evangelina but everyone calls me Nina." Not even my own parents had called me by my full name.

He squeezed my fingers before gesturing toward the adorable menace at his side. "That's Agnes, and that's Pascal."

I nodded and smiled, glancing up to make sure Matti was doing fine as he carried who I now knew was Pascal in his arms as he led us through the forest. We had decided it would be faster and easier to drive us all back. I just hoped one of their pack didn't come looking for them before we got there, thinking we were trying to kidnap them. That would be a great introduction.

Shiloh squeezed my fingers again, and I focused down on him. His eyes went so wide, so dreamy, I couldn't tell what he was thinking. It definitely wasn't what he said next.

"Are you a forest princess?"

Up ahead, Matti tried to muffle a sound. I pretended I didn't hear him. "I'm not, but thank you for asking."

"You look like one," he told me in a small, timid voice.

I jiggled his hand in mine. "Thank you." If things worked out here, he was definitely on my Christmas list.

Shiloh kept looking at me with that innocent, curious face. "What are you?" he whispered.

It was a taboo thing to ask someone what they were. Either you offered it, or you didn't. It was a sign of trust to tell another person your heritage if it wasn't obvious by scent or feel. I'd been told that all werewolves smelled slightly similar, and I could confirm that they all felt a certain way, like all ogres, trolls, and other beings like that. The same way an accent would give you an idea of where someone was from. Magic was the same in its way.

But, as I knew firsthand, a lot of people were very, very protective of that information for their own reasons, and I again wondered how many of those beings sometimes just didn't know *what* they were—look at me and Duncan. Regardless, asking a person's heritage was the equivalent of someone asking what color your nipples were or how big your penis was. So, it was rare to ever have someone just *ask*, if they had manners.

But Shiloh, who was holding my hand like we were old friends, eyes glittering when they met mine, looked so guileless . . .

I'd give him my bank account numbers if he looked at me that way when he asked.

"Back there . . . with that . . . you know . . . you smelled like . . . you smelled like—" His shoulders went up and down as he struggled to express himself. "—a birthday cake."

That was a new one.

I think I might have blushed.

"I don't know for sure," I whispered back, honestly. "I never met my real mom or dad." I had some ideas, sure. One was a very, very good guess, but most of the people in my life had all agreed that it was better for me to never actually voice my guess because of superstition with saying certain names out loud. The man and the woman who I considered in every way to be my parents didn't share DNA with me, but that didn't mean much to anyone. Like Matti had said: werewolves didn't care.

Big brown eyes blinked before the child frowned. "Never?"

I shook my head, grateful that this wasn't a sensitive topic for me. It was like talking about a celebrity, in a way. Or characters I'd read about in books.

"What do you look like?" He meant in my other body, like how he could go from half goat to human.

"I don't change. I can't," I answered, trying to explain it as simply as I could. "I always look like this." I was average, medium, in almost every way. Wavy dark hair, brownish peach skin that was a clue of who I'd inherited it from, and light hazel eyes that were another clue—but a really broad one. My bone structure was a hint of my possible parentage, I thought, but the rest of me was pretty ambiguous.

From the way he blinked, the concept of not having another form was unheard of to him.

It was to the majority of people. Myths were myths to some, and legends were simply legends to others. But they weren't.

My parents had explained it to me once when I'd been sixteen and that special thing in me had woken up and changed me. I hadn't understood why or how I could be so different from them. From everyone in my life. Why I couldn't turn into something too. *Shift*, some people called it. To me, it looked like a shimmer more than anything.

My parents had sandwiched me between them and explained that if there was *something*—magic—in this world that had created all those beings in mythology, that there was no reason to believe that *something*—that magic from a meteor—couldn't be capable of creating *all* the other beings in the world that had stories and legends written about them too. That they were all intertwined for a reason.

"We're in the same books but our stories are different, Nina," my mom had assured me. *"Why would only some be real but not the others?"*

And then we had gone to our window and, through the blinds, watched our neighbor across the street: a tall, very old man with an eye patch who had two pet ravens that he tried to play off like they were wild when all the magical people in the neighborhood knew better. He was usually sitting out on his porch. I had always known on some level there was something different about him. He'd worn a bracelet most of the time, but when he didn't? His magic had been staggering. He had been nice to Matti and me, but I remembered how much he had loved Henri. That was when my parents had mouthed to me who they thought he had been once upon a time.

They had never used the word "immortal" to describe him, but rather said "long-lived." From an old, old pagan culture. One of the few ancient beings whose existence hadn't faded from memory.

I would never forget that they had no sooner mouthed his four-letter name than the old man, who went by Otis, had turned his attention in the direction of our house and smiled in a way that made the hair on my arms rise.

We left for the store an hour later and bought a puzzle that I had dropped off on his doorstep.

Even now, thousands of years after magic had made its initial presence, some names, and the magic and the gifts that came with them, still evoked fear.

Nobody had called the puzzle an offering, but nobody said it wasn't one either.

The older man had left an impression on me, but that still hadn't been enough for me to accept who one or both of my biological parents might be. But when you're young, all you want to do is fit in.

And when you're older, you've accepted who you are, and you just want to be left alone. Funny how that worked.

In that moment though, Shiloh blinked, still confused, his gaze falling to my bracelet. It wasn't anything special. It looked like a normal bracelet, with one smooth, round obsidian bead strung to a fire obsidian and then a quartz. The pattern repeated throughout the length of it. It was the obsidian though that did all the work. It hid what I wanted to keep a secret.

"But . . . but the monster was scared of you," the little boy stuttered in confusion.

But he thought I was a princess anyway? There was no point in arguing his observation. I nodded. "You aren't scared of me, are you?"

His lips pinched together, and he shook his head. "No, you're nice."

"Thank you." I squeezed his little hand. "You're nice too."

Shiloh, the centaur/goat child, gazed at me for a second, the question about my identity lingering in his head before he used one of his two legs—hooves?—and kicked at a small twig. "My dad says you don't have to be the biggest to be the scariest."

"It helps to be big, but being small and scary works too. Like a spider." I dropped my voice. "My friend saw one and came running out of the bathroom screaming that he thought it was going to eat him. It was a tiny little spider too."

In front, Matti slowed down and glared at me over his shoulder but kept his mouth shut. That wasn't exactly what had happened, but I could be dramatic too. Just less often.

Shiloh's expression went pensive. "I was scared. Agnes was too, but she tried to fight."

"Don't feel bad for being scared. That thing was mean. You didn't run or cry. You stood up to it. You should be proud of yourself. I bet if you really wanted, you could have stomped on it. Broken a couple toes at least," I suggested.

Matti snickered.

"You think so?" little Shiloh asked.

"Definitely."

Maybe I shouldn't put that idea into his head.

He was quiet until after we'd jumped over a fallen log—him gracefully, me not so much—and then waited for crazy Agnes to take three tries to get over it too after she'd tried biting Matti again when he tried to help her. That time though, Matti had quietly growled at her and continued doing it until she'd stopped. I forgot there was a huge brown wolf under that 'stache.

Then Shiloh asked, freckled nose wrinkling, "But why was that mean lady scared of you?"

How was I supposed to explain that to a child, especially one who was holding my hand when I'd had full-grown adults who left campgrounds when I arrived? Plus, Shiloh wasn't a predator.

I guess I wasn't one either.

"I don't turn into anything like you all do, but I have magic that it doesn't understand. You liked the way I smell, but it didn't," I told him as casually as possible, not wanting to alarm him or give him a reason to ask more questions I wouldn't know how to answer.

"But—" he started to say just as we approached the visible signs of a road ahead. Matti gestured us to the left with his head, and I followed. He had to help all of us, minus the white puppy who dug a hole and belly crawled under the fence, and once we were clear, I spotted the travel trailer exactly where we'd left it.

"You're taking us home?" Shiloh asked with another squeeze of my palm.

"Yup," I told him. "We were going there anyway."

"Why?"

"Because I'm hoping your pack will let me and my pup live there."

"You have a pup?"

"Yeah. His name is Duncan, and he's over there with my friend, Sienna. She's a wolf like them."

Sienna wouldn't care if I told her secret—not that it really was one anyway, since the little boy could probably sense the similarities between her and his pup friends.

Shiloh's eyes widened in interest as Matti got to the spot where Sienna and Duncan had been waiting. He leaned in and kissed her, rubbing the top of my donut's head while he did.

Duncan leaned toward the boy, Pascal, and I was pretty sure they were smelling each other before my puppy gave the boy a lick. Sienna laughed and grinned before they made their way to the truck and opened the rear passenger door, loading Duncan inside first, then the child.

I squeezed my new friend's hand again as the white werewolf reached the truck and she barked at my best friends.

"Don't be scared," I told Shiloh. "None of us are going to hurt you, and I promise we're just taking you home. You're safe."

He gave me that spirit-soaring, dreamy smile. "I know," he assured me as more sharp barks filled the air. Agnes the werewolf pup was on the ground, her small face tilted up to the truck where Duncan was. She was wagging her tail and snapping her teeth at him. Sienna took a step between them.

"Stop, pup," she demanded, clearly aiming the command at the crazy one—but not that crazy because the puppy knocked it off and sat on her hind legs. That tone of voice usually had the same effect on Duncan, who hadn't made a peep to begin with. He was picky about what he was willing to get in trouble over.

Sienna smiled sweetly, and Matti and I both gave her an impressed face. I whistled at her, and she looked up, ready to say something when her mouth dropped as we made it to the truck. "Are you a satyr?" she gasped at Shiloh with sheer joy.

A *satyr*. That's what he was.

Shiloh leaned against my thigh. "Yes," he whispered, suddenly shy. Or maybe it was because she was a new predator he didn't know?

She squealed. "You're so cute!"

My new friend glanced up at me, his freckled cheeks pink. "You are very cute," I promised him. Then I focused on Duncan, who was too busy staring at Agnes to even notice I was back. "I missed you too, Dunky-Dunk," I called out with a laugh.

Bright red eyes moved toward me a split second before that fluffy tail swept from side to side. That warmth that felt like a hug in my chest flared in sudden greeting.

"*Yes.*"

I blinked, trying my best to get used to this ability that had popped up when his appearance had changed. He wasn't using it very often yet, but when he did? It was like a Christmas present. When I'd told Matti and Sienna about it, after we'd discussed the ranch, they had both looked at me like I was nuts. But I hadn't been totally surprised when he'd done it the first time; I'd had a feeling he would someday be able to communicate with me like that.

His mom had been great at it.

Duncan focused back on Agnes, his tail swinging around.

"What's that smell?" Sienna asked out of nowhere. She wrinkled her nose. "It's like sewage."

"I think we met a Jenny Greenteeth," Matti answered.

"A *what*?" we both said at the same time.

"Jenny Greenteeth." He scratched his nose. "That's what they call them in England."

"What's a Jenny Greentooth?" Sienna asked, reading my mind.

"Greenteeth, baby. An old crone that lives in a river and eats . . ." Matti's eyes flicked over to the truck, where the kids were. His lips and mustache went flat.

I took after Matti and scratched my nose. "I'm impressed you know that much obscure folklore, Matti."

"My roommate junior year of college was from Lancashire and had this book I read when I took a shit."

That explained it.

"You guys stink." Sienna wrinkled her nose. "Some more than others."

I didn't think it was us that smelled. I was pretty sure it was Agnes since she was the only one who'd gotten touched, but I didn't trust the puppy not to bite me if I talked about her. She wasn't barking anymore as she waited at the truck, her attention still on Duncan.

She was a wary one for sure.

But she was so dang cute.

I got Shiloh's attention. "Need help getting into the truck?"

He shook his head as he let go of my hand and jumped gracefully into the back seat, landing on the floorboards perfectly. "Come on, Agnes," he called to his friend. The puppy gave the three of us adults a mean look before backing up and jumping in too . . . barely making it. Duncan's tail waved faster, but he didn't lean down to smell or lick her like he had the boy, Pascal. He gave Shiloh space too, I noticed.

Matti held out his hand. "I'll drive the rest of the way, okay?"

"Sure," I agreed. I just wanted to give my boy a hug now. What if that child-eating asshole had found him instead?

He could have lit her on fire, but that was beside the point. I only wanted him to light things on fire that he *wanted* to light on fire—and that was a thought I didn't think I would ever have. This whole situation was one I never would've imagined either.

"I'll sit in the back with them if you want to ride shotgun," I offered to Sienna, who nodded.

It only took a second for me to get in and shut the door. Duncan settled into my lap and licked my cheek. "Hi, Donut."

His "*yes*" was soft and gentle. His form of hi. We were both still learning his gift. His voice was nowhere near as clear or strong as his mom's had been, and I wondered what it would sound like when he was older.

"Is that fire on his tail?" Shiloh whispered.

Pascal, who was leaning over, gawked. "Why are his eyes red?"

"The same reason why yours are gold. You got them from someone in your family," I answered him.

The boy seemed to think about that for a moment. "He smells like you, but he doesn't smell like you," Pascal the wolf boy argued. "You're not his mom."

Duncan licked my cheek in a way that felt like an argument against that claim. It sure felt like I was his mom, even if I'd never used the word out loud.

"He didn't come from my body, but he is my pup," I tried to explain, gently.

"He wasn't in your stomach?"

"Nope."

"Was he in his dad's stomach? Because my mom said that she wished my dad could have babies, and Dad said that seahorses do. And that maybe other animals do too, but not wolves," the boy rambled on out of nowhere before making an expectant face.

He actually expected me to answer that?

Sienna turned all the way around in her seat as Matti pulled us back onto the road. Pinching her index finger and thumb together, she dragged them across her lips. Freaking coward.

"I . . . I really don't think his dad carried him in his stomach either. I'm pretty sure it was his biological mom."

"What's biological?"

This kid hadn't said a word to Matti during the walk to the car, but now he had a million of them.

I wasn't exactly qualified to have this conversation. Duncan was the only child I'd spent significant time with since I'd been a kid, and he didn't argue with me or ask questions. He *could* push my buttons playfully sometimes, but that was different. He was an angel on four legs. And I just had to peek down at him, finding those big, sweet eyes, to know it was true. He was one of those puppies that looked like he was smiling.

But no one else seemed to want to answer the boy's question, so I guessed it was up to me. "Uh . . ." I started fidgeting. "That means . . ."

There were coughs from the front seat that sounded deceptively like laughs.

I guess I couldn't expect any backup from Matti or Sienna on this.

I cleared my throat. "To have a baby, the baby has parts from the mom and the dad. Like maybe you have your dad's eyes but you're funny like your mom? Because most beings can't have babies without someone else sharing part of their . . . bodies?"

Pascal frowned at me like I didn't make sense, and let's be real, it didn't really, but how did you explain biology and cells to what looked like a seven-year-old? I sure didn't know. I wouldn't even know how to explain the birds and the bees *using* the birds and the bees analogy. I hadn't understood the concept when I was thirteen, and I still didn't understand it now in my early thirties.

And I was not going to be the one to explain a daddy's pee-pee going into a mommy's privates. I would throw myself out of the truck first. "But Duncan is my pup. I take care of him, he takes care of me, and I love him," I told them before they could nitpick my BS explanation.

"Does he love you?" the werewolf child asked in a way that kind of sounded innocent but also pretty judgy.

I glanced at Duncan, who still had his attention on me, and smiled. "He does." I didn't doubt it for a second.

"My aunt says that moms and dads are great but other people are just as good as they are," my friend Shiloh butted in, wise beyond his years.

"Your aunt is a genius. As long as someone loves you, it doesn't matter." I paused and thought about something. "Do you want to call your parents?"

I'd never seen anyone go from being okay to looking like they wanted to throw up so fast.

Agnes decided right then to start growling again, and Shiloh had to scold her, which then led to the three of them arguing about whatever it was they were arguing over. Getting in trouble? Getting busted? The boys were talking over each other so much it was hard to tell what each one of them was trying to say while the white wolf pitched in her own thoughts through low grumbles that made me want to giggle from how adorable they were.

I guess nobody wanted to call their parents. If we weren't so close to the ranch, I would've insisted but . . .

I focused on Duncan then, grateful that he didn't talk a lot. Those red eyes were bright and attentive. I had already told him multiple times what we were doing and where we were going, and my gut said he understood, but I lowered my voice and palmed his back. "Do you remember where we're going? I'll be with you the whole time. Nothing is going to happen. This place smells so good, and I think you're going to like it. If you hate it, it's okay. You just have to tell me, all right?"

His *"yes"* was a touch to my soul. I could eat his telepathy with tortilla chips, I loved it so much.

I stroked the fur between his head and the base of his tail, then I did it again, trying to keep my thoughts on him. If I didn't focus on how this meeting was actually about to happen—how our future hinged on how it went—my body wouldn't react to the worry that came with it, and the exceptional noses in the truck would never notice I was ramping myself up.

Regardless of whatever happened, we were going to be fine. Duncan and I would figure it out. Matti had said something about Alaska, hadn't he?

The truck slowing down brought me back to the moment as Matti turned the wheel a hard left. Through the rear passenger window, the only things visible were massive trees and a fence taller than the one we'd jumped. The difference now was that there was an imposing iron gate ahead. Multiple signs were posted, claiming PRIVATE PROPERTY, NO TRESPASSING, NO SOLICITING, NO POACHING, YOU WILL BE PROSECUTED TO THE FULL EXTENT OF THE LAW, and YOU ARE UNDER VIDEO SURVEILLANCE.

They weren't screwing around. Good.

We slowed to a stop, and the driver's side window rolled down. There was an intercom-looking thing to the left. Leaning out of the window, Matti pressed a button on the keypad. It beeped. "Hello?"

Nothing.

He glanced at Sienna, who shrugged, before he leaned out the window one more time, making the intercom beep again. "Hello? This is Matti. I used to live here . . ."

Nothing.

The side mirror reflected his frown.

He did whatever he did to make the intercom beep for the third time. His mustache was flat across his upper lip. "It's still Matti. My cousin is Henri Blackrock. I found three of your children and have them with me—oh, the gate is opening now," he muttered in a voice that cracked with irritation.

On my lap, Duncan leaned to the side to peek out the window. I had already talked to him about how careful he needed to be around them. I didn't want to scare him or be so strict, but it was a necessary evil. I rolled the window down a crack. His shiny nose started twitching, taking in the air that somehow felt even more magical than before. Against my hand, his little heart started beating faster, so I stroked his chest. Did he sense the same thing I had when I'd gotten out of the truck? Nobody else seemed to be reacting to it, but . . .

Slowly, the gates finished opening, and Matti drove forward, giving me a close-up view of the black ironwork. Part of me had expected to see the outline of a wolf on them or something kind of catchy like that, but the only decoration on the iron was a half-moon on each side, which formed a whole one when closed. A full moon.

Duncan's nose kept twitching, twitching, twitching.

I glanced over at the kids and found Shiloh looking nervous. He was wringing his little hands. "Are you okay?" I asked.

Huge brown eyes blinked in the least convincing way ever.

"What were you all doing running away from home?" Matti asked from the front seat.

Those adorable eyes almost bulged out of his head as the most nervous laugh I'd ever heard came out of his body. "We weren't running away! We were going to look for—"

"Shh!" the werewolf boy hissed, putting his index finger up to his lips.

Shiloh gritted his teeth before offering almost glumly, "Stuff?"

That sounded *real* believable.

Sienna turned around in the seat as much as she could. "Were all of you born on the ranch?"

"No," the werewolf boy answered at the same time as Shiloh said, "Me, yeah. Agnes, no. Her mom—"

From the floor, the white puppy barked.

The satyr stopped talking.

I was learning real quick he might be sweet but couldn't keep a secret to save his life. I think I loved him already.

It was Pascal who leaned forward so his head would have gone between the seats if he was bigger and wasn't wearing a seat belt. "Are you really Henri's cousin?"

In the rearview mirror, Matti's face brightened. "He's my older cousin." He paused. "I'm his only cousin."

I wasn't sure Matti even knew the technicalities of their relationship, but I wasn't going to bring it up. If it had never mattered to him, why would it to me? I knew next to nothing about his dad's side of the family, and that was all right. If he'd wanted to talk about it, he would have by now.

"The one who used to pee his bed?"

My mouth dropped, and I leaned forward too, my head over Pascal's to get a good look at Matti's profile in person. He was focused on the road, but he wasn't beaming anymore. "*What?*"

"Henri said you used to pee your bed because you were scared," the boy explained.

"You were fourteen when you moved here . . ." I couldn't even finish my sentence. I started cracking up.

"No!" Matti shook his head. "I never—"

"He said you did it all the time."

Sienna reached back to blindly grab my hand, and then we were both cackling.

"No." Matti's face . . . "Why would he . . .?"

"All the time," the werewolf pup insisted, just in case we hadn't heard him. "Lots of pee."

Sienna and I were too busy trying to breathe to make a single comment.

Why would he make that up about Matti?

I couldn't stop laughing. *Henri had said that?* The teenage boy I remembered would not—*would not*—have said something like that. Ever. That made it even funnier.

"I don't pee the bed, and you both know it," he argued, way too defensively. We were still busy gasping for breath when the truck slowed down again just as Matti whistled, back to ignoring our BS. "This place has changed."

Wiping away my tears and saving the moment for later, I sat up and peered through the windshield, the laughter leaving my body almost immediately.

The ranch, the part of it I could see, wasn't what I'd expected.

There was no cozy farmhouse set on a desolate and dusty parcel of land. There were no pens of horses, or a riding rink surrounded by cowboys. There wasn't a single cow or steer in sight either, like most of the ranches I'd driven by.

In front of us was what seemed like a giant gravel parking lot that could have belonged at a sports stadium. Across from it was a building that was so large it resembled an old courthouse or a mansion . . . or basically a billionaire's gigantic cabin that was visited once a year. The walls were made of some of the most impressive logs I'd ever seen.

There were UTVs parked next to each other in between the lot and the building. To the sides and behind it, the woods cleared and opened a bit to show small homes in the distance. Most of them were also cabin-looking, but some of them were more traditional homes with muted neutral colors. There were multiple paths that branched out toward the dwellings from the huge building.

From the way it was all set up and the small number of cars parked in the lot in front of the main structure, it seemed like you had to leave your car there to get around.

"They didn't have this back then," Matti said, like he could read my mind. "The parking lot was here but not that building."

I opened my mouth to ask about the parking situation when a nudge at my chin had me tipping it down to find Duncan's pupils slightly dilated. "Everything is going to be okay," I promised him with a stroke of his soft, floppy ears. He didn't *look* all that worried, or even a little bit worried. Was it me? Was I giving off anxious vibes or something? "I'm fine."

"*Yes,*" he told me.

It was my nerves then. "I'm just a little nervous. Don't tell anybody." I winked at him.

"*Yes,*" he assured *me*. He pressed his nose to my chin again, and I gave him yet another hug, grateful I had someone who enjoyed them as much as I did.

He was worth everything—all the nerves, all the stomachaches, all the uncertainty. I couldn't think of a single thing I wouldn't do for these long ears and his big, loyal heart.

We had to make this place work.

"Might as well get out. They're going to have a million and a half questions," Matti warned as he opened the door.

Shiloh, the satyr, hesitated for a moment before opening the door closest to him and getting to his hooves before jumping out. Following him was the white puppy, and last went the werewolf child. I tapped Duncan's nose to get his attention one last time.

"Be on your best behavior. I don't want to put you in air jail," I warned him. He waved that fluffy tail behind him. We both knew, though, that he'd done enough stuff in the past that had required that kind of prison sentence.

But I didn't want him to know that staying here depended on him, and I definitely didn't want him to sense any pressure if he *didn't* like it and we had to figure out plan B.

That was a burden he didn't need to shoulder. He didn't need to know yet there wasn't a plan B.

I patted his head before turning and climbing out with him in my arms and then setting him down on the gravel. He wouldn't run off—I was pretty positive—but confidence was built by experiences. I had to trust him. He'd be safe here.

At least that's what Matti had told us, and I believed him despite the Jenny Greenteeth we'd encountered. I justified it by telling myself that she had been at least a couple miles away, and she'd taken off in the opposite direction. *But* I should probably get my fanny pack from where I'd left it on the front seat regardless. He rarely needed his leash, and I wanted to believe he wouldn't need it now, but . . . just in case.

I was thinking about that as I took a few steps around the truck after getting out of the back seat, standing close to Shiloh, who had made his way over while he spoke to Agnes beside him.

Pascal was saying something to Matti and Sienna on the other side of the truck. I swept my gaze around, too focused on the smell of the woods and the magic in the air to really listen to the low, consistent sound in the distance. The sound I would have recognized—if I'd been paying attention—was a heavy body running fast over fallen leaves.

Out of the corner of my eye, I noticed Duncan's ears perk up, his attention pivoting toward the trees. At almost the exact same time, Shiloh did the same.

Unfortunately, I missed their reactions, and I was going to blame the enchanted forest we were in for why I didn't sense the wrecking ball of a magical presence running like the wind through it.

And it had to be because of all those reasons that I was totally surprised when a huge black mass appeared in my peripheral vision.

It didn't click that it was running straight for us until it was almost too late, and I stepped in front of the two kids.

An animal the size of a Clydesdale took what I would call a flying leap at me not *twenty seconds* after I'd gotten out of the truck.

Matti shouted. One of the boys did too. Duncan whined deep in his throat.

It all happened so fast, and I barely had time to do anything but make sure it was me and not Duncan or Shiloh it was aiming for before gigantic paws hit my shoulders and tackled me to the ground like a pop star's bodyguard would take down a fan running on stage.

The only good part was that I didn't have time to tense and make hitting the gravel like a watermelon from a ten-story building even worse than it already was.

But that's what happened.

The massive black ball of fur tried to turn me into a pancake, and it wasn't until I gasped for air in shock as I barely managed not to crack my head on the ground that I heard the "No!" Shiloh yelled after everyone else's mix of noises. But all my lungs could do was rattle as my brain struggled to process what had just happened. It was at that point, despite my eyes watering, that I finally got to absorb the body standing over me.

Literally.

Two humongous paws were braced on either side of my head, and maybe a centimeter from my nose was a face that belonged in geographic magazines . . .

And the biggest wolf in the universe, who had somehow managed to survive the Ice Age or whatever time period wolves the size of the biggest horses existed, was snarling at me so deeply, *so pissed*, I should have been scared out of my mind.

I wasn't.

The most intense amber gaze I'd ever seen was looking down at me. I gasped, "Freaking hell, Henri, what have you been eating? Small children? Minor deities?"

The snarling werewolf suddenly went so quiet it was like someone had unplugged him from a power outlet. He dropped into a sitting position almost immediately, right by my feet. Even his almost-terrifying mouth closed.

Just as quickly as his whole demeanor changed, the wolf turned its head over his furry shoulder. *That's* when I caught it. The tiny growl I'd heard countless times, especially when it was within a foot of a raw meaty bone.

Leaning over, I gasped at the twelve-pound black puppy dangling in the air. Its jaws were clamped to the wolf's tail, the one red eyeball that was visible was wide, and the flame on the tip of his tail was the palest shade of blue I had ever seen. My sweet little Duncan baby, my donut, my joy, my boy, growled even louder, and I'd swear I could see his jaws clamp down even more around the bone and fur in his mouth.

He was attacking the kaiju of wolves.

To protect me.

But even as my heart stuttered in fear and my brain told me to do something, the huge werewolf only stared. At Duncan. Not aggressively. Not in preparation to eat him. In a way that made me think that *it* didn't know what was going on.

"Henri! What are you *doing*?" Matti bellowed. I was pretty sure I could hear him running over my wheezing.

The legs on either side of my feet shimmered for a fraction of a moment before the body looming over me was replaced by two work boots.

Big, human feet.

And above the double-digit-sized boots, which I'd bet were really sturdy, were long, thick legs, an upper body that could've created its own eclipse, and a face that . . . that . . .

The man there now was looking at me with the same intense amber eyes as before, and he was . . . he was . . .

He was holding my baby up by the scruff!

Honestly, I had no idea what came over me. Instinct? Maybe I had hit my head and wasn't thinking clearly?

I had no clue.

All I knew was that I made an unholy noise right before I rolled onto my side, grabbed the calf right there, and bit it.

"What the hell?" I heard Matti mutter just as I sank my teeth into jeans and muscle. Hard too.

I would've made a mama bear proud.

"The hell—" a husky male voice above me growled just as a much younger voice cut him off.

"She saved us! That's her baby!" I was pretty sure it was Shiloh who screeched, the voice of reason in the madness because I stopped biting the calf in front of me like it was a turkey leg at the Renaissance festival the second I heard it. Above me, the big man had moved his grip on Duncan so he had hands beneath his front legs instead of at the back of his neck.

And Duncan—bless him—was growling in the face of the werewolf man who had been ready to rip my face off seconds ago. If the growling wasn't enough, he started whipping his head and body from side to side like he was a rabid badger trying to escape. Like he was trying to help me . . . ?

Oh, Dunky. If this man didn't look like he ate only the best magical organ meat on the market to keep up his size, I might have cried from how proud I was. From how this act of love, of bravery, could be enough to support me through every bad moment I ever had in my life from then on out. He was so small in comparison, and it wasn't stopping him from putting himself at risk.

For *me*.

"What's this?" the man asked slowly, clearly referring to Duncan, before tipping his head down and aiming those familiar eyes back on me. He blinked. "Who's this?" he demanded, his tone somehow a grumbled mix between confused, irritated, and caught off guard. Mostly irritated though, I'd bet. "And what are you doing here, Matti?"

Someone was speechless again. Seeing your oldest friend almost get mauled by your relative might do that.

Or maybe he'd thought I was . . .

"Long time no see."

That took a second.

There was a pause of silence before Matti cleared his throat, his tone coming out *almost* normal next. One of us, or both of us, had scared the crap out of him. I could tell. "Can you please stop standing over Nina before she bites you again?" The laugh that came out of him sounded almost identical to the one that Shiloh had made when we'd asked him what they'd been up to in the woods, kind of high and shaky.

There was another beat of silence followed by a muffled snicker that had me leaning around the leg still on one side of my body to find Matti standing a few feet away, looking frazzled and amused at the same time.

But mostly freaked out and trying not to be. I snapped my teeth at him before smiling too, hoping to make him feel better. Poor Matti.

From the way his dimples popped from one moment to the next, I wasn't surprised when he snorted suddenly. "You bit him? Really?" He grinned like a fool, shaking his head.

I shrugged from the ground, eyeing Duncan still hanging there, supported by hands that had gotten bigger since the last time I'd seen them.

Henri had always been huge in my memories—people had confused him for an adult man at sixteen—but somehow, he'd kept on growing over the last almost twenty years.

From the few memories I had of him in his four-legged, magical form, he had been impressive. Now?

I peeked at him again to make sure I wasn't imagining it.

I wasn't.

Henri didn't move, didn't breathe, didn't do anything other than stare at me.

I almost became self-conscious, he did it so long.

Eventually, his nostrils flared, not much but enough so I noticed. He was taking me in, of course. I smelled differently than I had the last time we'd seen each other, and it had been a long, long time.

But that didn't change the fact that maybe he didn't remember me, even if he'd stopped when I'd said his name. *I* hadn't forgotten him. He was still my best friend's cousin.

Now, he was the adult version. The supersized one. Even more imposing than my memories did him justice.

And was that a smudge of blood on his face?

"Hi," I told the man standing over me. Then, before I could second-guess myself, I hugged Henri's shin and calf. Pressed my cheek against it and everything. Part of me felt just a little bit bad about biting him.

Not really though. He shouldn't have grabbed Duncan like that, but that wasn't how I'd planned on greeting him after so long. I'd expected a light hug or a pat on the back in a best-case scenario, maybe a nod at least, but not getting knocked off my feet and snarled at.

Or having my precious baby held up like a sacrifice.

That was where he'd screwed up, but that wasn't his fault. Werewolves were territorial. It was part of the reason why we were here. I wanted someone who would try to rip off a stranger's face to protect my boy.

And if that someone was a protective man with sharp teeth, what was I going to do? Complain? Say "no, thanks"?

After a one-second-long squeeze, I scooted backward and sat up, getting my legs under me and standing. It was only then, not panicking anymore, that I could finally sense the full impact of his magic. I could have swooned. He was not the strongest magical person I'd ever met—our old neighbor and Duncan's mom were—but holy bologna. It was close.

Where in the world had this kind of presence on him come from? I'd been joking before, but . . . had he eaten some old gods? Maybe gnawed on the magical trees surrounding us?

The old man who had lived across the street from us had masked his magic nearly constantly with a bracelet like mine—rumor had it, he'd worn two or three of them—and if I'd ever met one of the other old ones, I hadn't been able to tell for the same reason.

Henri, though, wasn't trying to hide anything.

That was the part that shocked me. My body was ultra-aware of the magic living in the woods and the magic that came from every person around me, signaling that they were more than human, but where the children were candles and Matti and Sienna were steady burning campfires, Henri was a bonfire. A funeral pyre. Whatever was the biggest burning thing I could think of short of a city-destroying bomb.

I didn't miss the way Henri's attention followed me, watching me watch him, nostrils again flaring softly on a deeply tan face. Henri's hair was a deep black that was the exact same shade as the glimpses of his coat I'd gotten when he'd been standing over me. He was *tall* and broad at the shoulders and chest. His hips were narrow in comparison but not slim. He was the epitome of a big man. And his face . . .

Yeahhh, no wonder I'd had a crush on him when I'd been a kid.

And that was definitely blood on him. The corner of his bottom lip was slightly swollen too. There was a tiny cut near the corner.

Hmm.

Even with the busted bottom lip, Henri's facial features were striking and masculine. He was no pretty boy, like I enjoyed teasing Matti that he was. Henri Blackrock was all cheekbones and a big, defined jaw. In a lot of ways, he looked like the manboy I remembered, except older and two or three times bigger. He was even more handsome than my memories recalled, that was for sure. I had pictures of my childhood, of one or two of Matti's birthdays with his older cousin sulking in the background behind a giant steak with a candle in it—he only had cake or cupcakes when his mom brought them to school to help him fit in, and he'd always forced down a single bite before handing whatever it was off to me to polish off.

Henri might not have been a fixture in my life like Matti had been, but he had still made an impact in his own way—mostly on my hormones and in my daydreams.

Right then, his nostrils flared some more, and I figured he was still trying to get a whiff of me, except he couldn't. He could smell my skin and hair, but not the parts of me that made me magical too. Only in a different way.

Tough.

Thick, dark eyebrows scrunched together on his ruggedly cut face. His voice sounded like rumpled velvet when he asked slowly, drawing every word out in a way that emphasized how confusing my presence had to be, "What are you?"

I smiled up at him. "A Pisces. You?"

Someone made a sound, and there was no way it was anyone other than Sienna.

Adult Henri's head jerked back at my answer. His forehead furrowed before that yellowish-orange-ish gaze raked my face again. "*Cricket?*"

I burst out laughing. "Wow. I haven't heard that in forever." *Cricket.* I grinned, so pleased he hadn't forgotten me after all. "Hi, Fluffy," I greeted him. "How have you been? Can I have my boy back?"

Henri Blackrock, the biggest wolf *and* man I had ever seen, blinked at me. He'd said my nickname, but it was like he still couldn't wrap his head around it from the way the lines at his forehead got even deeper. Even his nostrils flared a little more.

And on second glance, his clothing was a little dirty too. Too dusty for it to be casual. He looked how I did when I got done rolling around with Duncan.

What was up with that?

Henri's gaze took me in like he had no idea what he was seeing, his eyes roaming my face, then sweeping lower, then lower . . .

Two back-to-back choking sounds that I would have bet money were courtesy of Matti and Sienna were the cue his body needed to instantly tense even more than it already had been, and in the next moment, he held Duncan out.

"Thank you." My palms and fingers glided over the backs of his as I took my boy and pulled him into my chest, meeting Henri's intense gaze afterward. I smiled at him some more.

Short, dark lashes fell over incredible amber eyes. He was looking at me. Really freaking watching me.

It had to be driving him nuts not being able to smell my magic. Werewolves were very scent-sual creatures, after all.

Scent-sual . . . I needed to whisper that one to Sienna later. She'd get a kick out of it.

Chances were, he was trying to reconcile the girl he'd last known with the person I'd grown into. Even Matti had done a double take the first time he'd seen me after my magic presented itself. Except all he'd done to verify my identity was peel back my eyelid, then say, "*Let me smell your fart.*"

I hadn't—farted that was—but I did smack him in the gut with the back of my hand, and that had done the trick.

"I almost had a heart attack, if anyone cares," Matti shared before literally sliding between us, facing his older cousin. "How's it going, bro?" he said, his tone dry like this whole scene hadn't just been a shit show. "Thanks for not calling me back."

Off to the side, Sienna caught my attention while she stood by the kids, her face paler than usual. She mouthed, *You okay?*

Physically? I'd been better, considering it had taken everything in me not to groan when I'd gotten up, and I'd almost blacked out with rage at thinking Duncan was in danger, but otherwise? I gave her a thumbs-up before taking a step away from Matti's back to get a better angle of the two men standing a foot apart, taking in their similarities and differences since it had been so long since the last time I'd seen them together. Not since the funeral.

Matti wasn't short at six foot three, but Henri was taller by a couple inches minimum. Other than that, where Matti's skin tone was a tan slightly darker than mine, Henri's was a perfect mix of two very different ancestries—a heavily indigenous side that I *assumed* had to be Amarok based off his size and family connection to Matti, while the other was descended from Scandinavia . . . if my memory served me correctly.

Their hair color wasn't all that similar. Matti's was a dark brown, and Henri's was a distinct shade of black that might have a touch of gray in it, but I couldn't confirm because of our height difference.

The truth was, there wasn't much I knew about the man my best friend was related to. He was a decade older than us. When we were children, they hadn't spent a whole lot of time together, considering the age difference. Henri would come and visit for the summers before he'd moved in with Matti's family for almost a year after he'd graduated high school.

After that, it had become even rarer to see him. He'd joined something—the military, maybe? Or had he just moved away? I couldn't remember, and it wasn't as if Matti talked about him. I had only learned that he eventually lived on a special ranch after Henri had come around and become Matti's guardian.

Irises a color I hadn't seen on anyone else other than him flicked back in my direction over his cousin's shoulder, then landed on the puppy in my arms who was still growling like the tiniest chainsaw in the universe. The notch between Henri's eyebrows went nowhere. If anything, it got even deeper as the line of his jaw went even more defined, like he was suddenly gritting his teeth. His chest—very noticeably muscular under the dusty long-sleeved white T-shirt he had on with the sleeves shoved up his thick forearms—rose and fell as he watched us before returning his attention to Matti.

He had a wound on his elbow that was bleeding too, I noticed with interest.

There was no way he'd gotten that tackling me.

Look at me being observant. Sienna was going to have to start calling me Nina Holmes.

"What are you doing here?" the big man asked, his tone not exactly what I'd call welcoming.

That didn't bother Matti. "Hi, Matti. Missed you too," my friend mocked in a deeper voice than usual before holding his arms out wide.

The other man hesitated before raising his arms as well and wrapping them around his not-so-little cousin. One Henri cheek met a Matti cheek as they thumped each other on the back. They were so cute.

Just as quickly as the hug started, Henri pretty much shoved him away. "Why are you here?"

"Hi, Sienna." Matti chose to ignore him again, talking in that different voice, gesturing toward where his wife stood, still on alert.

Henri didn't look over, but he did raise his voice to call out, "Hi, Sienna."

Kind of rude, I thought, but Sienna didn't exactly seem all that disappointed not to give him a hug. "Hi, Henri," she greeted him in return. She was smoothing her hands up and down the front of her bell bottoms, one of her nervous gestures.

Matti hiked his thumb over his shoulder. "And you remember Big Jaws—Nina—and Mini Jaws is—" A scream tore through the air, cutting Matti off.

All of us turned to find a body that had two long, brown, slender legs and an upper torso that was very much a woman with a tank top running through the woods by the homes on the other side of the main building.

"Uh-oh," Shiloh muttered loudly.

"Pascal!" another voice, a male one, bellowed from another direction. It was a man in jeans tearing through the woods, heading over too.

I glanced at Pascal and watched his already small body deflate.

But only for a second.

His hands formed fists, and out of nowhere, he started speed walking . . . right on over to me.

Me?

He stopped at my side, hooked a foot around mine, and his fingers reached for my shirt.

Did he expect me to protect him?

When I tried to get Sienna or Matti's attention so they could see what was happening, I caught Henri's instead. His gaze swung to Pascal. Big Henri Blackrock frowned even more.

"What happened?" he asked slowly to no one in particular.

There was so much authority in his tone that even I felt the need to answer him. How did he do that? Was it practice or was it magic?

"You're going to be grounded for the rest of your life!" the satyr woman shouted at the top of her lungs while running.

"Not just this life but the next one too, Pascal!" the man on the opposite side of the woods called out, also not slowing down.

"What. Happened?" Henri demanded again, louder that time, voice even gruffer, his frown morphing once more to a scowl.

Time had been good to him, I noted. Real, real good, I confirmed, really taking him in. Henri looked like a mountain man now if I'd ever seen one. His massive size, all those muscles, his clothes . . .

He was the complete opposite of his cousin in his khakis.

I could admit it already: he was *unbelievably* handsome.

Was he married?

The tiny chainsaw in my arms got louder all of a sudden.

Stroking my hand down Duncan's side, I whispered, "It's fine, Donut. It's okay. Thank you for protecting me. I know you could've messed him up if you wanted to—"

Amber eyes caught mine, and I shut my mouth.

Sensitive hearing, *right*.

"I cannot believe you, Shiloh!" the satyr woman was still shouting as she got within twenty feet of us, her steps finally slowing down as she fumed. "What were you *thinking*, honey? We've been looking everywhere for you!"

"Somebody needs to tell me what's going on. *Now*," Henri demanded.

Somebody was bossy.

"They snuck off," the man who was approaching answered. "We've been looking for them. The elders called saying someone brought them back."

One glance down confirmed Pascal, the wolf boy, had his cheek pressed against my hip. I didn't need a good nose to tell he was nervous. I set my hand on top of his head, not sure whether to comfort him or peel him off me. If Duncan had pulled this crap . . .

I'd swear Henri stood up even straighter, and he was already crazy tall. "Again?"

I winced. It was going from bad to worse. Again?

"Again," the woman confirmed as she got to us, her face pale and strained. She was worked up for sure.

And wow, the bottom half of her *was* goatlike. She was shorter than she'd seemed at a distance. At most, the top of her head reached my shoulder. She suddenly blinked, her brown irises flicking in my direction, her nose twitching noticeably.

I lifted my hand at her.

The best approach when meeting possibly skittish strangers was to give the initial impression that you were harmless.

Because sometimes the absence of my scent also made people upset. They thought I was trying to hide something, which I *was*, but not in a way anyone needed to worry about, unless they meant me or my loved ones harm. And even then, I had hesitated to do what needed to be done before. Not once but twice. They weren't my finest moments.

Earlier with the swamp thing . . . it had been a step in the right direction, but . . .

"She's nice, Mom," Shiloh said softly, apparently reading the room. "Nina saved us."

The adult satyr didn't look convinced, but for once in my life, I felt about ten feet tall.

I had a child I barely knew clinging to me, and *two* defending me—one a stranger and the other my greatest treasure. I didn't think I'd ever felt so special before. Actually, I was sure I hadn't.

A warm nose nudged at my neck, and I stroked Duncan's side some more.

"Saved you from what?" the man who had been hollering at Pascal asked, his eyes darting around the group standing in the lot. His nostrils quivered, and I watched him glance at me, look away, and then look again.

His eyebrows went up. He took another sniff. His expression was a curious one. I raised my hand at him too and got a wave right back.

"We aren't completely sure," Matti spoke up, drawing my attention back to him, "but it might have been a Jenny Greenteeth."

"A what?" It was the man who threw out the question.

I couldn't believe Matti knew what it was, and I didn't, but I had never really looked into English mythology much. I was going to need to brush up on it some time.

"A river crone," Henri answered, the big frown still on his face. "You saw one here? *On our land?*"

He had a nice voice, mad and all, I decided. It kind of reminded me of a lion somehow, the way he managed to bellow and project.

The satyr woman stepped back, and he must have noticed because he wiped the frown off his face and replaced it with a neutral expression instantly.

Matti nodded. "She knew she was trespassing. I didn't ask her what she was, but she was tall and looked like half a Ninja Turtle. Smelled like shit too. She threatened all of them."

The thick line of Henri's brow furrowed, replacing the almost serene expression he'd worn for all of ten seconds. "What happened to the Jenny Greenteeth?"

Matti smiled. "Nina happened."

Every word that had come out of his mouth was the truth,

and yet he'd managed to keep a lot a secret too. I loved how sneaky he could be.

"She went east, if you want to look for her," my friend added.

Pascal's maybe-dad and Henri both visibly tensed, growls vibrating from their chests simultaneously. The other man was around Matti's height, his eyes light colored, his hair around the same shade. He was definitely magical; he felt a little wild, like all werewolves did.

"I don't think she'll be back, but—" He shrugged. "—we couldn't put the kids at risk."

Against my leg, the wolf boy poked at me. "She farted she was so scared."

Every adult looked at the boy who, by that point, was half hidden behind me.

The man, who I hadn't seen in forever, let his gaze roam the circle around him, locking on every single person, man, woman, and child. The muscle in his jaw tightened in the process. Then he said, using that impressive, demanding voice he seemed to have a master's degree in using, "Everyone"—those amber eyes again swept from person to person, landing on me for what I felt was a microsecond longer than everyone else—"has some explaining to do."

Chapter Four

"This wasn't exactly how I thought the day was going to go," I whispered to Sienna before taking a bite out of the piece of beef jerky in my hand. It was one of my best batches, if I did say so myself. Instead of using premixed seasoning, I'd started experimenting with making my own blend. It had either been that or spending a huge chunk of my paycheck buying Duncan treats every month. The idea of underfeeding him was something that kept me up at night; it wasn't like there was a growth chart on the internet for what I could expect from him.

He was a bougie little donut.

Sienna snickered from her spot beside me on the gravel ground with our backs to the front of my truck, both of us trying to avoid the bugs splattered on the grill, my puppy between us having a stare down with the white mini wolf sitting about six feet away, doing the same thing right back. I'd known he was on the small side, considering his growth had basically stunted after a few months, but in the presence of the white wolf, who was probably five times his weight, it was very, very apparent.

I didn't think either of them had blinked in a while, but I wasn't sure considering I'd been eavesdropping the crap out of the conversation that the satyr woman, Henri, and Pascal's maybe-dad were having as they interviewed Matti and the two boys on what exactly had gone down leading up to all this. From what I understood, the kids had, in the past, taken off on adventures that they weren't supposed to go on, and they had done it again.

Except this time, they'd come across a "river crone" who had been ready to eat them. The river crone was a mythical being who should *not* have been anywhere near here from what the escalating body language in the group confirmed—and from the brief conversation that Henri had with someone on a cell phone, telling them to "find her."

I was a *little* in awe of him. Who was this man asking for explanations, throwing out orders that people listened to, and demanding searches? He was not the man-boy of my memories that sulked and brooded quietly in the corner, too grown up to deal with Matti's and my BS.

Ripping a piece of jerky into thirds, I popped one in my mouth, held the second out toward Duncan Donut until he edged his head closer—not breaking eye contact in the process—and took his piece from the side. Only then did I toss the final chunk at the white pup. It hit her on the forehead.

She ignored it.

"What do you think so far?" Sienna whispered as the group conversation got even more intense when the wolf boy said something the adults must have not liked. Even Matti winced.

"I like the drama so far. It's almost as entertaining as campground parking lot dynamics are," I told her, letting my gaze drift to the black body between us. His tail was up straight, the flame back to a solid blue instead of the ice-blue one that had taken over when he'd been ready to fight MegaWolf in my honor. It wasn't that I couldn't believe he'd done it—I could. But it still shocked me.

This little bitty boy had defended me, outsized and all. He had risked his life for *me*. Me.

I would do anything for him, I thought once more.

Which was why I was hoping someone who lived here would consider marrying me.

A part of me couldn't believe I'd actually just thought that.

I was willing to marry a stranger to be here, in this quiet land with fencing, big gates, half-goat half-human children, hairy green monsters that wanted to eat them, and werewolves bigger than my first car who were also my best friend's family.

I had made a rare being fart. I'd had two children claiming I'd saved them. My boy with red eyes had bitten a werewolf's tail.

None of the fairy tales my parents used to read me at night could have prepared me for any of this.

Except that thought led me to another, and then another, and I turned to Sienna, remembering what I was pretty sure I'd overheard.

"Question. Did Matti actually talk to Henri before we drove here?" I whispered, trying not to sound suspicious but pretty much failing.

Her nose wrinkled. "Huh?"

"I swear Henri asked what we were doing here, and Matti said something sarcastic about him not answering his calls," I explained. "He said he was going to text him, but . . ."

Her face darkened, eyes getting squinty the longer she sat there. She plucked at the spaghetti-strap of her pale-yellow top—a color I could never pull off, but she could perfectly. "He never actually said he spoke to him, did he?"

We looked at each other.

"I'm going to kill him," I warned her.

And my friend nodded like the person I wanted to murder wasn't the love of her life. "I'll help you."

We both turned to glare at Matti, who must have sensed it from the way his attention shot over to us, and he waved like he'd never done a wrong thing in his life.

That was such a Matti thing to do if he was desperate, and I had been pretty desperate the night I'd showed up to their apartment asking for help. I wasn't really going to kill him, but I might get Sienna to twist his nipple for me.

In the meantime, we sat there munching on jerky from a silicone sandwich bag in my fanny pack, and I released some deep breaths, my skin feeling kind of tickly, my lungs sucking up the fresh air like they had been deprived all their lives. The magic that lived in my gut stirred in response, a ball of squiggly warmth.

What was it about here? I had traveled so much over the

years, and while some places had wonderful vibes and traces of magic, no other place had ever felt like this one. Not even close.

I peeked at her, but Sienna seemed totally unfazed. Even a little bored. What was she staring at?

She answered my question a second later. "If that satyr looks over here again, I'm going to get up and go have a calm conversation with her about how rude she's being."

That got me to beam. "You're so scary, but what she needs to worry about is my attack hound right here. Did you *see* him?"

Sienna patted the furry butt cheek closest to her. "I saw him all right. The boy needs a steak dinner for that."

The good boy's ears twitched, but he *still* didn't break eye contact with Agnes, even as he said "*Yes*" in my head.

Yes, he agreed he was a good boy and he needed steak. He was always listening.

I smacked his other butt cheek for good measure, just as the adult satyr turned to look over *again* real quick.

I didn't say a word, and Sienna pressed her lips together tight, smelling whatever emotion the woman was releasing. Wariness, more than likely. Possibly even a little bit of fear; herbivores were like that, from what I'd been told. I palmed my bracelet. If she was like this now, what would it be like if I took it off? Shiloh had been fine, more than fine, but . . .

A warm hand slipped into mine, and my best friend since the age of fifteen gave it a squeeze. "I love you, Nina. I'm glad we made it, and I hope things work out."

I let go of her hand and threw my arm around her, my head going to her shoulder. Somehow, she planted a kiss on my temple. "I love you too," I told her. "Thank you for coming with us."

Loud sighs came from the group, and we watched the woman put a hand on Shiloh's shoulder before leading him down a path that curved around the right side of the big building. The boy's head was down, his shoulders slumped, and I really didn't think I was imagining his hooves dragging behind him. The man stayed talking to Henri for a minute longer before they nodded in agreement over something. Henri dropped into a crouch and leaned in close to Pascal, cupping the back of the boy's head with his hand. He said something that had the little boy gesturing with his hands before nodding as well.

Then the werewolf man pressed his cheek to the top of Pascal's head, and the little boy tucked himself into his neck and gave Henri a hug. With a scruff to his hair, Henri stood and gave him an expression that was totally a chastising one. The boy and the other man turned and headed down another path, but I watched as Pascal paused, looked over, and gave me a wave before continuing his march. His maybe-dad glanced over as well, in the middle of a frown. He lifted his hand briefly, mouthed what I thought was *thank you*, and kept going too.

Only then did Henri turn to where we were; his lips started moving. He still didn't seem very happy. Matti gestured us over, his eyebrows up.

"It's showtime," I told Sienna as I stood, and beside me, Duncan got to his feet, attention *still* on the white wolf pup. Somebody was a little obsessed. He was too young to have a crush, wasn't he? Or was he just in love with the familiarity of someone who looked similar-ish to him? Anytime we'd been around a dog before, he had never really cared much for them. But this was totally different. He'd never seen Matti or Sienna in their wolf forms.

It was like he was seeing himself in the mirror for the first time and couldn't believe it.

"Agnes," Henri's demanding voice called out.

Uh-oh.

I wasn't sure how I was expecting him to react, but it sure wasn't the way he did.

"I'm glad you're back safe and weren't hurt," he told the white wolf in a voice that was somehow stern and careful at the same time. "But now it's your turn to deal with the consequences. Go inside, tell the elders what you did, and see what your punishment is. They're waiting in the library."

The ball of poofy anger had already gotten to her paws when my donut did, but she barked at Henri.

"Now," his reply was no-nonsense, sounding very much like a dad. "You knew what you were doing. We had this talk last time."

The amount of attitude in her body couldn't be ignored as she lowered her head and stayed in that position for longer than I ever would have imagined—she was pushing it, defying his orders, even I knew that—but then she took off in the direction of the main house, disappearing around the back of it.

Matti's cousin blew out a long breath, which didn't do anything to the tension padding his body. He focused on where we were, and the man I hadn't seen since he'd been in his twenties dipped his chin. "Thank you for helping the children."

He was talking to me. "Sure, anytime."

His hands went to his waist, his jaw—a very defined one—ticked to the side. "Now, you going to come over here so you can tell me what this visit's about or are we going to keep yelling at each other?" Henri drawled. Not just bossy but blunt too.

We're here for the pup who has a paw on top of my foot, who can't live around humans anymore.

Instead of saying that, I reached down, scratched the top of my donut's head, and held out both hands to him.

"*Yes*," he told me, using his gift more often.

I scooped him up before marching over, Sienna at my side. Then I did what I'd told Matti I would do: I let him handle it. For now.

Or that had been my plan.

It seemed like Matti wasn't fast enough with an explanation when his cousin got impatient two seconds later.

"You didn't come all this way by accident. What's going on?" Henri asked . . . all four of us, really, even if his attention in that moment was centered on the puppy balanced on my forearm, legs hanging off either side of it. His long ears drooping.

He was so cute. He looked like a prince. I would even go as far as to say he made me think of a god in that position, shiny black coat an obvious sign he was well taken care of. The fire obsidian around his neck a subtle flash of color against his body.

Duncan gazed at Henri steadily, making it very, very clear he was something more. He listened, and he understood everything that was said to him and in front of him. He always had. For his age, he followed rules more than I ever could have hoped for.

"It's not an accident," Matti agreed, finally finding his words. He made a funny face. "I explained why in the voicemails, if you'd listened to them."

The mountain of a man he was related to blinked.

"We're hoping someone might recognize what Duncan is," Matti kept going. "He's the pup in Nina's arms, if you didn't get that."

Henri didn't move a muscle.

"*And* we wanted to see if the elders would be willing to accept two new members to the community," Matti wrapped it up neatly, leaving the final part of our visit out in the open, just hanging in the air like a wish upon a star.

The whole marrying part implied.

I'd been watching Henri's face, and *that* got him. Dark eyebrows rose on caramel cream skin, and even his clear eyes widened. I wasn't sure a man who looked like him could peek at someone, but that was the closest word I could come up with to describe the way his gaze flicked over to me for a split second. "You're serious?"

Was he scoffing?

"Yeah," Matti confirmed.

"Here?"

He was definitely scoffing.

My friend nodded.

"You and Sienna?"

Matti shook his head, and his older cousin's expression hit a new level of disbelief.

"Cricket and the pup?" he asked slowly.

Sienna took a step closer to me, asking under her breath through the side of her mouth, "Why does he keep calling you that?"

I only whispered, "Later," because I felt the need to jump in, even though I'd told Matti I'd let him handle it.

"I understand the rules about getting married, and I'm okay with them," I spoke up, wanting Henri to be aware that *I* did get what was going on and was willing to do what was needed to get permission to stay here. Other than my two closest friends, I didn't have anyone or anything tying me down. My parents had retired to Mexico, and they weren't coming back. I couldn't exactly move there now, with Duncan being what he was.

Amber irises met mine, and I tried smiling at him.

Maybe I should've kept trying to hide my nervousness, but it was getting exhausting, and honestly, if Henri opened up his senses to smell how I was feeling, he was going to be able to tell anyway.

Henri's eyes narrowed in reaction. Not exactly nice. Not in curiosity or interest either. But in the middle of a thought that could have gone either way. Wary.

Once upon a time, I'd been his little cousin's friend who he had tolerated slightly better than his own relative, possibly because I was a girl, or maybe because he felt bad for me. We had never been *friends*, but he had been nice enough. Just the right amount of attentive that had lured me into hoping to run into him during his visits.

And with a face like the one he had now, I could understand why. The only modeling he would ever be qualified to do was maybe the new face for that paper towel brand with a lumberjack on them. But he'd be perfect at it. That bone structure, those forearms, and boots? Sold.

Matti cleared his throat, bringing everyone's focus back to him. "You see the pup, Henri. His eyes. His tail."

"I see 'em," Henri agreed a moment before scrubbing a palm over his forehead, the spot of red still bright near his elbow, threatening to stain his shirt.

I unzipped my fanny pack and dug around until I found what I was looking for, then I held it out.

Henri eyed my face, then my balled-up fist. But he didn't hesitate long before extending his hand, palm up against my palm down, cupping his fingers beneath mine. I dropped the

Band-Aid into it. I always carried a couple around in my fanny pack, along with ten other things, mostly snacks, a poop bag, a glove or two, and a couple baby wipes. "Your elbow is bleeding," I told him.

The muscle in his jaw flexed, but he took in the Band-Aid sitting in his palm, then shoved it into his pocket instead of using it.

It was the thought that counted, I supposed.

"Right," Henri went on as if nothing had happened. "There's no use in you telling this story twice, and this decision isn't just up to me," he said. That bold gaze worked its way down to what I thought was Duncan but realized it wasn't when he tipped his chin in the direction of my hand. "If that bracelet is doing what I think it's doing, take it off. Whatever the pup has on, remove it too. We can't help him if his magic is hidden, and I haven't seen you in a long time. I need to know what you're hiding."

Hiding was such a strong word.

But it wasn't like I'd expected any different. I'd want the same thing if I was in his shoes. Probably more. It had been obvious to me from the moment we'd gotten out of the car that the people here had something precious they were protecting: magical children for starters. A forest with so much goodness . . . power . . . magic, whatever you wanted to call it, that I wanted to roll around in the leaves. Pick up tree bark and tape it to my skin. Bottle the scent and take a bath with it.

This was a community of people who I was told wanted to live in peace as themselves in an adorable village setting hidden in a small nook of the world. They had so much to lose, more than I ever could have imagined.

So I nodded at him, then turned to Sienna and held Duncan out. "Will you take his collar off, please?"

She did just that, releasing the button with the tip of her nail. With it in her hand, I suddenly stopped sensing her magic at the same time Duncan's strong, subtle one pressed against mine. She reached for my other arm and tugged my bracelet off. She put it on too, twisting her wrist this way and that way, as if testing it, but it didn't make the person wearing it feel any different.

Here went freaking nothing.

Because there I suddenly was. We both were. Duncan and I in our full glories. More vulnerable than if I'd been naked, in some ways. I took the bracelet off from time to time, but it wasn't often, and never when I was around people like us, unless there was a statement I wanted or needed to make, like earlier. That was rare. I wasn't the competitive type.

I watched and heard Henri take a tentative sniff, then another. Testing. After a moment, his brawny chest literally puffed out as he took such a deep inhale it would have made a yoga teacher proud when he held it for second after second.

If I hadn't known he wasn't human before, I would have then. His eyes widened, then widened a little more. His thick throat bobbed.

A couple of times, when I'd been younger, he'd let me sit next to him on the couch or at the dining room table. But back then, my true heritage had been a mystery. In Matti's words, I hadn't smelled magical, but I'd smelled magical. Those around me had been able to tell I wasn't human-human, but what I was hadn't been apparent enough. The same way that Duncan had been before his own nature had exploded across him physically and mentally.

Henri released his deep breath.

That stubbled jaw clenched even more somehow.

Slowly, he turned to his cousin and stared at him, hard.

Matti looked at him right back. Straight-faced. But there was a glint in his eye . . .

I didn't think I imagined that Henri's voice came out different, maybe slightly hoarse as he reached out. "I'll take those, Sienna."

My friend took the bracelet off and handed it over, along with the collar, and at the same glacial speed that he'd looked at his cousin, Henri brought both up to his nose. His chest rose and fell again. Then again. And for the second time, his intense gaze returned to Matti.

Henri's attention slid back in my direction, and I smiled. *He needed to like us.* I rocked up to the balls of my feet and let the eighteen years of living among their kind help me take the next step. "Do you want to smell my neck?" I offered, thinking about how many times someone—werewolves mostly—had done that to me. With permission of course. It was like a crash course in getting to know someone, Matti had explained. You could learn a whole lot of things about people from their odor, and the least important of them was whether or not they used enough deodorant.

Henri's jaw flexed again. "Do I want to . . . ?" He sounded a little strangled.

Shifting Duncan's weight on my arm, I tapped my neck with my other hand. "Smell me," I repeated. Why was he making it seem like I was offering him a lit stick of dynamite?

I slid my gaze toward Matti, who was looking real funny at his family member.

Taking a whiff of another person wasn't unheard of. It wasn't weird. If anything, it was a formality. Good manners. An olive branch from me to him.

There was a lot I didn't want him knowing *yet*, but this was nothing.

At least it should've been nothing.

"Or not," I muttered, trying not to feel dejected.

Maybe I'd finally met the one werewolf who wasn't a Nina fan.

But I refused to give up hope. Slowly, I lifted my shoulders and asked, "What about a hug?" We used to know each other. A reminder of the past might help.

It didn't.

There was more staring. Eventually, he cleared his throat and looked away. "I'm going to hold on to these"—he moved his hand indicating our jewelry—"while we're inside. I'll give them back later. Let's find the elders."

I gave him a thumbs-up, not sure if he was wary over this whole situation, or just me, or Duncan, or what.

Henri had always been a serious potato.

But I guess it was a good thing he wasn't telling us to get back into my truck or growling because he couldn't control his dislike of Duncan or me. Henri didn't seem overly interested in my donut either. He hadn't focused on his tail half as much as I'd expected him to.

Maybe he knew something I didn't.

I guess we'd see.

For now, we'd head inside and go from there. I'd forgotten all about these "elders" that Matti had mentioned. They were the main leadership here, the decision-makers. He'd explained it on the drive in a short, vague way: Henri was the CEO of this place, and they were his board of directors. One couldn't act without the other.

With that, Henri headed in the direction of the main building. Matti followed, waving us to do the same. I held Duncan against my chest and took in the forest as we headed to the massive log structure. Nature was nothing new to me, but I couldn't ignore or get over how this place felt. From the way Duncan's sniffer was going too, tipped up high, maybe I wasn't the only one pleasantly surprised and soaking up whatever special stuff was around here.

Now, without distractions, I'd swear there was something different about the trees. The bark wrapped around the trunks had a texture I'd never seen before, almost iridescent at a distance. They also seemed bigger and greener than any others I'd ever seen. In a way, they reminded me of the redwood forests I'd stayed by several times—there was something epic and timeless about them.

Rumor and folklore claimed that there were places in the world where magic *was* stronger. Where it was embedded more deeply in the environment than in other places. Those stories told that it was where parts of the Great Meteor—the unknown mass that had supposedly been responsible for bringing magic to Earth, according to ancient civilizations across the globe—had landed and subsequently turned normal people into what they became: legends and mythological entities.

I'd heard arguments that there was a chance we had always been around and someone in the past had made up stories to better explain how magic was possible, and maybe that was true. Maybe there had been a meteor filled with something special that changed the very essence of the humans it had come into contact with and made them something different. Or maybe those magical beings *had* always been around, and people needed some way to explain it. Without a time machine, who would ever know the truth?

Maybe the very old ones, like my neighbor was supposed to have been.

Regardless, this place made me wonder if the meteor theory was true and fragments had landed here thousands of years ago.

Or I just needed something to help me understand how this may or may not be a real-life magical forest with mythical creatures running around in it. Which then got me wondering . . . *did authors and screenwriters come up with enchanted forests after visiting places like this? Were they based off reality?* Why had I never thought of that before?

"You coming?" Sienna set her palm between my shoulder blades, forcing me to shelve my questions for later.

I nodded.

We went along, going straight for the front of the main building where my friend held one of the doors open. Henri was waiting inside. Duncan stuck his neck out while his nose continued twitching, taking in all the scents. The foyer we walked into had two connected hallways, one to the left and right, another straight across from the front door, leading toward the back of the building.

"Follow me," Henri instructed after Matti closed the door, heading down the hall that led to the rear.

We did, the silence so loud within the quiet, plain walls. There wasn't artwork, a clock, or anything decorative. Not really a surprise. Every werewolf home I'd ever been in had been the same. Even Matti and Sienna, as bougie as they could be and with the exception of their clothing, were pretty minimalist. Now ogres? They loved their little treasures.

"How have you been?" Matti asked his cousin from all the way at the end of our line. I wasn't sure how it happened, but somehow, I'd ended up directly behind Henri. Duncan had his head stretched forward, trying to smell him discreetly without being noticed. With his floppy ears, it was so cute because it wasn't sneaky at all.

"Fine," Henri answered him in a clipped tone. "Busy."

That was informative.

Matti thought the same thing. "I figured that when you'd barely respond to my texts the last six months."

"I replied," Henri answered with a grumble that might have held a touch of guilt to it. "There's been a lot going on. We finished expanding parts of the ranch last month, and I've been putting in a lot of overtime."

"Still working at the sheriff's office then?"

"Still." Henri Blackrock was a sheriff? Or a deputy? "Still doing aviation consulting?"

My friend answered, "Still." There was a pause. "You get into a fight before we got here, or did you punch yourself in the face?"

The self-control it took me not to snicker . . .

That must have caught Henri off guard too because his pace slowed for a second. "It was more of a disagreement than a fight," he answered cryptically, and I didn't even know him and could tell he was being weird.

Mr. Curious wasn't letting it go. "With?"

"Dominic" was the one and only answer he provided.

There was another pause "Over?"

Nothing.

"Leadership?"

Henri's reply was a single low grunt.

How long was this hall? I wondered as we passed a smaller hallway, then another that branched out from the one we were on. This place was even bigger on the inside than it had seemed from the exterior. Peeking around Henri's frame, I found that we were almost to the back of the building, and with a few more steps, he turned suddenly to the right, through a doorway and directly into a room.

In it was the biggest living area I'd ever seen. Multiple couches surrounded a television, there was a small bar area with stools in front of it, and a table that belonged in a conference room. At it were older adults whose magic felt very contained and low. One of them had a single eye . . . in the middle of his forehead.

An enchanted forest, a green swamp thing, a couple of satyrs, a werewolf the size of Falkor, and a cyclops.

Where exactly had Matti brought us?

"Over here." Henri indicated toward the table and the empty chairs at it. "Sit."

It was time to shine and, like I'd told Duncan, be on our best behavior. I took a seat right in the middle. Matti slipped into the chair beside mine, while Sienna decided to play bodyguard and stand directly behind us. Henri stayed off to the side with his arms crossed over that chest the size of Rhode Island, his expression still that tight one that didn't tell me if he was aggravated about the Jenny Greenteeth, his cousin being here, my and Duncan's very existence, or maybe it always looked like that.

The six men, women, and cyclops stopped talking the moment we settled in.

Like a line of dominoes, each one of them slowly caught sight, or possibly smell, of my puppy. Every single set of eyeballs went wide. Then wider.

One of the females delicately gasped. The cyclops rubbed a hand over his single eye. A man with wire-rimmed glasses leaned forward, pushing his frames up his nose . . .

"Dear gods," the man exhaled as Duncan let out the cutest yawn, not even slightly worried about his audience.

But my body went on high alert anyway, especially when I realized the man was focused on *me*, not Duncan.

I hoped he wasn't one of those people. Some older magical beings were way more superstitious than younger ones. Nothing I could do about it though.

"He's a good boy," I claimed out loud, just in case anyone was thinking otherwise.

And *that* earned *me* the rest of their attention and similar reactions. The woman who had gasped did it again but slightly fainter, and the cyclops rubbed his eye—a blue one—one more time. It was a striking blue too. The man with the glasses sat up straight in his seat.

For some reason, I had a flashback of the time a woman had thrown holy water at me that she'd carried around in a necklace. I'd been seventeen and on vacation with my parents. Why she had holy water on her was beyond me, but she'd been sorely disappointed when all I did was frown. It had been shortly after that, that I started wearing an obsidian bracelet.

Some people had problems.

And it had only been years later that I'd regretted not asking why her reaction had been so violent. Maybe she had known something I didn't. She may have also tried exorcising me if I'd done that. I was never going to know.

Matti cleared his throat beside me. He clasped his hands together on the table and bowed his head. "Elders, thank you for allowing us this visit and for the gift of your time and attention. If you remember, I'm Matti—"

The cyclops waved a wrinkled, heavy hand. "Be quiet, Matti. No one here has forgotten the time you lit the kitchen on fire."

I'd never heard that story.

The one-eyed man snorted. "I'm sure I'm not alone when I say I would rather hear the young lady explain what you're doing here."

All right, I guess I was winging it then.

I pressed my lips together and tried to give the group the friendliest smile I had in me. "I'm Nina," I said. "Nina Popoca." I lifted my donut a little, grabbing his front legs in the process and then holding them up toward them. It made him look extra cute and like a stuffed animal. "This is Duncan. Thank you for allowing us to experience the magic in your community."

That must have been the right thing to start with because all the elders nodded. It was the man with glasses who spoke next, his eyes a little narrowed, as he smoothed his hands down the front of the vest he had layered over a button-down shirt. "Hello, Nina. You smell young, but sometimes our ages can be deceiving, can't they?"

That was . . . an interesting comment to make.

It meant he either already suspected something or . . . he was wondering about childbearing years. I hoped?

"Most of the time, I feel old and young at the same time," I told the man carefully, trying to read his body language. "I'm thirty-two."

Out of the corner of my eye, Henri shifted his weight and crossed his arms again.

The elder nodded stiffly, still too watchful. "Tell us why you're here."

As I adjusted Duncan on my lap, he set his head on top of the table, and I bumped Matti's foot with mine for moral support to get through this next part. "We're here, elders, because I need help," I explained. With my chin, I gestured to the puppy who was busy looking at them. "I didn't give birth to him, but we've been together since he was a newborn.

"Two months ago, he went from appearing like a normal puppy"—that was a subjective description, but hopefully they understood—"to his tail and eyes changing and becoming what you see now," I explained. "I need to know how to fulfill his needs as he keeps growing. I've tried figuring out what kind of being he is, and I have a few guesses, but I don't know for sure. The only knowledge I have of raising a pup is what I know from the wolves I grew up around, and they've all told me how important having a pack is at this age."

A few of the elders started whispering to each other. Glasses, I noticed, wasn't one of them. He was sitting very, very still.

"Matti said you're all very wise and accepting." He hadn't said that, not exactly, but I wasn't above sucking up. "More than anything, I really hope that you might let us live here since this is a secure community. The world out there isn't safe for him. I've already had people try to steal him, and I don't want to put him at risk. I want him to be happy, healthy, and safe, and I hope this place might be able to provide all that for him."

There was stirring, and looks were cast that didn't make me feel all that optimistic. Or maybe I was just expecting the worst. They had been polite so far, but they were picky about their privacy and community. That much was obvious.

The cyclops narrowed his eye. "You're in danger?"

"Not anymore, only in the moment," I explained. "On two different occasions recently, people tried to take him, but I took care of the problem." I paused and held Duncan's foot. "They won't be an issue again. We aren't bringing any danger or attention here."

Matti huffed beside me. He'd heard the whole story on our first day of driving, and he and Sienna had just about exploded over me keeping those incidents a secret for so long.

"How can you be sure of that?" one of the female elders asked. Her hair was so silver it bordered on pale blue.

"Because there's no way they knew my name. The incidents happened at campgrounds at night. I checked their phones and cars before they . . . were taken away. There weren't any pictures related to us, and there hadn't been any recent calls or texts they'd sent or received." I'd been lucky their phones' facial recognition had worked.

"That doesn't confirm that you can't or won't be followed," the cyclops argued.

They were really going to make me tell them more than I wanted to. But I couldn't say I didn't understand why they needed to make sure I wouldn't be bringing any drama. My hand trailed up to my neck, where it had still hurt up until yesterday. "Every person involved suffered a brain injury and some other wounds. If they ever wake up, the chances of them remembering . . . or being able to communicate again . . . are slim." I tried not to wince. "Very slim."

A small part of me still thought that I had no right to mete out any kind of justice, but another part of me knew it hadn't been justice at all. I'd done what I had to, and I felt bad about it, but I wasn't going to apologize for it either. Both of our lives had been at risk.

I stroked my hand down Duncan's side, his coat so, so soft. Probably from all the sardines he ate. To be honest, out of everything I'd ever done for him, scooping those tiny fish out of their containers was the grossest. Not pulling hair out of his butt after a poop or having him sneeze into my open mouth. Nope. Sardines. I didn't like fish, but I did it every day, and it *still* made me gag. But like the song said, I would do anything for love.

I was here, willing to do what I was willing to do, and Matti and Sienna had come with us, and if that wasn't the four-letter word that had started wars and maybe even ended them, I didn't know what was.

My hand kept going along his side, over his flank, until I could wrap my fingers around the middle of his fluffy tail. I'd teased him before, telling him he had to be half fox with that thing, and he'd given me the stink eye even though I wasn't even sure he knew what a fox was. It would look like a black dust sweeper . . . if it wasn't for the tiny blue flame on the tip of it. I pinched it and smiled as the color flickered around my fingers.

There were multiple gasps, and it was the woman who spoke that time. "But how . . . ?"

Maybe they were letting the incidents go for now.

"It only gets 'hot'"—I used quotation marks with my free hand—"when he's scared or protective." It had changed colors when he'd been trying to save me from the giant werewolf, but I was the only one who'd recognized the signs. "He burned a few of the men who tried to kidnap him. Those were the other injuries they received. But it was in self-defense." It had happened right before I'd taken action. Just thinking about that moment pissed me off all over again because it had been my fault for hesitating.

I reached with my free hand to rub Duncan's ears between my fingers. Multiple sets of eyeballs moved from his relaxed body to the hand I had on him and back. Several nostrils flared again as the elders smelled him—and maybe me too—all while staying quiet, hopefully just intrigued by whatever he was and whatever I was. Two mysteries wrapped in the same tortilla.

I knew better than anyone how much was at stake. It could have been so easy for me to have lived a lonely life. Love could have been something I'd only read about in a fairy tale. I'd thought about it often, how different my life would have turned out without the love of my parents, of Matti and his family, of Sienna and hers. Without Duncan's.

Everything I knew about love and loyalty was because of them and their presence in my life.

You don't spit in Love's eye, my mom had told me once before my body had changed. *You'll make her mad if you do.*

I don't think you can spit in Love's eye, Mom, I had argued.

The face she had given me had been only a little patronizing. *Sí puedes, Nina, and she's not as nice as you'd think.*

It had been an interesting conversation, but I'd taken her words to heart. When life gives you a true love, you keep it.

And that was Duncan for me.

He was special, and I'd known it from the moment I met him, which had been about a heartbeat before I'd fallen in love with him. Up until then, I had always thought love at first sight was BS. An excuse for being horny, if anything. Then he showed up, and I suddenly understood just how the universe could drop something into your existence that your soul recognized belonged there.

Sometimes you learned real quick how you could love something more than you loved yourself.

"How old is he?" the man with the glasses asked quietly but still kind of weird.

"Two years old."

There was a murmur among a few of the elders.

"His magic is strong," he noted softly, attention locked on my donut.

"I know. When he was a baby, he felt magical but faintly, universally. The way most young magical kids do. I had hoped he might be an iron wolf because of his dark hair, or a mix—"

Matti's foot bumped mine beneath the table.

"But since his tail and eyes changed, I started second-guessing that," I finished telling them.

The woman with the silver-blue hair cleared her throat and

leaned forward. "How did you manage to become the child's guardian?"

My life with Duncan started on the night of a full moon.

Which shouldn't have been a surprise, really. Full moons were the time when magic was the strongest. When it pulsed and resonated and reminded those with even the faintest trace of it in their cells that there was something greater out there. Something so powerful that, once a couple thousand years ago, give or take, our ancestors had thought the world was ending when magic streaked across the sky and fell to the earth, or so the stories from so many civilizations said.

It had always made me wonder if the first person to write about mysticism on full moons had been magical. Then I wondered if someone had taken them out for spilling a secret. That was the first thing we were taught the moment our brains could comprehend it: *Don't tell anyone.*

On those special nights, I always had a harder time falling asleep than usual, which was why I'd been awake in the first place when I'd heard something big moving around in the bushes outside of my camper. I'd only been at that state park for two nights at that point, and the first thing the employee who had checked me in had said was "Watch out for coyotes."

Animals didn't concern me. It was everyone else that moved around on two legs that I side-eyed, at least until I got to know them. As many good people as there were in the world, it always felt like there were ten times as many not-so-good ones.

But the truth was, I hadn't thought much of the noises going on outside my RV at first. By that point, I'd been living in it full-time for almost three years, and I'd heard and seen some things. For the most part, I liked staying at RV parks more than I enjoyed parking in the middle of nowhere. Being able to plug in to power and drain my gray tanks easily was a luxury I didn't like living without. Having access to Wi-Fi, a shower that wasn't confined to a tiny stall, *and* laundry facilities? If I'd wanted to rough it, I could have lived out of a tent, but I wasn't that simple of a person. I loved air-conditioning too much, and the twenty-foot travel trailer I pulled behind my truck was more than enough space for one person.

Which was why I had been there that night in the RV section of a state park in Arizona, my reservation good for a whole month. Depending on how much I liked a specific location, and the ages of the people also around, sometimes I would stay for a month or two. Every once in a while, maybe three, if there was availability, among other criteria.

When I'd been outside earlier that day, I'd overheard a couple two spots down talking to another couple about how they were pretty sure they'd seen a wolf the night before, the night I'd gotten there.

It hadn't been a wolf, but they wouldn't have believed me if I'd told them the truth. My nose might not be anything spectacular, but my night vision was. The chupacabra had slunk around in the dark, keeping its distance from my van before eventually finding its way back into the fifth wheel where it had come from. The trailer with New Mexico plates had been gone by the time I'd woken up the next morning.

I didn't take it personally. I had been busy replacing the elastic thread that held the beads of my bracelet together when I'd spotted it. I hadn't intended on running it off.

So honestly, when the rustling started on that bright night, I hadn't thought much of it. I wasn't sure what kind of predators lived in the area, but I'd figured chances were a coyote was poking around. It hadn't been until I'd heard creaking on the steps, followed by something nudging at my camper door, that I'd sat up in bed, which was wedged into the open space at the front of the trailer, and listened. The stairs only creaked when something human-sized or bigger was on them.

The hairs on my arms had gone straight up.

An awareness of magic like I had only felt around one other being before—my neighbor—had filled my chest in the next instant. That was the best way to describe what sensing other beings felt like. An invisible nudge hello—pressure, even. A sensation that said,

This person is a little like you, with most beings, but with this one, it had been a shout across a room, a *HELLO, HELLO, HELLO*.

The most startling thing of all was that I'd been able to *smell* its magic. Sweet and potent, it had triggered something in me that left me itchy. I had driven through areas with it sprinkled into the leaves of its trees. Diluted in the water that filled its rivers and creeks. Invisible to most, but not to those that kept its secrets.

But I had never felt it the way I did then, maybe because it was so close. I'd never been within ten feet of my neighbor when he let the full spectrum of his power out for the whole neighborhood to feel. The magic at that moment had made me lightheaded. My heart had pounded faster than ever.

And just as every single instinct in my body shivered in reaction to what was outside, I'd heard it.

"*Child*," the soft voice had whispered, a stranger talking directly into my head.

And I hadn't known as I got to my feet—my own magic boiling to life in my sternum in reaction, awakened, tickling my nose, my throat, my spine, and every nerve branching out from it—what I was going to find as I'd crept to the door that led outside.

"Hello?" I'd whispered, fully aware that I hadn't imagined hearing something in my head. The only voice that had ever sounded like that, felt like that, had been in my dreams, and that one had been different.

But I knew I hadn't been dreaming. Even if the voice had gone quiet, the magic had still been present.

Somewhere between scared and concerned for the first time in at least a decade, I went for the latch and opened the door, knowing dang well that whatever was outside wouldn't be stopped by some aluminum framing and fiberglass siding.

And as I swung the door wide, I braced myself.

I'd seen a lot. Bogeymen and sirens. Gray men and harpies.

I had known a man who could turn into a gryphon when he wanted to, and a woman who had told me once at a bar that she'd pulled a man into a part of the ocean that was so deep, his body hadn't known what to do with the pressure.

My parents had never held back from sharing stories about the beings they had grown up wary of and those their parents had revered, like Kukulcan and Hunab Ku . . . among others.

There wasn't a whole lot I genuinely feared, but the magnitude of the magic that had snuck into the campground undetected until then was right on the cusp. And it wouldn't be until months later that I realized she had done that on purpose. The magical being had let me feel what she was capable of to draw me outside, like a curious moron who would die at the beginning of a horror movie.

And at a little after midnight on that full moon in May, with a power so great making me second-guess why I would even be outside in the first place, *trying to find where the magic was coming from*, my senses still managed to pick up on a tiny trickle of something.

All it took was a glance down from my camper doorway to spot it.

On the dirt-packed ground had been an itty-bitty body covered in matted black fur that looked wet. The lump had made a sweet cry right at that moment that I felt in my bones.

I'd jumped to the ground and crouched in front of it. The wetness was something that looked more like gel than water, I'd realized as I'd wedged my hand beneath the body and lifted it, thankful for my near-perfect night vision. Crust-covered eyes were set above the smallest nose I'd ever seen.

"Oh my God, you're a baby," I had cooed in surprise. I'd felt its fragile bones and its scrawny little chest raggedly rising and falling as the four-legged creature learned how to breathe right in my hand.

A newborn baby—not a dog, I'd been able to sense that, at least not any kind of normal dog that I knew. And as I'd cradled it to my chest, this innocent life too young and defenseless to take care of itself, I had raised my head and looked around. My heart was back to beating so fast.

I saw it then, in the distance of the chaparral landscape. Two bright red eyes.

"Care for him," the silky, tired voice commanded in my head.

"What?" I had squawked like it hadn't been the middle of the night and a powerful magical being capable of telepathy hadn't been communicating with me and I wasn't surrounded by people who didn't know about how true folklore was. I'd glanced down at the baby that fit into the palm of my hand before raising my gaze to meet the two eyes moving further away by the second.

She was backing up.

It was its mother. I would've bet my life on it.

She howled so deep, long, and loud, there was no way anyone who knew anything about animals would ever believe it was from a coyote.

As I gulped, futilely waiting for an explanation that was never going to come, bright red eyes winked out of view . . . and the glow of power disappeared.

The fuzzy, wet creature in my hand had let out another newborn-sized whimper.

With the full moon overhead, I stood there for a very long time, hoping the creature would come back for her baby.

But she never did.

Chapter Five

I swept my hand down Duncan's back as he yawned. I'd only told this story twice before, but he knew it. "That was a little over two years ago, and we've been together ever since," I wrapped up our first meeting, impressing myself. I couldn't have explained that any simpler or to the point.

The learning curve I'd experienced afterward—having to figure out how to feed a newborn magical creature, how to clean him, teach him how to be alive—all belonged to me. I'd share those stories if they wanted. It didn't seem like they did based off the silence that followed our meet-cute. Him being the cute and me being the "meet" part.

"To make sure I understand," the man with the glasses said after a long, loaded moment, "you didn't see who spoke to you?"

I shook my head. "All I saw were red eyes in the distance. We stayed there for a month, but she never came back." At some point, I had gone from hoping and praying Duncan's mom would come back to dreading she would. His little nose bumped my inner wrist, those ruby eyes peering at me through his curly eyelashes.

I wasn't sure what it said about me that I hoped she never returned. And if she did? I couldn't even think about it, so I didn't.

"You never met the mother before?" Glasses asked after another minute, his expression watchful.

Too watchful.

"Not that I know of." There wasn't a doubt in my mind she had something that dampened her magic like we did, not after the way I'd felt her and then hadn't. Obsidian wasn't hard to get. Some versions of it were more expensive than others, but it wasn't astronomically priced. Most people just didn't care enough to hide themselves. But if I packed the kind of punch she did? I'd have five bracelets on me at all times, and I'd rob a bank to afford them.

"Does the child speak?"

"Not verbally," I answered. "He understands language. Soon after he . . . changed, he started being able to speak to me, to tell me yes and no, telepathically. We communicate as well as I could with a toddler, but he's more well-behaved, and he's potty trained. He's more mature than a normal two-year-old." He was perfect, dead food habits not counting.

That got me an unexpected lazy lick on my wrist that made me smile. *He was so freaking cute.*

"His form at the moment . . . that's how you met him, and he's stayed this way since?"

He meant the fact he looked like a black hound puppy, except for his red eyes and the blue flame at the tip of his tail.

I nodded. "Yes. He hasn't changed into a human form. I don't know if he can."

It made me feel slightly better that Duncan's magic was such a mystery. I had tried to figure it out on my own, spent hours and hours looking up whatever I could on certain beings. On some I'd never heard of. Some that were more well-known figures.

There was only so much information available.

Somewhere in history and time, it became dangerous to be different. The trolls left their bridges, the unicorns fled their forests, and the thunderbirds abandoned their great nests in the greatest mountains.

And gods that were once worshipped for millennia became names that you couldn't find in textbooks . . .

But people weren't ready for that knowledge bomb, and I had a feeling that it would take centuries before that was the case, and even then, whatever I was, wasn't something even most of those who were "different" could handle. Case in point: the Jenny

Greenteeth, the chupacabra two years ago, and a handful of other people I'd run into when I didn't have my bracelet on for some reason.

But this wasn't about me.

This was about the sleepy baby on my lap who was back to yawning. One of the modern wonders of the world, I told him. A myth of a myth.

He was no dragon, no chimera, no giant devil dingo, no Shisa, or white greyhound. He was missing two heads, otherwise I would have thought he was a Cerberus. There were a few other options I thought might fit, but the rarer the magic, the harder those beings would be to find. The magical people of the world were secretive for a reason after all.

And there was no master list of mythological creatures to check off. Every culture and civilization had its share, and there were a lot of them. Rumor had it, they overlapped and went by different names in different pieces and places of mythology. They adapted with time to survive.

The elders whispered among themselves again, their voices too low for my ears to pick up, but since Matti didn't seem to be getting tense and he *could* hear, I didn't worry about it too much. Either they would help us, or they wouldn't. I liked this place, so far, but I would never stay where we weren't wanted.

When they stopped murmuring, the man with the glasses got my attention. "We have some ideas on what the pup may be."

"You do?" I almost squeaked. Could it be that easy?

He inclined his head. "I would need to make some enquiries to confirm my suspicions, but I have reason to believe I may." The men and women around him nodded in agreement, and he kept speaking. "It will take some time and effort to validate, but once I get an answer, I'll share what I find with you."

I kicked Matti, and he kicked me right back. I hadn't expected it to be this fast. "Okay," I said. "Thank you. We would really appreciate it."

None of them said another word. The elders kept staring. Freaking Sienna coughed, and I almost turned around because that hadn't exactly sounded like she was trying to muffle a laugh. I'd probably misheard it; Matti didn't seem concerned about that either.

I waited, then I waited a little more, hoping someone would say something. But a minute passed, and then another, and I started counting in my head each second, so I had something to focus on. When the third minute hit, I tried not to feel disappointed that they couldn't at least let me know they weren't interested in having us join their community.

I wasn't going to pitch a fit or fight them . . . I understood.

Maybe they thought Duncan was a danger. Maybe they thought I was. Maybe they just didn't want someone new living here in this special place with them.

Duncan lifted his head at that moment to peer up at me. *We're here for him.* How could I have forgotten? It might take months until we found another safe place, if this one didn't work out. We *needed* this to work.

I'd beg if I had to, dang it.

We didn't have the luxury of letting them say no without trying. I couldn't forget that.

Someone across the table let out a long, long exhale. "I have so many questions," the silver-blue-haired woman suddenly admitted in a rush.

"I do too," another woman added. "It's taken all of my self-control to stay quiet, but I can't anymore."

What was happening?

"This is the most exciting thing to happen here in the last ten years, if not longer," the cyclops chimed in.

"Oh" was all I could say, because I didn't think "Are you messing with me right now?" was an appropriate or polite response.

But were they? Messing with me, that was.

"You seem surprised," the man with the glasses noted as I watched them, not sure what was going on. First, none of them could say a single word, and now, they seemed kind of excited. They were going to give me whiplash.

"I am," I admitted to Glasses. He was the worst of them all, in a way, with his extreme wariness.

"Why?" the cyclops asked, sounding genuinely perplexed.

"You were all being really quiet, so I was pretty sure you weren't interested in letting us join your community." My chest felt a little funny, but I figured I might as well keep being truthful. "Some beings don't always welcome me with open arms."

That got them to stir, and I took a second to sneak a glance at Henri. That tendon along his throat was strained again. He seemed to be focused on whatever the elders were whispering over.

I turned to Matti and tipped my chin at him. He gave me a thumbs-up beneath the table that I was going to take as a good sign since he could hear their discussion. It took a couple more minutes before they wound down.

"We are a community who intends to preserve the gifts we've been given," Glasses said after a minute. His eyebrows were knit together, giving him a thoughtful, if not uptight, face. "We don't shun any creature of any kind here."

One of the women gently cleared her throat. "Beings like you, like you both, are no exception."

I blinked at the same time Matti kicked me harder than before, and now I was going to have to get Sienna to twist both his nipples. My eyes watered as my leg throbbed.

"We will help you discover what the pup's origins are and allow you to join the ranch as long as you're aware of the commitment required to belong to it."

I kicked my friend back as hard as I could. But visibly, I nodded at the group. "The marrying part. I'm aware of it, and you can sign me up right now as long as I get to choose . . . don't I? Who to marry, I mean?" I asked, wanting to see if they were going to pull some arranged marriage on me. I mean, I wasn't going to be that picky. I couldn't be. I'd accepted that reality already. I liked an attractive person as much as anyone did, but all the people I had ever *liked* had great personalities, they had all been funny and likable, and it hadn't mattered how symmetrical their features were or how many ab muscles they had either. When you're used to being judged for things out of your control, you learn how to focus on the things that matter sooner rather than later.

I was also pretty sure I could come to love anything under the right conditions, but I still wanted a choice.

Multiple nods answered me from across the table, thankfully.

Henri's grunt wasn't subtle at all.

Why was he glaring at the elders all of a sudden?

"You're all skipping a hell of a lot of fine print right now," he said in that gruff voice.

Did he have a problem with me wanting to live here?

Henri's statement got the elders bickering. "Well . . ." one of the quieter ones replied as Silver-Blue Hair challenged, "This is a unique situation . . ."

The man I'd known as a child shut them down with a no-nonsense slice of his hand that had no business being so commanding. "You're all aware of our rules, and it doesn't matter how excited any of you might be—"

This was them excited?

"—we aren't changing the way we go about things. We don't talk about the ranch. We don't let strangers in. We don't talk about the children. *And everyone has to go through the trial period.*"

I suddenly didn't like Henri so much.

I was pretty sure from the way my eye was twitching, it didn't like him much either.

I'd been *so worried* about what these people were going to say, and *he* was the one throwing wrenches now? He was supposed to be on my team, wasn't he? He'd called me Cricket not even thirty minutes ago.

"Come on, Henri," Matti interjected, but his cousin shook his head.

"No. There are special circumstances, and you were one of them, but that's also part of the guidelines for living here. Children with no families and minors with relatives who already live here are always welcome. Anyone else has to go through a trial period before any unions happen. The way we've done things has worked for a long time, and we can't afford to put our people at risk," the big man argued. "No exceptions."

I blinked.

So there was a trial period before any marrying went on?

Everyone started speaking. They were loud too. It was only Sienna, Duncan, and me that weren't running our mouths from the sound of it.

I raised my hand, and Henri was paying attention because in a voice loud enough to be overheard despite the voices, he asked, "Cricket?"

I was Cricket again, but I hadn't been a second ago when he was making it more difficult for me to join this place?

That made about zero sense, but all right. If there was ever a time for me to be on my best behavior, it was now. Dang it. I tried to plaster on the most pleasant face I could and be the better person. "I'm curious. What exactly is the fine print I'm missing by asking to join and what's this trial period? Living here for a little while to make sure I like it before you all officially let us stay? How long is that for?"

The elders stopped bickering. It was Henri that answered though. "That's what it is. It's mandatory you live here for a minimum of three months before an official invitation is offered. It's to make sure you're a good fit and that you can live by our rules and values."

"Some beings have been known to change their minds," the man with the glasses added.

"Most," Henri corrected.

None of this sounded wild. They were protecting their investment and themselves. Plus, that would give me time to meet people and get to know them. Under normal circumstances, three months didn't seem long enough to get to know someone well enough to marry them for the rest of your life, but that was a normal-person thing. When you had different senses, it was easier to get to know the root of people, to see what they might not want you to if they had a choice. You could pretend to be a good person as much as you wanted, but when you could smell anger or frustration or attraction, or the million other emotions a body produced, there was no hiding that.

Or so I'd been told.

Sienna had sniffed out more than a few people for me before. "I understand," I told them.

Besides, the satyr woman had already been looking at me funny, and that was with my bracelet on. What if too many of the beings here reacted the same way?

They were going to need to suck it up because Duncan needed this place.

My donut's wet nose nuzzled the palm of my hand, his little teeth nibbling it. "A three-month waiting period is fine." I pet Duncan's tail with the hand he wasn't corn-cobbing. "After that, how long do I have before I'd need to marry someone?"

"One year," one of the women answered.

I kicked Matti before I could stop myself. A laugh burst right out of me, and I kicked him one more time for the hell of it. My leg was still throbbing. "A year is a lifetime." I was *relieved*. There were guidelines they had mentioned, but I wasn't worried about them. I'd bet I already lived my life with stricter rules than anything they could come up with.

We had bigger stuff to talk about than maybe having to pitch in around the community or whatever else they had in mind. They'd have to do some *Handmaid's Tale* kind of crap for me to second-guess being here, or every male resident would have to have an awful personality.

One year to marry someone. Wow, and here I was stressing over it. Would more time be nice? Sure. But I'd been mentally prepared to get hitched in a month. Realistically, I would've even done it tomorrow if I had to.

A whole year was a boulder off my chest.

Now, all that was left was that I needed to talk to them about the biggest elephant in the room after the sippy-cup-sized mystery on my lap. It was going to be the deal-breaker, and we needed to tackle it now so I could know for sure. I'd been vague with the explanation about what had happened to Duncan's would-be kidnappers, and I was well aware they were cutting me some slack by not asking how exactly I'd managed it. It was one of the benefits of the secrecy all magical beings widely embraced. I was going to milk it too.

"I appreciate you all agreeing to let us stay here on a trial basis." I shot a glance at the backstabber who had brought it up in the first place. A part of me still couldn't believe Henri had done it. It was hard not to give him a little bit of a stink eye. "I'm aware you already mentioned you welcome all people here, regardless of their heritage, but . . ." I scratched my throat as Matti kicked the living shit out of my foot.

We had agreed to disagree on this point. "No one cares," he whisper-hissed at me.

I gritted my teeth in pain. We'd never outgrown this part of our friendship. "More people care than people who don't," I muttered under my breath before kicking him back hard enough that he winced just a little. He had a high pain tolerance. I should have been proud of myself for putting in enough effort to get that much of a reaction. "It's going to come up, and I'd rather them be aware now."

My best friend growled.

I growled right back. Or at least, I tried to.

But it just made him laugh like it had since we'd been kids, like he thought it was so dang funny I "sounded like a chihuahua," as he liked to say. Fortunately, I knew I'd gotten my point across. I set my shoulders and began. "You're all being really accepting of Duncan, but I don't want to start here with secrets," I warned them as gently as possible. *Too many secrets.*

I took a breath and palmed my donut's back for support. He stopped nibbling and peered up at me. His steady breathing calmed me.

He loved me for who I was, and so did the man beside me and the woman behind me, and that gave me more strength than all the weightlifting in the world could have.

"Many beings don't appreciate what I am, but I can't change

that, no matter how much I might wish I was something else. If there's a name for what I am, I don't know what it is. I never met my biological parents. But there's something I need to be upfront about." I swallowed. "Women who spend a lot of time around me get pregnant easily. Is that going to be a problem?"

Someone snickered. Everyone else made a face that said they didn't understand or didn't believe me. But it was a real thing.

Beside me, Matti reluctantly nodded.

"Maybe I affect men's sperm count, maybe women are just more fertile . . . I'm not sure. But women between the ages of twenty and mid to late forties end up getting pregnant like—" I snapped my fingers "—when I'm around them." It was part of the reason why I moved so often and preferred to stay around people over certain ages. I wasn't making people have unprotected sex, and it wasn't my fault condoms and birth control weren't 100 percent effective on their best day, but . . .

Enough things had happened that had convinced me, and everyone who knew me, that this was a very real occurrence after a while.

When we'd lived together and Sienna had a boyfriend, she had been on birth control, bought mega packs of condoms, and had been a firm believer in the pull-out method. She hadn't put her whole trust into anything. I hadn't either, not trusting my body. I hadn't dated much, but when I had, I'd done the same as her. Since then, we hadn't been around each other long enough for me to affect her and Matti, but in her words, "You could never be too safe." They just didn't have sex when I was around.

The elders still looked to be in a state of confusion. Cyclops's eye was squinted. Silver-Blue Hair and another woman started whispering to each other. Glasses had his arms crossed over his chest, that wary expression plastered even more strongly over his features.

"I can't control it. It isn't something I knowingly do. I just want to be upfront. Maybe you can put out a warning so there aren't any unintended surprises." I laughed a little nervously. "Normal people, the magical . . . it affects everyone."

Murmurs spread among the members.

Eventually, it was Glasses again who spoke for them after clearing his throat. "Whatever effects your presence could have on our members—"

"I don't mean to cut you off, but it isn't a 'could have.' It happens. Sienna, back there, used to live with me when we were in an apartment complex. Eleven months after we moved in, almost every female tenant in the complex under the age of fifty and over twenty was pregnant. The same thing happened in every other apartment building we lived in after that." It wasn't every woman I lived by, but it was enough of them for it to be suspicious.

And people weren't always happy about it.

"We meant what we said. We're a community for all magical beings, especially those who have a harder time being accepted by the outside world, and I'm sure you'll see that here. Fertility is not an unwelcome gift."

So he said.

I wasn't sure he believed it from the way his eyes searched mine. Was I overthinking it?

I pressed my lips together, fully aware they weren't taking this seriously enough, and I would just need to warn anyone who spent a lot of time within fifty-ish feet of me. Shifting blame wasn't something I wanted to do, but I had tried.

Silver-Blue Hair nodded. "You don't need to 'classify' yourself to us if you don't want to."

But they had questions; it was obvious on their faces.

I thought about calling out Henri who had literally asked what I was when we were outside, but unlike him, I wasn't a snitch.

The thought of it made me smile, and I let the implication hang in the air. I was what I was, and they could only guess for now.

"You and the pup *are* welcome here," Glasses claimed, lifting a hand to mess with his eyewear once more. The movement made his sleeve slip down his wrist, showing off a hint of . . . a beaded bracelet?

Had I seen that correctly? There was too much magic in the room for me to filter out what belonged to who. If he was sitting beside me, I'd have an easier time, but . . .

"As long as you agree to the three-month trial period and the marriage stipulation. We can help, if you'd like. We have a good record in matching couples," the man explained. "As mentioned, there is a one-year period for you to find an acceptable mate."

Cyclops leaned forward. "You're under no obligation to explain your background to anyone unless you choose to. Your nature is yours alone, and you'll be accepted for who you are. We can assure you of that."

I got what he was saying, but I also understood that people were way more complicated than that.

Holding my breath, I peeked at the man I should have called Fluffy again in public just to see how he would react and found his attention already back on me. He wasn't smiling. He wasn't frowning. He was simply watching.

His nostrils were slightly flaring though.

He'd deserved that bite from earlier after this crap.

Maybe we hadn't been friends-friends, but *he knew me*. He had been my neighbor for a year when he'd lived with Matti's family. You didn't have nicknames for everybody, and he hadn't forgotten mine even after so many years.

Loyalty, man. Where had it disappeared to?

"Now," the man with the glasses butted in. His hands were beneath the table again, hiding what sure had looked like an obsidian bracelet to me. "About our other guidelines."

Chapter Six

"That was eventful."

I snorted at Sienna as I adjusted the leather toy Duncan was chewing on. We were spread out on the bed in the room that she and Matti had been assigned for "their short stay"—those had been the exact words of the elders. So they didn't get any ideas. It wasn't like I didn't know this time with them was temporary. I was used to living hundreds, if not thousands, of miles away from them at almost all times.

That's just what seemed to happen to real best friends. It was like the universe knew when there was a bond so strong that nothing—not distance, time, children, or responsibilities—could come between it. So, it proved it to you.

Life couldn't be *too* good all the time.

And like that saying warned, nothing good comes easy. Everything I valued in my life required work. This was just one of those things. My best friends and I had to put in effort to make our friendship still thrive after so many years. If things between us had only been one-sided, we never would have made it to this point.

"Tell me about it. That didn't go like I'd thought it might," I agreed with her, moving the toy from side to side as Duncan tried to lazily snap at it. If I had to guess, he was putting in about 5 percent effort. I could tell by the way his eyes drooped that he needed a nap. I dropped my voice. "I think I got a couple of gray hairs from the anticipation they made me go through thinking they were going to say no to us staying."

Sienna fluffed the pillow under her head as she lay on her side with Dunky between us. "They dragged that out, but you know how it is. It's an older werewolf thing. My grandparents are the same way any time they have news to share. They start off in this tone that sounds all doom and gloom, and then they tell us they're going on vacation and *can someone come by and water their plants?* It's a power play. They're bored."

I hummed and nodded, taking in her freshly washed face and wet hair. Did her skin color look a little off or was I imagining it? I wanted to ask if she was feeling all right but figured she had to be fine. The rooms had warm-colored light bulbs. Maybe that was it.

"Are you relieved they agreed to the trial period? Matti was telling me while I was showering that he forgot all about that part," she kept going.

"I get why they require it." I bit my lip and met her familiar gaze. "I'm hung up on that satyr woman this afternoon. I might be overthinking it." Or I might not be.

My best friend said nothing as she stroked a finger down Duncan's back. He paused lazily snapping and peeked at her over his shoulder for a moment before going back to it. "Don't mind them. They're herbivores. It's instinct for them to fear anything that might hurt them."

"I don't have sharp teeth. I can't hurt anyone like that," I whispered.

Light-colored eyes met mine, and even they seemed different than usual. Dimmer. "I know you wouldn't hurt anyone."

I wouldn't. There was no reason to let it bother me too much. Her son—if that's what Shiloh was—had liked me, and that was enough. Kids were good judges of character. If I'd listened to Duncan like I should have, I would have been on high alert around those people who had tried to take him before things had escalated.

That was the last time I was ever going to ignore his instincts. Or anyone else I knew with a fantastic nose. Which then got me thinking . . .

I lifted my head to see that the door to the en suite bathroom was still closed. It was. Franklin, the elder with the glasses, who I thought had been acting kind of weird, had explained while he'd given us the tour of the second floor of the main building—or the "clubhouse" as he'd called it—that each room on the second and third floor had its own bathroom. There were five rooms in total for "guests," and he'd stuck us in two right next to each other. They were comfortable, big enough for a king-sized bed, a nightstand on each side, a dresser, and a television across from the mattress. The bathrooms were identical with a large walk-in shower with some kind of stone tile and timeless accents that really tied in with the rustic and homey feel of the entire building. It was nice without making me nervous to damage something.

And while I would've rather stayed in my travel trailer, that had been one of the rules the elders had laid out during the final parts of our meeting.

We had to integrate, and apparently, my camper didn't count, but staying in the clubhouse for the next three months did.

It was fine. We had room for activities, and it would be nice to not be cramped in the tiny shower that worked just fine too. And from the way Duncan had been so attentive, he seemed to like this place already. The elders had given him a wide berth, but I wanted to hope it wasn't out of fear. There was a lot of new stuff going on in such a short time, and maybe they were giving him space before overwhelming him with attention. They had seemed interested enough there for a minute.

Except for . . .

"Matti?" I raised my voice, knowing he was listening from the bathroom.

He didn't let me down. "Yeah?"

I had to word this right. "What do you know about that elder with the glasses? Franklin."

My oldest friend took his time before answering. "Not much. I didn't spend any time with him when I lived here."

Hmm.

He kept talking. "There's no hierarchy with them, but Henri

mentioned once that they all seem to give him more of a say than anyone else. He looks the same too. I wonder what kind of skincare routine he has."

Freaking Matti.

It was only rude to ask someone what they were to their face, there was nothing technically wrong with wondering about it behind their backs.

"Do you not know what he is then?" I asked.

"I've got no fucking idea," he called out. "I bet Henri does."

"Why?" Sienna asked.

"I might be imagining it, but I thought he was acting kind of different from everyone else," I tried to explain.

She shrugged like she hadn't noticed. I guess that was a good thing.

Moving along, I decided to change the topic. "What's up with Henri?" I asked Sienna. I was rolling the dice talking about him in here in the first place, but I didn't care enough to be discreet. I wasn't planning on talking bad about him.

"What do you want to know?" she whispered.

There was a reason why I was asking her and not Matti. Sienna didn't love gossip as much as he did, and I wasn't sure if she knew about the crush I'd had on him when we'd been younger.

"Matti never talks about him, and you've only seen him . . . what? Three times in all these years? What's he been up to?" That wasn't the question burning a hole in my brain, but considering she and Henri barely knew each other, I was well aware she wasn't the person to interrogate about why he wouldn't want me living here.

I needed to ask him directly because that betrayal stung almost as much as when he'd taken Matti away without a goodbye.

"I've seen him for about half an hour three times in six years, Nina. Matti knows more because he's seen him more often than I have when he's had to come to Colorado for work and Henri's met up with him, but all I know is that he lives here, he works for the sheriff's department as deputy, he's bad at texting Matti back, and"—I had to read her lips because her whisper was so low—"he doesn't have a mate." She raised her eyebrows.

Hmm.

Her mouth formed a very flat smile. "You don't remember that I know?"

"Know what?"

Her lips moved, but nothing actually came out of her mouth. *"That you had a crush on him."*

I guess I had told her everything. I laughed. "When I was ten!"

She wasn't done. *"I saw you check him out."*

I rolled my eyes so hard as I laughed. "*Yeah*, because he's the size of a Jeep, and I haven't seen him in almost twenty years." And because I couldn't lie to her, I didn't. "He's really good-looking, but come on." That wasn't exactly a mystery, and I wasn't going to pretend otherwise and come across as even more suspicious.

"Ha!" She tapped the tip of her nose, and I knew what she was saying. She'd smelled my attraction to him.

Which meant chances were, so had he, dang it.

Unless he'd been too preoccupied, or had shut off his senses then, I could only hope.

The urge to argue that it meant nothing was on the tip of my tongue, but then I remembered exactly how I'd treated her after she'd met Matti and been all goo-goo-gah-gah over him, and I had picked on her relentlessly.

She could have this, mostly because it meant nothing. It had been a long time since I'd given her any kind of ammo to tease me with.

"Eh, he's all right. Matti got the good looks in the family," Sienna said after I stared at her for a minute. "He's too intense for me. He's kind of scary, don't you think?"

That made me laugh some more. "Henri? Scary? Why? What do you have to be scared of?"

Her eyes went squinty. "Did you not see the size of him when he was about to rip your face off?"

"He wanted to, didn't he?"

"Matti said he wouldn't have, but I don't believe him."

"He was not going to rip your face off, Nina!" Matti hollered from inside the bathroom.

"Quit eavesdropping!" I said in a normal volume as Duncan got up and did a little circle on the bed before plopping down with his toy in his mouth. He looked so tired, it made me smile. *Anyway.* "Once he knew it was me, I don't think he would have either, but when he didn't know? Definitely."

"I didn't know you knew him that well," Sienna went back to whispering. "Why does he call you Cricket?"

Before I could answer, a weird sound came from the bathroom that had all three of us turning toward the door. I raised my eyebrows at my friend, and she did it right back before calling out, "Babe? You all right?"

There was a short pause before he shouted, "Fine!"

Whatever that was hadn't sounded fine to me, even though I couldn't tell what it had been. It hadn't exactly been fart-like. But Si and I shrugged at each other, and I answered her question. "I don't know him that great. You know, he spent the summers with us, and then he moved in with them for about a year after he graduated." No one had ever mentioned why he'd done that. "He was always polite, and sometimes he was nice—nicer to me than Matti, but that's probably because I'm a girl and he didn't want to hurt my feelings," I explained, and she nodded. "Maybe he felt bad I was adopted?"

Sienna nodded. "But why Cricket?"

I grinned. "Because I talked a lot—"

"You still do!" Matti shouted, still not minding his own business.

I groaned. "Yes, yes, I still talk a lot, but back then I talked *a lot*. I had a chirpy little voice, and once I got going, there was no stopping me. So, Cricket was born, and it stuck."

She grinned. "That's cute." She made a funny face suddenly. "I've never heard him call Matti anything but his name."

"'Dumbass' is the only thing that comes to mind."

She nodded slowly like she agreed. Then she shrugged. "At least you know someone here, right?"

Someone who had made me moving here a little harder, but sure. I rubbed Duncan's soft ear.

At least I knew someone.

It was no surprise I couldn't fall asleep after we left Matti and Sienna's room. Neither one of them stayed up late. Under normal circumstances, they both woke up early to go running before starting their day. Duncan and I were the complete opposite; we were usually outside playing at midnight.

My mom used to tell me all about how, when I'd been a baby, I wouldn't sleep during normal hours and how she and my dad would have to take turns every other night keeping me company. *You never cried, Nina. We would find you sitting up in your crib, and later on in your toddler bed, looking out the window. Sometimes you looked so sad, we wouldn't be able to sleep, it broke our hearts, so we started staying up with you.*

It made me want to choke up thinking about how good they'd been to me. I'd gotten *so lucky* that of all the people I could have ended up with, it had been them. Two older werewolves who had never had children of their own, with hearts bigger than the state of Alaska.

Continuing to love others in the way that they had shown me by example was the most important thing I had learned from them. It was the best way I could honor their thousands of sacrifices. By raising Duncan.

And that's why, when the screen on my phone said it was eleven thirty, and I could sense my pup starting to get restless as he rolled onto his back on top of the bed of the room we were assigned to, I figured maybe now we could restart our nightly routine. We hadn't been able to do it since his physical changes. The risk of getting caught had been way too high.

I gently pulled his tail as his legs and paws stretched toward the ceiling of the room that was an exact replica of the one my friends were in. Duncan had crawled under the bed and checked everything out under there when we'd come in.

"Wanna go outside for a little while?" I asked.

A black head rolled toward me, his bright eyes so intelligent. "*Yes.*"

It didn't take long to slip him into his harness, put my fanny pack on, and grab a leash I rarely needed. I helped him off the bed. As quietly as possible, I opened the door and went out first with Dunky-Dunk right on my heels, nightlights set up along the hallway at every outlet lighting up the unfamiliar space.

Fortunately, as big as the building slash clubhouse was, the layout was mostly easy. It had seemed intimidating when we'd first walked in, but whoever had designed it had set it up to make a lot of sense considering its size. Franklin, or as I had called him in my head "Glasses," had given us a brief tour after we'd left the meeting. On the first floor, he'd gestured one direction and explained that the kitchen was there, along with other bedrooms—he didn't say whose. If you went the opposite way, there was a nursery and offices, along with a laundry room and supply closets.

Apart from the five spacious guest bedrooms on the second floor, with us taking up two of them, the uptight elder had explained that some of the community members lived on the third floor, but he didn't take us up to it or explain who those people were either.

At the staircase, I picked up Duncan again and went down them, taking in even more nightlights. He was still just slightly too small to take stairs easily. The front doors were down the hall, and we crept out, the building so silent.

I thought it was a little strange that they trusted us enough to let us stay on their property without supervision so soon after meeting us. I hadn't seen a single camera inside, and I wondered if there were any around the perimeter. There wasn't an alarm system set up either, I'd noticed when the four of us had gone to get our things from my truck. They must be really confident in who they allowed around here. That or maybe they had more faith since Matti had lived here in the past.

That had to be a good thing, I decided, as I cracked the door and Duncan snuck out first.

My donut waited as I closed the door. His head was tipped back. The moon was full tonight. I took a deep, deep breath.

My lungs expanded like I'd gotten a hit of that good oxygen casinos pumped through their systems.

My skin tingled.

The forest and village around us were mostly silent, other than an owl hooting nearby and a cool breeze moving through the trees.

It felt so good here.

What was it about this forest that felt like this? I wondered as Duncan backed up enough so that his butt settled on my foot, and for a few, quiet, calm moments, we took in the sweetness in the air that shouldn't have been so noticeable to me considering I didn't have a good nose. But that seemed to be the magnitude of this place.

Trees rustled.

Something big howled in the distance.

And my little donut gave me a loaded look over his shoulder right before he took off running into the evergreens.

"How are you so fast?" I panted a while later, lying on my back in the middle of some trees to the side of the clubhouse building. You'd figure I'd be used to running after him since it had been our daily game before his change, but I wasn't. We'd had to replace outside time with indoor mental stimulation for weeks, and my lungs weren't used to anything harder than a speed walk at this point.

I wheezed as he threw himself across my stomach, belly to belly, chewing on a stick he'd found at some point that was stripped of bark.

"I'm going to have to buy you a treadmill, man." I gasped some more, reaching blindly for him so I could run my fingers through his coat.

He was breathing normally. Show-off.

"I think I pulled my hamstring jumping over that log back there," I told him in between trying to breathe in through my nose and out through my mouth to calm down. Maybe I needed the treadmill too. Two treadmills. I might have to start doing some weightlifting because it seemed like we were going to get to the point soon where carrying him around was going to be impossible at the rate he was growing.

His tail swished through the air, resembling a shooting star.

I ran my fingers through his coat again, admiring its softness.

"Donut," I told him, letting my eyes settle on the full pie of a moon still visible through a gap in the towering trees surrounding us. "If you don't like it here, tell me, okay? I'm serious. I want you to be happy."

"Love," he told me, and it hit me the same way it had from the first time he'd projected that emotion. It choked me up.

"I love you too. With my whole heart. You know that, don't you?"

Duncan stopped chewing. A second later, he dragged his body the rest of the way over mine and jumped over my shoulder to stand beside my head, his ears so long they almost grazed the ground. My little black hound that was no puppy. He licked my cheek.

"Yes," he answered.

I framed his face with my hands and kissed his nose, knowing we were on the same page. Just as I let go, his body suddenly tensed and he spun around, a tiny growl erupting from his throat. I jackknifed into a sitting position. I hadn't heard anything, but I trusted him enough to know that he sensed something.

Duncan's tail stuck straight up in the dark just as a low voice murmured, "All is good, pup."

He sat, but his frame was rigid, and a long, low growl rumbled in his throat.

Matti had sworn we were safe here. There were tall layers of fencing closer in to the clubhouse. Plus, the scent of big predators should have marked this entire territory off.

But we were out at night, in an unfamiliar place, with strangers who held no allegiance to either of us. Anticipation and nerves came to life in my body as I caught sight of three figures moving through the trees toward us. Two were men and the other was a woman still a hundred feet away, their movements dead quiet as they crossed the ground.

No wonder I hadn't seen or heard them until the last second, they practically hugged the shadows and walked on air.

My puppy growled louder, staying in his seated position.

"Ah-ah," the deep voice corrected him. "You're safe. We're not going to do anything to you."

It was Henri, I realized, setting my hand on the bristling hairs of Duncan's back. That husky, bossy voice could only belong to him. "It's okay, but good job sensing them, Donut," I praised him.

His tail swished back and forth once, his whole frame tense and focused on the strangers approaching so dang silently. It was kind of impressive considering the fact that I'd put Henri at around six foot five or six, his build stocky and muscular. The man to one side of him was shorter and also well-built. The woman trailing behind them wasn't exactly small in comparison to either of them.

How long had they been creeping through the woods? They weren't exactly walking fast.

I'd tripped over a branch a little while ago—not that I cared if anyone saw me bust my ass playing with my pint-sized partner in crime, but I was kind of glad they hadn't arrived three minutes earlier, when I'd been on my back moaning and clutching my leg.

"Why are you bleeding?" the familiar-ish voice asked, somehow sounding even more gruff in the dark . . . and confirming that chances were, they'd witnessed my very fine moment.

Too bad for me. "My shin got assaulted by that branch you just walked by," I called out. It was the same leg Matti had kicked earlier too. When I'd rolled up my pant leg to see why it had hurt so much, there'd been a pretty good scratch there.

Matti's cousin slipped through the trees, clear, bright moonlight occasionally illuminating the shape of his frame as it moved through them in a way someone half his size shouldn't have been capable of.

But it was more than that, I thought, that kept my gaze riveted to him—stealth aside.

How was he so huge? I wouldn't call him burly exactly, but it was close. Thick neck, thick chest. Biceps? Thick. Thighs? Thick. He was . . .

My pride kept the gulp from climbing all the way up my throat.

Some women were attracted to six-packs made up of strict diets and three-hour gym sessions.

I'd always had a thing for a brawny, muscular build. In my imagination, the more I could grab on to, the better. The thicker the thighs, the better the prize—andddd that was nothing I needed to focus on.

If I wanted a big, beefy guy to ogle, I could pick a football game to watch. Or a rugby match. Not the man I used to call Fluffy who didn't exactly seem all that pleased to have me here, even if he had the exact body type that would've caught my attention in a crowded room.

"You injured?"

I knew he could see me, so I shook my head. "The only thing hurting right now is my ego if you saw me bust my ass." The words "help me, I'm dying" had come out of my mouth, mostly because I liked Duncan's attention as he climbed all over me, making sure I was fine . . . and because it had stung like an SOB.

"Maybe you shouldn't be running around in the dark, Cricket," he suggested, even closer now.

So we were back to "Cricket" again, huh?

And was that a *joke*?

I snickered, not sure how I felt exactly about this hot–cold thing we had going on. *He* had going on. I'd offered a hug. Offered to let him smell me up close. I was trying. Sure, he was teasing me now, but he'd thrown me under the bus hours ago.

I needed to talk to him about that. The sooner the better.

"I can see in the dark just fine," I told him; there was no point in keeping that a secret. "I stepped on my shoelace, it's my fault."

Henri kept coming, not commenting on my explanation. But the man beside him made a sudden rough sound. He stopped, and I watched him take a deep breath.

Henri hadn't given me back my bracelet after the meeting.

I touched the spot on my wrist where it usually sat, missing its weight. Missing what it meant. It'd been almost two decades since I'd begun wearing it full-time.

Henri gave the man a sharp look for some reason; it drew his eyebrows down flat. "Both of you can go home. We'll search again in the morning."

The small group whispered to each other, and the man and the woman changed direction when their chitchat was over. They headed toward the homes behind the main building. So many of them still had light coming through their windows, making the whole place even dreamier than during the day. It reminded me of something out of a postcard. The moonlight, the woods, the houses . . . all it needed was snow covering the ground. I bet it looked surreal during the winter.

I hoped we were here long enough to find out.

Unlike the two strangers, Henri kept coming toward us, stopping when he was a few feet away, so close his amber eyes reflected when he crouched.

He didn't look very happy. He didn't look very anything if I was going to be honest. I smelled different, but I was still the same person, just bigger and a little more mature most of the time.

I smiled at him. "Nice to see you again, Fluffy."

The only reaction he had to the childhood nickname was the slightest flick of his left eyebrow. He didn't say a word, which also meant he didn't tell me *not* to call him that either.

It also reminded me that he and I needed to talk. "Sorry I bit you," I apologized, hoping he could sense my sincerity. It seemed like a good place to start. The obsidian Duncan and I wore only helped keep our magic a secret; it didn't do anything against feelings or facial expressions.

His eyes swept toward Duncan, who was watching him like a hawk, his small body still on edge. *He had tried to take this man down for me. He had risked his life.* I was going to need a private moment so I could cry over that at some point soon, I decided. He was going to get whatever he wanted for the rest of his life, dang it.

For now, I focused on Henri. "Sorry if it hurt," I added.

That got him to snicker. "I've had stubbed toes that hurt more than that."

Was that another joke? I guess I'd expected him to pretend he hadn't heard me. But I could work with this. I'd rather have a joking Henri than a Mr. Rules and Regulations Henri. And that's why I said, "All right. Next time I know to bite harder."

That got me his undivided attention. "Excuse me?" he asked in that rumbly, commanding voice that I needed to get used to.

I laughed. "You heard me." Did he expect me not to mess with him back?

Those clear eyes moved over my face as his features gradually hardened.

He'd always been so serious. In my memories, he used to smile once in a blue moon and rarely laughed, unlike Matti whose first language was cackling. Where my best friend was a joyous handful, I remembered Henri as being the opposite: quiet, stoic, too responsible, even as a teenager.

I needed to try my best not to let his back-and-forth seriousness get under my skin.

So I smiled some more and drew my knees up to my chest, wrapping my arms around them.

"Did you go looking for the river crone?" I asked, keeping an eye on Dunky-Dunk, who hadn't moved a muscle other than the ones in his throat as he growled like a tiny chainsaw. The barest hint of white teeth peeked out from between his lips, his little nose working overtime as he tried to smell the werewolf attempting to be friendly and nonthreatening in a subtle way.

"We did," Henri answered, his attention still on my attack puppy.

I wasn't sure what to think about Duncan not breaking eye contact yet. The boy had balls of steel. "No luck finding her then?"

His gaze met mine for a split second before returning to Duncan just as fast. "No. We lost her trail a half mile from where you ran into her."

Someone sounded a little sour about that.

The defined line of his jaw flexed before he looked at me again with those sober features that I wasn't sure how to take. "What did you do to make her leave?"

Did he sound a little accusatory, or was it my imagination?

"They're known to be aggressive."

She had been a little b.

I hugged my knees closer, reminding myself of the importance of honesty. Of the roots the elders had briefly mentioned that were so important here. There was a chance that despite their assurances, one day they would ask for more specifics about what I was, and then nothing would be a secret.

And that made me think about the bracelet I know I'd seen on Franklin's wrist.

But wondering what he was made me feel like a hypocrite. If there was anything I needed to focus on, it was myself and my donut. And Henri's careful curiosity.

He definitely didn't know the one thing I was very careful not to bring up. The same thing Matti and Sienna and my parents also avoided like the plague. Nobody pretended anything, but we had all gotten really good at tiptoeing around the truth.

But these strangers were either going to accept me or they wouldn't. So I answered, "Nothing much." That wasn't a lie.

Duncan leaned forward a little bit, getting a better smell of the man patiently balanced on the balls of his feet in front of us.

I shared a little more. "I told her to leave and not come back."

His Adam's apple bobbed. He didn't actually raise an eyebrow, but there was something about his features that made it seem like he had. "You *talked* to her?" He paused, and I'd swear I felt him scoff. "That's all?"

He thought I was full of it.

I had an idea of what he saw when he looked at me. I wasn't short or tall. I was a handful up top and down below. The only part of me that anyone remembered, if they did, was my face, and it wasn't an intimidating one either. A drunk ex-boyfriend had told me once that I was "beautiful but not at the same time." My bone structure was a mix of the heritage I highly suspected ran through my blood and a very different one that softened my nose and gave me a lighter eye color.

I was the attractive equivalent of Brussels sprouts: some people were about it, and other people would rather starve.

Some people had soft faces that they could shape and make personalities for. Mine was angles and knew exactly who it was and made no apologies for it. Maybe one day I could learn from it.

"Yup," I confirmed. "That's all."

He scoffed as much as a man his size was capable of, and it was rough like the rest of him. He shoved his right sleeve up his forearm. "You want me to believe that?"

That was definitely a little bit of accusation in there.

I didn't *want* to take it personally, but . . . "Yeah. Why would I lie about that?" I asked, trying to keep my voice light.

"People lie about everything."

Ouch. "You're not wrong, but I meant what I said. I'm not going to start building bonds here based on lies." I thought about that a little more. "And that's such a dumb thing to make up. If I'm going to lie about something, it wouldn't be that."

Something flicked across the striking lines of his face, mostly in his eyes. He had thick, expressive eyebrows, his features all dark Viking. He was good at hiding what he was thinking, that was for sure, but I was excellent with body language.

I scrunched up my nose, taking in the scruff along his jaw and cheeks that had grown in from when we'd first seen each other. He'd stuck around the whole meeting, but right as the elder had offered to take us for a tour, his phone had rung and Henri had disappeared.

"Matti and I showed up, I volunteered to handle the situation so he wouldn't have to fight it in front of the kids—"

"He agreed to let you *handle* the situation?"

Did he have to sound so suspicious?

Yes, he did. He had no idea what one, or both, of my parents had passed along in their DNA. Henri didn't know who I was. Neither did I, exactly, but I had more information on the matter than he did. So I nodded. "Yes, I would've been fine, and he knows that."

I could see that it was on the tip of his tongue to ask how Matti knew that, but he didn't.

I kept going with my story before he asked more questions. "I went and talked to the river bully . . . Jenny Greenteeth. She wasn't nice. All I did was take off my bracelet, and that settled that."

His jaw did that flexing thing again. "You took off your bracelet?"

Couldn't he sense I wasn't lying? "You can ask the kids. Shiloh paid attention. He saw the whole thing."

Right there, without the slightest effort in being discreet, he took another whiff of me. A crease formed between those dark, full eyebrows. A muscle at his cheek went stiff as he processed whatever his senses and brain were both telling him.

He had more questions, that was obvious. Ones I wasn't really ready to answer unless I absolutely had to. But I didn't want to be put into the position of laying all my cards out this soon, not when he was being like this already, expecting the worst from me, or at least being so wary.

There were other things we needed to talk about.

As much as part of me wanted to let this go and pretend like he wasn't being all over the place with his behavior toward me, I couldn't. Henri was important here, and if he wasn't comfortable with my presence, then we had to figure this out. And it sure didn't seem like he was going to initiate it.

So I went straight for it. "Do you not want me to be here?" I blurted out.

Those light-colored eyes narrowed so much that they were basically slits on his striking face.

That wasn't a great nonanswer. "If you aren't, it's all right, but I'd like to know why." I lifted my shoulders. "I know it was a long time ago, but I promise I'm still the same Nina."

That didn't get me anything.

I tried again, hoping he wasn't preparing some speech on why he didn't want us to move here. "Is it what I turned out to be? Or is it something else?" My eyes slid toward Duncan, who was still going at his low, baby growling, implying with that look exactly what that "something else" was.

My precious, droopy-eared boy.

Henri's frown found a way to get even deeper. "I haven't seen you in almost twenty years," he answered in that husky voice, nothing about his tone giving anything away.

He had a point, but for whatever reason, I would have still trusted him. Trusted whoever he turned out to be. Because I might not remember a ton, but I did have clear memories of Henri making Matti and me snacks after school when he was the only one home, peeling and cutting an apple for me specifically because I hadn't liked the skin back then. Of him running off older kids who had picked on us. I had one particular memory of him giving me advice for riding my bike while I'd been learning.

I had thought a lot of young, teenage Henri.

Mid-twenty-something Henri, I had wanted to kick in the balls after what he'd done . . . even though I could look at his actions as an adult now and understood why he'd handled the situation the way he had.

But forty-ish Henri? I would give him the benefit of the doubt. I could believe in him, especially after watching him interact with the kids after they'd done something really stupid and communicating with their parents afterward. There had been genuine respect in those adults' faces, and those kids hadn't been scared of him. I didn't take that lightly.

"I have no problem with you." His gaze moved toward Duncan for a microsecond before returning to me. "Either of you."

"You sure about that?" I wanted to make it real clear that I couldn't sense lies the same way he could, but I wasn't unobservant. Body language said a whole lot where words wouldn't.

He frowned even more. "We have to be consistent with the rules in place," he started to explain, his tone somewhere between cool and polite. "Rules are bent before they're broken. What we do for you, regardless of your connection to Matti or me, can't be different than what we would do for anyone else."

I couldn't ask for special privileges, he was saying.

"It doesn't matter how much magic you have or who you're descended from. It doesn't matter what you look like. It's nothing personal."

He always did have a stick up his butt about rules, I remembered then.

And now he was a cop or something.

I wondered how well his uniform fit. I was pretty sure deputies had different types of clothing than police officers did. Hmm.

Both my eyebrows went up a moment later. "It doesn't matter what I look like?" I echoed.

There was no coyness on his face when he said, matter-of-factly, "Your face has changed a lot."

It had, but I still didn't expect him to make a comment about it. But at the same time, I had to fight the urge to stand up straighter. Was that a backward compliment?

I should leave it alone and not pry at the comment, and I dang well knew it, but when did I ever leave things alone? So I asked, drawing my words out, "In a good way or . . .?"

His eyebrow moved *just* a little bit. "What do you think?" he replied in that steady voice that held next to no emotion in it.

I blinked, shocked at his bluntness. "Thank you?" It didn't exactly sound like a compliment. Or an insult, for that matter. I wasn't sure what it was, but an invitation wasn't it either.

His gaze swept over me, and I could tell he gritted his teeth. I guess we were done talking about physical appearances. Fine by me. We could've been talking about a boring movie for all the emotion he was putting out talking about appearances.

Of all the things I'd inherited from my DNA parents, I would have given them all back except for my good health.

"Are you sure then? That you're fine with us being here?" I asked. "Because if you don't want us to join, all you have to do is say the word and we'll figure out another option. We won't stay where we aren't wanted, and that includes you, Henri. I would understand." It would hurt my feelings, and I might not want to see him for another two decades, but I would take it into consideration.

I wouldn't beg if it was him who didn't want us here.

"Understand what?"

"That you aren't comfortable." Around us, I explained silently. Or just me. Or just Duncan. It was honestly nothing short of a miracle that I didn't have self-esteem issues with those kinds of thoughts.

Those amber irises remained level on me. "There's nothing about either of you that could make me uncomfortable."

He said that now.

I pressed my lips together, trying to get a read on his careful expression. "Are you positive? Because I don't care if you hurt my feelings right now, but if you change your mind in six months, it isn't going to just be me that will be affected by your decision." I let the implication of who else could be hurt hang in the air between us.

His nod was slow. "I'm sure."

It sounded sincere, but . . . I still wasn't sure I totally believed it. I was going to have to take him at his word. There wasn't much else to do. "All right."

Duncan's growls suddenly got a little louder. He hadn't moved from his spot at my side, a mohawk lined his back, and those small, sharp white teeth were still very visible. Was he scared of him after what had happened?

"It's okay, Duncan." I reached out to pat his back. This was something else we needed to tackle. "This is Henri. He's Matti's cousin. He used to be my friend." I peeked at my old "friend," but his attention was on my puppy. "I know he was big and scary earlier, but he's not going to hurt us." That time when I turned to him, Henri's eyes were on me. "Right, Fluffy?"

"Right," he agreed.

Duncan wasn't buying it. This man had held him up like a ritual sacrifice earlier. I stroked my donut's back a little more, but convinced, he was not.

"It's fine," I tried again, stretching out with my other hand. I set it on Henri's arm, and what a forearm it was. My fingers couldn't wrap around it fully, not that I tried, but it was obvious. There were prominent veins along it. For being a man who could turn into a wolf, he was surprisingly not crazy hairy. "Henri's a friend."

Those bright red irises flicked toward me, and I took another turn petting his soft back.

"See?" I skimmed my palm up Henri's arm toward his shoulder, over bulging biceps, and then swept it back down to his hand, cupping my fingers over them and doing it all over again. He was warm, and the rest of his muscles were just as hard as I would have imagined. He could have been a modern-day Paul Bunyan with a handsome face, if I didn't know the truth. "It's okay, Duncan."

My boy's growling got a little better, but not much.

"I'm a friend, pup," Henri tried to assure him too, staying very, very still as I basically felt him up. "I'm not going to hurt you or your mom."

The knot in my throat at him calling me Duncan's mom . . .

Henri kept talking. "Watch," he told him before reaching very slowly out toward me—my boy's little growl revving up once more, but Henri ignored it—and setting his hand on top of my head. Taking his time, Henri swept it down the side of my skull, over my ear, and did it again.

Henri Blackrock was petting me.

"It's all right," I started talking again, scooting a little closer to Henri's frame and putting my palm back on that thick, corded forearm. "He's not hurting me. See? That feels really nice actually."

Duncan still wasn't convinced, and I met Henri's light-colored gaze and raised my eyebrows at him, not sure what else I could do to show Duncan we were safe with him. He'd never been this defensive . . . other than those two times.

But Henri seemed to know what to do from the way he gestured me closer.

I scooted over until my knee touched his thigh. Henri's arms opened, and in the span of a breath, he set one around me. He pulled me over to him. Then, in a fluid movement with the palm of his other hand, he drew my face to that notch between his shoulder and neck.

I got it. He was showing Duncan that he trusted me enough to get into such a close and vulnerable position with me. A parent might do it with a child, or possibly family members or close friends. I was honored, but I was even more surprised.

It *almost* made up for his BS with the trial-period situation earlier.

"Friends," Henri claimed.

"Friends," I agreed in the cheeriest voice I could muster. All the while, one of my arms was pinned between our bodies while *he* hugged *me*.

I would've climbed into his lap if he let me.

Cut it out, Nina.

Was I that hard up that a hug from a near-stranger, who just happened to be good-looking and my favorite body type, could turn me into a perv? My hormones needed to stop this crap immediately.

I needed to remember that everyone here more than likely had exceptional senses. I'd gotten lazy living around normal people for so long. It had been nice, having secrets, not being so vulnerable and honest *all* the time.

Plus, Sienna had already caught my attraction to him earlier.

If I acted weird now, that was going to send the wrong message to everyone. Plus, I would die of shame if my body did something it shouldn't be doing around not just someone I barely knew but *my best friend's family member.* Someone who might be a neighbor if things worked out in my favor.

I hope he hasn't opened his senses. Wolves didn't walk around smelling everything all day, every day, after all. I knew for a fact that Matti only opened his up when he was at home, or in situations where he was uncertain about other people and wanted to feel them out.

Fortunately, it appeared Henri's nose wasn't working overtime, and after a moment, he sat back, gaze staying on Duncan as his palm went to my face.

He wasn't done proving a point, and apparently he wanted to demonstrate that I was just as comfortable around him too.

Henri tipped my chin back—and I let him, like a doll—and the man wasted no time pressing his forehead to my neck. His movements were slow. The angle changed so his nose drew a line up the side to just beneath my ear. Finally smelling me from the soft puffs of breath that touched my collarbone afterward from his nose . . . some from his mouth . . .

If his senses hadn't been open before, they were now.

I couldn't shiver. I absolutely couldn't. This was a werewolf thing, through and through. It was what I'd invited him to do hours ago when he'd turned me down. Sort of. I wasn't sure anyone had ever had their arm around me while they'd done it before. Nor had anyone ever done it so *slowly*.

"He's just getting to know me again, Dunky," I explained, fighting for my life to keep my voice even as Henri's face switched sides. His breaths were there again. His cheek. His nose. All of it like a brand. I had to keep it together. I had to keep it together, and I did that the only way I knew how. I started blabbering. "We haven't seen each other in a long time. Back then, I didn't smell the same way I do now," I explained just as he finally withdrew, his face only inches away from mine when he did.

Henri's lids were low. His lips slightly parted. He had a strong jaw. A little cleft in his chin. Deep-set eyes framed by those heavy eyebrows that hugged his striking facial bones.

I winked at him, and before he could say anything else, leaned forward and wedged my face into the same place it'd been in before. Between his shoulder and throat. A spot that wasn't just warm but smelled like rain and something woodsy like cedar.

Good, so freaking good.

And I didn't want Henri to know that. Not if I had the choice. "See, Donut? Friends," I told my puppy, inhaling as discreetly as I could a little more.

When I pulled back, Henri was watching me, his eyelids still lower, but his mouth was pressed tight.

"He stopped," the man so close to me said.

I hadn't noticed. I pulled all the way back and smiled again, hoping it didn't look as tight as it felt. "You're *sure* you're fine with us being here?"

The face I hadn't seen in over a decade hovered there, and after a moment, he nodded tightly.

A low ring exploded from the direction of Henri's pants. He stood up and dug into the back pocket of his jeans. He started talking as he read whatever was on the screen. "Breakfast is at nine. Be careful with the branches. Our physician's assistant isn't here right now, and the nearest hospital is over an hour away."

"Okay."

Henri hesitated for a second. It wasn't until that moment that I noticed he'd changed out of the dusty white shirt he'd had on earlier. His lip was healed too.

He gave me a long look. "I don't need to worry about you, do I?"

We both knew what he was referring to.

I was and I wasn't like them, and I didn't want to let myself take it personally. I had once asked my dad why we lived across the street from our neighbor if they were scared of him, and he'd said, *"For that reason, Nina. His presence keeps the things we love safer than we'd be anywhere else."*

"How?"

He had patted my head. *"We're not the only ones scared of him."*

I understood now what he'd meant. There was fear and there was respect, and there was a gray area in between. And there was a reason why the only little pig who survived had hidden in the brick house.

I shook my head. "No, you don't need to worry." I lifted my hand, my fingers formed in a V-shape. "I come in peace."

For the second time that day, no one laughed at my joke.

His phone rang again, but he ignored it. "Just making sure." He pressed his lips together. "I'm sorry I knocked you down earlier," he claimed in that low voice, shooting me another expression I couldn't recognize, before swiping his thumb across the screen and bringing it up to his ear as he started walking toward the house with a barked, "Blackrock."

"Sleep well," I wished him anyway, not sure how exactly I felt about that interaction. About him in general, to be honest.

To Matti and Sienna, I was always Nina. They knew every single good and bad thing I'd ever done, and they loved me anyway. I thought they always would.

There were other people who liked what they did know about me. We could have a good laugh. We could talk. But I kept them at a distance, I filtered what their knowledge of me was because of my concern over how they could or would react to things that didn't need to be worried about. Wearing my bracelet around other magical beings had always made me feel like I wore a constant filter—like some people only got to see part of me, which was true.

A tipsy mermaid could tell me some of the darkest things she'd ever done, but I'd never been forthcoming enough to do the same.

And to Henri? In the span of just a few hours, I'd been Cricket, the girl he'd known, and Nina, the adult he didn't understand and was struggling not to judge too hard—at least it seemed that way to me. His fluctuation between those two people had already been evident. There wasn't much I could do about that other than just show him who I was, and I needed time for that.

On top of that, there was my attraction to him. Not just a little attraction, but more than I would've wished, if I had a choice. I didn't think I'd ever met someone I would describe as a hunk before, but now that I'd seen him, I understood how that word could be used.

In the middle of thinking about all that, Duncan climbed

into my lap, his attention on the figure walking away from us. I set my nose into the crown of his head and watched too, the low murmur of Henri's voice reaching us despite the distance; it was one of the good and the bad things about being out in the middle of nowhere: you could hear everything. The front door opened and closed soon after.

Only then did Duncan's nose move to the spot where Henri had rubbed his cheek. He sniffed it. He didn't get a mohawk when he did it, which I thought was a good thing.

Maybe Henri wasn't going to bend the rules for us, but he wasn't going to work against us either, it seemed. I needed to take that for the win it was. And maybe he could help me with getting to know some of the men here. Because I was going to need to work on that too: finding a mate.

Unless he was an option? I'd ponder that later. We had to get through the next three months first.

For the time being, we needed to focus on settling in.

Getting people to like us.

Not scare anyone along the way.

And hopefully get Henri firmly on our side at some point.

But for Duncan, I would do anything, and now I had to prove it.

Chapter Seven

"You both look like . . . how do I say this? S-h-i-t. You both look like s-h-i-t," I pretty much giggled in front of Sienna and Matti the next morning.

There were few things better than being right.

And even fewer than when you could be smug about it.

Duncan had already been awake for close to an hour by the time we'd left our room to find out why his second and third favorite people weren't texting us back. By that point, I'd been awake for almost two hours. I'd woken up feeling off, groggy and flustered, like there was something I should've remembered that had happened in the middle of the night, but I had no idea why.

I hadn't dreamt. I went years between dreams. So long, I forgot their details but not the way they'd all made me feel, or what the voice that talked to me in them each time sounded like. It made no sense, and the problem was that no one I'd ever spoken to about it had ever really believed me when I said I didn't dream to begin with. They all thought I just couldn't remember them.

That wasn't the case.

Whatever had happened overnight, I'd woken up earlier than normal, unable to shake off the imaginary spiderwebs that left me feeling off. Once I gave up trying to go back to sleep, I tried making a plan for all the small things I needed to figure out sooner rather than later while Duncan chainsawed it up beside me. Then I'd showered again, even though I'd done it last night after we'd come back inside. I used the unscented soap I always washed with, so used to limiting my scents around sensitive noses for most of my life.

Then we'd gone to pee, and finally went looking for these two, only to find them on their death bed.

Sienna groaned from her spot beneath the covers, next to Matti who had his arm thrown over his eyes as he made the same sound. "We both had loose stomachs. You didn't?" she moaned.

"No, but I told you not to buy those hot dogs at the gas station, didn't I? And didn't you tell me, '*We never get sick, Nina. I've got an iron stomach,*'" I reminded her with a tone that got me two middle fingers. I laughed and leaned against the doorframe. "You guys are gas station noobs. You never eat the hot dogs or get the nachos," I reminded them of the exact words I'd used at the time.

"Shut up, Nina," Matti muttered, lifting his arm just enough to give me a peek of a dull eye. "I feel like my ass gave birth to two ten-pound babies."

I snickered, and even Sienna snorted before moaning. "Don't," she got out in between her own pained sound effects.

"Yeah, Matti, don't make her laugh. She doesn't need to shart in someone else's bed. I'm trying to make a good impression here."

He groaned at the same time as she grabbed a throw pillow from the floor and tried to chuck it at me. It hit the floor between the bed and bedroom door. They really were sick to be that weak.

"Want me to bring you anything?" I asked them, deciding to be nice.

Their responses came in the form of more groans, which I took as a "no." From the glasses of water next to their nightstands, I knew they weren't going to get dehydrated. I should probably bring them some salt from my camper to replenish their electrolytes.

I'm turning into a mom, I realized right then.

I peeked down at the calm puppy sitting next to my right foot and smiled. His tail was wagging, the flame on it small and dark blue. He'd rolled over once in the middle of the night, he'd slept so good.

"All right, we're going to figure out breakfast. Henri said to be down there at . . ."

They weren't listening. Or maybe they couldn't hear me over their groans.

"I have my cell. Let me know if you need something, okay? I'll wipe Sienna's butt, but I'm not wiping yours, Matti, until you're at least in your seventies," I told them before backing out of the room as another throw pillow went flying through the air. "Love you, guys," I called out, shutting the door of their room before making eye contact with my donut. "Well, Dunky, I didn't want to go downstairs by ourselves, but we've got no choice. Might as well get used to it. At least we have each other."

He tilted his head, his *"yes"* a reminder that *we* were in this together.

We had changed tires in the worst conditions of every season, we'd come across brown bears on hikes, and we'd been stranded in the middle of nowhere once or twice overnight.

Duncan and I had been through some stuff.

Neither one of us might have been cowboys, but this wasn't our first rodeo, and we were a team.

Team Duncan Donut.

We were going to have to acclimate eventually and meet people without Matti and Sienna. That part was non-negotiable. So, with my boy by my side, we headed downstairs. There were sounds coming from every direction. I hadn't asked how they handled the whole eating situation with the people that lived here. Last night, the four of us had dinner in my trailer while we'd grabbed our bags. The elder with the glasses, Franklin, had been vague about how many people lived in this building. Did they all share food? Did everyone buy their own groceries and put names and labels on their things? I had questions. The only people I'd ever lived with were my parents and Sienna.

"Good morning, Nina and Duncan."

I turned in the direction the voice was coming from. Down the hall, the elder who gave us a tour yesterday dipped his head in greeting. I lifted my hand. "Good morning."

It was clear from the absence of puffy facial features that Franklin had been awake for some time. In a button-down shirt with a maroon vest over it, tucked into khaki pants, his glasses riding low on his nose, he made me think of a librarian. He looked so . . . disarming.

For some reason, I didn't trust that impression.

And I noted again, like I had confirmed during our tour yesterday, that I couldn't sense his magic.

I was confident I'd seen a bracelet on his wrist. His long sleeves hid any trace of one at the moment too. What was he? Would Henri tell me what he was if I asked?

"Was your room comfortable?" the elder asked.

"Yes. It's perfect, thank you."

His nod was a little stiff, at least I thought so. "I'll escort you to the kitchen. Henri is making eggs, and it's a real treat when it's his turn to cook for us."

I could not make a face at the idea of mountain man Henri making eggs for more than just himself. So I pressed my lips together and nodded. "That sounds great."

The older man waited for us outside a cracked door—with a smaller doggy door at the bottom—that a quick peek inside confirmed was a bedroom. His, I imagined. The only thing visible was a sliver of a bed a little bigger than a twin, and it was made. Franklin smiled when Duncan stopped at his feet. The older man reached down to scratch the top of his head. "How did the handsome boy sleep?"

The handsome boy stretched up to bump his nose against the man's hand in his own answer.

He couldn't be so bad if my boy was being affectionate, could he?

Plus, I was a sucker for Duncan compliments. He might seem suspicious, but he had good taste. "Great. He didn't want to get out of bed this morning." He'd slept across my chest for half of the night, and I'd barely been able to breathe, but I was never, ever going to complain about it.

Franklin nodded before gesturing for me to follow him to where he'd explained yesterday the kitchen was located. When we had gotten thirsty last night, we'd gone to my trailer and gotten water from the five-gallon jugs I refilled at grocery stores instead of wandering around. I wasn't shy, but I hadn't been ready to treat this place like home so soon.

"Do you have questions?" The elder turned to me. "We went over things quickly yesterday."

That was a relief. "I was actually just wondering right now . . . how many people live in this building?"

"Three of the elders call the clubhouse home, myself included. We're all on the first floor, along the hallway there where you found me. The others are both offsite at the moment, visiting their families. One of the children also has a bedroom by ours." He hadn't mentioned that last night. "On the third level, there are two unmated members of the community who either choose not to live with their family members or don't have that option."

I felt that comment in my soul.

"The homes we have on the property are reserved for members with family units."

"What counts as a family unit?" I asked.

"An adult and a child, or a married couple. Two or more constitutes a family," he replied. "You and Duncan would after your trial period."

We got to the end of another hallway, the smell of cooked meat getting stronger the closer we got.

Duncan even sped up to a trot, his nose tipped up high, his tail sticking straight up in the air. He almost looked like he was prancing.

I slipped my phone out of my pocket a little and snapped a picture of him.

Franklin kept talking. "Since there aren't many of us, we set up a meal schedule for breakfast and dinner. It's more convenient, so we aren't stepping all over each other and there aren't arguments about cleaning pots and pans."

I nodded, listening . . . but also keeping an eye on Prancer over here. His ears were so long they were inches from dragging along the floor. It was so precious.

Even more adorable was the way I could faintly hear him saying, *"Yes, yes, yes, yes,"* in excitement from whatever he smelled that he was thrilled about.

"There's a monthly calendar in the pantry where you can sign up to make breakfast or dinner when you can, along with what meal you're preparing. Our only request is that you decide twenty-four hours in advance. If someone doesn't want to eat it, they don't. We understand sometimes someone is busier than normal, so we don't have a minimum or a limit on how many times you do it as long as you do. Be fair about it, that's all we ask. Some days, everyone is on their own." Brownish-greenish eyes met mine. "Will that be an issue?"

"No. I like cooking," I confirmed, pondering over their schedule. "Are we in charge of paying for groceries ourselves or does everyone pool money together?" I made enough to live off without sweating small extra expenses too bad, but feeding other adults? Especially carnivores?

I didn't make enough for that.

Franklin looked startled. He pushed his glasses up his nose. "The community fund pays for the groceries for all residents. We have a shipment from a grocer supply that delivers food once a week. If you want something that isn't included in the staples, you're responsible for purchasing it yourself."

"There's a community fund? And it pays for groceries?" I asked just as we made it to the doorway that led into a spacious kitchen.

The room was the size of a commercial kitchen, yet still homey. Dark cabinets framed most of the walls, there were two giant islands, and at least four built-in ovens visible from where we stood. A big two-door stainless-steel fridge took up another wall, and there was another steel door off to the side that reminded me of the kind of walk-in refrigerators I'd seen in restaurants.

But most astounding of all was the man at the multi-burner range, a spatula in one hand, a white wolf puppy at his feet.

"... revenues from the community's businesses pay for certain things. What I mean when I say grocery staples are meats mostly, but also breads, some dairy, fruits, and vegetables. If you're looking for rare French cheese, that would be your financial responsibility."

Dang it, I'd missed part of what he'd said. I'd been too focused on Henri's back, taking him in as he'd turned while the elder spoke. He had a green flannel shirt tucked into jeans, his hair damp from a shower. He'd shaved since last night.

Smooth skin looked good on him too.

"Morning, Henri," Franklin greeted him. "Smells delicious."

"Cheesy omelets," the werewolf explained. His gaze flicked in my direction. "Morning," he greeted us. So polite.

I smiled. "Morning, Henri. Hi, Agnes."

The white puppy had angled her body to the side, keeping an eye on us. I bent down and picked up Duncan to show him to her, even though she would've already smelled him by that point. Both of their ears perked. Setting him down, I watched as Franklin headed to the double-door refrigerator and pulled out a container of orange juice that he held up. "Nina?"

"Yes, please."

"Water for the . . . oh, he found it," Franklin trailed off at the exact second the sound of slurping reached me, and I leaned over to find two bowls of water—one ceramic, the other stainless steel—on the floor. Duncan was drinking from the ceramic one. "We wash those throughout the day. If you see it dirty, please clean it."

At the stove, Henri asked over his shoulder, "Is he a picky eater?"

I couldn't help but shiver a little. "No. He just stopped trying to eat dead animals a week ago." A gag built up in my throat at the memory of the things I'd pulled out of his mouth. Part of me had figured that he wouldn't get sick from it—I remembered Matti eating all kinds of messed-up stuff when we'd been kids and he'd been in wolf form passing as a puppy—but I hadn't wanted to get too crazy, at least until he built up a better immune system.

Henri nodded before turning and pulling two textured silicone mats out of a drawer. Then my mouth dropped open as he pulled container after container out of the fridge, along with a short can. The man who had drawn my face to his neck hours ago spread out small, spotted eggs with the shell, a variety of thawed meats, and then sardines from the can on the mats, pushing the food into the grooves with the bottom of a fork. I had to lean over the side of the counter again to see that Duncan and Agnes had made their way over and were sitting at his feet, eager expressions on both their puppy faces.

And here Duncan had been growling at him a few hours ago. I had to hold back a laugh.

"Is this fine for breakfast?" Henri asked with his back still to us as Franklin handed me a glass of juice.

"Perfect," I told him, a lot breathier than normal, mostly in pleasure and surprise at what he was feeding them. It was almost an exact replica of what I gave Duncan for breakfast. It made my chest feel a little funny.

"Is there a problem?" Franklin asked as he took the seat beside me.

"No." Which was the truth, but honesty was the best policy. "It's just that I've been worried I'm not feeding him what he biologically needs. I feel a lot better now seeing that what I've been giving him isn't that different from what you all think it should be." Not that they even knew for a fact what he needed exactly, but I trusted them more than myself. I had just been going off what a nutritionist recommended for his weight.

The older man patted my back kind of awkwardly, or maybe reluctantly. I wasn't sure how old Franklin might have been. He could've been an older-looking fifty or anywhere up to eighty. His glasses gave him a grandpa vibe, but there was something else about him that just didn't come across very elderly to me.

Or maybe I was being distrustful because of that bracelet under his sleeve.

"He's in good health. You've done a fine job with him, Nina. He's happy and healthy, and your bond seems strong. All those things matter. You can feed a child a healthy diet, but if it's in an atmosphere without love and safety, that can be just as harmful to them as poor dietary choices."

"Thank you." I smiled at him, thinking his words over and seeing the truth in them.

He nodded, peering into my eyes carefully like he was looking for something. With a smile I thought was a little stiff, he dropped his hand. "I have existing commitments after breakfast, but we'll discuss the pup soon," he offered. "I'm going to begin looking into the matter of his possible heritage and get back to you once I have any information."

I wondered. Oh, did I freaking wonder. But we had waited this long for an answer. What was a little more time? "Thank you, Franklin," I said just as a plate was set down in front of him.

"I don't know what you eat, so serve yourself," Henri's husky voice explained as he met my gaze briefly before heading back to the range.

Had his eyes gotten prettier or was I imagining it? "Thank you."

"The calendar to sign up for meals is through there." Henri pointed toward the regular-looking door in the far corner of the huge kitchen beside what I was sure was a walk-in fridge.

Someone had overheard our conversation.

"I'll check it out," I said as I got up and headed to where he was busy piling food onto a cream-colored plate with flowers painted on it that were almost identical to the vintage ones my parents used to have. Duncan spared me a quick glance before his attention went right back to the counter where his breakfast was waiting.

I was going to need to get used to it not just being us from here on out. Every morning was going to be like this if we were going to be living in this building for at least a few months. Who knew how things would change after that? I couldn't be sad about it, about sharing him, about mourning the life we'd had, going to new places, eating breakfast braless, doing whatever we wanted around my work schedule.

Nothing ever stayed the same, and he needed to be safe.

We would start a new routine here. Build new habits. Make a different life.

More than anything, I needed to set a good example. He didn't need to sense my grief over our previous life and be confused over it. How could I expect him to move forward if I couldn't?

I picked up a plate from the stack and waited until Henri had moved aside to get my own servings, resignation and determination steeling my body and brain. Laid out like a buffet were the cheesy omelets he'd mentioned, along with bacon, some kind of hamburger patties, and a pot of what I was pretty sure were grits. That part was a surprise because every werewolf I'd ever known rarely ate anything other than meat, fish, and high-fat foods like avocados, butter, and small amounts of cheese. Fruit was tolerable—fruit juices were always welcome. Complex carbs like pasta or bread were rarely eaten. Maybe they'd tackle a plain potato or a couple fries.

"You don't like grits?" that grumbly voice asked.

I snuck another peek at Henri.

His features were so different from Matti's that it was hard to see their resemblance.

Their jaws and cheekbones were different shapes, their eye colors were also not the same; their builds were muscular yet complete opposites. The only similarity they had in common physically was that they were both tall. They were like day and night, on the inside and the outside.

Matti was big for a wolf in that form, thanks to his Amarok ancestry, but he looked like a scrawny teenager compared to Henri—not that I would ever tell him that.

"No, I like grits," I told him. "I was just surprised to see them. Before I came down, I'd been thinking about how I'd need to squeeze some fiber in during my lunch from here on out." I beamed. "Thank you for making them."

His jaw flexed, but he dipped his chin.

"I should have mentioned that everyone that lives here is mainly a carnivore," Franklin piped in, breaking my concentration from the man that I shouldn't have been so aware of. "For meal-planning purposes."

"It's okay, my parents are both wolves in their magical forms. I'm used to it," I told the older man.

His gaze narrowed, just for a split second, before he pasted a small, tight smile on his mouth as he nodded. "I see." Franklin's attention flicked down to his plate for a moment before he asked, "If you'd like oatmeal . . . don't we have some instant oats for the children, Henri?"

"We do," Fluffy answered, setting his plate on the counter before moving around me. He picked up one mat and set it against the wall closest to the walk-in refrigerator.

Agnes didn't move, but Duncan's tail swayed.

Apparently, my donut wasn't worried about Henri for the time being. Was it the fact he was making food? Or had what happened last night chilled him out?

Henri went for the other mat and placed it a foot away from the first one. "Agnes and Duncan, you can eat now." One white fluffball and a black one darted toward their breakfasts, no hesitation.

"You said he's two years old?" my best friend's cousin asked, watching the pups inhale their meal.

"He is. Two years and a couple months." Dunky was acting like he hadn't eaten in a week.

"He has good self-control for his age," Henri noted in a thoughtful voice.

Of course he did. That comment made me way too smug, but I tried to be humble and say, "He's a very good boy. How old is Agnes?"

"Eight," Franklin answered.

Sienna had said Henri didn't have a mate, but . . .

No, she wasn't his. Matti would've said something by now.

Come to think of it, unlike Shiloh and Pascal, she hadn't had angry parents or guardians come out after we'd gotten back to the community yesterday. Henri had told her to get her punishment from the elders. What was her parental situation? Was she the child who lived here? I decided I'd have to ask about it later. Definitely not in front of her. She seemed to be interested in Duncan, but I was pretty sure she'd flashed a canine at me when I'd been walking around her to get my breakfast. A part of me admired her for it.

She was a smart kid, already knowing you couldn't trust everyone that came into your life.

Most of us took a lot longer to learn that lesson.

I had barely finished eating when the elder pushed his stool back. "I need to get going." He dusted his hands off before pushing his glasses up his nose. His whole demeanor seemed so uptight, his smile at me forced. "Young lady, I leave you in good hands."

Whose hands?

The older man peered over at Henri. "Before I leave, Henri, what's going on? You've been surlier than normal this morning."

Henri, who had been sitting quietly while we ate at the island, grunted without looking away from his plate. "I'm fine."

From his narrowed gaze, I'd say Franklin didn't believe him, and neither did I. "Is it . . . ?" He trailed off, whatever he was implying hung in the air, a mystery I didn't understand.

But I wanted to.

"No," Henri answered tersely, clearly not wanting to talk about whatever was on his mind.

Deciding to be nice, I threw him a bone. I wanted us to be friends, and friends were always allies. "He's probably mad at me because I bit him," I offered as an explanation.

Two sets of eyeballs swung over in my direction.

Henri's forehead furrowed. "I'm not mad because you . . ."

I smiled.

The grooves between his eyebrows got even deeper. "You're fucking with me?"

It was like he couldn't believe it.

I held my thumb and index finger apart about an inch. "Little bit." But that confirmed it, he *was* in a mood over something.

He tipped his head to the side.

I was pretty sure that might have been his amused face, at least one of them. Or it might be wishful thinking.

"I don't understand what you're talking about." Franklin frowned before shaking his head. "I will take that as my cue to leave. Nina, if you think of any more questions, I can answer them later if Henri is unable to. I will see you both this evening," he finished quickly before exiting the kitchen like he was in a rush, his hands in his pockets while he left. Franklin had even left his plate on the counter.

Maybe he was running late somewhere, but . . . something still seemed fishy about him.

Real fishy.

"Is he okay?" I asked, even though I really wanted to know if he was always like that, but that sounded aggressive in my head.

He pushed his chair back. "He was fine to me."

If he said so.

Standing up, I shoved my stool back and picked up my plate, along with Franklin's, and went around to where the pups had eaten their food and collected their lick mats too.

"We have two dishwashers. You can load those plates instead of doing them by hand. It saves water consumption," Henri explained as he pushed his stool in. He'd been awfully quiet while we'd eaten; all three of us had been.

Both Agnes and Duncan had wandered over to sit by us after they'd finished their meal and drank more water. Duncan was curled up into a little ball, watching the white puppy.

Just as I set the dishes into the sink, Henri came up beside me. I tipped my head back to meet his eyes. "You can put the mats into the dishwasher too. I'll put the leftovers in the fridge, and you can load the pot into the dishwasher."

I could do that.

Halfway through loading the dishwasher, he asked from behind, "Where are Matti and his mate?"

I'd been waiting for someone to ask. "They're upstairs." There was no reason I couldn't give him specifics. "They've got the brown plague."

"The brown . . ." He went quiet, figuring it out.

I couldn't help but snicker, thinking about them. "They both looked about ten pounds lighter than they did last night, so I think that gives you an idea of how—"

Henri cleared his throat. "I understand."

I bet he didn't, but it made me want to shake my head picturing how sick they'd looked. They had been so confident about those hot dogs. And with their noses? I didn't understand how they hadn't been able to tell there was something wrong with them.

"When we're done, I'll give you a tour so you can get familiar with the grounds."

"All right." I stuck the skillet I'd handwashed, because it was too large for the dishwasher, under the faucet. "Just us?"

There was a pause. "Is that a problem?"

I made a face as I flipped the pan and rinsed the other side. "No, why would it be?" I turned off the water and peeked over my shoulder. He must have sensed me staring at his back because he slowly did the same and blinked at me. I lifted my chin. "You all right? It was only a question."

He turned back toward the range. "Fine," he answered, back to using clipped answers.

All right then.

When I was done with the dishes, I picked up Duncan, and Henri bent to pet Agnes, and I followed him down the hallway we had taken to get to the kitchen. His voice was loud enough for me to hear clearly, the white wolf beside him, looking so small in comparison. "Did someone explain our early school situation?"

"Franklin mentioned a nursery during our tour yesterday . . ."

Agnes's yellow eyes peered at us, not slowing down one bit while she did. I wiggled my fingers at her with the hand not supporting the majority of Duncan's weight. She flashed me *both* her canines.

"It is and it isn't a nursery. All the pups who are old enough to be away from their mothers attend it. Some of the parents refer to it more as preschool for the small ones until they're old enough to attend school," he explained.

"Some of the kids go to school? In town?"

"Most. A few are homeschooled or take online courses. We don't have enough children or qualified educators to offer classes on site," Henri went on. "We provide after-school supervision until six in the evening for the kids whose parents can't pick them up, but it's never a problem to find someone to keep an eye on a child if they don't make it by then. Most of the kids go home with someone after school."

Even I knew that daycare was something highly sought after.

"The kids are usually split into two age groups—the young ones, and the ones who are only around after school—but the member who used to care for the older children is on a leave of absence to care for his mother. For now, through the summer, they're mixed together until we can find someone else to take over the position."

We passed by the door that Franklin had been standing in front of when Duncan and I had come downstairs. It was closed now. Every door had a small doggy door. I hadn't noticed that until now. It wasn't only his.

I focused on the bundle in my arms. He was relaxed, curious, and very awake. I pulled him in a little tighter to me. "That's a great option—"

"It's not an option."

I focused on the back of Henri's head, his hair was shorter around the sides and longer at the top, like he cared but didn't really want to put in too much effort either. It was a good haircut for him. "All right. But do you think we should wait a couple of days until he settles in since we just got here?"

Henri had the nerve to glance over his shoulder, his dark

eyebrows arching slightly as he took in the puppy in my arms. "He looks settled to me."

I waited to bite the inside of my cheek again until he was facing forward. "I think he's doing great so far, but it hasn't even been a day—"

He cut me off. "He'll be fine."

I could not growl at a werewolf, especially one that looked almost nothing like every other one I'd ever met—size-wise. I had questions about that, but none of them I could ask in this building or without soundproof walls. I reminded myself that I didn't need to argue with Henri. We had to get along. I wanted to be his friend. "I don't want to stress him out or make him think he's being abandoned . . ."

We passed by the front door and headed toward the faint sounds of what had to be little kids.

I started to get a little nervous. "How about tomorrow?"

Henri stopped right in front of a door halfway down the hall. Like every other one we'd gone by, this one also had a puppy-sized mini door at the bottom. The only difference was that it was twice the size of the rest of them.

The serious man gave me an even more grave expression. "He'll be fine," he insisted.

I pressed my lips together, trying to stop myself from arguing with him again. I was trying to stay on his good side, dang it.

"He isn't nervous or scared, and you said he understands what we say, so there's no reason why he'd think you aren't coming back for him." His eyes moved to my chest area. "You understand what's happening, don't you, Duncan?"

Only I heard the *"Yes"* he projected.

There went my last hope. He'd been sitting here overhearing our conversation and hadn't made a peep to disagree about his nursery attendance. I guess he didn't mind . . . ?

I barely managed to hold back a frown. "He agreed," I admitted, knowing dang well how glum that statement came out. I looked at my sweetheart and only lowered my voice a little bit. "I guess you're staying, Donut."

"Yes," Duncan agreed, making me sigh. How could he be this mature already?

I hugged him two more times, and he gave my chin and cheek the same number of licks.

A throat cleared. "When you're done, let's take him inside."

Just like that, it felt like I'd swallowed a bag full of Warheads, and I would've been surprised if my face didn't reflect it.

If he felt any compassion for me leaving Duncan for the first time, it sure didn't reflect on Henri's face.

It wasn't that I hadn't believed him when he said the nursery was mandatory or that Duncan would more than likely be fine being away from me, but . . .

I had hoped that he would change his mind. I swallowed and clung to my donut tighter. How could he expect me to just drop him off?

There was a sigh, and I wasn't sure I imagined that Henri's voice might have gone *slightly* softer. "This'll be good for him. This environment promotes socialization, the strengthening of pack bonds, emotional maturity—"

The beginning of the end of him being my baby.

I suddenly understood why parents cried when they dropped their kids off at school.

Duncan had needed me for almost everything the last two years. He relied on me, and the truth was, I relied on him too. He was my shadow. My ride or die. The cilantro and lime to my carne asada tacos.

A knot formed in my throat, and it took everything in me to exhale. It came out strained. *This is what we were signing up for, for him to be safe.*

Even knowing all that, it really didn't help.

"Yeah, I get it." My voice was small. I didn't *want* to get it, but . . .

"Love."

I peeked at Duncan's face. He was sitting up in my arms, watching me, but his nose was busy twitching as he smelled what, or more likely who, was in the room.

Being here period was the end of a lot of things, but it could be the start of something new too.

The start of my heart breaking . . . Stop, Nina.

Lifting my gaze to meet Henri's, it took more effort than I ever would have imagined to keep the grief from my tone. "If he doesn't want to go in or he starts crying . . ." I threatened as the tank of a man watched me for a moment, then turned toward the door and pushed it open, slipping inside.

I could have used a hug or another word of reassurance. Even a nudge, but all right. Fine.

I could do this.

I barely got a chance to see Henri crouch through the window before the puppy in my arms started trying to lunge out of them.

Here I was, on the verge of crying, feeling so guilty for leaving him, and *he* was ditching *me*?

I dropped to a squat just as he wiggled out of my grasp, darting through the mini door to get into the room, leaving me standing there with my mouth open. I could not *believe* him.

A little bit of jealousy and disappointment that he'd left me that fast—at the first opportunity!—made my heart hurt for maybe two seconds total. But the sound of his familiar, playful bark reversed it almost as quickly. This was what I wanted for him. To be happy. To have people other than just me and our occasional visits to Sienna and Matti's.

I gulped.

My time of living apart, of being so solitary, was over—as long as we made it through the next three months.

Someone told me once that life was 10 percent of the things that happened in it, and 90 percent how you handled those things.

Now, I had to figure out how to handle this next chapter. If that had to be with my head held high, my heart open, and maybe a little teary-eyed, so be it. For Duncan, I'd manage.

Moving toward the door, I pushed it and went straight to stand beside Henri. He hadn't gone very far into the brightly lit classroom with lots of windows. Scattered around it were small beings of various heights. Most of the kids were human, looking between the ages of big toddler and elementary-school sized. Agnes was greeting the teacher, and Duncan was sniffing a small boy who was already scratching his ears, grinning wide.

Very, very slowly, I released a long breath as the woman who Agnes had been by made her way over.

She was very nice; she shook my hand and assured me that Duncan was going to be just fine, or something like that. Everything went in one ear and out the other. She might have said I smelled like a stinky dumpster, and I would have had no idea because I was trying so hard not to cry that I gritted my teeth and nodded a lot.

I didn't think I was fooling anybody because Henri patted my shoulder once halfway through whatever the teacher said.

I was leaving Duncan.

Everything was moving so fast.

In a daze, just as quickly as we'd come in, Henri shooed us out, and I tried to catch Duncan's attention, but he was busy being fussed by a boy with large ears and pale green skin. My donut had his butt in the air, his tail was swishing back and forth, and the boy, who I assumed was an ogre, was smiling at him.

That meant he was fine, right? That he felt safe and confident and knew that I would never, ever leave him until he was an adult? I could not cry.

This might be the worst moment of my life.

Top five at least, and I'd lived through losing Matti's mom and dad, who I had considered my second parents, and moving away from my own parents.

The door had barely closed behind us when Henri stopped, and I couldn't find the strength in me to do anything else but do the same.

I scratched my upper lip.

Henri lowered his voice. "You can cry outside but not in front of him."

I wasn't technically in front of him, I wanted to argue, but I nodded, all jerky and just once. "He used to wail when I locked him out of the bathroom because he'd bite my underwear and try to take off running with them, and he just dropped me like a bad habit," I told him, torn between laughing and tearing up.

There was a clear winner not even a second later. Shrugging my shoulder, I wiped my eye with it and sniffled. Then I did it again.

"It's fine. I'm fine," I tried to assure him. Then I waved my hand in front of the upper half of my face, but that didn't do anything. "You don't need to say anything. I'm not crying."

Henri's rugged face was neutral as he lifted his hand, set it on my shoulder, waited a second, and gave it a light squeeze. "He looks happy."

"He does, huh?" I whispered.

He nodded.

Then I nodded.

And he said, very seriously, "If you're done not crying, we can start the tour."

If I was done . . .

That did it. The grief left my body just like *that*. There was no way I didn't look like a goldfish as I stood there, trying to figure out how I could respectfully respond to that, while also trying to process whether he was teasing me again or not.

Henri didn't give me enough time to decide. He squeezed my shoulder gently one more time, a very werewolfy touch—and so unlike the man-boy I'd known who had never been very affectionate to anyone in my memories—and said, "Follow me."

Chapter Eight

"About half of the community who live in single-family homes own their own forms of transportation to get around the ranch. We don't allow full-sized vehicles beyond the parking lot," Henri jumped right into his explanation as we left through the door at the back of the building. It was next to the huge living room slash conference area where we had met the elders when we'd arrived.

Before the start of my tour, we had taken a quick detour after leaving the nursery and gone to check on Matti and Sienna. My conscience wouldn't allow me to leave without making sure they were okay. I'd had an upset stomach more times than I could count, but they hadn't. I'd peeked in the door, with Henri at my back, and found my friends passed out. After a quick refill of their glasses of water from the tap—Henri had explained they had an excellent filtration system for the whole building—I'd snuck back out without waking them up. They'd still looked like s-h-i-t.

Outside, there was a giant metal building directly behind the clubhouse that I hadn't noticed yesterday. Along the front of it were three oversized garage doors, one of which was open, revealing rows of golf carts, UTVs, and I didn't know what else. He gestured to it. "Everything in there is available to anyone who lives here, but we ask that you clean whatever you use if you get it muddy, plug it in to charge if the battery is low, and return it as soon as possible in case someone else needs to borrow it. No one will steal your belongings, but don't leave them in the vehicles."

I said, "All right," since he was ahead of me and couldn't see me nod.

"We'll take one now so we can get around faster," he said, entering through the opened bay.

Knowing exactly what he was doing and where everything was, he unplugged the first side-by-side two-seat all-terrain vehicle in the front row. It had a short bed in the back. From where I stood, there were multiple cables strewn across the floor, some of them connected to the sides of golf carts, but most of them were hung up on hooks along the walls.

"Are they electric?" I asked when I got to the garage door.

He kept doing what he was doing. "Some. The ones in front are. We replace them as the older UTVs stop working, and only when they're beyond repair. Nobody likes the smell of gas, but it's wasteful to get rid of them if they're still running. The tanks are kept low. If you use one, you need to put gas in it. There are portable tanks along the wall in the back. We write the dates of when we fill them up so we can use the oldest ones first when needed. Keep an eye out for that."

"All right," I agreed again. "Where does the gas come from?"

"Someone takes them into town to fill them up every week or two," he explained. "Leave the keys in when you return them. Back them in, if you can."

I pressed my lips together, fighting the urge . . . and I lost it. I smirked. "Yes, sir." My friend's cousin leaned to the side of where he was by the ATV, and I gave him a little smile.

Just as quickly as he'd appeared, he was gone again, setting the cord he'd been holding over one of the random hooks on the walls. "Ready?"

At the vehicle, I slid onto the bench and buckled the thick seat belt across my chest and lap. Henri did the same, then started the UTV and pulled out of the building, turning a hard right almost immediately onto one of the wide gravel paths that connected the structures in the community together.

The trees soared over us, old and majestic. I wondered what they'd look like in the fall. Some of them were bound to change color; they weren't all pine. The air somehow seemed even fresher and more inviting than it had yesterday. I wasn't subtle about taking in more than one big lungful of it, my skin reacting just as much as my nose did, goose bumps popping up along my arms.

But as I glanced to the side to ask Henri if the magic in the air affected him, I kept my question to myself.

He was glaring forward. The angle of his jaw was strained, and I was pretty sure the muscle between his cheek and ear was kind of bulging. His bone structure gave him a striking profile.

I had to stop checking him out sometime soon.

"You all right, Fluffy?" I asked him, noticing that his lips were pinched.

"Yes."

I called BS on that from the way his back molars seemed clamped together at the moment, but all right. "Okay."

He didn't want to confide in me? That was fine. He'd made that clear in the kitchen, hadn't he?

I focused on the homes and buildings that I'd only seen from a distance. For the most part, they were all the same size, with some slightly bigger than others. A woman standing outside of a small cabin waved as we drove by, and I was only mildly surprised when Henri greeted her back. I did too, figuring I needed to be friendly with my, hopefully, future neighbors.

Only after that did I let myself peek again at the broody-looking man to my left.

How does he feel about mating?

I looked away.

Ahead, the path we were on split. There were multiple ones that wound through the trees; none of them were paved, but they were all in good condition and free of debris. I'd lived at enough campgrounds to know how often weeds grew and overran *everything*. The gravel mini roads connected every building either to a main path or, in a few cases, to each other. There were even speed signs with the number 5 every hundred or so feet. While the forest was thick, plenty of sunlight snuck through, making the village seem just as unreal as it had the night before. It was adorable.

It was so adorable.

I couldn't help but "ooh" and "ahh." There were *so many* cabins and houses tucked in the trees. Most of them were log homes, blending into the surroundings perfectly, but there were a few that seemed new, painted neutral shades, with metal siding halfway up them.

The man behind the wheel drove a whole 7 miles an hour down the road. Eventually, we slowed down when we got by a house with a fenced-in garden. In one of the beds, a little boy was kneeling, and at the sound of us approaching, he lifted his head.

It was Shiloh.

With a white T-shirt covered in multicolored handprints, his satyr legs tucked under him, my new friend had the most mournful expression on his face. It managed to get even worse when he must have realized it was us, because he looked even sadder as he lifted his arm and waved, a small shovel in his hand.

"I'm not slowing down to talk to him. Part of his punishment for running off is that he's grounded, and that means no socializing. His family asked everyone to not come by their house until he's not in trouble anymore."

I winced, but I'd been grounded before. "Is Pascal in trouble too?"

"Big trouble."

Henri and I both waved as we drove past the house, and I snuck a glance over my shoulder afterward to find Shiloh staring after us.

I waved at him again as slyly as I could, and that earned me a cute smile and a happier wave.

"He'll be all right," the man beside me promised, probably noticing what I'd done but not bothered too much by it.

Soon after that, Henri pointed toward a newer structure that kind of looked like a home but didn't at the same time. There weren't enough windows. Two satellite dishes were mounted to the metal roof. "That's the teenagers' building. Anyone is technically allowed in, but we try to give them their own space in there."

The teenagers here had their own space? "That's so nice," I told him. "How many teenagers live here?"

We kept driving. "Between the ages of thirteen and eighteen? Eighteen."

"Wow."

He nodded and pointed at a discreet-looking brown building off into the distance. "We're on a community well. Someone is usually doing something to maintain it. We try to conserve water as much as possible. Keep that in mind while you're with us."

While you're with us.

Beyond all the homes, we came to a huge field with five massive greenhouses. He explained that they grew as much food as they could, that everyone was expected to participate in their upkeep, but that there were two members who worked in the greenhouses exclusively as a full-time job.

There were also several henhouses and another structure where they grew mushrooms for the community's herbivores and omnivores.

After that, Henri drove me to a field of solar panels and told me all about how the ranch used a mix of solar, wind, and hydropower from a nearby river to provide electricity for the entire property. He also stressed the importance—again—of conservation and how much work it was to keep this place running in harmony.

Henri hadn't exaggerated with his warning about everyone pulling their weight around here. In the distance, we spotted more vehicles that he explained were the ranch's employees getting around to do their duties.

We had just waved at an older man peeking through his front window when Henri asked, "Is there anything you're good at?"

Keeping my attention through the windshield, I folded my hands on my lap and made a decision. Then I peeked at him. "Making quesadillas. Kickball. I'm *really* good at whistling."

The way Henri turned to look at me . . .

I smiled.

Another muscle in his cheek, this one higher and further away from his jaw, flexed. "Being a brat too, I see."

I burst out laughing. "Are you kidding me? I've never been a brat."

He faced forward, that cheek muscle popping again. Was he trying not to smile? Because that's kind of what it looked like to me.

"I was just trying to cheer you up, you look tense, but shouldn't the elders have asked me about that before they agreed to let me stay? You're trying to figure out how I can help around here, aren't you?"

"No and yes." He wiped his expression clean the same way he had yesterday, like that was something he was used to doing, he did it so easily. Going from being a little amused to all business that fast was a talent. Or maybe it took a lot of practice. "Everyone contributes regardless of what they're comfortable doing." The side of his mouth twitched. "The kids are our road maintenance crew. They keep the paths clear."

I snorted. "Are you serious?"

He was. "They make it a game; it isn't child labor."

They'd thought of everything. Literally everything. This place was a well-oiled machine.

"There's another section where we have other buildings," he explained just as his phone rang. Henri pulled it out, took in the screen for a moment, and answered. "Henri."

Henri now. Not Blackrock. I catalogued that for later.

He listened, and his eyes narrowed by the second. "Where? . . . Send me the coordinates. I'll be there as soon as I can . . . I can't go straight there. I'm by the greenhouses, and I'll need to stop by the clubhouse first."

I cleared my throat, but nothing happened. I did it again, louder, in the middle of him doing a full U-turn with one hand. "Ahem," I tried for the third time.

Nothing.

I stuck my hand in front of his face and wiggled my fingers. That finally did it. "If this is an emergency, I can go with you."

His eyebrows slammed down, flat.

"You're wasting time," I told him like he didn't already know that. He'd mentioned the greenhouses and the clubhouse; whatever was going on was ranch business. "Let's go."

I could tell he was contemplating my offer from the way his eyes bounced from one of mine to the other, but so much faster than I would have expected, he nodded. "You won't get in the way."

Not a question but a statement, and I barely managed not to sigh or wink at him. "Yes, Fluffy. I will not get in the way, and we can pinky swear on it if you want."

He put the phone back to his cheek and said he'd be there soon.

Then the werewolf man broke the community's 5 mile an hour speed limit even more by 5 whole miles and took us off the path.

The smell and feel of magic got stronger and stronger with every minute we got deeper into their territory.

I felt like a superhero in the sun. Like I'd guzzled a couple of energy drinks back-to-back in a short period of time. My hands got twitchy, then full-on shaky, and I had to hold my breath like I was some kind of free diver who could do it for longer than fifteen seconds at a time. *Because this place . . .*

This had to be what a cat experienced around catnip.

I had to shove my hands between my thighs because I didn't know what to do with them. If Henri could sense that I was going through something as we traveled, he didn't say a word or even glance over, but that might have also been because he was driving over fallen logs and branches with one hand and holding his phone in the other while navigating using a map on the screen.

I thought of Duncan to focus on something else. I hoped he was doing okay. Making friends . . . the mini Benedict Arnold.

Part of me wanted to laugh at how he'd dumped me the second he could, and the other half was just a *little* bit still hurt over it. Little bit. Tiny bit. But this was exactly what I would have wanted if I'd had to pick. I didn't want him to cling to me and cry and be scared. He was only a baby for now, sure, but he would grow up like every other living being on the planet, and he'd be a young adult, then an adult, and someday he would leave—*nope*, I couldn't go there yet. Hard pass.

That was the worst thing I could have thought of. I needed to focus on the present. On the fact that he'd felt comfortable enough and safe enough to spend time with strangers after the things we'd been through. He seemed happy. Weren't those all signs of emotional stability?

The side-by-side slid to a sharp stop. By the time I realized it, Henri had already unbuckled himself and jumped out. Leaving me there.

"Don't get in the way," he called out over his shoulder.

I sat there for a second. Then I snickered. *That* was more like the Henri I'd known.

Taking off my seat belt, I slid off the bench. He'd stopped us on the other side of a fallen tree trunk that had to be two feet wide. He'd already leapt over it, as well as several other similar logs covering the forest floor, those long legs really helping him gain some distance.

What is going on *with me?* I needed to stop creeping on him. Have some dignity.

His face might belong to a Greek god—though as far as I knew he didn't have any of that ancestry in him—and his body might as well have been molded from an inspiration of Hercules, but—*Stop, Nina.*

It had to be this place doing something to me. The magic was making me horny. My hormones and I were going to need to have a serious talk later when the object of our fascination wasn't around and couldn't sense me getting squinty over him in fine-fitting jeans.

I wasn't ashamed of being attracted to him, but that would only complicate things. So, I had to keep it in moderation.

Unless he started openly flirting with me.

That would be the day.

He was barely talking to me now. And he hadn't even hesitated to leave me behind. I almost laughed.

Ahead, I could see in the distance there was a small group. Two people . . .? And they were . . .?

Were they talking to a tree?

I blinked and squinted when the tree seemed to bend in half a split second before the loudest roar I'd ever heard in my life erupted from it. It would have given a T-Rex a run for its money, I bet. It made the Jenny Greenteeth's growls sound like a hissy fit.

That was no tree though, I decided when one of the people leaned forward right back and growled loud enough that I could recognize the very werewolf sound.

What was that thing? I wondered. I climbed over a big fallen log, a branch poking me hard in the ass. I had to stop and make sure it hadn't torn my pants. Gaining distance from me, Henri's movements sped up as he literally prowled forward. How in the world a body that size could move so soundlessly was beyond impressive, and I kind of wished I wasn't so intrigued by the talking tree that I could settle for watching him in that denim.

But I was curious.

In less than twenty-four hours, I'd seen a river creature, a cyclops, and a satyr. What was the rest of my time here going to be like? The possibilities made me excited, and it wasn't like I hadn't occasionally met interesting beings.

I jumped and climbed over every other trunk as I tried to circle the long way around where Henri was going so I wouldn't break my word. He was too pissed to notice I was following, I thought, since he didn't tell me to go back. The direction of the wind helped too.

. . . or maybe he just didn't give a crap what happened to me. Hmm.

Another one of those T-Rex-like roars blasted through the forest, and I heard Henri snarl like he had in my face the day before but ten times louder. "I'm not in the mood for your shit today."

He was talking to the tree.

I inched closer, trying my best to avoid making more sound than I needed to. It wasn't that I thought I was going to get away with being sneaky—Henri had exceptional hearing and sense of smell since he was what he was after all—but hopefully he'd be too distracted to pay attention for a little while. If I was lucky.

"I am not in the mood for your shit any day," a low, inhuman voice replied. Deep voices were one thing, but this one was in a league of its own. If a mountain could talk, that's what it would sound like.

I finally got a good shot of the talking branch.

That was no tree.

What I'd thought was bark was hair. Lots and lots of long hair. Like a Yorkie on steroids. A bigger and less gross-looking version of the river crone with brownish hair.

And that was when I gasped. It was a bigfoot. A *bigfoot.*

Ohhhh, I wished Duncan was here to see this!

Now that I was close enough, I could tell the two figures I'd originally spotted were a man and a woman. I was pretty sure they were both the same people from the night before, the woman the one who had growled at the bigfoot after its first roar. It was right then, that the man turned his head in the direction where I was standing. His hair was shades lighter than Henri's, his frame closer to Matti's leaner build.

I'd made it five seconds trying to be incognito. Dang it. I lifted my hand. *No point in being discreet now*.

Something in his body language changed a moment before Henri got to where they were.

My childhood sort-of friend didn't even look tense as he took in the bigfoot like it was a child throwing a tantrum. "Oh? You're not in a good mood?"

Was he *mocking it*? Was freaking Henri *mocking* a bigfoot that was a foot or more taller than him?

"Because," he continued talking, "we've had this conversation before, and you damn well know you aren't allowed to be in this part of the forest."

He was mocking it. No doubt about it.

The bigfoot, who had to be around eight feet tall, was a pretty accurate replica of all the supposed sighting photos I'd ever seen of them. His dark eyes were kind of visible beneath the long hair framing its face. If he had a nose, it wasn't noticeable, and I could only see his mouth because every single sharp tooth in it was displayed when he pulled his lips back into a loud snarl.

It was almost scary.

The bigfoot stretched out arms so long they weren't proportional to his body, making the image even more impactful. "I *am* the forest—"

Henri laughed. This lumberjack-looking man laughed, *loud*. Right then and there in the middle of the being's spiel, in this forest that made my skin prickle and made me feel like I was a little high, he laughed. It wasn't ha-ha-funny, but more like the way I did when I was frustrated and wanted to kill someone.

Not that I would, but I wanted to—or at least give them a little strangle.

He even shook his head, like he couldn't believe the situation. "Your people are from the Pacific Northwest. We gave you permission to live on our land, Spencer"—*No*. The bigfoot's name was *Spencer*? S-p-e-n-c-e-r?—"You are not the guardian of this forest, *I* am," Henri told him in a strong, demanding voice that pulled at something inside of me. Something that made the goose bumps on my arms that much stronger. It had so much authority to it. "*We* are, and last time we talked about this, we made it clear that we weren't going to tolerate these tantrums you throw every few months."

"Tantrums? Do you know who you're speaking to, Little Wolf?" Spencer the bigfoot gnashed teeth that would've had a great white shark doing a double take.

The man I'd known decades ago did it again, he laughed. Even louder that time. Big and bold and—and then I did too a little, more like a giggle. Because *Little Wolf*? Had he *seen* Henri in his wolf form? Not even his eyeballs were small in that body.

The bigfoot was massive, but my money would be on Henri,

hands down. Calm, collected people in the face of high emotion were dangerous. They made less mistakes. They thought things through.

Every single head in the group swiveled.

I took a half step back behind the tree I'd been trying to use as camouflage.

"I'm out of the way," I called out to Henri, because I was. There were at least fifty feet between us.

The slightest breeze picked that exact moment to carry its way through the trees, making the group downwind from me.

Crap.

I grabbed my bare wrist.

An abnormally long arm stretched forward, a long finger extending out from it. "What is that?" the bigfoot asked in a way I honestly didn't appreciate much. I'd heard those words before. That tone too.

Nothing good ever came from it.

"None of your damn business," Henri snapped, his amusement gone, his attention laser-focused on the giant hairball pointing right at me.

A slightly stronger breeze blew through, going in the same direction as the last, and I took a second to get another hit of the rich, rich scent that seemed embedded in every part of this place. It was so much stronger here. I had to stick my hands in my pockets, it made me so twitchy.

But Spencer wasn't paying attention to Henri because I was the lucky winner. Then the bigfoot said it, the tips of his sharp teeth appearing as he did, "That smells like an abomination."

That? First of all, was I or was I not over here minding my own business? Sure, maybe I shouldn't have laughed when Henri had, but it was funny. I wasn't laughing at *him* but what he'd said.

But now?

A low growl crept through the spaces between the trees, and it was not coming from the bigfoot. "Watch what you say next," Henri threatened slowly.

I glanced at him for a split second, touched that he would stand up for me.

The hairy being took a step forward, drawing my gaze back to him. "Show yourself, demon!" it bellowed.

Of all the words in the world he could have picked, that term got under my skin like nothing else—and I mean nothing else. It triggered something in me that I wanted to think I was better than, after so many years. There were a whole lot of words that would never bother me again. Sometimes, people sucked. *Abomination* was mean without a doubt, but *demon* . . .

That thing that lived invisibly in my body, side by side with my soul and my organs, flexed, reminding me it was there.

That it was always there and always would be. Whether I understood it or not. Whether I wanted it or not.

But I was going to keep my promise to Henri, so all I allowed myself to do was lean clear around the tree so the mean bigfoot could get a good look at me. He already knew I was here. I might be a fraction of his size and didn't have his physical attributes, but I didn't need either to defend myself.

And that's why I let my anger and hurt get the best of me, and I yelled the first thing that popped into my head. "The only abomination here is your dry-ass hair, Fabio!"

You could get a lot done without stooping to words like "evil" or "asshole." If you made an insult personal enough, it could be almost as hurtful as something really nasty.

It worked.

"You dare tell *me* that *my hair* is dry?" the big jerk hollered back.

"Being insulted isn't very nice, is it?" I yelled again, focusing on the hairy being as I took a step back until I was a little more behind the tree. I didn't want to totally go back on my word.

"My hair isn't dry!" Spencer roared.

Some people couldn't take their own medicine. He could call me a demon, but I couldn't talk about his hair? The Jenny Greenteeth from yesterday wasn't the only little b around here.

"Do you have any idea what that is?" the hairy mythical being demanded, aiming the question toward the group.

I made the mistake of peeking at Henri again, but that time, his attention was centered on me. Just me. His eyebrows were a hard line on his tan forehead, and his expression . . .

Maybe I should've stayed in the golf cart.

The bigfoot let out a roar even louder than the ones before. The only person who reacted was Henri, who took a couple of steps so he stood directly in the path Spencer had to where I was. Was he blocking him from seeing me?

"You've allowed a curse onto this land," Spencer the Asshole spat, and I could literally see the muscles under Henri's flannel shirt tense.

Did he call me a curse? That was a new one.

"The only curse here are your split ends," I muttered, insulted all over again.

If the log that randomly landed a good distance to my right meant anything, I was pretty sure he'd heard me.

What a jerk!

It had barely landed when Henri bent over, picked up a log—not a small one, not one that he should have been able to lift singlehandedly or much less barehanded—and hoisted it onto his shoulder. In one fluid movement, he threw the log like a javelin. It landed several feet to the side of Spencer. I guess I wasn't the only person who thought Spencer may have just tried to hurt me.

"Enough!" Henri's dominant voice echoed through the forest.

I'd swear on my life that even the birds stopped singing at the sound of it. The wind might have stopped blowing too. Everything in our vicinity seemed to freeze for a moment. I was pretty sure the only thing I heard was Henri taking a deep breath before speaking again.

"If you have a problem with the agreement we've made, leave. This is getting old. Do this again, and I will escort you off this land. Threaten my people again, verbally or physically, and I'll still do it, but it'll be with two broken legs." The growl he let out was a freaking menace. "Am I making myself clear?"

The hairs on the back of my neck stood up.

In that moment, I didn't think I'd ever been so attracted to anyone in my life.

A strong breeze made the younger trees sway and sent dust motes swirling around us like a dream. I saw the moment the bigfoot really got a good sample of my scent. He must have had a crappy sense of smell if it had taken him that long to go from throwing around ugly words to looking uneasy.

I needed to ask about my bracelet.

Henri took a step toward the mythical being. "Are we on the same page?"

Spencer's beady black eyes flicked from where I was to the semicircle of werewolves he was surrounded by. He was silent for longer than I would've expected. "Yes," the bigfoot grunted.

It was kind of amazing how well he blended into his surroundings as he retreated one step at a time. How the color of his hair—coat?—matched the trees like natural camouflage. He never turned his back on us.

When he'd finally disappeared into the trees, the man who had been my first childhood crush slowly turned to face me.

I threw up both my hands. "I stayed out of the way."

He didn't say anything.

"He insulted me first."

Henri kept looking at me, and I kind of expected him to rip me a new one, or at least scold me—he had that bossy vibe going on after all—but all he did was stand there. Not glaring. Not staring. Just looking calm, cool, and neutral as I stood there in shorts and a big T-shirt that said "South Dakota" in cursive orange letters on it.

Dang it.

I shouldn't have done that. I shouldn't have reminded anyone that there was something in me that would scare a Jenny Greenteeth and make a bigfoot flustered. I needed to blend in. I knew that better than anyone. But . . .

"He hurt my feelings," I tried to explain, not that I expected them to understand that I was sensitive over his insults, but it *was* the truth. You could make fun of just about any other part of me or my body, but *demon*, *evil*, and *abomination* were my trigger words.

I wasn't proud of who I became when I heard them, but I also figured I could react a lot worse than I had.

Henri pressed dark pink lips together, and after a second, he lifted a hand, crooking his finger in a "come here" gesture.

That took me back to when I'd been a kid and he'd catch Matti and me doing something we shouldn't have been up to. He'd been bossing people around ever since then, hadn't he?

I pressed my lips together right back. I took my time getting over fallen trees and sharp branches. By the time I made it over to where they stood—Henri, the man, and the woman—Henri's face was still mostly clear.

I dropped my shoulders and tipped my face up at him. "Yes?"

His eyebrow shot up a millimeter, the gesture so small I almost missed it, his Adam's apple bobbing at the same time. His face was so grave, if I hadn't known him as a teenager, I would've thought he practiced it in the mirror, but he'd been good at it back then. He was just better at it now.

And why did he have to be this good-looking?

Those amber eyes bounced from one of mine to the other.

I smiled at him cautiously.

"You made fun of his hair?" His question was slow, like he hadn't been standing right there the whole time. Or maybe he thought he'd misheard?

I lifted my hands, palms up, at my sides and dropped them.

Henri Blackrock blinked.

The leader of this community, the sword and the gavel for its residents, stared down at me.

And it was so easy to picture him at that moment with a battle-ax in one hand and a sword in his other, a thick beard on his jaw, as he made his Scandinavian ancestors proud.

Had I screwed up already?

Was he that mad?

Out of nowhere, when I least expected it, the corner of his mouth hitched up and those eyes I hadn't been able to get over—orangey light brown irises weren't something you came across any ol' day of the week—glittered.

I was confused.

A dry, rough chuckle rumbled out of his chest, slow and steady, and out of the corner of my eye, I saw the man and the woman suddenly grin.

Henri wasn't mad?

"We were seconds away from a confrontation, and you *told a five-hundred-pound sasquatch he had split ends*." His smile grew bigger by the second, and he even squinted at me. "You lost your goddamn mind?"

He thought this was funny.

He thought this was funny.

Right in front of me, Henri swiped a palm down his face, cupping his mouth while he shook his head.

I wasn't sure I'd ever seen or heard him be this amused.

But I liked it.

I opened my mouth, closed it, and then shrugged. "Little bit, I guess. He hurt my feelings, and I wanted to hurt his back." I thought about that for a second. "Was it too much? Maybe I crossed the line."

Those intense irises met mine, his smile and amusement wiping away in a second once more. His expression resetting to that familiar, no-nonsense one that had handled everything that had happened yesterday like a professional. "He deserved it. He insults everyone. That's why he isn't allowed close to the community. We have a yeti that's a welcome member, but sasquatches are notorious assholes that are difficult to live with."

What was the difference between a yeti and a sasquatch? I was going to need to ask someone. In the meantime, I settled for nodding at him, like this whole situation wasn't mindboggling in the first place.

But that was *two* random mythical creatures in the woods in less than twenty-four hours. Two!

In my old life, I wasn't a stranger to running into magical beings from time to time. I'd run into a kitsune or two—a revered nine-tailed fox that went by many names in many cultures. I knew to expect aquatic-based beings when I was on the coast. There was a town in Maine that was full of selkies. But I could also go months in between coming across other magical people, so this was wild.

The man I had called Fluffy when I'd been too young for him to tell me to stop focused on me for another long moment before he turned to the two people who had been silent until then. "Randall, Ani, this is Nina. Nina, Randall and Ani are members of the community who handle our security issues. Randall lives in the clubhouse too."

I smiled at them, feeling my hands twitch with the magic high still coursing through me and the adrenaline from having a log thrown in my direction from a *bigfoot*, and I shoved my hand out first toward the tall, muscular blonde woman, then the strawberry-blond man. We shook. "Nice to meet you," I told them both. "I'm not usually that mean toward strangers, forgive me. Please let me know if I can help with anything."

Instead of judgy eyes, I got a smile from the woman. "He had it coming. Welcome to the ranch," Ani said, her eyes flicking toward her palm.

She didn't seem scared or concerned or uncomfortable, and the smallest amount of hope bloomed in my chest. "Thank you."

Her gaze moved from my face and across the rest of me, the same kind of curiosity I usually came across in werewolves radiating from her. A little notch formed between her eyebrows.

I only kind of braced my feelings.

"How do you get your skin to glow like that?" was what she decided to ask.

I blinked. Then I smiled. "Snail moisturizer, but I think it's mostly my genes." I wasn't going to say they were good genes because that was debatable, but they weren't totally awful.

This woman who had biceps the size of calf muscles groaned. "Do you use vitamin C?"

I shook my head.

She pursed her lips together. "Exfoliate?"

"What's that?"

Her lips parted, and I grinned.

"I'm just messing with you. Twice a week, every week," I shared.

Ani's laugh made me smile. It was loud and free, and I liked it. You could tell a lot about a person based on their laugh, and the freedom in hers said a whole lot. She had the same golden-brown eyes as so many werewolves I'd known. She had to be five ten minimum, I guessed. Everything about her seemed capable, and looking at her made me feel safer. No wonder she was part of the security team.

The man took a step forward. He had a short beard a shade darker than the strawberry-colored hair on his head. "Can I . . .?" He lifted his hand and tapped his neck.

He wanted to smell me the way I'd offered to let Henri do the same yesterday. I nodded, and he didn't need to be told twice, he stepped forward and started to lean in—

A hand landed on the redhead's forehead and shoved his face back. "No," Henri snapped.

I opened my mouth to tell him it was fine, that I was used to it, but he moved on from the topic too quickly to give me a chance, and the guy didn't argue with him over it.

"I'm going to guess, since I haven't heard from either of you until now, that you didn't find the trespasser?" he asked.

"No." Ani was the one who answered. "Nothing fresh. She has to be long gone by now. We would have found her if she was nearby."

"Good. We'll move on and deal with her if she comes back." There was an odd beat of silence. "Something tells me that won't happen."

I scratched behind my ear.

"I did some research on them last night. There isn't a whole lot of information available. They go by different names in different places, yadda, yadda, but they all seem to be aggressive . . ." The man, Randall, trailed off, his gaze sliding back toward me.

He was cute, I thought, and I was on a one-way mission. A very important one. I couldn't help but try and peek at his left hand, but it was on the side of his body I didn't have direct access to. I'd try and check again some other time, I decided, rocking back and forth on my heels as I listened to them.

I had to keep my options open here. Unless . . .

"We'll keep an eye out," Henri said. There was a pause. "Either of you seen Dominic today?"

Where had I heard that name before?

The man made a snickering sound. "Not up close, but I saw his black eye from a distance."

The guy who split his lip!

"He needs to be glad I only gave him one." Henri's voice was low. "If he doesn't show up for his patrol tonight, let me know. I need to get going and finish this before my shift starts," Henri told them. "Be safe."

That was my sign to quit playing dumb. I smiled at them. "It was nice meeting you both. If I can help with anything, please let me know. I'm staying in the clubhouse."

The Ani woman grinned again, and the Randall guy nodded. I was pretty sure I noticed his nose twitching discreetly. I'd let him smell me some other time, if he still wanted to. I didn't get why Henri had gotten so defensive. It wasn't rude to ask someone to smell them; it was only rude to ask them what they were.

"I'll take you up on that offer. See you around," Ani said. "Be safe, Henri. Dom's a dumbass."

Henri and I made eye contact, and I took that as my cue to get walking back to the UTV. He caught up to me almost immediately, and when his hand landed on the back of my neck, I got a little excited . . . until he steered me to the right instead of the direction I'd been going. I lifted my head at him and smiled.

He dropped his hand.

Ten minutes ago, he'd been defending me to a bigfoot. Now, I had cooties. Life was confusing.

Once we made it back to the off-road vehicle, we buckled in. I waited until we got a short distance away before saying, "Fluff? Thank you for standing up for me. I appreciate it."

His attention was still forward as he replied, "Sure." Like it was no big deal that he'd put himself between me and a giant, angry creature, then thrown an enormous log in retaliation.

"We can call it even now," I let him know.

"Even?" There was a pause. "For what?"

"I spent ten years telling myself that if I ever saw you again, I was going to punch you in the gut."

There was another beat of silence before he drew out, "Why?"

I had always figured he'd had no idea just how much his actions had hurt me. As I'd gotten older, I'd begun to understand why he'd done what he'd done, but I'd still been dead set on that punch. I would've settled for tripping him. "For taking Matti the way you did. That wrecked me back then, how you just left without letting us say bye. He was mine just as much as he was yours," I explained. "But you don't need to worry about that now. Like I said, we're even. You might have saved my life a little bit."

Those amber irises flicked in my direction again. He looked genuinely surprised. "Cricket, I . . . why are your hands shaking?" He let off the accelerator with a frown. "You don't smell scared."

I hadn't even realized they were back to doing it again. I balled them up into fists. Maybe it wasn't the best idea in the world to bring up that stage in our lives. I should probably drop it. "I wanted to ask you about that actually."

"Your face is red," he said, deciding to change the subject, thankfully.

I pressed my cheeks with the pads of my fingers. They were hot. "I don't feel sick. But since we got here, I've felt . . . wired? Like I've chugged a few energy drinks back-to-back." I had done that once, and it was a miracle I hadn't had a heart attack. I'd scared the crap out of Sienna so bad she made me promise never to drink even a single one again. "The magic here is intense, but I asked Sienna about it, and she didn't seem to be affected by it."

He slowed the UTV down some more. Big hands flexed on the steering wheel. Henri made a little grunt in his throat.

"It doesn't feel bad, but it reminds me of a high," I told him, struggling to explain it.

"Some people who come to live here are more sensitive to it than others."

"Really?"

He nodded, attention on the scenery through the windshield. "The more exposure you get outside, the more it'll help. You'll be fine in a month."

Hmm. I stored that food for thought. "It doesn't bother you?" I asked.

"No, but I've spent most of my life here. I love everything about this land."

His comment made me smile. Then I asked, "Do you have problems with other creatures regularly? Creatures that aren't members of the community?"

"Not often, but it happens more than I'd like."

"Do you think it's because of how powerful the magic here is? That they're drawn to it in a way?"

He steered the vehicle to the side, going around an incredibly thick log that had been sawn in half. "There isn't science behind it, but sure, I think so. The closer you get to this area, the more beings start to sense it. It's a magnet in a way for some. It's worse around a full moon."

"That must make it really hard to keep the people here safe and keep the land to yourselves." The more I thought about it, the more complicated it got in my head. How many creatures wouldn't come across this place and decide they wanted to be a part of it? Or wanted it all to themselves? And why were some of us and not everyone affected by it? For the same reason that some people liked the smell of lavender and other people thought it was gross?

"We take measures to prevent it from happening, but it's never-ending. We might go weeks without an issue, sometimes longer, and one day, the kids are running off, a river crone tries to eat them, and a sasquatch decides it wants to pick a fight because it's lonely and angry."

And *that* got me. "That bigfoot is lonely?"

The side of his mouth went tight. "They aren't a fan of that title."

I winced. Who was I to tell someone what could hurt their

feelings and what couldn't? I'd been ready to shave his head after he'd called me those ugly names, but . . . "He's still a jerk, but now I kind of feel bad."

It was more than that. I felt ashamed of myself. He'd gone for my emotional jugular, and I might have done the same thing. I'd wanted to hurt him because he'd hurt me, and maybe that made me as much of a mean person as it made him.

My soul wilted at the idea.

I didn't want to hurt anyone. Not really hurt them at least.

His hands did that thing on the steering wheel again. "He chooses to be that way," Henri said carefully. "I wouldn't feel too bad for him."

I felt bad anyway. Because I had forgotten, when I knew better. Some people were assholes just because they could be, but most people had deep, deep reasons why they behaved the way they did. You never knew what someone else was going through or what they'd gone through to make them that way.

On a separate note, who *was* Dominic and why had Henri given him a black eye?

And here I'd thought campgrounds were dramatic.

Chapter Nine

"Nuh-uh, park your dump truck over there. I don't want to catch your cooties," I told Sienna later that evening when she'd finally wandered into the kitchen for dinner.

Sienna's reply was a whine, still looking pale and weak, a very clear indicator of the condition she had been in. In all the years we'd been friends, I couldn't remember her ever being sick. I didn't think I'd ever heard her cough. And the more I'd thought about it, the more I was convinced she and Matti had contracted some terrible bacteria that would probably put anyone without incredible magical DNA in the hospital, if not worse. I'd seen Matti eat some things when we'd been kids that made the kinds of "organic matter" Duncan put into his mouth seem almost Michelin rated.

Because of that, I'd called the convenience store where I was sure the contaminated food had been from and warned them they might have a death trap on their hands.

And since I didn't want to risk her hacking germs into my eyeballs on the 1 percent chance whatever they had was contagious, I pointed at the seat two down from mine. A little distance was better than no distance, I figured. But if she tried to touch Duncan, I'd tackle her.

My best friend winced as she took the stool. We were the only two people in the kitchen at that point. I'd checked the calendar in the pantry, and Franklin's name and meal had been signed into the slot, so I assumed I would sous chef for him and keep learning where ingredients were and how they liked to do things. We were immersing ourselves.

The sooner we started, the better.

Based on how this afternoon had gone, Duncan was already doing a spectacular job at it. He had been so happy when I'd gone to the nursery to check on him. His teacher had let me stay after she'd spotted me at the window. He had jumped on me, sending me *"Love, love, love,"* even as he'd played with the other children, like he was singing it. His puppy smile had been radiant. The teacher had said he'd done great. All signs pointed at him having a good time.

I'd tried to convince myself that it was better this way. If he'd pitched a fit and had been crying, climbing on me, begging me not to leave him with those puppy eyes, it would have been so hard. This immediate independence and confidence was better.

Sure.

My little selfish heart just needed to come around.

Now, the black ball of fur was so exhausted he was curled under my stool, passed out from a long day of interacting in a new environment with new people. He was going to have to adjust to a new sleep schedule from now on.

"My butt is sore." Sienna winced as she propped her legs on the rung of the stool. "I didn't want to waste the day not spending time with you. This sucks."

I snickered as she planted an elbow on the counter. "I know, and I hope you and your butt feel better."

"Matti says he now understands why I've never wanted to try a-n-a-l," she whispered.

We had already gone over how Duncan didn't know his alphabet yet—at least I hadn't taught it to him, and he didn't watch *Sesame Street*, so I figured? More like hoped. "But maybe now would be the time to do it since all those muscles are blown out," I told her, and she groaned.

"No. Never. He's not even allowed to look at it ever again."

I laughed, and she smiled a little. "Where is he anyway? He's still really sick?"

"Uh-huh. I told him to fast, but he didn't listen and ate more of your jerky a few hours ago, and now he's paying for it."

We both scrunched up our faces and said, "Dumb," at the same time, making us burst into giggles.

"How was your day?" she asked, misery etched all over her features. "I feel so bad we left you with all these strangers."

"You should." I lifted a shoulder. "First off, someone—" I pointed toward the floor where Duncan was. "—forgot I existed. Did you know the preschool here is mandatory for the kids? Anyway, I dropped him off, and I was trying so hard not to c-r-y, and he ran in there like his butt was on fire. Real fire, I mean."

Sienna's laugh was as loud as it could be considering I was pretty sure she might have pulled some ab muscles on the toilet seat today.

"I'm o-f-f-e-n-d-e-d and a little h-u-r-t, but I'm really, really glad he seems to be doing well." I *was*. Deep down. I gestured with my chin toward the cutest donut on the planet by my feet. "See how tired he is?"

We looked down. The tip of his tongue was hanging out of his mouth. I was pretty sure I heard a snore. *So freaking adorable.* Traitor and all.

I wasn't going to get upset, so I changed the subject. "Anyway, all you missed out on was a tour of the ranch."

She made a circle with her hand like she wanted me to rewind. "Who gave you a tour?"

"Henri."

"Who else went?"

"Just us."

Her nose wrinkled. "Huh."

"What?"

Her shrug was pretty dang dainty. "Just you two. Huh. Hmm." She slumped even more across the counter, but her expression stayed attentive. "He doesn't have time to text Matti back, but he has time to give you a tour of this place."

"Franklin, the elder, pawned me off on him. I'm pretty sure he—Henri—only wanted me to be sure I understood that there's a lot of work that goes into the upkeep and that they expect me to help," I told her. "We had a chitchat over me moving here after that crap he threw out about the three months, and he said it was fine, but . . ."

But maybe that was in character with the way he operated, but maybe he was also trying to be diplomatic when he would rather me leave regardless of what he'd said.

I doubted it. Nothing about the way he spoke or acted, so far, gave me the impression he spent too much time screening his words or decisions. Just his emotions. He still seemed to be the same honorable Henri who had been so reluctantly chivalrous when I'd been a kid. Like if he'd catch me busting my ass, he'd lead me back into Matti's house and hand me a first aid kit. Or if Matti and I got caught playing too rough, he had never hesitated to remind him to be gentler. I'd had a crush on him for a reason. Once I'd discovered liking boys, he'd been one of my earliest victims.

He just . . . was a decent man. Maybe a good man now, was my guess. I figured I'd find out the more time we spent together. Talking to each other hadn't been a struggle so far. He'd called me Cricket multiple times. It was nice that he'd remembered.

On the way back from the bigfoot—I meant *Spencer* the sasquatch, who I still needed to tell her about—Henri had told me more about the situation with the children who lived on the ranch. How when they reached a certain age and were in control enough of their magic, they attended a normal school in the closest town, but not all of them did. Half the teenagers preferred to study on the property. For every question I'd shot at him, he'd had an answer. A good one.

He knew everything about this place.

And he'd told me a few other things that caught my attention.

There was a five-thousand-acre wildlife preserve located on the ranch.

Two weeks a year, some of the residents worked as tour guides for exclusive—he meant expensive—raft fishing tours through a section of a river on the opposite side of the property.

One of the mountains you could see from certain spots on the ranch was called Blackrock Mountain.

When we'd made it back to the building that stored the vehicles, all he'd said was, "Someone else will give you more details." Then he'd headed straight back to the clubhouse without another word, leaving me there outside.

Henri wasn't the first person to ditch me without a second glance, and he wasn't going to be the last. At least Duncan had given me kisses every time he'd run by while I'd spent the rest of the day in the nursery with the very nice teacher named Maggie, who had thanked me no less than ten times for helping out since I had no idea what else to do with myself. Even if that "help" had mainly consisted of me helping her pass out supplies for projects, tie shoelaces that somehow miraculously were constantly getting unraveled, and then playing board games with the older kids—who had been whispering about Shiloh and Pascal's shenanigans the day before—who were out of school for the summer, still.

I liked all the kids. They were well-mannered, a little mischievous, kind, and just good kids.

Even Agnes, who had snarled at me when I'd offered to wipe her face after she'd eaten dehydrated chicken necks for a snack.

And now we were here, in the kitchen, just the three of us. Agnes had left the nursery with a puppy a little older than her.

"It just seems a little convenient to me that he has time." Sienna tried to give me a smile that mostly made her look drunk since she wasn't feeling well. She dropped her voice. "He doesn't make you feel awkward?"

Awkward? "No. Why?" I whispered back.

She dropped her voice even more, to the point where I had to read her lips because her volume was nonexistent. "Because of the vibes he gives off. The way he talks. He feels like . . . *so much*, you know what I mean?"

Hmm. I guess I could see it. Everything about him seemed bigger, size-wise and personality-wise, than any other person I'd ever met. There was something imposing about him. Like if there was a werewolf I needed to roll over and show my belly to, he was the only one that would make me. "The way he was talking to someone today, I can see that. But I'm not like you guys, so it doesn't hit me as hard. I can still picture him as a teenager in my head, with his hoodie always pulled up, trying to be quiet and mysterious. Maybe that's it?"

"Yeah," she agreed. "And he isn't a warm person. Not like Matti at all."

I thought about the way he'd made the kids' breakfast so patiently and thoughtfully. *But* I barely knew him, and really, the more I argued about the goodness in him, the more Sienna might see something that wasn't there. He was doing his duty. In his ridiculous body. That was all.

"Who knows why people are the way they are and do the things they do. I only hope he's nice to Duncan and decent with me."

"He better be." She fisted her hand in the air between us.

I laughed at the same time as she did the same. "*Hopefully* other people here like me. So far, I've got most of the kids in the bag. I met some family members today who were friendly . . ." They had all been werewolves, except for Shiloh's mother. The ogre child had left with a werewolf pup and her parents. "I'll settle for no one calling me hurtful names." I crossed my fingers.

Like Spencer.

And there went the guilt again.

"They better f-ing not," she threatened in that way she always had when someone had been rude in her presence. People could be mean to her, but heaven forbid anyone hurt one of her loved ones' feelings. It was the werewolf in her. "You don't need to win anyone over. Someone having you in their life is a gift they should be grateful for."

I started to reach over to touch her, but I remembered she was sick and stopped with my hand halfway to her. "Have I told you today that I love you, Germs?" I asked, dropping my hand.

"You don't need to. I know." She smiled, and I tucked her love into my heart where it belonged.

"Before I forget, guess what I saw?" I didn't wait for her to answer. "A sasquatch!"

She sucked in a breath just like I'd expected. "You saw one?"

"I did more than see it. We pissed each other off, and I told him he had dry hair—"

"Nina!" she shrieked with a hoarse laugh, instantly regretting it from the way she broke off into a whimper, her palm going for her stomach.

"He was ready to end me. He threw a log at me, and I told him he had split ends, and now I feel bad because Henri said he's mean but he's also a lonely sasquatch."

"He threw a log at you?"

She sounded so concerned. "Henri threw one back at him. It was pretty epic," I explained, miming the movement of him treating the log like a javelin. "He made me promise to stay out of the way when we got to the area where we found him, but I didn't listen."

"Good," she grumbled, not seeming all that convinced.

Maybe I hadn't gotten lucky in a lot of ways I wish I would've been, but in all the ones that mattered, I'd won the lottery. I'd been raised by wonderful parents. I had two friends who loved me so much, I was their second favorite person after each other. And I had a little guy that might trade me for a chicken tender basket if he was hungry enough, but later on, he'd regret it. But for the first time in a couple months, I wasn't so concerned about the uncertainties of the future.

I told Sienna all about Spencer the sasquatch, and I gave her a hug anyway when we started cracking up over other dumb stuff we'd done that the incident reminded us of.

If I was going to get diarrhea, I might as well get it from one of my favorite people in the world, especially when our time together was running out.

"Shh," I whispered to Duncan at five minutes after midnight. The halls were as quiet as they'd been the day before, and I really didn't want to wake up anyone, even if the only person I'd met who lived on the first floor was Franklin.

I figured the elder needed his sleep. When he'd come into the kitchen halfway in the middle of Sienna reminding me about the time we had gotten into an argument with a neighbor at our apartment complex over his inability to park in a single spot, Franklin had already been yawning. I'd gladly helped him make five pounds of chicken while he listened to Sienna talking about issues within her family, which had taken up the whole dinner, and he'd even gotten in on the boyfriend troubles her sister was going through. Agnes had eventually wandered in, going straight for the elder, then Duncan, and ignoring the rest of us.

Dinner had given me the opportunity to study the elder, who I'd caught side-eyeing me more than once.

Did he suspect something about me?

I wasn't sure, but I wasn't going to overthink it more than I needed to. It'd been one whole day, and it had been a pretty good one, all things considered. And now, the donut and I were going to wrap up the night with a little game of tag, just the two of—

"Oh my *fuuu*—" I screeched, bending down before I could even think about what I was doing and scooping Duncan up into my arms, ready to take off running back up the stairs and lock us in our room.

"You said a bad word," the pale-haired girl standing in the hallway—the *pitch-black* hallway in the middle of the night—said.

For a second, I'd really thought the house was haunted by Victorian-era children, but I realized the little girl wasn't a ghost because her body wasn't translucent. *Thank you, good night vision.*

Duncan, unlike me and my instincts, wagged, not even slightly alarmed.

Why was he . . . ? Oh. *Oh.* "Agnes?" I whispered.

"What are you doing?" she answered in the exact kind of voice I would've imagined coming out of her mouth. Unimpressed, flat, high in the way girls that age were capable. The most surprising thing of all was that she had unicorn pajamas on. I would've expected her to have Wednesday Addams's pajamas from the expert-level side-eye she was capable of in her mini wolf form.

She was so cute in the way a jellyfish was. You could look, but maybe you should second-guess touching it.

Duncan's tail wagged some more against my side, and I set him down. He trotted over to his new friend. She gave him an affectionate pat, whispering something so quiet I couldn't hear. Just as quickly as he greeted her, he came back, pouncing on my feet before sticking his butt in the air, paws stretched out ahead of him.

God, he was so cute. I lived in a constant state of wanting to bear hug him. His ears grazed the floor, and I was going to need to give them a wipe. When he'd been really young, I'd used a hair tie to hold them back when he ate.

"I didn't recognize you." I gave her a little smile. "Are you okay? Can't sleep?"

Agnes shook her head, so I was going to take it that she was fine but couldn't wind down. She was too young to be filled with worries, but there wasn't much I could do about that. What I could do instead was be nicer to her.

Even if she seemed like a snitch and she didn't seem to like me.

But there was a reason for her distrust, I just didn't know what it was yet.

I hesitated for a second, watching her just standing there, silently. "Where do you sleep?" I tried.

She lifted her arm and pointed at the door next to her.

I had to take advantage of her in her human form. "Are you by yourself all night?"

"No. Liddie and Sera take turns sleeping with me."

I didn't know either of those people. "In the same room?"

"Yeah." She was so still, standing there. "They snore. They only wake up if you shake them hard."

"I see." That made me feel better, and it made a hell of a lot more sense than a child sleeping by herself all night, magical or not. "So one of them is in the room right now?"

She nodded, her eyes narrowing. "Where are you going?"

Duncan pawed at my feet, telling me to hurry up. "We're going outside. I would invite you, but I think everyone is asleep, and I don't know where Henri is." Or anyone other than Franklin. "I'm scared to take you, and then we all get in trouble for not asking permission." I didn't think waking up a stranger in the middle of the night was a great idea either; Liddie and Sera probably wouldn't appreciate it.

Wasn't she grounded anyway?

The pale blonde didn't say a word, and dang it, that made me feel bad. But I knew what it would look like to take a child that wasn't mine out of their home in the middle of the night. How would I feel if someone did that to Duncan without my permission?

But even being aware of how complicated the situation was, and that I was doing the right thing, didn't make me feel less crappy.

"I'll try and talk to someone tomorrow about it. Should you be in bed? Duncan took a long nap earlier, and I don't need a lot of sleep . . ." Oh, this child hadn't been my fan before, and she still wasn't. I could sense it, even though her expression didn't change. "I'm sorry, Agnes. I'll ask them about you coming out to do things with us—if we do anything—tomorrow. All right?"

The too-serious little girl stood there like the young ghost I'd initially thought she was.

Duncan pawed at me again, his front teeth biting my shoelaces and tugging at them. There wasn't much more I could do now. "We'll see you in the morning. Sleep good." How could I feel this bad twice in a single day? I was on a roll.

"Night, Duncan," the little girl called out.

Ouch. Well, I couldn't blame her, but I would make it a priority to talk to someone about including her in activities I did with the donut, if she wanted, especially if she didn't have anyone else.

Slightly deflated—at least I was—we turned and headed down the hall, and I waited until we'd made it to the front doors to finally peek back. Agnes was gone. That didn't necessarily make me feel better, but I had an excited puppy who I could do whatever I wanted with, and I'd make it up to her if I could. In the meantime . . .

I pulled the ball I'd stuffed into my fanny pack out when we were far enough away from the house and tossed it underhanded. Duncan took off like a rocket after it, his tail bright in the shadows. He picked up the ball, glanced at me . . . and then he took off toward the trees.

"Dang it, Duncan!" I laughed, knowing I shouldn't, but I couldn't help it.

He did circles around a few trees, still holding the ball, and slowed down to let me catch him. When I did, I took the ball and tossed it again. Pure delight came off him as he went after it, saying, *"Yes,"* over and over again. That time, he brought it back, and I pretended to throw it, then took off running the other way instead.

"C'mon, slowpoke," I egged him on, going around a trunk. He pounced on my heel and did a quick 180 turn so I could chase him. I did, or at least I tried. He was fast and only getting faster as he grew. "I'm gonna getcha!"

I wasn't, but we could pretend.

Those short legs pumped even faster, going around a pine with wide lower branches before he dove into them as a shortcut.

Something caught my foot, making me lose my balance, and I landed on my knees with a "shit!" and an "ow!"

"You all right?"

Snapping my head up as I brushed off my knees—noticing my unraveled shoelace as the culprit—I didn't know how I'd missed the figure coming from the direction of the parking lot. I hadn't sensed him at all. There wasn't a single outdoor light on, but every detail of the dark uniform covering his body was obvious. It took everything in me not to make a peep, not to make a *face* in reaction to the well-built man who had poured himself into black pants and a short-sleeved black polo that I *knew* didn't have enough stretch in the material to have any business fitting him that well.

He looked like the kind of law enforcement a woman might get arrested for on purpose.

Was I going into heat? Was I capable of that? Because . . .

I had never in my life had a thing for a guy in a uniform, other than a football one, but I was really, really reconsidering it.

I'd always found him attractive. First, he'd been cute. Then I'd thought he was hot. Now? He was handsome.

Too handsome.

Stop it, Nina.

"I'll live," I called out, retying my shoelace real quick, then tucking my legs under me and standing. He was the only one around, so I had that working for my pride. "Hi, Fluff."

A flash of blue stopped in place, Duncan's tail straight up in the air. He wasn't growling. That was good.

"Hey." Henri kneeled and held out his hand. "Hi, Duncan."

The puppy didn't move any closer, but he craned his neck, smelling his fingers from a distance. Henri's smile was visible through the shadows. Nothing could hide in them from me.

"You're a handsome boy. A good boy, huh," he murmured to my donut, keeping his hand extended as a little nose twitched. "I made your breakfast this morning, remember that?"

I watched them.

"We need to take you to stretch your legs," Henri kept talking to him in a low, calming voice. That small, pleased smile remaining on his features despite the fact Duncan hadn't inched any closer to him. "How's he done with Matti on runs?"

I crossed my arms over my chest and watched as Duncan's tail lowered just a little bit, like a hair, but a minor improvement was still an improvement. "We haven't gone anywhere together where Matti or Sienna felt safe enough to be in bodies that they could run freely."

"Why's that?" he asked. Henri stayed focused on my puppy, who was doing the same thing right back. "He's been with you for two years, hasn't he?"

"Yeah, but we don't see each other that often. We go a couple months between visits. Your cousin travels a lot, Sienna's busy with work, and I'm not usually close enough to Chicago to drop by easily."

He made a face.

What was that expression for? I wondered. What was wrong with that? It wasn't like *he* saw them that frequently either.

Whatever had come to mind wasn't that important though from the way he moved the conversation along. "If you're comfortable with it, Randall and I can take him out on one of my days off. We can bring Agnes for company since they seem to get along. Nothing long or strenuous. Just to let him run a bit."

I didn't have to think about it. "Sure."

Those orangey-brown irises met mine.

Why did he look surprised?

"What? Matti told me I could trust you, and if I can't, then there's no point in being here. And we used to know each other. You were always polite to me, Fluffy. Sometimes you were even very nice," I teased him.

His eyes moved toward Dunky-Dunk, and I saw his mouth stretch into a smile as he gave my boy a long, assessing look, which he got right back from someone a fraction of his size. Duncan was half an angel, but his side-eye game was strong. He was something else. "That's a good point."

"He did really good at the nursery today."

"Good job, pup," Henri encouraged him, using a voice gentler than any other one I'd ever heard from him before.

I had to shove every little bit of my attraction *down*.

I fidgeted. "Hey, about Agnes . . . she caught us sneaking out, but I didn't want anyone to think I was kidnapping her. No one has said anything about her parents . . ." I scratched my throat. "Is she yours?" They didn't look anything alike, but you never knew. Sure, Henri didn't have a mate, but . . .

That got me his attention. "Everyone here is mine."

The hardest part of living here was going to be learning how to suppress my emotions, I decided right then and there.

Somehow, I kept my face even, chained whatever sound was in my throat in place, and said the only thing I could. "Hmm."

But that wasn't an answer exactly.

His gaze flicked to me before going back to my donut just as fast. "She's bonded the most to me and Franklin, but we all take care of her. Every child here considers every elder extended grandparents, Agnes especially. In the same way that every adult is a guardian to every child," he explained. "You're included in that now. Their safety and well-being are the responsibility of everyone, not just a biological family member."

That made my chest feel a little funny, and my eyes feel even funnier. The situation was what I'd been expecting. What I'd hoped for. "That's nice." I heard the hitch in my voice that got curious amber irises back on me. "Then, you're saying I can take her out to play at night, if she's awake, and no one is going to try and bite my head off?"

His forehead furrowed. "No one here is going to hurt you, Nina."

Trying to keep from making faces was a whole lot harder than I ever would have imagined, especially when he was looking right at me—and in that short-sleeved, collared shirt that showed off tan biceps, no less.

Henri kept going. "Either of you. And yeah, you can take her out if you want."

"I do," I answered. "She's not grounded then?"

"She is, but . . ." He gave *me* a long look that had my eyebrows shooting up my forehead.

"*But?* Are *you* breaking the rules?" I whispered in delight.

Who was this man?

His facial expression didn't change, and I ate it up even more. "If you don't tell, I won't either. She's a good kid, and it was Pascal's idea. She told me she tried to get them to come back, and I believe her."

My mouth formed a little O in even more surprise, and one side of his mouth hitched up for a split second before he blinked and it was gone.

"Do you need to give me a permission slip in case anyone asks?"

The man, who kept surprising me, looked around. Literally, over both of those broad shoulders. "Are there more people out here right now that are gonna worry about it?"

I really didn't know who he was, not the same man-boy I'd known, but I wanted to get to know him. This part of him made me smile, not just because it was unexpected but because . . . I liked it. A lot.

I snorted. "Just because I don't see them or smell them, doesn't mean they aren't out here. You probably have people patrolling at all times, don't you?"

He made a gesture that said I wasn't wrong. "How are your friends?

"Sienna felt better enough that she came down and ate a little bit of plain chicken for dinner, and Matti was still upstairs claiming he's on his death bed. It's the first time either of them has ever had food poisoning."

That got his attention. "What'd they eat?" He hadn't asked about it after we'd paid them a visit. He'd seemed so distracted to me. "When we checked on them earlier, I thought they'd caught something viral. There's a few illnesses that do get us sick."

"Hot dogs from a gas station."

His forehead furrowed. "Why the hell would they eat that?"

I laughed. "That's what I said!"

Henri shook his head in disgust. "You remember the name of the gas station?"

Even more than a fit body, I had a thing for a good man.

I was in trouble.

But I shouldn't *have* a thing for this good man. It had just been too long since the last time I'd talked to one, I guess, that it felt so new. So rewarding. My last boyfriend had been BD—before Duncan. Before my RV life, even. My last boyfriend had been when I'd lived in Santa Fe.

It had been a while.

Anyway, I wasn't convinced this particular good man liked me as a person all that much to begin with. Tolerated? I could see that. Could be sarcastic with and maybe joke a little with? Yes, but I was also aware I gave those vibes off to most people, at least some part of me did. I was a weird contradiction in repelling some folks and strongly attracting others.

And there wasn't going to be a point in harboring a little crush on an attractive man if I was going to have to devote myself to finding someone here to marry me so I could stay. That was the most important thing I had to focus on. I needed to find options. Whoever I ended up with, we were going to make it work, come hell or high water.

Because, if it was a werewolf, they stayed with their mates. A werewolf's dedication to their partner was unparalleled. In sickness and in health, through sunny skies and tornadoes, they stayed together. And I liked that, I always had. But there was no point in thinking about that in front of Henri, even if a werewolf was my best shot since most of them seemed to like me just fine.

But some part of my brain wondered again about Henri being a potential mate. The other question was, did I talk to Matti about it or did I keep the idea to myself? He had a big mouth, and I wasn't sure how he'd react.

"I do remember. I called and spoke to the manager earlier, but I'll write down the number for you in the morning if you want," I told him.

He nodded, then asked, "Do I need to check on them?"

"I don't think so. Sienna and I won't let Matti die. I don't want him haunting me for the next sixty years."

His eyes crinkled at the corners, there one second and gone the next. "All right," he replied a little more softly than he had before.

"What?" I asked, tipping my chin up at him.

It took him so long to answer, I was half expecting him not to. But he did. "You don't look like the Cricket I remember or smell like her. Then you laugh or say something cute, and I know it's you." Henri met my eyes, and I watched his nostrils flare again for the briefest moment before he looked away.

I thought about my bracelet again and how he still hadn't given it back, but I didn't want to ask. If this was what they needed from me—to not mask myself for the time being—I could do it.

I'd just need to stay away from Spencer.

"Thanks, Henri." He wouldn't say something like that if he

hated having me here. "I need to ask you something since I forgot to ask Franklin earlier."

"What's going on?"

"I have to start working again soon. How do I fit in helping out around here? How do I know what you need help with? If there's a calendar for volunteering, I haven't seen one."

That got his interest. "What do you do?"

"I work remotely in customer service. I just need the internet. It's what I've done for years, since satellite internet got so good." I had zero plans of selling my trailer until the three months were up. Even after that, I might still not. What if one day Duncan could be out in public again? Maybe we could travel a little, and my trailer was paid off; the only monthly payment I had for it was insurance.

"Who do you work for?"

I told him the name of the major online pet company. "It's full-time, and scheduling is really flexible." I liked it, and the way the company was run was very customer-focused, so I rarely had to piss people off telling them "no." Plus, I got a discount for Duncan's toys, even though his favorite method of entertainment was animal carcasses, followed closely by any old stick.

"Most of us work away from the ranch. All that's expected is that you help out when you can. Download the app. It's how we communicate with everyone. There's a calendar, a forum, and a sign-up list . . ."

There was an app? They had thought of *everything* here. I didn't know how it was possible for my awe to grow every day, but it did.

". . . with different jobs and tasks that you can sign up for," he finished explaining.

Tasks. I didn't know what that meant yet, but I'd look. "Sounds good," I said. "Is it okay if I work in that room where I met the elders? I have satellite internet, but if I can avoid running my generator, I try to."

He got a funny look on his face. "Yes." The muscle in his

cheek flexed. "You live here now. The bedrooms and family homes are the only places that aren't free space for everyone."

"That was what I'd figured, but I wanted to make sure."

"For tax purposes, there's an address in the town you can use as your place of residence. I'll get it for you."

"Okay. Thanks." I smiled at him.

Those orange-brown irises lingered on me. On my face. The moonlight was hitting his features in a way that brought to life all those stunning angles and the beautiful color of his skin, all creamy golden.

His eyes flicked toward Duncan suddenly.

Stop checking out Henri.

We stood there silently for a minute, Duncan the center of attention as he kept on trying to sniff Henri from where he was. After a moment, my puppy ran for my legs, twining his way through them before sitting right on top of my feet. He leaned the side of his head against my knee.

"You're a good boy protecting your mom," Henri stated with a nod at my donut. "I need to get to bed." The werewolf man drew his palm down his face before sighing. "There are people out here. Nothing would dare come this close, but if you need anything, yell as loud as you can."

I smiled again. "I will. Sleep good," I wished him.

He looked at me for a second, throat bobbing before nodding. "'Night, Duncan," he called out before heading toward the house.

I didn't let myself watch him just in case he happened to turn around. He definitely didn't need to see me checking out his butt in those black tactical pants. I was already hoping he hadn't caught on to my attraction when we'd been out in the woods earlier. Instead, I bent down, poked Duncan in the side, said, "You're it, Donut," and took off running again.

Maybe another day, we'd invite Henri to play too.

Chapter Ten

"Quit looking at me."

"You quit looking at me."

"I'm not even looking at you!" I laughed, side-eyeing Matti as we walked to my truck.

"I can feel you looking at me," he argued with a sniff that had less to do with him being sick and more with him just being a pest. This was the first time he'd left the room since he'd gotten the brown plague the day before last. He looked like he'd been haunting abandoned hospitals for a century based off the dark circles around his eyes and the gauntness of his cheeks. This was the thinnest I'd ever seen him, and I had known him in his scrawny boy years.

And right at that moment, he was being the same pain in the ass I knew and loved because his heart was in the right place.

There was no hiding that I was sad they were leaving—not from his nose and not from eyes that had known me for most of our lives. I wouldn't cry about it, I didn't think. This wasn't our first goodbye—not even our twentieth—and it wasn't going to be our last either. It didn't mean it wasn't hard though. Every time was.

This time might just suck a little bit more because we'd lost two days spending time with each other while he'd been sick, and . . . for whatever reason, this goodbye felt different. A little more permanent. A little more scary, for me at least.

Duncan and I couldn't exactly load into my truck and drive over if we suddenly wanted to.

I huffed at him. "If I was, it's because you look like something that climbed out of a well."

He huffed back as we got to my car, but he didn't deny his appearance.

Maybe someone would try and exorcise him at the airport. "That'll teach you never to ignore me again." I nudged him with my elbow.

Matti snickered as I opened the truck bed and he grunted, lifting Sienna's bag, then his, into it. I'd offered to carry it. He elbowed me back before slamming the tailgate shut and raising his eyebrows at me. I raised my eyebrows right back at him, earning me a smile and a hand on each shoulder.

"Sorry we didn't get to spend more time together," my oldest friend apologized.

"It's okay." I set my hand on one of his. "Thank you for coming with us. For helping me find this place. For everything." That was the simplest way of putting it, wasn't it?

"You going to be okay?"

"I think so," I told him honestly, hearing the front door close. Sienna had gone into the nursery to tell Duncan goodbye one last time since he couldn't come with us. Leaving the ranch wasn't worth the risk, and he had a comfortable place to stay at the nursery. Matti had said bye when he'd gone outside with us in the morning. "The donut is happy so far, and I hope I will be too."

His perma-smile drooped. "When I first got here, everyone gave me a lot of breathing room the first few months, Nina, to give me time to get my bearings. Don't take people giving you space too personally, all right? They didn't say anything, but I remember them discouraging residents from getting too close to new people until their three months are up."

I nodded at him, not surprised at all that Sienna had relayed to him that other than some of the parents here and the few people Henri had introduced me to, no one had come by to say hello.

Even though Sienna still hadn't been feeling like herself the day before, we had gone to visit the two closest towns to the ranch after dropping Duncan off at the nursery. We'd spent the whole morning and most of the afternoon checking out the bigger town almost an hour away, buying groceries at the big box stores they had, and then stopped at the much smaller stores half an hour from the ranch, just seeing what they had so I could plan for future trips.

When we got back, I'd helped Maggie in the nursery again while Sienna checked on Matti and took a nap. After dinner, we'd spent time in my room, sprawled on the bed, watching television and talking while Dunky napped after another exciting day with his new friends. It had been a good last day with one of my favorite people.

Now I had to say bye to them for the time being.

The expression on Matti's face got even more serious. "I'd planned to go with you and see if we could find some of the people I knew when I lived here, but none of them came to say hi either." He scowled. "Glad I didn't waste my damn time keeping in touch with any of them."

I smiled up at his protectiveness, and he kept right on scowling.

"If anyone is mean to you—"

I took a step forward and wrapped my arms around the middle of him, pressing my cheek to his shoulder for maybe the fifty-thousandth time in my life. "I'll write down their names and you can bring some of those hot dogs to share with them."

His laugh was weaker than normal, but it was still all Matti. He hugged me back. "If you aren't happy, say the word and we'll figure out another option, yeah?"

I nodded against him.

Matti pulled back. "I'm being serious."

For once in his life, he was. "I know you are."

"We were talking already, and we're going to check our work schedules and see when we can come back."

"Just let me know. You know I get that you're both busy."

"I know you're more than capable of taking care of yourself and Duncan"—he thumped my shoulder—"but someone has to check on you."

"Yeah, we have to check on our Nina," Sienna piped in from a few feet away as she approached us from the direction of the clubhouse.

But it was the man following her that surprised me, and I knew I wasn't the only one when Matti's head jerked.

"I sent you a text. We're leaving," my best friend said to his cousin.

Henri, who I hadn't seen yesterday at all, stopped to the side of us, a beaten-up stainless steel water bottle hanging from his index finger. In jeans and another long-sleeved T-shirt, he looked like a different man from the one I'd seen running around the forest after a long shift with LOBO COUNTY SHERIFF'S DEPARTMENT stitched onto the breast of his shirt. "I got it." His gaze caught mine, holding it steady in a way that made me feel he was trying to figure out if I was still the same person I'd been the last time we'd seen each other. "I'll come with you, if you don't mind, Cricket."

I forced myself not to peek at Matti because I had to put all my effort into not seeming shocked in Henri's face. "It's fine by me . . .?"

He blinked. "Why are you asking it like it's a question?"

Play it cool, Nina. "Because I figured you're busy, and I'm surprised you're coming?" I tried again. I'd learned from Franklin at dinner that Henri had been working a ton of overtime lately—it wasn't just an excuse he gave Matti. I had also learned at the same time that the elder had made plans to leave later today. He had something he needed to "look into" had been the only explanation he'd given the night before, still acting sketchy, even though I wasn't sure if I was imagining it or if he was just a suspicious person by nature.

I really wasn't sure what to think about that bracelet he had on and what it might mean. I wasn't in a position to ask about Franklin though, and I knew it. It might just always have to be a mystery I lived with, unless he decided to share his backstory with me.

I wasn't going to hold my breath in that case . . . unless I could weasel it out of Shiloh once he was done with his prison sentence. He'd already proved to have trouble keeping a secret, and I wasn't above getting innocent information out that way. We'd see.

Henri raised that left eyebrow a millimeter. "You still answered it like it's a question."

I scratched my neck. "Okay?"

It was Matti who laughed, his head ducking down to give me a peck on the temple. "You're a pain in the fucking ass, Nina, but we should get going. I want to check my bag."

I said, "I'm not a pain in the ass."

And Henri agreed, "She's not a pain in the ass."

I smiled, pleased at him defending me again, even if it was unexpected.

Then he ruined it. "She's just a brat."

I looked at him, and he looked at me.

But there was that sparkle I'd seen in his eyes the other times he'd tapped into his unexpected funny bone.

Why he went back and forth between acting like we were familiar with each other—old friend-ish—and then acting like he could barely tolerate me was beyond my mental capacity. There was also the chance that I might have been overthinking it since I did that with everything else around here. Maybe it had nothing to do with me and it just depended on his mood. But people were complicated, and there was a chance, if I spent enough time pondering when he acted the way he did and who was around when he did it, it might bring those actions to light in a different way. He wasn't a mean man. I really didn't think he was *trying* to hurt my feelings.

And honestly, I wanted one single person here in my corner. Other than the kids I'd met at the nursery, and Maggie the teacher, who I really needed to have an awkward conversation with sooner rather than later, Henri seemed to be my only other "friend" at the moment. If this was how he wanted things to be, then that was fine. We were going to be a mullet, I guess. Business in the front and a party in the back when no one was looking.

All right, maybe it was going to hurt my feelings, but it wasn't anything I couldn't recover from.

"All right, in that case, let's go," I said, discreetly eyeing Henri standing there as I moved around them and headed to the driver's side.

"Shotgun," Sienna called out before hip checking her husband out of the way to get into the front seat.

The two cousins were already in the back seat by the time I got behind the wheel, and I handed Sienna my phone so she could put the address for the airport into the navigation app. The community parking lot was mostly empty, with only about ten cars parked.

It was strange how I never saw anyone walking to and from their cars.

I tried to keep the suspicion in my body so my friends wouldn't sense it and then ask questions about it, and it must have worked because the second we were through the gates—they were motion-sensor activated on the way out, we'd learned yesterday—Si put my music streaming app on, and we sang along under our breaths, the back seat oddly quiet other than the near constant buzzing of what sounded like incoming texts. One glance in the rearview mirror confirmed that Henri was glued to his phone. Beside him, Matti was sprawled sitting up, still looking like the ghost of Christmas past.

The airport wasn't close, and according to the directions, it was going to take over an hour to get there through the winding mountain roads. We made it about twenty minutes before Sienna snickered for no reason. I lifted my chin at her.

"Remember that time we went on the road trip to see my grandma and we got that flat tire and had to hitchhike because we didn't have service?" she brought up.

"Oh, that poor dog in the back seat was shaking and wouldn't stop crying, he was so scared of you, and the lady was worried he was sick," I remembered.

Matti's head appeared between the seats. "You *hitchhiked*? When?"

It took the rest of the drive to tell Matti the story about the trip we took across three states during a summer we spent with Sienna's grandma. We had done that twice, and each time had a funny story behind it that we cracked up about. How neither one of us had ever told Matti about it was surprising, but laughing with them was better than listening to all the music in the world.

Unfortunately, it also made the time go by too fast, and we were talking about an armadillo we'd almost gotten into a wreck trying to avoid years ago when I pulled up to the drop-off section of the tiny regional airport.

We got out, and Sienna pulled me into a hug the second she shut the passenger door. "We'll come visit soon," she promised.

I tucked my cheek against hers. "If, or when, Duncan figures out how to hide his tail or his eyes, we'll be the ones coming over." I hoped she wasn't holding her breath though.

"We're only a phone call away—shh," she dropped her voice suddenly. "Matti's telling Henri something."

If she could hear them, they could hear her, but I got her point. That was my girl. "What are they saying?" I fought the urge to peek at them too. That would be too obvious.

"He told him . . . that he'd appreciate it if he kept an eye on you . . . that you used to take care of him and . . . huh, that's true," she muttered.

"What?"

"That you'll take care of other people but not yourself . . . shh, I'm still listening."

Maybe there was some truth to that, but he didn't need to tell freaking *Henri* about it.

"Matti said that if things aren't working out, to tell him . . ." Sienna rattled off before suddenly kissing one cheek, then the other, acting like nothing had just happened. Her voice went back to a normal volume too. "Call if you need anything. Got it?" She winked, but her cheeks were pink.

What was that about? I narrowed my eyes at her. I'd text her later and get the scoop. For now, I kissed her cheeks right back.

"Yes, ma'am." I squeezed her muscular biceps. "Love you, Si. Thank you for coming all the way here with us."

Her eyes started glittering, and I was sure that if I had the ability to smell her emotions, I would've gotten confirmation I wasn't the only one who was sad. "We'd do anything for you and the baby. We love you. *I* love you."

We hugged again, holding on just a little tighter, a little longer.

Done with their conversation, Matti came over and held out his arms wide. "Be a good girl, Jaws."

"Shut up." I laughed and stepped into his embrace, hugging him tight. He'd definitely lost weight. "Love you. Thank you for everything."

I could feel him kissing the top of my head. "We're only a call away," he reminded me as he pulled back and gave me an intense look. "If anyone tries to hurt you, do what you have to, understand?"

Pressing my lips together, I nodded at him.

"I'm serious."

"I *know*," I told him. "I promise. I'll do what I have to."

He didn't look like he totally believed me—because he knew me well enough to feel that way—but he nodded after a moment. Then he lifted his finger and said, "Come here, I want to tell you one more thing."

I narrowed my eyes but stepped closer. "If you burp in my ear..."

"I'm not," he insisted.

I didn't believe him but all right. "Yes?"

"Closer."

Okayyy. I did.

He glanced to both sides—Henri and Si were behind him—and mouthed, *Get my cousin to marry you.*

"Huh?" I almost barked, pretty sure there was no way I'd read his lips correctly.

From the expression he gave me, I knew I had, in fact, not misunderstood. Then, with his face so grave, he said clearly, "You trust me, don't you?"

That was a stupid question, and I told him so with my own expression.

Marry Henri, he mouthed that time, not tiptoeing at all around it.

There was no hiding the way my heart started beating faster at what he was telling me to do, and we both knew it from the way he made his eyes wide at me before leaning in and giving me another big hug. I was so tense and distracted—and regretful that I hadn't talked to him about it even though I'd literally thought about it—I barely managed to sneak in one more hug of my own before he pulled back.

The loaded expression he shot me made a knot form in my throat before he turned and went for the bags in the bed of the truck, while Si scrunched up her face, clearly wondering what was going on. I could see Henri's attention on us, so I shrugged and hugged her one last time. My friends waved as they pulled their carry-ons behind them to the terminal.

Matti stopped halfway there and turned around. "Someone needs to give Henri a hard time. You got this, Nina?" he hollered.

He'd just suggested I marry him, and now he was telling me to give him a hard time?

I blinked and bowed. "It would be an honor," I told him with a smile that felt a little shaky on my face. I might kill him after all, I thought, as they kept going.

"Love you!" Sienna shouted right before going through the sliding doors. "Henri, take care of my girl!"

I blew her a kiss before we headed to my truck.

Exactly two seconds later, Henri, who had taken the front passenger seat, shifted to face me. I was staring straight ahead.

I couldn't look at him.

I couldn't look at anything.

"Why are you crying?" His voice was gruff. "And what'd Matti say that worried you?"

Pressing the tip of my middle finger to the outside corner of my eye, I sniffled. I opened my mouth to answer, had to swallow, then tried again. "I hate saying goodbye." I skipped his other question, not that I was expecting him to forget about it. I just needed to deal with one thing at a time, and right now, being sad was the winner.

"You were fine five minutes ago."

I pressed my finger to my other eye. "I know, but I'm not going to cry in front of them. They worry enough as it is." I sniffled again and attempted to hold back the tears while ignoring the way he turned even more in his seat, like he wanted a better view to watch me cry. "You never know when the last time you're going to see someone is," I tried to explain. "I think about that all the time with my mom and dad."

There was a pause, then, "They're both healthy, Nina."

I dabbed at my eye again. "I don't have your nose, so I can't tell that, but that isn't what I mean. You never know what's going to happen a week from now, much less two minutes from now. And I love them." That came out like a croak. I had to swallow to get my voice under control. "I get upset every time. Please don't tell them. I think they think I'm tougher than I really am." I stopped. "But they might also know and they let me get away with it." I could see that happening too.

He didn't agree not to tattle, so I had to peek at him.

"Please, Henri?" I whispered.

Those light-colored eyes narrowed, but he nodded after a minute. "You didn't live close to them even before Duncan, did you?" he asked.

"No." With my eyes blurring from the tears I was struggling to hold back, I was thankful we were still parked. "Because I don't like living in cities the way they do, and they don't like smaller towns, like I do. We compromise to see each other. *I need to stop tearing up.* Duncan hates it when I cry. I don't want him to worry." But with that thought, even more tears spilled onto my cheeks.

Silently, Henri kept studying me, and I sighed. "I don't want to make you uncomfortable. I'll stop in a minute."

"You aren't making me uncomfortable."

I bit the inside of my cheek as another tear spilled over my bottom eyelash.

I watched his gaze follow it down my jaw, his mouth going dang near flat. "You smell like cinnamon right now," he stated bluntly.

"I do?" I asked, sniffling. I hadn't cried a whole lot in front of people, but no one who had witnessed it had ever commented on the way it smelled. They would have said something... wouldn't they?

He made a positive sound in his throat.

"I'm sorry."

There was more shifting, another pause, then, "What are you sorry for?"

"The smell." I could feel his gaze on my skin.

"You're apologizing for smelling like cinnamon?" he asked slowly.

I used my knuckle to dab at the corner of my eyes some more. "The way you said it..." I tried to hold in the couple more tears threatening my eyeballs, but it didn't work. "You made it sound like you don't like it. It's just been a lot of change in a short amount of time, and it hit me all of a sudden, Fluff."

There went my voice again.

I could not lose it. I needed to drive, I reminded myself. What was I getting upset about? Missing my friends was one thing. But he didn't like the way I smelled? Since when was that new? I dried the parts of my face I could reach with my shoulder, then took a deep breath. "It's fine. I'm just emotional because I'm upset since seeing them from now on will be more complicated, and I'm worried it'll be a while, but we'll figure it out. We always do. I'll stop crying in a minute, I swear."

He didn't say a word, and when a minute passed and I still hadn't stopped, his sigh filled the cabin.

Stop it, Nina.

It's okay to be sad. It's okay to be worried about being on your own surrounded by strangers. It's okay to lose one more thing from a life you loved.

Maybe that's what I was really the most worked up about. Losing that one more thing so freaking soon. For all my big talk, accepting change wasn't one of my strengths in life. Maybe it was some trauma response from the time that Matti's presence had disappeared from my life without a warning, or maybe I just loved my friends, and everything going on right now was a lot to handle in general. It could be both.

I wiped at my face some more, that time not even trying to be dainty about it. I used my whole palm. Then I wiped it on my pants and did it again, trying so dang hard not to make some real unladylike sound. *Get it together.*

"Henri?" I asked in a wobbly voice after a second.

His "hmm?" came out like more of a grumble.

I moved my hand enough so I could peer at him through my fingers. "Sorry for biting you."

"You . . ."

I didn't think he believed me from the way he was frowning and glaring. And I must have been too focused on it—his dark pink lips—that I didn't see his fingers coming for me until his palm cupped the back of my neck.

Before my body could do anything other than process the fact that this man was being affectionate with me—nice to me—his voice came out all rumpled velvet as he murmured, "They'll be back soon."

They had both reassured me of the same thing, but coming out of Henri's mouth, it was soothing for some reason.

He kept going. "Matti said they were going to try for next month for a weekend."

Matti. That pain in my butt. What he'd mouthed to me was burned into my retinas. Get Henri to marry me?

What was he *thinking* dropping that on me and then walking away? We needed an hour-long discussion, minimum, to go over something like that. Some conversations couldn't be had over text, and now I was going to have to wait who knew how long to get him to explain why he would've brought that up. Why that would even enter his brain. Sure *I'd* considered it. Briefly.

But from Matti himself?

Unless...

My friend was a lot of things, but he was a realist. He was one of the most impulsive people I'd ever met, but at the same time, logic was known to steer his thoughts and actions when it mattered.

Hmm.

There had to be a reason he would throw his cousin into the ring.

What did he know that I didn't? I wiped at my face when a couple more tears beaded along my eyelashes. I hiccupped just as a very low growl and the flexing of fingers at the back of my neck had me flicking my eyes toward the man who was trying to make me feel better. His eyebrows were knitted together, lips pressed tight.

Or maybe Matti had lost his mind suggesting Henri tie his life to mine when he could barely sit beside me.

"I'm sorry!" I reached for the door. "I can't help it. Let me roll down the window."

His frown got even worse. "What do you need to roll down the window for?"

I grazed my fingers over the buttons on my door lightly, not pressing them in yet. "You look like you're mad right now." I paused. "Because of the cinnamon smell."

Or that was what I thought before those light-colored eyes bounced around my face. I watched his throat bob, his jawline getting more defined. There was no missing the way he seemed to force his teeth to unclench before gritting out, "That's not it."

It wasn't?

"I..." His thick throat worked, like even saying words was difficult. "You crying... your tears... makes me want to bite you."

I blinked very, very slowly.

"You smell like a cookie when you do it."

But werewolves didn't even eat cookies.

I lifted my face and wiped at it some more. Henri was looking right at me. Glaring, even. I pointed at him. "I swear, if you bite me, I'll bite you back."

I didn't think it was my imagination that some of the tension on Henri's face disappeared.

"Not as hard as you can bite me, but I'll try my best," I warned him. "I used to give Matti bruises when we were kids. You remember that?" Not that I ever got in trouble over it. His mom used to say a nip got a message across better than any word ever could.

"No," he took his time answering. "You bit him?"

"His mom told me to." I had loved her almost as much as I'd loved my parents.

He didn't exactly look like he believed me.

A honk from behind had me blinking and remembering where we were. I put the truck into Drive and pulled onto the road. I waited until I was back on the highway that would take us to the ranch to speak again. "Right after his magic presented and he started turning into a fluffball, Matti started nipping me. Duncan's gotten me too, and that hurt like hell. I'm glad we got over that phase." I imagined how much it would hurt to have those full-grown adult teeth do the same. "I don't like pain." I gave him a side-eye. "You could nibble instead?"

His lips slightly parted. "You're telling me to nibble on you?" He sounded like he'd swallowed nails.

"Instead of biting me," I clarified.

Henri faced forward. His hands fisted and then released over and over again as we pulled up to a stoplight.

Maybe I'd made this weird. That hadn't been my intention. I'd just been joking. "You know what you remind me of right now? There are these movies about vampires that you probably haven't watched, but I'm sure you've heard about them. The vampire likes the way the girl in the movie smells, and he's like, '*Grr, she's the best thing I've ever smelled,*' but he looks constipated instead of hungry."

Both of Henri's eyebrows rose up a whole millimeter if not more. "I'm not going to bite you or . . . nibble on you." He side-eyed me. "Vampires usually do look constipated."

My mouth dropped. "They're *real*?"

Those thick eyebrows stayed right where they were. "You didn't know? There aren't a lot of them, but they're around."

I made the closest sound to a squeal that I was capable of. Vampires! They were real!

Why wouldn't they be?

Like he could sense the million and one questions suddenly going through my mind, Henri raised a hand. "I don't know much about them other than they drink blood and they're more sensitive than allergic to light."

My next semi-squeal was a little quieter, but it still counted, and the corner of his mouth twitched like he wasn't totally irritated with my shock at *vampires* existing.

Were they good-looking? Were they immortal? How much blood did they drink? And why was that what I was curious about? "Can I tell Sienna about them?" I whispered, the secret feeling huge in my truck cab.

Henri shrugged, pinching the tip of his nose between his thumb and the middle of his index finger while he turned toward the windshield.

Another wave of guilt went through me. "Want me to turn the vents away from blowing on me so that my smell isn't circulating so much?"

He was still focused forward. "No."

"Are you sure?"

"I'm sure," he insisted, not really sounding that sure.

I reached over and moved the vent anyway, ignoring his sigh.

And here Matti wanted me to convince him to marry me. What was he thinking? What had I been thinking? Henri and I couldn't even sit in the front together.

That was kind of depressing because I really did want him to like me, at least as a friend.

I was going to have to tell Matti how dumb of an idea it was the second I could do it in privacy, because the last thing I needed was for someone to overhear us talking about *that*.

Plus, why hadn't he or Sienna or my parents ever said anything about my scent when I cried? I didn't get upset that often, but I had definitely done it around them, more than once. If anything, they hugged me tighter than usual when I was sad.

Dang it, just the reminder of my loved ones made me tear up all over again.

Change was *good*. Good change was great. We had gotten what we needed being allowed to live here.

What was going *on* with me? First, I was acting like the magic in the forest was catnip. Then I was acting like I'd never seen a man before while I was in Henri's presence. And now I was weepy?

This was a lot, and anybody would cry over everything that had happened and everything that would continue to happen over the next few months or years, I told myself, trying to feel better about why I was so all over the place emotionally.

I had to be strong and . . . I couldn't drive if I couldn't see through my tears, dang it.

Henri's sigh filled the cab, but his voice came out almost as gentle as when he was talking to the kids. "Why are you really getting upset, Cricket? Because of Matti and Sienna?"

He was making it worse being so nice. I scratched my throat. "Y-Yes and no."

Didn't I know better by now? It wasn't that I didn't think there was no one in the world who cared about me, there was, but those people had chosen to be there. Worked to be there. More than anything, they wanted to.

And then there was everyone else.

When you stayed away from people, you didn't give them the opportunity to push you away.

Being alone-alone was different than feeling alone in a place surrounded by people who didn't want you there.

Having to pretend to fit in when you knew you didn't, and so did everyone else, was hard. No wonder I couldn't stop my eyes from watering. *Stop it.*

"In two blocks, there's a diner on the right," Henri said, still using that same soft voice that was quickly turning into a weakness of mine. His cousin's way of making me feel better was to make me laugh. Sienna's methods included tickling. Henri wasn't the person I expected to actually *be nice*. "Pull in the parking lot."

There was no asking; he was telling me to. There was a clear difference between the two. But . . . "I'm fine," I promised, using my shoulder to dab at my face. "I just need a sec. I can still see."

A big hand came out of my peripheral vision, and for a moment, I thought he was going to put it on the steering wheel and try and take control.

But this man, who I knew and yet didn't know, set his fingers over mine and gave them a little squeeze. They were warm. "I'm not asking if you're fine or if it's safe for you to drive right now. Pull over at the diner," he ordered in his sneaky, bossy werewolf voice that made me feel like I needed to listen to him.

The annoying part? It worked. Sniffling, I drove the next block, finding the sign for Howling Hill Diner—was that on purpose?—and I turned into it. I hadn't even realized we were already in Lobo Springs, the small town closest to the ranch. We were on the outskirts of it, but we were in the limits, I was pretty sure.

The second I put the truck into Park, Henri reached for the keys, turned them, and followed that up by undoing his seat belt. Then he reached over, undid mine and sat back.

"When a pup is upset," he started to say, widening his legs as much as he could once he'd leaned back into place, "a cuddle usually makes them feel better."

I . . . I was no puppy, and I almost told him that, but it wasn't like he didn't know it already. Butttt I was never going to say no to affection, especially not from someone I knew, much less when that someone looked like Henri, *and* gave off the kind of comforting, stable vibes he did. The man was built to snuggle.

Which then reminded me about asking Matti why and how he was so big compared to everyone else. Amarok were bigger than every other kind of wolves I'd ever met, but Henri was twice the size that Matti's dad had been, and he'd been full Amarok.

"I don't want you to throw up on me," I told him instead of sliding across the bench right then and there. "It might break my heart if you did." Then I would have to consider moving away immediately, which I would have to reconsider because I wanted this to work for Duncan, and after that, I'd be forced to avoid Henri at all costs for the rest of my life.

He narrowed his eyes. "Why would I throw up?"

I tapped the tip of my nose, not really wanting to say the words out loud again.

A slow breath slipped from his lips. His head tipped to the side, those amber eyes regarding me carefully. "Nina," he was back to using his gentle voice, "I like the way cinnamon smells."

"You do?"

He nodded, splaying his fingers wide on those full thighs that seemed to be straining the seams of his jeans.

Was he sure?

"You're a human pastry," Henri told me, meeting my gaze straight on.

I wiped my face one more time, still not sure I believed him. My voice gave it away as much as my words did. "I am?"

"You are."

"A good pastry?" I asked, half joking, half serious. "Or the kind you get at the gas station?"

The muscles at his throat strained. "A good pastry," he confirmed.

So he didn't mind me in that way. Couldn't he have just admitted that in the first place? A little bit of relief loosened my body, and I'd swear his facial expression softened at the same time, not much but some. And it was really so unexpected that I couldn't help but smile a little as I dabbed at my face. All I said was "Oh. Thanks, Henri."

His sigh was so soft. "Don't." A short groan grumbled through him. "I forget you can't tell how I'm feeling without me saying anything. At the ranch, everyone is aware of everyone else's emotions at all times. I don't hide anything because I can't. I like the way you . . ." He sighed once more, piercing me with a look that was real close to being pleading. "Please. Stop crying."

I was a sucker for a few things. Big muscular men, puppies, children, and the word "please." And coming out of Henri? I didn't know what was wrong with me, but I couldn't stop brushing tears off my face.

He looked at me for another second, his expression going almost pained before he scooted across the bench seat until he sat right beside me.

I watched as he slipped a hand between my back and the cushion, and then, with his opposite hand, he gently wiped under one of my eyes and then the other. And while I sat there, in a mix of sadness for the past and the present, fear of the unknown future, and the most unexpected kind of surprise as the hand he'd used on my tears went to his nose. He took a sniff of his damp finger, the tendon at his throat flexing, and before I could ask what that was about, he moved again. That palm went to the back of my head, and he drew my forehead to his shoulder.

I let him.

I let my head fall to the spot along his thick trap muscle and neck, as he sighed, "Poor little Cricket."

My bones might have well been nonexistent the way I slumped against him even more. I was human jelly. Cinnamon jelly according to him.

He wasn't my parents, Matti, Sienna, or Duncan, but this didn't feel wrong. Didn't feel cheap. It made me feel better.

Henri made me feel better.

"You'll see Matti and Sienna again." His warm fingers on my skin felt like straight magic. "I haven't lived anywhere new in a long time, but I know it's hard. You'll settle in with time."

I'd been so caught up on keeping my shit together that I hadn't let myself appreciate the way *he* smelled again. How much I liked it. Up close, it was even better the second time around. It took all the strength in my body to act normal, to breathe like I always did when his natural body odor and deodorant smelled like rain and cedar.

His fingertips moved, skimming along my back through the thin material of my shirt. I could feel the heat of his palm on the back of my head. His breath was soft on my ear like he had his head bent toward me.

I wasn't starved for affection, but . . .

"You'll make more friends," he seemed to promise in a steady, strong voice.

I didn't trust mine, or really even myself, honestly, so all I did was nod. I wanted to tell him that I wasn't too worried about making new friends, but that was a lie. There were a lot of things I was uncertain about, things I was mourning that were human-shaped and not human-shaped, and that was the freaking truth.

And fortunately for me, he smelled good, and he was warm, and he was being so nice, and I knew he would have done this for anyone getting upset around him. He'd said everyone on the ranch was his, and I believed that he believed it. By default, I guess that made me the same, in a way.

One of many.

But it was something.

Being needed could be such a crippling thing, but it could also give you more purpose than you could ever imagine. It could make the crappiest day brighter. I understood that first-hand now.

So I wasn't going to pull away and not take what was offered. What I was going to do was sit there and soak up his scent and the reassurance his body gave me. He was no Matti, his presence was no warm, friendly hug to my soul, but it was something nice in a totally different way. Like hugging a domesticated bear.

And after a few breaths, he shifted a little, and I took it as my sign to lift my head. "Better?" he asked. He hadn't scooted back, and his nose was right there, inches from mine.

He was gorgeous with those cheekbones and square jaw.

"Much better. Thank you," I told him, giving him a real smile. I felt much better.

Henri looked at me for a second longer, like he was making

sure he believed me, then he tipped his chin after a moment. "You hungry?"

"I'm always hungry."

The muscles around his mouth didn't move, but his eyes crinkled a little. "Let's grab a bite then."

I nodded, patted my cheeks one more time, and got out. He was already waiting for me behind the truck, that stern, no-nonsense expression over his features. He was a real-life action hero standing there.

And then he reached into his pocket and pulled out a string of beads.

It was my bracelet.

Without doing more than briefly meeting my eyes, he closed the distance between us, took my right wrist, and slipped my bracelet on me. His palm covered the beads and my wrist. "You don't need to hide who you are," he told me, his thumb touching the soft notch where my hand met my forearm, "but it's your decision. I'll give you Duncan's collar later."

My lips were formed into a little O, but I nodded, meeting his bright gaze fully.

He didn't say anything as he looked at where his finger rested. His skin was a little creamier than mine, but very tan. When he let go a moment later, he stuffed his hand into his pocket, and we headed into the diner side by side, with him opening the door for me.

I hadn't been paying attention when we'd parked, and I was surprised to find the inside was a real retro 50s diner. The floor was checkered, the vinyl booth seats pink, the black tabletops sparkling. There was even a jukebox. A waitress assisting a table was dressed in a cute black-and-pink skirt and button-up, short-sleeved shirt.

But it was the magic coming from every inch of the place that struck me more than the décor.

It was coming from the waitress, from behind the counter—where there were two other women in the same uniform—and beyond them, from the kitchen.

They were all magical beings of some kind.

Fingers nudged at my forearm, and Henri gestured with his head toward the corner booth. I followed him, glancing around some more, taking in the handful of tables that had people at them. I took a seat across from him, my butt squeaking on the bench.

The employees were watching us. Staring, more like it.

One of the women behind the counter broke away from whatever she was saying to the other employee—a blonde who was making a face I wouldn't call friendly—and came over, picking up a single menu on the way. She was pretty with dark hair and big dark eyes, maybe in her early thirties.

Something about her seemed familiar.

"Hi," she called out while she was halfway across the restaurant. Her eyes flicked back and forth between Henri and me, almost . . . nervously?

My phone beeped with an incoming text, and I took it out of my fanny pack.

Sienna: Miss you already.

"You've got to be kidding me," the man across the booth muttered maybe a whole second after I'd finished reading the text.

I laughed, but I doubted either of us were surprised when it came out watery. I showed him the screen with one hand and wiped at my eyes with my other. "It's Sienna's fault," I explained as the dark-haired waitress arrived at the table.

She set the menu down in front of me, leaving nothing for Henri.

"Morning, Phoebe," he greeted her in a very polite tone, almost gentle.

She didn't *feel* like a predator to me, and the more I looked at her, the more that sensation that I was missing something got stronger. For some reason, her magic felt familiar, but I couldn't pinpoint where I'd sensed something similar to it . . .

I smiled at the woman named Phoebe, confirmed by the name tag on her chest. Her round, brown eyes met mine, and I knew there was no missing how shiny mine were. "Hi," I said, picking up the menu.

"Water for you, Henri? What would you like to drink, Nina?" she asked.

I read through the drink options, and said, "A vanilla milkshake, please."

She knows my name? I lifted my face, trying to figure that out too. "I'll be back with your drinks," she told us before I had a chance to guess.

The second she turned, I peeked around the side of her to see that the other employees were still eavesdropping and watching. The way they had their hands over their mouths told me one thing—they were talking about us. Or I might be inflating my own ego, and they were just talking about Henri.

I barely heard him say, "You don't recognize her, do you?"

"She looks familiar, but I don't know why," I whispered to him. It wasn't like I'd met that many people within a 100-mile radius of here to begin with.

"She doesn't have as many freckles when she isn't in her satyr form."

My eyes went wide. "That's why she looks different!"

Henri nodded.

It was Shiloh's *mom*. I went "ohhhhh" in realization. "I feel dumb." I laughed.

"I forgot again," he told me, tapping the side of his nose. She would've smelled the same.

I nodded. "I've never had your senses, so I don't know what I've been missing out on, but the more we talk about it, the more it feels like a lot," I joked.

"It can make life less complicated, but it can make it a hell of a lot harder too when you're forced to always tell the truth and deal with it because you can't lie about anything."

"And then if someone does lie, it makes it that much worse when you know they are," I agreed. When I'd been very young, I remembered how long it had taken me to get over trying to lie to my parents about little things I thought they would get mad about.

It made me feel like crap, and I still felt guilty over certain things I'd tried to get away with, even if they were small and inconsequential now. Having to confront issues might seem like a curse sometimes, but it really wasn't. Resentment built problems.

Henri nodded. "No matter how good a liar someone thinks they are, they're never good enough."

The way he said that made it seem like he had a lot of experience dealing with that kind of thing. Being in law enforcement and in his position in the community, he probably did.

Lowering my attention, I read through the menu. They had three different kinds of steaks, one with mashed potatoes, another with french fries, and a third option with a side salad. Bison and elk were also listed.

This was definitely a diner that catered to carnivorous magical beings.

As much as I enjoyed steak, I wanted comfort more. A BLT on the menu made my stomach grumble. I closed the laminated pages and sat back.

I clasped my hands together and smiled at the man across from me. I didn't want to ruin his lunch being weepy. "You already know what you're ordering?"

"Ribeye," he answered, his intense gaze unwavering.

"That's what your cousin orders every time it's on the menu."

"It has the best ratio of fat in the cut." He set his hands on top of the table, those long fingers linked together, his light, caramel skin popping against the counter. The only jewelry he had on was a military-grade watch with a shiny, digital face.

"How many times have you moved?" he asked, surprising me with his change in subject.

"Since I started living in my trailer?" I hadn't really traveled to that many places before I'd bought it. After leaving the small town where we'd grown up, Sienna and I had moved to Santa Fe, where I had learned the depths of my dislike of living among a lot of people. But for her, I had stuck around while we took six and a half years to finish school, both of us getting degrees in nothing we actually went on to use and barely passing our classes.

Working full-time and going to school was not for the weak. By that point, I had maxed myself out on Santa Fe.

But I knew that wasn't what he was asking when Henri dipped his chin. I still told him about it anyway. "I don't know if we have time to go over everywhere, but I'm pretty sure I've stayed at almost every RV or state park on the west coast at least once, a few multiple times. I spent a year in Arizona, another year in California, months in New Mexico, but not where we lived . . ." I shrugged. "Everywhere, Fluff. Northern Colorado. I'd never heard of Lobo Springs. I didn't know a place like this could exist. South Dakota and Wyoming are the closest I've ever experienced, but it doesn't compare to here. This place feels like a nuclear reactor of m-a-g-i-c."

Henri's fingers stretched on the table. "There's a place in Alaska that's rich. Banff and parts close to Thunder Bay feel the most similar, but still not on our level."

Matti had mentioned the place in Alaska already. "Really? I've never been to any of those places." What were the chances these places were all located in the wilderness? Or maybe that was why there was so much wilderness.

Ancient conspiracy theory there.

"It's where the majority of communities like ours are located, 'least the successful ones." He was back to talking so low I had to put all my focus into paying attention and reading his lips.

"Are there a lot? I know of this one because of you and your cousin, and one in Kansas that I can think of, but that was because I was eavesdropping on a conversation outside my trailer. They weren't saying good things about it."

"If it's the one I know of, the people running it are idiots, and it's a miracle they're still around," he replied. "There aren't a lot of communities. Only a handful around the same size; there are more that are smaller. Mostly extended family units. Streets in small towns where every neighbor is magical."

"I know about streets like that." Like where home had been. The whole street had been magical—not that anyone ran around in their other form or anything, but more than a few times, someone's "big dog" had gotten loose and been spotted. We'd had a lot of Irish wolfhounds that made rare but special appearances at night.

Wolfhounds. Whoever had come up with that excuse was clever. "Your family really left all this land to you?" I asked him.

Henri nodded. "My father's family, yes. My—Matti's dad relinquished his rights."

Something told me he probably wouldn't appreciate having that conversation out loud in front of so many nosey people. I moved on. "How do you afford the property taxes?"

This man looked me right in the eye as he answered, "With money."

I slumped forward, forehead hovering over the table, and started laughing. "Who *are* you?"

The faintest, tiniest little smile crossed that grave mouth when I peeked up at him.

I was in the middle of doing that—watching his serious mouth fighting a smirk—when Shiloh's mom returned. She set my milkshake down first and then the glass of water. "Do you know what you want to order?" she asked, her body language back to being uncomfortable. Maybe nervous.

The point was, she wasn't at ease. Whether it was me or Henri, I had no idea. She had gotten really startled that other day when he'd raised his voice. I'd had my bracelet on when we'd met, and it was back on now, but . . . dang it, I was going to need to get this conversation over with as soon as possible. Today, if I could. There was no reason for me to put this stuff off. I didn't want to tiptoe for the rest of my life.

I held the menu out. "A BLT with fries, please."

"Sure." Phoebe smiled almost shyly at Henri. "Your usual?"

"I'd appreciate it," he answered, back to using his softer tone.

"I'll be back with your orders." Her voice was low before retreating, and I wondered if that was how she usually spoke when she wasn't on the verge of strangling her child for making reckless decisions that put him in jeopardy.

I wrapped my hand around my opposite wrist where my

bracelet sat. "Henri, is she usually nervous around everyone, or is it me?"

He took a sip of his water, and I wondered if he was picking his words or if he was just thirsty. "Both, I think."

That helped.

He tilted his head to the side, raising one of his hands up to slide over the short ends of the hair above his ear. "She moved here before Shiloh was born. I don't know what her situation was like before, but I've met enough satyrs to know most of them are skittish."

He had a point.

"People are scared of what they don't understand on the best of terms." I smiled, half in resignation and half in acceptance of a universal truth. "I went out on an offshore fishing trip once, and we were able to jump into the ocean, a hundred miles from shore, and I was scared the whole time. I didn't know what else was in the water, under my feet. Imagine sleeping next to someone that all your instincts tell you is a danger."

"That's never made sense, why people waste their time being scared of things they can't control. Isn't it worse knowing something is coming and you can't do anything about it?"

I stopped in the middle of peeling the wrapper off my straw.

He took another sip of his water.

"I've never thought about it like that." I balled up the paper and set my straw into the glass. "Scary is scary, I guess, regardless of whether you can see it or you can't. If it's logical or not. Maybe the only thing you can do is learn to manage the things that you fear. You know? Break them down. Reason them out if you can." I thought about it some more. "But there's some stuff that no amount of reasoning will make more bearable." I took a sip and raised my eyebrows in surprise. Ooh, it was good.

I looked around the diner one more time. The waitresses, including Phoebe, were behind the counter. Some of them were doing a crappy job at being discreet as they peeked at us. Or attempted to listen in to our conversation.

"Did you say scary is scary?" Henri asked, drawing my attention back to him.

I nodded. "Yeah. It is."

He didn't say anything for a moment as he watched me from across the table. "What scares you?"

"Lots of things."

"Like?" He drew the word out.

It was unnecessary how much pleasure this conversation was bringing me. I wanted to think it was mostly because this version of Henri Blackrock at forty-ish was someone new and unexpected, so different from the serious introvert that hadn't exactly avoided responsibilities when he'd been a teenager but definitely hadn't been an overprotective or overly affectionate person. He had always just . . . kind of been there, when he was around.

So maybe it was his growth that drew me to him the most, wanting to see just how much he'd changed over time. How he was a member of law enforcement who considered other people his responsibility, under his protection, with a visible soft spot for little kids. Who lowered his voice around skittish people. Who would comfort someone upset.

A man who was curious and had a sarcastic and funny streak in him too.

Buttttt I wasn't going to overanalyze it or make more out of it than I needed to. Not in front of him, at least.

"Taxes," I answered.

He leaned against the back of the bench.

"Late fees."

The muscles in his right cheek twitched.

"Ticks."

Was that really the start of a smile on his face?

I lifted a shoulder. "Mortgage interest rates?"

Yeah, it was.

"My credit score. That thing scares me too."

It wasn't just his cheeks giving him away, it was the glimmer in his eye, too. The crinkles at the corners of them. "Your score is good, but you should open another credit card."

I dropped my voice. "You checked my credit?" I wasn't *mad* about it, but . . . I hadn't expected it . . . and how had he gotten my social?

"Had to. We can't have bill collectors or the government poking around." He looked so nonchalant. "The elders told you we would do a background check in the meeting—" Henri's mouth slammed shut in the middle of his sentence. His head whipped to the side, to where there was a wall of windows between us and the parking lot.

I did the same, wondering what could make him react like that.

A man stood beside a truck parked a few spots down from mine, arms crossed over his chest, glaring in the direction of the building.

A slow, deep rush of breath left Henri's lungs on an exhale right before he slid out of the booth. His expression and tone were icy when he met my eyes. "I'll be back. Wait here."

It was on the tip of my tongue to ask if he wanted backup, but this man was six foot six, close to three hundred pounds was my guess, and I wasn't about to insult him.

Plus, I didn't want to get involved in things unless I had to . . . or if he asked.

Now, if the man outside did something really stupid, that would change the situation, but in the meantime, I sat there and agreed.

I ceased to exist as he walked out, and I watched him cross the parking lot and come to a stop a few feet away from the stranger. The man was tall, but not on the same level as the one who had comforted me earlier.

Henri had sat there, held me to his shoulder, and cuddled me—his words, not mine.

Henri Blackrock had cuddled me.

And now he was out in the parking lot, in front of a silver truck with wide tires and shiny rims, arms loose at his sides as the blond stranger said something angrily, the muscles of his biceps and forearms bulging as he expressed himself. I couldn't sense his magic from this far away.

But he was worked up about something. His face was turning red.

I set my hand down on the bench beside me, ready to start scooting out.

A plate stacked high with a three-layer sandwich and fries slid onto the table in front of me before a different meal was placed directly across from it. Phoebe stood there, her big brown eyes focused on the two men outside. Her lips were pursed.

I'd always known I had very little shame. "Do you know who that is?" I asked her.

I thought it said something that she glanced over her shoulder, toward her coworkers, before whispering, "Dominic."

This was him? The guy that Henri had let punch him? I frowned and squinted out the window, finding them in the exact position they'd been in before. With *Dominic* prattling on, and Henri resembling a volcano about to erupt. I thought I could see a hint of a black eye . . .

I glanced back at her and frowned some more. She seemed concerned. "Do I need to go save Henri?" I whispered back.

Her eyes widened. "Save Henri?" She gave me a look that said she didn't think I could save anyone. It was all pink cheeks and raised eyebrows. "No . . . I don't think so."

"You just seem a little worried," I told her, though she'd seemed concerned the last time I'd seen her too.

Phoebe glanced over her shoulder one more time before saying, "He's . . . difficult."

I'd gotten that already.

But this was *Henri*. He'd only gotten hurt before because he'd let it happen, so he'd said, but I believed him. More than anything though, I'd bet on him being able to take care of himself, especially in public. It was more than the inches of height and weight he had on the other man too; it was just that sense of being so capable that radiated from him at all times . . . the whole two days we'd seen each other before now, but I didn't doubt my instincts, not where he was concerned at least.

He'd gone head-to-head with a sasquatch a couple days ago and not given a crap.

And since I didn't know the next time I'd have an opportunity to talk to her in private, I figured I had to take advantage of it. There wasn't much he and the other man could do other than fistfight. The blond was still ranting.

I dropped my voice again. "Phoebe, I just wanted to tell you really quick that I'm sorry if I've alarmed you." Most people would never want to admit their fears to anyone, especially not a stranger. I sure wouldn't. "I don't mean anyone at the ranch any harm. I was only trying to help the kids that day with the river creature. I don't even kill ants if I can help it.

"I hope that you're willing to get to know me. I know I smell different to some people, and you have no reason to believe that I'm a good person, but I think I am." I offered up another smile, a smaller one. "If you don't feel comfortable with me, I'm more than willing to talk to you about it. This place is your home, and you were here first." There was no way I was going to go straight into offering to leave, not without trying to win her over, but I wanted her to be aware that I was willing to try, so she would feel obligated too.

At no point did I expect her to sigh or for her body to visibly relax at just words, but that's what happened. This woman, who was also a satyr, honestly seemed a little relieved. "I'm sorry, Nina."

It was hard not to smile a little.

"Shiloh has said nothing but the nicest things about you. He's told me the story about the day with the creature at least ten times," she said. "I trust his intuition more than I do anyone else's, even my husband's, because he's a sensitive boy."

"He's a very nice boy," I agreed.

She glanced over her shoulder one more time before continuing. "I'm not comfortable around strangers, and that has nothing to do with you." Her hands fidgeted at her waist. "I should have told you thank you that day, or any day since, but my mind was in full-blown panic. Shiloh has a thank-you card he made, but he's grounded right now . . ."

Phoebe blew out a little breath, like she was calming herself down. Her hands came up to her chest, one overlapping the other. "From the bottom of my heart, and my husband's, we're going to be grateful to you for the rest of our lives for what you did for him and the children. If there's ever anything my family can do for you, please let us know. We're in your debt."

My face had started going pink from the moment she started with her gratitude, and I couldn't imagine what color it was then, but I still kept my voice low and said, "You're welcome. Any time. Except I hope they never do something like that again." I paused. "But we're okay then? Or at least we will be?"

Phoebe the satyr gave me a shy smile. "Yes. I appreciate you talking to me about it. I've been here for six years, and I still can't make eye contact with Henri or most of them, really."

I looked her dead in the eye and said, "If they scare you, bite them."

She went pale. "B-bite them?"

"Sure. I bit Henri when I first saw him and he scared me," I admitted, stretching the truth just a little. He had scared me in the way that I had panicked he would hurt Duncan.

Her eyes went round. "I thought Shiloh made that up!"

I shook my head.

Phoebe giggled, and it was a good laugh, very cute and fitting for her.

Might as well egg it on, I figured. "It was like biting Clifford. I found hair in my mouth hours later." I hadn't, he'd been in his human form, but she didn't need to know that.

She smiled before one of the other waitresses called her name. Her narrow face went resolved. "I know you don't know anyone, and I don't have a lot of time, but I was wondering . . . maybe one day, if you have time . . . we could . . . like you said, get to know each other. Go grocery shopping? Or run errands . . ."

I was nodding before she'd even finished her offer. "I'd like that." That sounded way less pressure-y than getting coffee or something else. The more I thought about it, the more I liked the idea, and I nodded some more.

Then I remembered.

"Actually," I dropped my voice to the tiniest whisper. "There's something I need to tell you before we make plans."

That made her nervous.

"I already told the elders, but—" I scrunched up my nose. "— you should know that women who spend a lot of time around me become pregnant. I told them to tell all of you, but I'm not sure they have."

The woman, who had to be around my age, dropped into a crouch, one hand on the table, the other on the bench. Her eyes were wider than ever. Her voice so quiet I barely heard her. "It's true?"

So people had been told. What a relief. I nodded.

Her eyes roamed my face, like she was searching for a lie or trying to confirm some other way that I was pulling her leg. After a moment, when the same waitress who had called her name did it again, a small smile came over her mouth that was somehow the brightest one of all of them. "We heard, but . . ."

"It's true. I just need to throw the disclaimer out there. If you talk to anyone else about it, around the ages of when you can get pregnant, please tell them. I don't want to wear a shirt with a warning sign that says 'Stay Back 50 Feet or Get Pregnant'," I told her with a small smile.

The concern disappeared. Phoebe looked *happy*. "I'll spread the word, but that's not . . . I don't see anyone complaining about that."

She hadn't heard my neighbors in the past when they'd found out they were unexpectedly pregnant. Sienna's excellent hearing, and our thin apartment walls, had kept us in a lot of loops. Some days, we'd sit on our couch and instead of watching TV, she would eavesdrop on the neighbors and repeat what was going on.

Dang it, I missed her again already.

"Thank you, Nina," my hopefully-friend-in-the-near-future whispered. "Thank you," she repeated, backing away as her name was called once more.

I hadn't expected that, but it lifted my spirits to the freaking skies, maybe beyond.

And I'd forgotten all about Henri.

Through the window, I saw the two men were still out there. The other man was *still* talking, and Henri stood there like he might be listening, but he might also be contemplating murder. I ate a fry and watched him shake his head at whatever the blond was saying.

I ate more fries, taking a bite and then another of my BLT while the man kept going and going, and Henri got more visibly frustrated by the second. I swear his ears were turning red. When I was halfway through my fries, Henri said something that had the other man's face going redder than his ears before the werewolf turned and came inside without a second glance.

He was definitely pissed when he shot a dirty look toward one of the waitresses—the blonde who had been making faces—before sliding into the booth.

Matti ate fries sometimes . . .

Pushing my plate across the table, I used my clean fork to scoop three onto Henri's plate before pulling it back toward my side.

I kept my gaze away from him while I started eating again. He sighed after a minute, ate each of the fries, then picked up his utensils and started in on one of his two steaks. Nothing else. Neither of us said a word while we finished our food, and it wasn't until he set his knife and fork down that I peeked at him.

I couldn't help myself. "So that was the infamous Dominic?"

He sipped his water, his throat bobbing with the swallow. His cheek was tight again. "Yeah," the fountain of information answered, gritting his teeth the whole time, the action saying a hell of a lot about what had happened out there.

Did I want to know? Of course I did, but it wasn't my business, so I didn't ask more intrusive questions. I'd already overused my needy card today. So instead, I folded my napkin into a little accordion while Phoebe brought the check. I put cash down, which got me a look from Henri, who hesitated while he alternated between me and the receipt. After a minute, he put his card down along with the cash.

"I'll text you," I told Phoebe after I'd typed in her number, which had been on the check, into my contacts.

"Okay," she agreed with another shy smile. "See you, Henri."

He nodded at her, then tipped his head at me. We got out of the booth and headed outside and got in my truck. I pulled onto the main street through town. Lobo Springs, my new home.

The population was 3,000, the sign coming into town said. Elevation 7012, though it had to be higher at the ranch. They had an elementary school and a small high school, but I hadn't seen a middle school. There were even two churches. I wasn't sure why, but that got me thinking about other things.

"What is it?" Henri's voice was loud in the cab.

"What's what?"

"That look on your face."

That got me to side-eye him. I patted my cheek with my fingertips. I hadn't made a face. I hadn't even been thinking negative thoughts or even good ones, not enough for him to pick up on. I wasn't sure I wanted to tell him what had been on my mind either, not with the mood he was in after his visitor.

I tried to think of something believable, but nothing came to mind fast enough.

"It's still there," he accused. "We've got a thirty-minute drive left, you might as well tell me." He paused. "I can try to guess too."

This man . . . he looked so gruff and serious, and beneath that rough exterior, the sarcasm ran deeper than the Styx. Why couldn't he pretend not to notice my mind was on other things? Not even Matti and Sienna called me out on my crap constantly. They let me get away with things from time to time. It was called privacy.

"Cricket . . ."

I bit the inside of my cheek. "When did you get to be this chatty, by the way?"

That got him.

"You think I'm talkative?" He sounded surprised.

"Compared to teenage Fluffy? Yes."

There was a pause. "I can't get a whole lot across grunting at people all day," he claimed.

He had a point. "Nothing's bothering me," I clarified.

He didn't say a thing. He sat there, his eyes burning a hole into the side of my face.

I blew out my breath, realizing he wasn't going to drop this. "If you're going to insist, everything is all right. I was just thinking about how I don't know anything about what happened to you after you graduated and lived with Matti and his family for a while. I never even knew why you moved in with them in the first place."

The snicker he let out wasn't what I was expecting. Neither was the "Nina" he kind of chuckled in that ridiculous velvet voice, that was warmth and richness. "That's what your mind was on?"

I waved my right hand at him. "Yeah. You're so secretive about some things." I thought about it. "I'd like to be friends, Fluff. I don't want you to hate having me around for asking a bunch of questions or making you talk about stuff you don't want to." I shrugged. "And you have a cute chuckle, if you want to know that too. There? Are you happy now?"

There was a moment of silence so strong I considered opening my car door and tucking and rolling on the way out.

But before I could consider all the reasons why I wouldn't do it, he asked in a funny voice, "You always this honest?"

I snorted. "No, but you weren't going to drop it, and I figured I might as well get it off my chest and save us both time. What have you been doing for the last eighteen years?"

He angled his body against the corner of the door and the seat, attention still on me. He crossed his arms over his chest, flexing those arms that belonged on a men's health magazine. "Matti hasn't even been gone a couple hours, and you're already giving me a hard time" was what he replied with.

"I was minding my own business. You're giving me a hard time." I glanced at him real quick sitting in my passenger seat.

He gave me the most nonchalant look. "You can ask whatever you want to ask. I don't hate you being here, and we are . . . friends."

There had been a pause there, and a part of me wanted to pry at it, give it a little poke, see what happened, but a bigger part of me, the part that was scared what might come out if I did that, said I better not. It said I should take what I'd been given and be happy with it. If Henri said we were friends, then we were friends. That needed to be enough.

I shifted in my seat. "Does that mean you're going to tell me what you did in all those years?"

Part of Henri's mouth formed into a smirk, and that same man I knew, and yet didn't know, shook his head. "Nope, but it doesn't mean you can't ask."

I snickered, and I didn't imagine his smirk getting a little wider before he said the one thing I needed to hear more than anything else.

"You're going to be just fine here, Nina," he predicted. "I've got a good feeling about it."

Chapter Eleven

"I think you've gained at least two pounds this week," I told Duncan as I carried him down the stairs, positive I was straining more than I had the night before when I'd done the same thing. My right arm was getting tired, and I was huffing. Huffing!

When he'd shown up in my life as a newborn, he'd weighed a little over a pound. Over the course of the first year of his life, he'd reached twelve pounds and stayed at that weight for the next year. He'd had a little puppy belly, a soft innocent face, and he'd been all paws and preciousness.

But in the month since we'd arrived at the ranch, he'd gained *six* pounds.

Six!

He was taller, his feet were definitely bigger, and the boy had been asking for more food after meals. There was no doubt about it, my donut had thrived over the last four-ish weeks, physically and emotionally.

Me? I wasn't exactly blossoming into a new person, but I hadn't been unhappy. Things were going okay at the ranch—as long as I didn't take into consideration how I still spent almost as much time alone as I had when it had only been the two of us in our RV.

It was all right, and that was exactly what I'd told Sienna when we'd video chatted a couple of days ago. "We're good," I'd promised.

She'd just blinked at me.

But it was the truth. Since dropping her and Matti off at the airport, I'd started working again, and when I wasn't doing that, I volunteered at the nursery slash summer day camp, as I liked to call it. Shiloh and Pascal had gotten an early release out of prison—being grounded—and were now spending a few hours a day with me. When I wasn't with the kids, Duncan and I did a lot of walking around the property at night. Mostly, we spent time in our room, doing the same things we'd done in our RV— playing tug, we did nose-work games around the clubhouse, we watched television, Duncan did puzzles, and then we headed outside for our midnight games of tag.

Which was what we were doing at the moment.

"I'm going to need to start lifting weights at this rate," I kept talking to him as we went around the short landing before the other half of the staircase. I peeked at his face. "It's all right. I'll start bodybuilding if I have to."

The cutest puppy in the world blinked ruby red eyes at me.

"Yes," he told me.

He was worth lifting weights for. Having denser bones would just be a bonus.

"I've been thinking about it, Dunky, and I'm pretty sure you know you're some kind of rare magical prince who has lived a hundred other lifetimes having people cater to you, and this time, it's my turn, so you don't expect any different. Say yes if I'm right."

Duncan put a paw on the arm I was using to support the top half of his weight. *"Yes,"* he communicated, and I laughed.

That was another change, other than the weight gain, his telepathic abilities had gotten stronger.

He'd been communicating with me a lot more often, and his "voice" was louder and clearer. That part, I loved.

"I'm glad you know your worth." I snickered as we came to a stop on the first floor. Leaning forward, I peeked around the staircase, down the hall where Agnes was usually standing— trying to scare the crap out of me, I knew it in my gut.

But she wasn't there.

That was another of the biggest changes in our lives over the last month—Agnes had turned into the third member of our Musketeer party.

To be honest, she was mostly in it for Duncan—*only* in it for him—but it had been almost two weeks since the last time she'd snarled at me in her puppy form.

The little girl, who stayed in her wolf form 80 percent of the time, had joined us for the first time the day that Matti and Sienna had left. Since then, she went out with us every night we played tag. She was still as quiet and moody as she'd been on day one, but Duncan had worked his magic on her, and she'd turned into his poofy bodyguard. And even if that hadn't been the case, I would've been nice to her, but her devotion to my donut made me like her so much more.

She was the person from the ranch I spent the most time with, since Franklin was still on whatever trip he'd taken that no one seemed to ever talk about. The three of us had breakfast together every morning, dinner almost every evening, and then our midnight playtime. Some days after the nursery, she went home with a different pup and their family, but she was back before we started eating most evenings. Then Duncan and I hung around in the kitchen until Liddie, one of her nighttime caretakers, showed up to get her, or the other one got there, and Agnes went to her room to find her, before we reconvened later on.

Deep down in that tough little body, she was a good kid. And right then, she was a missing one.

Hmm.

From the way the hallway was illuminated, it seemed like the light in the kitchen might be on. *That had to be where she was.* In the time since we'd started our post-dinner adventures, she hadn't missed a single one. We could check the kitchen and then knock on her door to see if she was okay. That sounded like a good plan to me.

With Duncan Donut still in my arms, we headed in that direction first.

Half the lights were on, I realized soon afterward. I hadn't been able to hear voices while we'd been making our way over, and if Duncan had, he didn't give me a sign, but I wasn't totally shocked to find Henri with a hip against the counter beside the range. Leaning against his leg was Agnes. Henri's gaze was already on the doorway when Duncan and I walked in.

And just like I'd told myself every other time I'd been in his vicinity over the last few weeks, I did it again: *Keep it together, Nina.*

I hadn't seen Henri much since our trip to the airport. When I had, it'd been in the mornings during breakfast on his days off, and a couple of times I'd seen him at a distance when Duncan and I went for walks. He'd sensed me and waved, but I could tell he'd been busy and hadn't wanted to bother him. Unfortunately, that had been all the time we'd spent together.

I wasn't going to say it hurt my feelings, he was a busy man, but . . . in my truck, he'd *said* we were friends. He'd even joked with me. I didn't want to second-guess it. In my heart, I knew Henri wasn't the kind of person to say something he didn't mean. He was too serious, too polite, too used to having to say what he felt because there was no other choice when everyone around him at the ranch had a BS meter, but . . . it would've been nice to see him more.

Now though, Henri was out of that body-fitting uniform, and in black sweatpants and a dark gray T-shirt that said "LOBO COUNTY SHERIFF'S DEPARTMENT" in faded black letters.

At least they weren't light gray sweatpants, I thought with a silent prayer of gratitude to the universe.

If I'd thought that I'd get used to the impact his face and body had on me, I would've been wrong. If anything, he got more attractive every time I saw him, and I'd been trying my best to wrap those thoughts up tighter than my ponytails.

"Hi," I greeted him as Duncan wiggled in my arms, the universal sign to let him down.

I did, and the puppies ran toward one another like they hadn't eaten dinner together. Or been within twenty feet of each other in the nursery for most of the day. Two tails—one dark and very fluffy, and the other light and slightly less puffy—wagged.

"Hey," Henri finally said.

"I told you to marry him because he could use someone like you in his life," Matti had told me on the phone a couple of weeks ago, after he'd purposely ignored my texts regarding the comment he'd dropped on me outside of the airline terminal.

"That makes no sense," I'd argued, sitting on the step leading up to my trailer. I had wanted to keep an eye out on who was around so my chances of being overheard were smaller.

"I always make sense."

We were both silent for a minute before we'd laughed.

"When he's not at work, he's still at work. He's always fucking working. I'm not exaggerating. I don't think he's ever taken a real vacation. The times I've seen him in Denver were because he took days off to handle ranch shit because he only does business with people he meets in person. He has no chill. Think of it like this, Nina, he's the principal, and you're summer vacation," he'd explained. *"I think he'd be good for you too. He'd be loyal. He works hard . . . I know he'd take care of you."*

He'd take care of me. That had done something interesting to my insides. The point was, it had been a long conversation, and one I couldn't get out of my head weeks later.

I could feel eyes following me as I circled the island and went for the fridge, opening the freezer and pulling out a few different popsicles. I'd found some naturally sweetened, organic popsicles at the grocery store in Lobo Springs that the kids liked. Agnes came over first, and I smiled as I crouched to offer her a choice.

I held out the popsicles, and the mini wolf nudged the one in the middle. I looked at Henri as I got up. His facial hair had grown in a little, and a light scruff covered his throat, jaw, and upper lip, making him look like the borderline mountain man I'd met when we'd first gotten here. "Want one?"

Short, thick eyelashes fell slowly over his eyes, and it took a moment for his shoulders to go up. "I'll take whatever flavor you don't want."

I bit the inside of my cheek, thought about arguing, and picked a pink one—watermelon—to spice it up. Then I held them out again as Agnes pounced on Duncan, and he tried to nip her tail. Henri picked a green one—a surprising choice—and I kept the red one for my pup. I hesitated. He hadn't been around before for our nightly expeditions. I knew he knew about them, but . . .

"I was going to take the kids outside. We usually play a little while and then have our popsicles . . . Can I still take Agnes?"

He tilted his head to the side. "You don't need to ask." He wiggled the popsicle in his fingers. "I'll go with you."

"You sure?" I paused. "You're not too tired? I heard you've been working a lot."

"No." He palmed the back of his neck. "I'm not too tired to play."

He was going to play too?

I couldn't do anything but smile at that idea as I nodded at him.

He just looked at me.

Was he being weird? Had I made him uncomfortable after all with the cinnamon smell and the cuddling before? That had been on my mind the last few weeks. Dealing with people was so complicated, especially when I didn't have a magical nose. Because you could say whatever you wanted, but your body couldn't lie about what it was feeling.

But I was the one who couldn't hide anything, so too bad for me. I didn't mind him coming. It'd give me an excuse to get a feel for him without the hectic pressure that came with breakfast. Just because we'd been in the same room together during that time hadn't meant we'd gotten to talk a whole lot. On the mornings he was around, he'd been on his phone the majority of the time, sometimes answering his calls with "Blackrock," but the majority of it being "Henri."

Randall, the security guy I'd met in the woods right after we'd gotten here, hadn't had a problem telling me all about how busy Henri was. The strawberry blond, I'd learned, was the only other person, apart from Henri, Agnes, MIA Franklin, and the other elders who were away, living in the clubhouse at the moment. We didn't see each other often because he worked different hours almost daily, and he had family living at the ranch who he ate with often. He was a really nice guy, and my favorite part was that he gossiped as much as Matti did.

These freaking werewolves. There was a reason I loved them so much. I might not be willing to dig for details directly, but if they wanted to share that Henri hadn't had a girlfriend in over a decade, I wasn't going to tell them to shut up. But that was a thought for later.

For the time being, I decided to focus on the most important person in my life, not the one I wasn't sure about. "Dunky, want me to carry you outside?" I asked as I put the popsicles into Agnes's lunch bag, like we did every night. It had a unicorn on the side of it.

Red eyes met mine, and I felt that brush of consciousness touch my own. *"No."*

I winked at him and focused on the little girl towering over my donut.

It was a shot in the dark, but I went for it anyway. You didn't get anywhere in life unless you put yourself out there. Because my friendship with her might not have improved much yet, but she wasn't someone I was giving up on, even if I was pretty sure she weighed about fifty or sixty pounds. "Agnes, would you like me to carry you?"

Her dead-eye glare said no, and I didn't take it personally. What it did was make me smile. She was a tough cookie, but that was all right. Tough cookies didn't crumble as easily.

If she let me, I was going to be one of the eggs that helped this snitch cookie stick together, because the little girl had gotten me appreciating who I'd turned out to be.

My story might not have been one that took place in an animated movie, but that was all right. I knew that my story was more of a gothic fairy tale than one with a castle in a sunny state, and I was okay with that. None of those princesses had puppies who could light someone on fire for them.

"All right then, come on, Donut and Mini Wolf. There

aren't too many clouds tonight, and maybe we'll get lucky and see some shooting stars," I told them before meeting Henri's eyes and smiling a little again, just in case he was feeling awkward.

I turned and walked out of the kitchen, sidekick at my feet. Henri and Agnes followed behind us, the little girl carrying her lunch bag. The building was as empty as always. I led us down the hall and out the front door, warm fingers grazing mine on the doorknob when Henri almost beat me to it, gesturing for us to go ahead. I did, bending to pet both pups—Agnes only side-eyed me—before we kept going, through the yard and toward the familiar clearing where we'd had our snacks before.

Agnes set the insulated bag down, and I felt the tension radiating from the kids, who were used to our schedule, ready to play. We had our routine by now. It was Agnes's idea to have popsicles afterward to cool off, and who was I to say no? Her bag kept them from melting.

I pointed at myself. "Eenie." Next I gestured to Duncan. "Meenie." Third was Agnes. "Miny." Now we had a new player, and I pointed at Henri. "Mo."

"Are we seeing who's going to be 'it'?" he asked.

"Shh," I hushed him as I kept pointing at a different person with every word. "Catch a tiger by its toe. If it hollers, let it go. Eenie, meenie, miny, mo!" I hadn't even finished pointing at Henri when the kids took off in opposite directions. Cheaters.

I made eye contact with him and winked. "You're it, Fluff."

That neutral face brightened just slightly, his eyebrows going up a fraction of an inch, but he knew what to do. He looked at me standing there, light-colored eyes glittering under the navy sky, and he went after Duncan.

"This one is for you, and this one is yours. Donut, give me a second and I'll get you yours," I said, handing popsicles out. We hadn't played for very long, just enough for me to get out of breath.

And that was how we'd found ourselves sitting in a loose

circle around Agnes's lunch bag. I had my legs crossed, and the length of Duncan's ribs were pressed against my thigh, while an arm-length away was Henri, with Agnes beside him.

I wasn't sure why it hadn't ceased to surprise me how good he was with the kids, how much he genuinely seemed to like them. It was more attractive than the biggest biceps.

Henri had been smiling too. Grinning, even, while he'd been running circles around a tree, "trying" to catch Agnes, then attempting to avoid being tagged by Duncan's paw. I'd heard him laugh, his happiness so soft and sweet, if I'd had slightly better senses, I was sure I could have tasted it.

But it was that little, joyous smile that took him from being handsome to unbearably gorgeous. Dang it.

So what if I thought he was attractive? Who could blame me? I mean, other than Sienna. Non-magical people were all I'd ever dated before, and when I'd thought about settling down, it had always been with one. But then came all the other BS. I would have to lie, and we wouldn't be able to have kids because I wouldn't be able to tell my partner why his child could do the things they could do.

I'd known enough beings who had avoided having children, and it wasn't difficult to understand why. It was a sacrifice you had to make unless you were willing to explain things that you shouldn't. That you *couldn't*. Each culture and species had their own tales about the truth going so wrong.

They were handed down every generation.

There was an old story that Matti's mom had told us once, how her great-grandfather had married a human and they had a child. At the age of seven, the child turned into a wolf one night without warning, and when the husband had tried to explain to his wife that it *was* safe, that the child wasn't evil, it had gone horribly wrong for the woman. Her heart had failed out of pure shock, or fright, probably both.

Stories along those lines could be found everywhere.

It was why keeping the truth a secret was the one universal burden that everyone could agree on. It was necessary because no one knew how to keep things to themselves, not unless their own butts were on the line.

Life was complicated, or at least it could be.

Fortunately, it wasn't at that moment, and I was grateful for it.

I took the wrapper off Duncan's treat, then started opening mine, holding the stick of his between my teeth. Just as I was about to lay flat on the ground to take in the stars that were brighter than usual, something in Henri's body language changed out of my peripheral vision. Before I could begin to guess what was going on, he murmured, very, very quietly, so low I barely heard him, "Do you see them, Cricket?"

I turned my head just enough to face the direction he and Agnes were staring in. There was an awed look on both of their profiles. On my lap, Duncan's body went rigid after he moved around to look too. He must have been too focused on his treat to smell everything else around us, but I could tell the moment he noticed them.

Gnomes.

The size of a box of macaroni, if not shorter, one small figure after another were coming out from little caverns along the bottoms of trees in the distance. There was no way I would've been able to see them if my night vision wasn't what it was. But I could, and the scene stole the breath from my whole body.

Gnomes with tiny multicolored hats were coming out of trees. A few of them held torches with green fire burning from them, their skins were wrinkled and various shades of brown, their noses large in comparison to their bodies. Covering their limbs were clothing in shades of browns, reds, and a bluish purple that reminded me of blueberries. And they were marching straight for us.

Where in the world had we moved to?

Sure, I hadn't seen anything out of the normal in a month, but *gnomes*?

"I didn't know there were any here," I whispered, straight shocked. The gnomes moved effortlessly around wide tree trunks.

"I'd heard they existed, but . . ." I couldn't believe it. A quick peek told me that I was pretty sure Henri couldn't either.

Gnomes.

I wished I had something to offer them. Back home, our ogre neighbors had been the ones who told Matti and me about them. I knew all about the offerings the ogres left them in return for their mining efforts in nearby mountains. The gnomes were hard workers who used what they needed of the gems and minerals they excavated and shared their excess with the other magical beings nearby.

They were rare and wonderous, and I couldn't believe they were here in person.

"Look, Duncan," I whispered. "They're gnomes. I read about them to you, remember?"

His *"yes"* even felt like it had a touch of awe to it.

Henri shook his head slowly, as if doing it too aggressively might scare them off. "They haven't been seen in these mountains in fifty years," he explained. "We thought they had left."

Duncan didn't move an inch, eyes trained on the small people, his tail a candlestick in the night. I stroked a palm down his spine. "It's okay," I assured him. "I won't let anyone hurt you." I thought about it. "Or Agnes or Henri."

Out of the corner of my eye, I could've sworn Henri glanced at me.

"Yes." Dunky's trust all there, heavy in my heart.

None of us could keep our eyes off them. They were so small!

"I can't believe it," the man beside me whispered in definite wonder.

Caution came at me out of nowhere, and *I* suddenly didn't know how I felt about these mythical beings reappearing. My body made a decision before my brain did though, and I wrapped a forearm around Duncan before scooting to the side. Closer to Henri.

Maybe this was a coincidence.

But maybe it wasn't.

Maybe this had nothing to do with Duncan.

But maybe it did.

What I knew for sure was that I wasn't taking any more chances with his safety.

Not even around people less than a foot tall.

I would grab Agnes after I got Duncan and run, then I'd leave Henri to fend for himself while we got away, I decided at that moment, feeling only a little guilty but not enough to change my mind about that plan.

He'd be fiiine. I'd come back after hiding the kids and help him. I doubted he'd be in mortal danger.

Henri's knee bumped into my hip when I got close enough to him. I wasn't the only one moving around either, Agnes crawled around on her belly, hiding behind him. She had faced off against a cannibal river crone but was hiding from a gnome? What did she know that I didn't?

I tried to remember any other details or information I could about their kind, but with them in person, coming over, with their little green fires, I couldn't do much more than watch, torn between being absolutely awed and being really overly unsure.

A weight touched the middle of my back, and I looked over my shoulder. Fluff was palming my spine. There was a serious expression on Henri's features, those amber eyes were still directed on the creatures making their way. They literally almost looked identical to the garden gnomes I saw at the store, only smaller. I noticed then that they weren't focused on the white wolf or the huge one in human skin.

Every single gnome had their attention on Duncan and me. And when the first of them got to within three feet of us, they started to line up in rows of six. One after another until I was pretty sure there had to be close to fifty of them.

I held Duncan a *little* tighter.

Henri's body shifted beside my knee, and I didn't imagine that his voice took on a different tone as he said, with a strength and that deep-knit presence that had me glancing at him, "It's an honor to have you here."

He sounded the way I'd imagine a king greeted another visiting monarch, all grand and certain.

"We have returned," one of the gnomes in the front replied in a voice that crackled with grit and a depth that was at odds with his size. "This has been our home nearly as long as it has been yours, Great Wolf."

I peeked at the "Great Wolf" beside me and slowly turned back to our visitors. I was coming back to that title later. Yes, I was.

"I speak for everyone here when I say that I'm pleased you consider this your home. Is there something I can help you with?" Henri asked, still using that commanding voice. "We closed your mine off decades ago, but it's there for you whenever you choose."

In synchronization, every single one of the gnomes turned to the donut and me, and the beings stared as the green glow of their torches somehow brightened enough that I had to squint until the light wasn't so blinding.

They kept looking at us.

This wasn't exactly making me feel better.

I didn't know what to do. No one was saying anything. Henri wasn't doing anything other than watching them watch us.

So I did what felt right, what my ogre friends had brought up before. I reached into my unzipped fanny pack and pulled out a packet of almonds I'd been saving for a snack and held it out to them. It wasn't a proper offering, but something was something.

The green torches flared even brighter. The gnome closest to the package took it; it was almost as big as he was. He turned and passed it to the gnome behind him, and that one did the same, and they did it again until someone in the back row held the almonds.

Still unsure what to do, I stuck my hand out to the being who had originally taken the almonds, and without missing a beat, he wrapped a hand much bigger than I would have imagined—his skin was really rough—around my index and middle fingers, shaking them.

"I'm Nina, and this is Duncan," I told him. Them.

The gnome to the right of the original one stuck his hand out just as his neighbor let go, and I stifled a smile when he shook mine too. I was so surprised when the whole front row put their hands out and wanted a shake as well. In my lap, Duncan stretched his neck out maybe half an inch, his little nose twitching hard. He wasn't tense though. His tail stayed the same safe shade of blue the whole time, reassuring *me*.

"We rejoice in your presence," the main gnome, the one who had taken the packet said, adding a word or a name that sounded so gurgled in another language, I couldn't recreate it to save my life. It sounded like he'd hacked up a phlegm or two getting it out.

I smiled cautiously at the serious faces standing there. "Forgive me, but I think you might have the wrong person. I don't remember ever meeting any of you." I'd remember meeting a gnome before.

They didn't reply.

What they did was keep staring, until, as a unit, the gnomes pivoted toward Henri again and said, "We thank you for your greeting. No assistance is needed at this time." Then they all took a step back and said, "May the moon guide your way." In the reverse order of how they had arrived, each and every one of them returned to the trees where they had come from, disappearing into the gnarled caves inside them that shouldn't have been deep enough for so many of them to go into.

I'd watched satyrs become humans and humans turn into majestic wolves, but nothing had ever blown my mind like their tree system just did.

Henri didn't say anything else until the last gnome was gone. "You're safe, Ladybug. No need to shake."

That got my attention. The white wolf was huddled against Henri's back. She was trembling, and it made affection bloom in my soul. She was just a little kid, after all.

"We would never let anything happen to you, Agnes." I tried to make her feel secure too. Safety in numbers. Plus, I was so close to Henri that she could use my body as a shield if it came down to it.

He said who knows what else to her, and soon afterward, her shaking eased for the most part.

And that's when I finally exhaled like I'd been holding my breath for half an hour. That encounter didn't make sense or make me feel any better. I didn't get kidnapper vibes from them, and neither did Duncan from how easygoing he'd been, but you could never be too sure. I wouldn't.

I turned to Fluffy. "That was weird and amazing, wasn't it?"

The last thing I expected was for him to look troubled as he palmed the top of Agnes's furry head. "Yeah . . ." He trailed off.

A nudge at the hand holding a half-melted popsicle—when had I dropped the other one?—had me lowering it so Duncan could lick it since he had already moved on from the experience of meeting magical gnomes. "Why are they back?" I asked, like he'd heard something I hadn't.

The question got Henri to snap out of it. "You tell me. What did they say?"

I glanced in the direction they'd gone. "What do you mean?"

"I heard them, and I understood what they said to me, but whatever they told you wasn't for my ears," he answered, narrowing his eyes the same way he'd done when we'd first gotten to the ranch.

"You couldn't understand them?" I was so confused.

Henri shook his head.

"What? You think they spoke in a different language?"

He did that head shake again.

What the . . .? "My Spanish is excellent. But that's it. I don't know any other languages."

His head turned back toward the trees. It took him more than a moment to say, "You know more than that."

How was that possible, and what did it mean? I wondered as Duncan licked at the remainder of the popsicle, like rare magical beings coming in and out of his life was no big deal. I was glad someone was resilient.

I looked around the clearing like I was trying to find a clue that would help me understand what had just happened and what it meant. But the only thing I found was what was left over of the popsicle I'd dropped on the ground before we'd scooted closer to Henri. It was covered in dirt and pine needles.

Something nudged at my hip.

Henri was holding out what was left of his. He lifted it an inch higher. "You can have two bites."

I met his eyes.

"Only two," he specified with a straight face.

We'd just been approached by rare gnomes, and Duncan had acted like it was no big deal while Agnes shook like a leaf, and Henri and I were in shock, and the gnomes had spoken to me in a language that he didn't understand . . .

And this man . . .

This man . . .

"Two whole bites? That's how much you'll let me have?" I cracked up.

One corner of his mouth went up a millimeter. "Half," he compromised.

That made me snort. "That's so generous, but I'm all right, thank you."

I was the only one still stuck on the gnomes, it seemed from the way he'd moved on. "Take a bite. There's not much left anyway," he egged me on.

He would share with Agnes if our roles were reversed. It was a pack thing. Sharing. Community. It was great and exactly what I was familiar with and used to. How many times had I shared food with every werewolf I'd ever cared about?

I leaned forward and winced as the cold hit my teeth, the faint taste of lime slipping over my tongue. "Thank you," I mumbled around the ice.

He kept holding it out. "Take another."

I shook my head. "That's perfect, Fluff, thank you."

He shot me a look as he bit into the rest, savoring it as Agnes started in on what was left of hers too, even while her eyes flicked around nervously, especially in the direction of where the gnomes had gone.

"They won't hurt you," I told her, even though I didn't know that for sure. I *did*, but I didn't. "It's okay, Agnes."

Her eyes slid to me, but I was pretty sure I saw a sigh leave her lungs after a minute.

Everything was good, and there was no reason to think the gnomes were going to sneak out and kidnap Duncan. Henri would be able to sense them, and so would Agnes and the donut himself, if he wasn't too focused on a treat nearby. *I* needed to tone it down.

I wasn't weak or defenseless. And Henri was here. Every instinct in my body told me he'd protect the kids. He'd stood up for me in front of Spencer before, hadn't he? I winced thinking about the sasquatch.

But I still didn't need Henri if it came down to it. I forgot that part sometimes. It wasn't that I was alone here, but I also couldn't expect to rely on anyone else, not when we lived with hundreds of people and I'd only met handfuls of parents, who were polite but kept us at a distance—or kept me at a distance.

Matti had mentioned again during our last call that they hadn't been that friendly when he'd first moved to the ranch, and I reasoned with myself that they were more than likely doing the same.

But that didn't change the fact that until we were accepted by more than Maggie, the nursery teacher, and Phoebe the satyr and her husband, who had been very, very kind, and the children I spent so much time with, that we were on our own.

Hopefully only two months longer.

I couldn't expect Henri to have time for us. He had a lot of other people that relied on him. Take a number, right?

Rolling down to lie flat on my back, I stared up at the sky as Duncan relaxed enough to trample over me, paws going places that had me huffing and puffing and groaning until he settled, lying across me, still having access to my hand. The stars were crazy bright, brighter than any other night so far. The Big Dipper was there, as well as the little one, the Milky Way a line of sparkles that split one part of the sky from another.

I'd always loved looking at them. If I could take a spaceship, I would, I used to think. Now, the thought of leaving my boy was unfathomable, and I was okay with that. The weight of him on me was a reminder that things might be changing, but he still needed me, and I was going to drain that well dry until he didn't.

My one hope was that it was decades from now.

Two shooting stars later, when Duncan finished his popsicle, he wedged his way between my arm and the side of my body, rolling onto his back so he could look too. I could hear Agnes and Henri moving around too, and from the way the leaves crackled, I figured they were doing the same.

What had to be a comet, it was so bright, shot across the sky. "Did you see that one?" I asked the puppy tucked in next to me.

"Yes," he told me.

I reached for his back leg and wrapped my hand around his paw. *"Love, love, love"* filled my heart.

As much as I liked the gnomes, they better not even side-eye Duncan if they knew what was good for them. And that thought led me to another one. A less stressful one. "Henri," I called out. "Why did the gnomes call you Great Wolf?"

He didn't reply, and I slowly sat up. He was already looking at me with a deceptively blank expression that I knew was BS.

"You know who I was raised by," I reminded him, knowing he was aware that my parents had been descended from nahuales—shapeshifters. "And they taught me alllll about wolf mythology. I know what *that* means, Mr. Wolf God," I whispered as a grin took over my face.

The tale of the Great Wolf was one handed down throughout North America, of a monstrous but noble wolf who roamed the plains. A protector. A shield for the weaker. There were stories of great battles it faced in centuries past, against epic thunderbirds, who it ripped from the skies, and giant pumas who preyed upon villagers at night, to name a few.

The Great Wolf was a hero and a legend.

And I couldn't help but grin with freaking glee at the fact I was sitting inches away from the man recognized with that title.

Henri's jaw ticked to the right instantly. He even blinked twice. "I knew you were going to give me shit for it the second they called me that."

Was he *blushing*?

I laughed. "I didn't know I was in the presence of royalty."

He groaned and looked away, which made me laugh harder.

That was definitely a blush on those cheeks. Too bad for him, it was *adorable*.

"I'll keep that in mind when addressing you from now on, sir," I joked, watching as he shook his head . . . but there was a slight, *slight* smile on his face. Feeling generous, I decided to give him a break for now. "Was that an ancestor of yours?"

The way he shrugged bordered on embarrassed . . . but he nodded.

I smiled and laid back down, pleased and surprised and . . . a thought came out of nowhere. "Wait, does Matti know about that?"

"Does Matti know that he's related to him? Yes, he does."

And that son of a turd had never *hinted at it before*? It hadn't occurred to me that *Matti* could be related to him too. I guess I had automatically assumed that the Great Wolf would be on the other side of Henri's family, not the shared one.

Like he could sense my outrage, Henri added, "It's not something we advertise. Matti never met the . . . original one, and I think his dad might have met him only once."

That made me slightly feel better, but I was still going to give him shit about it the second I had the chance. I couldn't believe he'd never even dropped a hint. *But maybe it's because that is actually a big secret and not something most people should know.*

Hmm.

His voice rumbled unexpectedly through the dark. "You really don't know anything about your birth parents?" The question was so delicately laid out, it was like he'd set it on eggshells. Was he trying not to hurt my feelings?

It wouldn't, but how would he know that? He and I had never discussed my family situation before, other than my comments in front of the elders. I never really talked about those people, period.

I took a deep breath of mostly Duncan's scent and winced. He was going to need a bath soon. "Not much. Not enough to mean anything," I answered, keeping my voice light so he wouldn't get the wrong idea that this was a devastating conversation for me.

"Tell me what you know."

I hugged Duncan a little closer. "I know that I was left outside of my parents' house as a newborn." I thought about it. "All I had on me was a blanket. I didn't even have clothes on. The doctors guessed that I was less than a month old." I took another sniff of Duncan. "You know that though, don't you?"

His grunt echoed throughout the trees, and I thought about what he'd said before about how grunting didn't get things across.

I tipped my head. He was on his back too, the part of his face that was visible looked tight. Concerned? Maybe just thoughtful? Despite his silence, maybe he was still worried about the gnomes too . . . and why they'd spoken to me in a different language and how I'd understood it.

Sneaking my forearm under my head, I propped it up as I focused on the sky again. My breathing was loud in my ears, so I kept talking. "That's pretty much all I know for a fact. No one has ever recognized what I am, not for sure, you know? Some people just . . . know they don't like it." Hated it, more like, but there wasn't much I could do about that other than wear a bracelet that almost made me invisible.

Like I was telling the world that they could like me, but only when I was someone else.

I scratched behind my ear before I thought about something. "My parents had their guesses."

"What did they suspect?"

"My mom's family can trace their roots back for generations. Back to the days when the Mayans built their pyramids, did you know that?" I didn't wait for his answer. "My mom is a devout follower of a few of their gods, and so was her mom, and her mom before that... the list goes back centuries. Anyway, because of my fertility gift, she thought there was a chance that I might be..." Her superstition of saying their names out loud almost kicked in. She used to spell them out instead. But I tamped that urge down, thinking, *Let her hear me say her name.* "Ix Chel's."

Ix Chel, the Mayan goddess of midwifery. Some lore referred to her as the goddess of the moon, of love and medicine, among other things. The Aztecs, they had revered Cihuacóatl. And I was sure, I could've gone back in history or gone to another continent and found other fertility gods that maybe, just maybe she might have been known as.

It would explain a lot of things, internal stuff and external stuff... *if she was my DNA mom.*

I peeked over to find Henri side-eyeing me.

I gave him a small, flat smile.

"If a god was going to leave something as valuable as a child with someone, it would be a devoted follower," he agreed steadily, his face a neutral mask that really made me assume he was still attempting not to hurt my feelings.

"That's what my mom said, that it would have been thought of as a gift to raise her child." I shrugged. "Who knows though? She didn't leave a business card with me."

Henri didn't seem to like that response much.

I didn't want to talk about her anymore though. I turned my attention upward again. There were other things to spend my time and energy on. "Anyway, there is one other thing that might mean something, but might not." I might be dumb for bringing it up, might be oversharing after everything else I'd already admitted, but he was asking, and there was no reason not to bring it up to him. "I don't think anyone has ever believed me, but I've never been able to explain it either."

The way he asked, "What is it?" made me smile. Somebody was nosy.

"I don't really ever dream."

"Dream?"

Maybe he didn't believe me after all. "Yes, dream. I've never had normal dreams. Not really. Not like everyone else," I answered, half expecting him to give me the same lines other people had. *You just don't remember them. I'm sure you do. Everyone dreams.*

Sure, everyone probably did, but not as rarely as I did. The thing was, I wouldn't call what I did experience "real dreams." I never had some epic fantasy while I slept. Never woke up terrified after being chased by zombies. I'd never been naked in front of people or been lost in a maze of my own imagination or met a celebrity while I slept.

But Henri was listening, so I kept going. "When I have, there's been someone talking to me in the dark. Every single time. Whoever it was, whatever it was, I remember thinking it felt familiar. I can't tell you what they looked like, but I've always thought it was a man. And there was something in those dreams that felt more real than . . . not. I'd wake up and feel like I'd spoken to someone I should know." Then I told him the same thing I'd only mentioned to Sienna and Matti before. "When I was little, I used to think it was my dad talking to me, but I don't remember why I thought that, and it's been at least ten years since the last one.

"Chances are it doesn't mean anything. Who understands how the brain works anyway, right?" I bit the inside of my cheek. "It isn't like anyone ever came looking for me. If my biological family wanted to find me, I'm sure they could have. But they didn't."

Silence crept its way between us. Pity had that effect on people. What did you say after that? I wouldn't know what to do either, to tell the truth. Say I was sorry? Give someone a hug?

"Anyway," I told him, "everything turned out great. I've got the most handsome boy in the world. My mom and dad are the best, even though I don't get to see them or talk to them that much anymore, but they're happy. The weather is nice. It smells so good out here . . ."

"But?" he asked.

"But what?"

"There's something off." Henri made a sniffling sound. "You don't smell as happy as you did when you first got here."

There was no hiding anything. I lifted a shoulder. "I'm fine."

"Are you though?"

I hesitated for a second, knowing he'd pick up on anything other than honesty. "I'm a little lonely, I guess, which doesn't make sense since I'm not used to having a lot of people around normally. And when Duncan's around, I'm fine. I can't be lonely with my boy close by. It's just that so many things still feel up in the air? Maybe? I'll be okay."

"You're being given time to settle."

That had been what Matti had implied. "I know, that's what your cousin said too."

There was a long pause where the only sounds around us were the kids' loud breathing. "It's more than that, Cricket," he tried to explain. "Most people who come here don't stick around. Nobody mentioned that, did they? New residents rarely make it the three months. Half of them leave before the first month. Almost all of them are gone by the end of the second. Our residents don't want to invest in people who aren't going to stay," he said very matter-of-factly. "Three years ago, a giant came with her three children, and they were gone two weeks later without saying anything to anybody. A year before that, a goblin made it six weeks before he left and tried stealing a UTV while he was at it. People being distant right now has nothing to do with you personally. I should've explained that before, I'm sorry."

That made so much sense it was annoying. It was my turn to frown. "Well, I'm not planning on going anywhere or stealing anything. Maybe it's wishful thinking but, for some reason, this place feels . . . right. This forest, I mean. But I might be magic-high." I snickered, hoping I didn't sound defensive. My hands *were* feeling less jittery now, but on the inside, I was still hopped up on magical energy. "Has anyone else ever said that before?"

"We're family at the ranch. All of us," he told me. A little grumble rolled at the base of his throat in the stretch of silence after that. "There's no reason to think you aren't supposed to be here, Nina. Maybe you are. Maybe . . . this is where you're supposed to be."

Rising onto my elbow, I watched him do a crunch, his head angled just the perfect amount to make eye contact with me. *He's so handsome.* "I needed to hear that. Thank you, Henri."

Amber eyes moved slowly over my face, his expression a deeply guarded one that I wanted to understand. For the millionth time, I wished I could smell what he was feeling. Maybe one day, Duncan could speak more telepathic words, and he could give me the inside scoop.

"What is it?" Henri asked after a moment.

"I was thinking I wish I could smell what you're feeling right now."

The slow smile that came over his face made me blink. I might've even braced myself a little. "I'll tell you what I'm feeling if you tell me what Matti said that day at the airport that had you looking like you'd seen a ghost," he offered.

MFer. Why did he remember that a month later? Didn't he have better things to do? And how bad did I want to know what he was thinking?

Pretty bad. I wanted to know pretty bad. I nodded before I could think twice. "Deal."

Was I going to regret it? I hoped not. He was an adult. I was an adult. Maybe he would laugh.

And maybe there was a .001 percent chance he might surprise me.

My money was on a side-eye though.

"What are you thinking?" I asked, half expecting him to tell me to go first.

He didn't, and I thought that said everything about him. "I was thinking"—he wiped his face clear—"that whoever your biological parents are, they really missed out on knowing you."

It took me two tries to say, "That's a beautiful thing to say, Fluff. Thank you for that," without croaking it.

"I mean it," he said in that serious voice, watching me closely.

And now it was my turn. I was almost tempted to try and cover myself with leaves and hide so he could forget I was there, but nooo, I'd agreed. *Worst case, he'll roll his eyes.* "Don't be weird, all right?" I warned him.

"I'm never weird."

Maybe not, but I wasn't betting on that after I told him what he thought he wanted to hear. I squinted. "I wasn't planning on telling you, but you asked for this," I went on with my caution.

He tilted his head to the side, holding on to that crunch so long it would have been impressive if I wasn't just about to say what I was going to say. "Nina, I know what Matti's capable of."

The snort came out of me, because there was no way he knew Matti as well as he thought he did.

He had the nerve to make a face. "There's nothing he could say that would surprise me. I had to deal with him when he went through puberty."

I shrugged. "All riiiight," I sang. "Don't be weird."

"I'm waiting," he grunted.

No matter what happened, I wasn't going to let him be too awkward about this, I decided. He'd asked, and we both knew his cousin was nuts. *Mostly, he'd asked.*

So I looked him dead in the eye, smiled a little, and said, "Matti told me to marry you, Fluff."

Chapter Twelve

The kids and I were on our way to the nursery room the next morning when we heard it—voices coming from the back of the house, where the meeting room was.

And whatever conversation was going on, it had to be heated for me to hear them as well as I did. The funny part was, I wasn't the only one drawn in by the argument. Duncan stopped right where he was in the middle of the hallway to listen. He just plopped his little butt down, his ears twitching like he wanted to listen better.

It made me smile.

"What are they saying?" I whispered, even though he couldn't actually reply in a way that would give me any valuable information.

"They're talking about the gnomes," the little girl surprisingly answered in her normal volume, like she didn't care if we got caught. We'd found her in the kitchen earlier, already eating her protein-rich breakfast when Duncan and I had come downstairs. We had gotten into the routine where I walked both of them to the nursery afterward, at least the five days during the week, when it was in session.

I'd wondered where Henri had been during breakfast but had figured he was busy doing ranch stuff. Not because he was avoiding me or anything.

Riiight.

I wasn't going to say that I regretted telling him the night before what Matti had suggested, but my execution could've been better. Then again, if I would have done it professionally, he might have taken me seriously. He'd asked, and I'd warned him. I had even grinned at him afterward.

All Henri had done was blink, then he'd laid back down. When it had been time to go inside, he'd gotten up and held out a hand to help me to my feet too. His expression had been normal, I'd thought.

Only a very small part of me had died inside after I'd admitted what I'd admitted, but I was still here and still refusing to be awkward about it. It hadn't been *my* idea to tell him, and in the one or two moments I'd thought about it since, it wasn't that crazy. Not really. The difference in age between us wasn't huge. There hadn't been a single sign he was anything other than single, and so was I. I didn't think he found me unattractive, and I thought he might be the most handsome man I'd ever seen.

Matti was known to say some ridiculous crap, and his comment was on that level, but it wasn't *that* crazy. But I might have also been delusional to think it wasn't.

A voice louder than the ones before it had us all staring down the hall again, only to spot a face pressed up against the glass of the back door, hands flat on either side of it. It was Shiloh... eavesdropping?

I lifted my hand and waved, and from the other side, he had to see me, because he waved back before disappearing.

All right then...

I scooped Duncan into my arms, even though I wanted to listen more, and said, "Let's drop you off, and I'll tell you anything I find out later."

His floppy ears drooped, and it made me laugh just as we arrived at the door to the classroom.

"I'm sorry, Donut. We'll be nosey later," I told my puppy. "I'll tell you, if you'd like to know too, Agnes."

All that offer got me was a mini glare tossed over her shoulder as she left us behind and went inside, and I set Duncan on the ground.

He licked my forearm.

"Have a good day. Love you," I told him, ignoring that itty-bitty sense of grief that still hit me when he left for "school."

But it was what it was, and his happiness was more important than anything. New normals weren't supposed to be easy, and one day, I would look back on this period in our life and be grateful for just getting to carry him to his classroom. One day, he probably wouldn't let me go near it.

That was the single worst thing in the world I could have thought of.

Those red eyes peered up at me suspiciously, but then he sent me *"love"* and turned on those growing feet to push through the doggy—or was it wolfy?—door. Through the window, I peered in, met Maggie's brown eyes, and waved. *I'll be back later*, I mouthed to her. She smiled. Other than Randall and Henri, she was the most interaction I had with anyone here. We hadn't gotten very personal with each other yet, other than the uncomfortable pregnancy conversation I'd forced on her, but she invited me back every day, and when I'd asked Duncan if he thought she liked having me around, his answer had been a solid *"yes."*

Not for the first time, I wondered what kind of magic was in Maggie. Whatever it was, it was real subtle. She didn't feel like a werewolf, but she had their height.

Besides her, I'd also talked to some of the parents when they came to pick up their kids, just not for long. But now that Henri had given me his explanation for the distance the residents kept between us, it didn't bother me so much.

A touch to the middle of my back had me flinching like someone zapped me. That's what I got for zoning out. I hadn't been paying attention to the magical presence coming down the hall.

It was Henri.

Henri who had irritation stamped all over his face, and I meant a lot of it. He was in normal clothes—jeans and a T-shirt. He must not have shaved that morning because his scruff was thicker than normal.

He tugged at the collar of his shirt. "Can you come with me?" he asked, not beating around the bush.

"Morning," I greeted him, trying to read his body language some more. "Sure."

Henri blinked. His tone was a little softer after that. "Morning, Nina."

Setting my hand on his elbow, I gave his forearm a little rub. "You okay?" He was so tense.

His eyes flicked down to where I was touching him before meeting mine again. "I'm all good," he answered, actually sounding sincere. Maybe not *all good* but better than he'd been a second ago.

He cleared his throat after I dropped my hand. "One second." Henri leaned toward the little window built into the door, lifting his hand, a brief smile flashing across his features that made *me* smile. A second later, he stepped away, his expression melting off like it had never been there in the first place. He was so good at doing that. "The elders are in the media room."

I followed him down the hall. "It sounded like there was some arguing going on in there a minute ago."

Henri didn't even try and muffle his growl. "You heard that?"

"Little bit."

I wanted to ask what they'd been arguing over, but I figured the elders could probably hear us, so I kept my mouth closed and focused on following him, which reminded me of what he'd looked like from behind when we'd gone back inside the house last night. Those sweatpants had hugged tight, high muscles just right . . .

I put a lid on that thought just in time to spot multiple elders seated at the table. All of them minus Franklin, who was still missing in action.

These people had allowed me to join their community, then disappeared without a trace until now.

I wasn't sure why it hit me then, this sense of hurt, but it did. Did they all really think we weren't going to last?

Almost instantly, a solid weight landed between my shoulder blades. "What's going on?" Henri asked against my ear.

The urge to make something up was in my mouth, but I squashed it when his breath puffed against my skin. This was the wrong moment to answer him. The wrong place to say what was in my heart, so I glanced over my shoulder and shook my head.

He didn't need to say a word for me to know he didn't like me not explaining, but what was I going to do? Tell him that I was disappointed everyone thought we were flakes? I'd just told him last night that I'd been lonely.

Hoping he understood the timing being off, I reached back and patted his leg before taking the same chair across from the elders as in the past. This time though, I was alone. I missed Matti and Sienna. We had been texting as much as we always had—video calling once or twice a month, which was also the normal—but it was different now.

I eyed Henri as he went to stand in almost the same spot as before too. I thought he was a little closer to the table this time though.

Pushing my chair forward, I said, "Good morning, elders," in the most non-hurt voice I could come up with.

They murmured something in return that sounded like "good morning," but it didn't exactly sound enthusiastic.

"Nina, tell them what happened last night," Henri demanded, his irritation back in its full glory.

One of the women aimed a narrowed look at him through her tortoiseshell glasses; it was the woman who had spoken the most after Franklin our first day. Silver-Blue Hair. She coughed delicately. "I will handle the questions here, Henri." She offered a smile that was deceptively encouraging. "Nina, tell us what happened last night, step-by-step and word for word to the best of your ability."

The faster I did this, the faster I could get it over with. I started. "We were outside, Henri, Agnès, Duncan, and me. We had just finishing playing tag and were eating our popsicles, sitting there talking—"

"About what?" the cyclops asked.

I slid my gaze to Henri.

"That doesn't matter," he answered for me, his tone cool.

I didn't smile, but a part of me wanted to. What I did do was tell them about the gnomes coming out of the trees and coming straight for us, like something out of a fairy tale. I told them about the color of their clothing and the way they had spoken in unison and what they'd said, at least how I remembered it, which was something I hadn't even shared with Henri. I guess we'd both been too overwhelmed by the miracle of their appearance to notice. I told the elders everything, except for how we'd shared Henri's popsicle and our conversation about my parents afterward. To me, those discussions weren't any of their business.

The cyclops elder spoke up. "How do you know their language?"

"I don't," I replied. "I didn't recognize that they were even speaking a different one until he mentioned it."

"You have never met them before?" the woman with the glasses asked.

"Never."

"Not even in a different location?"

I shook my head. "I've never seen, spoken to, or dreamt of a gnome in my life. I've only read about them."

More stirring. More whispering.

A man with a faint green tint to his skin leaned forward. "Gnomes have long lifespans and equally impressive memories," he noted, like that meant something to me.

It didn't.

There were more murmurs from the group in what seemed like reluctant agreement over his comment.

"Now that you've heard that we both had the same experience, can we discuss something else?" Henri's husky voice engulfed the room, less of a question than a statement.

"We only wish to understand why they would return after so long," the woman said.

"If there's more to it, they didn't share it with us. Like I said," Henri went on. "There's no need to drag this out and have another meeting over it when there are other things around here that could benefit more from our attention. The gnomes are back, and it's a good thing. We can leave it at that."

The woman waved her hand. "We should continue this discussion. I would expect you of all people to be more understanding about our desire to understand *why*, Henri. This is unlike you."

I was on Henri's side with this. They could discuss hypothetical reasons and answers all they wanted, but if these were old, mysterious magical beings who could travel through a system in trees we couldn't begin to understand . . . did it really matter? They hadn't given either of us a single clue.

From the tension in the air, I could sense another round of arguing on the verge of starting, and there were other things I'd rather do. "Do you all need anything else from me?" I asked before they could begin.

"No, Nina," a couple of them answered at the same time, dismissing me without a second thought before they turned on themselves and multiple people started talking at once.

Pushing the chair back, I slid out and went for the door, undisturbed. Forgotten again. I headed up to my room, grabbed the small cardboard box that had arrived a few days ago, and swapped into my hiking boots before I went right on back downstairs. The voices echoed from the library as I went in that direction, but I passed the doorway and ignored what was happening, going straight out the back door. The air was clean and sweeter than it had been earlier when I'd let Duncan out to pee, and I smiled wide when I spotted Randall, the redheaded security person for the ranch, outside of the building with the vehicles.

The man, who I had started getting to know over random meals the last few weeks, was leaning against the building, texting on his phone, but when he sensed me, he dropped his hand and gave me a friendly smile. "Morning," he called out.

"Hi, Randall. How's it going?"

"All right." The man who had told me he was one of the few people who had been born at the ranch tipped his head toward the clubhouse. "They wrangle you into their gnome discussion?"

"Yeah . . ." I trailed off, not being willing to talk badly about the elders.

I figured he understood when he grinned. "What's going on?"

"I wanted to ask, could you tell me how to find Spencer the sasquatch?"

You would have figured I'd told the nice man a few years older than me that I had proof Santa was real from the way his entire body reacted to my question. "You want to find Spencer?" He made a face. "Why?"

I held up the bar of conditioner, feeling about an inch tall. "Remember I hurt his feelings when I first got here? I wanted to apologize and give him conditioner to make up for it. I should have done it sooner, but it took a long time to get here. The conditioner I ordered, I mean."

"*You* hurt *his* feelings?" Randall couldn't believe me.

But he needed to.

I nodded. "Can you tell me where to find him?" I thought about it. "I'll be all right. He can't hurt me unless I let him." I wanted him to understand that, otherwise he might be worried that this could go wrong.

It *could*. Only if I let it.

I wanted him to forgive me, but not at a risk to my safety. I wasn't that dumb. "Please?" I tried again.

The redhead thought about it for a second. "Sure, but I might as well take you. Someone needs to head out that way to check some batteries, I'll switch."

"Okay," I agreed, so grateful. "Can I help?"

"I got it. Let me swap the UTV for the side-by-side, and we'll get going," he offered, and I nodded.

It didn't take him long to change vehicles, and I heard the door to the main house open and close before a voice I recognized spoke up. "All good?"

It was Henri making his way over, all six-foot-six, prime rib of a man.

How did normal people not tell he was something else just by looking at him? Did they assume he'd played football at some point in his life? Or imagine that he'd been a wrestler? People just weren't built the way he was.

I put a lid on that thought too.

"Everything's fine," I answered him as Randall wandered out of the warehouse.

The other man lifted his chin. "Hey, boss. We're heading to the western side of the property. Probably be gone a couple of hours. You mind taking the north—"

Henri's steps slowed, and those dark eyebrows crept up a millimeter. "You're going together?"

Did his tone come out a little . . . different, or was I imagining it?

I nodded. "I asked Randall to go with me to run an errand." It wasn't that I didn't want him to know where we were going, but I didn't want to risk getting a lecture on why I didn't need to apologize, or whatever else he could come up with.

But I was underestimating the curious nature of a werewolf, and that was always a dumb thing to do. Henri asked, "What errand?"

"We're checking batteries along the fence and going to see Spencer," Randall answered.

"*Spencer?*" He sounded even more surprised than Randall had.

I gave him a weak grin. "Yes, Spencer the sasquatch, formerly known as the bigfoot."

"Why?"

This was why I always explained everything at once to my parents. I was going to have to remember that. "I have a conditioner bar I want to give him that's good for his hair. I feel bad about making fun of him."

To give him credit, Henri looked perplexed for about two seconds more before his features smoothed back into that serious expression that was standard for him. His boss face. He held out his hand to Randall. "I'll go."

Dang it. "I want to go. I want to apologize to him," I explained. "Not just give him the conditioner."

Amber eyes slid toward me. "I understand. I'll take you, and we'll check the western fence line."

Under no circumstance had I meant for this to turn out so complicated. "I can go by myself. You both seem busy . . ."

"No" came out of both of their mouths.

All right, I'd probably get lost anyway. I was going to need to learn to navigate with their map app and coordinates if we were going to be sticking around, which *was* the plan, contrary to popular belief.

Henri caught the set of keys Randall tossed and didn't say a word from the moment we got into the side-by-side.

We traveled slowly through the parts of the forest closest to the residential areas, all the sections I'd become familiar with on weekends with Duncan. Soon after, we left the gravel road, then the dirt-packed one, until we made it to an area that was more remote. He did it on his own without any kind of GPS or navigation to lead us either. Henri knew exactly where we were going.

I rubbed my hands on my thighs, made it maybe two more minutes, and then I blurted out, "So? Are you being awkward, or are you frustrated with the elders right now?"

He didn't look over, but "I'm not awkward" was what he decided to reply with.

I scrunched up my nose at him.

His jaw, though, looked even more defined than it'd been a minute ago. "I've got a lot on my mind." He hesitated, then pressed his lips together like he was catching other words that wanted to come out too.

Reaching across the seat, I set my hand on his forearm one more time and gave it a squeeze. "You can talk to me about whatever you want. The only person I might tell is Duncan, and he can't tell anyone."

His eyes slid over to me before they moved forward again just as fast. Those tan hands flexed around the wheel, opening and closing. He did it for so long that I thought he was ignoring me. Then he said, "I'm busy. Here and at work. When it isn't one, it's the other." His exhale was soft, and I thought he was done before he suddenly huffed. "And I'm not being fucking awkward around you. Give me a break."

Give him a break?

The urge to joke about why he might be being weird was strong, but I had a vague idea of what this slice of honesty from him meant.

Henri Blackrock had opened up to me a little.

He'd *complained*.

I didn't need to know him better than I already did to realize that had to be a once-in-a-lifetime event.

And now I felt guilty for taking up more of his time.

I slid my hand up and squeezed his elbow. His skin was nice and warm. "I'm sorry you're swamped, Fluff. Being responsible for one person is a lot of work, and I haven't spent that much time with you, but I've seen how busy you are. Your phone is always ringing, you're always talking to someone about something at the ranch . . . I don't know how you do it." I thought about how Matti had mentioned his dad leaving here because of the responsibilities that came with it, then shoved that topic aside for the time being. The last thing Henri needed was to be reminded about how much he had on his plate, even if I sympathized with him. "Will work get better, or is that just part of it?"

His hands did that flexing thing again around the steering wheel. "As soon as we hire another deputy they will, whenever that is. There aren't exactly a line of people moving to the county with the right qualifications."

I kept massaging the muscle on his lower arm with my thumb, I was pretty sure the tension was slowly easing from it in the process. "I see."

"It'll happen at some point, but we're all getting tired of working so many hours until it does. It isn't just me," he explained before clearing his throat, maybe getting a little self-conscious about what he'd admitted.

"Well, I don't know how many of the other deputies have to deal with elders and giant hairy creatures with attitude problems on top of everything. I wouldn't be too hard on myself."

He dipped his chin like he thought I had a point.

"I'm sorry," I blurted out.

His forehead wrinkled. "For?"

"I used to think that you were always so serious, but I get it now. It's because you've always had to be. You knew what you were going to have to bear in the future, huh? When you were younger?"

He met my eyes. I smiled at him.

"I know I haven't been here that long, and my opinion doesn't mean much, but I think you're doing a great job, Fluff. I mean it. The kids are happy, and they love you. They're always 'Henri this and Henri that' in the nursery. All of them. Don't tell Pascal I'm telling you this, but he's been drawing a lot of pictures of you the last week. He told me you're his hero. It's the cutest freaking thing. Plus, the ranch is in great shape . . ."

"Your opinion matters." Henri's jaw muscle did that ticking thing some more. His hands flexed. Then a frown came out of nowhere. "Don't say shit like that."

It took me a gulp and a second to react. "It matters to me, but you know what I mean."

"I know what you meant, but I don't care." He shot me a look. "Don't."

I gave his forearm another squeeze, so touched I wanted to put my hand over my heart. "In that case, thank you. I appreciate it." I smiled at him even though he was focused in the direction of the windshield again. "You're a good man, Henri Blackrock."

When I let go of him, the way he turned to me . . .

"Don't make that face. I'm not flirting with you." I squinted at him. "I said you're a good man, not . . ."

"You're not asking me to marry you?" he cut me off with a straight face.

The gasp that came out of my body was a borderline shout. "And you tell me I'm a brat." I shook my head, so completely caught off guard by the fact he'd bring it up, especially like that. Like in a joke. I laughed even harder. "I thought we were pretending I didn't tell you what I told you!"

"It happened," he muttered, his mouth twitching.

He thought this was *funny*?

I groaned. "Hear me out, I did *not* ask you to marry me. Your cousin—"

"You said he was yours just as much as he is mine."

This was happening. Henri was messing with me. "He was yours first, and I only told you what he said because you asked!" I laughed some more and shook my head. "I knew you were going to make this weird after I told you, I knew it."

This man who had just finished telling me all about how he was overworked and tired, smirked. Right then and there. I might have even called it a semi-smile.

I liked this version of him.

I liked it a lot.

He wasn't at all what I expected, with all these different facets of him.

I was thinking about that as he slowed the UTV to a crawl when we got to an even thicker section of forest with slim trees clustered so close together it was impossible to drive any further.

"We'll have to go by foot the rest of the way," he explained, shutting the side-by-side down and unbuckling his seat belt.

I did the same, meeting him at the front of the off-road vehicle. We had to split up to get around the aspens, the gaps between them too narrow. There were branches and rocks of all sizes scattered everywhere, and I slipped on wet leaves more than I was proud of. Half the time, he made sure I was mostly standing, but every once in a while, he pretended not to hear me mutter "shit" to myself.

"We're almost there," he let me know after a while.

"Okay."

What he considered "almost there" was not what I considered "almost there," that was for freaking sure. We came up to a steep incline that had to be a hill or a mountain hidden in the trees that I'd never seen before from the clubhouse. My calves and thighs burned sooner than my ego would have expected, and I started holding my breath for longer and longer periods so he wouldn't hear me gasping.

"Do we need to take a break?" he asked from up ahead after a few more minutes.

Breathing through my nose had never been harder, and I really wanted to know what altitude we were at because my lungs were under the impression we were at eighteen thousand feet. "Are we almost there?"

Henri stopped. His face wasn't red. He wasn't even sweating, while I was sure he noticed that my face probably resembled a tomato, and I might need an inhaler. "Breathe through your nose."

"Where else am I supposed to breathe from?" I gasped.

His eyebrows rose. "We'll be there in five minutes. You going to make it?"

Swallowing hard, I waved him forward, really, really wishing I'd brought some water with me.

Henri's eyes twinkled for a moment before he continued up the dang hill. He had the nerve to talk in a perfectly even voice. "His home is up ahead. If he's rude, we're leaving. If you feel uncomfortable, we're leaving. Am I clear?"

"Got it, your Royal Wolfiness," I confirmed.

He slowly turned to look at me. His nose wrinkled a little.

I smiled at him, trying so hard to breathe normally when I wanted to wheeze.

His nose stayed scrunched, then he did that "come here" gesture with his index finger that was way more attractive than it should have been.

Maybe I should have asked what he wanted, but I didn't. I stepped right up to him, so close I had to tip my head back. Henri dipped his, and at least half my brain cells stopped working as he lowered that masculine face—I knew he wasn't going to kiss me, I knew it like I knew the exact shade of Duncan's eyes—but still, the brain cells in my skull decided to make my heart race right then.

It wasn't every day a gorgeous man got this close to me.

But instead of his mouth touching some part of my body, it was his cheek that moved across the top of my head. He tilted his neck so that he rubbed it across my ear and my own cheek . . . a little over part of my mouth too. He did the same with his other cheek on my other side.

Henri Blackrock was covering me in his scent, and I just stood there.

After maybe the longest minute or two of my life because I was trying so hard not to react, he looked down and nodded. "Good," he grumbled.

Good?

His nostrils flared just a little. "You smell like mine now."

Not choking right then might have been the hardest thing I'd ever done, because I *knew* what he meant, and at the same time, some part of me couldn't help but take it the way it sounded.

"Spencer's less likely to get aggravated if you smell like me. He'll know if he messes with you, he messes with me." He said it so nonchalantly, dismissing the moment like he did this kind of thing all the time. "Let's go be nice, Cricket."

Oh, sure. I was fine. Like nothing had happened.

I settled for a single nod and followed after him—pretending not to be in a state of shock—the side of the hill getting steeper with every step. I guess a part of me had expected to find a cave nestled in a rock formation, but what we came up to was a small but tall log cabin with solar panels on one side and a *satellite dish* on the other.

My mouth dropped open as wide as it had wanted to when Henri had started rubbing all over me. "What in the magical hell . . . ?" I whispered.

The chuckle at my side got me. Henri was semi-smiling again. "He has a refrigerator."

I couldn't believe it. "He has *TV*?" I recognized the name of the company on the dish.

"Basic service. He doesn't want to pay extra for more channels," Henri explained. "It's what comes standard with being a member of the community. We get a corporate deal."

Before I could wonder about what kind of shows a sasquatch might want to watch in his cabin in the middle of nowhere, a big door opened and a booming voice called, "You're on my land."

The man beside me sighed. "Your land is in the northwest. This is my land, and you're allowed to live on it. Any member of the community can venture out here whenever they want. You agreed in blood, and you aren't old enough to start having memory issues unless you have a medical condition you need to see someone about."

The level of confidence it took to talk back to an eight-foot-tall being . . .

The sasquatch stepped out of the house and into the clearing in front. Even with all the hair on his body, it was obvious he was irritated. "What do you want? I haven't 'wandered' close again. I've kept my distance," Spencer argued.

"Someone wants to speak to you."

"The abomination?" the sasquatch huffed, those dark eyes landing on me.

I—oooh. *Ooh*. This was going to be harder than I thought. The urge to say something I'd regret once I stopped being mad lingered in my mouth, but the part of me that was trying to be nice reminded me to rise above.

But I still had to grit my teeth as I said, "That's a really mean thing to call me when I came here to apologize, *Spencer*." I was going to treat him like a person, even though he couldn't do the same for me. *Yet*.

"You're here to what?" the sasquatch barked like he hadn't heard me correctly.

I looked at him. "I'm here to say I'm sorry for what I said before. You hurt my feelings, so then I retaliated, and it's been bothering me since it happened."

Those dark, beady eyes moved back and forth between Henri and me, like he wasn't sure we weren't pulling his leg or something. It made me feel more guilty. It also made me more resigned to saying and doing what I needed to.

I tried again. "You have a lot of beautiful colors in your hair. Look at mine. There isn't a single highlight in it—"

"It is plain," Spencer agreed, way too easily.

I blinked. "Sure, plain—"

"It isn't even chestnut colored. *That* is a nice shade," the sasquatch threw in.

I nodded slowly and bit the inside of my cheek.

The compliments kept coming though. "Dark auburn, I would say." He shrugged. "Meh."

"Meh?" I echoed, not sure I was hearing him correctly. Was this giant legend with dry hair making fun of me? I didn't have split ends. It was healthy, dang it.

A hand landed on my shoulder and gave it a squeeze, and I made the mistake of looking at Henri. He had a smug expression on his face. He wasn't even trying to be discreet about it either.

I was glad someone thought this was funny. "I appreciate you sharing your opinion," I lied in a flat voice, dang well knowing he could tell I didn't mean it.

"You're welcome, demon."

Demon?

All right, I was done.

"It is shiny. You do have that going for you," Spencer added just as I was about to grab Henri's wrist and pull him in the direction we'd come.

I touched the ends of my hair. "Thank you." I'd *known* he was vain about his appearance. "I stopped using shampoo two years ago, and it made a world of difference for me."

I was surprised when Henri murmured, "But it smells good."

A compliment. I dropped my hand. "I still wash it with castile soap, just not shampoo. And I use a vinegar rinse and a good conditioner. It's a whole method." And actually this was a good segue into why I was here. I took the little box out of my fanny pack—realizing then I should have gotten him multiple ones since he had so much hair—and I tossed it.

The sasquatch caught it and read the box, which was something I was going to have to tell Sienna about. Or ask Henri over.

How did he know how to read? Did he walk around in human form sometimes? "Conditioner?"

"Your hair is fine despite what I said, but that's a good conditioner. I can help you order more if you want." Did he have money?

How I could tell a being covered from head to toe in hair was surprised was something I didn't totally understand, but I did.

"If you want," I offered, so he wouldn't feel any pressure. Maybe he'd hate it, but I'd tried.

Spencer's voice was loud. "Okay." Not thank you, nothing else. Just *okay*. At least he hadn't called me a demon again. I needed to quit while I was ahead.

"I'm sorry again for what I said in anger. Hope you like the conditioner." I turned to Henri and raised my eyebrows, telling him I was ready to go if he was.

He nodded. We started hiking back in the direction we'd come. We hadn't gotten very far when Spencer called out in his big voice, "Henri?"

"What?" the man beside me hollered, not slowing down.

"Tell Maggie I called her a traitor!"

"No!" Henri yelled back, shaking his head.

Maggie? *Nursery Maggie?* What in the . . .?

Going down the hill wasn't any easier than going up it. My knees cracked and started hurting, and I slipped more than once again on damp leaves but managed to stay on my feet. But it was faster than going up had been.

We had just gotten to where the land levelled off when the rich voice that was becoming more and more familiar by the sentence spoke again. "You didn't need to do that, you know."

"What? Say I was sorry?"

"Yeah."

He was a little further ahead of me, so I couldn't see his face, but he couldn't see mine either. "Maybe not, but I don't know what his life has been like, who has hurt him. I don't need to be one more person in a line of shitty people."

That got him to stop between two aspens. He lifted his head but didn't do anything else.

"It makes sense, doesn't it? I just don't think you get that distrustful or rude because it's fun, unless you're a psychopath." I kept walking, catching his eyes when I got to his side. I shrugged up at him and that thoughtful, handsome face. "The people who are the hardest to love are usually the ones who need it the most. Funny how that works, huh?"

Chapter Thirteen

Sienna: How's my baby doing?

Lying across the bed after dinner, I eyed Duncan who was busy gnawing away on a bone while hooked on an action movie with immortal soldiers who were being hunted down.

He was too much.

The fact he loved television, and especially action movies, never failed to tickle the crap out of me. But just about everything he did had that ability. He could sit there snoring like an exhausted dad after a theme park visit, and I thought it was precious. His farts, ignoring the smell, were adorable. At least half the photos on my phone were of him in various stages of sleep. With his paws in the air, on his side, with one lone paw extended, with his butt on me and the rest of him on another surface.

It was crazy what love could do to a person. They could pick up and change their entire lives for it. And even if things weren't absolutely perfect, and maybe they'd been better—or at least more familiar before—sacrifices for love had never been less painful.

Maybe they couldn't even be counted as sacrifices. I had that in mind as I texted Si back.

Me: The baby is doing great. He has more friends than I've had my entire life, and he's going on his first run tonight with the pack finally.

Henri had given me the news that morning over breakfast, and maybe Duncan didn't really seem to care—because he had no idea what he'd been missing out on—but that was all right. I was excited enough for him. I'd talked to Matti during his lunch break, and he'd mentioned how much fun they were and how good they would be for the donut. Running around playing tag and ball was fine and all, but a pack run was *different*.

I'd also given him a tremendous amount of crap for not telling me about his Great Wolf relative, to which he'd sputtered and explained that it was something his dad had told him never to mention to anyone. *Long lived beings have long memories*, and the Great Wolf had done some things that certain beings would never forget. Enemies probably remained enemies forever. Apparently, Sienna knew about his family tree, but I didn't get the story about how she'd found out. I let it go, figuring that if there was something my dad had asked me to keep a secret, I would do it in a heartbeat. And I knew dang well that Matti had loved his parents as much as I loved mine. Of course he'd do the same.

And when I'd asked Matti if anybody would ever call him by that term, he'd laughed his butt off. His "*no*" had been half a hoot. I didn't understand why that had been so funny, but all right.

Who was I to give him too much crap about family secrets?

But he had seemed way too interested to find out Henri had shared that information with me.

Another text came through.

Sienna: Duncan ☺
Sienna: But how are YOU?

I missed her, I was still a little lonely, and I was struggling with how fast my boy was sprouting up. But I didn't tell her that over text. Maybe the next time we talked and I was far away from the ranch.

Me: I'm fine. Just getting used to this new normal. 😄

I cringed inside right after sending the text. What were my chances she was going to buy my BS with a thumbs-up emoji? It was like I'd forgotten she'd known me most of my life.

Her reply came through even faster than I'd expected.

Sienna: 😒
Me: I'M FINE. I promise.

It wasn't a lie. I was healthy, work was fine, Duncan was good. What more could I ask for?

A lick at my ankle had me glancing down my leg at the puppy who was resting his chin on top of my foot, his toy wedged between his paws as he peered at me.

"I'm all right," I promised. "Just texting Sienna. I miss her and your uncle Matti. That's all." Those bright red inquisitive eyes didn't blink, and I booped the tip of his nose. "I love you, Dunky," I said. "I'm good."

"Yes," he told me. *"Love."*

I smiled, trying to push down the little bit of frustration that had caught his attention. He gave me another lick before his head suddenly turned to the left where the wall was. His tail rose straight up in the air a second before there was a knock.

"It's time," Henri's voice carried through the door.

Duncan's fluffy black tail swayed, making me smile. I wouldn't go as far as to say that Duncan really liked Henri, but it had been weeks since the last time he'd growled at him. Whether my donut had been won over by how often he made the puppies their breakfast, or that one game of tag, I didn't know, but the Great Wolf had slowly but steadily been winning my boy over.

When we got to see him, at least, which still hadn't been a whole lot.

It had been a week since Henri and I had visited Spencer, and over that time, we'd had breakfast with him twice and dinner once. Poor Henri had needed to leave early all three times after getting phone calls that had him squeezing his utensils so tight his knuckles had gone white, but it still counted. It was something.

"Okay, coming," I called out, already rolling off the bed. "Let me put my shoes on, and then I'll go drop you off," I told Duncan, moving to the row of shoes lined up next to the door. I put on my hiking boots, fanny pack, and a thin jacket as he jumped down. With a touch to the top of his head, I opened the door to an empty hallway. "Matti said you're going to have a lot of fun tonight. You get to run around with a few other members of the pack. Howl at the moon; that'll be great. And don't worry that yours isn't very loud because you're small, so it's in proportion to your size, buddy. Your howl is my favorite howl I've ever heard."

His tail brushed my calf as we took the stairs side by side.

He'd gained another two pounds and at least an inch in height over the course of the week.

I was okay with it. Just ecstatic.

"Henri will take care of you, and Randall said he would keep an eye on you too when you're out there. Agnes is probably already waiting, too. I'll stay outside the whole time until you're back."

He nudged my leg when we got to the bottom of the stairs, his "*yes*" strong.

The hallway was empty as we headed out the front door. In the same clearing where we sat every night to look up at the stars, which were dim at that moment with the full moon shining so brightly, were a handful of adults with not one but two young wolves.

Where was everyone else?

Duncan glanced up at me, and I gave him a nod before he took off, running straight for the white wolf and the slightly bigger and darker one that I had a feeling was Pascal from the color of his coat. I hadn't seen him in his pup form since the incident with the Jenny Greenteeth. He hip-checked my boy when he got there, and it made me smile as I went toward them, recognizing Henri, the tallest adult of the group. Randall was by him, Ani to the side, Pascal's dad, and another man who looked a little familiar. He was younger than Henri, not as tall, a dirty blond and—

Glaring in my direction?

All right, maybe I wasn't going to be making a new friend tonight.

Sticking my hands in my pockets, I was halfway to the group when Ani glanced over. I waved. "Hi, Ani."

The woman who I'd spent some time with in passing when I'd run into her at the UTV warehouse beamed. "How's it going, Nina?" She greeted me with genuine kindness. I'd learned she was forty-two, had two children, and was married to a Mexican wolf.

"Pretty good, how are you?" I asked as I came to a stop in a gap between her and Randall. "Hi, Randall. Hi, Pascal's dad." We had never done more than politely greet each other with nods and smiles at the nursery. Pascal had whispered to me that his mommy got jealous, so I didn't take his distance personally. Now when his mom came to get him? That was a different story, and I could see where Pascal got his personality from.

Even though I didn't want to, I aimed my attention at the stranger. I didn't hold out my hand though. "Hi. I'm Nina."

His hand stayed right where it was, just as unfriendly as I'd expected. "Hi," the stranger muttered, his posture stiff, his glare definitely intense, maybe even a little confrontational.

With a sinking feeling in my chest, I turned to Henri. Him, I couldn't help but smile at. "Thank you for taking Duncan out."

There was something about Henri's expression right then. This wasn't the joking man who had rubbed his face all over me for protection days ago. This was bossy wolf Henri. Great Wolf Henri with his coolness and neutrality. That Henri dipped his head like we were strangers. "I'll talk to him, walk him through what we're going to do, and then we'll get going. We'll be gone about an hour."

I nodded.

Henri approached the kids, crouching a few feet away from my puppy, and I could see his lips moving as he talked to them.

"It's easier to keep track of the pups in a smaller group, so it's only going to be us. The rest of the pack is meeting later," Randall explained beside me. "We'll keep an eye on him. We do this every time one of the pups hits a certain age."

"Thanks," I told him, trying to ignore the man who was burning a hole into the side of my face. He wasn't trying to hide it either. But no one else seemed worried about his mood, so chances were, he had very good control of his emotions and maybe I was overthinking his body language since I was hyper-aware of it. Henri looked serious almost constantly. Maybe resting bitch face was this man's normal.

A moment later, Henri called out, "It's time."

Taking a few steps back, a wave of magic tickled my skin as the group went from five adult humans to five big wolves standing in their place.

Duncan pressed up against my leg, a small, uncertain *"love"* grabbing my attention.

Was he worried? "You're fine, buddy." I bent over as he lifted his head and met my eyes. "You know Henri and Randall. Agnes and Pascal are your friends."

He pressed closer, the strip of hair between his tail and the base of his neck rising up.

Moving somewhere new hadn't made him nervous, but this was? *My donut.*

"This is your pack, Dunky," I promised him and the universe. "Henri won't let anything happen to you. He's been really nice to you since we got here, hasn't he?"

Duncan looked at me, and it touched some huge part of me when I felt his *"yes."*

A soft howl had me focusing on the biggest of all the werewolves standing with the kids. The rest of them looked like huskies in comparison to the black wolf. It made so much sense right then that the gnomes would call him Great Wolf. Under the moonlight, surrounded by the towering trees with their magical bark, circled by other wolves of every size, Wolf Henri, with his thick, dark coat and regal head and build, was something out of a fantasy novel . . . or a romance novel.

I gave him a thumbs-up.

Another howl rose out of Henri's chest at that, starting off low and quiet and gaining depth and volume with every second. From the adult group, two other voices joined him, weaving through the air together as a high one erupted from the children. It was Agnes. Another adult entered the chorus before a small one did the same.

Their voices made me think of my parents. Made me miss them. Miss my childhood and all the people who had been my whole world. I hoped they called me soon. The last time we'd spoken, they'd said one of my mom's sisters was going to pick them up for a mini family reunion, but they hadn't said which sister, and she had six of them. I'd give them another week to check in and then I'd start trying to track them down.

A small, crackly howl came from my feet before it cut off, and Duncan gave it another shot. He tipped his head, his neck an elegant line, his ears the highlight of his whole body. His lips pursed together as he tried to sing too.

My boy. My donut.

His voice was thinner than the others, but he was no wolf, and he was a baby, and love filled my entire body when his little lungs ran out of breath so soon and he had to start again, the cutest howl to ever be heard in the world. You couldn't have paid me a billion dollars to think otherwise. It was magic and life, and I couldn't imagine what it would sound like when he was older.

A small paw landed on top of my foot, and Duncan gave me this look as he arched his neck some more . . .

"Love," he told me, those red eyes intent, trying to tell me something else . . . Lifting his paw, he stomped on my foot once more.

I laughed. "Oh, you want me to howl, too?"

His *"yes"* so joyful, I laughed again when he set more weight down on me.

"Yes, yes, yes."

"Okay, okay," I told him as the adult wolves' song started to rise once more.

"Yes, yes," Duncan's telepathic touch urged. Like I could tell him no.

I might have not been a four-legged creature in any fairy or folktale, but I'd been a member of a pack before.

I lifted my face and howled with them, my donut's weight settling even more against me, his voice gaining volume by the note.

I howled, and when I ran out of breath, caught it, and howled even louder, not letting myself feel like a poser because I knew who I was doing this for.

For this sweet child who was mine. Mine to keep. Mine to protect. Mine to love.

And as I looked at the growing boy who I'd centered my whole world around, I projected the same thought at him, at the universe in general, that he sent me. LOVE, LOVE, LOVE, I sent him. ALL OF MY LOVE.

One day, I hoped he'd feel it the way I did when he shared it with me.

I lifted my head and howled some more, like I had done dozens of times over the years with my loved ones, and almost instantly caught the amber-colored gaze of a wolf the size of a horse. The deep foundation of Henri's song suddenly seemed to get lost for maybe a second before he found it and awoo-ed an awoo that was both werewolf magic and so much more. I wasn't the only one who felt like it was a call to the rest of the world to howl even louder.

And the moon in her infinite beauty and greatness seemed to shine even brighter as we sang and sang to her together.

I was lying on my back in the clearing when I heard something. Not the frogs and owls that usually filled the night or the rustling sounds that made me paranoid something was going to try and crawl into my ears. These were small, creaky noises.

Sitting up slowly, I instantly spotted the single small green fire bobbing along, heading in my direction from a big tree maybe twenty feet away. On either side of the torch were two gnomes, their wrinkled faces intent and serious. Did they look like they meant business or was I imagining it?

"Greetings," the one without the torch called out.

"Greetings," the one with it added.

My hands were already fumbling at my fanny pack as I smiled at them. "Greetings."

They moved so fast for how small and old they seemed, but

appearances were deceiving. Honestly, I thought they looked a little mean. A little grouchy. Adorable in their own way.

"How are you?" I asked when they stopped a few feet away from where I was sitting.

There was a pause that told me they hadn't expected my question, but the one without the torch replied, "Pleasant."

I smiled at them, not sure what to do next. After a second, I pulled a couple pieces of dehydrated sweet potato from my fanny pack and held them out. I'd made them the day before our latest jerky batch. The gnome without the torch reached out and took the rounds, one he put in his pocket and the other he nibbled on before passing it to his friend who finished it off.

When a minute went by and nothing else happened, I cleared my throat. Now this was a little awkward. I didn't want to put my foot in my mouth, but sitting here being stared at made me squirmy. "The . . . wolf you spoke to last time isn't here right now. He'll be back soon."

The gnome with the torch made a short grunt. "It is not the Great Wolf we've come for. We are here for you, child."

I pointed at myself.

They nodded simultaneously.

That wasn't intimidating. This wasn't nerve-racking at all. They wanted to talk to me? "What do you want to talk about?"

"Talking is unnecessary, we only seek to be in your presence," the one with the torch answered with a hard stare.

Huh?

"Your obsidian hides nothing from us. We are attuned to elements of the earth," the other gnome explained, Torch Gnome nodding.

Ohhhh. I thought I understood, at least that part. "So you . . . want to hang out?" I asked them, hoping not to sound too confused and insult them.

"Yes," Torch Gnome answered. "We are the oldest in our clan. It is our duty to continue our line."

I blinked. Just as I was about to ask if they were implying what I thought they were, the talkative gnomes kept going.

"It was a surprise to hear from our brethren in the north that your father is doing well," Torch Gnome said almost conversationally. "We had believed he had passed on some time ago."

"It isn't often they send news," the other added with a nod.

I wasn't sure I'd ever been so caught off guard in my life.

And I couldn't control how high my voice came out. "My . . . father?"

Both gnomes nodded in sync with each other. "The son of the night, yes."

My blood pressure might have dropped. I might have even lost my breath for a moment. "I . . . I've never met my biological father. My dad, who raised me, has never met a gnome, as far as I know, and he's never hid from anything or anyone, so I don't think you're referring to him, are you?"

They exchanged a glance.

"In this case, we speak of your true father, not the one of your heart," one of them explained after a moment.

My stomach churned at their words, at the small clues they'd dropped in front of me in a convenient little pile that felt very, very huge all of a sudden.

"You might have me mixed up with someone else." For a moment, I hesitated and looked down at my bracelet. Tugging it off, I set it on the ground, watching them both lean forward just a little, filling their lungs once before releasing their breath, even though they'd already implied it didn't hide anything from them.

They knew something. I'd bet my life on it. I swallowed hard.

"Do not be frightened. There is no confusion. You are his young," the one with the torch announced.

They sounded so sure of themselves . . . but it didn't change the fact whoever my parents were had left me. Both of them. Not just one or the other. And neither of them had ever bothered to check on me. Not in a way that mattered, if they ever truly had.

When I'd been younger, I'd clung to the idea that something tragic had happened to the people I liked to think of as my DNA donors. Only once had I ever brought that up to my parents, and

I could still remember the way pity shaped their faces. It hadn't taken me long to stop believing that.

But I was older now, and I thought I'd come to terms with all the possibilities that could have led me to end up with adoptive werewolf parents. I'd been lying to myself though, I realized, because the idea that my DNA dad was somewhere out in the world, living his life, and that these gnomes could get an update on him?

I didn't like the way it made me feel.

I didn't like the thoughts it put into my head.

And I had to take a ragged breath in through my nose and shove the magic stirring in my sternum into the pocket where I usually kept it.

"We meant no harm," one of them murmured. "We appreciate your offering, child."

The urge to ask for more information, for a *name* was on the tip of my tongue, but no.

No.

What did it matter? What did it change? Nothing. That's what.

The gnomes had already started to retreat before I thought of something I wanted to know. "Wait!" I called out and watched as they stopped. "Why can I understand you but my friend the wolf, the Great Wolf, said he couldn't?"

Smiles crept over their lips.

And I had to try not to flinch because in their mouths were sharp, needlelike teeth. I'd always thought they were herbivores . . .

"You may be your father's daughter, but you are also your mother's daughter. Our brethren to the south lived among her people for a time," they answered.

I wanted them to elaborate so bad, but that was all I was going to get when the gnomes deemed our conversation over and marched in the direction of the tree they had come from. The light from their torch gradually disappeared into the darkness in a way that made no sense because the trunk didn't look deep enough.

I stared at that tree. I stared at it for a long time. Until twigs snapped and leaves crackled in the distance. Until red eyes and a blue flame came running straight at me from a distance.

And that—he—was the only thing in the world that could have made me smile when my nose felt funny and my fingers tingled over the conversation I'd just had.

Duncan charged over, leading the way with Agnes at his heels, Pascal behind her, his tongue hanging out. The adult wolves were further back, loping gracefully through the trees without the urgency that my donut had.

I held out my arms, and Duncan jumped into them, knocking the wind out of me when he landed.

"YES, YES, YES, YES."

He was real. He mattered. He—

"Dunky, *why is your face wet?*" I cried out as he licked my cheek, hoping to the freaking universe that he'd found a creek and that it wasn't bodily fluids that had his snout soaked. "Oh," I whimpered, not moving an inch or trying to stop him from licking me but fully aware I was rolling the dice letting him rub all over me like this.

He kept licking, and it was a warm nose nudging at my right hand and the feel of fur at my other that distracted me from what could be water, blood, or worse. Pascal was sniffing my fingers, and Agnes . . . I didn't know what Agnes was doing, but I thought I had felt something brush my leg.

"Oh, fine," I laughed, giving up. Dewormers and antibiotics existed for a reason. There was soap and water, and clothes could be replaced.

"LOVE, LOVE, LOVE, LOVE, LOVE."

Duncan licked and licked my chin and temple, his tail a flutter of emotion and happiness as he jumped and pounced. Little paws pressed down on sensitive places of my body, but it didn't matter. If joy caused some bruises, it was a small price I was more than willing to pay. And then Pascal must have joined in because someone was pressing a bigger body against my back and sides, and I opened my arms and hugged the puppy bodies that were . . . yeah, they were both wet and I still *really* hoped they'd found a creek in the last hour.

"*YES, LOVE, YES, LOVE, YES, YES, YES, LOVE, LOVE,*" Duncan pretty much shouted, he was that pumped.

"Did you have the time of your life?" I asked, still laughing, soaking up his excitement.

I scruffed up their sides. I hugged them. One body then another. Then I did it again, affection and happiness making me smile. No wonder these puppies were raised by everyone. How could you not love their love?

And I kept on smiling as a reddish-brown wolf trotted over, his snout nudging one pup, then another, Agnes—who at that point was hanging out off to the side—getting one too. Familiar eyes met mine, and I squinted, "Randall?" I asked.

One of its ears twitched, and I grinned.

There was a low woof as a dark wolf lumbered over on ridiculously long legs, and I watched Randall edge away. Wolf Henri's amber gaze was bright and glowing as he came up to us, a skyscraper in a village. His head dipped, and that long snout nudged at my arm.

"You want a scratch?" I asked slowly, surprised.

A face that would have made Little Red Riding Hood wet her pants stretched close until his warm nose grazed my cheek in the gentlest brush.

I didn't move. "Yes?" I asked, making sure.

That soft, warm nose edged back toward me, going right for my neck. *He was snuffling.* Soft puffs of breath had me almost shivering as he smelled me.

"I'll take that as a yes," I warned him.

Wolf Henri's nose grazed my neck a little more, and it wasn't fear that made me tense up exactly, but it was one thing to let human Henri smell one of the vulnerable spots on my body, and it was a different thing to let His Royal Wolfiness do it. For one, because I'd seen his teeth. I had survived Duncan's teething stage, but just barely. I could only imagine what adult wolf teeth could do. Then there was the other reason—it tickled.

And maybe it did a little more than tickle.

Fortunately, Wolf Henri moved his face, touching his nose to my ear very gently at the same time one of those massive paws nudged my leg.

I reached up, still surprised at him instigating this, and stroked my hand over his shoulder, sneaking my fingers in as deep as I could, not able to reach his undercoat, and followed that up by scratching a spot on his ear that none of the wolves I'd met before had ever complained about having touched. A low rumble worked through his throat, so, so close to my face.

He smelled good even like this.

I scratched him and scratched him, until Duncan jumped onto my legs and almost licked my eyeball, and I cracked up too hard to do anything else. "Okay, okay," I laughed, opening my eyes to find that all the adults were back in their human bodies. Duncan dropped onto my feet, his pink tongue hanging out of his mouth. He was so happy.

I wasn't sure I'd ever seen him happier.

"I'm so glad you had fun," I told him, feeling so right, like all my worries and insecurities over this huge step had been worth it for this moment. For this reaction from him.

"We're going inside for a snack," Henri called out. "You coming?" he asked over his shoulder, with a human Randall next to him.

"Sure," I answered.

Did they not sense the gnomes? Maybe I'd wait and bring it up to Henri in private later.

I gave Duncan a kiss on the top of his forehead before freezing. I touched my mouth and nothing colorful came off. It wasn't blood, just sweat . . . I thought. I sniffed my fingers; they didn't smell like pee . . .

Out of the corner of my eye, I saw Agnes take off, catching up to Henri and Randall, then continuing on ahead to the clubhouse. We followed the group inside, but instead of going to the kitchen, everyone headed to the living room. Three charcuterie boards of meats were already on the table waiting—pepperoni, salami, carved chicken, and more pieces of meat that I couldn't totally distinguish. Who had brought it, I had no idea, but no one acted like it was out of the ordinary.

For once in my life, I wasn't hungry—I could thank the gnomes for that—so I hung back as the pups rushed over, devouring the food that Ani handed out while they sat; unlike the adults, they hadn't changed back to human form. Less than ten minutes later, three full puppies were piled together on the hardwood floor, passed out and full.

I snorted at the same time Ani did. "So freaking cute."

Pascal, the biggest of the three, was in the middle. I could already see Duncan's mouth beginning to open, his signature move before his chainsaw snoring took over. Agnes had her back lined up to Pascal's, and my donut was tucked up to the other boy's chest. I took my phone out and took about ten pictures.

Gratitude I could barely handle made me so happy ... so thankful that we'd found this place. That Duncan had not one but about a dozen other puppies who were so good to him, despite their age differences. I loved each and every one of them.

"You want something to drink?" Randall asked just as two ringtones went off.

Both Henri and Pascal's dad pulled their phones out. The other man didn't hesitate to answer his, but Henri stared at his screen for a moment before walking out of the room, turning left to go toward the front of the house with a barked, "Blackrock." I'd learned already that was how he answered when someone from work was calling. If it was someone from the ranch, he answered with his first name.

By the time both men had left the room, Randall was holding up two different bottles. "We've got beer."

I eyed the pile of puppies on the floor and pointed at his left hand. He popped the lid and held it out with his friendly, but not too friendly, smile. He'd never asked again about smelling me, and I hadn't brought it up either. Randall was very, very nice, but it hadn't escaped me how fine of a line he walked with me. Unlike Ani and the puppies who were very handsy and touched me all the time, he kept his hands to himself, and his body at a solid three feet away almost constantly.

I'd marked him off my imaginary list of potential mates already because of it.

I eyed the silent blond man sprawled on one of the couches, legs extended out in front of him, as I took the bottle from Randall. I'd purposely been ignoring him. He had his own bottle already in hand, and like before, he wasn't being discreet about the way his gaze followed me across the room.

Why did he look familiar?

Another cell phone started ringing, and that time Randall pulled his out. "Randall . . . Yes . . . yes . . . we'll be there soon . . . yes, I'll bring help." He chuckled, then ended the call. "Constance fell and needs help. Ani, will you come with me? She needs to get dressed and doesn't want me to see her naked."

"Yup." Ani slid a look toward the other man, their eye contact lingering, communicating something I wasn't sure of. She turned to me with a smile that almost seemed brittle. "We'll be back in a little bit, Nina."

"Sure," I said. "I'll be here."

She winked. Then she glanced at the man one more time and made a face that didn't put me at ease.

He glared at her right back, taking a long pull of his beer before Ani and Randall left, turning right to go out the back, the door slamming shut behind them.

I managed to take one single sip of the nearly frozen bottle before an unfamiliar voice asked, "What the fuck are you?"

I almost wanted to snicker at the predictability. People, people, people.

Instead of answering him or wasting my time giving him any attention, I took another sip that I didn't enjoy half as much as I should have.

Unfortunately for me, he didn't take the hint.

"Did you hear what I asked?" the blond man tried one more time.

I thought about ignoring him some more, but my gut said

that wasn't going to have the effect I wanted it to. So, without looking at him, I replied, "I heard you."

"So?" he asked in one of the most annoyingly entitled tones I'd ever heard in my life. One of those voices that had the ability to instantly get under my skin by how demanding it was. There was bossy and then there was passive-aggressive.

I wanted people to like me. I wanted to fit in. But at what cost?

Since we'd gotten here, no one had asked me what I was—other than the kids—and no one had visibly shunned me. It had been nice.

But this was the exact reaction I'd been dreading when we got here.

And he wasn't going to drop it.

"You listening? I have a right to know," the werewolf claimed.

He had a point, to an extent, but I still wasn't ready to answer his question, regardless of how much he believed he wanted to know the truth.

He didn't.

He just didn't know that yet.

And that realization was what I was trying to avoid.

Which meant I had to put my polite face on while I said, "I'm not anything you need to worry about," even though he was being so rude. Plus, my bracelet was on, it wasn't like he could smell me in the first place.

"That doesn't answer my question."

I bit the inside of my cheek and tried to hold on to my patience. Tried to hold on to my understanding. "It doesn't, but what you're asking is personal and rude," I told him, trying my hardest to be polite. I even looked at my instant serotonin boost—Duncan—lying there, sleeping, to remind myself why we had to make this place work.

It helped, but not enough.

Especially not when the man scoffed.

I took another sip of my beer and tried again, for Duncan. "Look, your elders said I didn't have to share that information with anyone, and I hope you can respect my wishes." See how nice I could be?

Not nice enough though.

"If you have nothing to hide, then why can't you tell anybody?"

I focused on the bottle in my hand, trying not to let frustration get the best of me. I didn't like being ambushed. Confrontation wasn't my thing either, at least not when I was having a perfectly good day. It was one thing for Spencer to call me something that hurt my feelings, and it was another to deal with someone annoying . . . very annoying.

"Folks hide things when they have a reason to," the blond kept on.

I should've seen that coming.

He wasn't wrong. At the same time, I thought about the elder with the bracelet that I knew I hadn't imagined. Did he give Franklin shit about it? I doubted it. But just thinking about the elder rekindled my curiosity about his magical nature. "I understand why you think you should know," I tried to reason. "I'm not like you. I'm not going to pretend like I am, but I hope you understand that you can trust me. I'm here for the same reason everyone else is. I just want to raise my boy in a nice, quiet community where he can be safe."

The man's expression went dark, *and I did not like that*. "I don't know you. I don't need to trust you," he just about spit.

My magic fluttered in my chest. "No offense, but I don't know you either, and I have no reason to trust you. And what you're doing is the same as me asking how big your balls are, the only difference is that I don't care because I don't want to see them, the same way my ancestry doesn't affect you either," I replied, clenching my teeth almost the whole time.

The man's ears started turning pink. "You're going to have to marry one of us. Whoever it is, is gonna have to know."

"He will, sure, but not everyone else needs to, and that includes you."

His eyes went squinty, his mouth almost pouty, and it sure seemed like he gritted his teeth.

If he thought I was going to cower, he was out of freaking luck. Was this what Phoebe had meant about being nervous around werewolves? If some of them acted like this, it was no wonder. This guy wasn't just being pushy, he was being a dick.

And I really didn't like bullies.

The man leaned over, elbows going to his knees, his whole face, his energy, so aggressive. "You don't get to tell me what I should know and what I shouldn't."

I wasn't going to win this argument. I knew it. I couldn't. Not when this MFer was this hardheaded.

Butttt I needed to play nice. I didn't want an enemy, no matter how rude he was. *This is for Duncan.* Who had just had the time of his life. Who was thriving here. Who needed this place.

When people said being a parent was hard, they never brought up the little things like having to be the better person. Marrying a stranger was nothing compared to having to suck crap up.

Forcing my best impression of Henri's neutral face, I focused all my attention on the blond. I knew I'd seen him somewhere. He was handsome in his way. He was fit, had more facial hair than Henri, but there was a mean glint in his eye that was very, very obvious.

There was no hiding it: he was definitely an asshole.

"What's your name?" I had to ask.

"Dominic."

I wasn't sure I managed not to flinch. *That's why he looked familiar.* It was the same man from the diner. The thorn in Henri's ass . . . paw. No wonder. I didn't even need to know his name to not like him on principle.

Phoebe's reaction to him explained a lot.

If he could get under Henri's skin, no wonder he could do it to other people.

"So?" the guy who had punched Henri weeks and weeks ago asked, crossing his arms over his chest. "They say you smell sweet. You a gingerbread woman or something?"

I deserved a medal for not rolling my eyes. "No, I'm not a

gingerbread woman." Was he going to ask me if Pinocchio was real next?

I swear I could feel the condescension radiating off him.

"You a bogeyman?" *Dominic* goaded after a minute, with a nasty little sneer. "'Cause that's what everyone thinks."

He was mocking me, saying "bogeyman" like he was convinced there was no way that was possible. I wasn't sure I'd ever wanted to smile smugly so bad ever before in my life. But I didn't. Instead, all I said was, "I'm too old to care what anyone thinks."

His sneer became even worse. "Henri had us running around like dumbasses looking for that river monster, and you conveniently show up the same day. Nobody knows anything about you, and they're letting you move in? How does that make any damn sense? You're going to be helping raise our kids. How do we know it isn't them that need protection from you?"

I wasn't about to let *anyone* make me do something I didn't want to, especially not this asshole.

Not like this.

As much as I might want him to tolerate me and might want everyone else here to do the same, I wasn't going to bend over backward to get that to happen. I decided that right then.

I would do anything for Duncan, but I wasn't going to let some dickhead be rude to me for no reason.

I looked him dead in the eye and blurted out one of the last things I probably should have said, "I'd never do anything to the kids. But people who hurt them? Who hurt me? I can't say the same for them."

If his face had been pink before, it was bordering on coral by the time I finished talking. "You threatening me?"

"I'm not threatening you. I'm telling you." There was a big, big difference.

And I should've shut up or walked out of the room when he'd started, I knew that then, but it was too late, so now I had to ride this out.

Across the room, he rose out of his seat. Six four to my five six, I guessed. He had to have at least fifty pounds on me.

"That sounded like a threat to me," he argued as he stopped a couple feet away from where I was standing.

Maybe it was, but he needed to get out of my face. "I don't need to threaten anyone."

He took another step, and there was no way I was going to be breaking eye contact now.

I knew I was daring him. He was an agitated werewolf with an attitude problem. For most people, this whole situation would be a terrible idea.

But if he was this pushy and rude with me, how would he be with other people? Did he try and bulldoze them too? Something told me this wasn't anything new. He was too good at it.

Dominic took *another* step closer. "Do you know who the fuck you're talking to?"

I had my head tipped back to keep making eye contact. Anger pulsed deep in my stomach, and my magic flared again in me, reminding me of the part of it that was always there. *You don't need to take this shit*, Matti would have told me.

There was nothing I needed to prove. Not to anyone. Especially not to him.

But despite knowing all that, I couldn't help myself. I couldn't turn off how much I disliked a bully.

And I dropped my voice to say, "The problem here is that *you* don't know who you're talking to, precious."

Something funny crossed his face as he stared down at me. I'd surprised him. Shocked him, maybe.

"What's going on?" Henri's voice cut through the room like a battle-ax.

I *almost* stepped back, but I refused to risk having Dominic think I was doing it because of him. In front of me, his forehead furrowed. He was still angry, but there was something else there too in his eyes. Something that hadn't been there before.

"Dom was trying to intimidate Nina," Pascal's dad answered from the back of the room.

When had he come back? How long had he been here? I hadn't noticed or heard him.

"And you're just standing there?" Henri shot back as he stormed into the room.

"She didn't need my help," the dad countered as a familiar body got right in front of me, so close I had to shuffle backward to give him room.

But he wasn't listening anymore. At least not to Pascal's dad.

His attention was on Dominic.

"What do you think you're doing?" Henri demanded, his voice flat and cool, and I leaned over, my cheek going to the side of his arm.

He was standing almost nose to nose with Dominic.

Henri was in his space, all in his face, a few inches taller, his build bulkier, Henri's expression even fiercer than the one he'd had when he'd dealt with Spencer the day he'd been a jerk.

He was *pissed*.

I might even use the word *infuriated* to describe him at that moment.

But as much as I would've been willing to pay for a front row seat to Henri going big and bad on someone—because I knew, *I knew* he had it in him, that quiet intensity wasn't fooling me—this wasn't what I wanted. I'd been trying to stand up for myself and all the other small potatoes that this asshole intimidated. Fluff had enough reasons to dislike and argue with this jerk. I didn't need to add on to it more than I wanted to avoid being a pushover.

More than anything, I didn't need to be one more person who made Henri's life harder. I refused to be that kind of friend unless I had to, and in this case? It wasn't worth it. Dominic wasn't worth it. Maybe I'd given Dominic something to think about, and maybe I hadn't, but it didn't matter anymore. I set my hand on the carved biceps beside my face, and whispered, "I'm okay, Henri. He doesn't know I'm not the little pig in this story."

At my words, his head turned. Those clear eyes met mine, and I saw the strain on his face. The *anger*. It wasn't just him being mad or annoyed; he was dang near furious.

That couldn't mean anything good.

I had done this, and I needed to fix it. So I did the first thing I could think of when he leveled me with his attention: I oinked at him. Then I squeezed his arm.

Fluff blinked.

"He hasn't heard the myth of Big Jaws," I whispered, still trying to deescalate the situation.

His blink was even slower the second time, and just as I was about to try and come up with another comment to distract him, Henri grumbled in a voice so low I felt it along my spine. "Get the fuck out of here, Dom."

"I didn't do anything," Dominic started to argue before Henri snarled, his head whipping around to face the other man.

The sound made my hands tingle, and not in a bad way. There was something wrong with me. I leaned around Henri's arm to peer up at him.

"You and I are going to talk about what you have and haven't done," Henri murmured in that deadly tone.

"She's fine," the asshole replied. "She was talking shit back. She wasn't scared."

Henri's face darkened, and I was pretty sure his pupils went wide like a great white shark. "You're goddamn right she wasn't. If she had been, this would've gone down a whole lot differently." He sounded even scarier, all flat and emotionless.

And here I'd thought him controlling his facial features so well was impressive. He was even better at being intimidating at a low volume. I had to fight the urge to tug my collar away from my neck.

My newest protector leaned forward so he was nose to nose with the other man again. "Go home before I change my fucking mind about letting you leave."

Since I wasn't looking at Dominic, I didn't see if he made a face as he left. From the sound of his footsteps, he was pissed, but screw that guy. The second I stopped sensing his magic, I finally took a step back, only to find Pascal's dad had moved closer to us.

Just how much had he overheard? Did he hear me threaten Dominic?

I opened my mouth to apologize, but a small, very careful smile crept over his face when we made eye contact.

I closed it.

That careful smile turned into a full-blown one. Was there a tear in his eye? "That was pretty badass how you stood up to him."

Who were these people?

It took me a second to get my reply together. "Thank you . . .?" My face felt hot.

"You ever thought about a career in—"

Henri's hand rose between us, and he pointed at Pascal's dad, his "No" sharp. The other man rolled his eyes but held up both hands.

Henri eyed him for a second before dropping it, the lines at his throat flexing. "Help me put the pups up, would you?" he asked, his tone still all grumbly but not anywhere near as intense as it'd been when he'd been dealing with Dominic.

I wasn't sure who he was talking to, but Pascal's dad and I both moved toward the puppies.

But halfway to Duncan, I happened to notice Agnes's eyes were open. She closed them the second I busted her. I wished she hadn't heard all that. I didn't want to be a bad example.

The one small blessing was that Duncan, at least, had slept through everything, which was a surprise since he was usually so in tune with me. When he wasn't exhausted, that was. Pascal's dad collected his son, Henri hoisted a fake-sleeping Agnes over his shoulder, and I carried my donut. Pascal Senior went out the back door, but Henri and I went the other way; the silence not stifling, but it left a little knot in my stomach.

I hoped he wasn't mad at me.

While Henri headed to her room, I took the stairs with the small body that was getting heavier by the day.

I cuddled my boy, my thoughts drifting back to the asshole wolf who liked to pick on people smaller than him.

If only he knew . . .

Back in our room, I set Duncan on the foot of the bed and covered him with his blanket. Then I took my phone and snapped a picture. I was in the middle of texting it to Sienna when a knock came at the door.

I sighed.

"Why are you sighing?" Henri's voice came through the other side, reminding me yet again that there was no hiding anything living here, much less from him.

Nothing in this world could have prepared me for Henri Blackrock becoming the nosiest person in my life.

And he was right there when I opened the door, arms crossed over his chest, looking like . . .

He raised his eyebrows, asking me again with them what I was sighing over.

My shoulders dropped. "I was expecting you to give me a hard time for what I did," I answered.

His eyebrows went up a little more. "Why would I do that?"

I shrugged.

"Knowing Dom, he asked for it." Henri tipped his head to the side, showing off that strong jaw. "I'm glad you didn't back down."

"You are?" I squinted. "Why?" This sounded too good to be true, or maybe I was that paranoid.

"Because now everyone is going to know the truth."

"That I'm stubborn sometimes?"

The muscles at his cheeks tightened. "That you shouldn't be fucked with," he explained.

That wasn't what I'd been expecting him to say. Not today, not tomorrow, not in a million years.

"We admire strength." He nodded to himself. "Good for you."

I didn't say anything. I was too surprised by his support, even though it made sense. He was right, werewolves took strength as a gift, though they accepted those weaker as well. It had been easier before, when I'd been a kid. The rules back then had been totally different though. Children were cherished and protected, above all else.

Now? I had no idea where I was, and at this point, there were still a couple of things I wanted to keep a secret . . . which was why Henri had put himself between us.

He'd been trying to protect me again.

I lifted my chin. "Thank you for standing up for me against that . . . person." More like a moron, but I was trying to be diplomatic because of ears.

The man I liked to think of as my friend looked at me. Really looked at me. It was a long, serious inspection that made me want to squirm because I couldn't tell what was going through his head despite the fact he had just said what I had done was a good thing. His forehead scrunched and his voice was low. "I used to wonder what you were going to be when you grew up."

He had?

He drew his palm down his mouth. "How old were you when your magic finally kicked in?" he asked.

Here I was, feeling shy all over again. "Sixteen."

That seemed to surprise him as much as it had me when it had finally happened. I'd started to think it never would, that maybe that "different thing" everyone else had always brought up with my scent was a fluke. I had assumed I was half human, and because of that, I'd kept my expectations low. That maybe that was why I'd been given up to a magical couple.

Mythical beings didn't have kids with humans because there would have been no hiding what they inherited and would eventually become.

As for children of other magical beings who could pass for human, there wasn't a whole lot on them. Most of the stories I could find of demigod kids in mythology didn't have happy endings. For all I knew, maybe nothing about them changed either. Maybe for some of them, depending on who their parents were, they never even realized there was something different about them.

Then it had happened.

My parents had burst into my room in the middle of the night, the moon bright and full in the sky, because they'd smelled something different in the house. Something that shouldn't have been there. That had never been there before.

I wasn't sure who'd been more shocked to find that the only thing that had changed was me.

One moment, I'd been awake, the same as I'd always been. Then I'd fallen asleep, and when I was woken up, there had been this feeling in my body that hadn't existed before. This thing that felt like a very calm butterfly in my stomach.

It hadn't left me since. It had gotten easier to ignore, or maybe to live with . . . as much as I could. When we'd learned just what my magic meant, I'd had to accept real quick that while I could pretend it wasn't there, I had to keep control of it at all times.

Fortunately for me, I didn't have a temper; the most I did was talk a whole lot of crap when I was mad. I never really wished ill on anybody, and I was definitely a lover more than I would ever be a fighter.

At least until a loved one was endangered, then, even if I didn't have in me what I had, I would've found a way to torture someone.

"I'm not asking what your magic means, but I am asking how much control you have over it," he explained, probably seeing the borderline panic on my features. "You said something about the fertility aspect being involuntary. That's not all though, is it?"

I hesitated, but then I shook my head.

The fact he wasn't asking about my ancestry said he might have some vague suspicions. Or maybe he thought I was a chihuahua; I might not be the biggest or the baddest, but that wasn't going to stop me from going after your ankles and whatever else I could reach.

Henri didn't look concerned though.

But I was. Because I hadn't wanted to talk about this, and he might have a good feeling that there was something in me that was different from most other magical people. I could tell everyone here not to worry as much as I wanted, but he'd made it clear from the beginning that he protected the ranch's residents.

He wanted to know if my bite was as big as my bark or if I was just bluffing. So what was I supposed to say?

I couldn't lie.

So I fidgeted, and I shrugged. "It's more complicated than just having control over it, like how all you need to do is think you want to be a wolf and it happens. Right? Then how, when you want to be this version of Henri, you come back to it and your clothes are on. My body doesn't change. The fertility, I have no control over." That reminded me of the gnomes' comments. We could circle back to that. "The other parts of what I am? I do feel that in me, and I choose whether to let it... make my hands tickle or not." Did that make sense?

I wasn't sure it did. Not entirely, and he confirmed it when he murmured, "Your hands tickle?"

I nodded.

He wanted to ask. He wanted to know so bad, but I wasn't willing to tell him yet. We were on the right track to being friends, and I was sure he liked me. We'd spent too much time together to think otherwise.

I liked him. I wasn't going to deny that. But none of those feelings were enough to share the one small truth that could change everything—the other active part of the "gifts" I'd been given.

Henri rubbed a hand over the back of his neck, his face watchful. "Most people don't like Dominic. He's got a temper, and he's been used to getting what he wants by talking enough shit. Half the residents here avoid him. But there you were, squaring up to him like you knew there was nothing for you to be afraid of."

The smile I gave him was so freaking weak, and he knew it.

His nostrils flared, and he stared at me for so long I was sure he was about to lecture me on why *he* deserved to know what I was hiding. He didn't though. "You have nothing to prove here, Nina, no matter what anyone says." His jaw went tight before he lowered his voice. "Has Agnes said anything to you about her parents?"

"Nothing." I tugged at the collar of my orange T-shirt that said "OREGON" in block letters. "I've *wondered*, but I haven't brought it up. We're still working on our relationship."

"I should have said something about it to warn you."

Warn me?

"Dom is Agnes's dad." That sounded like it cost him to admit it. "It's complicated."

"The blond hair makes sense now, but . . ."

Somehow, his jaw went even tighter. "He and Agnes's mom weren't in a relationship when they had her. Her mom was young and couldn't raise her. She gave her to Dominic, who . . ." His palm came up and dragged over his mouth before he palmed his throat. "She's ours now," he summarized.

"He gave her up?" I whispered.

"We made him sign away his rights."

I took a step closer to him, lowering my voice even more. "Does she know?"

"She knows. She can smell it," he explained. "We've never kept it from her."

"I can't believe that dickhead is her dad," I told him even though . . . I kind of could. Maybe that's where she got her attitude from. But just as quickly as that thought entered my head, I realized it went deeper than that, maybe to an extent it was genetic, but I'd bet it had to be her reacting to her situation in the first place. Maybe.

What would it be like to see her father around, knowing he would rather she live in a clubhouse by herself than be with him?

Just when I thought I couldn't dislike that asshole any more, I proved myself wrong.

It was my turn to grit my teeth. "They don't spend time together? At all?"

"Other than pack runs and the twice a year he had to agree to spend some time with her—if she wants—no." Henri took the baton for teeth clenching again. "The only reason he goes on the runs is because he's part of the security for the ranch and it's mandatory."

"Doesn't he have other family here that could've taken her?" I thought about the blonde woman who worked at the diner.

Henri's face clouded over. "They declined."

Wincing, I wanted to give Agnes a hug so bad it made my

throat hurt. "Is that why he's such an asshole to you? Because you're more of a dad to her than he is?"

Henri's body straightened, and I watched his eyes bounce from one of mine to the other. His mouth went a little flat. "That's . . ." It looked like he poked at the inside of his cheek with his tongue. "That's not the whole reason why, but I'm sure it's part of it. He doesn't agree with a lot of our rules, and he thinks he can run the ranch better than we already do."

"So he's always been an asshole?" I muttered.

That got Henri's mouth to twitch at least. "Basically."

I smiled a little. "But where is Agnes's mom now?"

"She's not from around here. They met when she was visiting. She might be from Denver, I don't know." He didn't care, it didn't make a difference to him, was what he was implying.

I sighed. "Well, now I feel terrible for her, but that man . . ." Lifting my hand between us, I shook my fist so he could silently get my point.

He smirked again. "He doesn't deserve a conditioner bar."

"He deserves some spit in it, more like," I snickered.

The corner of his mouth hitched, but just as soon as he did it, the expression disappeared again. "Keep your eye on him. He's been all bark, and he's good security, but I've broken up him and Ani getting into it. You might not be scared, but I don't like the idea of somebody getting in your face."

"I'd be fine, Fluff," I tried to assure him, but he started shaking his head before I'd even finished my sentence.

"I don't want you getting hurt, and I don't mean just physically," Henri said, looking me right in the eye while he did.

I regretted going into that room with them tonight to begin with. All of this could have been avoided if I'd walked away when Dominic started his BS. If I'd been an even bigger person.

He was being really nice worrying about me.

"I understand. I'll try to keep my distance from him," I promised.

His features twisted. *He wanted to know what I was.* It was one thing not to fear him or Spencer at a distance. One thing to scare a swamp crone, but that moron had been in my face. I could've smelled his breath, and that hadn't been enough to get me to step away.

And that made me mad the more I thought about it because how many people had he intimidated before by doing the same crap he'd done to me?

Those bright orange-brown eyes moved over my face, his forehead furrowing all over again. "You make people fertile, but you also scare the shit out of beings four times bigger than you," he stated, walking the intrusive line perfectly.

A small part of me wished I could have denied it, but in for a penny, in for a pound. I shrugged to play it off. "Something like that?"

My answer rolled around in his head, and he plucked my words apart, trying to figure out how they fit together. How they could make sense. I couldn't tell him because I didn't know either.

"I don't want anyone to be scared of me," I admitted. I didn't want *him* to be scared of me, more like. Matti wasn't. Neither was Sienna. But they *knew* me.

Henri, though, didn't say he was scared. He didn't say he wasn't either. The only thing he did was keep watching me. His mouth formed a flat little line after a moment.

"Look." I hoped I didn't regret saying what was about to come out of my mouth. "Dominic can think whatever he wants. He can paint runes on his door to make himself feel better, but . . . I don't want *you* to be scared of me, Fluff. That's all."

The way his eyes widened, maybe I shouldn't have said that, but for some reason, admitting that to him felt kind of relieving.

I gave him a little smile. "But you probably aren't scared of a whole lot, huh?" The nerves were there, in my voice, in my skin, in my soul. "I guess there isn't a whole lot that could scare you or bully you. Agnes, maybe. The way she looks at me sometimes is intimidating. She's got her glare locked in."

Look at me trying to change the subject.

Fortunately, he either felt generous or the idea of him

being scared of me was so ridiculous he could move on from it that fast.

"I wasn't bullied when I was young. Now . . . ?" The corner of his mouth gave the world a faint half smile that I liked as much as I liked a full-blown one. "The pups make up for it."

I hoped the universe would bless him ten lifetimes for letting me move on from talking about myself. "I guess it's a good thing Duncan can't talk back yet."

Henri's eyes flicked around me to the side of the door, taking a peek at the puppy passed out on the bed. "He's a good pup."

"He is," I agreed. The best one.

He focused back on me, jaw tense. "I didn't want to bring it up in front of everyone, but the elders are going to want to talk to you about the gnomes' visit tonight."

Ah. That's why he was here. "Right." I stood up straight. "I was planning on talking to you about them, but then all that happened downstairs . . ."

"They say anything I need to know about?"

"They said so much stuff I didn't understand, Fluff," I trailed off, going through the list in my head. "It was two of them today, the oldest of their clan. They said that they were there to be around me?"

He raised his eyebrow that mini amount that was standard for him, and I nodded.

"I might be imagining it, but that sure sounded to me like they thought I could help them have kids or something. Then they brought up my father—my DNA dad, not my werewolf one—and how they thought he was dead but they were happy to hear that he isn't?" I rambled out in a single breath, feeling as overwhelmed as I had in the moment when the conversation had gone down. "I said that they probably had the wrong person, and they claimed that they didn't. That the person they're talking about is him."

I bit the inside of my cheek and threw out the last part. "Did you know that obsidian doesn't hide magic from them?"

That dark eyebrow went up another millimeter, and he must

have been used to dealing with people on the verge of hysteria because he didn't seem bothered by my rambling at all. "I didn't know that," was what he decided to respond with first.

I remembered something else. "They also mentioned that their 'brethren' in the south lived with my DNA mom at some point, and that's how I understand them. How does that work?"

"I don't know," he answered. "Gnomes have been said to have long memories. There's a lot we don't know about." He paused. "I met a man once who could do things to plants that you wouldn't believe. I've heard of other beings who could do things there aren't explanations for." He said that looking me right in the eye. "Do you remember the man who lived across the street from you? With the eye patch?"

"Oh yeah. I know who my parents thought he was."

Henri nodded slowly. "He's who they thought he was, Nina."

That's what I'd been afraid of. Not actually afraid, but . . . "You really think so?"

"I know he was."

So had I, but it had still been wishful thinking. If that man had done half of what stories said he had, no wonder he'd been feared and revered at the same time. A benevolent god, he was not known for being.

And how or why the man who had once been called Odin had ended up in a tiny town in New Mexico was something I would never understand either.

Henri had already moved on though. "The gnomes didn't say any names?" He almost sounded hopeful.

"No, but they called him the son of night." I shrugged.

Henri stayed quiet for a minute before saying, "The elders are going to ask about what you talked about. We'll have to tell them you saw them, but the rest can wait."

Was he telling me to lie?

He must have seen the question on my face because he added, "You know what? You told me about it. That's good enough. If you want to say something, I don't see how them wanting to be around you would change anything or give anything away."

I focused on his thick throat, covered in short, dark hair that needed a shaving before he went to work again. "I don't want to do something that ruins us being here," I admitted.

"It won't." He shook his head. "You're not lying about anything. I'm telling you it's fine; if they have a problem, they can talk to me. All right?"

My gaze slid up to meet his again, and I took in every bit of that ruggedly boned face that got better looking the more I saw it. "I don't want you to get in trouble either."

"I won't," he seemed to promise, his expression so serious. "And you don't need to put up with other people's shit. Nobody has a right to pressure you into telling them anything, even them, not if it isn't their business. You'll let me know next time there's a problem."

He wasn't asking me. He was telling me I would.

The urge to insist I could handle it was in my mouth, but his offer did something to the part of me that wanted him to like me, so I kept my mouth shut and asked, "You'll back me up?" Like I couldn't believe it.

Maybe because I couldn't.

That muscle in his cheek flexed, and those beautiful irises burned straight through my flesh and into me. "I will," he confirmed.

I took his offer to heart and nodded.

And then he said the words that were going to get stuck on a loop in my head for probably the rest of my life. "I don't need to know what you are, because I'm seeing it, and I'm not worried about you, Cricket." The chest that had stood as a barrier between me and that asshole minutes ago, rose and fell. "There's nothing scary about you at all," Henri Blackrock claimed. "Got it?"

Chapter Fourteen

I had an idea something was going on when I dropped Duncan and Agnes off at the nursery and caught Pascal waving at me shyly.

From what I'd learned about him in the time we'd spent together, the shy bones in his body were the size of the tiny ones found in people's ears . . . if he had any to begin with. I didn't count how quiet he'd been around Matti the day of the Jenny Greenteeth incident because I had a feeling that had been more shock than shyness that had stolen his talkativeness.

I didn't put too much thought into his wave though. There were other things on my mind. Things like my biological parents, the gnomes and their mysterious desires, Henri, Duncan, and that asshole Dominic. Agnes too. And I'd needed to start my shift right afterward.

That afternoon, after working in the room where all the action had gone down the night before, I'd realized without a doubt that something was definitely up when I made my rounds to the nursery. Because when I got to the little window of the door, every single puppy had been sitting properly, some on their hind legs and some on their human butts with their legs crossed in front of them.

But they were *all* facing the door. Each and every one of them. Little ears pinned back and down. Eyes bright.

I'd never seen *all* the kids on their best behavior at the same time.

Standing there with her arms crossed was Maggie, their teacher. She waved me in like she'd been expecting me.

I opened the door like I was going to the principal's office, and every puppy tail started wagging. The blackest one of them all was the fastest, and I couldn't help but blow a kiss at Duncan first before saying, very slowly and cautiously, "Hi? Is everything okay?"

Every pitch of "awoo," from small squeaky ones to some much deeper, answered me, and it made me grin. I wish I could've saved it as my ringtone. It was so cute.

"Everything is fine," Maggie answered. She was tall, around six feet, her build reminded me of a pin-up model, and I wondered again what kind of magical being she was. Then I asked myself why such a nice person could be on Spencer's radar. That was another question on my list for Henri. "I made a deal with your fan club, and I promised to hold up my end of the bargain if they held up theirs."

I scratched my cheek, not sure what half of that meant. "All right . . . what's going on?" Had she said "fan club"? The tails in the room wagged even faster.

It was sweet Shiloh, still one of my favorite of all the kids because he was the kindest and most patient one, who spoke up. "We heard."

He was in his human form today in shorts and a T-shirt for a popular kids' video game. I could see the signs of his pretty, graceful mom in him when he was like this. He didn't know it, but the thank-you card he'd made me for "saving his life" was on my nightstand. Phoebe had delivered it the day after we'd spoken at the diner.

I crossed my arms over my chest and hoped I didn't regret the next question out of my mouth. "What did you hear about?"

"Love!" Duncan sent me, kind of surprising the hell out of me with the potency behind it. When had he learned how to do that? He'd started projecting louder and more clearly but not like that.

"About . . ." Shiloh's big brown eyes widened in a way that seemed like he wanted me to guess.

"The gnomes?" I tried.

Pascal, who was beside my sweet buddy, made a farting sound. "No! You stood up to Dom!" he shouted, throwing his fist in the air like it was a battle cry.

"Yeah!" what sounded like a dozen different voices agreed.

"No yelling," Maggie shushed them.

I just looked at them. "I stood up to Dom?" How did they know about that? How did *he* know about that? He'd been asleep.

Hadn't he?

"Yeah! Everybody is scared of Dom," Pascal answered at a normal volume with a nod like it was a fact.

"Nuh-uh, not my dad," a boy around five added, one of the ogre children.

"Franklin's not," someone threw in.

"Not Henri," another of the younger boys argued.

Pascal nodded so enthusiastically, I couldn't believe how or why any of them could be so excited about me standing up to someone. Was Dom really that much of a jerk? Could his personality be so infamous that they were celebrating me talking back to him?

A terrible thought came to me. *Had that MFer been mean to my little friends?*

"How did you do it?" an older boy in the back shouted before wincing. "Sorry, I'm not yelling, Miss Maggie."

"Thank you for apologizing, Jurgis." Maggie's expression toward me seemed apologetic. "I only promised them that they could ask you what they wanted but you were under no obligation to answer anything. It's all they've been able to talk about all day."

"My dad said Dom was so mad . . . and my dad was a Navy SEAL, and he's more tough than almost anybody, and he doesn't like him . . . and Dad said you didn't do *anything* when he got in your face," Pascal spit one word out after another, rapid-fire, his face so wide and innocent and excited. "You didn't move. You didn't blink. Nothing."

I smiled, and then I smiled even wider. Because when you put it that way . . .

"How?" the little boy asked. "Why aren't you scared of

anybody? How can I not be scared of anybody? Because my mom scares me a lot. She scares my dad too." He didn't mention the river crone, and I had a feeling that was on purpose.

I laughed. This was exactly why I loved coming in here after work. The kids said the craziest stuff. "I'm a little scared of your mom too, Pascal. I'm scared of some things but not a lot of them."

Definitely not people like Dom.

A couple of kids yelled, "Like what?"

Now that they asked, I couldn't think of a single thing that would be relevant to them.

I made a face. I didn't kill spiders, the dark was pretty much my friend, heights were fine. They wouldn't get my joke about taxes and credit ratings. Why couldn't anything come to mind?

"See!" Pascal shouted, laughing like a maniac. "See!"

I swear, there was something wrong with werewolf children. They were insane. The older ones were nuts, but the younger ones were even worse. No wonder I had loved Matti so much.

I missed him. He had planned on coming to visit, but he'd had contracts come in that were good business, and we were postponing our reunion. It wasn't the first time it had happened, and I was glad he was making money.

"Listen, I am scared of things, I just can't think of anything right now. And there's nothing wrong with being scared. But why are you scared of Dom?" I asked, trying to keep my tone light and not like I might have to escalate what had happened last night depending on his answer.

"Because he's mean!" someone in the back shouted.

I tried my best not to react, but . . . "So mean!" someone else said. "He broke my bat!"

"He told me I was annoying!" another child added.

Who in the world could be mean to these little sweethearts?

I was going to have to put water in someone's gas tank.

Pascal started scooting over. "Do you," he dropped his voice to the barest whisper in the middle of scooching even closer, "have superpowers?"

I leaned forward and wrapped my arms around the small, big-mouth wolf with the crazy imagination. And the small, big-mouth wolf hesitated zero seconds before wrapping his scrawny arms around me.

He whispered, *again*, "Do you?"

So I whispered back, "No, but I wish I did."

His body sagged, and I had to fight not to laugh.

"I'm sorry."

He hugged me tighter. "It's okay."

A damp nose nudged the side of my head, and I lifted it to find Duncan there. He put a paw on my knee. Was he jealous? I released one arm from around Pascal and wrapped it around my own pup, bringing him in close.

And before I knew it, there were multiple puppies surrounding me, and I somehow gave them all hugs—minus Agnes, who stayed back, but I made sure to make eye contact with her and smile.

I hadn't even thought about how this conversation might affect her. Dang it. I'd make it up to her. It was my goal to bring her along to do more things with us. I wasn't going to let her continued wariness stop me.

For the time being, I hugged and I cuddled, and then there were a few more children and pups that came in for thirds and fourths, and who was I to say no?

The entire time, Duncan sat halfway on my lap, possessive but not demanding and licking the occasional friend when they wandered over.

Maybe I didn't need everyone to like me. Maybe I just needed a few who really mattered. That was something to think about.

"This is the life, Dunky," I sighed with pleasure later that night.

A piece of jerky was hanging out of Duncan's mouth when he turned toward me. *"Yes,"* he agreed, his mouth shaped the way that made it look like he was smiling. *"Love."*

I held back a sigh at the familiar but different face sitting across the bed from me. His ears were longer, his jaw a little wider. And there was no denying the fact he was taller and his ribs were thicker. Even his flame was bigger.

Growth was a good thing, I reminded myself, taking in the boy who had been the center of my life for the last two years.

And today had been a great day. A part of me was still riding high from the scene in the nursery earlier, getting more hugs in the matter of an hour than I'd probably gotten in an entire year at some points in my life. The kids were the best, and I wanted to thank all of their parents for raising them to be so great.

Now, with my favorite kid of them all, it had turned into an even better day, I thought, as I wiggled under the covers even deeper, snuggled up all nice and comfy with him beside me, tucked up against my legs as we watched a movie about an accountant who wasn't really an accountant.

I scratched his butt with one hand and angled the pillows behind my back and head better so I could be propped up higher.

"I was thinking we should make some chicken jerky this weekend. What do you think?" I asked, reaching for the bag of jerky on my lap and taking a piece out. To my side, there was a plate of apple slices and sweet potato chips made with coconut oil. Dunky's favorite snacks.

"Yes," he answered immediately, back to gnawing on his jerky.

I dropped my voice. "Is it okay if we give Agnes some?"

"Yes," Duncan replied without breaking his focus on the TV.

Love bloomed even brighter in my chest. "You're a good boy, you know that?"

His head turned toward the door a moment before there was a knock.

"Henri?" I called out, finally sensing the strong presence of his magic. It was different from everyone else's, big and bright, wild and solid at the same time. Just like him, in a way.

The door cracked, then went wider as the man I'd expected it to be appeared in the doorway. It was clear he'd showered from his glossy hair. His dark green pajama pants and white under shirt were a surprise though. I'd never seen him ready for bed so early.

"Hi, Fluff. I wasn't expecting visitors." I indicated down at the blanket tucked up under my armpits and the snacks scattered around my body, the beef jerky literally sitting on my chest.

From just inside the doorway, Henri nodded. "I can see that."

He looked tired; he sounded like it too. He hadn't been around for breakfast or dinner, and I'd thought he was supposed to have the day off.

I sat up a little. "Everything okay?"

His gaze moved around the room, landing on Duncan, the photographs of my parents, and us with Matti and Sienna on the nightstands, and then the toys piled on the dresser. Eventually those orange-brown eyes made their way back to me just as he cupped the back of his neck, hard muscles clinging to his thin white shirt in the process. I pretended not to notice that his nipples were hard. "I wanted to make sure you were all good after yesterday."

"Yeah, I'm fine, thank you." I watched him for a second, then contemplated for another second. "Do you want to watch this movie with us? It's only been on ten minutes." I gestured to my chest and to the plates. "We have snacks, and I washed the sheets today." I patted the bed beside me and smiled at him. "No funny business. Promise."

The faint smile that came over his mouth was one that touched my heart more than it had any business doing. Especially when he had the closest thing to dark circles around his eyes. How much sleep had he been getting lately?

"If you want," I offered. "No one will come looking for you here. We can wedge something under the door so no one can open it."

"They can still call," he let me know, touching his pocket where the unmistakable angles of a phone pressed against the cotton of his pants.

"*Yes*," Duncan said out of nowhere. It wasn't that I thought he was scared of Henri anymore, and I realized he liked him more than Agnes liked me at this point, but I hadn't noticed that he liked him *this much*, enough to invite him to hang out with us.

That's interesting.

"Even Duncan is inviting you," I translated for Henri, trying not to let the surprise show on my face. "No pressure though, Your Fluffy Highness."

I saw the moment he made a decision, and I shifted closer to Duncan as Henri came straight over on those long legs, pulling the comforter back like he'd done it a million times and climbing into bed.

Into my bed.

Not on top of the covers but *under*.

He took a second to adjust the pillows, propping them up so he had his back to the headboard like I did, but straighter, all while Duncan and I watched him without even trying to pretend like we weren't.

Part of me hadn't expected him to actually say yes, but I smiled when we made eye contact and held the bag with jerky out.

He reached in for a piece and took his time eating it, his eyes lighting up halfway. Those orangey-brown irises slid toward me.

I held out the bag again, and he took another two strips.

"Why's it so good?" he asked, after he'd finished one of his pieces.

"I don't add liquid smoke or sugar to it." I winked.

Gaze still locked on mine, he took another bite with those strong white teeth.

Setting the silicone bag between us, I faced the television again and knit my fingers together over my chest. Duncan glanced over twice, and I handed him another piece of jerky before he turned back to the television, holding the dehydrated meat between his paws.

Out of the corner of my eye, I saw Henri take an apple slice after a little bit. The sigh he let out was so deep it could have inflated a hot-air balloon. Poor Fluff.

No one said a word until two commercials later.

"You ever take that bracelet off?" he asked out of the blue.

I startled and touched one of the beads, like I didn't have them memorized. "Sometimes, but not that often."

His "hmm" caught me about as off guard as his, "You don't need to wear them around me, you know." There was a long pause. "It's only us in the clubhouse right now."

Hooking my finger beneath the band, I gave it a tug. But . . . I left it. "Thanks, Fluff. Maybe some other time."

His lips parted a little before his attention jerked toward the door at the exact time Duncan's did too. Except my donut's tail went up. He wagged.

"Yes," he called out telepathically at the same time Henri raised his voice, "Ladybug?"

Agnes?

There was a pause before the doorknob turned, and a small face appeared in the crack.

I kept my expression as even as I could despite the fact my heart felt funny at the remote expression on Agnes's features. She was so stoic for her age. Too stoic. "Come in, Mini Wolf," I called out, waving her in.

Her body language was all serious shyness as she shuffled inside, her eyes bouncing from Duncan to me to Henri.

Whether it was Henri that reached for my fingers over the covers or it was mine that went for his, the backs of them touched, and I didn't need Duncan's telepathy to know we were on the same page. We both recognized why she was here.

And we both wanted her to stay.

I should not like him this much. I knew it. It was a waste of time and energy, and I had too sensitive of a heart for it. But, in that moment, telling myself not to have feelings for him, to not admire the kind of man he was, seemed like the hardest thing I might have ever done. Like telling myself to write with my left hand for the rest of my life. Like putting on mascara without squinting to do it.

"What do you need?" Henri asked, his tone kind.

Dressed in lilac pajamas with teddy bears on them, she went

up to her tiptoes. "I was looking for you," she replied, her voice quiet and very unlike the side-eyeing child who tried to bite people she didn't trust.

"Does Sera know where you are?" he asked her.

She peeked up at us quickly before looking back down at the floor. "I told her I was going to the kitchen."

"We talked about you disappearing on them," he scolded her, already pulling his phone out with his free hand.

The one that wasn't still touching mine.

"I'm sorry," she said, not sounding that sorry at all . . . just hesitant.

"You're not in trouble, Ladybug, but you can't be doing that. It worries us if we don't know where you are at night." Henri unlocked his screen and pulled his messaging app up.

I knew because I was looking.

I cleared my throat and slid my gaze back to her before I got busted. "Mini Wolf, do you want to hang out with us?"

I tried not to smile as I patted the space to my right. "There's a perfect, Agnes-sized area right here." The movie was going to be gory, but I'd overheard kids younger than her in the nursery talking about what kind of video games they played, and they were not PG.

"*Yes*," my donut agreed, his tail still wagging at the sight of his friend.

"Duncan said you should," I translated.

An adult would have played hard to get. The child that she was, didn't. She nodded instantly and made her way over to the side of the bed where Duncan was. Agnes petted him, giving him a kiss between those incredible ears, and with a careful avoidance of meeting anyone else's eyes, she climbed up onto the spot I'd pointed out. I set the apple plate between us since I knew she was the only one who didn't care for jerky much.

At least my jerky.

Pretending like I didn't see her going for the fruit all sneaky-like a second later, I put my hands on my lap.

But I almost flinched when a fingertip grazed my cheek.

I turned my head to the man beside me, trying so hard not to seem shocked by his touch. *Please, body, don't do anything embarrassing.*

He wasn't helping.

Henri's thumb slid across my jawbone.

Thank you, he mouthed, flicking my earlobe with a rough thumb.

I didn't dare freaking breathe.

And I was super grateful for it when he leaned over and pressed his mouth to my temple for all of point two seconds before pulling back.

I didn't want to know what my face looked like in that moment.

While I was reeling over the fact that his mouth had *touched my face*, he said in a very low voice, "After high school and that year I lived in New Mexico, I moved up to Montrose to get my bachelor's, spent two years working for the police force there afterward, and that's when Matti's mom died." He paused, the silence so loud while his throat bobbed. "I didn't know what to do, so I got Matti, and we moved here. I took a job with the county, finally took over my responsibilities, and I've been here ever since."

He was finally answering my question from the car ride after the diner. Wow. Wow. Wow. "Thank you for telling me that, Fluff. I always wondered," I admitted, trying my hardest not to make a big deal over him sharing personal information.

His head rolled to the side so he could look at me. "You really didn't know?"

"No, Matti almost never talks about anything family-related anymore." I paused. "He never talked much about your side of the family to begin with."

He frowned. "Not his mom or dad?"

I shook my head. "I can count on one hand the number of times he has in ten years."

"*Matti?*"

"Big-mouth Matti, yes," I confirmed, since he knew the magnitude of that behavior from his cousin.

His frown got deeper, his expression going thoughtful. "I'm not surprised he wouldn't talk about me—"

"Why's that?"

"Because . . ." He suddenly looked a little uncomfortable.

"Because?" I whispered.

Henri wiped a hand down his mouth, and I almost expected him not to answer, but he did what I'd forgotten was a part of him—tell the truth. "I did a shit job watching over him back then. I didn't know what I was doing. When I was grieving—"

When had he grieved? Who had he grieved?

"—I wanted to be left alone, so that's what I gave him. It wasn't until after he left that I thought that might've been the opposite of what he needed from me."

"He's never said a single bad word about you to me or Sienna," I told him. "He loves you. I'm sure he appreciates what you did. It was a s-h-i-t-t-y situation."

One of those brawny shoulders went up and down. "He wasn't happy here. He left as soon as he could."

"That had nothing to do with you," I tried to explain. "He loved his parents, Fluff. His life changed overnight. That was all. I don't think there's anything anyone can do for someone else's broken heart." I winced. "If it makes you feel any better, he's a city boy. He told me he can't live without food delivery and two-day shipping. *He has a white couch.*"

He rolled onto his side. "A white couch?" he repeated in disbelief.

I nodded. "The interior of his car is white too, if you can believe it."

He grimaced. "He doesn't get it dirty?"

"I found a steam cleaner in their closet."

A huff left his mouth, but the corner of it tipped up right after. "He's such a little fucker, still. My first grays came in when he started living with me."

I reached over and touched the side of his temple where a couple of silvery strands were mixed into the blacks of his hair. I'd never really noticed them before, but he also just didn't have that many of them. But I couldn't let this opportunity go. "Was it these . . . ?"

The way he narrowed his eyes told me exactly who Agnes had learned her expressions from. "I bet I have a few on the other side from you talking shit to Spencer and having a tree thrown at you."

We were joking then? "Sorry?" I tried to give him an apologetic look.

"The only thing you're sorry about is being mean to him."

I couldn't argue that.

And if I thought it was adorable he knew me well enough to recognize that . . . I guess there were worse things in the world I could think were cute.

Chapter Fifteen

I was going to blame Sienna for why I was so distracted a few nights later.

Sienna: You met any cute guys yet?
Sienna: Any future Mr. Popoca's?

I had not, in fact, met a single cute guy at the ranch . . . not any that counted. I wouldn't refer to Henri as a mere "guy," and my feelings toward Randall unfortunately didn't run in that direction at all. None of the dads I'd met at the nursery made the list either—they were all mated.

So, I hadn't needed to type more than two letters back at her.

Me: No
Sienna: What are you waiting for then?

And it was that question I had on my mind when a short whistle had me spinning around on our way to dinner.

What *was* I waiting for?

I didn't have any more time to think about it though when I found Henri coming down the stairs, looking fresh out of the shower in dark jeans and a long-sleeved T-shirt that said "Lobo Springs" on it. The man, who had stayed and watched not one but two movies with us the other night, looked great.

Like always.

Lifting my chin, I gave him a smile. "Hi, Fluff. Just got off work?"

"Hey." He nodded before glancing down and smiling a little. "Hi, Duncan."

The tip of my donut's tail twitched.

"Just got home a few minutes ago," he explained warily, telling me everything I needed to know about how his shift had gone. "Where are you going?"

I hooked my thumb down the hall. "I was going to fix something for dinner."

"I was headed that way too," he said, brushing my shoulder.

I guess we were going together, I thought, as we headed in the direction of the kitchen.

"Agnes is eating dinner with Ema and her family tonight," he told me, his nostrils suddenly widening, a frown coming over his face as he seemed to smell . . . something.

Ema was one of the elders, I remembered. Silver-Blue Hair lady.

I slowed down right when we were beside the door to Franklin's bedroom. Were those voices coming from the kitchen or was I imagining it? *No*, I could sense a concentration of magic coming from across the house.

Werewolves, a lot of them, if I was right.

I peeked at Henri to see what he thought, but his expression was more confused than concerned, so it couldn't be anything or anyone bad. It was probably the elders. They hadn't approached me about the gnomes after all, and I'd kind of been waiting to get bombarded any time.

Which made me think about the other things I had been waiting around for.

I scratched behind my ear. "Do you know if Randall is eating dinner here tonight?"

He glanced down, his bone structure stunning in the overhead light. "Yeah. Why?"

"I wanted to talk to him about something."

People thought cats were curious. They had nothing on werewolves. "You can talk to me."

How could he make my life so complicated without even knowing it?

I peeked at him out of the corner of my eye . . . and he caught me, a suspicious expression already shaping his features. *There is nothing to feel guilty over.* "I was going to ask if he could help me meet potential mates here, since they're all lining up to get to know me." I snickered. "Get it? Since the only people I know are the kids and their parents?"

Henri literally slowed down. His eyebrows went up along his lightly lined forehead. He looked . . . he looked . . .

I squinted. "What?"

"You want to meet . . ." His cheek did that thing it did when it flexed. "Men?"

I might as well have named some demonic creature.

"Yeah?" I answered. Why did I want to start fidgeting? Why did I feel guilty? I wasn't doing anything wrong, and yet . . . "Sienna just got into my head, and it hit me that I'm kind of on a time crunch. It's been over a month since we got here, already. A year will go by like nothing. I need to find a way for us to stay. I know some people think we might flake, but we aren't, and if it takes me being the forward one, then"—I lifted my arms—"I'm game."

If I'd thought I had ever heard his voice come out funny before, it was nothing compared to how it sounded next. Like he'd sucked on something sour. "What does that mean?"

Had he said that awful slow too or was I imagining it?

And there went the guilt again. I didn't want to clarify. I also didn't want to look at him when I answered, so I focused on the wall ahead. "You know what that means."

"I don't," he argued.

How could I feel so uncomfortable so fast? I was doing what I had to. What their guidelines, or bylaws or whatever they were called, asked for. Was I being weird because I found Henri so attractive . . . and liked him more than a little . . . and *he* was the person I was asking for help?

Possibly. But . . . it had to be done.

It was one thing for me to recognize that Henri liked me as a friend and maybe didn't hate looking at me, but it was something else to expect him to *marry* me.

Especially after the way he'd reacted, literally not responding, when I'd told him what Matti had suggested.

There had been that peck on the temple the other night, but that had been it.

And if I thought that was a shame, then it was on me.

I shoved the urge to fidget as deep inside of me as I could. "*You know.* I need to put myself out there. Maybe I need to go buy a push-up bra or walk around in a bikini or . . . do something to stir up some interest." I dropped my voice and my shoulders. "I need to meet people."

My best friend's cousin stared down at me.

Was the vein by his temple throbbing or was it an optical illusion?

But really, what did he expect? I was the one on a schedule. I was the one riding a whole lot of hope into this whole ordeal. I meant what I said. This had to work, and I was going to do whatever was necessary to make it happen. I could put it off a little while, but the sooner I met someone, the sooner I could get to know them, that was a fact.

Why did I want to squirm justifying that?

Henri's jaw worked from side to side very subtly.

I blinked.

"Do *not* walk around in a bathing suit," he said through clenched teeth.

I couldn't help myself when his cheek muscle started throbbing. I'd used up all my self-restraint for the month on Dominic. "But go buy a push-up bra?"

Somehow he managed to clench his jaw even harder, so I poked him in the forearm.

"I'm kidding, Henri." I beamed at him. "I just won't wear one."

His eyes flicked up to the ceiling, and I laughed.

"I'm kidding!" I poked him again, because why not?

He scrubbed his hand down his face without lowering his chin. "You're not going to ask Randall how to meet potential partners then?" he asked in a voice I swore made him sound like he was being strangled.

"No, I'm not kidding about that. I was kidding about the bra and the bikini . . . and the braless thing. I want someone to like me for me, not because of my skin suit."

That got me his attention, narrowed eyes and all. "Skin suit?"

I nodded. My chest wasn't small enough or big enough to fall into a fetish category. "I know my strengths are my sense of humor, that I'm willing to have kids, and I like taking care of people." I ticked each off with my fingers.

The way those bright eyes trailed from my face, dipped to my collarbone area, and went back up made something funny happen to my chest. "You think those are your strengths?"

"I don't know how I feel about your tone of voice right now, Fluff," I deadpanned.

His hand started to rise toward his face again before he dropped it, but his flaring nostrils gave him away.

Someone was irritated.

"I gotta do what I gotta do." I tried to ignore the unsettled sensation in my stomach. I bent down and picked up Duncan, who had settled at our feet at some point, with a grunt. He was heavy. His red eyes were aimed at our werewolf neighbor. "C'mon, Dunky, we need to find you a stepdaddy," I mock-whispered.

The *"yes"* he sent me was strong and clear. At least we were on the same page. He really was my ride or die.

But a hand on my forearm stopped me before we got anywhere.

Henri's warm palm skimmed up my arm, stopping right below my elbow. His voice was low. "I get why you think you need to do something"—he squeezed the words through his teeth—"but there's no need to rush into anything. You've got time."

I was ready to argue, but his hand slid down to my wrist and back, and my brain kind of short-circuited while he did it. "I just . . ." *Get it together.* I tilted my head toward Duncan, who was watching us. "I want to stay, Fluff. The longer I have to get to know someone, the better, right?"

Those incredible eyes narrowed again, and that muscle in his cheek started popping all over again. "Listen to me."

He had a nice voice, and that wasn't a hardship, so I nodded up at him.

"No one is kicking you out of here," was his big speech.

"But—"

His hand gave me a light squeeze right before his thumb grazed the inside of my elbow where my veins were. "No one, Cricket," Henri insisted quietly. "You're going to be fine. Duncan is going to be fine. Wait your three months."

The urge to disagree was so strong. I got what he was saying, and I was grateful that he was reassuring me, but my plan made sense too. The fact was, time wasn't on my side, and I didn't want to wait around to get my life started.

But I felt so freaking guilty for some reason, like I was cheating on . . . someone . . . just thinking about dating faceless people.

Maybe I needed to get over this and get to a better mental state so I could meet someone and not compare them to . . . other people.

I was going to have to think about it some more. Another week or two of weighing pros and cons wouldn't kill me, I guessed. As long as another woman didn't show up wanting to marry in, that was. I could freak out then, if it happened.

I nodded and watched Henri dip his chin right back, like the matter was settled.

For now at least.

Turning back toward the kitchen, I asked over my shoulder, "You coming?"

"Against my better judgment," Henri muttered, following behind me so close, it was hard to ignore the heat from his body and the potency of the magic that radiated from him.

I *was* going to think about it, and if it came down to it, I'd ask Randall for his opinion.

Henri meant a lot to me. He was a tie to my past, to one of my favorite people in the whole world, and he was . . . a shield here, even if I thought I was almost bulletproof.

He was my friend.

My very attractive, very mature, caring, steady, and responsible *friend*.

And why that idea made my shoulders want to slump wasn't something I was going to pick at, I decided, as the voices coming from the kitchen got louder with every step.

I stopped walking and felt Henri's arm brush mine when he did the same. His expression was concerned. "What is it?"

"Why are there a bunch of people in the kitchen?"

His eyebrows drew together. "I've been wondering that."

"But you have an idea?"

He shrugged, but his face didn't come across all that casual.

I held Duncan a little tighter. "No one's here to try and tell me to leave, are they?"

His focus went over my head. "I doubt it."

Dang it.

Weight landed on the back of my neck, and Henri tipped his head close, so close I could see the dark ring between his pupil and much lighter iris. "What did I tell you already? I'm not going to let anyone mess with you. Either of you." The hand on my neck slid down to land between my shoulder blades. "Are we clear?"

I nodded.

"You haven't done anything wrong," he reminded me, apparently knowing I needed to hear that.

I nodded again, turning my attention back toward the kitchen doorway; the pressure on my shoulders got a little heavier.

"Nina, look at me."

I did.

Did he have to be this intensely good-looking? Some people won the genetic lottery, and Henri had somehow scored a record-breaking Powerball that I didn't exactly struggle to pay attention to.

"You haven't done anything wrong," he insisted, lowering his face just a little more.

I knew that, but did everyone else?

Henri looked at me for another minute before he blew out a

slow, minty breath and touched my forearm. "Let's see what's happening in there. Together."

When his hand didn't fall away, I let the presence of it soothe me as we made it to the kitchen. Duncan's nose started twitching, and I could hear him smelling the air. His tail went so, so still but the color didn't change.

There were men. A lot of them. A couple were seated at one of the islands, two more leaned against cabinets, and three were in the process of cooking, Randall being one of them. On second glance, I realized one of the two at the island was Dom.

And they were all focused in our direction.

I hadn't even realized I was backing up until I stepped on Henri's toes, and whispered, "Save the baby."

"What?" He got even closer to me. I could've sworn I felt his lip graze the shell.

"Take Duncan," I repeated, tilting my head to look at him.

I wasn't joking, but he must've thought I was when he got squinty. Before I could insist I was being serious, he eyed the room over my head, and then asked in a huskier voice than normal, "What's all this?"

A chorus of "hey" and "hello" answered us, but I didn't miss how some of the men stirred as they glanced between each other.

Did they seem uncomfortable all of a sudden or was it my imagination?

"We're here for dinner," a man with tan skin answered, smiling so wide and excessively welcoming, I scooched even closer to Henri, until I was basically tucking myself under his armpit.

A noise that sounded an awful lot like a growl vibrated through the chest beside my ear.

At the range, Randall held up his hands. "I told them to go home."

I should have been pleased that people—men—were finally being polite enough to come visit instead of being nonexistent before this, but I couldn't. No, sir, I could not. This was way too convenient.

Why now?

But if there were negative feelings in the room, Henri would've been able to sense them, and so would Duncan. My donut wasn't doing anything out of the ordinary, just resting in my arms, casually taking in the room. Nothing bad seemed to be setting his radar off.

And since they'd all been polite and greeted us . . . I lifted my hand. "Hi," I called out.

More "hi" and "hello"s echoed around the room in a range of deep voices, but it was Dominic who stood up and called out my name like we were old friends. "Nina?"

This asshole had been in my face not too long ago. He'd also punched Henri, the kids had nothing but terrible things to say about him, and he was basically not going to be on my Christmas list in this lifetime or the next. But I also didn't want to start crap, so I said, "Yes . . . ?"

"You and your answers that sound like questions . . ." Henri muttered under his breath. I would've glanced at him, but I had my eyes on our mutual enemy across the room. *Agnes's biological dad.*

"I've decided I like that you didn't back down from me," Dom proclaimed, smoothing his thumb and index finger along the sides of his mouth.

I stared at him. What did he want me to do? Thank him?

But then Dom said what really made me choke. What had Henri making a hoarse sound in his throat *and* palming my lower back. The man who had stood nose to nose with me nights ago—and not in a good way—said, "I'll mate with you."

"You all good?"

I didn't need my eyes to know it was Henri talking. I'd heard the front door open and close. Sensed the bright flame of his magic. On top of that, I'd caught Agnes's smile when she'd done all those things too.

So far, there was only one person worthy enough of that reaction from her, and I'd seen her get picked up by almost every parent with a child at the nursery. She didn't growl at them or anything, but there had definitely never been elation on her face. Not anything close to the kind of expressions she made for Henri every time she saw him.

Plus, there was no hiding the sound of his weight crunching over grass, pine needles, and tiny twigs . . . unless he'd wanted to. But Henri hadn't been attempting to be stealthy as he made his way to where the three of us were lying. We'd just finished our popsicles, and we were on our backs, staring at the stars, soaking up the sounds of all the life surrounding us. The magic in the air wasn't as strong as it could get, but it still felt like a gift to the senses.

It had been easy to cast aside the real-life TV show that had gone down in the kitchen hours ago.

It almost made me want to laugh, if I wasn't still in shock, which I figured was exactly what Henri was asking about.

"I'm all right," I answered him . . . and then I finally freaking broke. I propped my elbow under me to sit up and found him directly to my right. "*What was that in there?*" I gasped, cracking up.

A part of me expected him to smile, but he seemed about as amused as he'd been earlier, which wasn't amused at all. If anything, he was cranky, from the way his jaw was clenched and his eyebrows were all flat and sober. Even his reply bordered on monotone. "A bunch of fucking idiots being idiots."

He'd been quieter than normal during dinner. Twice, his phone had rung, and he'd peered at the screen with a scowl, then shoved it back into his pocket, which was something I'd never seen him do before. I'd heard all about him not answering Matti's calls and taking forever to text him back, but I figured it wasn't him because of the time of day. He usually only had time to talk around lunch time or midnight unless he was traveling.

Before that, Henri had stood in the kitchen after Dominic had made his unhinged declaration, which had surprised the hell out of me and made the men start talking over each other, and said in that commanding werewolf voice, "No."

No. That was all that came out of his mouth. *No.*

His palm had then cupped the back of my neck, and when none of the strangers moved an inch, he'd raised his voice, "Everyone other than Randall needs to go home."

I had stood there and taken in the tension in the room, those men I'd never seen before all exhaled deeply before, one after the other, they drifted out of the kitchen almost immediately. The only person who said anything else was Dominic, who on the way out, had one last thing to suggest, "Think about it," before he'd disappeared.

Fortunately, being raised around werewolves had taught me they were all nuts. Every single one of them. It didn't matter how reasonable or wonderful they were, or could be, they were, at their baser nature, nuts, and they followed their instincts more than anyone else I'd ever met. And once they got mad? Forget about reason.

And I needed to marry one of them. At least chances were, that's who it would be. I was fairly certain every man that had been in the kitchen tonight was some kind of wolf.

After they'd left, there had been an awkward tension in the room as we helped Randall cook. Only when we'd sat down did he tell Henri that he'd spoken to Franklin and that the elder was on his way home. All the while, I'd sat there, half listening and halfway trying to remember what the men who had come into the kitchen looked like.

As sneakily as I could, I'd taken my phone out and jotted down some notes while I was at it, feeling like I was doing something illegal.

I wasn't dumb. It hadn't taken me long to figure out why they had shown up. Did I know for sure? No. But I could put most of the puzzle pieces together, especially after Dominic's super-romantic offer.

Henri had said it best—werewolves admired strength.

And these crazy bastards *would* take me standing up for myself as an attractive trait.

I hadn't cowered in front of a member of their community who was known to be a pain in the ass, and they admired me for it. It was annoying, but also a little funny. Talking crap to a Jenny Greenteeth and Spencer hadn't been impressive enough, I guessed. That said a whole lot about Dominic though.

I snickered, casting a look at Duncan, who was on my left, his focus on the man on my right. His tail was down. I wasn't sure if Henri noticed that or not, but I did.

"I was so confused," I told Henri, shaking my head with disbelief.

He looked about as serious as a heart attack. All narrowed eyes, his mouth a hard line. "You understand why they were there?"

"Dominic offered to mate with me because I didn't pee my pants or back down when he got confrontational with me. Now, there's a bunch of werewolf men who show up for dinner? C'mon, Fluffy, I'm a werewolf in everything but magic and DNA." And the nuts part. I paused as I thought about it. "Unless I'm wrong, and I should go ahead and feel like the biggest dummy on the planet."

There was a short, steady hum in his throat. "You're not wrong."

Whew.

"I figured word would get around fast, but I didn't expect it to be that fast." That muscle in his cheek clearly popped over and over again, like it was spasming. "I bet it'll be worse tomorrow."

To an extent, I was horrified. Being the center of attention went against the way I'd been living my life since hitting puberty. Blending in had been my motto almost from the moment I'd learned how different I was from everyone around me—the magical and the non-magical. It was better to not bring too much attention to yourself, which came easily to me. I wasn't very tall or short, very thin or curvy. At a quick glance, no one would do a double take if I walked by.

But now these crazy asses were interested.

All I could do was laugh. This wasn't exactly what I'd wanted, but at the same time, it was exactly what I'd been ready to question Randall over before—how to meet people.

Be careful what you ask for. I wondered if whoever had come up with that saying was a magical being.

I laid back down and followed the line for the Milky Way splashed across the deep blue sky. I sighed. "Henri?"

"Yeah?"

My hand was clammy while I formed a fist. "Are any of those men from the kitchen decent guys?"

There was a clear pause before he replied, stretching the short word out. "Why?"

"Because." There was no reason for me to feel bad. Uncomfortable, possibly. But this was for Duncan. "I'm going to wait like we talked about, but there's no harm in doing background checks on some of those men." I reached over and sank my fingers into my donut's coat instead. The softness and the heat of his body was just the reminder I needed of why I was in this situation in the first place. "I don't want to end up with a closet butthole."

Henri sucked in a sharp breath.

"I don't need an answer tonight, but think about it, would you?" I asked. "Please?"

He didn't reply, but I knew in my heart that he was a decent enough man that he would keep an eye out for me regardless of whether he wanted to or not.

Maybe I could sneak in the suggestion to Matti, so he could pass it along the grapevine for me. I doubted he could really guilt-trip Henri into anything, but maybe his influence would do something. At least a wink or a thumbs-down. That wouldn't take too much effort.

Or . . . I snickered.

"What?" Henri pulled that word apart by the syllables too.

"I was just thinking . . ." I tilted my head so I could get a good look at him. His attention was up on the sky, but I could see his cheek still glitching. Maybe I'd talk to him about having a magnesium deficiency one day. "My life would be way less complicated if you wanted to marry me, Fluffy."

Henri didn't even blink. There was almost no reaction on

his face of any kind. It was only his cheek that stopped its shenanigans.

I wilted a little.

"Or not." I only let my feelings hurt for a second before I laid back down so I could stargaze more. And maybe so he'd have a harder time finding any disappointment on my face. If it was there. "I'm messing with you."

I'd been joking.

Hadn't I?

So that my feelings wouldn't project anything they had no business sharing, I focused on the way Duncan's chest rose and fell under my fingers and told myself that I wasn't embarrassed.

I wasn't going to bring it up again, him marrying me. Not even playing around. Not ever. Period. I promised myself that right then and there.

This was going to be the last time I talked about mating with Henri.

My face burned, and I tried my best to ignore it.

But in the way Henri seemed to like throwing surprises around when they were the least expected, after a long stretch of slightly awkward silence, he cleared his throat. Then he said my name. "Nina."

He was going with Nina. That meant business.

Fortunately, I excelled at customer retention even when I was frustrated with a grumpy customer and answered in a way that didn't sound like I would've buried myself under leaves if I had the chance. "Henri?" I sounded so nonchalant, I would've given myself an award for my acting skills if I could have.

"I promised Matti when you were younger that I would always keep an eye on you," was what his cool, neutral voice decided to share.

"Why?" I fought the urge to roll over and look at him. He was trying to make me feel better about shooting me down, I knew it.

"You remember the summer he went to stay with his uncles in Idaho?"

"No." I remembered his uncles from Idaho—they were so nice and fun—but him going to visit them? Never.

"You were about seven. He went to stay with them . . . it doesn't matter. He was worried about leaving you alone for two weeks. He asked me to take care of you."

I made a sound in my throat that I would never be able to describe, but it was pure love and emotion, and I suddenly wanted to hug my friend more than anything. That was the most Matti thing ever. Even back then, he'd been the best best friend.

"He wouldn't drop it until I agreed," Henri went on, his own voice very casual. "I did, eventually."

I tried to side-eye him without moving my head. "Is that why you were nice-ish to me?"

The man did a crunch to look over. "Nice-ish?"

My laugh caught *me* off guard. But I wasn't really the grudge-holding type. And what was I going to do? Be mad because he didn't want to marry me? At least he hadn't laughed when I brought it up. I could take that as a win.

I did a crunch too and met his eyes. "Whoa, whoa, whoa. I mean, you didn't baby me or treat me like a princess or anything, Henri. You were never mean. If I fell down and no one else was around, you'd tell me to wash my cut off and hand me a paper towel. You didn't put a Band-Aid on me and kiss my boo-boos. You were always polite. Patient. *Nice-ish.*"

There was another long pause of loaded silence. We stared at each other, and I would've given a day of my life to know what was going through his head while we did. But all he said was "I see" in a really weirdly tight voice.

It didn't sound like he saw anything to me.

"It's okay. You've always been a reliable person. I knew that if I really needed something, I could have asked you." He'd been close to the bottom of the list, after my neighbor across the street, but what did I get admitting that out loud? "That was a big ask, so thank you for agreeing to keep an eye on me."

He hadn't committed his life and sword to my honor, but it

was more than something. More than most people would have. Especially from a teenage boy.

I could have sworn he mumbled under his breath, and it made me smile up at the stars when I laid back down. "What are you grumbling over?" I couldn't stop myself from asking, purposely trying not to focus on our awkward marriage conversation a minute ago.

"*Nice-ish*. I was saying nice-ish under my breath."

Someone was testy. "Are you mad?"

"No. I see your point now that you mention it."

I lifted my head again to find him flat on his back, fingers knitted together and resting on his flat stomach.

But the expression on his features . . .

There I went feeling guilty again. "I'm not talking crap or being unappreciative. I know that you were nicer to me than you were to Matti—"

Henri Blackrock literally grunted. "Not helping."

I grimaced. "I'm making it worse, huh?" I could've sworn the side of his mouth curved up. "What I'm trying to say is that . . . yeah, wow, every way I try and word it, it still sounds like an insult. How is that possible?"

He grunted again like he agreed.

I'd dug myself into that one, even if it was true, and I didn't mean anything *that* negative about it. I tried to think of something nice, and then winced right after it came out of my mouth. "You were like . . . the big brother I never had," my freaking mouth offered.

Of all the things I could have said . . .

That got him to do *another* crunch. His eyebrows were basically a unibrow, they were so furrowed. His jaw so defined, I could see the striations of muscle beneath his skin as he snapped, "I'm not your big brother, Nina."

Ouch. "I said *like* my big brother. Back then." But ouch again. The good thing was, my little crush secret got to live another day.

Even though he had more than likely always known about it back then.

I wasn't going to worry about it.

Stretching my arm out, I reached for him and touched the top of his hand, noting that his fingers were long and thick. "I was messing with you, Henri. Thank you for telling me that about Matti. I meant what I said about always knowing I could count on you if I needed you. I still think that way now."

He didn't say a word, and I winced.

There went my big mouth again. "If it makes you feel better, when the gnomes showed up the first time, I was ready to run with the puppies and leave you with them because I knew you'd protect us."

His blink made me snicker, and the reappearance of Teasing Henri soothed what was left of the hurt from his polite way of shooting me down. "Thanks for making me your sacrifice?" he muttered, but there was a slight twitch at the corner of his mouth while he did.

"You're welcome," I told him sweetly, relieved we'd worked our way back to this point.

His lips twitched a little more. "You're a real brat, you know that?"

"Only around you, I guess."

He huffed, and it made me smile.

Not two seconds later, the familiar sound of his phone ringing filled the night. His "Blackrock" was sharp.

That was my sign to sit up. I was brushing off my back when Duncan climbed into my lap as Henri spoke to whoever was on the other line, the frustration on his face evident when I peeked over.

I poked Duncan, who looked up at me with those brilliant red eyes, and I tipped my head toward the man on the phone. Hunching over him, I cupped his ear and whispered, "Tell him he's it." We had already played, the three of us, but another quick game wouldn't hurt.

My donut's red eyes were bright. "*Yes,*" he confirmed.

I smiled and stroked a long line down his back, noticing that he hadn't just gotten taller but there was definitely more spine to touch now too.

Henri said something sharp, rolling up into a sitting position. He ran a hand through his hair aggressively, meeting my gaze quickly. Reaching out, I set my palm over his trapezius and kneaded the muscle there for a second before pulling back.

If he ever made a face at my affection . . . I'd keep my hands to myself at that point.

His gaze stayed on me as he wrapped up his call, then slid his phone back into his pocket.

"You okay? Do you need to go to work?"

"It's all good." His nostrils flared softly. "Just an administrative call that could've waited until tomorrow."

I nodded and discreetly poked at Duncan. My brilliant genius didn't miss a beat. He stood up, stretched his front legs out, going into downward dog, and real casual-like, trotted over to Henri.

The normally serious man watched him closely, even smiling a little when the puppy stopped right beside his knee.

I got my legs under me, and I caught Agnes getting up slowly too. She must have recognized the signs. Or eavesdropped.

Duncan stared up at Henri for a moment, that incredible tail a candle in the darkness.

Very gently, my donut set a single paw on the man's kneecap. His head was high, his tail as straight as any pointer's. Everything after that happened really quickly. Dunky barked, sharp and sudden, and in the next blink, he took off running.

Agnes sprinted in the opposite direction.

And I crouched there, smiled at His Royal Fluffiness and said, "That was him tagging you, if you didn't get that."

He blinked, and I watched his smile start at one corner of his mouth and stretch to the other side. "I got that," he confirmed.

I hopped up. "Just making sure." I grinned at him before walking off in another direction from where the kids had gone. We both knew he wasn't going to go after me first.

I'd only managed to make it a few feet when I heard "You're still a brat" over my shoulder.

I might be a brat, and he might not be interested in me enough to marry me, but at least I'd helped make him smile.

That was something.

And it would have to be enough.

Chapter Sixteen

For the record, I'd genuinely believed that Henri had been messing with me the night before. "*I bet it'll be worse tomorrow*" had seemed like a joke.

So, the next morning, when I'd been heading downstairs with Duncan, and I'd asked him, "What do you think, my little donut? Are there going to be a bunch of guys in the kitchen today trying to sign up to marry me?" I'd said it with a cackle. And from the way his tail had slowly swayed and he'd nudged my ankle so sweetly when he said, "*yes,*" I thought he'd been playing along too.

The only warning I got was when we were halfway to the kitchen and I finally picked up on the strong presence of magic coming from it again.

Except this time there were eight or nine tall men, with Franklin in the middle of them looking baffled.

"Good morning..." I trailed off as Duncan leaned against my leg. His tail had slowed, and he didn't *look* defensive or worried, but his little head was swinging from side to side, taking everyone in. He stepped on my foot.

A round of different versions of "good morning" answered.

Meanwhile, Franklin's eyebrows were knitted together behind his glasses. He looked well for someone who had been missing for over a month. I'd never gotten around to asking where he'd gone.

"Hi, Franklin," I greeted the elder specifically, taking in the half-zip baby blue sweater layered over a striped button-up shirt and dark brown slacks. "Welcome back."

His answering expression was a little too bright, I suspected. "Good morning, Nina," he replied in a tight, contradictory voice. His gaze swept the kitchen, and his bushy eyebrows pinched together even closer. He gestured generally around him. "How long has this been going on for?"

I made eye contact with a handsome man with green eyes for a second and then forced myself to focus back on the elder. "Them? Since last night."

He peered at the group some more, his hands going to the pockets of his pressed pants. "Is there a reason they're here?"

I hadn't forgotten about his bracelet.

A man with medium brown skin and hazel eyes loudly cleared his throat. "Can we introduce ourselves now?"

Franklin glared at him.

And me? I stood there, not sure what to do. Was this my time to shine? Should I be friendly and talk to them? I wasn't *un*friendly by nature . . . but that guilt came back with a vengeance for some reason.

I'm not doing anything wrong.

But time wasn't on my side, and there were only so many single men in the community for me to choose from to begin with—even less who might be interested. As much as I might want to, I couldn't back out and disappear into my room. Dominic had made it clear there were rumors going around about me.

People liking me wasn't something I would have normally wanted, but . . .

"*Again?*" a deep voice growled.

I didn't even have a chance to turn around before a warm, dry palm cupped the nape of my neck, a thumb and index finger landing on the tendons on either side of my throat. I'd been so distracted, I hadn't been paying enough attention to sense him.

For one brief moment, I thought about stepping back into him, into his side. Into the familiarity and comfort that was Henri . . . and then Duncan started nibbling on my shoelace, and I stopped myself from moving an inch.

Henri had made a promise to keep an eye on me, not to marry me.

It was what it was.

So all I allowed myself to do was smile at him weakly over my shoulder—he was in sweatpants and a long-sleeved T-shirt—and say, "Morning."

Some of the men started muttering curse words.

"No, no, no," Franklin spoke up. He was shaking his head. "I don't like this. If there's going to be any courting, we're going to do it the way we've done it in the past." I didn't miss the way his eyes sliced in my direction.

The fingers on my neck skimmed up to my hairline, the warm palm flat against my skin.

"This is much too soon," Franklin continued as I forced myself to stay exactly where I was. "I will set up a schedule, and if you want to spend some time with our potential resident, you can sign up for a slot." The older man hesitated before sharing a smile that seemed borderline grim to me. "If that's acceptable to you, Nina. We're accustomed to starting this process after the three-month mark."

These people and their schedules.

I almost blew out a relieved breath, and my nod could have been more enthusiastic, but . . . I didn't know these people, and all their attention was on me . . . and Henri was here, witnessing it . . .

It was too much.

Or maybe I was being a chicken. There was that.

I had to meet them—eventually—and get to know them, but I didn't want to do it like this. This was worse than a job interview.

I nodded as the rough pad of Henri's thumb grazed the underside of my jaw, and my chin instinctually went up in reaction. There was no reason that should have felt that nice. And I needed to pretend it wasn't happening.

Franklin pushed his glasses up his nose and clapped once. "It's settled. Everyone out. You can make your proper introductions another time, not when you're crowding the kitchen and some of us have things to do." He gestured to the door. "Out with you all."

No one made a peep, and the man with the green eyes happened to catch my attention again, smiling just a little when he did.

I smiled back—a deep, low growl by my ear had my head jerking to the side.

"You good?" I asked the underside of Henri's chin before leaning over so I could see his face.

I blinked. His eyes were narrowed, his jaw clenched. Even the tendons at his throat were standing out way more than usual, and I'd seen him aggravated and pissed before.

I tapped his chin twice.

Amber eyes landed on my face, that muscle in his cheek pulsing one single time before smoothing away. "Fine," he just about barked.

That tone didn't seem fine to me, but if that was the story he wanted to stick to, then who was I to tell him he was full of it? I was in the middle of a shrug when one of the men walking out of the kitchen—they all had their heads down for some reason, I noticed—stopped and flicked his eyes over to meet mine quickly. "I made breakfast today," he announced quietly.

His irises were even prettier up close. It was almost as if there was a starburst around his pupil. A little gold, brown, and green all mixed in together.

Beside me, Henri took a single step toward the guy right before Franklin butted in again in an even more irritated tone.

"Do I need to repeat myself?" the elder snapped. His lips kept moving though, but the only thing I heard after that was something, something "death wish," I thought.

Hazel Eyes looked startled, then quickly nodded and dropped his head again before he kept moving.

Werewolves weren't normally so submissive . . .

My eyeballs followed the man with the pretty eyes out of the room, at least part of the way, before Henri startled the crap out of me. His voice was sharp. "What are you doing?"

I jerked, busted. "Whoa, Fluff, checking him out."

Right in that moment, I learned that Henri Blackrock had a vein in his forehead that could bulge. I reached up and dragged the tip of my index finger across it before meeting his gaze and asking, "Where'd this come from?"

Then he did something I never, ever would have expected.

He nipped the side of my hand. Not even a little hard, but a nip was a nip, and I yanked my hand back in shock. I hadn't been nipped in years. Decades!

I laughed. "I'm sorry. It's just so . . . bulgy."

Fluffy didn't seem impressed with my observation, not even a little bit.

Somebody was touchy.

I tried to make him feel better. "It's cute?"

Franklin let out an exasperated sound that drew both of our attentions to him. "Can we have breakfast now? I have news and questions."

Henri wasn't the only grumpy one.

I said, "Yes," at the same time Henri agreed too.

No one said much as we went to the range where there were different dishes already prepared.

Henri served up a plate for Franklin with a little of everything while I made the pups their breakfast as Agnes strolled into the kitchen on four legs. I was in the middle of portioning out a serving of eggs when a warm body leaned over me, and there was a nudge at the top of my head.

I blinked at Henri being right beside me, so close. Was he . . .? "Whatcha doing?" I asked.

Had he been sniffing my hair?

There was another nudge. "Marking you."

My lips parted as he dipped his head lower.

He was rubbing his scent on me like he'd done when we'd gone to see Spencer.

It took me a second to get my words together, and when I did, there was only one I could come up with as he pressed his cheek to my crown. "Why?"

Henri didn't let me down as the side of his throat grazed my ear so nonchalantly. "For protection."

I almost freaking choked. "From the big bad wolves that just left?" I croaked.

He didn't answer.

What he did do was lean forward and touch his cheek to mine, a soft puff of his breath hitting my ear while he did it. And just as casually as he'd done it in the first place, like he did this type of thing every day, Henri straightened, looked at me once more, and then cupped my cheek. Then he nodded one last time and turned to the range like that just hadn't happened.

That sure hadn't seemed like it was just for "protection," but . . .

This wasn't the time to overanalyze it, especially not with Franklin right there.

Trying to pretend like it was no big deal Henri just rubbed his face all over me, I finished serving myself and took a seat on the stool next to the elder I thought was still being really suspicious. More suspicious than Henri, who came and sat on my other side, his thigh crowding mine in.

I left my leg where it was.

"I'd like to be caught up on what I missed while I've been away, but first, I have some news you might be interested in, Nina," Franklin said after we'd all eaten a little.

I barely managed not to drop my fork as I swiveled on the stool to face him. "About Duncan?" I might have sounded deranged.

A heavy hand settled between my shoulder blades, and I turned my head to meet Henri's gaze. His expression didn't change, but his touch said what his mouth didn't—he was there for me—and that touched me so much I had to fight the urge to throw my arms around him.

The older man forked food into his mouth like he hadn't just teased the crap out of me. He made a pleased face while eating his eggs, and I understood. They were delicious. They were buttery and fluffy, and I understood why Hazel Eyes had wanted to take credit. I would have too.

I should add him to my notes app. I poked at the eggs when that thought made my stomach hurt worse.

"Yes. I had some success with the pup's background," Franklin began to explain between bites. "I reached out to an old friend, who steered me to someone else, and I was able to get in contact with a man in California who I was told might have very specific knowledge. He wouldn't admit a word over the phone, so I took a trip to visit him."

That was not what I'd been expecting him to say. He'd gone to California *for Duncan*? After barely meeting him?

"He told me about a set of brothers in Alaska who might have answers." Franklin didn't stop eating or chewing as he continued with his story, but I'd swear his voice got funny. Maybe a little flat? "They live in a community there."

It had to be the one that Matti had mentioned as a backup to here.

Franklin kept talking, "I took a trip there—"

"They allowed you to visit?" Henri asked, sounding surprised. "I was under the impression they don't allow guests."

That question had the elder pausing. His hesitation was evident, and I wondered why. "I . . . have a family member who calls the community home. I am an exception."

Was that something worth being secretive about?

"As I was saying." That was quick. "The magic there is rich, but not as strong as ours. They have less land than we do. Their community is much newer. Their organization is mediocre; it's run as a monarchy for now. They have some things to sort out." He made a slight face. "They didn't ask for my advice, and I didn't provide it, but there are some issues they'll have to address one day," he told us with a huff.

"I digress. It took some coaxing to get the brothers to speak with me. Once they agreed, they had several questions. I answered them to the best of my ability. When I shared the pup's physical description, there was a reaction there. I attempted to get them to admit what they thought the pup might be, but they refused." He sniffed and gave us a pleased and almost smug grin.

"It took some time, but fortunately, we were able to reach a compromise."

What did that mean?

Franklin paused his story as he ate a breakfast sausage, and once he was done, added, "The brothers are older and avoid traveling. They would like to send a representative of the community first to confirm the information I provided. At that point, the pup could travel back with the rep, or they would consider coming here, under the right circumstances. Those circumstances being that they strongly believe in certain signs regarding the pup's parentage."

I sat up straight, and I mean real straight. From the wall where he was eating his breakfast—at least I'd thought he was—I felt Duncan's *"no"* shoot across the room at the same exact time.

And if none of that was enough, Henri's almost scary, cool voice said, very carefully, "They aren't taking Duncan, no matter what he is or isn't."

My body and brain were well aware that, to some extent, I couldn't violently react to what Franklin had just announced. I couldn't cry, I couldn't get mad, and I couldn't freak out. *I wanted to.* Over my dead body, and a whole lot of others, would my boy be going anywhere without me.

I couldn't control my heartbeat speeding up a little, but I managed, just barely, to keep from getting upset.

I didn't want Dunky to know.

But my hands balled up into fists as I tried to rein in every curse word I knew. I was so busy focusing on not freaking out that I almost lost my balance when the stool I was sitting on got spun around.

That perfect face that I was learning every inch of, with its clean-shaven jaw and those orangey light brown eyes that shouldn't have been possible, was suddenly right there, inches from mine. "Don't lose your shit," he ordered quietly.

I pinched my lips together, fisting my hand tight.

His eyebrow rose about a millimeter before the hand that had spun my stool landed on top of one of mine. "Listen to me, Cricket," he instructed, prying my fingers open with his dry, warm ones.

"I'm listening," I said, trying to ignore the fact I was gritting my teeth while I did it.

"He's yours, and you're his," Henri reminded me, taking my other hand and starting to peel those fingers open too. He didn't break eye contact. "*No one* is taking your boy."

"Nobody," I emphasized with a little nod.

"And I told you every person here is mine, didn't I?" he went on, giving my pinkie a jiggle when he was done spreading my fingers.

"Yeah." I sounded like Pascal answering that, kind of pouty, kind of resigned.

His eyebrow went up to be parallel with the other one, and I wondered if he recognized the tone. If he did, he let it go. "And you're a member of this community, aren't you?"

I nodded slowly.

"That includes you and Duncan, and I'm not letting anybody go anywhere," this gorgeous man assured me. "Right?"

He didn't have to be this nice to me, and I knew it, but I sure wasn't going to bring it up. So I dipped my chin and agreed, "Right."

Henri's thumb swept over my knuckles. "You're upset, and he's alarmed. Neither of you need to feel any kind of way, but you want to know what he is, don't you?"

The selfish part of me wanted to say that I didn't, not at this cost, but . . . "I do."

"Then they need to come and meet him, but that's all that's going to happen. Got it?"

I didn't want to say it, didn't think I *could* to begin with, but I had to.

I knew it.

I just had to dig in deeper than I ever had in my life to find the totally unselfish part of me. It was buried under layers and layers of emotional greed, stubbornness, and fear of losing something precious and irreplaceable. Because that's what Duncan was to me. He was my treasure, and nobody wanted to lose what they valued the most.

Nobody.

"Unless he wants to go," I made myself mutter, knowing dang well that I might have said the words, but they sounded so, so forced.

The soft padding of feet warned me that my boy was coming over, and my donut's chin went straight for my knee.

He gave me a look that had me sighing. He had his smiling face on. How could he be this mature at his age?

"It's all right," I reassured him, reaching down to stroke his soft cheek. I gave it a gentle pinch; it was so squishy. "Nothing is going to happen unless you want it to."

I really hoped I didn't sneer when I said that last sentence, but if I did, Duncan didn't have a way to tell me.

But his *"love"* right then was the fuel that kept my heart beating, and I loved him so much, looking at his devoted face. At those long ears that were now getting further and further away from the floor with every inch he grew. He was the cutest boy in the entire world.

The best one.

And I had to do right by him, no matter the cost.

"Finish your breakfast," I told Dunky with a blown kiss. "It's you and me forever." I paused. *And maybe a future stepdaddy*, but I kept that tidbit to myself with Protective Henri over here covering me with his scent.

I was going to talk to Matti about that when I had the chance.

My puppy gave me another long look that was pretty suspicious, but he reluctantly trotted back to his mat, that incredible tail swinging from side to side.

When Duncan was eating again, I faced Henri. "That's the only way he can go—if he wants to."

"No" came at me from across the kitchen and eased some more of the tension in my chest. It also made me smile because he was such a stubborn, nosy donut.

"Unless he wants to," Henri agreed, not looking like he totally believed me.

I dropped my voice. "But if they try to take him against his wishes, you'll rip their spines out?"

He lifted a hand and dragged it down his handsome face before pinning me with his amber eyes. Henri almost huffed. "*No*. No one is ripping out anyone's spine, Nina."

I blinked. "But if they try and kidnap him?"

"Then we'll talk to them and make it known they can't," he replied, squinting a little.

It was a sign to me I was feeling better about the situation because of Duncan's insistent "*no*" that I lifted my chin at Henri. "But what if they're pushy? Would you?"

His eyes were slits by that point, but his mouth was a funny little line when he said, "I can't tell if you're fucking with me right now or if you're being serious."

I was being only a little serious, mostly because I didn't need to rely on him to get people to stop doing things I didn't want them to do, but he didn't know that. He might guess it, but he didn't *know*, so I kept my mouth shut and played along if only to lighten the mood.

"You're a vicious thing," Franklin chuckled in a drawn-out way, reminding me he was listening. He almost sounded proud. "I can assure you that no one will be taking anything or anyone without permission."

Grudgingly, I turned my stool back around. "Can you tell me what your suspicions are before they come?"

He hesitated.

"I understand you don't know for sure."

Franklin thought about it for a moment, then shook his head. "I would rather not speculate."

Son of a . . .

"They'll be here soon," he said in a way that made me think that was him trying to make me feel better instead of making me panic even more.

I barely, and I mean *barely*, managed not to shout, "How soon?" Tomorrow soon or three months from now soon?

"I explained that I needed to speak with you before we could agree to any kind of invitation." His eyes slipped in Duncan's direction. "For the sake of the child."

A graze at my lower back had me sitting up straight and appreciating the affection that Henri wasn't being stingy with when I needed it the most.

Because I really did right then. As much as I was trying not to overreact, my heart wasn't getting the memo as it pounded slowly but steadily against my sternum. But having your whole life on the line might have that effect on anyone.

"I need names and flight information before they arrive," Henri demanded in his Great Wolf voice.

Franklin went back to eating, apparently not bothered by the bossy tone. "I'm aware, Henri. I'll send you the information when I receive it." His movements paused after he speared a sausage with his fork. "There was some excitement on their end at the possibility of Duncan's ancestry."

I didn't like the sound of that.

The last time people had been excited to meet him, I'd ended up with a bruised neck, sore vocal cords, and had made decisions that wouldn't haunt me exactly but that I'd wish that I hadn't needed to make.

But I was never falling for BS like that again. Henri didn't seem willing to rip out any spines to protect Duncan—a disappointment—but I would carve them out with the little blade on my nail clippers if I had to. I'd use my fingernails if it was my only choice.

"Is that plan agreeable to you?" the elder asked.

I didn't want to say that it didn't sound like I had much of a choice. I wanted to know what Duncan was, mostly just so I could care for him the proper way. It would be good for him to have that knowledge too.

There was a *small* chance he might meet people like him and prefer to live with them. I was aware of it. I hated the idea with the passion of a thousand suns, but it was a risk I was willing to take if it benefited him.

It might kill me, but what was love if it wasn't a freely given gift?

Plus, if Duncan ... left ... without me ... before the three-month trial period was up, what would I do? There wouldn't be a reason to stay here unless something drastic changed. What if he decided to leave after I'd gotten married? Then what? I'd be tied to someone for the rest of my life for no reason?

Those variables complicated things so much it made my heart and my brain hurt.

Maybe the community knew exactly what it was doing with their trial period. Maybe I should wait until the three months were up before getting to know anyone. It didn't mean I couldn't do research and take notes in the meantime.

Just in case.

I bit the inside of my cheek and tried to keep my voice level. "Sounds good, Franklin. That works." I dug my fork into a sausage and paused when the tines touched the plate. "Now, would you explain what this whole schedule thing you mentioned earlier means? I just kind of went with it, but I don't understand."

"Ah, yes," the elder answered, his attention briefly snagging on something behind me. "In the past, when a new member joins the community and is in the process of meeting a potential mate, we've found that having specific, short periods of time where partners can speak to one another in privacy works the best. Unless you want an audience during every conversation you have?"

This was the modern-day equivalent of a dance card. "Can't you all hear everything anyway?"

His forehead wrinkled. "We could, but the idea of there being privacy makes things more comfortable."

I wasn't sure how you were supposed to forget you were surrounded by people who could hear every little fart if they wanted to, but ... sure.

"We typically ask our new members to wait until their trial

period is over before we take that step . . ." The elder trailed off, his eyes darting back and forth between mine and whatever he kept eyeing over my shoulder. "I don't believe you have much longer left. When you're ready, choose the days and times that you would want to meet with interested parties, and we have a schedule where they can sign up."

This suddenly felt very, very real and very, very unreal at the same time.

"Like how mealtimes are scheduled?" I asked in a dry voice.

He gave me a tight little nod.

I'd always said they'd thought of everything here.

"What do you think about that? Do you have a problem waiting for that period to be up?"

The hand on my back fell away. It'd been so steady there for a minute that I'd forgotten Henri was still touching me. My spine suddenly felt lonely and cold.

But too freaking bad.

I picked up my speared sausage and bit into it. Only after I swallowed it did I say, "Sure. That works. I think . . . I think I'm going to wait until then. The three months, I mean. I'm about halfway through. It should be here around the corner, right?" The weak smile that took over my face fell off as quickly as it had arrived.

The suspicious old man pushed up his glasses, but he nodded.

Child?

Are you there?

I woke up with a gasp—a wild, sucking gasp that had my heart beating like crazy in the confines of my chest. It felt like I'd just gone down a steep drop on a roller coaster, except I was in bed with Duncan snoring away by my feet.

It hadn't been him. It hadn't sounded like him. That . . . that voice had been louder and too clear. Way deeper than my donut's.

But it had definitely been male.

Had I dreamt it? I tried shaking away the grogginess clouding my brain. I didn't think I'd been asleep long.

I'd heard it though. I knew I'd heard it. It hadn't been a dream.

"Hello?" I asked out loud, more hesitantly than I should've been considering I usually thought so highly of myself for not being scared of things.

The only answer I got was in the form of Duncan's snores getting even louder. There was no voice coming from under the bed or in the closet. Not out loud, not in my head, like how Duncan and his mom could communicate.

Nothing.

Shoving the covers away, I stood up and slipped my feet into my shoes before opening the door. Duncan still didn't stir, so I turned and took the staircase, trying to listen. My gut said I hadn't imagined it.

The hallways were just as empty as I'd expected them to be at this time of night. Agnes had to be dead asleep, and I didn't expect Franklin to be roaming the halls either. At the front door, I threw it open.

"Hello?" I called out, looking around, for a sign? For red eyes? For someone randomly standing there? For *something*. "Hello?" I was louder that time.

"What was that?"

I screeched, flinching so violently I almost pulled a muscle in my abs, as I whipped around, ready to fight for my life . . . only to find Henri standing in the doorway, looking sleepy and grumpy.

And only wearing sleep pants.

Loose sleep pants. There wasn't a shirt in sight. Just . . . muscles.

Lots of muscles.

Broad, bulky pectorals that had chest hair sprinkled across them before tapering into a flat, hard stomach with another sprinkle of dark hair there too, his waist thick but firm—

Quit it.

I snapped my gaze up to a safe zone. "Did you hear that too?" I asked, a little high-pitched from him surprising me, not from his chest hair. "Or am I going crazy?"

His eyebrows came down on his forehead as he frowned. There was a crease across his cheek from a pillow that was way cuter than it had any business being. It made him look so... normal. "I heard... something." Those clear, bright eyes flicked down to my pajamas—a faded T-shirt that barely reached the tops of my thighs.

Oops. I'd been too distracted to put shorts on.

His jaw tightened before he lifted his eyes and asked in a slightly funny but sleep-rough voice, "You all right?"

"I'm fine." A shiver came out of nowhere, racking up and down my spine. "You heard something then too? Because I still feel like I'm imagining it."

He dipped his chin even as his irises roamed from my face down the rest of me one more time, lingering low for longer than I would've expected. I didn't need to touch my legs to know there were goose bumps up and down my thighs. "Sounded like someone talking in my dreams." He frowned even more. "You scared?"

I shook my head, thought about it, then shrugged.

It was one thing to have Duncan talking to me telepathically, but a stranger?

Being vulnerable... helpless... was a shitty feeling.

A really, really shitty feeling.

As if he could read my mind, Henri's brawny arms opened, and he gave me this look, this invitation...

He didn't have to tell me twice. I walked right into him. Right up to the living wall that was Henri Blackrock. Straight into his embrace, plastering my front to his, and let him wrap his arms around my back as I threw mine around his ribs like a freaking leech. And like a leech, I had zero shame about clinging to him.

"You're safe," he grumbled into the top of my head as he drew me in even closer somehow, meshing our fronts together.

"Okay," I muttered, my cheek flat to the skin and hair on his sternum.

He was so warm, and he smelled *good*. Better than with

clothes on. Like cool, fresh weather that couldn't be soap or cologne because I couldn't think of a single werewolf that would willingly use something scented since their noses were so sensitive.

A hand skimmed up my back. "What exactly did you hear?"

I'd swear his voice sounded deeper.

"It said 'child.' It—he—asked if I . . . someone . . . was there." I didn't want to say it sounded like it had been for me. That was ridiculous. Wasn't it? He'd heard it too, after all.

"You heard 'child'?"

I nodded, slipping my hands to land on the sides of his waist, right over the material at his hips. It was soft cotton. Thin too.

His heart beat under my cheek. "That's all?"

I nodded some more, trying my best to take another discreet sniff of him. *How can he be so toasty with no clothes on?* I wondered, making sure to keep my grip on his waist loose and easy, while some part of my brain was ready to just . . . drape myself over him like a blanket.

"Ever heard it before?" he asked, not struggling to keep his thoughts straight, like I was.

"I don't think so." That . . . that might have been a lie. Already the memory of the speaker's tone was leaving me. "Maybe? Remember I told you about that voice I've had 'dreams' about before? It might have been the same one, but I don't know. It's been a really long time since the last dream I had."

The palm on my back stopped right in the center of it, his fingers molding to my spine. I wondered if he could tell I didn't have a bra on, because I could definitely tell he didn't have underwear on. But I'd run out here half dressed, and so had he. I'd gotten used to living around exhibitionist Sienna. I was pretty sure that after Matti and her mom, I might have been in third place for the person to have seen Sienna's butt the most.

And now, I was thinking about Henri's butt cheeks. Whether they were high and tight, or meatier at the bottom. Were they tan like the rest of him, or did he go without a shirt often enough that there was a nice tan line where his pants met his shirt?

Stop it, Nina.

"That's all you heard?" Henri asked, oblivious to me daydreaming about his heinie while trying my hardest to pretend like his quarter chub was no big deal.

"Yes, just 'child' and 'are you there?' That was it."

A thought strong enough to have me stop thinking about what was pressing against my stomach hit me.

Could it have been Duncan's dad?

My knees almost went weak at the possibility.

"Do you smell anything in the air?" I asked Henri, instead of sharing my concern. "Anything close by that shouldn't be there? I couldn't see or sense anything out of the normal. The trees aren't pointing fingers."

"No," he answered right before the sound of his inhaling filled the ear I had pressed to his chest. He held his breath for so long I was tempted to look up at him to make sure he was fine. His exhale only lasted a fraction of what his breath had. "There's nothing close by out of the normal." The hand on my back slid up a little, and I was sure this had to be considered a cuddle at this point. "What are you worried over?"

I wilted at getting busted again. Might as well admit it. "I was thinking . . . remember I told everyone that Duncan's mom communicated with me telepathically?" I didn't wait for him to answer. "Do you think that could've been his dad? Maybe he has something blocking his scent?" My legs felt out of sorts all over again, and my arms might have clung a little tighter around Henri's waist.

His body went solid. "I see what you're saying." He pulled back, concern written on those hard, dark features. "I'll look. Go inside."

Go inside? Was he kidding? "I'll get a golf cart and go with you."

He shook his head. "I'll travel faster on my own."

"But what if you need help?"

"No. We don't know who or what that was," he argued before a very faint smile slowly crept over his mouth. His eyebrows scrunched together. "You worried about me?"

I made a face. "What do you think?"

"I think you're not such a brat after all." Before I could give him crap, the werewolf took a step back. "If you hear anything, holler. I'll hear you."

Unfortunately, I was too hung up on him being out here with me without a shirt or underwear on to do more than stare as he stepped off the deck, his form shimmering briefly before his other body. The gorgeous black wolf shot off into the woods, his stride reminding me more of a horse than what he was.

I had the strangest urge to hug him.

And I suddenly missed my parents so much. I hoped they'd call me soon. Sometimes they forgot they had a needy kid who liked hearing from them while they lived their isolated and quiet lives, just the way they wanted to.

And then I wondered where I got it from.

I waited and watched Henri disappear in the distance between trees that seemed even taller and more unreal in the darkness. Moonlight reflected off some of the bark, giving it that shimmering quality that I'd seen the first day we'd gotten here. It was faint, but it was there.

Minutes passed. Then more minutes, and I slowly realized just how quiet it was out here. There wasn't a hoot, a howl, or frogs.

It was spooky silent.

But that got me thinking about how I wasn't really alone. How . . .

I took a couple steps off the deck before calling out, "Mr. Gnomes? You never told me your names, but are you there?"

Nothing and no one answered, and I felt a little dumb for thinking they would have. What did I expect? That they were waiting around, listening?

Rustling at the tree closest to me had me looking down to find four sets of eyeballs through a small circular knot in the wood.

How did they do that?

I crouched. "Hi." I felt like a jerk for bothering them, but not enough of one to tell them never mind. "I'm sorry for waking you up yelling," I apologized instead.

"We were not in slumber," one of the gnomes answered. They all had such similar features that I wasn't sure whether he was one of the ones I'd spoken to in the past or not.

"We prefer to work under the cover of the moon," one of the others explained.

"Oh, all right." I still felt bad for being so impulsive. "Thank you for coming. I don't have an offering tonight, I'm sorry."

The gnomes peered at me.

I guess I was forgiven?

"I called you because I wanted to know . . . did you happen to hear anything? A few minutes ago?" I asked, feeling a little—or more than a little—foolish. They had literally just explained that they hadn't been sleeping. Henri had said he'd heard the voice too, but it had been in his dreams.

"What is it that you expected us to hear?" one of them asked.

"I thought I heard a man calling out for a child."

"In your dreams?"

I nodded.

The two in the front blinked at the same time. "Your kin, we would suppose."

My *kin*?

My butt plopped down in the dirt and pine needles without my control, like some imaginary being had swept my legs out from under me. "You . . . think it was someone in my family? Why?" I croaked.

The gnomes exchanged the same kind of glance Sienna and I did when something extra ridiculous came out of Matti's mouth and we were trying to decide who was going to give him crap about it. "Who else could traverse dreams?"

Of all the things that had happened in my life, this felt the most unreal. And I had a puppy with red eyes and a flame on his tail. And I'd sent people to the hospital.

"Did you respond?" one of them asked.

I squinted. "No . . . I thought . . ." The truth was, I wasn't sure what I thought when they were implying I had relatives—parents—who could speak through dreams.

How was that possible?

"Do you think it might be my . . . father?" I squeaked, since that was the family member they had been so focused on before.

There was no hesitation when they agreed. "Could be him."

I went lightheaded.

"Could be another member of your kin," they suggested.

This wasn't helping.

"I would answer if I were you," the other one claimed. "The old ones don't take well to being ignored."

They'd gone there. The old ones. My hands started tingling for the first time in weeks.

Could they be right? Could it be a biological relative of mine? It didn't add up. *It didn't.* Not when I took into consideration that I was in my thirties and had never known anything about anyone I shared blood with. *But . . .* "I want to make sure I understand and that I'm not hallucinating. You're saying that whoever is calling out for a child . . . I'm that person?"

"Yes," the gnomes answered in unison.

"But Henri, my friend, the wolf, said he heard him too."

They shared another glance before their small eyes landed on me. "Yes."

This didn't feel possible. Pressing my palms together, I tucked them under my chin and whispered, "My friends . . . can I call you that?"

"You may," they agreed.

"I don't know what any of what you're saying means," I admitted. "I was abandoned as a baby. Whoever left me didn't care enough to put clothes on me. I highly doubt that anyone who could do that, who could go over thirty years without ever having anything to do with me, would suddenly care now."

I wiped at my face without thinking about it, without realizing that my eyes had started tearing up at some point. In anger, mostly. Maybe a little in frustration.

I had gone through a phase early on after my magic had presented itself, where I'd been scared of myself. That had been the only real, genuine fear I'd ever known—other than the incidents with someone trying to take Duncan. But there was something almost terrifying about feeling helpless, and that's the effect the voice talking to me had. It told me that this person was strong enough to *communicate with me while I was unconscious*, to get into not just my head, but Henri's too. It was almost unfathomable. If they could do that, what else were they capable of? I'd heard stories. How the oldest magical beings, the ones who had been there at the beginning when the meteor fell, how much more potent their gifts were. How they were the gods we still knew about from the oldest tales.

Just because their followers stopped writing their stories doesn't mean their books were finished, my mom had told me once. *It only means we got to see some of their chapters.*

Something big moved through the forest as the small, wrinkled faces scrunched up even more as the gnomes stared at me in silence. Then each one reached a hand through the knot in the wood and placed a cool palm on the part of my leg closest to them. "There is no excuse for abandoning a child. Your pain and hurt is not unfounded."

I wanted to argue that it wasn't pain I felt but anger. Annoyance. Frustration. The ugly stuff, but before I could, the gnomes kept going, ignoring the sounds of heavy weight crashing over leaves and debris.

"All will be well, child," one of the gnomes predicted. "There is nothing to fear. The old one may anger, but the dreamer has returned."

What did that even mean?

Before I could get another word out, they were gone . . . and where their faces had been, bark had replaced the spot.

The sound I'd heard approaching from a distance came to a stop behind me, deep breaths filling the silence. I whipped around and stared up at the colossal wolf standing so close I could count his eyelashes. The dark creature dipped his head and snuffled against my throat, all warm comfort and sharp teeth I didn't fear.

I threw my arms around his neck.

I hugged Wolf Henri so tight. So freaking tight. Because maybe he didn't want to marry me, but he'd said I was one of his people.

And right then, I needed a hug more than I needed anything else.

I leaned into him and pressed my forehead to the side of his snout, right beneath his eye. Grateful for this. Grateful for him. This had to be what hugging a bear felt like, or the equivalent of a land shark.

He didn't have to be out here. He hadn't needed to comfort me earlier or now. He hadn't even needed to roll out of bed.

But he had because he was that kind of person.

And dang it, this wasn't the time to think of just how much I liked him, but I did. I liked him so much. Everything about him. The physical part was the smallest factor of it all.

Henri, bless his soul, didn't deny me anything. I clung, and he let me. I sucked up his strength, and he said it was fine.

What might have been five minutes or ten went by before his body changed. Fur and muscles turned into smooth skin covered with a touch of body hair. Arms wrapped themselves around my back. Face to chest, hips to legs, that strong hand palmed the back of my head, holding my cheek to him in what I might call tenderness.

I hadn't planned on saying it, on telling him, but apparently some part of my conscience decided it was a good idea to blurt it out, not even trying to be easygoing or funny about it. "I don't know what it is about you, Fluff, but you make me feel safe." I cuddled *him* closer. "I know you won't rip any spines out for me, but it's still nice." I moved my cheek just enough to feel the crisp hair on his pecs slide across my face. "Thank you for this."

It *felt* like he curled around me more in response, but maybe it was my imagination or wishful thinking. And after a while, after he'd ignored my comment long enough—which was all right too because what was he supposed to say? That I was welcome?—he asked, "What happened? Did the gnomes do something?"

It was probably for the best that he let my comment go, not that I would take it back anyway. He *did* make me feel safe, and I owed Matti even more gratitude than I already did for bringing this man, with this capacity of protectiveness, into my life. Especially now when I needed it the most. When I needed it more than I ever had before, because life didn't revolve around me anymore.

"They didn't do anything," I replied. "They just confused me."

"That all?"

He knew that wasn't all. He had to be able to sense it. "Sad too," I admitted.

A soft touch stroked down my bed head. "Why sad?"

I wasn't proud of the way my inhale went in shakily through my nose. Nothing had happened. I had never been the kind of person to focus too much on ifs or coulds. But here I was clinging to Henri like someone had actually kicked me while I was down. "After you took off, I wondered if maybe they heard something, so I called out for them, and they actually came. I saw them in a knot in a tree over there."

His pec muscles went hard, and I tried not to be impressed. "What knot?"

"I'll show you. I don't know how they did it."

"What'd they say?"

"They weren't sleeping, so they didn't hear the 'child,' but as soon as I mentioned it, how it happened in a dream, they said it had to be my father or my 'kin,'" I told him.

"Your family?" There was a delayed kind of interest in his tone. Or maybe it was wariness.

"That's what they said, and then they told me that I'm the child the voice in the dream was calling out for, and I told them that that didn't make any sense because whoever my biological parents are, they didn't want me in the first place—"

He growled.

I had faint memories of my dad—my werewolf one—growling when he'd hug me after something had made me upset. He hadn't liked me being sad either. But it had been a long, long time since I'd experienced it so up close and personal.

It was awesome. A little chainsaw-y, but better.

I smashed my cheek against him even more. "It's stupid to be sad over people who never wanted to know me and never gave a crap about what happened to me in the first place, especially when I ended up with a family who did, but . . ." I shrugged and tightened my fingers around his waist. "If it is someone I'm related to, why would they be doing this? Could it be my dad? Do I have siblings? And why now? And how, Henri? In our *dreams*?

"They said . . ." I didn't think I could keep what they'd suggested to myself. I found that I wanted to tell him. "They said the old ones don't like being ignored. And something about a dreamer returning?" I whispered. "I don't get it."

The growl hadn't gone anywhere while I'd talked, but it had lowered to a hum that reminded me of the volume Duncan reached when he snored, quiet and steady. "I've got my suspicions," Henri murmured.

My body tensed, but I refused to let go of him. I'd been raised by the belief system that you avoided talking about the beings once called gods. About the magic in the world that was even more difficult to explain than a person turning into a four-legged being. About the magic in the world that had left such a sour taste in so many lives, that fear had guarded the gods' secrets even more closely than anyone else's.

"What do you think?" I asked him, gulping while I did it.

All those hard muscles, even the parts of his thighs touching mine, went solid. Then I heard and felt him take a deep breath. "Let's sit for a minute. The twigs are annoying."

I'd forgotten he was barefoot. Nodding, I pulled away before he sank into a cross-legged position right where we were. He set his hand on his thigh. Before I could wonder if that was the kind of invitation my brain was telling me it was, he tapped the cotton stretched tight over his legs. "Come here, Nina."

This was . . . new.

"You don't want to get a splinter," that velvet voice warned.

I wasn't sure I was slick enough to hide my reaction—my eyes going wide—but I tried to make it seem like it was no big deal to the best of my ability. His reasoning made sense, and did I really want a stick digging into my butt? Not so much. So, I did what he said and sank onto the inner thigh of the leg he'd patted, tucking my feet into a spot under his opposite thigh, my knees to my chest. If the position gave me a really, really good view of his bare chest, it was just a bonus. Like a triple Yahtzee.

His chest grazed my arm, and I tried my best to pretend it was no big deal.

Maybe this was a bad idea.

Out of nowhere, he lifted me up and adjusted me on him before sliding an arm low around my back, like he was helping prop me up. "I think you should tell me what you think first, and then I'll go. I'll be surprised if we aren't both on the same page," he tried to compromise.

Discomfort was a javelin straight into my sternum at what he was asking.

But I forgot that nothing got past Henri. "We don't need to talk about it if you don't want to."

I didn't, but at the same time, sticking your head in the sand and pretending something wasn't happening didn't mean something wasn't happening. Sure, I wanted to go on with my life like someone wasn't calling out in my dreams—and Henri's—but the truth was, this wasn't just affecting me.

But all I could get myself to do was grunt at him.

I didn't want him to look at me differently.

"Nina," Henri murmured, and I could've sworn I heard affection in his voice, or at least amusement. "We both know at least one of your parents was someone who somewhere, at some point, was called a—"

I put my hand over his mouth. "I don't like that word."

He raised an eyebrow, and it was more than a millimeter. His fingers went to my wrist, and he tugged my hand down. "I don't like it either. Too many preconceptions, but you know what I'm talking about—an old one, does that work?"

I nodded.

His eyebrow dropped. "Then there's no disputing that—that one of them is very old. There's a chance both of them might be. Am I right?"

I met his eyes and found only curiosity there. I jerked my head at him once. Then I agreed to things even my parents had never wanted to admit out loud, or at least not without spelling them out instead. "I think so." I made it sound like the dirty secret it had always felt like.

"You *think* so?" this man decided to tease right then.

I realized at that moment who I was talking to. The same man the gnomes had called the Great Wolf. A descendant of a wolf god. Which made him a wolf god. Probably. There was a big difference between him and Matti, and there was no hiding that. It hadn't escaped me that not once had anyone *ever* brought up Henri's parents. I still wanted to ask for details, but even for me, that felt like crossing the line with privacy.

Now I felt like a hypocrite.

"We can come back to it," he offered. "All we're doing is guessing anyway, aren't we?"

I nodded, then so did he, tiptoeing right along with me.

"Someone is talking to you in your dreams, in mine—in who knows who else's—for a reason. I'd bet there's a list of figures that have that ability, and I bet we could narrow it down. I bet you've had ideas, and this incident might have narrowed them down."

I grumbled and dipped my chin in agreement, squeezing my knees, my shirt tucked between my legs to hide my underwear.

His gaze slid to what my hands were doing before meeting mine again. His throat bobbed with a swallow, and I felt him shift his weight around below me. "There are stories that have been around for longer than I've been alive. Longer than the elders and their ancestors, too. My family, the ones who moved here, who made this their home and inherited this land, would tell us about how there was so much magic embedded into everything that makes this place *this place*. I don't think they had a word for atoms back then, but it's that idea . . . Your hands aren't shaking anymore, are they?" he asked suddenly.

I smiled up at his face, touched he'd remembered. "They stopped being jittery on their own a few weeks back."

"Good. I knew it'd go away eventually." He paused. "I've noticed the more magical someone is, the more strongly they experience the magic here." His gaze flicked back toward my hands again lightning quick. He blinked. "Where was I?"

"You were saying that there's so much magic in the land." Something I had already reasoned for myself, but I liked hearing him talk.

He sat up straighter, bringing his chest into contact with my arm and side even more. "Right. The stories I was raised on say that this land is special. That it heightens everything that lives within it . . . What are you smiling at?"

I couldn't control my facial muscles; I was grinning so hard it sort of hurt. "You're good at storytelling." I squinted. "Why? You want me to stop smiling?"

"No." He looked at me one more time, then continued on. "Everything that was born and raised here is bigger, stronger, than it is elsewhere—"

"Is that why you're the size you are?" I interrupted.

"Yes and no," he answered cryptically. He moved on real quick. "I think that whoever it is doing this can communicate with more than just you because you're here. Maybe it's projecting into you . . . whatever gift it is that he's known for."

I gasped, already figuring out what he was implying: dreams. But, more than I wanted to know about someone I hadn't given a crap about in decades, I wanted him to keep talking, so I snapped my mouth shut even though I was positive I was at least a tiny bit bug-eyed. What he was saying made sense.

Too much sense really.

He noticed. "I don't know, Cricket. I might be wrong about it all. The gnomes might be too, but at the same time, why not? Why now? *They* sensed you. The elders might not want to face it, but they didn't come back here for no reason." Henri looked me dead in the eye. "They made that comment to you. Maybe they want to reproduce. They brought up your biological mother too."

"I did wonder about that . . ." I trailed off.

"Why not?" He repeated it like this wasn't an unreal conversation that included old, magical beings and gnomes who wanted to have kids.

And now, I was even more confused.

My shoulders slumped at how much I knew, how much I could guess, and how much could be a sheer matter of luck and coincidence.

"When you were small, everyone called you 'Honey Bun' because you smelled so sweet," Henri told me quietly, surprising me with bringing it up out of nowhere. "Now . . ."

"Now I'm like cilantro. Some people love it, some people hate it." From the way his eyes lit up, I was pretty sure he hadn't expected that. Part of me wanted to joke and ask if he liked cilantro . . . but my mind went blank when our eyes met. I bit the inside of my cheek as some invisible force landed smack in the middle of my chest.

I could've sworn my ears started ringing, but that couldn't have been true because his voice was clear a moment later.

"Part of me still can't believe that you and Matti didn't end up together," he admitted.

The comment wasn't exactly a bucket of ice water, more like tepid water, and it made me snicker.

"When he told me he was mating Sienna, I tried to talk him out of it," he said.

My whole body jerked. "No! You didn't!"

"I did. You two were always drawn together, and he'd mention that you were still friends . . ." Henri was watching me closely.

I shook my head. "I think my parents thought the same thing for a while, but there was never a chance. To me, he always felt like my twin in another body." I shrugged. "Sienna is my right hand, and Matti is my left. I love them. They love me. All three of us have worked hard to stay close."

"I didn't understand until I saw the three of you together now, in the present." His voice went a little funny. "You don't love him other than as a friend."

"No. I'd give him a kidney if he needed it or find a way to get him one. I know he's not ugly, and I'll be the second person to argue with someone if they said he was, but it's not like that." I smiled at him, taking in the rough structure of his masculine face. *He* was so handsome to me. And the way he smelled, the way he felt . . .

The tiniest little growl built up in his throat a moment before his features twisted into something between a scowl and a frown. A scrown. A frowl.

Crap. There was no hiding anything from him. Not when we were this close. Not when what I felt was so strong.

So I did what I had to do, and that was own what my body had just done to betray me. "I'm sorry, you're attractive, but it doesn't mean anything." My voice went a little high, and I had to fight the urge to nervous laugh. "I know we're only friends. You're just . . . you're gorgeous, and you're nice, but I'm sure everyone thinks that about you, so . . . please ignore it and take it as a compliment, all right, Fluff?"

Henri Blackrock, law enforcement officer, werewolf, protector of this land, leaned back. It wasn't much, but he definitely tilted his upper body away from me. But before I could get offended or worry I'd screwed up by being so honest, he blinked. Then he let out a huff through his nose that counted as a laugh.

"What?" I narrowed my eyes.

"You," was all he said.

"I'm just trying to ease the tension," I told him warily. "No need to make it weird."

There was that frowl again. "*I'm* making it weird?"

Did he sound offended? "You laughed. Your tone just now. All you needed to do was say 'okay' or 'that works for me,' and we'd both move on and pretend you didn't just smell me thinking that you're a good-looking person when I'm sitting on your thigh and we both have less clothes on that usual." I raised my eyebrows. "Be uglier. There. Problem solved."

He made another one of those huff-laughs from his nose, that one a little louder than before. It was adorable.

"I'm trying to let you off the hook. You don't need to embarrass me." I eyed him. "I already have to work so hard to keep what I can to myself, thanks."

He made another huff-laugh! "*I'm* trying to embarrass *you*? Why would you think that?"

"Because you're laughing at me." I pointed. "Right in my face."

He started full-on chuckling, and I didn't know how I'd missed the glimmer in his eyes, but it was there.

What did he have to be so amused over? Me admitting he was a hunk of a man out loud? Really? "It's a compliment, you know," I muttered.

His body sobered slowly as his gaze moved around my face some more and he sat up, bringing his chest back in touch with my arm and side. "Thank you for the compliment." His mouth twitched just a little like he couldn't help himself. "I'm not laughing at you. I'm laughing at the dumb shit coming out of your mouth. That's what's funny."

Was he teasing me again? "I don't say dumb shit."

"I think you just proved a minute ago that you do sometimes."

I blinked. "You looking to get bit again?"

His eyes lit up, and Henri leaned in to me. "You threatening me?"

I took in the rough bones of his face, the signs of humor in his eyes, in his body language. "Not very well if you're smiling." It was my turn to smile too. I couldn't help it. Not when he was being this Henri. Dreamboat Henri. Half naked and playful and protective and everything anyone could ask for.

"The first bite was a freebie," he warned. "The next one, you'll be getting one right back, and I know exactly where it'll go."

I almost fell out of his lap.

The way my voice came out strangled and more excited than it had any business being would probably haunt me for the rest of my life but too bad. "Excuse me?" I howled, eating up his playfulness, boxing it up and planning on eating some more of it as a snack later.

Somehow, he leaned in a little closer. "Try me, Nina. Find out," he seemed to tease me . . . threaten me . . . or maybe it was a goad.

Was it?

I wasn't sure, but my nipples were hard.

I thought there might have been a good chance a part of me might have gone a little slick, a little wet, at what my brain was trying to interpret at this mythical-like specimen of a man flirting with me.

I needed to think about something else. Needed to talk to him about anything else. But . . . I was my own worst enemy.

"Are you going to tell me why you were laughing at me, or am I supposed to figure it out on my own?" I asked instead as I absorbed even more of the tiny details of his face that I'd never been close enough to notice before. A small scar below his lip that was slightly paler than the rest of his skin. One of his eyes was slightly darker in color than the other. How hadn't I seen that before?

Had his bottom lip always been that full too?

"I don't know if you want to know," he said carefully.

"Cut me some slack, Fluff. You can keep most of your secrets to yourself. I'd like to know," I tried.

"Sure about that?"

I nodded.

His eyes narrowed just slightly. "I keep forgetting your nose is the only thing not special about you."

He wasn't helping me not like him.

Henri didn't wait for me to croak something, because that would have been the best I was capable of when he was being like this, touching me like this. "It's funny to me," he started to say in a rough, quiet voice, "that you would think—"

He stopped talking, his head turning in the direction of the clubhouse a moment before a high-pitched voice called out, "Henri?"

It was Agnes.

She was on the porch in bubblegum pink pajamas, looking ruffled and sleepy.

A small, small part of me deflated on the spot as disappointment ran through my veins because she couldn't have waited ten more seconds to wander outside. What had he been about to say? *And had he been flirting with me?* It felt like it. Where was Sienna when I needed her?

I didn't wait for him to gesture that he needed to get up, I stood with a gulp and held out my hand.

Henri met my gaze before taking it, his long fingers curling around mine, and I helped him stand too, as much as I could, considering he outweighed me by at least a hundred pounds.

"Everything is all right," his voice carried to the little girl, sounding more than a little different, hoarser than it'd been a minute ago. "I'm coming, Ladybug."

I had never really asked for more than I had or more than I needed. I knew in some way that I'd always had more than most people could or would. The things I might have wanted, I knew to an extent could never *really* be mine.

But all of a sudden, right then, I thought about one more thing that I wished I could have. One more thing I wanted. So, so much.

This stunning, strong-willed, teasing man.

Amber irises didn't leave mine even when he towered over me. His face sober. His smile gone.

I tried to muster one up for him, but I didn't think my effort was that convincing. He had to be able to see right through it. He could probably see right into me—the longing, how much I'd just enjoyed the moment. How a part of me wished he would've finished saying what he'd been in the middle of.

And more.

But it had ended and everything was back to normal, and I knew in my heart that I was never going to hear the end of his sentence. More than that, I was never going to get what I wanted either. Even if I really wished I could.

Chapter Seventeen

"Put me on Zoom when you go on your dates."

I leaned away from my phone, my back bumping into the massive tree trunk behind me and burst out laughing. "The hell I will."

Matti's familiar face took up my entire screen, showing me that he'd regained all the weight he'd lost when he'd gotten sick. He'd announced a couple weeks ago that he was never going to look at a hot dog again. "I can help you screen them," he insisted, leaning even more into his camera. He had been eating his lunch right up until I told him about all the men in the kitchen and the schedule that Franklin had mentioned. I hadn't gotten around to sharing that I wasn't sure how I felt about any of it though.

He'd claimed he didn't remember that part—the speed dating aspect. I believed him, but it wouldn't have made a difference to me being here or not if I'd known ahead of time. I was just happy to see his face for a little bit. It had been weeks since our last video call. I'd been busy, he'd been busy, and we'd been texting every few days and sending funny videos on our social media accounts that we only used for that reason.

"I don't need you helping screen them from a distance. If you were here and you could smell their intentions, that'd be a different story, but you're off living your big-city boy life." I shook my head. "I'm not video calling you."

"Record the dates and we can analyze them afterward," he tried with a straight face.

I scoffed. "I want to think you're joking, but I know you're not."

"I'm not," Matti confirmed. "Sienna and I both agree we deserve to have a say in who you mate with because we're going to have to put up with them too. Ask her."

I tilted my head to the side.

He huffed. "At least tell me their names before, and I'll give you my input, if I know them or not."

"Fine, we'll start there. I have a list going already, but I don't know anyone's names, just what they look like," I explained.

He laughed before suddenly sobering in a way that reminded me of Henri going back and forth between being Teasing Henri and Serious Henri. Matti leaned forward, so close I could only see his lips. "Nina," he tried to whisper, "don't let Henri see it."

"Why?" I whispered back for some reason, confused.

His lips kept taking up the screen. "Just trust me."

I trusted him with my life, but . . . I kept my voice the same volume. "I already talked to him about what you said. Two or three times. He's not . . . he's not interested."

I wanted to tell him about that yearning little thought that hadn't left me since the night Henri and I'd been alone outside together, but this wasn't the time or the place, and that wasn't a conversation I could see myself having with Matti. He could know all about me being bloated and having terrible gas from eating raw broccoli, but about my feelings toward his cousin?

I could just imagine it: *Hey, Matti, I think I might be a little in love with your cousin, but just a little bit. What do you think?*

Best-case scenario: he'd probably fall out of his chair laughing.

But before anything else could be said, he made a face. One I recognized. It was a young Matti face. The one he'd made when he knew he'd done something wrong and was trying not to get busted.

It put me on red alert.

"What?" I drew the question out.

The camera panned back. He reached for his throat and adjusted the pale gray tie tucked into a slate blue vest. He gave me a side-eye that confirmed I wasn't in the wrong for getting wary. "My cousin is an idiot." He squinted. "Don't tell him I said that."

"Why is he an idiot?"

Matti's expression left me feeling more suspicious than I already was. He looked constipated for a second, grimaced, then finally opened his mouth. "I wasn't going to say anything, and Sienna and I talked about it, and we agreed to let things happen naturally, but . . ."

"You sure are dragging this out," I muttered.

"You didn't sense his reaction to you that first day," my best friend just about blurted out.

"Explain."

He gave me another classic Matti smile that might have fooled somebody else. It was his "look how cute and innocent I am" face. "See . . ." He trailed off again.

"Dang it, Matti, quit dragging it out." I was freaking bracing myself here.

"Listen, *listen* . . ."

I leaned back against the tree and threw my hands up in the air.

Matti *laughed*. "Nina, listen to me. Two seconds after I thought about you and Duncan moving to the ranch, I thought about how you were going to need to marry someone. Right after that, I thought '*hey, she should marry Henri,*' but I didn't bring it up because he's not a martyr. He's not going to marry someone because they need him. He isn't that generous."

I felt my face going a little hot because I'd learned that the hard way.

"I'd *hoped*, but I figured chances were slim. I didn't want you to be disappointed if he told us all to fuck off," he explained while I brought my cell back down so I could peer at his face.

And he'd still told me to do it anyway, but I let him keep going.

My best friend's face was sober as he kept rambling. "But you didn't smell what Sienna and I did when he first saw you. Those first ten minutes." He whistled low. "I don't ever want to scent that off him again, but I know how he felt, and so did she, and that's why I told you to marry him, Big Jaws. Because you can't hide that, and I don't know what the fuck he's thinking." He paused, then whistled again. "He's always been real uptight. He'd be the last person I'd expect to have some biting kink, but you did it, and he didn't hate it."

My mouth opened a little, and I tried to process what in the world he'd just admitted. What it meant. Or how it made me feel.

But I'd known this MFer felt something!

And that thought had barely entered my brain before another reality smacked the initial thought aside. It took the wind out of my sail almost instantly, too. And that brief little flash of hope, of awe, disappeared, and I slumped.

On the screen, he tipped his chin up at me in question.

I gave him a half-hearted shrug. "Whatever he might feel, it isn't enough to get him to . . . you know. I told you. I've brought it up more than once." I paused. "Except, the other day, he did something I thought was sneaky. A few guys from the ranch showed up for breakfast, and right afterward, he started rubbing his face against my hair and my cheeks and everything."

Matti's face was almost incredulous. "I told you, he's a—"

My body became instantly aware of magic, the sensation getting stronger by the second, and I held up my finger, cutting him off.

He knew the drill and shut up.

Sure enough, heavy footsteps crunched over gravel before I heard a familiar voice. "I'll see what I can do, but I can't promise anything."

I raised my eyebrows at Matti, aware he would know based off my expression who was coming. I wasn't wrong when Henri walked right by where I was sitting, phone up to his cheek as he listened to whoever was on the other end. He got two steps past me reclining against a big tree off to the side of the clubhouse before he stopped and looked over his shoulder. He blinked, the phone still up to his ear.

I smiled at him, and he turned his whole body to face me. I flipped my phone toward him, letting him see who was on the screen. Matti must have made some kind of gesture because Henri's eyebrows dropped before he sighed and grumbled into his phone, "Like I said, I can't make any promises, Margaret."

Margaret wasn't someone I'd met yet, but Randall had mentioned her before, and I was fairly certain she was a senior member of the community.

I turned my phone back.

"Call me later," Matti said in a voice lower than the one he'd been talking to me with.

"I will. Love you, bye."

"You too, bye," he replied, flashing another Little Matti smile before his face vanished and my background image—baby Duncan with a stick in his mouth—appeared.

Tucking my feet beneath me, I pushed off the trunk and stood up.

Henri held up a rough-looking index finger.

He wanted me to wait?

"Yes, I'll get back to you . . . as soon as I can . . . yes . . . yes . . . sure." He kept talking as I brushed off my butt and spent a moment taking him in. Dressed in a long-sleeved T-shirt, dark jeans, and boots, he seemed to me like he had the day off.

And how did he keep getting more handsome every day? I wondered before my brief conversation with Matti swept that aside. It was something and nothing at the same time.

This wasn't going to go well for me.

Henri's bone-deep sigh was the first sign he'd hung up, followed by the way his hand dropped to his side.

I raised my eyebrows. "People driving you nuts?"

He released another breath that seemed like it came straight from his soul. "It's been a long day."

I looked at my phone's screen. "It's ten in the morning."

He rubbed his hand over his mouth before slanting me a look. "Exactly."

"Poor Fluffy," I told him with a grin. "Anything I can do to help?"

"It's all good. I'm off from work the next two days," he tried brushing it off. "Margaret's having a problem with her hot water and thinks it's faster to call me than it is to call our maintenance man." His gaze moved over my face, down my white shirt, black shorts, and fanny pack. A little notch appeared between his eyebrows. "What are you doing out here? Where's Duncan?"

I scratched my cheek. "He and Agnes are with Phoebe and Shiloh. I just dropped them off, got sad on the walk back, and I called your cousin to cheer me up. I forgot he's on a work trip in New York."

Henri made a face I wasn't sure how to interpret before looking me over again. Just as he seemed to be about to say something, that ringtone, the one I had memorized by that point, went off. He closed his eyes, made a hum in his throat, then very visibly—and only halfway failing—tried not to snarl, "One sec," before bringing his phone to his ear. "Henri," he answered, all traces of whatever frustration or irritation he'd been feeling gone, at least from his voice.

His face on the other hand? It was a good thing he wasn't taking a video call.

"I'll be there as soon as I can," he snapped into the phone. His features were like thunder, all dark and sharp. Henri's body became tense.

He was angry.

"What's wrong?" I asked.

He was already stepping back. "Someone smelled something that doesn't belong, and there's only a few things that come across the way it was described. I need to check."

"You think the Jenny Greenteeth is back?" That little b better not be back with her BS.

"I don't know, but I need to see for myself," he explained, taking another step backward.

I didn't even think about it. "I'll come with you."

He stopped. "You don't need to—"

"I want to." I smiled. "I'll be your bodyguard."

Henri's head jerked at almost the same time as amusement glimmered in his eyes.

But I wasn't going to give him time to tell me why I couldn't protect him. I reached for his wrist and started pulling him toward the golf cart building. "Two sets of eyes are better than one, and I would rather hang out with you than do nothing in my room. I'm trying to not helicopter mom Duncan while he's with his friends. And if it's the Jenny Greenteeth again, I want to tell her what I think about her trying to eat my friends."

The cutest little expression twisted Henri's mouth and even touched his eyes as he let me pull him for a minute, at least until he was walking right beside me. When he got there, he didn't tug his arm out of my reach.

I didn't let go either.

In less than a minute, we were on our way in one of the newer electric UTVs, and the coordinates for wherever we were going were on the screen of his cell phone, which he held in his right hand while he drove with his left. What we were going to find, I had no clue, but I could tell he was concerned by his tenser-than-normal body language, so I kept quiet and let him concentrate.

I looked up at the sky while we drove by the clearing in front of the clubhouse and parking lot.

It had been over a week since someone had tried talking to me in my dreams. Since Henri and I had sat in the forest, wrapped in shadows and silvery moonlight, talking about things that still felt like a secret and probably always would. Since that incredible yearning I'd felt in my soul had me hoping for things that weren't destined for me.

I cut that thought off at the knees and focused on the rest of what had happened that night, because that was a safer topic than the latter.

I peeked at the latter out of the corner of my eye. Now wasn't the time. No time was the time, no matter what Matti had said.

Anyway.

The gnomes.

I had purposely tried not to think about anything that had to do with my past or with anyone I could potentially be related to by blood over the last week. Because the more I thought about someone waiting *thirty years* to find me, the more it pissed me off. What excuse could anyone have to justify that?

There wasn't one.

I had enough stuff to worry about. The last thing I wanted was to have some annoying voice speaking to me in my dreams, which was the reason why Agnes had woken up that night. She'd heard it too. When I'd asked Duncan about it the next morning, he had confirmed that he hadn't, and I had wondered if his telepathy had anything to do with it.

And thinking about Duncan made my stress shoot up even more because it reminded me of the person from Alaska coming to visit, according to Franklin.

I felt sick thinking about all those balls I was trying to juggle hanging in the air . . . when I had no idea how to juggle in the first place.

It was a testament to how on edge Henri was, or maybe it was the breeze hitting us head-on, that he didn't comment on my yo-yoing moods at the moment. I'd gotten used to him picking up on everything and forcing me to talk about it. Maybe it drove me a little nuts, but I sort of liked it.

I am my own worst enemy, dang it.

Much sooner than I would have expected, he pulled the UTV off to the side. Henri got out, then stopped. He turned to me, and the light slipping through the trees, golden and beautiful, struck him at the perfect angle, illuminating him like some angel who had just fallen to Earth.

But more like a warrior angel than a guardian one.

The gorgeous man held out his hand. "I don't know what we're going to find, and I don't want you getting hurt."

I stared at his fingers, then at that incredible face, and walked over to set my palm in his. I gave it a squeeze.

Look how freaking cute he was trying to protect me. He didn't squeeze back, but that was all right.

I had to walk faster than normal to keep up with him, but it was worth it. Despite holding my hand, Henri was totally focused on scanning the area, his nostrils flaring ever so slightly every time I happened to glance over at him. We hadn't gone very far when he caught a scent of something that had him tensing. No wonder he was irritated and whoever had called was concerned. We were too close to the clubhouse and all the houses.

I whispered, "What is it?"

His eyes swept across the wooded area, his nose clearly working harder. "Smells like something rotting, but not in a natural way. Not how dead bodies usually smell."

I wanted to ask how he knew the difference, but unfortunately, I knew exactly what he was talking about. I'd smelled something like it before. "Bogeyman?" I asked quietly.

He glanced at me. "You smell it?"

"No, but I've come across them before, and that's how I'd describe them." It had been once in Maine at a campground. I'd had an upset stomach and needed to go number two, which I never did in my camper, and had gone out to find the bathroom in the middle of the night. I'd seen the figure skulking around the campground, sticking to the shadows, trying his best to hide, which had been ballsy because what was a campground if it wasn't clusters of people separated by feet? I hadn't known for sure what exactly I'd seen, but I'd sensed his magic and smelled him, his odor had been so strong. He hadn't been peeping through windows, and I'd watched him long enough to make sure he wasn't doing axe-murderer stuff. At some point, the figure had caught me watching him and then just about basically melted into the shadows of one of the RVs.

The next morning, while I'd been coming out of the shower facility, I'd brushed by a well-dressed man in his seventies whose magic had felt identical to the being's from the night before. He recognized my face and must have instantly identified my bracelet for what it was, because he apologized for being seen. One thing led to another, we had breakfast together a couple of days, and he'd explained what he was.

A bogeyman.

Henri hummed in response. "We're getting closer." He squeezed my hand. "Want to go back to the UTV?"

This man. I went up to my tippy toes and gave his cheek a peck. He'd shaved that morning, and his skin was smooth and warm. "You're a good man, Henri, but I'm coming too. I'll be fine."

The expression on his face said he wanted to argue, but something else won because he nodded. If it was a bogeyman...

Bogeymen didn't just smell like the streets of a city in times when people would toss their crap and pee out of their windows. They were what most people would call a monstrosity in their magical forms, and to most, just looking at them made them sweat, if not have a meltdown in panic. They terrified adults and children at night for a reason. I wasn't sure if they sucked up their fear like a succubus was supposed to feed off sex, but from all I'd heard, they did thrive off it. The older man hadn't spilled his beans to me, so I never got clarification on how exactly his magic worked.

Henri and I didn't go far before I spotted something ahead—multiple somethings. Two wiry bodies were shuffling through the trees and foliage, the normally sweet air tinged with a hint of day-old vomit and decay.

If I hadn't already become desensitized to pulling long strands of grass covered with poop out of Duncan's butt from time to time and having to gag on the few occasions he'd thrown up a carcass he shouldn't have eaten, I might have started retching.

Maybe I wouldn't be able to eat dinner tonight after this, but I'd worry about it later. A breeze picked up from behind us, going straight for the two figures.

The bogeymen whipped around.

I didn't like to call anything ugly, but... *damn*. With splotchy pale gray skin, thinning hair at the tops of their heads, and a build that was borderline emaciated, they weren't attractive beings. Small, membrane-like wings, that didn't look like they could carry five pounds, were dark and tucked against their bony, hunched bare backs. Apart from their body odor, I could confirm that they had terrible breath in both forms—the one I'd met as a human man had apologized for his halitosis from the beginning.

There was a reason why rumors said they didn't mate often.

I lifted my hand and waved at them.

Thin mouths parted, and beside me, Henri went still.

"Hi," I called out.

Henri's head swiveled in my direction, but he didn't tell me to stop.

"Forgive . . . us . . ." The first one slurred through large, too blunt teeth. He might have had an overbite.

Before our eyes, the air shimmered and two lean men, about average height, appeared. They were both dark-haired and dark-eyed. They were okay-looking, but there was nothing memorable or striking about them.

One of them started wringing his hands. "We tried the gate, but no one would let us in," the bogeyman claimed, his eyes nervously sliding to Henri. "We parked at the road and used our magic to follow a trail."

I wasn't sure what to expect, but it wasn't Crown Prince Wolfiness standing there, silently, breathing loudly through his nose, the muscles at his arms flexing as his hands formed fists.

Their throats bobbed, and the men glanced at each other.

The second one seemed to steel himself before his voice came out strained. "We mean no harm. We're looking for . . ." The man, who looked to be somewhere in his thirties or forties, glanced at the other guy, who, now that I could see them well, had some physical similarities that made me assume they could be related, even brothers. "We heard a rumor of a young one . . ."

Henri took a sidestep in my direction, his hand palming my lower back.

"One who smells like life," the bogeyman finished, his lean features expectant but clearly nervous.

I didn't need visual confirmation to know Henri was pissed, and if they had decent noses, they'd be able to tell that too.

"We want to have kids," the other man almost blurted out, his voice emotional. "We were hoping for a blessing. We'll pay for it! It would mean the world to us. We mean no disrespect. We tried the gate so many times, and we leave tomorrow . . ."

The fingers on my back went from flat to clutching the material of my T-shirt from Idaho.

"What is it?" I whispered, peeking up at him.

His left eyebrow went up that signature millimeter he wasn't allowed to go over without special permission. He seemed to be thinking real intently about something. His attention was on the bogeymen, but I knew he was talking to me when he finally replied, "They're not looking for me, young one."

I wouldn't say I smelled like life. I wouldn't say that at all. No one had ever given me that idea. Not in any way. It had always been the opposite—except for the kids and Henri telling me I was the equivalent of a pastry, that is.

But right then, Henri was standing there like he was waiting for me to say something, to do something . . .

He peeked at me right back I guess, when I didn't reply.

I did that "come here" gesture he was so fond of with my index finger and was pretty pleased when he leaned in close enough that I could ask straight into his ear, "You think they're talking about me?"

He stayed right where he was with his earlobe a hair away from my mouth. "There's nobody else it could be," he answered, and I'd swear I felt his skin graze my lip for a millisecond.

"You're sure?" I whispered, backing up an inch so I wouldn't do it again.

His head twisted, and those amber eyes roamed my face when he was at the right angle, and . . . was that a tender little smile on his mouth? On that serious face? "What do you think fertility is?" he asked before lifting his hand and touching my chin with light fingers. "You don't need to do anything you don't want to."

"I can't do anything; that's not the way I work," I explained, forcing myself not to stare at his lips so close. The top one had the most perfect little bow to it. How had I never noticed that before?

"Tell them that, then, because I've been ready to drag their asses off my land for the last fifteen minutes, and they're lucky I'm feeling more generous than I ever have before with a trespasser." That time, he didn't bother lowering his voice. Not at all. "They're risking their lives coming onto my land, and they know that."

He did have murder eyes a couple minutes ago. I grimaced.

The pad of one of his fingers slid to the corner of my mouth, and he did that scowl-frown thing again. "I'm running out of patience. Do what you're going to do, or don't, but decide. Their odor is starting to give me a headache, and I've been told I get grumpy when I get one."

I smirked at the idea of him being grumpy. Serious, often and frequently. Broody, every once in a while. But grumpy? Aww.

But the weight of his words settled into my heart, at what he thought they knew they were risking by trespassing. At what they wanted. Just reproduction. No biggie. *Sure.*

I nodded at him and turned to the men. Might as well be up front about it. "That's not the way my magic works," I called out and scratched my cheek.

Two sets of eyeballs went wide, and I tried to ignore the fact that even they didn't believe me. "You're the one?"

That was definitely a touch of disappointment in their voices.

I smiled. "Neo is the one. I'm just Nina." I shrugged. "But I think it's me you're talking about. Maybe. I can't just . . . you know . . . it isn't like that. I haven't done a study if I work on men or women, or both."

There was a sigh beside me. "It's her," Henri assured them, the slightest little growl in his tone.

If we were doing this, we needed to hurry up. He wasn't exaggerating when he said he was losing his patience.

The men turned to each other. One of them bobbed his head. "A blessing . . . a touch . . . anything would be welcome."

"Anything," the other reiterated.

A blessing?

"Please, we would love a son or a daughter. Would do anything for one," the bogeyman on the right pleaded, his wish so heartfelt even if I wasn't convinced they believed us.

A slightly louder low growl started up in Henri's chest, and I made a decision right then.

Telling myself to hold my breath, I started marching over there. At least I tried. I made it two steps before a hand landed on my shoulder. Before the momentum could stop me, Henri's velvet grumble muttered, "Hold on a second, cowboy. You're not going over there alone."

I was such a sucker for Protective Henri. That was an undisputed fact.

And Matti's admission came back right then and there, trying to lull me with a false sense of hope. Maybe my smile dimmed a little as I put a lid on it, but . . .

Henri was just trying to take care of me in his own way. And that was going to be all right with me. I smiled up at him so hard my cheeks hurt, and I didn't miss the way his features softened. Only for a second, but they did.

Side by side, we walked toward them together. Henri was so close, his arm brushed my shoulder when we stopped a few feet away from the two. "I can't do anything like what you're asking for on purpose, but what about a hug?" I offered, telling myself I wasn't wasting their time. I'd been up front about it. They'd insisted.

"A hug?" Right Bogeyman asked carefully.

All right, guess not that. I thought about it and held out my hand. "A handshake . . . ?"

A thought made me straighten, and I took off my bracelet and bent to set it on the ground. "Or maybe I'm not who you're looking for." I raised my head and they . . . they . . . they both looked stunned all of a sudden.

Not a little stunned but s-t-u-n-n-e-d. I might even say flabbergasted.

And in the blink of an eye, whatever adjective that could've been used to describe the one bogeyman's face turned to pure excitement, and before anything else came out of my mouth, they both threw their arms around me.

These two strange men with questionable body odor, whose names I didn't know, who I had never seen or sensed before, hugged me.

Hugged the crap out of me the same way Sienna did after we hadn't seen each other in a couple months.

The same way my parents did every time we were reunited since we'd moved away from each other.

Their frames trembled as I closed my arms around them too, trying to hold my breath in case I smelled something I couldn't hide a reaction from.

I didn't want to hurt their feelings.

"Oh," Left Bogeyman said in a way that sounded so... relieved? The arms around me tightened, their shaking intensifying. One of their hands curled into my T-shirt.

"That's enough," a deep, snarly voice barked at the same time a palm landed on my lower back one more time.

The bogeymen reacted instantly, releasing me, and one of them bowed. Then the other one did the same, their unremarkable, lean faces bright and shining and so hopeful it made my heart squeeze.

Was one of them tearing up?

"Thank you, thank you," the one on the left choked out with another bow that made me uncomfortable.

Right Bogeyman reached into his back pocket, earning a clear, loud growl from Henri that was anything but human, and the man lifted his hands, palms toward us, holding his wallet. "I mean no harm," he gulped as he dug into it and started pulling out cash.

I watched as he held out a handful of bills. Hundreds and twenties it looked like. "Please, for your blessing," Right Bogeyman explained.

The hand still on my back twitched, and I could see Henri's face out of the corner of my eye. He was gritting his teeth, so I shook my head at the stranger. "No, you don't have to. That wasn't . . . I told you, that's not how it works."

The bogeyman eyed Henri, before rushing out, "In the old days—"

"I'm only in my thirties!" I cleared my throat and lowered my voice. "The old days for me was having a flip phone," I told them with a slight laugh.

"But—"

The human chainsaw beside me got louder.

For their sakes, I took a side-step closer to Henri, the hand on my lower back moving with me, and the next thing I knew, his arm was draped over my shoulders.

And the man who I'd been thinking less than an hour ago that I might be developing serious feelings for, drew me in to his side, tight, so much tighter than I ever would have expected, my shoulder nestling perfectly under his armpit while he literally tucked me *into* him. Fingertips grazed the exposed skin of my arm before he wrapped his whole hand around it. Lifting my head, I found him glaring at the strangers with narrowed eyes and a . . .

That was an interesting face.

He reminded me of Matti when we'd been young and a human kid in school who didn't know any better would try stealing food off his plate.

That poor idiot had no clue how close he'd been to getting bit.

"My patience has run out," Henri spat through clenched teeth. "Pretend this never happened. That can be your payment." He looked at them through slitted eyes. "If I catch you anywhere near here or hear that you've told someone about what happened today, I will find you. Both of you. Understood?"

The bogeymen bowed immediately, the one holding his wallet stuffing it back into his pocket. "Thank . . . thank you for your graciousness," the left one stuttered before he focused on me with his simultaneously nervous and joyous plain face. "Thank you for your kindness, your gift—"

"Get off my property before I change my mind and show you what I do to trespassers." The hard body lined up along mine pointed at a specific direction and growled, "Be fast."

The men took off.

We watched them, or at least I did for a minute before tilting my head up.

Henri hadn't been paying them any attention anymore. That focus was down. On me.

His mouth was already flat, his gaze narrowed. He was thinking. He was thinking long and hard, all right. His cheek was doing that pop thing. Pop, pop, pop.

Reaching for him, I squeezed the fingers that were holding my other upper arm. "You okay? You're sure you're fine letting them go?" I asked, not positive what I would do if he said he wasn't. I didn't want him to hurt them, not as long as they were really leaving and would keep their word.

"I'm fine," he answered, staring me right in the eyes with that sober freaking face.

"That's good," I said before biting the inside of my cheek and coming to a decision. "About that . . ."

Henri was taking me in like he'd never seen me before.

It made me nervous.

"Don't finish that sentence. The last time I met one of their kind, it didn't end well," he cut me off. It was what he said next that had me blinking. "You did a nice thing. Hope in itself is a gift."

He wasn't wrong about that, but it didn't make me feel less self-conscious. A part of me wanted to pretend that hadn't just happened, so I did what I usually did when I wanted to change the subject.

I poked Henri in the solid wall that were his abs. "See? Told you I was going to be your bodyguard."

He blinked, and it made me grin.

But a thought occurred to me suddenly. My stomach dropped. "I'm not worried about myself, but if someone in the community is talking . . . are they going to spread rumors about Duncan?"

"No." Henri sounded so certain. "You don't need to worry about that. The children are the greatest treasure we have in our community. No one would say a word. Not even Dominic. To put a child in jeopardy is to sacrifice your life."

I almost sighed with relief, trusting his every word.

"Come on, let's—" His ringtone went off, irritation taking over his face as he pulled his phone out. "One second," he warned before touching the screen. "Henri," he answered, his tone deceptively polite. The person on the other line would never know his jaw was clenched the whole time.

Since his focus was still on me, I tipped my head in the direction of where we'd left the UTV, and he nodded. He didn't say more than "yes" and "correct" the entire walk back to it. Even when he picked up my bracelet where I'd dropped it, he only handed it to me. Something else came out of his mouth when he got behind the wheel that sounded like he'd ended the call, but Henri had barely pulled the phone away from his cheek when it went off again. It was another call from the ranch based off his "Henri."

No wonder Matti and his dad had left this place behind.

Did they ever leave him alone around here? Did he ever get a day off to relax? I deflated at the idea that he didn't, because every time I racked my brain for a sign that he got time off, not including the few play sessions outside and the night he'd watched movies with us, I couldn't get any solid evidence otherwise.

Which got me thinking . . .

He stayed on the phone the entire way back to the clubhouse, shooting me an occasional apologetic face, his hands flexing and gripping the steering wheel, his knuckles going white on and off the whole ride. When we got to the warehouse, he pulled in, still listening to someone ramble on the other end.

Those amber irises slid toward me after he parked, and he shook his head, his whole expression just . . . tired.

Almost pained.

I held up my index finger just like he'd taught me and got out, leaving him there to run into the clubhouse. It didn't take me long to get up to my room and get what I needed. My trip to the kitchen didn't take long either, and neither did jogging out to the parking lot to back my truck up to my RV and hitch it up.

It might have been about fifteen minutes max by the time I circled back to the warehouse, not sure I was going to find Henri still there, but *he was*.

In the same position I'd left him in. One hand was cupping his forehead, eyes closed as he said in a flat voice, "I know you're upset that your water heater can't be repaired today, but if Shane said you need a new one, then you need a new one, Margaret. You're more than welcome to stay in the clubhouse until then."

He lowered his hand and gave me a flat smile when I slid onto the bench seat beside him.

A few more things were grumbled, and about five minutes of reassurances and apologies later, he dropped his hand with his phone in it on the seat between us.

He blew three normal-people-sized breaths out of his mouth at once.

I gave him a second to decompress before setting my keys beside where his hand was resting on the seat. The movement caught his attention, and he gave me that neutral expression he was so good at. I flicked the keys a little closer to his fingers.

"Right now, there are a whole bunch of leftovers sitting in the fridge of my RV. There's enough gas in the generator and water in the tanks for maybe two days, if you don't flush the toilet every time you pee. My best guess is that there's two days of drinking water in bottles, if you don't stop and get more. My trailer is already hooked up to my truck, ready to go. We can trade phones, so you aren't without one in case of emergencies, and I'll deal with whatever calls come in while you're gone," I explained my plan to him in a rush.

Henri blinked.

"I'll tell everybody you got called into work, and if your work reaches out, I can contact you on my phone and pass the message along," I went on, hoping I'd covered all our bases. "*And* nobody will know I'm lying because it'll be on the phone."

That bottom lip slowly unpeeled from his top one in what I would call the closest thing to his mouth gaping as he might ever get.

I kept on going. "I know I'm not qualified to handle running this place, but I can listen to someone complain just as well as you can. Plus, I have no problem telling them to call whoever gets paid to do that specific job, Fluff. I work in customer service. I'm a professional at resolving issues," I told him with a straight face. "If you want to look at it like this: I've kind of been training for this, not my whole life, but for a long time."

Henri blinked again before his attention dropped to my keys sitting beside his hand again, and his throat bobbed.

I pushed them closer. "I've got about half a tank of gas in my truck," I let him know.

Another very, very deep breath left that incredible body. And I almost didn't hear him start to say in a strangled voice, "You're . . ." He paused, his forehead wrinkling. "You'd do that?"

Did he have to sound so surprised?

I pinched my lips together. "Your Furry Highness, you're tired, you're overworked, and I think you might have needed a vacation five years ago. Go. If it's life or death, I'll call you. I'll lie out of my teeth if I have to first though. I promise to exercise sound judgment. I won't let you down. You can trust me," I told him seriously, meaning every word and hoping he was aware of it. "You're the one always taking care of everybody else. Let me help you out this time."

He was quiet for so long, his expression so blank, so still, that I honestly had no idea what he was going to decide.

Then those amber irises caught mine, and he started shaking his head. "I don't—"

"You don't have anything to feel bad for. From everything I've learned around here, it's a well-oiled machine. Residents don't bother you when you're on shift, and I've heard some of your work conversations—they're not that important. Right? If it's an emergency, I can call you. The only people who might text or call are Matti and Sienna. I talked to my parents last night, so you won't hear from them either. My phone won't go off much if you have it," I told him.

That chest I might have been becoming obsessed with rose and fell, and . . . he nodded.

Henri freaking nodded.

Those long fingers curled around my keys, and he palmed them. "I don't know where I'm going," he let me know. "I won't go far."

"I don't need to know." I shooed him. "Go. I've got this. My job is dealing with upset people. It's a science, and I'm nice, but I'm not that much of a pushover. The customer isn't always right when they're shopping at the Nina Trading Company. A little tough love never killed anybody. Go."

He didn't go right then; he hesitated with my keys in his hand, thinking it over, and probably thinking it over again.

But Henri gave me a look—a warm, nice one—that made me beam at him.

At this hardworking, loyal man who made the bones that made up my chest feel too small for my heart.

"Thank you," he said quietly, and in the next second, he was gone.

"Yes, ma'am, you have a great day too," I said into the phone the very next day, only partially paying attention while holding out my thumb at Pascal who was waving his arms like the lunatic he was.

He was trying to get my attention again. The little boy had a radar for knowing when he wasn't someone's sole focus, especially when it counted, which it did at that moment because the kids were having a cartwheel competition, and I was the lucky judge. There was a small whiteboard on my lap, and someone had already tried to bribe me. That someone being Pascal. With a piece of onyx he'd found in his pocket.

Except I was scoring all the kids 9s and 10s. The 9s were given out if they couldn't complete the cartwheel, but as long as they landed on their feet, they got a 10. They were adorable. And with the weather being amazing and a steady breeze keeping the area where we were at cool, I was having one of my favorite days yet with the kids. But with everyone else?

I waited until the other end of the line went totally dead before I did my best Henri impression by keeping my features neutral as I set his phone back into my fanny pack. Heaven forbid someone see me rolling my eyes, figure out who I'd been talking to, and it get back to them. The truth was, I had no clue how Henri did this crap every day, having to keep cool while dealing with people acting like their issue—no matter how big or how small—was life or death.

I'd made a list of the problems people had called with. Some of it had been important, but some of it hadn't been. The list was saved in the notes app on Henri's phone as: MFer. Someone's satellite TV wasn't working. Someone else couldn't log on to their Wi-Fi. Margaret needed to vent about her hot water heater again. Someone wanted to know if they could add on to their house. Another resident burned themselves and the PA wasn't answering her phone. Someone thought they sensed something they shouldn't have. A teenager called to complain about their parents grounding them. Margaret called again to complain some more about her water heater.

And that had just been in the first four hours.

"Nina! Nina! Watch this! Watch this!" Pascal shouted until I gave him another thumbs-up and he threw himself into a cartwheel.

I drew the number 10 on my whiteboard and held it up.

The little boy started jumping up and down like he'd won a gold medal.

"He's so dumb," Agnes muttered from a few feet away. She had decided from the beginning she wasn't participating in their competition—the prize was two strips of my beef jerky—and had sat off to the side, drawing with markers.

In between us, Shiloh let out a little laugh that had me peeking at him. He had done a couple of cartwheels before wandering over and plopping down so close to me that he'd kneed me in the thigh. He was stacking flat rocks on top of each other, or at least that's what he was trying to do while wearing my bracelet.

That was a new thing with the kids, them taking turns each day wearing it when they got home from school. I wasn't sure how they decided who was going to get it, but I went along with it. I loved it because I got the cutest reaction from them every time I took it off. *"You smell soooo yummy, Nina,"* Shiloh had cooed as he'd let me put it on him.

They liked the way I smelled with my bracelet on, but without it?

Their comments were good for my soul.

One of the ogre boys, Billy, did a beautiful cartwheel. I wrote 10 with a smiley face beside it.

"We're gonna do one at the same time!" two very sweet were-wolf twin girls yelled before they chatted for a moment, nodded seriously at one another, and twisted into their own cartwheels. They got a 10 with two hearts.

The ogre boy and Pascal huddled together, and I wondered what they were planning on doing. You never knew with these crazy asses.

Agnes's head shot up, her upper body twisting around just as I felt a familiar presence from the same direction.

"Nina!" Pascal started shouting. "Nina! Nina! Check this out!" He and the other boy high-fived and did *two* back-to-back cartwheels as the strength—and proximity—of the magic behind me got stronger. I drew them a score of 10 with two stars on either side, and the way they did some dance I had never seen before made me grin.

A figure approached and crouched beside Agnes, speaking to her softly, and out of my peripheral vision, I saw Shiloh set his rocks down and get a hug from our visitor.

One of the twins yelled, "I can do a roundoff, Nina!"

To which Pascal shouted, "Me too!" before he froze. "What's that?"

Snickering, I watched the girl do a cartwheel but land with both feet instead of one at a time. I wasn't sure what the boys told them, but she did another, and that got them trying to replicate one—they looked like cartwheels to me though.

Two hands landed on my shoulders then, and I turned my head to see the face I'd been expecting. The eyes I had memorized at this point. The cheeks and jaw I might be able to draw from memory too.

I couldn't go as far as to say that he looked different, but Henri did somehow. Maybe it was his energy, maybe it was the brightness in his eyes, or it might have even been the faint curve to his mouth. He looked better than ever.

"Hey." I grinned at him. "You're back soon."

"I missed home," he admitted.

Before I could ask him where he'd gone, how it had gone, or if he wanted his phone back, this wonderful man leaned toward me and pressed his lips against mine, softly, sweetly, a smooth touch that lasted a single second, but it might have been the longest second of my life.

"Thank you," he murmured after he'd pulled back, his voice just about a whisper.

"For what?" I practically gasped, not sure what year it even was when my mouth could still feel the pressure from his lips, and he was looking at me like I'd brought a loved one of his back to life.

"For the nicest thing anyone's done for me," he replied.

I'd do nice things for him every day if that was what I got, I thought. I'd answer all his phone calls. At least most of them.

From the corner of my eye, I saw Shiloh's head angled to watch us, his mouth wide open.

Henri must have seen it too because he let go of my shoulders like they were hot potatoes. His throat bobbed, and in the blink of an eye, his face had smoothed into his neutral one. "Did I miss anything?" he asked, all evidence of his affection gone.

Right.

All right then. I forced a smile like my mind wasn't still centered on him kissing me a minute ago. There was a lot you could blame on being a werewolf, but *that* wasn't one of them. And

I wasn't sure I could handle trying to guess why he'd done it, much less what it meant.

"Everything went fine," I told him.

I would break my own legs before I complained about how needy the ranch's residents were and how around midnight, when Margaret had called for the millionth time, I'd considered running his phone over.

He raised an eyebrow like he could tell there was something I wasn't telling him. There was a lot I hadn't told him, but I shrugged and gave him the only piece of honesty I was willing to share with him in front of the kids. "I made some friends, maybe some enemies, and I might've considered calling a priest to come and exorcise M-a-r-g-a-r-e-t, but you have nothing to worry about, Fluff. I handled it." I clutched my whiteboard. "All that matters is that you had a good break."

And I would do it again if I got another kiss for it.

Not that I would tell him that.

Chapter Eighteen

It wasn't very nice, but I was this freaking close to groaning the next morning when I walked into the kitchen, because sitting at one of the islands were Franklin, the elder woman with the silver-blue hair, and the cyclops elder whose name I still didn't know.

"Morning," I greeted them, trying not to sound reluctant while I went over all the reasons they might be here this morning. I didn't think I'd pissed anyone off too bad answering Henri's phone. I hadn't taught the kids any bad words either.

Was it something about the dreams? Or the gnomes? Other than Henri, no one else had brought them up with me after that first visit.

"Good morning," the cyclops began to greet me before the woman, named Ema, cut the BS before I'd even made it halfway into the kitchen.

"We were hoping to discuss—" she started to say.

"An incident was brought to our attention regarding some unauthorized visitors," the cyclops announced, cutting her off with a side look.

"What—" *Oh.* I tapped into my inner Henri and kept my face blank to finish my question. "Visitors?" It wasn't that I was playing dumb, I just wanted to make sure we were on the same page.

"That's what we'd like for you to tell us. Another resident informed us that they came across a peculiar scent, as well as yours," Cyclops answered.

It was only at that point that I noticed the dirty glare Franklin was aiming at the cyclops and Ema. He was annoyed. For the twentieth time, minimum, I wondered what was going on with him. Last night during dinner, he'd been extra quiet, his body language had come across as tense, and he'd left the kitchen the second he'd finished eating.

Even Henri had mentioned how off he'd been acting, but he'd assumed that Franklin had been mad at him for leaving overnight without a warning.

"A resident told you they smelled me and someone else?" I asked, mostly just to see what they knew.

"Yes," the cyclops answered. "In the forest, close to our residences. That's an expressly forbidden—"

I glanced at Duncan lingering by my feet, my boy tall and gangly, and I couldn't help but smile down at him and his smiling face.

LOVE, I tried to tell him.

One of his ears twitched.

Dragging my attention back to the elders, I wondered where Henri was. After he'd gotten home the day before—and kissed me, which I was still overthinking and yet trying not to think about—he'd surprised the crap out of me by sticking close by for the rest of the afternoon and evening.

It had been so nice.

We'd spent another hour outside with the kids, where he'd helped me judge their gymnastics by drawing his own score right next to mine. Then he'd followed us to the nursery and spent the next couple of hours in there, which all the kids had been over the freaking moon for. A few of the youngest puppies had even cried while they'd climbed into his lap and tried to claw their way up to his face. It had been so dang cute, I'd taken pictures.

We'd had dinner together later on, then a call had come through that had drawn him away, but we'd met up outside with Agnes and Duncan to play tag and have popsicles before bed.

And the whole time he'd acted like he hadn't kissed me on the mouth. He'd acted like normal, likable Henri. A Henri who treated me like I was every other person in the world.

It was a travesty—one I wanted to analyze under a microscope but wouldn't. Because if he was going to act like it hadn't happened, then so would I. I could pretend he wasn't giving me mixed signals.

I could pretend him putting his lips on mine was no big deal.

The point was, I didn't think there had been time at any point between the bogeymen and now for him to tell anyone about the incident. Now someone had ratted only *me* out? It kind of seemed like some BS to me.

"We would like to hear your side of the story before we discuss the situation," Cyclops ended.

Franklin's glare toward the other elders went chilly. Even his tone had frost hanging off the syllables when he said, "There's no need for threats, Yiannis."

Was he defending me?

The cyclops looked insulted. "I am not threatening anyone."

The man, who I thought might be my new champion, scoffed. "Do you not hear yourself? To make the situation worse, you won't tell us who approached you with this rumor. If you can demand to speak to Nina about it, I can demand to speak to the gossip."

"I don't see why that information is necessary," the cyclops argued.

Not knowing what to do, I held up my hand like I was back in elementary school, and that was enough to get all three of the elders' attentions. "I don't need to know who tried ratting me out, but I don't think I did anything wrong," I rushed out. "I'll tell you what happened. I don't want to pack our bags."

"Why would you need to pack your bags?"

A body that could only belong to one man came up beside me, and I almost did a double take at the uniform that had to have been poured over Henri. Black pants and a polo shirt had never looked better on anyone in history. I think I had a new favorite outfit over football uniforms.

Then I remembered how his mouth had felt touching mine, and I smiled at him, but tried to keep it within reason.

"Did you hear everything, or do you want me to tell you what happened?" You never knew with him.

His eyelids dropped low over his light-colored eyes as his arm brushed mine. "I meant it more along the lines that you didn't do anything worth packing your bags over." His eyes slid across the elders at the island, his expression melting into his flat one. His tone was thick. "Who was it?"

There was an odd moment of silence.

"Hello, Henri, I don't see how that's relevant," the cyclops answered with a sniff.

The increasingly familiar feel of Henri's palm skimmed up my spine to land just short of my nape. "It is when they left out one important fact in their story. If they could sense the 'other' being and could recognize Nina in the same place, then there's no way they wouldn't have been able to tell I was with her the entire time."

The cyclops didn't look so comfortable all of a sudden. "*You* were together?"

"Who do you think invited her to come along? *I* got the call, and you can contact the greenskeeper who was on duty, because I can't remember which one I spoke to, to confirm. Nina rode over there with me and helped me take care of the issue," he explained in a low, steady voice. "It was an unauthorized visit, we dealt with it, and the visitors left. If there's a problem with that, then there's a problem with my decision-making it sounds like."

Franklin shifted in his seat, still irritated with the cyclops, but more interested in what Henri had finished admitting. "Who were the visitors?"

"Two bogeymen," Henri answered.

"Bogeymen? Here? Why?" the woman elder squawked, alarmed.

Amber irises found mine, and I shrugged. It wasn't anything I hadn't warned them about already, and maybe they would back up on the threats if someone put in a good word for me. I didn't like whoever this snitch was, but . . .

"Rumors have made their way out of the ranch, which is something we need to address with everyone, because that information shouldn't be shared with outsiders, and that *is* part of our guidelines." He sounded so saucy, I almost called him my hero in front of everyone. "The trespassers came looking for a blessing from our fertility g—"

I whipped my head up and started shaking it. "I'm not... that's an exaggeration."

Franklin very clearly shifted in his seat.

Henri pretended I didn't say anything. "They met Nina with my one-time blessing, under my supervision, and left a minute after they were done. Nothing inappropriate happened, and I don't appreciate rumors." The hand he'd left between my shoulder blades slipped down and spanned my lower back. That time, I did lean back into it just a little. "Tell me who I need to have a discussion with."

The Great Wolf was back.

Franklin's gaze discreetly swung toward me, and even though I didn't know him well enough to recognize the little nuances that might reflect on it, it was obvious that his eyes slightly widened.

"I will give you that information in private," Cyclops amended, looking *almost* remorseful.

Maybe he felt guilty.

The muscle in Henri's cheek popped, aggression in his tone as he asked, "Was it Dominic?"

The cyclops didn't need to say "yes" because his face did. "The resident said they recognized Nina's scent along with another. I suppose we can close this matter now."

Franklin's voice was interesting as he agreed, "I suppose we can."

I blinked, the silence so thick I wondered if that was what floating around in outer space had to be like. It was almost suffocating on the ears and heavy on the soul. I wanted to fidget so bad. Whistle maybe.

The female elder made a delicate sniffling sound. "Have you arranged a schedule for your suitors?" she asked me, and I had a feeling she was just trying to change the subject at this point.

The guilt came back with a vengeance the second the word "suitors" came out of her mouth. The urge to glance at Henri had never been so strong. But I didn't. "The men. *Yeah*. Franklin and I talked about it, and we were planning on adding a calendar to the app when my trial period ends."

I couldn't believe I'd agreed to set up mini dates with mythical beings on an app for a secret community I lived in, in front of a man I had more than a giant crush on. A man who had kissed me and currently had his palm mapping parts of my spine.

Fourteen-year-old me, who couldn't get a boy other than Matti to look at me twice to save my life, would have shed a tear of joy.

Thirty-two-year-old me, who had feelings for a good man, a *great* man, the most attractive man I'd ever met, who was also the wrong man, also couldn't believe it, and it wasn't in a good way.

"What are you going to do with Duncan?" It was Franklin who brought up the question, even as he continued glaring at the cyclops elder with an expression that was strangely intimidating for his size and age. He was somewhere between average height and a couple inches short of six feet. He had the body of a man who used to be a runner and still maintained his fitness. And then there was his usual business casual clothing.

There was more than met the eye to him, that was for sure.

But that was something to ponder later.

And his question was a very good one, even if it made me even more uncomfortable than Ema's had. I fought the urge to glance at Henri again. "I have time to think about it, but I guess take him with me if he wants. He needs to like whoever I end up with too." I hadn't thought that far ahead. I didn't like the idea of him meeting every person I met, to be honest.

"He can visit with me," Franklin offered, that borderline scary glint still in his eye as he shot the cyclops another quick glare. "He and I should spend some time together. He needs to get to know the other members of the community since very few seemed fit to do it in my absence."

The cyclops and the woman had the decency to look ashamed—not much but some was some. And me? I tried not to react to him calling them out. I was glad I wasn't the only one annoyed about it.

"I would be willing to watch the child as well," the woman volunteered.

"I could also spend some time with the pup," the cyclops said, definitely sounding sheepish.

Out of the corner of my eye, I saw Henri scowl, but whether that was over the elders being guilt-tripped into being welcoming or not, or the gossip on the ranch, I didn't know. I elbowed him and tipped my chin up. He just shook his head.

We were back to that, I guess.

He could keep his secrets if he wanted to.

I turned forward. "Thank you for the offers," I said to them. "I'll let you know when the time comes." That was so weird to say. In the grand scheme of the last few months, it wasn't even in the top five though.

That was something to think about.

What wasn't was the hard expression that came over Henri's features before he made his way to the range and started loading up a plate of food, his upper body clearly tense beneath his black, long-sleeved polo shirt.

"Where is Agnes?" Franklin asked out of the blue.

"Sounded like she was in her room when I went by," Henri answered in a gruffer tone than usual.

It was strange she wasn't already out here. It had been taking her longer and longer to come to the kitchen the last few days. She had been in her human body a lot more often lately. "Should I get her?" I offered.

"Please," Franklin replied.

"I'll be right back then." I raised my voice. "Duncan, do you want to come with me?"

His *"no"* came as he trotted over to Henri and—was he leaning against him?

He *was*.

Good. Heading out of the kitchen, I went straight for her closed door. Even without excellent hearing, I could tell there were sounds coming from inside. "Agnes? Are you all right? Ready for breakfast?"

I stared at the swinging door at the bottom, but there was no movement.

"Agnes?" I tried again.

Still nothing.

I fought the urge to crawl on my belly and stick my head through the opening, but I wasn't going to invade her privacy like that, not when we were still working on our relationship. We were getting somewhere slowly, very slowly, but there was only so much push she could take.

But just to be on the safe side . . .

"Did I do something?" I asked out loud. "It's okay to tell me if I did." I didn't think so, but . . .

"No," the grumpy, small voice answered, surprising the crap out of me.

"Are you sure?"

"Yes," she replied, still touchy.

All right. "Do you need help with something?"

Another moment of silence stretched so long, I was convinced she was done answering again, but just as I was about to try another tactic to get her to talk, she spoke up. "You don't know how to do it."

"How to do what?" I asked, already offended by her lack of faith in me.

"Braid my hair."

"I know how to braid hair."

There was another long pause. "Then why does your hair always look messy?"

Not scoffing right then might have been the hardest thing I'd ever done in my life. That was mean. "Because I don't care what my hair looks like." I stopped myself from rolling my eyes at the door. She was a child. *She was a child.* "Would you like me to braid your hair?"

"No."

She hadn't thought about that answer at all. That time, I couldn't help *but* roll my eyes. "Want me to try another hairstyle then? Space buns? Pigtails?" How did little girls like their hair? My mom had let me run around like a feral animal. I didn't think I'd used hair products other than shampoo until I'd turned fifteen.

"Can you make them straight? Sera always makes one too high."

I barely held back a snicker. "I can try my best," I promised.

There was another very long moment of silence before she grudgingly said, "Okay."

I reminded myself again that she was young. Very young. "Can I come in?"

More silence then, "Okay."

This kid was making me work for it. Of all the nursery kids, she was still the only tough cookie. The only one who kept everyone she didn't love at a distance, and there weren't a whole lot of people who made the cut. She tolerated Pascal and Shiloh, and a couple other kids—which I figured was the equivalent of friendship. But Duncan she was always sweet to, always so patient and kind with.

Like she was with Henri.

And that just made me even more determined to win her over, even if it took years.

All good things required work after all, I thought, which had my mind straying to my mom. She had told me more than once that people were a lot like plants, and that life in general was very similar to gardening. Some people were thorny, and other people had very weak stems.

As she would remind me in this situation, some plants took a whole lot of water to grow, some plants were cacti that needed just a little to thrive and flourish.

And Agnes, despite her sharp teeth, was more like a bonsai, I guess. Her conditions had to be perfect for her to flourish. But I had a feeling that when she did, she'd be the most beautiful girl in the entire world.

Turning the knob, I opened the door. The room was a little bigger than ours, the walls a pale purple. She had a practical full-sized bed with a plain wooden headboard painted white. Across from it was a big matching dresser with a few knickknacks that ranged from a toy race car to a jewelry box with a ballerina in the middle of it. There was also a picture frame with her and Henri at what looked like a carnival.

On her neatly made bed were so many stuffed animals I wasn't sure I had enough time to count them.

It was those that touched me the most. She might be a tattle-tale ready to bite someone's fingers off, but she was a little kid. A girl who was cared for by a community of people.

But why hadn't any of the families on the ranch adopted her? It didn't make sense, and that just made me sadder. But there was no way I could let my eyes water in her presence, so I was going to have to do this on her terms, at least until she tolerated me better.

She stood beside her bed in bell-bottom jeans and a pink sweater, her cute face twisted into a very, very watchful one, almost like she was expecting me to give her a reason to kick me out. But it was gonna suck to be her because I wasn't letting that happen. We could play by her rules. I was going to water this little bud.

"I'll sit on the bed, and you can stand between my legs while I work on them, deal? If they don't look good, we'll try again," I offered the blonde.

Agnes's nose wrinkled and she squinted, but she nodded in a way that reminded me a lot of Henri, all brisk and no-nonsense.

This was a test. For whatever reason, the idea of it made me more nervous than when I'd taken my SATs. I didn't care if most people didn't like me, but I wanted her to.

Everyone deserved love, especially the difficult ones.

This could have been me. This could have been Duncan. This could've been Matti or even Henri, here, without an adult they trusted enough to ask for help with a hairstyle.

I couldn't cry.

But I blinked a whole bunch of times while I sat on the end of the bed and the girl came to stand between my legs, holding three different kinds of elastics.

She only made me redo her pigtails twice.

* * *

Child?

Can you hear me?

I gasped awake, jackknifing up into a seated position.

A low pulse of pain, a baby headache, pressed against my forehead, directly above my eyebrows. My heart was racing. My throat felt dry.

That hadn't been a dream.

It hadn't been a freaking dream in any way.

My bedroom door swung open, my sleeping puppy lifting his head groggily at the intrusion, his tail doing the same as a familiar body slipped inside.

"Cricket?" Henri's voice was soft, navy blue sweatpants clung to his hips for dear life as his long legs brought him to my bed. He wasn't wearing a shirt again. I wasn't too out of it not to notice that.

Duncan took one look at him, peeked at me through bleary puppy eyes, and set his head back down.

I opened my mouth to say I was fine, but the only thing that came out of me was an exhale. It was a shaky one too. I tried again, and the same thing happened.

I felt . . . not scared, but worked up?

"I heard it." Henri frowned as he sat on the edge of the mattress, his butt literally pushing my legs aside. "You all right?" he whispered.

My fingers were shaking. But nothing had happened. No one was hurt.

A warm hand covered mine, right where it was on my lap, jittery like I'd had the scare of a lifetime.

"Hey, you're good." Henri's fingers curled over my own. His forehead wrinkled. "You're here. You're safe. You listening?"

I opened my mouth again, but another shaky breath was the only sound that left my body.

Fingertips touched my chin, tilting my head back.

Henri's face leaned in so close, his cheekbones and eyes filled my vision, becoming my whole world in that moment. "I'm not going to let anything happen to you," he told me.

The logical part of my brain was aware there was nothing to be worked up about.

But the rest of me wasn't convinced of anything.

How the hell could someone be talking to me while I slept? How powerful was this MFer? *Who* was he?

"Same thing happen?" His thumb drew a line from the knuckle of mine up to my fingernail.

I nodded, feeling dumb for acting like this when I was fine. Duncan was fine. Henri was fine. That was what mattered. I was here, and I was safe, and whoever this person was, he wasn't Freddy Krueger, and he didn't *seem* to be wanting to hurt me.

He was just . . . asking for someone.

For maybe, possibly, me.

I had to pinch my lips together at that.

After a second, I said, "Yeah, it sounded like the same voice from before." Flipping my hand up, I snuck it under his palm, shaken up but ultra aware of this man in only sleeping pants, inches away from me. His chest got better every time I saw it, covered in creamy tan skin and dark chest hair that I would've wanted to focus on if someone wasn't visiting me in my dreams.

I didn't want this. I wasn't a child anymore who was different from everyone around her and needed some way to identify. I definitely didn't need someone poking around, ruining my chances here.

I squeezed my eyes together and swallowed hard. "I'm sorry, Fluff."

There was a soft touch to my jaw that had me peeking at him. Any sign of his neutral face was gone. He looked . . . concerned. "Why are you apologizing?"

I let my head droop forward, my forehead grazing the bare skin on his shoulder, nestling into the perfect crook right there. "Because you're being woken up, and it might be my fault. I know you got home late. You need your sleep." I'd happened to be standing in the hallway at the window, holding a heavy Duncan in my arms, while we'd been nosy. Henri had gotten home an hour later than usual. While I'd been outside with Agnes and

Duncan, I'd caught the little girl sitting there, staring off at the parking lot almost expectantly.

And the truth was, she hadn't been the only one wishing he'd gotten home earlier.

I pressed my lips together, thinking again about that peck that shouldn't have meant so much to me.

"It's all right." The fingers by my jaw slid so he cupped the nape of my neck. "Agnes used to have nightmares, and she'd come knocking on my door with an excuse every time." I could hear him take a deep breath. "Everything is all good."

Was it? Because it didn't feel that way, waking up in the middle of the night, panting like I'd run a marathon. All because someone was invading not just my sleep but other people's too. Just how many, I had no idea. No one had brought it up, other than Agnes, and I hadn't wanted to ask and bring attention to myself in case the gnomes were right.

A faint growl rumbled through Henri's chest. I felt it on my forehead. "You smell like cinnamon again." Those callused fingers gently kneaded my neck. "There's nothing to worry about." I would've sworn he leaned in even closer. "We'll figure out who's doing it, and I'll deal with them."

That had me lifting my head. He was *inches* from me, and I peeked at him from under my eyelashes. "You'd do that?" I whispered.

The way he nodded made me feel like it was a promise. "I would," he confirmed quietly.

He wasn't doing this to protect *me*, I reminded myself. He would do this for anyone. I had to remember that. Him rushing around to comfort me was going to be a memory sooner rather than later. If this kept happening, I'd wake up with someone else in bed next to me. Someone else would be making me feel better.

I suddenly felt sick.

His scowl came out of nowhere. "What?"

Crap. "What?" My voice came out a little higher than normal.

"What did you just think about? Your scent got stronger."

He was on to me again. "Just . . . just thinking about the future," I tried to keep it vague.

He could tell, and he wasn't going to let me get away with it, like usual. "Why are you lying?"

Dang it. "I didn't want to, but I felt like I should," I answered him honestly. "Just thinking thoughts I shouldn't be, that's all." Not even I believed my BS.

"Which are?"

I shook my head.

There went that half frown, half scowl again.

"Do you bother everyone this much when you want to know something they don't want to tell you?"

"No," he replied, watching me closely. "What were you thinking?"

I shook my head some more.

He wasn't going to drop it. "Tell me."

"I don't want to." I bit the inside of my cheek. "There's no point, Fluff. Trust me."

"I do trust you; that's why I want you to tell me what got you worked up." Those amber eyes bounced from one of mine to the other. "Trust *me*."

I did, damn it.

He said he wanted to know, but I really didn't believe he was going to want to afterward. He didn't look away though. He just sat there, touching me, like he hadn't kissed me and then acted like he hadn't. Sitting here with every line of his body insisting he wanted honesty. Maybe even needed it.

All right.

So be it. I shrugged. "I was just thinking that in a few months, if this happens, there'll be some other man in a bed probably just like this one, having to talk me down from this, and . . . that made me feel disgusting inside, Henri. You're my friend, and I understand why you don't want to be more than that. I get that you don't. I told myself I was never going to bring this up with you again, but . . . but I like you a lot, and I'm not going to apologize for that." I tried to smile, but even without seeing it, I knew it was weak. "That's what I was thinking, Your Hairy Highness, since you insisted on knowing. Don't say I didn't warn you."

Henri leaned away like I'd cursed his ancestors or something, and I thought . . . I thought I'd screwed up. That maybe this wasn't something he could brush off after all. That there was a chance I wasn't going to be able to smile my way out of this situation.

I tried to think of a way to salvage this and not make it so awkward. He *knew* I was attracted to him. I'd never been subtle about it, and there was only so much I could hide. Liking him as a person couldn't be so out of this world he was shocked by it.

Sienna had told me once that love and affection were some of the loudest emotions people could emit.

He'd asked for my honesty, and I'd freely given it, but . . . I took in his features, his jaw covered in scruff, his short hair with its shorter sides. I lifted my chin.

He was used to getting his way, but I was an only child, and so was I.

I knew he liked me. And if I had to choose anyone on this ranch to mate with, it would be him. Without a doubt, Henri would be every number on my top ten list. The idea of marrying someone else . . . The more I thought about it, the more I hated it.

And if you don't like something, do you know who's going to change it? Only you will.

So before I could talk myself out of it and remind myself why I shouldn't, why I'd thought "never again" already, I snagged his gaze and *held on*.

"Unless you've changed your mind," I told him with a wobbly smile. "I'm good at snuggling, and I'm pretty good at brushing coats out." It was only a tiny victory *that's* what I decided to say instead of telling him the ten other inappropriate things that I could have gone with, like having strong fingers and how I used to own a shake weight.

But that small mercy didn't seem to do much for him.

I'd watched a lot of storms roll in over the years. Big, grayish purple storms that bubbled over mountaintops and beautiful hills. And yet, I hadn't seen one move the way I watched his expression literally morph in front of my eyes. He seemed... frustrated? Maybe angry?

But I'd swear his gaze flicked down the front of me for one second before he zeroed in on my face again, and his voice was low and rough as he murmured, "I see."

Yeah, I bet he saw.

Or maybe he was annoyed that I was still bringing this up after he'd let me down.

I could tell he was bothered from the way his body tensed. Then his hands fell away from where they'd been on me, and he leaned back. Away. From me. "Wake me up if you hear anything again, Nina."

He might as well have tossed a bucket of warm water on me.

I see.

I wouldn't wake him up. His room was on the floor above mine, but I didn't know which door was his. But even if I did, I wasn't going to bring the dreams up in his presence, not when he was looking the way he was right then. Uncomfortable, mostly. Frustrated and possibly angry. But I nodded.

And when Henri got up and left my room a couple heartbeats later, taking his warm, comforting presence with him, I watched it happen with a knot in my stomach.

But it was what it was. I'd tried to put myself out there one last time, just in case, hoping, and hoping, and hoping some more. He was going to do what he wanted to do.

And I had to do what I needed to do.

Relying on him so much, expecting anything from him, was only going to hurt one person in the long run, and that person wasn't going to be him.

It'd only be me who got hurt.

Chapter Nineteen

"How's the number two love of my life?"

I melted on the other side of my phone's camera, torn between so much love my body could barely handle it and wanting to slap my hands against my face so I could muffle the scream that had been steadily building in my body over the last few days. I hadn't purposely kept things from my two closest friends in the entire world, but there were some things that were easier to explain verbally than through text.

Plus, I knew Matti and Sienna; they were going to want the *whole* story, not just part of it.

And Sienna showed me just how well she knew me when she lunged forward, so close into her own phone's forward-facing camera that all that was visible was a single green eye and a perfectly plucked eyebrow. "What happened?" she demanded.

Did she have any idea she'd picked up Matti's video call habits? I let it go for now as I leaned against the seat of my travel trailer's dining room table slash bed, not sure where to start even though I had already planned parts of this conversation out so we could cover everything. That's why I was in the trailer, to give myself the closest thing to privacy I could get without driving an hour away. Nothing I had to say was worth the gas. And too many people came in and out of the clubhouse for that to be a proper venue for our conversation.

"That good?" Sienna's eye got even closer so I couldn't see anything but a blurry iris and pupil.

"'Good' is a stretch," I told her honestly, slumping into the refinished seat. I had redone it myself four years ago when I'd parked outside of Sienna's parents' house and spent a month and a half refurbishing my trailer with the help of her dad.

She whistled long and low. "I had a feeling about this two nights ago." Her eyeball flicked to the side where Matti was sitting. "Didn't I tell you my sixth sense was going off?"

"You did, baby," he agreed from out of the shot.

I smirked, and Si nodded.

"See? I'm ready when you are," she let me know.

The smirk fell off my face. "You pick. I don't know where to start. My maybe biological father waking me up in the middle of the night—"

She gasped, and it was my turn to nod.

"The bogeymen and the gnomes who want to have kids." Her eyebrow arched at that. "Or do you want to hear about how *someone's cousin* is ignoring me now because I haven't been able to stop asking him if he wants to marry me, even though he kissed me . . . or he gave me a peck, if we're going to be technical." It was not my finest moment. But I didn't want to regret not putting myself out there, especially not when the only person I wanted to mate with to stay here was him.

I held up my finger. "He also rubbed his face all over me after a bunch of werewolves showed up to cook."

I was suddenly really glad Sienna wasn't around to smell the despair that I had to be emitting at the acceptance that I wasn't going to get what I wanted.

The thing I wanted being Henri.

"You didn't," was all she said.

"I did."

"*Nina.*"

I shrugged.

The camera zoomed back, and she shook her head slower than anyone I'd ever seen before. "That. I pick that. I want to hear about that son of a bitch DNA donor, but later, and you having a bunch of werewolves wanting to mate with you has been old news before it was even news. I've always known you were boner material."

I beamed. "Have I told you lately that I love you?"

"No, but thank you. Now tell me what's going on with *someone's* cousin. *Henri* kissed you?" Her voice went high and everything.

Out of view, Matti muttered, "Ugh."

Even though I'd told Matti some of what was going on, and I was confident he'd shared it with her, it took about two minutes to rattle off the first brief mention I'd made to Henri about Matti's suggestion. I followed that with the most recent and wrapped it up with a brief explanation about him being stressed, letting him borrow my RV, and him coming home and giving me that smooch that was still haunting me.

It had been three days since I'd last seen him, for the record.

I told her almost everything but skipped out on him being half-naked and all the stuff with my father since this was a three-part miniseries. "He's avoiding me now."

She scrunched up her face. "Why do you think that?"

Holding up a finger again, I peeked through the blinds behind my back and then got up and checked the other windows. There still didn't seem to be any other community residents walking around; for the most part, none of them got home until late in the afternoon anyway. Once I was back at the table, I leaned forward and whispered, "Because I take the kids—Duncan and the white wolf, Agnes—out every night for a game of tag and a popsicle, and we look at the stars. We go out at the same time, and I know he knows that because there were a few nights before all this that he would come home and sit with us when we were out there. Since that night when I'd asked him if he was sure he didn't want to marry me—" I realized then I'd forgotten to tell her the part of me telling him he was attractive. "—he's purposely gotten home fifteen minutes after we would've gone back inside the clubhouse. Same time every night." I'd timed it.

"You sure it isn't a coincidence?" She squinted. "Matti's said before he's blunt. Wouldn't he tell you if something was going on instead?"

"I know one night his shift ended an hour earlier because one of the other wolves called him and asked where he was."

That had left a little knot in the center of my chest. The idea that Henri might be avoiding me, hurt.

But I'd taken a risk with him that night in my room, even though I hadn't actually thought he would say yes, no matter how much he seemed to stare at me sometimes, or touch me, or how helpful or kind he could be.

Or how playful he could be with me. Or affectionate. Or protective.

Or regardless of what Matti had smelled coming from him.

I'd been doomed.

On the screen, Sienna got even more squinty, and Matti was blinking very casually at the screen—he'd slid closer to her at some point—and I knew I needed to change the subject.

"Can I tell you about my father now so I can tie in that story with Henri avoiding me?"

"Proceed."

Only with them could I grin through this conversation. "My DNA dad may or may not be waking people at the ranch up in the middle of the night, in a dream that's not a dream, asking for his 'child.' The gnomes think it's him or a family member."

"*What?*"

That sounded as outrageous as it was. I told them what happened.

Moving the camera back to only focus on her, she mouthed *whatttt,* and I nodded again. "There's a lot to unpack here, but let's back up a couple steps." Sienna leaned forward again. "What exactly would you do if he said yes?"

We were back to that. "Do it," I told her instantly.

She leaned away, then zoomed back in. "Really?"

Did she have to sound like it was that crazy? "Yeah."

Her eyes slid from side to side. "I haven't gotten the full story, but it sounds like you might have options, and if you do, then why wouldn't you explore those instead of him?"

I'd known this was coming. I sat up on the bench seat. "He's very handsome. He's so good with all the kids. He bickers with me but in a fun way. He works hard, but too hard. He's very protective—"

"Henri?" She couldn't believe it, and I laughed.

"Yes." Not that she could see, but my shoulders dropped. "Henri. He ticks all my boxes. Every single one of them." I paused and told them the truth, even though I couldn't see Matti at the moment. "I like him a lot." Saying that out loud made me . . . it made me sad, because I did. And nobody was indebted to like anyone in return, but why couldn't that be the case? He was the first man I'd ever felt this level of attraction to, on so many different levels, not just physically and . . .

Sienna narrowed those green eyes at me, but all she said was "Huh."

I shrugged, and I knew my struggle had to be evident. I more than liked him, and if I couldn't admit that to them, then who could I say it to? Raising my eyes to the ceiling, I told her without moving my lips, "I think I'm a little in love with him." I bit the inside of my cheek. "Sorry, Matti."

Sienna didn't say a word, and I peeked back down at the screen.

She had the saddest look on her face. "I'm sorry, Nina. That doesn't explain that kiss, but . . ." Si shrugged. "It's his loss, and I kind of hope he regrets it when you mate with someone else."

It said something that she wasn't telling me things would work out, and it said even more that Matti stayed quiet too.

The low-key grief was there in my tone. "I kind of hope so too." I shrugged. "It's fine. I saw a couple of the wolves who did seem interested, and they were nothing to be disappointed over." I could love anyone. If I gave it time and watered the love, fertilized it . . . it could grow. That rang true for every kind there was.

Just because one person couldn't love me didn't mean someone else couldn't.

There was no reason for that thought to hurt me as much as it did, but it did. My stomach, though, revolted like it always did when I pictured that.

My oldest friend leaned in front of his wife. "Give me names. I'll do backgrounds checks."

The three of us were smirking, but something that felt exactly like disappointment took a little bit more of my joy away.

At least I knew what I was working with. At least I knew where I stood with him. With Henri.

At least . . . I had another chance to be with someone else in the future.

Child. Nina?

I sat up.

My throat hurt. My nose stung. It was the grogginess, though, that was the worst of it all. Duncan, fortunately, was sleeping peacefully against my leg. Safe. Innocent. Undisturbed.

I took a breath in through my nose and let it come out shaky. And when a minute went by and then another and there was no knock, no barging in, no handsome man coming to save me, no nothing, I told myself it was for the best while wiping at my eyes and my nose with the back of my wrist. I did it again before I put my elbow on the mattress and crawled out from beneath the covers. Duncan lifted his head up from where he was on his side, and I curled my body around his. And my sweet, perfect puppy wiggled his way up to tuck his head beneath my chin, and he gave me exactly what I needed right then.

"Love," he told me.

LOVE, I tried to tell him right back.

". . . farted in my eye, Dunky. If I end up with pink eye, it's going to be your fault," I rambled to my donut who was on his way to being a bear claw, as we made our way down the staircase.

A red eye set in a dark face peeked up at me, and I gasped.

"Did you do it on purpose?" I asked him, referring to the way he had woken me up by passing gas with his butt inches from my face earlier. My whole eye felt funny now. And from that little side-look he'd just given me, I would have sworn he'd done it on purpose.

My boy didn't say yes, but he didn't say no either. It made me laugh before I reached down and tickled his neck as we kept going. He was taking the stairs so easily now.

"That's rude, if you did it on purpose," I kept on going as we approached the closed door where Agnes's room was. "But your firepower was impressive."

We hadn't even gotten to it when the door opened and a blonde head of hair stuck out like she'd been waiting.

I slowed down and smiled. "Good morning, Agnes."

Duncan trotted ahead to stick his face in the doorway, and I could see the little girl duck to give him a hug as she replied, "Hi."

"Everything okay?"

There was a pause longer than it needed to be before she peered up at me, her face pretty much pinched. "Can you fix my hair?"

I couldn't let myself blink.

Agnes hadn't been acting differently during the day or at night when we met up in the hallway before going outside. She was still quiet. Still self-contained.

But now? She was *asking* me to help her. Me.

It had only taken two months.

"*Love,*" Duncan's familiar voice had me flicking my eyes toward him.

My donut and his moral support. I puckered my lips and blew him a kiss. He knew me well enough to sense I was going through something, and he was telling me it was okay.

How in the world had I gotten so lucky?

"Sure," I agreed, still trying to keep my features even. This had to be the equivalent of the popular boy in high school being interested in me. I had to play it cooler than I ever had before. "Pigtails again or would you like me to try something else?"

If she noticed that my voice came out pitchy, it didn't reflect on her face. "Pigtails are okay," she answered a little warily.

One day, she was going to let me braid her hair, I decided right then. That was my goal, which meant I should practice my braids, so I'd be ready when we got to that stage in our relationship. Because we would, even if it took ten years. I had never met another child like her before, and I still had no idea what had led to this, but as long as I was here, I was going to be there for her.

Agnes backed up and opened the door wide, and Duncan darted inside, his nose to the ground, smelling one way and then the other, drawn the most to the twin-sized bed closer to the window with a plain white comforter on it. It was where the women who took turns sleeping in her room stayed. I hadn't made friends with either of them exactly—they were polite yet not what I would call friendly—but I wasn't worried about it. All that mattered was that they were good to her, and so far, I hadn't heard a single complaint.

While Duncan snooped around, I sat on the bed in the same spot as last time and the little girl backed up between my legs.

"Did you sleep okay?" I asked, taking the comb she handed me and drawing it through her thick but very straight hair.

"Sera snores a lot," she answered, not sounding any grumpier than usual.

"You know . . ." Would it be too much too soon to . . .? Should I talk to Duncan about it first and see how he felt about it? I was overthinking it, I decided. "If you need anything in the middle of the night . . . or can't sleep . . . or if you want to have a sleepover, Agnes, you can always come upstairs with us. We all fit that other day with Henri."

"*Yes*," the puppy on the other side of the room told me again, confirming my thought that I'd been overthinking my offer to the little girl. Red eyes were peeking at me from over the edge of the bed.

Oh, this donut knew exactly what he was doing and when he was doing it best. After holding him for a while, I'd eventually fallen asleep the same way we used to when he'd been a newborn. On his back with his butt tucked into my armpit, legs straight up in the air.

I winked at him before parting Agnes's hair straight down the middle.

I'd just perfected the spot for her right pigtail and gotten the elastic around it when she whispered, "Henri said the man in the dream is looking for you."

My hands stilled. I had a choice here, and I made my decision. I'd hoped for a miracle, that he hadn't woken anybody up, but that was wishful thinking. "That's what people tell me, but I don't know for sure, Agnes. I'm sorry he's waking you up." I wrinkled my nose for a second. "I promise there's nothing for you to be scared of."

"I'm not scared," she chuffed like I was dumb. I could've pointed out how she'd been shaking around the gnomes, but it was enough for me to know the truth.

"Good. Because you shouldn't be," I assured her. "None of us are going to let anything happen to any of you." I would do whatever I had to to keep Duncan and the rest of the pups safe. I would even include Henri, Randall, Ani, and Maggie, too, on my list of people I was protective over here. There was Phoebe the satyr too. She was the one parent who talked to me the most. We had gone grocery shopping together the day before, and she was still quiet but very sweet. We'd made plans to go again.

Then there was Franklin, who might get there someday after he'd gotten bent out of shape on my behalf with the other elders, even though there was something still suspicious about him. Since getting back from Alaska, he'd been quiet when we shared meals together and also super tense. More than once, I'd caught him watching me discreetly, but I'd played it off like I didn't see him. When we did talk, it was usually about the puppies at the nursery, and every once in a while, he might ask a personal question, like where I had grown up, where my parents lived, and where I'd lived before.

Everyone else here though? I'd think about it. It would probably be a case-by-case basis.

"Why's he doing that?" Agnes asked, bringing me back to the present.

"Waking us up?"

"Uh-huh."

"You have pretty hair, Agnes," I told her, drawing the brush through it. "I don't know why."

"Who is he?"

Her own family situation went through my head, and I knew I had to be careful. "I'm not sure. Remember the gnomes? They told me it's my dad, but I don't know any of my family," I admitted. This was the first time she'd asked me something personal about myself.

That got her to peek at me over her shoulder. She didn't resemble Henri physically at all, but her expression couldn't have been any more Fluffy if she'd tried. I wanted to tease her over it, but it was too soon.

"You don't know your mom or your dad?" the little girl scoffed like she couldn't believe it.

How did I explain this? "No." I pressed my lips together. "When I was a baby, these two werewolves found me and decided I could be their daughter. They were my mom and dad, but I came out of other people's bodies. I don't really count my birth parents because my werewolf parents did everything for me. They raised me and took care of me and loved me. I was their baby, and they're my family. I love them very much. Does that make sense?"

She faced forward again. "Uh-huh."

I didn't want to call my biological parents my "real" mom and dad because I didn't think of them that way. "Real" parents were the ones who did the work and put in the effort and love, but that would be way too complicated to explain to a child, so I was going to have to go with it. "But my mom and dad, who are like me, I never met. Or anybody else, not my grandparents, aunts and uncles, cousins, no one. All I'm trying to say is that I don't know why that voice is waking us up. I am sorry that he's bothering you, though."

I managed to start her pigtail before she spoke up again, her own voice more careful than I ever would've expected. "So you have two dads?"

She still wanted to talk about me? "Sure, I guess," I answered.

"And that's okay?"

I had to pretend like I had no idea how she was relating this to her own life, because if I did, it would make me cry, and I could not cry in front of this land shark. "I don't see why it wouldn't be. One was in my life and the other wasn't. One wanted to be my dad, and the other didn't. There's no law that says you can't have two."

Another long minute went by before, "So sometimes . . . dads don't want to be dads?"

My tear ducts activated.

It took me a second to say, in a voice I thought was pretty even considering I was real close to weeping, "Sometimes, Agnes. I wish I could tell you why, but I have no idea." I touched her hair. "But like with my parents that weren't a part of my life, it wasn't my fault. It wasn't anything I did for them to not be with me. I didn't do anything wrong. I try not to let it hurt my feelings." I swallowed. "Sometimes it does though. But I was lucky like you are; I had people who loved me and wanted to be in my life. They're the ones who matter the most. Some words, like *mom* or *dad*, are just words. It's how someone makes you feel that matters."

The little girl didn't say anything after that. And when we were done, Dunky strolled over, planting his chin on my leg, and I strained picking him up, and even though I knew she was going to say no, I held out my hand to Agnes.

"No, thank you," she answered but opened the door for us.

She was a salty little peanut, but fortunately for her, I liked savory things just as much as I liked the sweet stuff.

And if anything else, she reminded me of what it was that mattered.

I hugged Duncan just that much tighter, relishing the feel of his frame and his weight because I was running out of time with moments like these. The good thing was, he didn't mind as he licked my cheek.

"*Yes,*" he told me. "*Love.*"

My heart was going to burst one of these days, and I couldn't think of a better way to go.

"What happened to your mom and dad?" Agnes asked

suddenly, tipping her face up at me in the hallway. Her eyelashes were almost white, her eyebrows almost a light brown that made her cute face so striking.

This was the most we'd ever talked to each other at once. I loved it.

"My werewolf mom and dad?"

She started walking right alongside me. "Uh-huh."

"They live in Mexico now." I held Duncan tighter as the words came out of my mouth. "I still see them, but not a lot. I can't drive to visit them anymore. They live somewhere without cell phones and internet, and calls are expensive. They're older, and it's harder for them to travel." I would never blame Duncan, but his presence had put a stop to our easy visits.

Her eyebrows were at her hairline when she glanced up at me. "You miss them?"

"I miss them so much," I told her gently, not sure where she was going with this.

I wasn't sure she did either when she seemed to ponder that a while before asking, "But are they still your mom and dad? Even if you don't see them?"

How could I explain such a difficult concept? And how in the world did I get myself into this position so much? "Some people are so important to you that nothing, not time, not being far, not life or . . . death, will ever take them away. I don't see my best friends all the time either, but I still love them so much, and they love me, and they're always going to be there for me."

"But . . . how do you know you aren't gonna forget them? Since you don't see them?"

This was the last person in the world I ever would have expected to break my heart, and it took me a moment to get myself together. "Some things you just can't forget. Think about Henri. He calls you Ladybug, right? So I bet, for the rest of your life, any time you see one, you're going to think of him. There are probably a lot of things you two have talked about and been through that will make you think of him forever."

She grumbled under her breath, but that was the best

explanation I had. Fortunately for me, we made it to the kitchen, and I could see her pressing her lips together, that sharp mind racing with who knew how many thoughts. I hoped she'd ask me more about anything she wanted, even the difficult topics, even if I didn't know how to answer them.

At the doorway though, I spotted a man leaning against the island, the rest of the kitchen empty.

There I went not paying attention again.

But it wasn't Randall's red head or Henri's black color, much less Franklin's more-salt-than-pepper hair.

It was a blond man.

And coming off him was werewolf magic.

It was Dominic, who looked up with a scowl from the phone he'd been focused on.

Honestly, I'd almost forgotten all about him. I hadn't given him a single thought in a while. I considered it a blessing that he hadn't been by again with his offer to mate with me.

I'd move to the South Pole before that ever happened.

And from the face he made, he didn't exactly seem thrilled to see us either.

Not even his daughter, that rotten asshole.

As if the same thought hit her at the exact time it did me, Agnes set that stubborn chin, clenched those fists Maggie had mentioned she'd gotten into fights with in the past, and she marched right up to him, a freaking bone to pick written all over that small face. The eight-year-old girl went straight into intersecting a man that adults and children were intimidated by, like it was nothing to her. She was an army of one right then.

Pure pride went through my system, even though I had nothing to do with how tough she was.

I must've not been the only one surprised by her actions because even Dominic made a face like he didn't get what was going on.

The girl I'd gotten to know, who was only scared of gnomes, steeled her titanium spine and said, in her snitch voice, "You're not supposed to be here. Franklin said."

I didn't think my mouth had ever formed the shape of an O faster.

Out of the corner of my eye, I saw Duncan's tail go straight up in the air, but he didn't move an inch.

Dominic's face contorted into a sneer. "What did you say to me?" he snapped in a way that had me taking a step forward.

Maybe he was her dad, but that didn't mean shit to me.

But Agnes wasn't even a little intimidated as she tipped that little chin up and *said it again* even louder. "You're not supposed to be here. Franklin *and* Henri both said. I heard them."

She tapped her right ear, and I almost howled.

Just like that, she got promoted from protector to badass.

But it was the wrong thing to say to a man with an anger problem.

Dom's face went red. "Franklin and Henri are not the fucking boss of me."

I moved around the island and slid in between her and the man who was supposed to take care of her and protect her.

But I knew better than anyone that sometimes biology failed in that aspect.

But you know what didn't fail? Love. And for as prickly of a cactus as she could be, I did love Agnes, and so did Henri and all the other people who included her in their lives. She had her own chat in the app.

Maybe this asshole had gotten away with being mean to kids before, but that was over.

"You need to go," I said in a flat voice as anger like I hadn't experienced since the days those people had tried to take my donut flared inside my whole body, my ears ringing.

The asshole's lip curled. "I'm not talking to you."

I didn't think it was possible to get angrier, but it was.

"You must be talking to me because I know you're not talking to her like that," I told him through gritted teeth, ready to shave his eyebrows off.

We were shocking him left and right tonight. He reared. "What?" Dom snarled.

Wasn't used to someone talking back, was he? "You heard me," I answered, refusing to tiptoe around him anymore. "It's time for you to leave." What was he doing here in the first place?

Angry pink streaks formed across his cheeks. "You don't get to tell me shit."

"When you talk to a child like that, then yeah, I do get to tell you when you need to go, and that's right now."

"Fuck you."

"Okay?" I shrugged. "I'll do that, but you still need to leave."

A confused expression spread over his features at what I could only imagine was me not being devastated at his incredible comeback. It only lasted a second. "No. *No.* I don't need to do *shit*," he claimed. "I don't give a fuck who you are and who you're banging. You're fucking *nobody*."

If he thought he was going to hurt my feelings, he was going to be in for a huge disappointment.

And how could he say "banging" in front of the kids?

Dominic's eyes dropped to my side as Agnes leaned around me. Not peeking. Not even trying to be discreet, but literally clearly hanging out. And her DNA daddy didn't like that.

His face turned even redder before he exploded. "Neither of you get to say *shit* to me. I don't care if you're under Henri's protection or not. He's a fucking spineless—"

I'd heard enough. It was one thing to be rude to me, but Agnes? And much less Henri?

Not on my damn watch.

A sharp knife was only dangerous when you used it in the wrong way, after all.

At that moment, the magic in my stomach said, *Here I am*, and I said, *There you are.*

Use me as you need, it told me, and I welcomed it.

Maybe it was a gift I didn't necessarily want, but it was there, and it was mine, and I would do what I could with it.

I leaned forward, my voice steel and night. The past and the future. Life and death. "Dominic?" I murmured.

Out of the corner of my eye, I saw Agnes's face tip up to look at *me*.

Dom's eyes slightly widened, and I wondered what he saw in mine. Probably exactly what I wanted him to.

A part of me I didn't like sharing. But he'd forced me to come this far. Forced me to do this. And now we were all going to ride this out.

"Do you know what happened to the last person who threatened someone I care about?" I asked him.

His throat bobbed, and I watched goose bumps prickle along his neck, saw the way his mouth parted as those irises, very similar to Agnes's, scanned my face.

He was seeing me again for the first time.

Seeing a part of me I'd only shared with a handful of people.

"Last time I checked, they were still in the ICU," I explained, knowing it wasn't low enough for Agnes to not overhear, but I couldn't care at that point.

I clenched my magic tight. It was a warm, dark night with a full moon blazing down on it. It was powerful and timeless, and it was *mine*. And maybe I hadn't wanted it for most of my life, but it wasn't going anywhere, and now it was my time to use it for a good reason.

"You ever wondered what life looks like?" My chin went up another notch. "It looks like a spark, like the flame on Duncan's tail. But inside. Beneath your skin and ribs and all the organs that keep a body functioning. It's hidden *right up in there*.

"For most people, it's the biggest and the brightest when they're young. As they get older, it loses size and gets duller. It's not everyone, but it's most people. Nice people, happy people, are always bright and beautiful," I explained, holding his searching gaze tight.

"It's easier, the older someone is, to make that spark even smaller though, a little dimmer . . ." I dropped my voice even lower, but I didn't doubt he could hear it. "To pinch it between magical fingers and extinguish it completely."

Dominic's lips parted even more, and I caught him licking

them, caught his gaze moving from one of my eyes to the other. And I didn't imagine that his voice wobbled, "But . . . you get people pregnant . . ."

He was finally seeing the full picture.

"Most people don't know there's a very, very fine line between life and death. Between creating and erasing. One of them is easy to control, and the other one . . . not so much. Want to guess which one is which?"

A harsh breath left the man in front of me, but I wasn't done.

He'd had his chance to walk away, and now he was going to regret not taking it.

"I want you to think about that the next time you threaten someone that you think is weaker than you. That you think can't stand up for themselves or won't retaliate. Because maybe they can't, or won't, but someone else might. Someone else would. Maybe someone else might feel a little bad about doing what they have to do to protect their loved ones, but at the end of the day, they'll be able to sleep just fine," I warned him softly.

Because like I'd told Shiloh, you didn't have to be big and have sharp teeth to be scary.

Then I gripped my magic even tighter, and I showed him, just a little, just enough. I brought it to the surface.

He saw it. I let him get a real good view of it too—of the other side of my parents' gifts. The opposite of life. I showed him the death that ran through my veins, in my eyes. Some might think it was cold, but it wasn't, pulling at it was like tugging at an inferno in my chest, in my soul. I could crush the life out like a crumpled piece of paper: that was what he saw. Color drained from his face in a split second, and there was something in his eye that would have made me feel awful if he'd been anyone else.

But I was sick of his shit, and I was done playing nice.

Sometimes good men could be misunderstood men, the same way good women could be. But he was not a good man. He was jealous and petty, and it went against a werewolf's nature to not care for those weaker.

He might be under the impression he was still the baddest fish in this pond, but I was the box jellyfish here and everywhere.

And this was no competition.

I took a step closer to him and softened my voice that much more, even as that dark, ancient magic that coursed through my body flared throughout it. "I want to make sure you understand this isn't a threat. I'm only sharing a fact with you, and you can share it with whoever you want." My nostrils flared as I thought about my friends at the nursery and the wounded look on Agnes's face and remembered the way Phoebe hadn't wanted to be overheard when she'd told me about him.

"Tell whoever needs to hear it: death isn't one person. Death doesn't walk around with a scythe and a robe. Sometimes it has long hair, sometimes it has short hair. Sometimes it comes in an accident, and sometimes in the middle of the night when you're asleep." I dropped my voice and looked him right in the eye. "And sometimes it likes wearing a fanny pack."

Dom swallowed hard.

Very, very hard.

His coloring went even more pale when his gaze dipped to my waist, where a brand-new silver fanny pack rested around my hips.

He blinked.

I felt like I was in a daze as I watched him leave the kitchen without another word. Some part of me recognized that I had to tell Henri what had just happened. What I'd admitted.

But before all that, there was another conversation I needed to have first.

For all of a disappointment as Dom might be, he was still Agnes's dad, and she was still too young to process why people were the way they were, and maybe I shouldn't have handled this in front of her.

Spinning around, I took in the features I'd gotten to know. It was the same level of serious as it always was. She didn't seem mad, but . . .

"Mini Wolf, I'm sorry for talking to him like that in front of you," I told her, ready to apologize some more, ready to figure out how to explain just what I'd implied.

But in front of my face, her eyebrows knit together, and she shrugged in a way that seemed familiar. Then she shocked me for the third time in a matter of minutes. The girl who'd tried to bite a green river crone shrugged. "It's not my fault he's mean." She even blinked while she said it.

My eyebrows shot up my forehead, and I blinked right back at her. "No," I agreed, "it's not."

Out of my peripheral vision, I saw Duncan look back and forth between us, and I had to fight the urge to smile when he was looking up at me like that.

"Are you okay?" I asked her, taking in all those small features for signs that she might be traumatized. But . . . there weren't any?

"Yeah," she scoffed, like I was dumb for asking, right as Henri and Franklin both walked in.

What were the chances he didn't smell Dominic's presence in the room?

"Morning, Franklin. Morning, Henri," I piped up, taking in Henri's uniform. He had the black on black again, black tactical-looking pants, and a short-sleeved black polo. If someone was going to twist my arm, I'd say it was my favorite of all his outfits.

Other than his sleeping pants one with no shirt.

Henri stopped dead smack in the middle of the kitchen, halfway to the island and the range. His expression was already suspicious. "What's going on?" He drew the question out as his eyes narrowed. "Why was Dom in here?"

I was too busy trying to think of an appropriate response when Agnes answered, "He made Nina mad, and she was gonna kick his ass."

I choked on freaking air.

But before I could laugh—or do anything else—Henri replied, "Thank you, Ladybug." He paused. "Say 'butt' instead, okay?"

"Okay," the little girl agreed in a cheery voice.

I almost didn't want to glance in his direction. I didn't need a good nose to know he was mad. But I peeked anyway. *I had just been thinking about telling him everything that had happened.*

And from the barely contained expression on those sharp features—he was definitely mad—there was no time better than the present.

I scratched my cheek and reminded myself that I'd done the right thing and now I had to live with it. "Henri, can I talk to you for a minute?"

His attention shifted toward me, his mouth flat, that cheek muscle popping, but he nodded. It was his slow nod though. His angry one. He was already expecting the worst.

"Franklin, do you mind watching Duncan for a few minutes?" I asked.

The elder looked like he had no idea what was going on as he stood by the main island, but he nodded.

Now or never. "Duncan, stay here, okay?" I told my puppy, who was still standing beside his friend.

"Yes," my boy answered.

It made me feel like a coward, but I purposely avoided making eye contact with Henri as I walked over to him, and neither one of us said a word as we left the kitchen. Out the front door, we went as I led him to my trailer. It wasn't much, but something was better than nothing. I opened the unlocked door and waved him in with a small, uncertain smile, not sure how he was going to look at me after this conversation.

Henri reached over my head to hold it open, and he tipped his chin toward the inside of the trailer. I went in, and he followed. I took a seat at my dining room table, and he stood in front of it instead, arms crossed over his chest in a way that reminded me of my first day here.

"Wanna tell me what happened?" The werewolf didn't bother wasting time. He'd smoothed his features into that neutral expression that was my least favorite version of Henri.

"Not really." I hesitated. "But I need to."

That wasn't the response he'd been expecting from the way

his eyebrow went up a millimeter like usual. "Why don't you want to?" he asked.

I squirmed in my seat. "Because I don't want you to look at me differently." Well, more differently than he already was, avoiding me, and just . . . retreating.

But maybe this would be a good thing. I didn't want to hide myself from whoever I ended up with. It was bound to come out anyway. And maybe I'd have a better excuse as to why Henri would pull back and stick to being polite with me from now on.

That would make things easier to an extent. Moving on, that was.

I didn't think he liked my answer, though, from the way he frowned.

"Dominic was rude to Agnes, and I said some things I don't regret, but I'd rather you hear it from me than from him," I told him, crossing my arms over my own chest, hugging myself. "I owe you that much."

His face went even broodier. "Was he rude to you too?"

"I don't think he knows how to be nice. From everything I've heard, he's mean to everyone," I explained. "But I got mad, and I may have threatened him a little." A grimace shaped my mouth.

"A little?"

I nodded and held up my index and thumb apart. "Little bit."

"How?" Henri asked, his tone cooler and flatter.

I bit the inside of my cheek, but I had to own it. Nobody had made me do what I'd done. "He got in my face for telling him to leave after he got an attitude with Agnes. I may have said that he can bully some people, but there are other people who wouldn't put up with his BS." I swallowed. "Other people who might make him pay for his actions."

Henri shifted his weight, his expression still sober. "Make him pay how?"

I scratched my cheek, but there was no hiding me. No hiding who I was, and this was something else I shouldn't be too ashamed over. Did I wish it was different? Absolutely, but I was the knife, and I could cut a cake, or I could stab someone. And

I'd warned Henri already in bits and pieces. There was a good chance he might have already deduced what I was about to admit.

I could only hope.

"You probably already have an idea," I said. "I've told you more than I've told anyone else in a really long time . . ."

I couldn't say it. It was one thing to threaten Dominic. To insinuate heavily. But it was a whole different ball game to tell Henri. To tell anyone, I wanted to believe. Matti knew because he was Matti. I trusted him more than anything and anyone. He would never look at me differently, and because of that, his reaction could never have been devastating.

If Henri did . . .

Why had I done this to myself? Why had I given another person so much power over my feelings? Was it because I wanted him to like me? Was it because I more than liked him?

Amber eyes burned a hole straight into me. "You can tell me anything," he claimed, like he could read my mind.

I lifted both my shoulders, pressing my lips together.

"I'm not scared of you. I thought we went over that already," he went on, steadily.

But I still hesitated.

Sure, he *thought* that. Sure, we'd faced two bogeymen and he hadn't batted an eyelash with them or with Spencer, and who knew what other beings he'd come across in his life. But . . . that was different.

His thick throat worked, and I didn't think it was disappointment that came over his features, but it might have been something close to it. "You don't need to tell me if you aren't ready."

Would I ever be?

Planting my elbows on the table, I palmed my forehead and released a low, long breath. "You're going to hear about it. I don't think that bigmouth is going to keep it to himself, and you don't deserve to find out from someone else."

His voice was so deep. "Tell me then."

I closed my eyes. "Remember I told you about those people who tried to kidnap Duncan? How they had brain damage?" I didn't wait for him to answer. He wouldn't have forgotten, it was a stupid question, and I was trying to avoid getting to the point, so I kept on going.

"I know about their injury because I called the hospitals in the areas where we were and pretended to be related to them. They're all at the ICU, or they were last time I checked, which was a month ago. I didn't know for sure when I did what I had to do, that that's what would happen if I used my magic on them. I honestly thought they would have a heart attack, if anything." I pressed my forehead tight into my palms. "I took a little bit of their life away from them."

Silence stretched long in the trailer between us.

Until, "How's that?"

I couldn't hear anger . . . or disgust . . . or anything that would've inspired me to risk looking at him.

What if he seemed disgusted? Or afraid? Or some other emotion I wouldn't be able to forget?

"I think"—saying that I was sure made it feel too real even to me—"one of my parents is some kind of death god," I blurted out for the first time in my life. It wasn't a relief to announce it exactly, but I still had to fight the urge to peek through my fingers when he didn't respond immediately.

There was a long moment of silence. The breath he let out was loud. "A death god?" was what he chose to repeat in a nearly emotionless voice.

I nodded, still refusing to open my eyes. It was easier this way, not knowing how he felt, and for the first time since moving here, I was grateful not to have a werewolf's nose. "I realized it right after my magic manifested itself. I hugged my dad and let my magic go a little, and I saw . . . I don't know how it works, but I . . . I told Dom that life looks like a flame. Like this light that I can see with my magic, and I can pinch it off if I try hard enough." That made me drop my hands and lift my head. "Not that I have! Not all the way, but . . ."

Henri had uncrossed his arms at some point. His face was clear and open, so carefully neutral. His muscles weren't bulging. He wasn't sweating or pale.

Was that a good thing?

I leaned back and hugged my arms tighter around myself. "But I can. I know what it means if I do it; I can feel it. I saw what it meant when I did it to those men, and I didn't go to ten even though I had sort of wanted to. But I always . . . knew, Fluff. Henri. My parents and I talked about it, and they both agreed. Doing it feels wrong, but I can, if I have to." Easily.

Shaking my foot beneath the table, I watched him stand there, the Great Wolf heir, the leader of this community, as I kept talking. "I showed that to Dominic, a little bit. I know I shouldn't have. I know I was picking on him, the same way he bullies everyone, but you know how people like that are. They think they're tougher than everyone else. They think no one would ever stand up to them, and I'm sick of it, and I've only been here a couple of months. Now I'm worried I might have made things worse. I should've told you before anyone, but . . ."

Henri's nod was slow. Too slow? Was he disappointed in me? *Please no.*

Planting my elbows back on the table, I cupped both sides of my neck. I shouldn't care so much what anyone thought about me. I couldn't help myself though. He *was* the one person at the top of the list that I didn't want to run off. I wanted Henri to like me. To keep liking me. Even the parts I kept hidden from just about everyone.

And I felt that reflected on my face—fear, hope, earnestness— as I caught his attention and held on. "I'm sorry, Fluff. I shouldn't have taken it that far. But that's why I scare people off. They can sense that there's something wrong in me."

Henri's whole body jerked, and his voice came out harsher than I'd ever heard it, a scowl storming over his mouth and eyes and his whole body. He even took a step forward. His tone was sharp. "There's nothing wrong with you, Nina."

My lips parted, my heart was touched, but . . . realistic. Maybe

I tried to sometimes live in a fantasy world where I hoped for the best, but I could be real too. I could. "You said it: I scared a child-eating crone." My voice cracked just a little. "Spencer hates me."

"Spencer hates everyone," he snapped almost as ferociously as he had a second ago.

I shook my head. "I've had holy water thrown on me, Fluff. Henri. I'm not under any delusions—"

If I thought he'd been mad before, I would've sworn death rolled over his face right then. Tight skin over striking bone structure, eyes narrowed, neck muscles tense. "Who . . . ?" His nostrils flared. "Who did that to you?"

"It's fine." I waved him off. "Some lady. But that's why I stayed away from other beings for so long. Because I don't know how they'll react, and I can't be mad at them for being scared. I don't even use my magic anymore to look at people's flames unless I have to. I can see when people are really sick—terminally ill—and it's terrible. The coloring changes, the flames get so weak . . . It all seems like an intrusion to me now. It feels so personal to see it. To know that kind of thing. Maybe I'm a coward, and maybe one day I'll change my mind, but I don't want to know when someone is dying." My face went hot at admitting this to him, at giving him every reason to shun me, too, like so many others had. Even my eyes started to sting a little, as I thought about the fear I'd witnessed from all those people before. As I thought about how sad it had made me to know someone was coming to the end of their life. "I don't want to hurt anyone."

My voice cracked, and I had to swallow to reset it, hating that it still didn't come out normal. "I wish this wasn't in me, but it is. I've tried to come to terms with it, you know? This is who I am. I can ignore it, but I know it's there. I just . . . I thought you should hear it from me, instead of that asshole."

The vein at his temple started throbbing as his jaw got even more pronounced.

"You know the kids hate him? Even Phoebe mentioned he was a jerk a long time ago. He had the nerve to raise his voice to Agnes," I tattled.

Henri stood there, staring over angrily. There was no clear sign if he was mad at me for what I'd done, mad at the fact no one might have told him how much of an asshole Dom was, or at Dom for being Dom.

Or at me for being me? Just thinking that broke my heart and made my eyes sting. But it was what it was, and even if I cried afterward, I was going to hold my head up high. Apologizing for my magic would be like saying I was sorry for not having blue eyes. Wasn't that what I would tell Duncan if he ever worried about what he looked like and who he was?

Even if Henri couldn't love me or appreciate me, that didn't mean no one else could.

Henri lifted his hand and scrubbed it down his face before pinning me with a look that made me want to squirm. His voice was thick. "First off . . ." he began, and I braced myself, "there is nothing wrong with you. Do I need to say that again?"

I held my breath and shook my head.

He was just getting started. "You, of all people, should know," he glared at me hard, and I mean *hard*, "without life, there can't be death, Nina."

I swallowed and stared right back at him, wanting to hear what else he had to say, but I was scared too. Scared he might break my heart without even knowing it. Without meaning to. Scared he would make me second-guess myself more than I already had so much of my life. Scared he would make me regret moving here, and I didn't have the luxury of feeling that way.

But he was on a roll, and he kept going, his hands forming fists under his armpits as he crossed them over his chest again. "We don't need to talk about that right now. It wasn't my place to bring it up before, but it is now. Tell me exactly what happened with the people who tried to kidnap Duncan."

Dang it. I should've known he was going to ask for details. I would have too.

And of all the crap I'd just brought up, this was what he wanted to focus on? It wasn't like I could argue with him over it. I leaned back and squeezed my arms to my chest, and I told him.

I told Henri about being at a campground in Oregon and having a group of men carrying obsidian come over while Duncan had been peeing.

I told him about how they'd snuck up from behind and gotten me in a chokehold, a knife to my throat, while they had grabbed my boy as he did his business.

How I'd magically pinched and I'd pinched, and I'd pinched again, not fully, but enough when that knife had grazed my skin.

Then I told him about how almost the exact same thing had happened again about a week later, at a different campground in rural South Dakota. Instead of a knife, it had been a gun. Instead of three men, there were two.

Another pinch and another.

And while I told Henri about it, I watched his face. It stayed plain and grave. His only movement had been a bob of his throat. And only after that, after he'd blinked at the end of my story, did Henri murmur, "You did what you had to do to protect your boy. There's no shame in that."

I shrugged, aware he was right and not regretting my actions but still wishing I hadn't put us into that situation in the first place. It was still something I was probably going to have to think about from time to time for the rest of my life. But it wasn't like I had made those people do what they'd done.

That didn't make me feel any better.

And as he stood there, I also wished I hadn't needed to tell him everything.

Despair, discomfort, and sadness at the idea that this might change what was left of our friendship after I'd been pushy with him the other night made my stomach feel funny. I hugged myself even tighter, like it would help the rest of me stick together as I laid out piece after piece for inspection. Hoping I measured up.

And it was with that thought in my head that the vein at Henri's temple got even more bulgy as he shifted his weight in front of me. By his armpits, his hands opened and closed. "I don't like how you've been smelling since we left the kitchen," was what he stated.

Here we go again.

But before I could apologize, Henri opened his arms.

I blinked.

He opened his hands next, doing another "come here" gesture.

He didn't look happy; he didn't look sad. He didn't look disgusted or even inviting, apart from his waiting arms.

I lifted a shoulder that sagged back down just as quickly as it had gone up. "We don't have to if you don't want to," I sort of whispered, sort of sighed.

His face went wary, but his right hand did that thing again. "You need a cuddle," he told me, just to be clear.

Maybe a stronger person would have insisted that they were fine. Anyone would have been nervous to admit what I'd just told him. But I thought I was strong. Strong enough to admit that I did need a hug. That I had done something that went against every instinct in my body, and I felt vulnerable and maybe upset because of it.

I needed that hug though.

From him especially.

That's why I didn't hesitate more than another heartbeat before I got up and went straight for him, slipping into those arms that became a blanket of muscle as they closed in around me.

I let Henri hug me. Cuddle me. Let him soothe my nerves with his rain and cedar smell and the vibrant energy emanating off his body and his soul that seemed to overpower mine in a way.

A leader and a protector, that was him.

And for the last time, because I swore it would be, I really did—I wasn't going to think it anymore—I wished that he was mine as I hugged him tight.

I wished things were different.

I wished . . .

The familiar sound of his ringtone went off, and it was me who pulled away first. Henri's eyes briefly met mine before he stared at the screen for a solid five seconds before saying, "Hold on." His eyebrows scrunched. "I need to take this."

"Sure."

His finger swept across the screen, and he brought his phone to his cheek, answering, "Henri."

Turning around, I faced the window behind me, where the sink was, and pretended not to listen to him talking, saying things like "yes" and "someone can come out" and "you want me to?" So when he hung up, I already had an idea of what was happening.

I just wasn't expecting him to say, "There's something I need to deal with. Want to come with me?"

The "yes" was on the tip of my tongue, on the edge of my heart. This was his olive branch. His way of telling me things were okay.

But I didn't know who was more surprised when I replied, "That's okay," instead.

I might as well have punched him in the stomach from the face he made.

"Maybe some other time. Thank you, though," I rushed out, forcing a smile that he had to know wasn't genuine.

The truth was, I wasn't ashamed of my feelings for him, but that also meant I needed to be realistic about things between us, once and for all.

I'd tried getting my way, I reminded myself. I'd brought it up enough. Wished for it enough.

But just because you really wanted something, didn't mean you were going to get it.

Which meant that now, I had to go with plan B.

Not that I even knew what it was . . . other than it didn't include Henri.

Chapter Twenty

I was folding my clothes in the clubhouse's laundry room, surrounded by five commercial washing machines and an equal number of dryers, when I heard someone coming down the hall, with some speed.

Not werewolf fast, but fast enough.

I couldn't sense their magic though, and there was only one person here I'd met so far who was like me in that aspect—the tightlipped, suspicious elder who lived a floor below me.

I'd just finished setting the navy blue shorts I'd folded in half on top of another pile of bottoms when Franklin appeared in the doorway. It took about half a second to dread his expression. It was a mix between a grimace and a concerned one, and somehow it got even grimmer when we made eye contact.

"Are you all right?" I asked the man who had been nothing but polite toward me since he'd gotten back from his trip, but I *still* couldn't help but think there was something off about him. There was something about the way he watched me, like he was sizing me up, but not with ill intentions. Duncan would have warned me if there was anything to really worry about.

Plus, a few nights ago, I'd watched him slicing a roast into thin slivers and had definitely seen a flash of yellow gold on the clasp, and I was pretty sure even the chain the beads were looped through had been too.

I still hadn't managed to get around to taking a chance and asking Henri if he knew anything, mostly because I had barely seen him since the incident with Dom over a week ago. From comments Randall and Franklin had made, I was pretty sure there had been some kind of staffing issue at work that had kept him away and working odd hours, but it wasn't something for me to worry about.

What was on my radar, and deserved to be there, was the expression on the elder's face as he stood in the laundry room.

That was another thing I'd noticed the same day as his golden jewelry. I had always assumed Franklin might be in his seventies, but the more time we spent together, the more I realized that he couldn't be. His hair was graying, that was for sure. There were lines at his mouth and eyes, but not as many as a man his age would typically have.

While he was thin, he wasn't what I would call skinny either—not like my dad, who was in his late seventies and had been lean as far back as I could remember.

It had made me reconsider how old Franklin could be. And hadn't Matti said something about him not having aged much since he'd lived here? It could be good skincare and good genes, but . . .

"Ah, yes," Franklin answered, everything about him still radiating unease. He tried to smile, but it just put me even more on edge. Like when someone tells you there's good news and bad news, but the good news is really just slightly better than the bad news. "We're in the middle of a slight emergency, Nina."

"We?"

"Yes." He plucked at the sleeves of his button-down striped shirt, and I watched how steady his hands were, though his face said otherwise. "I need to apologize for not giving you more notice, but the leader of the Alaskan community contacted me five minutes ago and explained he'll be at our gates in five minutes."

I couldn't feel my legs anymore. I wasn't even sure I felt my eyelids either, but I somehow blinked. There must have been a rock in my throat, because when I tried swallowing, nothing happened at first. I had to try again. "He's going to be here in five minutes?" I finally squeaked. Hadn't he told me and Henri that we would have notice?

There's no reason to freak out.

The only way anyone was taking Duncan against his wishes was over my dead body.

That thought actually made me feel a little better.

"Yes," the elder confirmed, still pulling at his sleeve—the same one that covered his secret bracelet. "They gave me no warning. Under normal circumstances, we could turn them away, but I fear we would offend our visitor . . ."

He trailed off for a reason.

If we offended him, he might not come back. If he didn't come back, then I'd be one step short of ever finding out the truth about my boy. And he deserved to know for his own sake. For his own identity.

If anything had been made clear over the last couple months, it was that knowing your magical heritage might not be necessary, but it might save a little bit of heartache along the way.

Duncan could grow up and be whoever he wanted to, but I didn't want the mystery that had weighed me down for half my life to do the same to him.

Not if we could avoid it.

And *no one* was taking my donut, dang it.

"What do you say?" the elder asked, watching me closely, tugging at his left sleeve.

I wasn't sure I'd ever seen him fidget so much, but I didn't have the mental capacity to worry about him at the moment.

On numb legs, I reached deep inside of myself for strength—thinking of Agnes facing down her asshole dad, remembering Shiloh trying to stand up to the Jenny Greenteeth in his own way, and I thought of those bogeymen risking their balls trespassing on werewolf land, on *Henri's* land to get what they wanted—and I set my chin. If they could put themselves in uncomfortable situations, so could I. "If they're here, they're here. Let's do it."

Franklin's eyes narrowed just the tiniest bit, but he nodded back seriously. "We'll meet him outside."

My arms joined my legs in the numb department as I followed

him out. I tried to get my body under control on the chance that whoever was coming could smell my emotions. Fear wasn't for the weak, but I needed to put up the best front I could and show that there was a reason why I'd been picked to care for my boy.

Without doing any pinching.

With my opposite hand, I toyed with the bracelet on my wrist. I rubbed my finger over one of the beads. Did I leave it on or . . .?

Henri had said I didn't need to hide who I was, hadn't he?

Setting it on the corner of the deck, I kept my chin up and made a face that would've made Agnes proud as Franklin and I both silently waited and watched as a red car pulled into the lot and parked. Based off the lack of tint on the windows, I assumed it was a rental. Behind us, the front door opened and closed.

I recognized the heavy, bright energy that approached us right before a familiar frame stopped at my side.

Henri's arm brushed mine as he braced his hands on his hips. I couldn't help but peek at him real quick. He was in his normal clothes.

"You're home early," Franklin noted as he, too, stared at the parking lot as a man got out of the car and started walking over.

He seemed tall from over here.

"I've worked nine days in a row and finally told Waller, if he doesn't hire somebody soon, I'm quitting," Henri replied with a grunt. "Who's this?"

I had to fight the urge not to glance at him again. He'd threatened to quit? Randall had explained to me that the elected sheriff of the county was actually a member of the community—Pascal's dad. Apparently, they kept a magical being in the position to keep things running in the town, and here, smoothly. Since the town had been incorporated, there had always been one in office. Sometimes it was a member of the Blackrock family, but sometimes it wasn't.

"I know I should've given you a warning, Henri, but the leader of the Alaska pack called at the last minute, and I barely managed to give Nina the news before we rushed out here.

I would've called you in a moment," Franklin explained, not sounding that apologetic.

To me, he sounded stressed, but I didn't know him well enough to confirm it.

Henri's head slowly turned to the side, and even I could feel the glare radiating off him as he focused on the older man, but Franklin wasn't bothered by it at all from the way he ignored him and stepped off the deck, calling out, "Hello!"

I clenched my hands and released as much of the tension in my body as I could. I was strong, I was capable, and I had so much love in my body. I was Duncan's mom, for all intents and purposes, and I would flay someone's skin off with my teeth for my boy if I had to—throwing up the entire time, but I'd do it. I'd do it over and over again if it came down to it. This was just a meeting. Just a confirmation.

"He's a firebreather," Henri murmured as Franklin shook hands with our visitor.

I narrowed my eyes and fought the urge to look at Fluff again. "Really?"

There were several of those in mythology, so that wasn't a whole lot to go off of. The closer the visitor got, the more I slowly started being able to sense him, and his magic was different from any other kind I'd ever felt before. There was a lot of it too. More than most beings.

In a way, it felt similar to Henri's. Big, powerful, and very special.

And he was also a lot younger than I'd expected—somewhere between my age or Henri's. I figured he was about Henri's height, just not built as thick through the frame, though he wasn't small in any way. His skin color was lighter, eyes a pale blue. He was handsome, but not as handsome as Henri.

And those blue eyes, that were almost glacial, narrowed by the second at me even as he spoke to Franklin. I was suddenly very aware that I'd taken my bracelet off. *Too late to put it back on now.*

Pushing my emotions down, I headed toward them. I didn't

smile, mostly because the stranger didn't either. He was being discreet, but I could tell his nose was engaged. Whether he didn't mind what he smelled or not, I had no idea, but there was nothing I could do about it.

"Ilya, this is Nina, the pup's guardian," Franklin introduced us, his tone kind of brittle.

I held out my hand. "Hi," I said simply. "Thank you for coming." *A warning would have been nice, but . . .*

The man named Ilya didn't say a word, but there was no hiding the intensity in his attention as he shook my hand. Not in interest really, but . . .

Henri's body brushed mine as he held out his own hand.

"This is Henri, the leader of our community," Franklin said.

They exchanged a quick, tense handshake. "Thank you for allowing me to visit on short notice. I had a last-minute trip that brought me into the area, and I wanted to take advantage." He had a deep voice. "I don't leave much."

Henri's expression stayed that neutral one as he nodded.

"You're welcome to spend the night," Franklin claimed, even though I could've sworn he didn't sound thrilled, and I watched Henri's head swivel toward him. "For now, we can take you to see the pup, or you can meet him later. The choice is yours."

Franklin was being so weird.

But Ilya nodded, his bright blue eyes flicking back in my direction.

I pretended not to notice.

Henri moved. He angled his body halfway in front of me. "Follow us," he said, setting a hand on my shoulder and guiding me to go in front of him.

All right then.

I led our small group back into the clubhouse, turning right to go down the hall. The nursery door loomed ahead like a portal into another dimension I was scared to see, but the heavy palm on my shoulder stayed right where it was. I told myself everything was going to be fine.

Duncan didn't just have me now. He had Agnes. He had

friends at the nursery. Maggie, his teacher, adored him. He had Henri. And even Shiloh would stomp on some toes for my boy if he had to.

At the door, I stepped off to the side, while Franklin gestured our visitor over. "If you come to the window, you'll see the pup the exact way I described him," the elder told him.

He didn't need to be told twice. He went up to the door and peered in.

He moved his face muscles even less than Henri did, I thought, spying on him. The man didn't even blink. His eyes, though, followed someone around the room, which from the sounds of it, made me think the kids were chasing each other.

What did he think?

The man named Ilya backed away from the door after a minute or two. He nodded with that carefully blank face, then met my eyes. "Tell me how you found him."

Henri bristled at the same time I blinked at how freaking bossy that sentence had come out. What did Ilya think he was? The boss of me? Fluff agreed from the way he said very calmly—too calmly— "You're a guest here, but that'll be the last time you demand anything from one of mine."

Our visitor narrowed his eyes, and even his nostrils flared, but after a second, he bent his head.

Fluffy stared at Ilya, then looked at me and winked . . . in encouragement?

Henri had winked at me.

I realized in that moment that he'd always have my back, awkwardness or not, and that made me feel a little better about the future of our friendship. It wasn't what I wanted, and it definitely wasn't what I would've wished for if I had a choice, but I'd take it with open arms. I didn't want to lose him.

So if all I would ever get was Teasing Friend Henri . . . so be it.

I pressed my lips together, then I told Ilya the story. All of it.

"Shh, Dunky, *shh*," I whispered to the tap-dancer wiggling his butt down the stairs as we headed outside.

I had two beef tracheas in my hand that he was losing his mind over. Except, when we turned to go down the hall, Agnes wasn't waiting for us in her usual spot. This was the first time in weeks that she hadn't been right outside of her room, waiting, with her hands on her hips. We always went out around the same time, unless it was raining.

I thought about knocking on her door, or at least opening it to check if she was okay, but I didn't want to invade her privacy. Her behavior toward me hadn't changed much since the day Dom had been an asshole, but I'd swear there was a different glint in her eye when she was around me. I wasn't going to say it was respect or even affection, but it was something.

Taking my phone out, I opened the app for the ranch, then went to the Agnes specific chat to see if maybe she was spending the night with someone. The last entry had been from earlier, where Phoebe had said she was taking her with them for dinner. Maybe she was still at their house. I'd save her trachea for another day.

Figuring she was in good hands, the donut and I headed outside. The moon was tucked behind thin, narrow clouds as we made our way to our clearing. Before we managed to do anything else, something caught Duncan's attention, his tail snapping up straight right as a voice called out, "I didn't mean to scare you."

We found him at the same time. Ilya from Alaska was leaning against a tree maybe twenty feet away. His arms were crossed over his chest.

I hadn't sensed him, and when I checked to see if maybe I just hadn't been paying attention, I realized that the strong magical presence I'd felt when he'd shown up was missing.

I was starting to understand why my bracelet bothered other people so much. Even I wondered what other people were hiding when they used them. Dang it.

Duncan didn't growl, he didn't even get a mohawk, but his tail stayed in that upright position, his eyes locked on the stranger. I'd introduced them during dinner, which had consisted of the other man talking to Henri and Franklin the entire time. From what I'd gathered, after the scene at the nursery, they'd invited him on a tour, while I'd gone back to the laundry room, trying to pretend like everything was normal.

I made it ten minutes.

I'd ended up calling Matti from my bathroom to tell him what had happened.

The man pushed off the tree when I handed Duncan his treat. My donut took it but held it in his mouth instead of plopping on the ground like he usually would have as he kept watching the stranger make his way over to us.

Duncan had seemed a little interested in him during dinner, but more in a cautious way. He hadn't run over to him or tried sneaking around to smell him from behind. But a few times, I'd caught those red eyes peering at our visitor.

It was rude to be relieved over how much he hadn't cared about him, but I'd been *thrilled*.

That was part of the reason why I'd busted out the beef tracheas tonight—for being such a good freaking boy.

"Is this a coincidence or . . .?" I trailed off, already knowing the answer as I took in the man's strong features and suntanned face. I didn't *think* I had anything to worry about with him, but there was no way I could forget how he'd looked at me earlier, just as warily as I had him.

Except I wasn't a risk to what he loved the most.

He didn't BS me. "No. I overheard the wolf tell the little girl not to leave her room tonight. He doesn't trust me," he explained, bright blue gaze snagged on mine. His features still weren't giving anything away. "It made sense you'd be awake late."

Blood rushed from my head. "Why's that?"

"Because of what you are."

I blinked. "You . . . you know what I am?"

There was still nothing on his face. Not amusement. Not surprise. Not even smugness at what he'd just implied, just total facts. "Of course I know."

I opened my mouth and closed it just as fast.

Ilya slid his hands into the pockets of his black jeans, all casual. "You don't get the cinnamon from him, but the rest of it . . ." He whistled. "You smell exactly like him."

Him? What the hell did that mean?

Duncan pressed against the side of my leg, and it took everything in me not to pick him up and hug him. "Excuse me?" My right leg might have started going numb. "Who . . . do you think I smell like?"

Ilya's eyes flicked toward the clubhouse. There was surprise in his voice, I thought there might have been a touch of it on his face too. "You don't know?" he asked, eyebrows rising slowly on his forehead.

"I don't know a lot of things," I admitted as Duncan leaned even more deeply against me, and I reached down until my fingers could stroke the top of his head.

"Love," my boy told me, like he knew I needed it.

"I love you too," I whispered to him even as I kept my eyes on the man Henri had said was a firebreather. There were so many mythological ones, I couldn't even begin to imagine what kind he could be. A dragon, a chimera, Jormungandr, Gaasyendietha . . .

Eyes narrowed in my direction. "How old are you?"

"Thirty-two," I answered, but he wasn't going to distract me from what he'd just dropped on me. We needed to circle back to that. "You know who my father is?" That had to be the "he" he'd mentioned. It had to. There was no other possibility.

And what were the chances that not one but *two* different sets of beings could be bringing him up since I'd gotten here?

One of those blue eyes had the nerve to wince. "I could tell you . . ."

I didn't like where this was going.

"But he should be the one to do it instead," Ilya said. "He knows more than I do. He's your best bet for getting answers to the rest of the questions you're going to have afterward."

Was he talking in riddles, or was I imagining it? Because now that sounded like another "he" that wasn't my father. I squinted up at him. "Who should tell me instead?" I asked to be sure.

Ilya's eyes slid toward the clubhouse again, and I frowned.

"Henri?" I asked as Duncan stepped on my foot but said nothing.

A different glint sparkled in his eye, and something told me I wasn't going to be a fan of what was about to come out of his mouth. He confirmed it a second later. "I'll tell you, but I have a few questions first."

I raised my eyebrows but shrugged. Fair enough. We could trade.

"Why are you here?" was what he asked. At this ranch, he meant.

"Because it's a safe place for him," I answered.

"Do you like it here?"

I didn't see why that would be any of his business, but all right. "We haven't been here long, but it's growing on me, and Duncan loves it."

He'd caught on to the nuance in my words, but his face didn't reflect what he thought of it. "Why don't you?"

Another shrug had me hunching my shoulders. "I don't have deep bonds here yet, other than one . . . and the children." And that "one" was a stretch. "I'm new, and they're all nice enough, but that kind of thing takes time. It's easier to get settled when you're young. You know what I mean?"

The man named Ilya nodded slowly, and if he was the leader of his Alaskan community, I figured he'd be aware of that. He shot off another question. "How long are they giving you to marry someone? Is it a year?"

How did he know that? Or was it common knowledge? "Something like that," I answered.

The man nodded before glancing down at Duncan. The silence stretched and stretched, and I wondered what he was thinking and what he was going to ask next.

But he didn't. Those blue eyes levelled on me, and even though his features didn't change, it was obvious he was thinking about something. It just wasn't what I expected.

"Come to Alaska."

I was going to need a Q-Tip. "Excuse me?" I repeated, hearing a scoff in my voice, and even Duncan put more weight on my foot.

Ilya repeated himself. "Come to Alaska with me. We have the same policy they do here, but you can have three years to choose a mate. You wouldn't have a problem finding one with us. I can promise you a worthy partner, a home of your own, protection, and you would both be welcome there with open arms," he shot out one sentence after another. One explanation on top of another.

I rocked back on my heels. Surprised. Stunned really.

He wasn't done either. "You wouldn't be feared there."

I scrunched up my face. "I'm not exactly feared here either."

He tilted his head and got squinty. "But you aren't exactly welcome here either, are you?"

I got squinty right back. What made him think that? "What do you get out of both of us going with you?" I asked, trying to figure out why he'd be making this offer. We'd been trading questions for information. He wasn't a fool. I had a feeling he'd known dang well what he was doing when he'd made the offer.

The corners of his lips tipped up, and that small gesture made him slightly more handsome. "You are what you are, Nina. Only an idiot wouldn't welcome that."

My whole body stilled.

"There's a chance they don't know better because some of them aren't aware of what they have with you. But you ask me, and everyone who lives with us, and there's nothing to deny. You wouldn't have to keep who you are a secret around us. You and the child would be safe." He didn't smile, but he made a face that projected acceptance. "And more."

His words didn't exactly rock me, but they did slide into a place in my heart that was on edge and uncertain. Three years was a hell of a lot longer than one. But all I had to do was take a deep inhale, taste the magic surrounding us, and . . .

There was only one way to answer his offer.

"Thank you," I told him. "Really, thank you, but we're here and . . ."

Ilya took a step forward. "Think about it. The offer doesn't expire. Franklin knows how to find us. We're a small community, but it's by choice." He paused. "There's a reason why both of your kinds have called our community home."

I pressed my lips together, caught off guard by his reasoning, just as his hand came up and cupped the side of my neck.

I raised my eyebrows at him; at the same time, the paw on my foot put even more pressure on it.

His blue eyes searched mine, his magic feeling so bright in my chest.

What was going on?

"I don't have much of a sweet tooth, but may I?" he asked, gesturing in the direction of my neck.

"Smell me?"

He tipped his head slightly downward.

I'd forgotten I'd left my bracelet on the deck earlier. I needed to pick it up on the way back in. But in the meantime . . . "Sure, since you asked so nicely," I told him, tilting my head to the side, not seeing the harm in it. Duncan didn't seem too wary of him, which reassured me too.

But to be safe, I reached for my magic with one invisible fist and searched for the flame in his chest, finding it instantly, and nearly letting it go at the same speed.

The thing was freaking—

The side of Ilya's mouth curled up in a half smile that eased some of the severe soberness to his face as he reached over to touch a spot beneath my ear at the same time he leaned forward.

He was very magical, and he smelled nice, I thought, warily.

But not as nice as Henri, who was now my benchmark.

I felt a hint of his breath—

"Get your fucking hands off her," a familiar growl almost scared the crap out of me.

Hadn't I literally just told myself to pay attention?

Over my shoulder, I caught Henri storming over from the direction of the clubhouse.

He looked *pissed*. Pissed times one hundred if the bunched muscles at his shoulders and arms said anything. He looked a flex away from bursting out of his shirt.

It was unfortunate how much I kind of wished it happened.

Was the vein at his temple and his cheek popping at the same time?

Ilya, though, stepped back almost immediately, throwing his hands up, but . . . why was he smirking?

"Touch her again, and I'll—" Henri snarled, his incredible eyes blazing, his face literally thunderous.

Was this Murder Henri?

"She gave me permission," the other man explained.

"I did," I added, not sure why the hell Fluff would be so mad. Was he worried he would hurt me? Hadn't I made it clear that would be really difficult?

Or was *someone* . . . no. *No.*

But maybe . . . ?

That familiar body slid between us, but instead of facing Ilya's direction . . . Henri focused on me.

The paw that had been on my foot eased off, but I didn't dare look at Duncan when I had a six-foot-six man staring down at me.

I frowned up at him. "What?"

A low, deep growl formed in Henri's chest.

He tipped his head down in a movement that was almost identical to the harmless and common one he'd just busted us in. I didn't move as he went further than Ilya had, his nose brushing against my neck. Warm breath wafted over my collarbone before he dragged the tip of his nose up the column of my neck a fraction of an inch by the second.

I could hear him breathe. I could feel it.

Henri's cheek pressed flat against my throat, and there was no ignoring how he rubbed the bristly side of his face against me in the same way he had done twice before, with Spencer and after the men had been in the kitchen.

There was no stopping the shiver that racked down my spine or the goose bumps that erupted along my skin at the contact. Even my hair follicles seemed to wake up as Henri marked me.

Because that's what he was doing.

Again.

Tagging me with his scent.

Replacing the stranger's with his—not that there had even been much to begin with.

I stood very, very still.

And my heart went very, very fast in something that was either delight or excitement or both.

"Ah," the leader from Alaska sighed from behind Henri. "I see."

The man rubbing his stubbled cheek on me snarled, the heat from his breath getting that much stronger. "Shut the fuck up," Henri snapped at him, and I would've sworn I felt his lips brush my skin.

I gulped.

"No offense, sweetheart," Ilya started to say, "but, Henri, she's not my—"

"You're goddamn right she isn't yours," Henri roared, lifting his head away from my ear to shoot a glare over his shoulder. "She isn't your anything."

Was he shaking?

There was a long pause. "*Regardless*, the offer still stands, Nina."

Henri was still turned away from me when he demanded, "What offer?"

I leaned around the side of him.

Ilya was smirking again. He had his hands in his pockets to top it off. "To join our community in Alaska."

Henri's whole body went rigid. "No," he spat out.

"It's not your call," the other man replied in a voice that almost sounded cheery. "She wouldn't need a trial period to join us, Duncan would have room to roam, and I wouldn't ask her to marry anyone she doesn't want to marry. She would have three years to find someone suitable. There wouldn't be a lack of available mates either. Nina wouldn't be single long; the three years would just be a safety net."

Very slowly, Henri swiveled his head to glance at me over his shoulder.

If looks could kill, I might have been on my way to the ICU after the one he shot me right then.

I raised my eyebrows at him. "I didn't say I'd go," I clarified since he seemed to be looking at me like he'd caught me talking about him behind his back.

"But you didn't say you wouldn't either," Ilya, the stirrer of the shitstorm, added for some reason.

Was he *trying* to piss off Henri?

Could he not read the room?

And why would Henri get this upset?

When I didn't deny it, Henri's forehead furrowed, and he faced the other man again. His voice came out even gruffer. "She's not going to Alaska, and neither is Duncan."

I reached for him—for his hand, specifically—and when I hooked my index finger around his pinky, he closed his fist, trapping it there. Trapping *me* there. Not that I fought to take it out, anyway.

"Do they have a reason to stay that I don't know of?" Ilya asked curiously.

Henri squeezed my fingers. "Sure." He exhaled deeply. "Me."

My eyeballs had to be on the verge of bulging out of their sockets. The urge to snort and call BS climbed up the back of my throat with a little parachute, ready to jump out at a moment's notice. But no one understood how important a united front was better than I did. Loyalty wasn't just a word you used to describe standing by someone during big, important moments.

Loyalty was staying true to people even when they said dumb crap. You just waited until the right moment to tell them they'd lost their minds. That was loyalty.

And I might not understand Henri's actions from time to time, but I did know that he was the only person here that I held an allegiance to, regardless of his feelings toward me. Because that was loyalty too.

So even if I wanted to roll my eyes, I kept from doing it—at least until we were alone again.

The man from Alaska made another sound in his throat before he caught my attention from around Henri's shoulder. Something in his blue irises almost seemed amused. "You change your mind, I meant what I said," he told me.

I might not want to move to Alaska unless I had to, but I appreciated his offer. So, so much, and so, I nodded . . . and I ignored the way Henri's head turned toward me. Then I got down to business again. "I have two questions first. What is Duncan? And are you going to tell me who I need to talk to about that thing you mentioned?" I made sure not to side-eye Henri right then.

"Duncan's heritage is not my news to confirm. My people in Alaska will come meet him to be sure. They should be who tell you."

Dang it.

"And it's Franklin you need to speak with," Ilya announced, ripping the ground from under my feet with just that one name. I hadn't actually expected him to tell me about my donut, but I figured I had nothing to lose by trying. But just as quickly as he'd dropped that bomb, Ilya moved on. "I'll be gone in the morning. I'll make arrangements for my people to visit soon," the man went on before he focused back on my boy. "Goodbye, Duncan. I hope you visit when you're older."

Dunky, who hadn't made a peep until then, let out a low "awoo" that echoed through the forest as Ilya walked off. Only I heard the *"yes,"* but I wasn't going to worry about his future plans for now.

In that moment, I had something else to focus on. Multiple somethings.

I started with my immediate priority.

I poked Henri in the stomach. "What was that about?" I griped.

That frowl had returned to his face, half a frown, half a scowl, and his tone wasn't much better as he tried to bite my head off with his, "What?"

I blinked. "*That*. What was that about? I appreciate you being protective, Fluff, but he was being nice, offering to let us stay with them."

"You think that was him being nice?"

"Yes. That was more than anybody else has done for us," I told him, not believing his BS. "If things don't work out here, I don't want to burn the only other bridge we might have."

Henri's eyebrows climbed up his forehead, and there went that bulging vein in his temple again. His voice came out like an earthquake. "Why would things not work out here?"

I scowled at him right back. "I don't know. I'm just saying, what if—"

"There's no 'what-ifs.'"

"There's always a what-if. I want things to work out here, but I have zero promises that things are going to—"

"I'm promising you that things will work out," he had the nerve to argue while baring his teeth.

"You of all people, Fluff, can only promise me so much, and we both know it, and that's okay." I held up my hands. "I'm not giving you crap about it, but that doesn't give you a right to sabotage my backup plans."

His eyes became literal slits on his face, his nostrils flaring wider than I'd ever seen. "Going to Alaska isn't a goddamn backup plan—it's okay, Duncan, your mom and I are just having a discussion." Henri whipped back and forth between talking to me and my donut. Did he sense him getting worked up? "You're not moving across the country, Nina," he barked, back to talking to me.

"What is happening?" I laughed, and not because I was amused, but because I wanted to strangle the thick neck in front of me. Just a little strangle, but still a strangle. "I don't want to move across the country, but I will if I have to! Why are we even talking about this? Nothing happened!"

"Nothing happened because you're not going anywhere, and I don't know why you're not dropping it," he gritted out.

I poked him right in the chest again. "I'll go wherever is best for him, and I'm only asking you to be nice to Ilya so I can sleep better at night knowing I have another option."

If I'd thought he'd been mad before, he was seething then. "Here is your only option!"

"No, it's not!" There went another poke. "I can't stay here if I don't get married, Henri. You know that as well as I do. He promised me—" He growled, but I ignored him, so frustrated I could spit. I really could. Right in his eye too. "I've got no promises here and—what the hell are you growling at me for?" I snapped.

Henri's eyes were bright, his nostrils still wide, and now he was breathing heavily.

He was so mad!

I looked him dead in the eye anyway. "You were my first choice, and I've made that clear. I'm not asking you anymore. You don't want me? You don't want me—"

A loud, rough guffaw exploded out of him. He sounded . . . he sounded like a psycho, honestly. That was the sound I made when I was about to snap, and hearing it made me narrow my eyes.

"What's so funny?" I demanded, confused. I hadn't done anything to him, dang it.

"I'm not laughing, Nina," he said through clenched teeth, still doing it.

"It sure sounds like a freaking laugh." I squinted at him. If he didn't want to explain it, I wasn't going to beg. Not today, not tomorrow, not ever. "Look, Fluffy, *you* kissed *me*, and you're always so nice, and you're over here rubbing your face all over me and I let you, but let's get one thing straight. To keep my family safe, I'll find someone who wants me, and that someone might be in Alaska," I told him in another hiss. "Understand?"

Henri Blackrock's eyes skewered me, that not-a-laugh gone with the wind. His skin was tight over his features, eyelids dropped low over those incredible amber irises, and I'd swear something about him changed right in front of my eyes.

Henri wasn't standing in front of me anymore.

The Great Wolf was.

And he said, "I understand, all right."

He didn't look like he understood anything. And from the step he took toward me, those boots bumping into the toes of mine, I was sure he didn't.

I didn't let myself break eye contact. I had to say what I had to say, do what I had to do. If I had any chance of making things work here . . .

I retreated, one step at a time. The words burned in my throat and in my soul, but they had to be said. I'd promised myself. "You'll always have my loyalty, Fluff, always, but we can't keep doing this."

"Can't keep doing what?" His irises moved over my face.

I gestured to the space between the two of us as I took another step away from him. "This. It's hard for me right now because I have feelings for you. I know you know. And that's not fair to whatever my future holds." I swallowed. "Whoever my future holds. You're a good man, Henri, but you don't need to worry about me. Duncan and I will be fine. Please don't do anything to ruin our chances though."

His face clouded with every word out of my mouth. He looked . . . he looked . . . Pink lips parted, and I could see the argument forming in his mouth.

But it was like all the airline safety talks implied, you had to take care of yourself first before you could take care of someone else.

"Look," I sighed. "I don't want to fight with you right now. I don't want to fight with you ever. You're getting mad over a hypothetical situation that I hope I never have to pursue. I don't want to move to Alaska. The days are too short, and I wouldn't like being locked up indoors all day for months. I respect people who can handle it like champs, but I'm not cut out for it. I don't like the snow *that* much. And right now, I have other stuff to figure out. I need to go wake up Franklin—"

He reared. "What was that about?"

"Ilya hinted that he knows who my father is," I admitted.

"Franklin?"

I nodded. "I've thought he was suspicious from the moment I met him. He's very watchful. Very thoughtful. I don't know how to explain it." I shrugged, a small part of me relieved we'd changed the subject. "He has a bracelet like mine. Did you know that? It's made out of gold."

Henri nodded at that, his expression pensive.

"Do you know what he is?" I finally blurted out, not sure what I was hoping for. I didn't know his background. He could be from a dozen different mythologies and folktales. Chances were, I might not even recognize whatever name anyone could use to catalogue him.

But I needed to know now.

He seemed to think about it. "No. I don't think anyone does. I've never been around him without it on." He frowned.

"What do you know about him?"

He still looked mad, but he answered. "He's been here since before I was born, but I don't know who he came here with or who his family was. I don't know if my family made an exception for him. As far as I can remember, it's only been him."

That was so sketchy.

"He hasn't really aged at all in all the time I've known him. I think he's a long-lived being," he added thoughtfully. "He never talks about his past. I can only tell you he's been reliable while he's been here, and I've never had a reason not to trust him."

I nodded at Henri, disappointed he didn't know anything important either. "Thank you." Setting my shoulders, I glanced down at Duncan, who had lost interest in Henri and me arguing and had . . . he was halfway done with his beef trachea. I didn't even remember giving it to him. But his bright eyes were on me, his little mouth pulled into that partial perma-smile.

"Donut, when you're done, will you come with me to talk to Franklin?"

"*Yes,*" he answered at the same time Henri said, "I'm coming too."

I thought about telling him that wasn't necessary, but Henri gave me a look that kept me from actually saying it out loud. I didn't feel like arguing with him anymore.

So I guess he was coming too.

We were going to find out what Franklin had to say.

Chapter Twenty-One

"You don't need to come with me," I told Henri under my breath as we made our way to Franklin's bedroom.

He peered down at me, that frowl-scrowl still plastered on his profile. Murder Henri was gone, but I wasn't sure how much better Grumpy Bear Henri was in his place. "Yes, I do," he argued.

"*No.*" Between us, Duncan stepped on his foot, capturing both of our attentions.

I blinked. "Even Duncan said no." Why was he saying no though? There weren't many things he had a strong opinion about, but this . . .

"You're wrong this time, pup," Henri disagreed, his expression lightening just a little as he focused on the donut. A hint of a smile crossed his face as he looked down at him, but all that wiped away the second we made eye contact. "I could tell he'd been anxious the last few weeks, but I thought he was concerned about you."

"You mean afraid," I clarified.

He gave me a look that might as well have been an eyeroll. "Wary," he compromised. "Now, I'm rethinking every conversation I've had with him about you and what it might mean. Ilya didn't say anything else?"

That perked me up. I shook my head. "That's all. What has he told you? Franklin, I mean." I didn't bother trying to keep my question a secret. I was coming for him, and I didn't care if he was sleeping. If he'd been purposely hiding something from me, I deserved to know what it was, and we both knew it.

"Nothing that would've set me off. What I knew about you, your relationship with Matti." Henri gestured toward the door to our left.

We were here. At Franklin's.

I clenched my fist.

"I can hear you in there," Henri called out, not even bothering to try and press his ear to the wood. "Are you going to open the door or are you going to make us knock?"

The doorknob turned and the elder appeared in button-down flannel pajamas . . . which were an odd choice because most people after a certain age used the buttons that popped together, or didn't use buttons at all. Just like his shirts . . .

But the strangest thing was the resigned expression on his face. The hair he usually had neatly combed was all over the place, kind of scruffy, pretty messy. Somehow it made him look younger.

A lot younger.

Nervousness seemed to lurk in the corners of his eyes as he stood there. "I was expecting this, come in."

I glanced at Henri, who gave me a squinty look.

I still couldn't believe how much of a hissy fit he'd thrown over Ilya inviting us to Alaska, and I definitely couldn't believe what he'd said to him about it.

He'd been so . . . possessive.

But I couldn't think about that now, I told myself, walking into the room first, with Duncan following next, and Henri taking up the last position.

The room was larger than mine, but instead of a full-sized bed like Agnes had, Franklin's was much more modest. His frame was a twin, and next to it was a comfortable recliner. There was a television on the opposite wall, framed by huge bookshelves—four of them, stuffed full with all kinds of paperbacks and hardcovers and more.

In front of those books were knickknacks in bronze, some that glittered like they were gold, and a few that looked . . . ancient with how faded and in poor condition they were.

"I meant to have this conversation with you before Ilya arrived, because he might not talk much, but he always seems to say the wrong thing." Franklin sighed as he settled into the recliner with almost a plop. "Please sit."

Henri gestured to the one other chair in the room, a simple wood one in the corner, with a surprisingly delicate design on the back, and he took the edge of the bed. Duncan curled up at my feet, having demolished the rest of his trachea before we'd come inside. The elder set his palms flat on his legs, his eyes watchful as he took in the pup and then me.

He was uncomfortable. There was no denying that.

I had so many questions.

"He told you?" the elder finally asked, catching my eyes full-on.

That was a strange opening question. "All he told me was to ask you about my DNA dad, because he made it seem like you should be the one to answer my questions," I replied, watching him closely. Franklin had hazel eyes, a proud nose, and skin a particular shade of honey that wasn't light or brown, but somewhere in between. His ancestry could have been from dozens of different places, I thought again. But the surface of his skin was oddly smooth, and if he colored his hair, I wondered what age he would actually look like.

Franklin nodded slowly, his gaze never leaving mine. At his knees, he wiggled his fingers. *He was nervous.* "I didn't mean to avoid this conversation, but . . ."

"But?" Henri piped in from the bed. He sounded irritated.

The elder shot him a side look. "I convinced myself I could put it off." He almost harrumphed. He was building this up big-time.

He was definitely hiding something, and it sure felt freaking huge.

"What are you not telling me?" I went right out and asked.

Franklin's fingers fidgeted some more.

I gestured toward them. "I'll be specific. What is that bracelet keeping from everyone?" If he thought I was going to take it easy on the questions, he was delusional. This was the most personal question I had ever asked in my life, and I couldn't find it in me to regret it.

The elder hesitated before picking at his wrist, then folding up his sleeve and revealing *two* bands of a variety of obsidian beads linked together with a gold chain and clasp. From the color of the gold, it wasn't 14 carat either. He turned his wrist one way and then another. Those hazel eyes flicked up to meet mine, and he seemed to come to a decision. The fingers of his free hand came over the top, and he undid one clasp after another with surprising dexterity and ease, taking them off, then setting both on the table beside him.

It was like being swallowed by a tidal wave.

His magic . . . it was strong and subtle at the same time. Not a punch like Duncan's mom's or my old neighbor's had been, there was a smoothness to it that was unlike theirs.

From my feet, Duncan rose up like the dead in a single, fluid motion, ears up high, posture straight. His tail did that candlestick thing it did, though the color of it didn't change.

On the bed, Henri shot up to stand. "You son of a bitch," he just about spat.

The elder rolled his eyes before picking his bracelets up and putting them back on.

"What is it?" I asked, fully aware that I was missing something. He was some kind of long-lived being, all right, but I figured he'd been a god from some ancient, small pagan religion.

Henri's teeth were gritted as he glared. "Tell her right now or I will."

So it was like that, huh?

Franklin glared at Henri before he focused on me again and said in a very careful voice, "First, I want you to understand, that I, at no point, was aware of your existence"—I sat up, and Duncan peeked at me over his shoulder, sending me *"love,"* and I leaned over to pet him—"until you arrived here. If I had known you were in the world, I would have found you, child," he warned.

The way he said "child" . . .

"Cut to the chase," Henri growled low, still standing.

There was a pause. Then, "You and I are family," Franklin admitted, staring straight into my eyes when he did.

Henri scoffed, but I couldn't look at him.

Franklin wasn't nervous, I realized at that moment. He was being cautious, but not because there was any dread going through his body. No, he wasn't afraid. The elder kept right on meeting my gaze as he said, "Your father is my brother. I'm your uncle, Nina."

I hadn't seen that coming, not in any way, in any universe, in any kind of folktale, and I could feel it on my face and in my soul as my eyes widened.

When I had thought he was hiding something, I'd assumed it was his background. I'd imagined that he was some god that had been around for a very long time who wanted to live in peace—still a sketchy, secretive MFer, but not *this*.

I had never, ever, not for a second, expected him to say he was my *fucking uncle*.

I was so damn surprised not even my jaw could manage to drop.

No part of me knew what to do with itself.

"You smell similar to him, the sweet note you must get from your mother, but your magic feels very strongly like my brother's. I struggled to comprehend it at first, how he could have had a child at his age, but . . ." His shrug was almost delicate, but still wary. "My main focus when I left shortly after your arrival *was* locating information on the pup. It was sheer coincidence that I could handle both situations at the same place."

I took Duncan's ear between my fingers and let the softness of it ground me when it felt like I'd just been emotionally sucker punched. No matter what happened, what this man said, my relationship to my boy would never change. He wouldn't love me less. I would always have him, and there was a foundation to that knowledge that kept the world from spinning out of control.

"Nina's biological father lives in Alaska?" It was Henri who asked.

"Her father, yes—"

"My dad who matters lives on a farm in Mexico," I butted in through stiff lips.

Franklin nodded slowly. "Correct, I understand. I'll refer to him as my brother, if that works for you, but his blood runs through your veins."

"Love," Duncan told me again, and I sank off the chair completely to crouch over him and give him a hug. My boy tucked his head under my chin and nuzzled it.

"Love, love, love."

"Love you too," I murmured, taking in his reminder for what it was. Proof of real love. A titanium infusion into my spine that said I could handle this conversation. It was all those things that allowed me to sit back up and manage to ask, pretty dang professionally, "Did he try and claim he didn't know about me either?"

Franklin's fingers fidgeted again on his legs. "*I* didn't know about you. Before this trip, I hadn't seen my brother since . . . the Chicago World Fair," he answered almost casually. "That was in August 1893, give or take. We kept in touch with letters for the most part, a few calls here and there. We don't tend to move often, and not now at this stage in our lives. He's even more of an isolated homebody than I am."

"He left his house long enough to get someone pregnant thirty years ago, so he's not that much of a homebody," I muttered under my breath.

Henri snickered, and I glanced at him. A corner of his mouth twitched, and he winked at me. Hadn't we just been arguing half an hour ago?

We had, but he was still more on my team than this secret keeper was. Just like I'd told him, he would always have my loyalty no matter what. I could never forget that.

"I agree." Franklin grimaced. "Initially, when I confronted him . . ." His fingers started tapping faster, and he was beginning to look even more uncomfortable by the second. He seemed to be having some kind of internal struggle. "I don't want to hurt you more than you've already been, Nina."

That was surprisingly thoughtful. "I've known my entire life that I wasn't wanted. I don't think you can hurt my feelings much more than they've already been," I said with a shrug.

Henri grumbled.

Franklin winced. "I see—"

"Choose your words wisely," Henri murmured from where he continued standing, except now his arms were crossed over his wide chest.

The elder nodded. "*My brother* attempted to claim that he wasn't aware of you at the beginning. He insisted that I didn't know what I was talking about, but I've known him my entire life. I would recognize an essence of him anywhere, and I decided that I wouldn't leave until he admitted the truth. It took longer to wear him down than it did to find out what I was able to about Duncan, but eventually, he confessed."

"He knew about me," I deadpanned.

"He knew about you," Franklin confirmed, his eyes flicking toward Henri briefly, then returning to me. "Would you like to hear what I learned?"

I nodded, a small part of me appreciating the fact he was asking me for permission.

"My brother met your . . ." He raised his eyebrows.

"DNA donor," Henri suggested before I could, and I smiled at him weakly before shrugging at Franklin.

"He met your DNA donor when she was visiting the area on a cruise ship. There's a fishing town a few hours from their settlement that gets tourism, and he happened to be visiting when he came across one of our kind. A very strong, very bright, beautiful woman."

I felt one of my eyes go squinty at the description, but I let him continue his story.

"My brother has always refused to hide what he is, and she recognized the same thing in him that he saw in her."

He meant magic, I thought.

"They struck up a conversation, the cruise ship was on an overnight stay there, and at some point, between that afternoon and the next morning, relations were had that resulted in your existence."

My jaw found its way to persevere that time and it dropped as low as it was able to.

I was the child of a one-night stand between two gods.

I . . . I . . .

I laughed.

I laughed, and I bent over to pet Duncan again because I didn't know what else to do. My boy gave my arm a lick in reply. I didn't think he knew what to do with me either.

Fortunately, Franklin continued the second my laughter waned. "One month later, my brother received a letter in the mail—which I read, he has his sentimental moments and kept it—from the woman stating that she was expecting. Verbal contact was made, and your DNA donor, who called herself Isha, made her wishes known. She believed she wasn't in a position to have a child, my brother felt the same, and they agreed that she would find . . . adequate parents to raise the child."

"They were more than adequate," I said, not sure if I was angry, sad, or both, mixed in with some surprise. But I needed to make that point real clear.

"I'm very pleased to hear that," the elder acknowledged almost gently. "My brother eventually admitted that he reached out to you over the years, though he stipulated that it has been some time since his last visitation—up until his most recent, I suppose."

"Visit?" Henri asked in a dull voice.

"Those terrible night visits he's been subjecting us to," Franklin huffed. "The obsidian blocks him from reaching out to Nina directly, and he has no finesse with dream walking. Before you started hiding yourself, he was able to find you more easily and directly." He grumbled, "Dreams are not his natural domain."

My brain ran through his info dump. About the bracelet. About the visits in dreams that weren't dreams that I'd always known were more than they seemed.

I lined up the events in my head. The last time I had had one of those "dreams," they had been before I'd started wearing my bracelet. Since then, I rarely slept without it. If that had been blocking him from "finding me" directly, there would've been no way he'd been able to dream visit again. Hmm.

"So that is him waking us up in the middle of the night?" I asked.

"It is. I've made it clear he's to stop that immediately."

I bit the inside of my cheek, thinking about the gnomes' hints. "Why's he doing that? And how can he if I wear my bracelet? Because he knows where I'm at now?"

"I may have given him my thoughts on his choices. I may have told him what he and that Isha did is unforgiveable." Franklin stopped fidgeting. His expression went intent. "You have the right idea, Nina. He knows where our ranch is, and because he can't find you directly, his telegraphing in sleep is more like . . . using a sledgehammer with a gift he could never use well in the first place. Think of it as him screaming into the abyss in a way." A slight sneer tilted his mouth. "Or a grown man throwing a tantrum at being ignored."

That made surprising sense, but a part of me refused to react to him going out of his way. But the first part of Franklin's statement raised a question that I couldn't keep to myself. "Do you know if he has other children?"

"Not still on this earth. His last child was easily a millennia ago." A stricken look crossed the elder's face. "It's difficult."

Seemed to me like there was more to that, and the elder didn't let me down.

"After your first child, you have the groundwork for what to expect. You know in advance that they'll age while you don't, that they'll pass on, while you have to continue to live with a part of you missing . . ." The older man's throat worked. "It never gets easier. No matter how many times you go through it, losing a child doesn't become more bearable. They don't start to mean less even being aware of the inevitable.

"Each loss takes a bite out of you, and eventually, there isn't much more you can afford to lose," my biological surprise uncle stated carefully.

Too carefully.

I'd swear his eyes sparkled in the dim lighting.

"A thousand years ago, when my last daughter passed, and my brother's son did as well, we made a vow to each other, while we were at our lowest, that we were done with children, who would only grow up to break our hearts. And I'm sorry for that, Nina. I don't think our agreement had anything to do with the decision he and your . . . DNA donor made, but if there was the slightest chance it did, I beg you to forgive me."

I couldn't help but look down at Dunky Donut and imagine what losing him would be like. To spend a lifetime of joy and happiness with him and eventually have it ripped away. Then have to live after that, with his absence.

That was . . . No.

No.

My eyes teared up trying to imagine it, and my imagination was poor because I couldn't even get far enough into that horrible fantasy to do it. I would be a shell. I would be a fraction of the person I was now, knowing I would never see him again. Knowing what I was missing.

It was one thing to know he existed somewhere, even if we weren't together, and it was a totally different thing to be aware I could never hug him again.

And Franklin was right that my father's decision might have been impacted by his vow, but it also might not have been. But if it was, then a small part of me got it. It didn't mean I had to forgive anybody, though.

But I sure wasn't going to sour my life holding on to resentment toward people I didn't care much for to begin with.

Just as I opened my mouth to reassure him that his brother was an adult who could make his own decisions, Franklin slid forward in his recliner, elbows on his knees, and said, "Your life is a gift. Simply knowing of your existence has brought *me* so much joy. I don't believe in suffering through possibilities, but if I had known that you were out there, I would have found you, and I would have raised you."

That got me to shut my mouth like nothing else could have, and got my eyes to water in a way that I wasn't expecting. Below me, Duncan scooted between my feet and leaned against my calves, his *"love, love, love"* a drumbeat alongside my heart.

"I don't expect you to be happy with me for keeping this a secret from you, but I want you to understand the statistical chances it took for my brother and your DNA donor to meet over so many, many years. I haven't known you long, but I can sense the goodness in you. I've seen it with my own eyes and heard it with my ears through the mouths of others. You are life and you are death, Nina, and I have never met anyone like you in the millions of days I've been on this earth. I consider myself blessed to know that I have a child like you in my family," he told me like I was made of tissue paper.

In that brief moment, I felt like I was.

He sounded so earnest too.

With the back of my hand, I wiped at my eyes—I hadn't even noticed them getting watery to begin with—and nodded. What could I say to that? Thank you? He didn't want to hurt my feelings, that was clear, and I didn't want to risk hurting his either. This situation wasn't his fault. But I didn't feel ready to give him a hug and call him Uncle Franklin or anything.

This was a lot.

I'd like to think it would've been a lot for anyone.

What he'd just said had been so nice, and I appreciated it. His words had touched me, but . . . I didn't know what I wanted. I didn't know what I was supposed to do with all that. But suddenly, I was very aware that what I didn't want was to sit in front of him and weep with the confusion taking hold of my body and feelings.

It wasn't like I hadn't known my parents didn't want me. That they hadn't gone out of their way to let me go into the world. I'd been at peace with that knowledge for most of my life.

And it was because of that, feeling that absence so strongly after more than thirty years, that made the situation so much more confusing.

There was no reason for me to feel betrayed and confused, but my soul and brain didn't get the memo.

"I need to . . ." Duncan placed his head on my knee, and I dipped mine to peck the top of it. My voice came out funny, but I refused to beat myself up over it. "Thank you, Franklin, for telling me all that. I have a lot to think about, but just . . . I don't blame you for any of it. All right?"

He nodded as I got up, my donut getting to his paws too. But I hesitated. To ask or not to ask?

We were here though, weren't we? He was telling me things now, wasn't he? What better time than now, right?

Maybe there was a list of things I had no interest in being aware of, but this was one I did. I looked him right in the eyes, and I went for it. "Did an ancient civilization have a name for you and your brother?"

His eyes sparkled through the lenses of his glasses, and his voice was very, very still when he said, "They called him Thanatos, and I was known as Hypnos."

The god of death, and the god of sleep. I should've known.

I nodded at him before turning to walk out of the room.

I didn't make it past the bed when a hand caught mine, a moment before amber irises did the same. His eyes roamed my face as I looked up at Henri. Concern was etched over the strain at his mouth and the creases at the corners of his eyes.

I wasn't the only one upset.

And his worry did something to me I had no business spending too much time on.

"I'm all right," I tried to tell him. "I just need a cuddle right now." I caught myself, not wanting him to get the wrong impression. He was the one who'd taught me that word. He was the person whose face came to mind when I heard it now. But . . . I wasn't doing this with him anymore. I couldn't. I shouldn't. "A Duncan cuddle, I mean. I'll be fine. Today was a long day." Flipping my hand in his, I squeezed his fingers for a split second before slipping them out of his hold. "I'll see you later, Henri. Thank you for coming with me. You're a good friend."

His features darkened at the same time his head jerked enough I could have called it a flinch, and it made me feel bad.

But I didn't have the emotional capacity right at that moment to make him feel better.

Instead, telling myself it was all friendship, which was what he was sharing with me being there, I leaned into him and pressed my lips to the part of his arm level with my mouth, avoiding his eyes while I did it. Then, with my boy at my side, we went upstairs.

I laid on my bed, took out my phone and searched through my messaging app for the group chat I was looking for. It only took a couple minutes before one of my aunts replied with who I could contact. My parents didn't leave their house often, but I was grateful they were visiting someone I could reach out to easily at that moment.

It didn't take long for a loud female voice to answer my app call and talk to me for a moment before she called out, "¡Marcela! ¡Felipe!"

And somehow, I managed to hold on to my tears long enough to hear my mom's familiar voice on the other end. "Nina?"

"Hi, Ma."

Chapter Twenty-Two

I blinked at the two furry faces currently staring at me from their spot on top of my bed.

So different and yet so alike. One was dark, with a short coat, long and narrow features, and brilliant red eyes. The other the complete opposite with a pale, longer coat, shorter and fluffier, and bright blue eyes. One loved me, and the other . . . let me do her hair sometimes. They both blinked at me again.

One of the things I had never, ever considered was how often—as a guardian—I was going to be stuck being stared at by a bored face, expecting me to help entertain it. I was well aware that I was lucky Duncan enjoyed watching TV, wasn't high-energy, and napped a good amount throughout the day.

But every once in a while, he got ants in his imaginary pants, which was going on at that moment. Only it wasn't just one set of puppy dog eyes boring a hole straight into my soul, it was two.

Neither one of them were vocalizing that they wanted to do something, but words were unnecessary.

I could feel what they were asking for, and that was for me to figure out something to keep them busy.

It was the weekend, after all.

And maybe they didn't need to forget things that were going on in their lives, but I wouldn't have minded.

It had been a long week, and I'd spent more time trying not to think about men than I ever would have imagined. Men as in Henri, Franklin, Ilya from Alaska, and Franklin's freaking brother. When I'd been younger and dumber, boy problems would have sounded like fun.

They weren't.

But I'd been trying my best not to let any of them get me down—I had promised my parents after all when we spoke on the phone for an hour after my conversation with Franklin—which meant I'd been keeping myself as busy as possible since the night that had changed everything and nothing at the same time.

"It's only eleven. Do you want to go for a walk?" I suggested, standing in the doorway between the bathroom and the bedroom.

Nothing.

I tried again. "What about an ATV ride? We can have a picnic, play hide-and-seek?" They both had such good noses, it wasn't exactly challenging, but Duncan hadn't outgrown the game yet.

My donut stared at me, but I felt his *"yes"* after a moment.

One down, one to go. "What do you say, Agnes? Want to come?" I asked her.

How she managed to be able to glare at me despite being in her mini wolf form was honestly a talent, but she was doing it. Her short, little growl, I took as a yes.

Phew. "All right, let's go then," I told them, cocking my head toward the door before they changed their minds.

Both pups took flying leaps off the bed, and I winced when Duncan's was a little less than graceful and he landed sprawled out on his stomach, but he got up like nothing happened. Agnes disappeared through the small door, but he waited for me. A two-year-old magical boy was the most reliable male in my life—my dad not included. It made me love him even more somehow.

After brushing my teeth, smoothing on some deodorant, and taking a quick pee, I put my boots on and slipped my phone into the fanny pack I had hanging off the doorknob, clipping it on and giving Dunky a scratch behind the ear before we took the staircase where Agnes waited on the landing. We had just gotten to the first floor when both puppies' heads cocked to the right a moment before the clip-clopping of feet echoed and a satyr woman appeared around the corner from the direction of the kitchen.

It was Phoebe.

The frantic expression on her face put me on alert. "Have you seen Shiloh?" she called out in a shaky voice.

Since Agnes and Duncan couldn't exactly answer, I did. "Hi, Phoebe. No. Not today." After school yesterday, sure.

"Pascal?" Phoebe tried.

I shook my head, hoping this wasn't going where it seemed like it was.

She managed to look even more sick, and her hands went to her face. "Do you know where Randall or Ani are?"

Nothing good could come from her asking for two of the ranch's security people. "No." It had only been us three at breakfast, Franklin and Henri had both been pretty scarce lately, and I let that thought go as soon as it entered my head. "What happened? Can I help?" I asked.

Phoebe sniffled, her big brown eyes widening. "I can't find Shiloh or Pascal. They were playing outside of the house while I was on the phone with my sister . . . I can't find them. They didn't warn me they were going anywhere, and I checked Pascal's, but no one was there because I said I would watch him . . . but now I can't find them."

I walked right up to her, barely containing the urge to hug her or put my hands on her shoulders to tell her everything was going to be okay. "I would be freaking out too. I'll help you look for them, all right?" I glanced over at the puppies. "You two will help, won't you?"

"*Yes*," Duncan answered as Agnes stared at me with her bright blue eyes.

"I don't know where anyone is right now, but I'm sure someone will help you find them faster than they would help me if I asked. I'll start looking with these two, and you can get other people to help." I took her hands. "We'll find them. How long do you think it's been since you saw them?"

She whimpered, clutching my fingers tightly. "I don't know, Nina. We were on the phone longer than I'd expected."

"It's okay. I have my phone. I'll come back in an hour if I don't come across them, and we can reconvene here. Sound good?"

We would try our best. I had a baby wolf and a baby Duncan, and they could smell things from much further away than I was able to. When he was even younger, Duncan had found some stuff that was genuinely impressive—if you could be impressed by finding dead animals.

"We'll start looking. Please call me if you find them, all right?" I told her.

Phoebe nodded quickly, and in no time, she was down the opposite hallway, close to where the nursery was. Meanwhile, the pups and I headed down the main hall that went by the living area and out the back door toward the vehicle warehouse.

Agnes stopped for no reason, the air around her changing before her human form appeared.

"Do you want to stay?" I asked.

"I told them not to go," she blurted out, managing to look grim in gummy bear pajamas and two pigtails that were half undone.

"Not to go where?"

"To look for the waterfall."

"What waterfall?" I'd never heard about a waterfall.

"*The* waterfall." The way she said it made it seem like I was an idiot for asking for specifics. Like there was one that I should've known about.

I crouched. We could talk about the waterfall later. "You think that's where they went?"

The unflappable menace didn't look so unflappable. She started wringing her hands. "Maybe."

Maybe wasn't "no."

I nodded. "Do you know how to get there? Or know what

direction it's in? We can take the ATV. And even in this form, you can smell better than I can, so you can help me find them, if you want to go." I looked at Duncan. "You smell too and tell me if you sense them close, okay, Donut?"

"Yes," Duncan agreed, his tail swinging behind him.

"Are they gonna get in trouble?" the little girl asked.

"I have no idea," I told her. "But it would be better for them to get in a little bit of trouble than get hurt, or worse. Right?"

I'd known she was a logical child, but I definitely knew it when she agreed almost instantly.

When we got to the warehouse, there were a few vehicles missing, which wasn't uncommon since it was the weekend. I got into the first one that fit four to six people. Agnes jumped on the bench seat to my right, and Duncan got in too, opting for the floorboard. I didn't see a single person after I pulled out of the garage, so I tried to call Henri. He didn't answer, and his voicemail was full. I tried calling Phoebe, but she didn't answer either, so I left a voicemail.

"Hi, Phoebe, there's a chance the boys might have gone looking for a waterfall. I don't know where that's at, but I'm going to follow Agnes's lead. Please call me. Bye," I rattled off before hanging up. I guess it was just going to be us. "Point where you think they might have gone, Mini Wolf," I instructed the girl buckled into the seat next to me.

Duncan would figure out a way to tell me if he noticed anything, that went unsaid.

She pointed straight out into the woods to the side of the warehouse, but what was I going to do? Ask her if she was sure? I had no idea where to start, and one place was just as good as any other when we had no other leads, I figured.

Shiloh and Pascal were going to be dead meat, and I couldn't say they weren't going to deserve it.

With my two companions sniffing the air, we were off down the gravel road, going in the direction that Henri and Randall had both taken me on the times we'd ventured out into the more remote parts of the forest. Fortunately, the vehicle we were in was electric and quiet, other than the tires going over small rocks and loose branches too small to be relocated.

"Pascal! Shiloh!" I started yelling once we'd gotten some distance from the clubhouse. The road was getting less maintained and more dirt-packed but still visible enough to follow. Duncan and I hadn't come out in this direction much when we went for walks. The paths were rougher over here than they were everywhere else on the ranch. "Do you smell them?" I asked the kids.

Agnes's eyes swept the area. "Not close."

"*No,*" Duncan answered.

I slowed down and stuck to the road that was getting narrower and bumpier the further we got from the residential part of the ranch. The trees were becoming slimmer and in thicker clusters, the magic in the air getting sweeter.

A small hand touched my arm eventually. "Around here."

I let the UTV come to a stop, and Agnes unbuckled her seat belt and got out before I did the same, Duncan following. Agnes moved through the trees like she knew each and every one of them by name, taking big inhales through her nose as she walked forward a little bit, then turned one direction then another, visibly sniffing. Her face was pinched in concentration.

"Shiloh! Pascal!" I yelled again.

"This way," Agnes instructed, her hand rising to point, before frowning. She looked so much like Henri making that face, it would have made me smile under any other circumstances.

Duncan and I followed her, walking on and on and on, further and further from the UTV. I really hoped I could remember where I'd left it. Eventually, we came up to a river. It was raging, gurgling over half-buried boulders, pushing an unimaginable amount of water every second.

"What are they doing coming out here by themselves?" I asked. "Why are they looking for the waterfall? Because they're bored?"

That got her to glance at me, her eyes wider than normal.

"I just want to know. I'm not going to ground them. They're already busted."

She didn't answer, but she did keep going, waiting a little bit before muttering something under her breath.

I asked her to repeat herself. "I'm not going to get them in trouble, Agnes. I promise. I just want to understand why they keep wandering off into the woods."

"They want to see the waterfall," she answered in a huff.

The urge to ask *what freaking waterfall* was on the tip of my tongue again. Matti, not Henri, nobody had ever brought up a waterfall of any kind. But the kids wanting to see it . . . that made sense. If no one wanted to take them . . . I could put the dots together.

I wanted to see the dang waterfall now.

"Is that what you all went looking for before? The day you came across the swamp thing?"

She didn't hesitate to answer that. "Yup."

Hm. "Is it a nice waterfall?"

"Yes, Nina." She slowed down to side-eye me. "It's the magic one."

A magical waterfall?

I blinked.

How could a waterfall be magical? The trees here looked different, sure. I'd noticed during my walks with Duncan in the past that their trunks had kind of a glittery sheen to them, their leaves ranging in shades of green, and even Henri had suggested that things were special because of the magic in the land. Maybe the trees around the waterfall were more epic? Maybe there were magical fish in it?

I definitely wanted to see it now too.

Agnes stopped so abruptly it was like she ran into an invisible wall.

"What is it?" I leaned around her and squinted into the distance.

But I didn't need to look far.

Spencer the sasquatch was leaning against a tall pine, looking about as pissed off as he had the other times I'd run into him.

"The dumbasses are in the river," he growled in that inhumanly deep voice.

I was about to argue that they weren't dumb and that he was being rude, but the hairy mythical being huffed.

"If the river doesn't get 'em, I will, their wailing's that annoying. I was trying to take a nap," he grumbled. "I'd get to them soon if I were you."

The urge to argue with him was on the tip of my tongue again, but he was warning me for a reason.

I didn't miss that part.

Spencer deserved to have someone explain to him why he should care about children, but that person wasn't going to be me.

"Thank you," I told the sasquatch with an attitude problem, twisting my body enough to see through the split in the tree line. Light glinted off the surface of the river to our right, the sounds of the water rushing so much louder now. The river seemed even wider in this spot.

Agnes, Duncan, and I all started moving again, even faster that time. Soon, Agnes's hand went up, and she violently gestured ahead. "There! They're over there!" she shouted just as a scream pierced through the forest.

Out of the corner of my eye, I caught the bright flame of Duncan's tail go vertical.

"Help!" a shrill voice wailed.

I recognized it, and that alone had me pointing violently at the ground, making brief eye contact with both Agnes and Duncan, who looked as freaked out as I suddenly felt. "Stay here!" I commanded before I turned and ran parallel to the river. If I went down to the embankment, I'd lose too much time and not be able to cover the distance as fast.

The shouting got louder, shriller, and more frantic, and I tried to find where it was coming from, but there were so many trees, and I was the wrong person to run in the forest in a panic. But I was the only person in the forest other than Spencer, and I wasn't about to expect him to turn into anyone's hero.

"Help!" a clear, high-pitched voice shrieked.

I ran. I ran and I ran like my life depended on it. I'd looked on the map shortly after we'd moved here, and now that I thought about it, I couldn't remember seeing any bodies of water so close to where the actual ranch was. There was a river further away by where the nature preserve part of the property was, but that wasn't close. And that was something to wonder over later . . . when I wasn't running toward a river raging in early fall, when every other one I'd ever seen had usually been starved from rainfall and snowmelt by this point in the year. But why should that surprise me? Since when had this place made any sense to begin with?

My legs pumped under me, and I was pretty sure I heard trampling from behind, but I couldn't worry about Agnes and Duncan when they were more responsible than Pascal and Shiloh, at this point. Just as I was about to yell at them to stay again, a figure appeared by the riverbank.

And my stomach sank a split second later when I cut down to it.

Shiloh stood on a boulder just shy of the edge of the river, shivering and soaked, and Pascal . . .

Pascal was balanced on a rock jutting out of the water, maybe a couple inches at the most. *In the middle of the fucking river.* A river that had no business flowing the way it did, like it was early spring after a heavy winter. Pascal's teeth were visibly clenched, his arms were at his sides for balance, and he confirmed he was the one screaming when he let another piercing one out.

"What the *fuck*?" I hissed under my breath, not wanting to yell and scare either of them. But they must have smelled me or heard me because they both looked over.

I wanted to hold up my arms and ask what they were thinking, but I realized then why Spencer had said what he'd said.

If Pascal fell into the river . . .

I couldn't let that happen.

Leaves and bushes rustled along my legs, and just to the side of them were Duncan and Agnes. They had followed me. My ride or die and the girl who I was pretty sure saw him as a little brother.

I would die before I let anything happen to them.

"Stay. Here," I repeated, pointing at the ground. "Please. Don't go in the water for any reason. Do you understand? *No matter what happens, you don't go in.*"

"Yes," Agnes answered.

"*Yes*," Duncan told me, meeting me with those bright red eyes. He was worried.

"*Please*. I'm serious. Stay here where it's safe. I love you so much. I love you both," I said, taking my phone out of my pocket and thrusting it toward Agnes. "Stay here," I repeated as Shiloh shouted something that sounded really close to "Shit!"

Forcing myself not to look behind me—because I had to trust them; I did trust them—I scrambled closer to the river where Shiloh was, the bank grassy and muddy and getting steeper the further down river I went. I moved from one rock to another, some boulder-sized, some barely big enough to fit my toes, but I didn't have time to worry about busting my ass.

It was faster to get to a shaking Shiloh than I'd expected, but I figured being led by pure panic helped. When I got close enough, I reached out. "Grab my hand, Shiloh," I called out.

The little boy shook from his spot maybe two feet from the bank. "I'm scared!"

The water was high and looked deep, even though he wasn't that far in, and I didn't blame him, but . . . "It's okay. See? I can reach you."

Opening my hand, I coaxed him to grab it, trying to ignore Pascal wobbling on the rock he was perched on. *One kid at a time*. I couldn't freak out this soon.

"You can do it. Come on, Shiloh!" I egged him on.

His little hand trembled, but he stretched, reached out, and grabbed me. "On the count of three, jump, okay?" I told him. "One! Two!"

I didn't get to three and almost slipped when he jumped early and I wasn't ready, but I managed to pull him into me with his momentum, and we both stumbled when he landed in my arms.

We didn't have time to celebrate though.

I picked him up, set him higher up on the bank, and ordered, "Don't move an inch."

Damn, that water is high, I thought when I was facing the river again. It didn't help it was muddy, which made it impossible to see the bottom.

Eyeing the distance between us, there was no safe way to get across to Pascal that way. My legs weren't long enough to safely jump to where he was. I wasn't even sure how he'd managed it. There was a log halfway jutting out of the water thirty feet along the river, but it was way too far to reach him from it . . .

"Nina! I'm scared!" the little boy wailed in a frantic voice that was probably going to give me nightmares.

"I'm coming!" I yelled back as Shiloh made a distressed sound, but I couldn't reassure him. I had to act fast. Act now.

But I swear I decided right then, that if I died, I was going to come back and haunt Pascal when he was older and it would be less traumatizing

I can't let that happen. I couldn't leave Duncan. I didn't want to never speak to my parents again. I didn't want to miss out on Matti and Sienna's lives. And damn it, I wanted Henri to mark me again with his cheek on my throat.

Before I could waste more time or overthink this crap more than I already had, I leapt to get to where Shiloh had been perched. The water flowed aggressively around my feet, but I couldn't focus on it. Holding my breath, I hopscotched the last few embedded boulders I could reach before the wide gap that separated me from Pascal. And that was when he screamed again, thrusting his hands out at his sides to keep his balance.

"Nina!" he hollered, wobbling so hard he almost fell in.

Fuck, fuck, fuck, fuck, fuck. I had to act. I had no idea what the hell I was doing, and someone with better survival instincts was more than likely going to call me an idiot, but . . . I squatted until my butt hovered over the surface of the water and called out, "I'm going to try and walk over to you. If I get swept away, don't jump in after me, Pascal. Stay right where you are as long as you can. Do you hear me?"

His face was white, his expression so totally different from the cocky, mischievous boy that cackled over the weirdest stuff. "Yes!"

"If I get to you, I want you to get on my back, and we're going to try and get to that log over there. You see where I'm pointing? The fallen one halfway across the river?"

"Yes!"

This had to be the worst idea I'd ever had. Why didn't I have rope? Why wasn't this river low?

What the hell had they been thinking trying to cross it?

"If you fall off—" I started.

"What!" he screeched. "I'm gonna *fall*?"

He was making this worse. "If you fall off of me, *if*, I want you to float on your back with your legs up and try to grab on to a branch or swim to the side with your arms. But only *if* you fall into the river, do you hear me?" I yelled, trying not to get angry he'd gotten us into this situation.

How in the world had he managed to get all the way into the middle of the river in the first place?

"Yes!" He was so scared his shaking was visible, but that wasn't going to stop me from wringing his neck if no one else did.

"And nobody jump into the water if anything happens to me, okay?" It was my turn to shriek—sounding deranged—so that hopefully Duncan would hear me. He was the only one I was worried would risk his life to help me if something happened.

Someone shot back a "yes," and I was going to take it. I didn't have time not to. Knowing I was more than likely going to regret this, I settled my butt on the rock beneath me and slid my legs into the water, gritting my teeth the whole time. It was so cold. I touched bottom sooner than I'd expected, but the power of the water rushed between and around my legs. It was only about waist high, but the current was strong. Too strong.

"I got this. I got this. I got this," I said out loud to myself as I started my journey with a single step. Which I realized was a strong word when I twisted around to see how far it had gotten me. It was more like . . . a small shuffle. A very small shuffle. My feet grazed the slippery pebbles beneath them, not wanting to break too much contact with the bottom. The last thing anyone needed was for me to trip over something, and the current was hard enough to ignore in the first place.

I took another small step with the same leg, then dragged the other one forward.

Careful.

It was so freaking hard to move. I held my arms out at my sides to keep my balance, my legs slightly bent.

This was a horrible idea, and maybe I was descended from Rumpelstiltskin, because this kid was going to owe me his firstborn, I decided at some point.

Something hit me in the calf, but I managed to keep standing. I shuffled, then shuffled a little more, regretting so much right then. I couldn't decide what in the hell I'd been thinking doing this. *Getting into the water, Nina? Dumb, dumb, dumb.* I was pretty sure that was the first thing every single raft guide I'd ever met had stressed: do not stay in the water.

And you know what? Pascal wasn't just going to owe me his firstborn. I was going to get his second and his third, and every child his children had. This was going to be my supervillain origin story. I was going to start claiming children's lives and futures after this. They were all going to owe me.

My foot slipped, and I had to wave my hands in the air to keep from going under, my heart fluttering. Someone from the direction of the bank yelled as Pascal started crying louder, but I had to ignore them all. I had to focus. I had to get to him *and make it back*.

Fuck, fuck, *fuck*.

I could do this. I could do this. This was a magical river. Maybe it would give me nicer skin or add a couple years to my life the longer I was in it. People paid a lot of money for cold therapy bathtubs, and here I had this river for free.

It's not that cold, I tried to lie to myself.

What felt like ten minutes later, with water rushing at my

hips and my entire back soaked, I made it to Pascal, who was still making a scene with his tears and sobs. Snot ran down his mouth, literal tracks of tears down his cheeks, and he was wailing louder than La Llorona I'd heard once when I'd stayed by a river in Texas. I never went there again.

"Get on my back, Pascal," I told him in a voice that would have impressed Henri, refusing to meet his eyes because I had to stay focused. If I thought about it too much, I was going to get scared. It wasn't just my life I had to worry about.

The little boy didn't hesitate; he jumped on my back so fast and aggressively I almost lost my balance. But Pascal didn't stop there, even though that was exactly what I'd asked for. He climbed me like a jungle gym. Knobby knees hit either side of my face as he scurried up my body instead of just piggyback riding me. *This is going to be harder than I thought.* The other bank was closer, but then how was I going to cross over again? We were going to have to go back the way we'd come. It was our only option.

"We're okay. We're okay," I repeated out loud as Pascal's fingers gripped the sides of my face so tight, I was sure I looked like I'd had bad plastic surgery. I wanted to tell him to crawl back down a little because doing this with him wrapped around the middle of my body would make it easier for me to distribute his weight but knowing him, he'd poke me in the eye or make the situation worse than it already was somehow if he tried getting off my shoulders. That would be when he fell into the water, dang it.

I managed two shuffle-steps before everything went to shit.

Agnes yelled at the exact same time Duncan went "awoo" a second before something hit me on the butt. So hard on the butt, I flailed for a second before what had to be a big branch or a log took my legs out from under me because there was nowhere else for it to go with the force of the current being what it was.

I fell backward. Hands gripped my head and my hair for dear life as multiple voices screamed. The river gushed over my face as I went under.

Fear took over my soul as I sucked in water, and something else in the river hit me as I tried to get my legs under me, but fortunately whatever it was, it wasn't as big, so it wasn't as painful. I came up sputtering and gasping, and somehow, Pascal was still on my shoulders as he ripped hair out of my head to hang on. He was shrieking at the top of his lungs. And I must have been under longer than I'd thought because when my head broke the surface, we were coming up to the fallen log that now seemed like a hazard instead of help.

If I face-planted the trunk . . .

LOVE! I tried to send Duncan. "Grab it!" I shouted out loud to Pascal. "Grab the log!" I didn't want to die, but I didn't want Pascal to die more than I wanted to live.

That just meant we had to nail this.

Because I didn't want this to be what took me out. I wanted to hug Duncan again. I wanted to grow old with Sienna and help Matti wipe his butt when we were elderly if I had to, and Henri—

With all my strength, I reached up, sinking beneath the water with the shift of my weight, and literally tried to toss Pascal toward the tree. His weight left my shoulders, and I had to pray he'd made it as I blindly reached up the moment after he was gone and scrambled to grab something.

And grab something I did.

It was a broken-off branch that might have impaled me if I hadn't gone under water when I had, but I held on for dear life with one hand as I went under again before using it to pull myself up. I sucked in a big breath and reached for something else, thanking the universe that the trunk must have not been in the water long because it wasn't slick with algae or moss, like it should have been.

I was gasping and panting, and my hand hurt, but I found a short, thick stub, and clung to it with my other hand.

"Pascal?" I coughed.

It was the whimper I heard first, then, "Ninaaaa!" really close by. Over the top of the tree, a wet, dark head of hair appeared, and looking like a drowned rat, Pascal's small face was one of the best things I'd ever seen. There was a cut on his cheek, but he looked fine.

He was alive. Everything else he could heal from. The urge to cry hit me just as strongly as panic had when I'd gone underwater.

But this wasn't the time. We weren't safe yet.

"As fast as you can, crawl off the trunk," I told him.

There was an "awooo" that spurred me into finding another broken branch along the trunk, then another as I managed to get my legs under me, my feet grazing the pebbled bottom.

Pascal's face disappeared, leaving me there, but I watched him crawl across the trunk in the time it took me to move a foot closer to land. When he finally made it to the bank, I clung to the damn tree, ignoring the way sharp nubs and tree bark dug into and scraped my chest and stomach, but there was no way I was relaxing my grip and risking falling back in. Slowly, I shuffled one leg after another, the water shallowing to midthigh, then my knee, and finally my ankle, and I let out the most violent shudder of my whole life.

My legs gave out on the muddy and rocky slope, and I propped myself up with my hands as I panted. *That had been close. That had been way too damn close.*

Arms wrapped around my waist as a wet body pretty much tackled me, sobbing, "Nina," and from the other side, a warm, furry body slammed into me too.

"Love, love, love," Duncan told me as my arms shook and he wound his frame—on his belly—around them like a cat.

I was crying, I realized. *I was crying.* Water dripping from my face onto the rocks wasn't from the river; it was from my eyes.

A lick at my cheek, at my chin had me sucking in the breath I hadn't been able to take before. Wrapping an arm around Duncan, who was making this frantic sound in his chest, I set my hand on Pascal, tears blurring my vision.

As I rolled onto my butt, both of them climbed on top of me, and another set of arms wrapped around my neck. It was Shiloh, I thought, and from the sound of it, he was crying too.

"I'm sorry," Shiloh whimpered.

"I'm sorry," Pascal hiccupped, crying so loud it was hard to tell what he was saying.

"You okay?" Agnes asked a moment before she must have patted the top of my head.

"Love," Duncan told me, licking my cheek before licking my other cheek, so frantically. *"Love, love, love."*

I'd been so damn scared.

So freaking, freaking scared, I could finally admit it in my head. I clung to the kids just as tightly as they held on to me.

It took me a minute to notice they weren't the only ones shaking. I was shaking like a dang leaf too.

And if that was what fear felt like, I never wanted to experience it again.

Chapter Twenty-Three

"Are you mad?"

I peered down at the little boy clutching my hand tightly. The same little boy who hadn't loosened his grip even a little bit from the moment he'd taken ahold of it over twenty minutes ago, all damp palm and slippery fingers, clinging so hard my hand hurt more than it already did from the scrapes and the tiny puncture wounds from clutching at the fallen log that had probably saved my life and Pascal's. One day I'd go back and give it a hug.

"I'm not mad," I assured Shiloh, squeezing his hand. It was taking everything I had not to let my teeth chatter.

There was a poke to my forehead a moment before the top half of a familiar head appeared in my vision. "Are you mad at *me*?" Pascal asked from his position perched on my shoulders again, where he'd been holding on to my ponytail like it was reins on a horse. He was basically a cold, heavy brick on top of me. He'd taken off most of his clothes, and I'd wrung them out as much as I could, same as I'd done to mine. The difference was, he seemed perfectly fine. His skin wasn't even cold.

I was still shaking. My bones and skin literally hurt. Every muscle in my body was wound so tight, they felt on the verge of tearing.

But in a weird way, I felt more alive and more dead than I ever had before.

Not that I wanted to relive that incident again.

For now, my whole focus was centered on us making it to the

golf cart, and the sooner I got us back to the clubhouse, the sooner everything would be fine.

Because what I needed more than anything at that moment, more than warm clothes, more than a hug, was a cry in the privacy of my shower. I didn't want to traumatize any children more than I already had. We'd been a spectacle, and I was glad no one else had been around to witness it.

Shiloh and Pascal had wept all over me on the bank, and Duncan had done the puppy equivalent. He had let out these little "awoo"s that had the potential to scar me for life. Agnes had managed to keep her tears in check, standing off to the side of us, her face tense. Her arms, on the other hand, had been crossed over her chest.

A violent shiver went through my whole body right then, and Pascal grabbed on to my ears to hold on better. When we'd realized he'd lost both shoes in the river, I'd been under the impression he would just change into his werewolf puppy form, but he said he was too tired. Then, I'd asked him if he wouldn't prefer a piggyback ride on the way back to the UTV—because of his barefoot situation—and he'd hugged my head and said very earnestly, "No, thank you."

I must have been a sucker because I didn't insist on him not riding my shoulders. But I did grit my teeth when he pinched my right ear too tight. "No, I'm not mad at anyone." *Maybe* I was a little, but I wouldn't say it out loud to him after we'd all just gotten done practically wailing until I'd forced myself to be an adult and calm them down enough to figure out our next step. "I was just scared someone was going to get hurt."

And worse.

"I'm mad," Agnes threw in from where she was walking close to my other side. Her hand kept brushing my thigh, and I was trying so hard to pretend I didn't notice just how purposeful it seemed. But I'd seen her face when I'd taken my clothes off to wring them out. Maybe she hadn't made an actual peep, but there had been no hiding the emotion coming from her either. She'd been just as scared as the rest of us. "You're dumb!"

"Who's dumb?" Pascal asked, sounding offended and not like he'd been blubbering for his mom and dad minutes ago.

"You're dumb. You and Shiloh," the little girl accused.

"I'm not dumb. You're dumb!" Pascal claimed, leaning over my head again so I had to reach up and grab his hips so he wouldn't topple over and send us both headfirst into the ground. A concussion was the last thing I needed. And if we didn't find the UTV soon, I was plucking him off my shoulders regardless of what he wanted. He was too dang heavy.

"I'm dumb?" Shiloh sounded more than a little hurt.

The universe was balancing out my perfect Duncan with these agents of chaos. It had to be. It's what I deserved.

Almost like he knew I was thinking about him, a nudge had me glancing at Duncan trotting beside me. "Love you," I told him as my calf cramped so hard, I wanted to stop and massage it, but if I bent over, I might not get back up.

"*Love*," he told me in return, watching me carefully with those incredible, observant eyes.

Shiloh and Agnes froze at the same time Pascal tensed up on my shoulders.

No. I couldn't deal with this right now, I thought, as I paused right where we were, expecting the worst. If this was some magical being that liked eating people, I was going to scream. I wasn't going to break something; I was going to—

"You're gonna be in sooooo much trouble," Agnes cooed as something big crashed in the distance, getting louder and louder, closer and closer.

I couldn't deal with another catastrophe right now. *Please let this be help. Please don't let this be a Mothman or whatever other cannibalistic asshole might be in this forest.*

"Is it someone we know?" I asked, ready to lower the kids and hide them if I had to. It didn't sound small. Or friendly.

But I sensed the wrecking ball of magic before anyone answered.

A flash of a coat appeared in the distance, and the sight and color of it relaxed me as much as my frozen body could handle. Massive, fluffy Henri was flying across the ground, his long strides eating up the distance. He looked like something out of a children's fantasy book, all imposing and menacing and just . . . unreal.

But he was very real.

Because at that exact moment, on my shoulders, the boy shook. "I'm sorry, Henri!" Pascal shouted in a broken voice.

The black wolf slid to a stop a few feet away, head held high, his posture regal. His coat was so glossy I would've sworn he got regular baths. He was beautiful.

The air shimmered, and in the place where a colossal, black wolf had stood, there was now a man with the same color hair. A very pissed-looking man whose amber eyes slid from one child to another before finally landing on me. The muscle in his cheek popped.

I'd barely seen him since my talk with Franklin, and the times I had, had been through the window across from my room that faced the parking lot. He'd been working extra-long hours again, and when he wasn't, from what Randall told me, he was dealing with ranch stuff. The same old story.

Matti had been right when he'd called him a principal.

Regardless, I liked to think Henri was giving me space to deal with the news Franklin had shared, but there might have been a chance he was still mad at me after our conversation with the Alaskan leader. Not that that conversation had even made all that much sense in the first place, but he hadn't made the effort to bring it up again so chances were that maybe he'd seen my point. Maybe he was fine now with letting me keep Alaska as a backup option.

I didn't let that possibility hurt my feelings. It was what I'd asked for. It was what I needed.

And he was *here*.

Glaring, but he was here.

Taking us all in while we looked like a million bucks.

There was a drowned rat on my shoulders, a protective puppy at my side, Shiloh looked like he'd been haunted by ghosts for a century, and Agnes was about ready to fight someone.

And I was more than likely a mix of all of them.

I kind of wished someone had a camera so I could remember this moment forever. Me and my band of magical menaces. I loved them.

Weakly, I smiled right as a shiver hit that had my whole body shaking, even my teeth chattered.

Henri's cheek popped again. His nostrils flared, and I watched his throat bob. As much as he was trying to hide it, he was mad. "Is everyone fine?" he asked slowly, like he was chewing on glass with every syllable.

Two small heads nodded, and it felt like the one above mine more than likely did the same.

Amber irises locked on me, his eyes going a tiny bit squinty. "Are you?" His attention swept over my clingy, wet clothes briefly, nostrils flaring.

I nodded, not trusting my voice or my teeth to not give me away even more than they already had.

Bright eyes crept over all of us one more time, lingering on each person as that muscle in his cheek kept on flexing. It was clear he was pissed . . . but there was something else in his eyes. Worry?

"Where are you heading?" Henri asked after a loaded moment of silence, his focus lingering on the little boy who was doing his best impersonation of an opossum on my shoulders.

Here went nothing. "Looking for the UTV. I don't remember where I left it," I explained in my own funny voice—crying did that to vocal chords—only feeling a little sheepish I hadn't left a trail behind that Hansel and Gretel could be proud of.

Lids a shade darker than the rest of his face dropped over those stunning eyes of his as the rest of us watched him, not sure what to expect. It wasn't Henri holding out his arms though. "Come here, Pascal," he ordered.

To give the little boy credit, he launched himself off my shoulders like it was an Olympic event and into waiting arms, only stepping on my chest a little bit. For all he was worried about being in trouble, here he was jumping ship the second he could. Henri easily settled him on his shoulders. He didn't seem worried he was wet, but then again, he was a werewolf. He handled cold better than I ever would.

I sniffled.

"Let's find the UTV and someone can tell me exactly what happened," he informed us, still taking his time with his words.

Not that he could see it, but Pascal grimaced. Shiloh's hand went even slicker somehow.

"What happened is that they're dumb." Agnes threw them under the bus.

If we ever got to the point in our friendship where I wanted us to get to, I was going to have to teach her about snitches. I was all for honesty and understood that it was pointless to lie to a werewolf, but she could've stayed quiet and given the boys a chance to confess first.

But she didn't know that, and her claim set off a chain reaction.

I stayed out of it as the kids talked over one another, their story going backward and forward between getting to the river, falling into it, and walking. Someone said someone else cried. I was pretty sure Pascal shouted that we almost died. Not a single word left my mouth. Part of the reason was just because I liked hearing the kids bickering, and the other part was because I didn't want to bring any attention to my shaking hands or the wobbliness that I was pretty sure would take over my throat if I gave it a chance. I didn't fool myself into thinking that Henri couldn't tell I was worked up—he would've smelled it way before he got to us.

And despite having the entire forest that could have been between us, Henri walked so close to me his knuckles kept brushing mine. I wanted to take his hand, but I didn't. All my energy went toward trying not to wince or groan with how miserable I felt and how much soggy shoes sucked. Another shiver shot down my spine, so violent, my donut lifted his head to peer at me.

I gave him a grim smile and winked.

"*Love,*" he reminded me again.

"I see it!" Pascal hollered like he hadn't just about had a meltdown recently, pointing in the process.

Sure enough, the camo-colored UTV was there. Henri set Pascal on the ground, and I dipped down to hug Duncan tight. His warm, gangly body made me feel instantly better.

"Grab the emergency blankets in the glove compartment and put one on, Pascal," Henri instructed in a gruff tone.

The little boy turned and frowned. "But I'm not cold."

Must be nice.

"I don't care, put it on anyway," Henri instructed, using his no-nonsense voice.

Pascal looked like he wanted to argue but did what he said. Quietly, the kids ran over to the UTV, and only then did Henri's attention swivel to me again. His cheek was still doing that thing. But when he spoke, the words were for the kids. "One of you get a blanket for Nina."

There was going to be zero argument at my end. I pressed my lips together and kept my chin up, thinking about what I was going to name the future children I was going to get from Pascal. Sticking to a "D" theme might be cute. Duncan, Derek, Desiree . . .

A hand landed on my lower back, and I flinched as it brought the cold, damp clothing into direct contact with my skin. Henri's hand retreated almost immediately. I was pretty sure I heard him curse before he moved to stand in front of me. His Great Wolf face was on, and so was his tone. "You need to take off your clothes."

There was something wrong with me when the first thought that came into my head was an inappropriate joke to make in front of the kids.

"I already . . . wru-wrung them . . . out," I stuttered instead.

That bulge at his temple started throbbing at the same time as the lines on his face went tighter than they'd already been. "You're freezing, and the seat's too small for you to sit on my lap so I can warm you up," he informed me, like he wasn't insinuating he would've snuggled me half naked if he could slide the seat back on the UTV.

A part of me wanted to argue, or even joke around with him because I'd missed him the last few weeks, but I didn't have it in me. I was barely holding on from the cold, the shock, my discomfort from whatever had hit me in the water, and that freaking fear that had dumped through my body and brain. I watched as the boys climbed into the back seat and was surprised when Agnes came around, dropped to her knees, and took my shoes off, one at a time. She didn't even look at me as she climbed into the back seat with the other two when she was done. I wrestled my shorts down my legs one more time, struggling to get them off my ankles, and then pulled my shirt over my head, trembling the whole time.

A silver emergency blanket went around my shoulders before I stood up straight. A foot pawed at mine, and Duncan stood there, holding the package for another blanket in his mouth. But it was Henri who had wrapped the first blanket around me and him who reached to take the second one from my boy. He shook it open and tugged it around my hips like a tiny towel, those warm hands almost making me hiss when they came in contact with my exposed skin.

He looked at me, and I could barely say, "Why . . . is your eye . . . twitching?"

His mouth went about as flat as his voice did. "Get into the UTV."

So, somebody was still mad.

"Then, we're going to drive back, and after that, you and I are going to have a conversation about why my eye is twitching, Cricket."

I blinked, and he blinked.

All right then. I climbed into the front bench. Henri leaned over and reached for the seat belt, clicking it into place for me, his warm fingers brushing the sliver of skin exposed between the blanket on my shoulders and the one around my waist.

It hit me for the second time at that moment.

I'd been this freaking close to never seeing his face again.

And I almost told him that, but instead, I whispered, "You could've just let me borrow your shirt, you know."

His nostrils flared, his body jerking unexpectedly, and the hand that had lingered on my hip came up, and he tapped me under the chin. "Brat," he whispered back, his jaw clenched so hard while he did it.

I gave him a tight smile as another shiver made me shake.

He frowned. Henri pulled back and started issuing orders to the kids, checking them in the back seat, before circling around to pick up my bundle of clothes and finally ending up in the front of the UTV to get behind the wheel. Duncan jumped between my feet and braced himself there as Henri turned on the off-road vehicle and got it going.

No one said a word the entire ride back to the clubhouse. No one even breathed loud, and if they did, I couldn't hear them over how bad my teeth were chattering. I wanted to tell Henri he should call Phoebe and let her know the kids were fine, but my jaw felt too tight. My tongue lazy.

I'd really gotten the shit scared out of me.

I had been scared when those people had tried to hurt me to get to Duncan, but I'd known in my gut that I'd be fine. I had been able to control not just my destiny but theirs too. There was safety in that.

The river though? There was no amount of my magic that could have saved me or them from it. I'd known exactly what I was risking.

Everything.

And I would do it again if I had to, but *please no.*

No one was waiting for us when we got back to the clubhouse. My legs shook as I got out and put my wet shoes back on, while Henri helped and then carried barefoot Pascal. His expression went troubled as his eyes landed on me standing there in two tiny blankets that covered me as much as some of my swim coverups did. Agnes was holding my clothes in her arms, and

Duncan leaned against my bare lower leg in a way that felt like he was guarding me.

Henri tilted his attention up to the sky, his Adam's apple bobbing harshly in his throat once. Just once. He had a beautiful throat.

Pressing his lips together hard enough that I could see the white line form between them, he dropped his gaze back down and pinned me with it.

"I'll carry you to your room," Henri called out, sounding dead serious.

I crossed my arms over my chest, trying to stop another shiver from working its way down my spine. I shook my head. "You need to deal with them first, Fluff." But that sounded nice; I would've loved it in another universe. A hug would've been great, but . . . the rat-werewolf boy was a mess, Shiloh looked on the verge of crying again any second, and Agnes was . . . she was breathing hard beside me. I didn't know what that was about, but I'd deal with it when I wasn't out here in my underwear. "Want me to stick around?" I offered the man I wanted to believe was still my friend.

He did that frowl thing—a half frown, half scowl—even as he just about glared at the two kids who were about to be grounded for the rest of their lives. One of them was stuck to his legs like glue, and the other had already wrapped his arms around his neck like he was much younger than he was.

We both knew I was right.

But he still hesitated. I could see his jaw clenching and unclenching even at this distance. "Nina." His voice was all crushed velvet, his expression so pinched, so raw . . . I didn't know how to describe it. It couldn't have been anguished.

Could it?

The shrill ring of his cell phone erupted the way it always seemed to, at the worst moment, and Henri grimaced toward his hip before pulling it out of his pocket with his free hand. Whatever was on the screen made him close his eyes, made him sigh. His forehead was furrowed when he lifted his head again.

Murder Henri was in the process of reactivating.

And it was my job to reel him back in.

"It's okay, Fluff." I wanted to make him feel better when he seemed so torn standing there. "I can make it to my room."

My comment didn't help.

But he lifted his chin, his mouth a flat, harsh slash across his face that told me Murder Henri still lurked somewhere in his body, but he was trying his best to wrangle him in. "Go shower. I'll come for you the second I get them to their parents," Henri told me through clenched teeth.

Was there something else he wanted to say?

I didn't know, but I lifted my hand, trying to tell him it was okay. They were kids. And they'd had the shit scared out of them even more than I had.

"I'm glad you two are okay," I told the boys simply before turning and moving toward the clubhouse as fast as my stiff legs would let me.

Agnes's fingers grazed my thigh so lightly while we walked, her touch resembled a feather. I had to fight to keep a neutral expression; too much and I would scare her off . . . but I couldn't help myself. I touched the top of her head for the same amount of time she'd touched me. Just a second.

I'd only taken two steps when a hand cupped my hip and turned me all the way around.

It was Henri.

Henri who used his other hand to palm the back of my head, tilting my face up. His head dipped. His mouth and nose *right there*, inches, *inches*, from mine.

"What is it?" I croaked, surprised. "What's that look on your face for?" I raised my hand, ignoring the scrapes and tiny puncture wounds from the tree that peppered my palm, and pinched his chin. "Fluff, the kids are fine. If I was going to die from hypothermia, I would've already," I tried to assure him with a slight smile . . . that melted off at the fire that rose up in his eyes at my comment.

His hand took mine, and he drew it away, staring down at my

injured palm. A knot formed between those dark eyebrows. Henri's chest rose with a single deep breath, a moving wall in front of my eyes, before he exhaled, roughly.

I was going to die of shock, I figured out right then, when his mouth pressed against my palm. "If they were anyone else"—Henri lifted his eyes, his lips grazing the broken skin of my hand—"I'd be following you back right now."

Every part of my body seized up.

"Tell me you understand." It almost sounded like he pleaded.

Something happened in my chest. Right in the middle. Right in the center where my heart was. And I found myself nodding, giving him a smile that probably looked near death but was more overwhelmed than anything.

Because I finally understood that we had scared the shit out of him.

This man I felt so much for, who I knew I needed to feel less for, closed his eyes for a second before he opened them again. He pressed his lips to my palm for the second time in the sweetest kiss I'd ever experienced, and it wasn't even on my mouth. "Go get warm. I'll find you as soon as I can," he seemed to promise in a harsh whisper.

I nodded more out of reflex than anything.

A hand on my thigh brought me back to the girl who had touched me, her head ticking toward the clubhouse in a reminder of what I needed to do, and I gave her a weak smile of agreement as I took a step away from Henri.

From the frown he gave me, he didn't seem to like that very much but . . .

When the three of us were halfway to the clubhouse's back door, I stopped and peeked over my shoulder.

Henri was where we'd left him, watching us, with Shiloh and Pascal whispering to each other behind him.

I tried to give him a little smile, but it felt hollow.

By the time I made it to the building where we lived, Agnes was holding the door open for me.

No matter how stoic she came across, she'd gotten the shit

scared out of her too. My mini wolf. But before I could say more than "thank you" after I went through the doorway, she asked in that high voice that was young and old at the same time, "Why'd you do that, Nina?"

I slowed down until she was beside me. "Do what?" I asked her.

"Save them. They're not yours." The way those sentences came out of her mouth was so matter of fact, they might have broken my heart if it wasn't half-frozen.

I didn't touch her often, but I couldn't help but nudge her shoulder. Her eyebrows were almost touching from how hard her face was. I smiled at her, one that wasn't bitter or confused, just as we made it to the end of the hall and turned right. "They're all mine, Agnes."

Duncan glanced at us, and I winked at him.

But of all the things Agnes could have replied with, what she actually did say would've been on another page, in a different book altogether. I wasn't even sure she did it willingly when her eyes went slightly wider afterward. She asked it though, and there was no taking it back.

"Me too?" came out of her mouth.

It was so innocent, so curious . . .

I almost freaking melted. My mouth and the rest of my body were on top of it though. I nudged her again, smiling wider than I would've expected I had in me considering the day, and said, "Of course you too, Mini Wolf."

There was no way I could ever go to Alaska now. I'd have a polygamous relationship with every gnome to stay here. I wasn't going to be one more person to disappoint this child, I promised the universe at that exact moment.

And my thoughts were repaid a moment later when the little girl stopped when we got to the staircase to go upstairs and an arm wrapped itself around my thigh.

She might as well have hugged my heart.

And in a rush, she whispered what sure sounded like a deep, dark, dirty secret. "I was really scared."

I didn't want to touch her too much and send her scrambling

away, but I set my palm on the top of her head. "I'm sorry, Agnes," I told her, imagining how deep she'd had to dig to admit that out loud. And because she could, so could I. "I was too," I told her. "It's a crappy feeling."

"Yeah, it's shitty," she agreed.

I stared down at her head. I wasn't going to be the one to say anything; hadn't I been meaning to talk to her about snitches? Instead, I fussed her head while I made eye contact with the bright red eyes watching us intently from the first step on the stairs.

"*Love,*" he told me, and I blew him a kiss.

I waited until the arm around my thigh loosened and Agnes had taken a step away from me before I moved. She didn't make eye contact again, but when she started walking, so did I. We went up the stairs together and into the bedroom. I crouched after I closed the door and gave Duncan another hug while Agnes dropped my wet clothes into my laundry hamper.

"You okay, Donut?" I asked him, stroking along his spine and then one of his front legs, noticing how much longer it was now. He was growing up so fast.

Those big ruby eyes took their time staring at me before he answered, "*Yes.*"

"Are you sure?"

My puppy took two steps forward, his head proudly back, those propeller-like ears hanging low, not so close to the floor anymore either. And my emotionally mature puppy, who had been very concerned earlier, answered the same. "*Yes. Love.*"

I narrowed my eyes at him, and he put his paw on my foot, staring right at me the whole time.

"Fine." I smiled again, sneaking down to press my cheek to the top of his head. "Tell me if you're not," I said into his ear.

Duncan lifted his paw and set it back on the top of my foot. "*Yes.*"

Agnes was already on the edge of the bed when I stood up, reaching for the remote. Kids were so resilient, and someone had to protect that. That someone being me.

That had never felt as obvious before as it did in that moment.

But I could think about that later, when I wasn't feeling cold down to my bones. At my dresser, I pulled out clothes, settling on sweatpants that would have been way too warm under normal circumstances and a toasty sweater, along with clean underwear and fuzzy socks. Duncan jumped on the bed while I did that, scrambling up to his favorite spot on the end while Agnes turned on the television, her back propped by pillows and the headboard.

"I'm going to shower," I told them, even though it was obvious. That might be a magical river I'd been forced to take a dip in, but wildlife didn't get the memo not to take a pee or go number two in it, so . . .

A nod and a *"yes"* answered me, and I ducked inside the small bathroom.

I made it as far as rinsing the shampoo out of my hair before my eyes got watery, and it wasn't because I got soap in them.

I hadn't been exaggerating when I'd told Agnes I had been scared.

Some part of my brain recognized that nothing had actually happened, *but* it hit me hard how much I had to lose.

And that was so freaking much.

Not once had I ever consciously taken my life and everything in it for granted, but it had never truly hit me just how easily I could lose all the precious things I valued the most.

Duncan, my parents, my best friends, *my* life, the other kids.

I had so many questions I still wanted to ask Franklin.

And then there was Henri, whose every action made it seem like he cared about me, even if he wasn't doing anything about it.

I wanted him to do something about it, dang it.

When the water finally washed away my tears, ones that fortunately didn't come from my soul but from my brain, I let out a long, long sigh and finished my shower.

Once I was dressed, with the towel wrapped around my hair, I checked my face in the mirror. My eyes were red, a little puffy, but they had to have been that way since our Sob Fest at the river. If I looked half as bad as Shiloh and Pascal had, then there was nothing to be done about it. How bad were they going to get in trouble this time?

Agnes and Duncan were both asleep when I opened the door. My donut was on his side, and Agnes was on hers too, curled into a little ball. I had just taken a picture of them when a soft knock came at the door. Neither of the kids lifted their heads, and I crept over, pushing my senses out and not picking anything up.

There was only one person it could be.

Franklin stood in the hall, his arms loosely at his sides. Today he had on a baby blue button-down shirt tucked into khaki pants with a brown belt. He backed up as I closed the door behind me.

"The kids are napping," I explained, crossing my arms over my chest to preserve my warmth. "Did you need something?"

The man, who seemed younger every time I saw him, shifted his weight around. I wouldn't go as far as to say he'd been *avoiding* me—I didn't think someone who had to be thousands of years old would do that—but he had definitely been scarce since the day he'd dropped one truth after another on me. I really wasn't upset with him, specifically. How could I be when he'd seemed so sincere in his anger toward his brother for keeping me a secret? For trying to be kind when he'd repeated what he'd learned?

I couldn't.

But it was still a lot to take in, and he *had* kept things a secret.

Like I wouldn't have done the same, but I could be a hypocrite and ignore that.

"I know that you're upset with me," my biological uncle started almost somberly. "I'm also aware I have no right to scold you—"

"Scold me?" I cut him off.

Franklin nodded, his old and young features strained. "Yes. Scold you. But I blame myself, and your ... donors ... so I'll refrain."

"What exactly did I do?" I asked, rubbing up and down my arms, still so cold.

"My child, despite your parentage, you are not immortal," he chided me, giving me a stern look that made me think of my mom. "You aren't long-lived either. Only those of us who were around during the fall of the Great Meteor are. Magic isn't kind enough to give our children long lives for whatever reason. And contrary to whatever you may have heard, we do not have nine lives. If you were to drown, you were to drown. Your magic is death, not reanimation."

I blinked at him.

Just when I thought Agnes's and Henri's behaviors were going to be the most stunning part of my day, here went freaking Franklin. "I had a feeling, but thank you for confirming that?" I muttered, not sure how to respond to him. He sounded so . . . aggravated.

Then he continued giving me that no-nonsense expression that was one I'd gotten dozens of times from my mom. "Your donors might not deserve anything from you, and I respect and understand that, but *I* didn't make or agree with their choices." He paused. "You've just come into my life. I would like to get to know you, Nina, but I can't do that if you put your life at risk."

This ancient man had been worried about me?

"I couldn't let anything happen to the kids," I replied, carefully.

Franklin looked at me for a long while before sighing, his body almost deflating a little. "You must get that from your parents, because you don't get that from my side."

"I'm sure I do. My parents are wonderful," I agreed.

Neither one of us said anything. He watched me, and I watched him, trying to find signs in him that might show some kind of physical connection. My skin had more brown in it, and my nose was a little sharper than his. If my guess was correct, my hair was darker.

I couldn't see the resemblance strongly.

Our eye colors were kind of similar, if I had to pick something.

"I'm sorry for what happened to you," he rushed out. "I'll understand if you don't want to have a relationship with me, but it would bring me great joy." His hand went to his opposite wrist, where he usually wore his bracelets, and he rubbed at them absently over his shirt. "It would mean quite a bit to me," he added quietly. Even hopefully?

I was too easy. "I understand why you didn't say anything until you knew for sure, but I don't get why you waited to tell me, Franklin. It had been weeks since you got back."

The older man made a face that seemed regretful—not a whole lot, but some. I could give him the benefit of the doubt. "I was worried that once you knew, you might leave. When you mentioned your parents when you first arrived, how you didn't know them, there was clear detachment on your face." He rubbed his hands together. "I wasn't sure how to tell you. At my age, you would think I would know everything, but that's not the case." He huffed.

"I was angry thinking that they didn't give a crap. My biological parents," I told him. "But I don't care about either of them enough to be resentful." I bit the inside of my cheek. "*That* resentful."

He nodded.

"And I do have a lot of questions, not about them, but in general . . . Uncle Frankie." I looked him dead in the eye for a second before smiling a little.

The older man's mouth pinched.

"Or is Uncle H-y-p-n-o-s better?" I whispered.

He ticked his head to the side, this funny, relaxed expression coming over his face that I'd never seen before. "I prefer we kept the latter between us. An old man needs to have some secrets." Something powerful moved in his eyes. "It would be an honor to acknowledge you as my niece when you're ready. That's not something I'm unwilling to share."

For the third time, my eyes watered, and I nodded. "That would be nice." I hesitated. "Maybe in the future?"

The way his eyes lit up would stay with me for a long time.

"Will you tell me one day how old you really are? Or tell me about the meteor and how that happened?" I asked.

The elder took a step forward and held out his hand, palm up. An olive branch if I'd ever seen one. A step forward too, in a way.

It felt like I was accepting something. All the parts of me I hadn't known what to do with, maybe? The parts I had struggled with for half of my life.

I was telling myself, telling the world eventually, that I was this man's biological niece.

That I was descended from the night—his mother.

That his brother's death blood ran through my veins—my DNA dad.

That my uncle was an old god of sleep trying to parade through this time in his life under wraps.

I didn't know without a doubt if this "Isha" was who I thought she was or not, but that part didn't matter so much.

Not then.

If I wanted Duncan to accept who he was when the time came, how could I not be an example for him?

We *could* defy the paths that choices others made set up for us.

I could take this man's hand, or I could shun it all.

There was really only one choice.

I took Franklin's hand, noting how it felt like every other hand I'd touched, except maybe a little more callused.

My . . . uncle's gaze was steady on me as he said, "There isn't much I would enjoy more."

Chapter Twenty-Four

I yawned as a star shot across the sky.

There had been a lot of them tonight, more than usual, and other than on cloudy days, there were always plenty to admire. Small, thin ones that disappeared almost as quickly as they had appeared, and others were bigger, brighter, leaving a trail behind them that I could admire for seconds. I couldn't remember the last time I'd seen so many back-to-back.

I wished Duncan was out here with me, appreciating them as much as I was, but he and Agnes were at Ema's house. The elder had showed up after dinner with a container full of cookies that she'd handed over with tears in her eyes. She had thanked me for taking care of the children, and I'd learned that she was Pascal's grandmother.

The elder had invited the kids to her house for a sleepover, which Agnes had immediately agreed to, and my not-a-traitor-but-a-confident-boy had aimed those bright eyes at me, saying, *"Yes."*

And that was how I found myself alone, sitting on the steps of my RV under a shower of stars, contemplating a whole lot of stuff.

My past, my present, and my future.

The sound of a car warned me someone was coming before the headlights did. It was late, and everyone who had left for work for the day had been back for hours. There wasn't a whole lot of entertainment in Lobo Springs after dark, from what I'd heard. There was a bar and a small bowling alley with an arcade, but that was about it.

I didn't move as the car parked and the headlights turned off a few rows back from where my RV was parked. A door opened and closed before whoever it was walked a bit, then stopped. The walking started again, and I caught a shadow circling around a big red truck next to mine, and ... it was a man, and he was coming my way.

It was one of the guys I'd seen in the kitchen weeks ago. Green Eyes, as I'd called him in my notes for obvious reasons.

"You good?" the startlingly good-looking man asked on his way over.

I gave him a little smile and lifted my hand. The worst of the shivers had finally faded a couple hours ago, but I still kept my arms tucked in close to my sides for body warmth. "I'm fine," I told him, taking him in. He was probably close to Matti's height and musculature. His skin was about the same shade, but this man's eyes were emerald green.

He felt like a werewolf.

When he got a few feet away from where I sat, he stopped and gave me a faint smile. I held out my hand. "I'm Nina," I greeted him.

The man's smile brightened, his body language surprised. "Keegan." He took my hand. "I'm not supposed to be talking to you, but I smelled you the second I got out of my car." He glanced over his shoulder briefly. "Had to come see if you were all right."

Did I smell the same to him as I did to Henri?

Stop.

It had been hours since we'd split up after he'd driven us back to the clubhouse. Hours since he'd looked me in the eye, touching me so tenderly, and claimed he'd come find me as soon as he could. Since he'd said if the kids had been anyone else ...

He had other things to worry about.

"I won't tell if you don't tell," I told him, pushing up to my feet so I wouldn't have to stare up the whole time.

Keegan, with some of the prettiest green eyes I'd ever seen, smiled even wider. "Too late for that. When I get home, my nana is going to smell you on me. You're kinda famous around here."

Famous?

My smile dropped.

No one had said a word about what I'd told Dominic, and I'd held out hope that maybe he hadn't believed me and hadn't told anyone . . . That Pascal's dad hadn't either, and Agnes . . .

So many people knew, now that I thought about it. I couldn't comprehend how I hadn't heard a word about it. None of the parents had started acting differently either. Literally, nothing had changed since.

But now . . .

"I didn't mean it in a bad way," Green Eyes backtracked. "I'm sorry. The kids, all they do is talk up how you smell like a cake—and they don't even like cake usually, but you smell good to them—and nobody else around here has a scent like yours."

I felt dumb. "No, I'm sorry. I jumped the gun," I apologized, wincing. I needed to quit being so sensitive and expecting the worst. I was what I was . . . and now I knew what that was, didn't I? "I've gotten a lot of crap for it, and I'm sore about it."

"There's nothing to apologize for," he claimed before something caught his attention, and he seemed to scan the area around us. He suddenly looked tense, staring hard into a spot in the distance, in the direction of the clubhouse.

"Something out there?" I asked, going on alert. Today was not the day . . .

"No." His gaze was definitely locked on something. "Henri."

"Oh," was all that came out of my mouth.

Those pretty emerald eyes met mine, and his smile that time was smaller than the one before. More restrained? He swallowed hard. "Henri's the best of us all," the man said carefully. He even shrugged a little. "Just so you know. Everybody understands."

I was about to ask what he meant by that, but he was already walking away.

"See you around, Nina," he called out before turning directly right and disappearing in between cars.

That had been weird . . . hadn't it?

On the bright side, he'd been nice, and just as handsome as I remembered. Before he'd gotten distracted, he'd seemed interested in talking to me.

And I felt nothing. A pretty face was usually just a pretty face. What a bummer.

I slumped just as I heard heavy footsteps and picked up on the feel of a big ball of familiar magical energy.

All coming toward me.

Henri wasn't *trying* to be discreet.

I thought about waving at him, but my arm stayed where it was.

He didn't owe me anything. I had been fine. The kids had needed him more than I did. Fact, fact, fact.

But accepting that those statements were all true didn't do much. The best I could do was give him a little smile and hope he assumed I was tired. Which I *was*, but . . .

He didn't smile back anyway. He must have been too busy grumbling, "What was that?"

I raised my eyebrows. "What? Me talking to Keegan?" There went my big mouth. Hadn't I literally just told the guy I wouldn't tell anyone? "He was checking on me because I was sitting out here."

Unlike someone else I knew.

And *that* was an unfair thought. I wasn't *mad*. I wasn't trying to punish him for anything.

Henri's nostrils flared, and his mouth went flat. "He shouldn't be talking to you," he replied, his tone deeper than usual.

"I didn't mind," I explained, watching his features. "He didn't do anything wrong."

Someone didn't like that answer, and the closer he got, the more I could read the lines of stress and tension in his whole frame, not just his face.

"If I didn't want to talk to him, I wouldn't have. He was nice. It's fine," I added. Did I sound as defensive as I felt?

Henri didn't like that either, and I figured right then that

I wasn't the only one who'd had a long day. It made me feel slightly bad. I didn't want to argue with Henri. I didn't want to be frustrated with him either.

Not today.

I had missed him, and the only thing I'd wanted all day, other than love from my donut, had been a hug from Snarly, Emotional Henri. And just like I'd thought a moment ago, maybe I wasn't the only one not having the best day of their life. If I wanted to think about it from an optimistic perspective, other than the cuts on my hand and some scrapes, I had probably gotten more injured in the past chasing Duncan around.

"There's no reason to be a grumpy wolf, Henri," I tried reasoning. "Nothing bad happened. We were just being friendly."

I struck out again.

"Is that what you think?" he asked too slowly as he came to a stop directly in front of me, all the fine lines of his body even more imposing in the darkness. He was a physical mountain, and I was a tree in its presence.

One of those tan hands scrubbed down his face, taking its time around his mouth. Then he slowly lowered his chin. His eyes shone in the darkness.

He looked at me.

He just freaking looked at me.

Then he lifted his arm, palm up, between us. "Let me smell your hand."

I pulled it in close to my chest. "No." I thought about it. "Why?"

"I want to know where he touched you," he answered with zero hesitation, his eyelids low.

But why? I clutched my hand closer to my body and shook my head. "Look, Fluff, I appreciate you keeping an eye on me and wanting to protect my honor, but that ship sailed a long time ago."

Why? Why did I say that?

I kept on going and ignored the face he made at my poor choice of words. "I already told you. Nothing happened that you need to worry about. We were only talking, give me a break."

Those orange-brown eyes slid over my features. "I like to worry."

"I don't know why."

Why that comment shocked him, I didn't understand, but from how tight his face went, he made it seem like I'd kicked him in the shin.

But that wasn't what I wanted either. I really wasn't trying to be petty.

"You all right?" I asked, keeping an eye on him. "The kids okay?"

"Kids are fine."

I wanted to ask more about them, but I'd wait a second. That had only been a partial answer. "Are *you* okay?"

"You're asking if I'm okay?"

I nodded. His face had haunted me for the first hour or two after we'd gotten back. He had seemed so upset. Self-contained, responsible, had-zero-doubts-he-could-stand-his-own-against-a-sasquatch Henri. Sure, he'd been worried about the kids, and I would have been hurt if he hadn't been worried about me too, but . . .

"I'm not used to seeing you so concerned," I told him. "And you seem like you're in a bad mood."

"I am in a bad mood." The thick column of his throat bobbed. "I'm not used to feeling . . ." He did some up and down gesture with his hand.

Something in my chest stirred. "I don't know what that means."

There was a pause. His palm swept down his mouth. "Torn."

"Over what?"

"Doing what I should instead of what I want," he answered.

I squinted at him.

He raised his chin. "Tell me you didn't jump into the river, Nina."

Those bigmouth kids. I'd only been partially paying attention when they'd retold the story about what had happened, but maybe that had come up afterward with their parents. "I didn't jump into the river."

He looked down his nose at me. "How exactly did you end up wet then?"

I wished, not for the first time, that I could lie and get away with it. "A log hit me in the back and swept my feet out from under me," I muttered the explanation.

Henri's eyes went so wide, I was surprised they didn't fall out of their sockets.

Where had Neutral Face Henri gone? I wondered as I bit the inside of my cheek and figured I might as well keep going. "I climbed in, to be specific. I was on a rock, and I sat down into it, and then kind of . . . shuffled over?"

"Then the log in the river hit you?"

Did his voice have to be that flat? "Exactly."

His right eye was the part of his body that decided to react. "You didn't see how deep the water was or . . . ?" he asked, crossing his arms over that impressive chest. His biceps were so lined, I wanted to drag my fingertip across the overlapping muscles.

Instead, I tucked my hands under my armpits, grateful I'd changed into fleece pants and a warm sweater. But I dropped my voice into almost a whisper. "No, I couldn't. I didn't want to cross half the dang river to get to him, but what was I supposed to do? Wait for someone with longer legs to reach him and risk their life too?" How was that fair? What made my life more valuable than someone else's? Randall had a family on the ranch who loved him. Ani was a mother. And so was I.

"Yes," he tried to argue.

The face I gave him was the equivalent of rolling my eyes. "No, Pascal was scared, and I was scared, and Shiloh was crying. It would've been so much worse if he'd fallen in." I pinched the material of my sweatshirt between my fingers. "Don't be mad. I had to make a decision, and I did, and we're all still here."

A low growl formed in his chest that might have been intimidating if I didn't know by now how great his self-control was. "But you got hurt."

"I could've gotten hurt *worse*," I tried to compromise.

His eye started twitching even harder. "You think I didn't see your back? Your hands and arms?" Henri took a step forward. "It's a goddamn miracle that log didn't hit you in the head and kill you."

Oh, I knew that better than he did, but . . . I shrugged. "I had to try."

His nostrils flared, and for one brief moment, his nose wrinkled. Those light-colored eyes bore right into mine in a way that made me think some part of him wanted me to look away, that he was trying to do some dominating crap. He might be mad at me for risking myself, but I wasn't scared of him.

"I did what I had to. You said it. They're all our kids. And I did try calling you and Phoebe, for the record."

That muscle in his cheek went even tighter, and his eyes went *really* narrow, eyebrows dropping low to frame them. "I was taking care of some matters. I tried calling you back five minutes later, but it went to voicemail," he told me. Those tense shoulders he'd come over with finally lowered a little bit. "I'm sorry."

"You didn't do anything," I told him, gently. "Thanks for worrying. For coming to find us." I gave him a little smile, tugging at a tease to help the situation. "I'll make sure to tell Matti you've done a good job keeping an eye on me."

That didn't have the effect I'd intended it to. Another growl rose from his chest through his throat.

He stepped even closer, his chest bumping mine. "I'm not taking care of you for Matti, Nina."

I felt my eyebrows rise.

"You scared the hell out of me," he sounded so accusing.

I hadn't expected him to actually admit that out loud. "I scared the hell out of myself," I agreed.

"I could smell how worried you were from half a mile away. How terrified the kids were." Henri's throat bobbed. "It would've taken me longer to get there, but Spencer was waiting, and he told me where to find you." His volume dipped. "I've never run so fast in my life."

The way my body reacted to him talking to me like this . . .

"He told me to hurry up and look for them," I admitted. "He could've helped them, but something is something, I guess."

There was a light huff that was only partially from him being amused. I'd been right earlier about him being scared for us. Poor Fluff.

"Are the kids in big trouble?"

"I don't want to talk about them right now. They're not in as big of trouble as they should be for risking their lives and yours. If it was up to me, they'd be grounded until they're eighteen," he said, staring down at me. "It took me too long to get in contact with Phoebe. She didn't have service where she was looking for the boys, and none of Pascal's family was around, so I had to wait for them to get home. It . . ." He shook his head, his forehead furrowing. "It all took too damn long to handle."

So that's what happened. I nodded. "A-g-n-e-s said they were looking for a waterfall. Is there one around here?"

He nodded.

"No one's ever mentioned it. I thought she was making it up."

"No one's told you about it because we wait until the trial period is over to," he explained, watching me carefully.

"Oh," I sighed. "Okay?"

Henri lowered his voice. "It's a secret waterfall. Even the children only see it on special occasions."

"Why's it secret?"

"You have to see it to understand." Those eyes of his were intense, but his next words weren't. "Want to visit it?"

He didn't have to tell me twice. "I want to see what I risked my life for."

That brought the scowl back.

"Too soon?" I winced, feeling another little spark of humor rise up in me.

"What do you think?"

I lifted both my shoulders, watching him.

He dropped his head just a little more. "Next time you have to do something dangerous, you'll tell me first?"

It was my turn to swallow, the urge to say that I'd be calling whoever I mated with in the future instead of him was there and present in my thoughts and in my vocabulary. I guess I felt like being mean. Felt like reminding him of what he was being so wishy-washy with. How he could kiss me and be nice to me, and then just . . .

Remind me that he'd never promised anything. On purpose.

These hurt feelings were my fault and only mine, and dang it, that *still* stung.

"You're not agreeing with me," he brought up, being the observant man I knew and cared for.

The urge to look anywhere but at him was so strong, I couldn't ignore it. "I don't want to make any promises I might have to break," I warned him, tugging on my bracelet like I didn't have every inch of it memorized.

He let out a long breath. "There's no reason for you to break any promises to me."

I took a step back and lifted my head, my calves bumping into the step I'd been sitting on earlier. "No, and I don't want to start." This had turned back into a depressing conversation, and another reminder of just how things were. Which meant, there was no point in putting myself through it.

I'd made my decision. So had he.

"Well, I guess I'm going to go back inside."

He stepped in front of me so fast that I jerked my head to stare up at him. Henri's head was bent, his solemn face harder than normal. "You scared the hell out of me today—"

"I know—"

"Listen." He took my hand and tugged on my fingers with his. His tone imploring, his face freaking concrete. "Today was one of the worst days of my damn life."

I stopped moving.

"All I wanted since we got back, since I saw you carrying a kid on your shoulders, shaking and pale, was to check on you, and I couldn't." He gritted his teeth. "I've never been resentful about the things I've inherited with the ranch, but today . . . I was today, Nina."

As much as that meant to me, and that was a whole lot, so, so much . . . this was the last thing I'd wanted from him. I didn't want him to feel bad. "It's okay," I said in a small voice.

"It's not. I should've been with you." Those long fingers linked through mine. "The reason we have elders and employees is to spread the work out. *I should've been with you.* There's no excuse to justify how the day went down—"

"Fluff, it's all right. You were busy—"

Fire burned in his irises. "It's almost ten at night, and I'm barely checking in on you!"

This was exactly what I'd wanted, but it made me feel guilty. I squeezed his hand. "They needed you more," I tried to reason.

The way he exhaled, so forcefully, with so much emotion, made me blink. "They did, but *I* needed to make sure you were okay."

My whole body jerked. "Henri . . ."

He shook his head. "I never *want* anything. I never ask anyone for anything. My entire life has been in preparation for taking care of everything and everyone, and for the first time . . . for the first time, I've got someone around that feels more mine than anybody else I've ever met. For the first time, I've found something *I* want." I felt my lip drop a little. He stepped even closer, his chest pressing into mine. "And you know what I get instead? I finally make it back, and I find you talking to fucking *Keegan.*"

"What are you doing?" I asked, staring up at him as my breasts pressed against the wide expanse of his chest.

Those incredible eyes moved from one of mine to the other, and in the time it took me to wonder again what he was up to, one of his hands came up to trap my chin. In one swift movement, he dipped his head and brushed his lips against mine. The pressure was featherlight.

Henri Blackrock pulled back a centimeter after a second, then he did it again.

He kissed me.

Softly, with so much feeling in the way he pressed his lips to mine, that I shuddered, not sure what in the world to do until the last second, when he and that dark pink mouth were retreating, I went up to my toes and kissed him back before rocking back on my heels. Holding my breath. Staring up at him as he hovered there so close to my mouth, looking just as surprised as I felt by not just what he'd done, but what I'd done too. We'd surprised the crap out of each other.

Maybe even ourselves.

I searched his face for a sign, an explanation, something, anything. "What was that?"

His lips parted, and I didn't miss the way he licked his bottom one, his eyebrows drawing back down on his forehead like he was frowning but not.

"Henri?" I tried again, keeping my voice low.

That muscle in his cheek worked from side to side.

"Fluff. What was that?" I poked him in the stomach, getting frustrated with myself. Why had I done that? Why had *he* done that? We weren't supposed to be doing this anymore, dang it. I poked him again. "You can't do that. We talked about this. I'm trying to be a good friend. I'm trying not—" I cut myself off, but it was too late.

I didn't want to love him. There was nothing platonic about my feelings, and I had to get over that. It's what I'd been trying to do, hello.

But I could see something reflected in his irises.

I raised my eyebrows at him. Held in my breath too. "*What?*" I asked slowly, not sure I wanted to know what was going through his head.

Murder Henri was gone. Teasing and Grumpy Henri wasn't on the same block either. Great Wolf Henri was the one staring down at me.

And that version of him wasn't impulsive. He was just . . . *Henri*. A mountain. An ocean. An immovable force of nature that did what he had to do, even if he didn't want to do it.

And it was while I went over that idea that he reached for me, a hand curling over my hip, and he said softly but very clearly seven words that had me flinching. "I don't want to be your friend."

He might as well have slapped me.

But he wasn't done. "I want you to marry me," Henri said.

Chapter Twenty-Five

My ears were failing me. They had to be.

The lunatic with his palm molded to my hip just looked at me. He rubbed his thumb along the bone there, his face straight. His head dipped so close I could count his eyelashes if I tried. "You're supposed to say, 'Yes, Henri.'"

What was this voice he was using? Where was it coming from? Did he have recessive mermaid genes in him I didn't know about?

I . . . "*What?*" I snarled . . . or squeaked, it could have been either considering I didn't know how I felt. Not when we'd been arguing two minutes ago, and I'd thought we'd been on the verge of drawing a final line in the sand once and for all.

Now? I wasn't even sure there was sand.

"'Yes, Henri' was the response I was looking for," Henri said, his expression so serious. More serious than I might have ever seen him before. "I'd take you giving me a hug too."

I tilted my head even further back, taking in all his features, thinking about what in the universe had just come out of his mouth . . . and then I dropped my forehead forward so hard and fast, it practically bounced off the layers of skin and bone of his sternum. It hurt.

But I was in too much shock to feel pain. And for some reason, my forehead didn't want to go anywhere. It stayed right where it was, on his chest. "You want me to . . . *marry you*? Is that what you just said?" I asked the spot on his body between his pectoral muscles.

"Almost word for word," he confirmed.

"What the . . .?" I blew out a breath before sucking another one back in. My mind spinning. "Why are you suddenly offering?" I reared back. "Why are you telling me this *now*?"

His eyebrow went up his signature millimeter. "Which question do you want me to answer first?" Apparently Teasing Henri was making an appearance from his tone and the glint in his orangey-brown eyes.

"I don't know!"

He laughed so softly I felt it more than I heard it. Thumbs rubbed circles on my hip bones, the skin callused, and I had no business enjoying his touch so much. "Well, you made it really clear several times. You need someone to marry you, and I'm sure as hell not letting you marry somebody else," Henri had the nerve to murmur.

This was not, *not* how I could have, or would have, ever pictured this day, much less this moment happening. Even my ears didn't know what to do with themselves because they started ringing. I might have even lost my balance there for a second. Maybe they were more than a little in shock at what they'd just stood witness to. My forehead went back to that spot between his pecs. "You . . . want to marry . . . *me*?" I asked his chest, not trusting myself to have this conversation with his face. "Why? Why now?"

We'd already had the conversation that I *didn't* need to rush into anything. That I should wait until my three months were up to start figuring things out. That was what *he'd* suggested. *Strongly* suggested, damn it. And we were close to the three months, but we weren't there yet.

Warm, solid pressure landed on the back of my head, and I shivered, but that time it was at the smell of him, the feel and strength he emanated. Part of me expected him to give me a reason or two why he was offering to tie himself to me for the rest of his life. Because he thought I was brave or loyal or . . . something nice.

But instead, Henri's finger tipped my chin up, and he looked me dead in the eye, to say, "Why wouldn't I want to?"

My pride was the only reason my knees didn't buckle.

The same hand that had touched the skin beneath my chin seconds ago went to my shoulder, and he palmed that body part too. "Is that a 'yes'?"

"You brushed me off every time I've brought this up before," I reminded him, thinking of the roller coaster—a children's roller coaster to be fair—he'd put me on. "And *now* you're asking me to mate with you? I don't even . . . I don't even know who your parents are! Or where they are! Or anything about your family. Really, every single one of you is so guarded talking about it. You said you grieved someone once, and I don't know who that was. I don't even know who raised you, or how Matti's dad and everyone else could have just . . . left you here to deal with all this by yourself."

That was something that had been on my mind from time to time the longer I was here. How they could have all just left him with his huge burden without looking back. I knew Matti inside and out, and in my heart, I knew without a doubt that he wouldn't have abandoned Henri just like that. But that didn't feel like a conversation my best friend and I could have over the phone.

None of my questions or points fazed Henri even a little bit. "I grieved my brother and his wife when they died. They were both much older than me. They were who raised me. Matti's dad was their son, and he was my older brother in every way that mattered, but we always knew he was going to leave. This land didn't call to him the way it did to my brother and me. He invited me to go with him when I was old enough," he explained gently. "We called Matti my cousin because he and I are closer in age than his dad and I were, and that term was easier to explain."

Before I could say I was sorry, or ask about them, or bring up the fact that he wasn't actually Matti's cousin, he moved on.

"The whole purpose of the elders was supposed to be for them to help those in my family run the ranch. Every generation of my father's descendants had less and less children. Until I was born, my brother had been an only child, and Matti's dad was an only child. Things were fine when my brother handled everything with the help of the elders. They were who took care of things when I left for New Mexico and went away to school. Everyone knew I wasn't leaving forever.

"It was my decision to take on so much when I got back. Matti is his dad's son, and there was no way I could've ever guilt-tripped him into staying here," he admitted. "I have a hard time delegating work or asking for help. It's my fault things got out of hand, but I never had a reason to want more time for myself until now," Henri went on to explain.

I blinked.

And if everything that had come out of his mouth hadn't been enough, he dropped yet another secret on me.

"My mother was once known as Fenrir."

Fenrir? *The* Fenrir? *The Norse monster wolf?* Maybe it was no wonder he didn't talk about his family. We could come back to all this some other time.

"My father is the original Amarok—the Great Wolf, like the gnomes eventually came to call him. That's how I'm related to everyone here. All the Amarok are descendants of his descendants, but I'm his direct flesh and blood," he explained without even blinking. "He doesn't live here and neither does my mother. They used to check in once every few years—time means something different to them."

My lips parted in awe. "Are they together?"

"No. I think their relationship is an arrangement I don't want to begin to understand. I'm not the first child they've had together, but it's been centuries since. My brother raised me, and his brother raised him. None of us shared a mom."

Just when I thought that my DNA parents were out of their minds . . .

"I was told that our father has sons and daughters so that they can care for the land. In the past, every thirty to fifty years, a baby will show up, and his last child will raise it. It's been the cycle since he found this place. But I haven't seen or heard from him in almost a decade. No one knows where he is. I might be the last of his kids, or in a few years, he might show up with a baby he wants us to raise."

Us.

Henri leaned forward then. "Does that bother you?"

I frowned. "Why would that bother me?"

The face he made was just short of smug. "That's what I thought, but I needed to make sure. We have to stop assuming things about each other."

"That's dumb. You know I wouldn't care." I dropped my shoulders, vulnerability piercing my sternum. I wanted to pick apart him already signing me up to raise a child with him in the future, but really, there were so many other important things I wanted to discuss. I would do anything with him, and I was pretty sure we were both aware of that. A child would be a given. "But what about what Franklin said? My DNA dad can kill people. It was one thing when we guessed who he was, but it's a totally different thing to know exactly who he is. To know . . . that they didn't want me."

"I don't give a fuck who your biological anyone is," he argued gently. "And I'm never going to."

His words made me release a sharp breath.

"*You* are a good person," Henri went on. "And I want you enough for both of them. For all of them."

Cupid might as well have shot me in the heart. "But you didn't act that way, not until now," I reminded him, trying so hard not to say that shakily.

"Nina." He made a sound in his throat, and one of his thumbs did another circle over my skin that I had to try really hard to ignore. "We're supposed to wait for the three-month period."

Was that what all this shit was about? The three months?

"I don't hold myself above any of our guidelines. I needed to wait. You deserved the time to settle in," he tried to explain. "I thought we were on the same page—"

My scoff wasn't exactly quiet. "We haven't been in the same book, Fluff, if you think this is supposed to not surprise me."

Henri stroked my hip a little more, all his features pursed with intent. "You liked me, I liked you, and I could tell . . ."

"Tell what?" I asked slowly.

"That there was more there. More than attraction. More than surface feelings." His eyes moved over my face. "I *thought* you knew that."

My voice was a little flat. "How was I supposed to?"

"You think I kiss every member of the ranch?" he asked. "You think I tell all my friends to fuck off and go sniff around somebody else for just anyone?"

He'd told his friends to fuck off? What friends?

"You have to understand how many people have come here over the years and left before their three months were up. I didn't expect you to stay either, not at the beginning. I was trying to do the right thing, dammit." His eyebrows dropped on his forehead. "Why the hell do you think I told you to wait to start dating?"

I sputtered. "I mean . . . it was wishful thinking . . ." Had he been *jealous*? Had he been trying to sabotage my dating efforts for his own benefit?

I leaned back and looked up at him, totally caught off guard by this conniving MFer.

One side of his mouth curled a little, his thumb continuing to do that circle thing as he held me against him. "From the moment you made fun of Spencer, I knew I was in trouble."

I squinted so warily. "Go on."

His mouth curled a little more. "Then you made us go visit him so you could say you were sorry, and that was it." He exhaled. "Liking you would've been enough, but . . . you had to be you."

The sound that came out of my nose was as unexpected as the smile that took over his lips, and I think I might have gone a little lightheaded again for a second. "Are you telling me this right now because I almost died?"

The way the growl crept up his throat gave me the good kind of goose bumps. "*Don't remind me.*"

I raised my eyebrows, and he growled again.

"Yes, I was trying to wait for the three months to be up. We're two weeks away. What are they gonna do? Kick me out?" He had the nerve to snicker.

Just when I thought I had him figured out, he'd admit something like this. I poked him again. "But you still pretended I didn't say anything every time I brought it up."

He almost looked regretful. "Cut me some slack. I don't get proposed to on a regular basis."

My body wasn't prepared for Funny Henri. The skin on my arms prickled. "Who did you tell to fuck off anyway? Those men who came into the kitchen?" I asked him.

His palm slid up and curled around my waist, beneath my shirt. "Yes." His tone didn't say he felt bad about it either.

"Really?"

"They should've walked out the second I came in. Randall tried to tell them. I was a minute away from doing something no one was going to like."

Maybe some people thought you shouldn't be attracted to possessive people, but I wasn't one of them. It fueled my soul. Fed my spirit. If I could've glowed, I would have.

I just shook my head at him, smiling a little bit because I couldn't help myself. Plus, I'd known he was up to something rubbing his face all over me!

Henri closed the distance between us even more, his mouth hovering above mine. "I'd lay down my life for every single member of the ranch, but I was on the verge of forgetting about that. I had a talk with most of them afterward and made things real clear. You're the only person I was trying to keep anything from, Cricket, and the truth is, I can't go through you going on a single date," he told me somberly. "Attraction is important, but respect, loyalty . . . strength . . . those are the traits that matter the most to my people. If we're lucky, we might meet a few people in our lives that our senses are drawn to without ever talking to them. But it's everything after that that matters most."

That sounded an awful lot like how every werewolf before

him had explained how mating someone worked. Basically, biology had a small say in it: the same way you might prefer apples over oranges, you smelled someone you liked more than someone else. Then every once in a while you might meet a strawberry, your absolute favorite fruit. The one who lit up your taste buds and your sense of smell like nothing else.

Then you had to get to know a person, and that was what you fell for. It was like . . . a filtering process, kind of. A process of elimination helped by biology.

And the person my biology seemed to favor over everything and everyone before palmed my lower back with his warm hands. "You know damn well that I like you just fine. More than fine." His eyes searched mine. "Nina . . . you smell like my mate. Feel like it too . . ."

"And?" I asked, my voice wobbling, high and stringy.

Henri's brows furrowed before he dipped down to kiss me again, but this time, it was more than a hard press of a warm mouth. His lips captured mine, parted them too, and his tongue swept into my mouth with an ease and finesse of familiarity. His tongue sliding and meeting mine like they were old friends, and my body wasn't trying to pretend otherwise. When he pulled away, he only made it a second before he swept back in and did it again. And then again, followed by another one, a million more I would have taken before his breath wafted over my lips. He gulped when he pulled back and pierced me with those incredible eyes. "The more I learn about you, the more I like you, and there's not many people I can say that about."

My lips parted as I watched every line on his face.

He kept going too. "Nobody has ever made me as happy as you do, and the idea that somebody else would be spending their free time with you, hearing you laugh . . . I can't fucking do it. It's unbearable to me."

Someone had a way with words, and I was suddenly grateful that, while he wasn't quiet, he didn't drop things like this on me all the time, because I didn't think I'd be able to survive this Henri in large portions.

"Hmm," was all my brain could conjure up as a reply.

It made his eyebrows go up. "That's all you have to say?"

"This wasn't the conversation I was expecting to have with you today, Fluff," I breathed. "It's not every day your childhood crush kisses you, then says they'll marry you, makes out with you, and finally admits you make them happy. I'm processing."

I didn't think he liked that response much.

And there had to be something wrong with me, but I felt like I owed it to myself to do what I was about to do.

Even if it went against every instinct in my body.

"I should probably think about it," I told him. "I've spent the last couple of weeks thinking I needed to move on."

He reeled back. "You're going to think about whether or not you'll mate with me?" Henri asked slowly, surprise in his tone and his eyes.

"Yeah." I nodded.

"What's there to think about?"

The urge to mess with him ran so strongly in me that I couldn't even try and have a serious conversation with him, not after he'd had me considering a future where he was just in my peripheral. So, I blinked at him and said, "I'd already been trying to decide whether I could picture my future children having green eyes or blue ones."

The growl that rumbled in his chest was going to stay with me for the rest of my life. Maybe I'd make it my ringtone.

It took all my self-control to keep my features even as I kept messing with him. "My coloring with those eye colors . . . I want my kids to be cute." I raised my eyebrows and shoulders at the same time. "I have options, Fluff."

Henri's growl cut off as his eyes searched mine. He *almost* looked amused. "You can't even finish that sentence with a straight face, you little brat."

I couldn't. I really couldn't. I was already cracking up. I wiped my eyes and sighed. "Look, two months ago, I would have signed up for this"—I pointed back and forth between the two of us—"in a heartbeat. I was ready to marry anyone to stay here and make this work."

His nostrils flared at that comment, but I lifted my hand.

"You're the only man I've ever propositioned," I tried to soothe his ego.

It wasn't enough. "And I'm the only one you're ever going to," he tried to snarl.

I smiled and shrugged. "Probably, but I've seen the best relationships with your kind, Henri, and there was never any hesitation in any of them—"

He grunted, ready to argue, but so was I.

"It seems to me like you just made this decision right now because you're jealous."

"I've been jealous since before we walked into the kitchen and found people I thought were my friends wanting the only thing I've wanted for myself in a long time," he agreed, surprising me again, especially with the emotion in his tone. "I've been jealous since Randall tried to get near your neck."

That was a statement to store away for later, but I had to focus. "But maybe you need to think about it too some more when you aren't worked up."

"Cricket," he grumbled so deeply I felt it in my chest.

"Fluffy, listen. We have too much history for you to jump into anything. Your cousin is one of the most important people in my life—"

"And now I'm going to be," he cut me off, wrapping those brawny arms around me, collecting me. I stared up at him. "We both know what there is here between us, and we aren't going to insult each other by pretending like we don't. There's a choice to be made, yeah, but is there? The first thing I thought when I saw your face was that you were so damn pretty. You smell like my favorite thing in the entire world. The sound of your voice makes me smile.

"A wolf knows when it knows, and I haven't been able to stop looking at you . . . looking for you . . . since you got here. Matti's always going to be one of the most important people in your life, the same way he is for me, but what you and I are going to have is going to top that."

I was going to have to consider at a later time that I might have a heart problem from the way it started beating so fast and hard since I'd gotten here.

And Henri didn't have any mercy on it. "A mate is the foundation for the present and the future. I've made my decision, and you made yours before I even did. *This is going to happen.* You're not the kind of person who's going to give me shit for trying to do what I thought for a minute might be what's best for you." He lowered his face as he whispered, "There aren't going to be any green-eyed or blue-eyed babies for you in the future unless they need to use contacts."

I opened my mouth to try and disagree, but he shook his head. "You liked Dieter and Keegan just fine, but not anywhere near as much as you like me," he said slowly and carefully. "When you're scared, you come to me because you know I'll protect you. When you're worried, you come to me because you know I'm going to be there for you. You trust *me*. You love *me*. I know it, and so do you."

I squinted up at him, my heart still continuing its racket.

And Henri decided to finish me off. "And neither of them are as funny as I am."

Why was he talking to me in that low, raspy voice, all bossy and perfect, *and what was happening to me?* Was I sweating? Did I start panting?

Some small pesky part of me wanted to argue with him for the sake of arguing with him, because who was he to tell me how much I'd liked Green Eyes and whoever Dieter was, compared to him?

But I knew the freaking truth.

He was right.

Physically, Henri was a wet dream. Personality-wise, he was a wet dream. He was He-Man, Prince Charming, and a god amongst men all rolled into a bossy, serious package that made my world. And I'd never met anyone I found half as attractive as I did him.

I wasn't sure what a mate was supposed to feel like, but he checked off the boxes I figured needed the most attention.

He ticked off all of them, all right.

That had been my problem since I'd gotten here.

I'd been attracted to him from the start, and it had gotten worse.

I eyed him, my poor little heart still going at it—in fear, in excitement, a little bit of confusion. Some part of me said, "*This is very soon*," and, "*This is too good to be true, and he'll change his mind*."

But it *didn't* feel like it. It *didn't* feel too fast. And wasn't this exactly what I'd wanted?

I poked his stomach. "I think . . ."

"What?"

I poked him again. "You could have said something, you know. Every time you got home late on purpose to avoid me, it hurt my feelings."

He scowled, busted.

"This has been a kiddie ride at the fair that I didn't know I was a part of. *I told you*, to your face, multiple times, how interested I was in you."

His jaw clenched. "Ask me how many new members I've spent more than five minutes with after they got here."

Playful Henri was back, and I narrowed my eyes at him. We could play if he wanted to. "How many new community members have you spent time with other than meeting them, Fluff?"

"Zero. The elders deal with accepting and dealing with all of them. All I'm here to do is explain what'll happen if they do something to endanger our community," he said before his features softened. "I'm sorry I hurt your feelings. I scented them every night and went to bed feeling like an asshole, but I was trying to stick to the rules, dammit." Henri lowered his head. "I don't want you to go anywhere. I want you to stay. And if your nose was better, you'd know how I felt when you were talking about your little backup plan that was never going to happen."

I groaned again. "That's why I use my words, because I'm used to not being able to tell what people want unless they actually say it out loud, dang it. All you had to do was say, 'Nina, yes, let's wait three months.' Boom. Done."

"Nina, yes, let's wait for your three months to be up," the man holding me repeated.

I growled in my throat, in frustration, and he chuckled.

Henri's palms clutched my hips. "I know you're not going to complain about how long it took me to come see you today to my face, but I needed to work some things out first, after I got the kids squared away." He paused. "Are you going to ask me what things?"

Teasing Henri was going to be the end of me. I blinked. "What things?"

"I had to talk to the elders about how we're going to be doing things differently from now on. My mate isn't going to come second to me, and neither is my family. I'm not going to spend the rest of my life doing things that can be delegated."

That wasn't the answer I'd been expecting. Something lit up in my chest, and I whispered, "What did they say?"

"Most of them weren't happy." That didn't seem to bother him. "But Franklin was supportive." He smirked. "Very supportive."

"Then what happened?"

"Three hours and a few threats later, we came to an agreement. I'm turning my phone off at eight, and we're getting a cell exclusively for ranch use. We're all taking turns with it, someone has it for a day, and they pass it on to the next person the following morning," he explained.

"That's a good plan."

He lowered his chin. "We'll implement more changes as we go along, if we need to." If he needed to, he meant, and I blinked.

Tipping my head back, I gripped his shirt in my hands and took in his features—his wide brow bones, his broad cheekbones, all those striking features that made him so handsome.

And here he was telling me I was his.

I clenched his shirt tighter in my fingers. "I want to tell you yes, you know that, don't you? But I really need to talk to Duncan first, and I think . . . I think you should sleep on it—what?"

"Talk to Duncan" was the only thing he agreed with. He squeezed my hip, his words low and hoarse. "Can I kiss you now?"

I nodded faster than I'd ever nodded before, knowing dang well our conversation wasn't over, but . . .

I had a one-track mind sometimes, especially when that track was shaped like an epic statue in a museum and had the only other face I'd ever thought I'd want to look at every day for the rest of my life.

Henri must have known I didn't have any plans on letting some things go and decided he was going to distract the hell out of me in that case, because he didn't waste a second taking my mouth. Warm, soft lips closed over my own. I shivered again, opening my mouth just a little at the same time he did, his tongue meeting mine halfway like they were long lost lovers reuniting after decades instead of minutes.

He tasted just as good as he smelled and felt, that was for freaking sure.

Henri Blackrock kissed me harder, his tongue going a little deeper, and mine didn't want to be left behind. I reached up, my hands going for those wide shoulders, and I leaned into his frame. The kiss deepened, his tongue stroking against mine without an ounce of hesitation, his hands finding my ribs and waist over my shirt.

He pulled back, exhaling deeply, his gaze burning mine.

"A little more?" I asked him, already breathing harder than normal.

Those light eyes blazed. "You don't need to ask," he murmured. "Kiss me any time you want."

When he put it like that . . .

I did what I had to, and that was literally press every inch of my front against his, plastering myself to him. I even wrapped my lower leg around his, and Henri didn't let me down. Those capable hands slid down my sides, grabbing my butt and lifting me. I swung my legs around his hips, locking my ankles behind his back.

Henri wasn't messing around either.

We started moving.

One step after another led us up to my trailer, and I heard him messing with the latch, opening it before carrying me inside, his mouth never leaving mine, his tongue spearing against my own, kissing me like he was marking the inside of it, claiming it for himself.

The hands on my butt flexed as he groaned and lifted me up higher on him, my groin dragging over his.

My eyes went wide as I clutched him for dear life. Henri was packing as much as I would have imagined, if I ever had. The girth in his pants was unmistakable.

We groaned together, and I couldn't help but hike up my hips, rubbing them up and down against the part of him that was *right there*. He said something that sounded like a curse word under his breath as his hands and arms helped me, grinding my center over his through our pants. I pulled back, trying to catch my breath, but he only gave me a second before demanding another deep kiss, with tongue and lips and clingy hands.

"This all right?" he breathed when we broke apart, his hands shifting to my thighs, where he lifted me up, rubbing me flush against his erection some more, up and down twice, like he couldn't control himself.

I humped him eagerly, because I couldn't either.

"Please," I answered, wrapping my arms around his neck and helping him as much as I could as he kept doing it.

A whimpering moan tore from my throat as he grinded against my clit perfectly. His chest was a wall against my breasts, his muscles teasing my nipples through my shirt and bra. I kissed him even harder, grabbing a fistful of the back of his shirt as I moaned into his mouth more.

I worked my hips, pressing tighter against the length of his hard-on. His strength was beyond impressive. I wanted to hang on to him for the rest of my life. I needed to pull his shirt off and get my fill of that body I'd had to force myself not to ogle daily. Touch everything . . .

He groaned right against my ear. "You smell good when you're sad, but when you're wet? Fuck, Nina." Henri sucked my earlobe between his teeth, and I almost orgasmed right then and there. "Makes me want to rub my face between your legs."

That did it.

It was the easiest orgasm of my life. Pure ecstasy shot through my center, my thighs flexing and trembling around his waist while I rocked against him through my orgasm. I panted. I shivered. And Henri held me tighter to him throughout it, his forearm holding me up across my butt, his other arm at an angle at my back, our chests smashed together.

"Feel good?" he asked, grazing his lips down my neck.

I nodded almost dreamily, my muscles still flexing and spasming. "So good." I lifted up in his arms a little, his erection long and hard between us. "So good," I repeated, smiling, palming the back of his head. "You're still . . . Want to set me down? Let me help you out?"

His lips brushed the length of my neck, and I felt him take a big, shaky breath. Felt *him* tremble. The huffy laugh he let out was shaky. "I don't think I've ever wanted anything more in my life . . ." He kissed me under my ear, then found another spot his lips liked right beneath that one, and I arched my neck to give him more space. I'd pay him to keep his mouth on me.

"But?"

His arms tightened as his lips skimmed my neck some more. "But I hear two cars coming. We would have to be really, really quiet."

I groaned, and he let out a husky, pained laugh.

"I know," he grumbled. "Trust me, I know, but as much as I'd love to see your little lips spread—"

"Which ones?" I teased, feeling him tense around me.

His growl skipped my ears and went straight for my clit. "What the fuck, Nina?"

I couldn't hold it in. I burst out laughing.

The sound of my phone ringing, for once, had us both freezing and looking around. I didn't even remember carrying it in, or holding it, or anything, but the screen illuminated off the counter right beside the camper door. Instead of setting me down, Henri carried me over and handed it to me. Ema's name appeared on the screen. I'd given her my number before she'd left with Duncan and Agnes.

"The kids are with her," I explained before answering and hitting the speaker icon. "Hello, Ema. Everything okay?"

There was a moment of loaded silence that had Henri and me both looking at each other before a young voice said, "Nina, Duncan wants to go home."

It was Agnes. Henri and I both frowned.

"Hi, Agnes," I greeted her, still making eye contact with him. "Duncan wants me to come get him?" I asked, trying to figure that one out.

"Uh-huh," she replied matter-of-factly. "Right now. I think he's scared."

I pressed my lips together and squinted at him, and he nodded. I highly doubted Duncan had suddenly learned how to say that much in the matter of a few hours, which only meant one thing: it wasn't him that wanted to leave. *And she called me.* Not her nighttime nannies, not Franklin, not Henri. *Me.*

Probably just because of Duncan, but I was going to take it as a win.

She'd touched my leg, given me a hug, and *called me* all in the same day. I wasn't planning on risking my life any more, but I could see the appeal if it helped me win over my favorite salty peanut.

"That's okay if he is," I assured her, keeping my tone as neutral as Henri had shown me was possible, by example. "Tell him I'll be there in—" I almost said five. "—twenty minutes?"

Henri lowered me to my feet and rubbed a hand up and down my back. It made me want to curl against him. *Cuddle him.*

I almost whistled imagining it.

I'd just dry humped him. People said life could change in a minute, and I now knew from experience that there was more than a kernel of truth to that. Funny how that happened.

"If you want to leave too, you know you can come with us," I told her as nonchalantly as I could.

"Okay." There was another moment of silence before she whispered, "Duncan doesn't want to tell Miss Ema he wants to go home. He said he doesn't want to hurt her feelings."

Across from me, Henri grinned, because we both knew what she was trying to do. "I understand. If you want to give her the phone, I'll tell her that I changed my mind, all right?"

"Okay," she agreed immediately. "Here's Miss Ema."

It only took a minute to vaguely tell Ema I was coming to pick the kids up, but from the sound of it, she was trying to hide her amusement too. I didn't think Agnes was as slick as she thought she was. The elder didn't sound surprised at all that I was going to get them. Werewolf hearing, after all.

I'd barely hung up before I looked up at the hunk of a man towering over me, still holding me with his hands on my hips, his chest barely grazing mine. "Want to come with me to get them?"

Those amber eyes swept over my face, and his fingers kneaded me in a way that felt more erotic than it did soothing. "Sure." Leaning over, he took my top lip between his with a quick suck before pulling back an inch. "Do we get a popsicle and to play tag afterward?"

I stared up at him. Love and tenderness filling my entire chest cavity. *He* wanted to mate with *me*. This nearly perfect man wanted to marry *me*.

I wasn't sure whether to hug him or cry. Or both. I chose option 1.

And 3.

With my arms wrapped around his thick frame, I said, "They'd love that, and I would too." I smiled. "But let me change my underwear first, Fluff, and then we need to do something about that log in your pants."

That snatched the breath right out of him. "What are we doing?" he exhaled.

Hmm. My underwear could wait a few minutes, I guessed. Pulling back, I set my palm on the flat slab of his abs and peered up at his face. "We're going to do something about your situation. We've got a good fifteen minutes."

His eyes went wider than I'd ever seen before, his throat bobbing wildly . . .

But he wasn't saying no.

"We don't—"

Dragging my hand down his stomach, I let it rest over the top button of his pants. "If you don't want to . . ."

He grabbed my wrist. "That wasn't what I was going to say," he let me know, his breathing raspy.

"We'll just have to be really, really quiet." I slid my hand a little further down, palming the erection pressing tightly against his zipper, and I shuddered for about the hundredth time that day. Because *wow*. Wow, wow, wow. Watching his eyes, my fingertips found the tab of his zipper, and I tugged it down as far as it could go, Henri's fingers still wrapped around my wrist. But he didn't stop me or move as he swallowed harshly one more time as I slipped my hand through the front opening of the striped boxers barely containing him. I found him immediately. Warm and thick, long and eager as I pulled him out, squeezing him tight as I did.

I was going to need to erect an altar to worship his penis the way it deserved.

"Fucking hell," Henri gasped, his hand sliding a little up my forearm but not letting go.

He groaned deep in his chest as I stroked up and down against an erection that was going to need two hands when we had more time, and I didn't have scrapes. If I had a toothbrush in here, my plans could have been different, but . . . we would have time for that later.

Maybe.

"Look at you," I breathed, working my hand over his hard,

hot length. "What am I going to do with all this?" I asked him, tipping my head to make eye contact with him.

Henri's eyes burned as they moved back and forth between meeting my eyes and glancing down at the hand I was holding him with. "Whatever you want, whenever you want," he groaned.

I smiled so hard my face hurt as I jerked him up and down, his erection getting harder in my hand by the second. "You don't understand how much I wish we had more time right now, Henri," I whispered, still working my fist along him. "What I wouldn't give right now for you to pull my panties to the side a little and sink inside of me."

"Fuck, Nina," he moaned under his breath, his breathing going irregular, his chest rising and falling quickly.

"You like that? Because you're not the only one who wants to rub their face between some thighs. I'm going to want to bite yours, you should know that right now."

His hips arched at the same time as his hand cupped the back of my head, tilting it up, and he slanted his mouth over mine, as the hand he had on my forearm slipped down to cover mine, and he worked both of our fingers up and down over his erection. Faster, squeezing harder . . .

"Come all over my fingers," I told him before going up to the tips of my toes and catching his lips.

I felt him throb under my grip before he grunted and groaned into my mouth, hips thrusting, warm come spilling over my digits and knuckles. There was so much of it, it made me groan right alongside him, sucking on his tongue while I did. It was the dirtiest kiss of my entire life, and I *loved it*.

Henri pulled back just a little, his breathing heavy, but his eyes were bright and attentive, and I wasn't ready for him to slant his mouth over mine again, sucking my tongue that time, eating at my mouth like it was his favorite place in the entire universe and his job from then on was to kiss me like that forever.

I gave him one last, soft, wet stroke before I tipped my head back and watched in slow motion as he gave my forehead a soft kiss. And only then did I ask, "So, are you saying I can do whatever I want to you?"

He looked me dead in the eye and confirmed every fantasy I could've ever imagined. "Whatever, whenever."

Chapter Twenty-Six

There were a lot of things in this world I was good at, even more I was decent at, and more than I'd care to admit that I was absolute crap at.

Controlling my emotions fell somewhere in the middle.

During our walk to pick up the kids, Henri and I hadn't said a whole lot to each other. He'd taken my hand, then smiled down at me when I'd caught his gaze in surprise and pleasure. It was the same hand I'd worked him up and down with. But because you never knew who was listening, instead of talking about what we'd done to each other, I asked him about what exactly had happened with Shiloh and Pascal, and he'd gritted his teeth and given me an in-detail report of how their parents had reacted.

Phoebe had cried her eyes out, then claimed she was going to put a tracking device on Shiloh. His dad, the nicest ogre I'd ever met, and I'd known a lot of wonderful ones, had also gotten teary. My quiet little buddy, who I would never have imagined could be such a rule breaker, was going to be grounded for the next five years minimum.

To sum up what I'd learned about Pascal: I wasn't going to see him for a decade or two, if he was lucky.

When I brought up putting in a good word for them with their parents, Henri shook his head and asked me to wait a few months. Everyone was disappointed and furious with the kids. I understood. It was one thing to do mischievous stuff, but it was another to do something that risked your life. If they didn't cut that crap out now, how much further would they take it as they got older?

Right around that twenty-minute mark from when Agnes had called, we'd picked up the kids, with the three of us adults playing along perfectly that it was our decision. Then we'd walked back to the clubhouse, got some popsicles, and played tag. Since Agnes's sleeping buddies thought they had the night off, I invited her to stay with us in my room and had been very surprised when she'd agreed.

The way she'd whispered, "Good night, Nina," before I'd turned off the lamp had probably etched itself into my brain for the rest of eternity. I'd fallen asleep with a smile on my face, both from her and from the man that she adored who called her Ladybug.

Which led us to this moment.

I had planned on putting this conversation off with Duncan until I thought about it some more, but I made it all the way until half an hour after we'd woken up, when Agnes—in her puppy form—trotted off to her room and left us alone on the bed, yawning.

The truth was, I hadn't been able to stop thinking about my conversation with Henri, and how we *might* have agreed to *maybe* mate with each other.

It was only the rest of my life.

And Duncan's.

And the lives of my future potential children.

Henri was only, possibly, the man I would wake up to and fall asleep next to for the next fifty-plus years, telling me things that made my whole body feel like it'd been lit on fire.

Henri Blackrock, the Great Wolf according to the gnomes, had proposed to me in his way.

I had wanted to call Matti and Sienna and tell them everything, but I wouldn't. There were things I needed to figure out on my own first—and not when there was someone I needed to talk to more than both of them combined, no matter how much I loved them. Because whatever I decided would have a direct effect on him.

And that was what was on my mind when Agnes left the room and my beloved donut gave me those intelligent red eyes, like he was well aware I wanted to talk to him about something.

I could've put it off a little longer, but I wasn't good at keeping things from him.

We knew each other too well. I could tell by his ears how he felt about something, and I didn't even have to sigh for him to know when something was bothering me. It was one of the greatest gifts of my life being known so well.

I focused on my puppy and smiled over his beautiful coat and perfect head. He looked more and more like a black bloodhound every day, minus the eyes and tail. "We need to talk, Donut."

He blinked. *"Yes."*

"I know you know you're the most important person in my life, and no matter what happens, you'll always come first."

"Yes. Love."

See? He deserved all my devotion. "I talked to Henri last night, and he said he would marry me. We talked about that, remember? How I have to marry someone to stay here?" I asked him.

"Yes."

Just what I'd expected. "What do you think? You like him, don't you? I saw you sitting on his foot last night." He'd done more than that too. Duncan had wiped his face against the side of Fluff's leg after finishing his popsicle. Even Henri had noticed before he'd met my eyes with a smile on his face, pleased by it.

"Yes."

That's what I'd thought. I stroked the side of his head. It was so much bigger than it'd been a month ago.

"If you like it here, I have to do this. I have to marry someone. I think you know how I feel about him. But if you really don't like him and you don't want him around, you can say it." I meant it, but at the same time . . .

I knew what I wanted.

His tail swayed in the air, *"love"* pulsed at my heart, and I smiled at him.

"We would be a family. He'd be your dad someday, if you wanted. I know he would be there for you and protect you. Same as me." I reached over and touched one soft ear after another. "You can think about it. Maybe you need to spend more time with him. I don't need an answer this second, but I'd like to be with him. I'd like for us to be a family."

Duncan's cheek turned, and he licked my wrist. *"Yes."*

I raised my eyebrows, and he repeated himself.

"Yes."

"Yes, you're fine with it?" I drew the question out.

"Yes. Love."

"I love you too, Dunky-Dunk, but you don't need to say anything now. You can spend time with him by yourself, or us together—"

He pawed my leg and looked at me with those big, round eyes. *"No. Yes."*

"Or not." I laughed a little and petted him again. "You sure you don't want to think about it?"

"Yes."

I was talking to a two-year-old puppy about the future. I couldn't let myself forget that part. On the other hand, though, there was no reason for me to think that Duncan couldn't grow to trust and love Henri with time. There really was zero doubt in me that Henri would rise to the occasion and earn it.

Could it be this easy?

I tried to look into my boy's soul, but I knew every part of it already. He had the most brilliant flame of life in him. Strong and steady, a lighthouse at the edge of a dark and misty sea. His soul and lifeline were just as beautiful as I ever could have imagined.

And that made me smile at him even as I squinted and tugged at his ear. "Are you suuure?" I asked my donut.

"Yes," he told me, rising to his growing feet. *"Yes. Love, love, love."*

I watched him stretch, then pad over to my lap and plop down on it, so big now he didn't fit as well as he had two months ago. He stretched up some more and licked my cheek as he did. And my boy tucked his head beneath my chin, and he said it again.

"Yes. Love. Yes."

* * *

Henri wouldn't stop staring at me.

He wasn't being discreet about it either. Not even *trying* to be from the way Franklin's eyeballs pinged back and forth between us throughout dinner, his expression going from thoughtful to confused to intrigued. I was almost certain he didn't have the olfactory senses that told him things, but I figured when you'd lived as long as he might have, you learned a whole lot from body language.

I would've been shocked if I hadn't been putting off crazy faces the whole meal, but you try sitting through dinner with Henri Blackrock staring at you after saying he'd marry you.

In front of your ancient dream god of an uncle and your magical pup.

I wasn't much better when I stared at him every chance I thought I might get away with it in return, which was zero times, actually. Either Henri or Franklin caught me peeking every single time I tried. I couldn't help it. His proposition felt real, his sincerity more than believable, knowing what I knew about him. I was still so overwhelmed that it was like my brain needed to catalogue every inch of his face and body for research purposes.

And I was trying so hard not to think about what we'd done the night before in my camper.

I had zero doubts that if the kids wouldn't have been waiting for us, I would've wrapped myself around him like a naked spider monkey.

"I can't stand it anymore. What's going on?" Franklin blurted out just as I picked up his plate to take it to the sink.

Henri, who was busy picking up the kids' mats, answered casually over his shoulder, "Nina and I are getting married."

The way air whooshed out of my lungs . . .

Franklin's reaction wasn't much better. "*Excuse me?*" He even took off his glasses, wiped them down with his sleeve, and settled them back on his face.

"Is that going to be a problem?" Henri asked, not sounding like he actually cared.

Amber irises caught mine as he headed for the sink, and I froze at the smirk playing on his lips.

I pointed at him. "Are you being funny?"

"I wasn't expecting to feel like a weight has been lifted off my shoulders, Cricket," he said. "It does."

I wasn't sure who squawked louder, me or Franklin.

"Breathe, Franklin," Henri ordered as he came up to me, the side of his arm more than brushing against mine as he focused down on me. "We're a good match."

Out of the corner of my eye, I saw the older man kind of gaped.

"It isn't set in stone," I started to explain, even as Duncan piped in.

"*Yes,*" he argued, shocking me.

"This isn't . . . exactly a surprise." Franklin went thoughtful in voice and expression. He looked younger today somehow, I thought, but I might have been imagining it. "I'd hoped you wouldn't be a fool, Henri." My biological uncle made a small humming noise. "This is a good match," he agreed.

"Thank you . . .?" I muttered, catching Henri's attention and his amused expression. I was going to guess he hadn't expected otherwise.

Franklin made another thoughtful sound before nodding with purpose. "In that case, I'll watch the children while you two discuss whatever else you need to to make this official. Take some time, or the whole night, it makes no difference to me," he said with a wave of his hand.

Did Franklin look determined or was it just me?

My ears went that much hotter. "It doesn't need to be tonight . . ." I trailed off.

"It should be," Henri argued at the same time as Franklin added, "The sooner you know, the better. I'll deal with the elders who might have a problem with it."

I thought he meant because of the whole three-month period, but I'd let them deal with that, I guess.

If we got there.

Which meant we needed to talk first.

All right then. I blinked and turned to Duncan, who was sitting there looking innocent and not like he'd ganged up on me for a moment there with Henri. "Duncan, do you mind spending some time with Franklin?"

I wasn't sure whether I felt betrayed or pleased at how quickly he answered, *"No."*

"Are you sure?" I asked.

"Yes."

A warm brush of an arm had me turning to Henri, whose expression was back to a quietly serious one that was all furrowed forehead and a defined jaw. His voice came out soft. "Let's wrap up the dishes and go after that."

"Go where?" I asked, not bothering to lower my voice since they could all hear anyway.

"For a drive."

We were going to go for a drive? I thought it over as I helped him load the dishwasher and clean the counters. Once we were done, I crouched next to my donut, running my hand down his back.

He licked my wrist.

"I'll be back in a little while," I assured him.

"Yes. Love."

He was getting so good at using multiple words now.

I smiled and turned to Agnes, who was a foot away in her wolf puppy form. "We'll be back, Mini Wolf."

A hand appeared out of the corner of my eye, and I recognized the thickness of those fingers. The length of them too. I took it, his hand, all warm, rough skin, and let him help me to my feet. He didn't let go as he led me out of the kitchen, saying, "I have my phone on me. We'll be back later, pups. Thank you, Franklin."

The older man called out, "You're welcome," but when I glanced over my shoulder, he had the most thoughtful expression.

Henri's fingers laced through mine.

I let it happen, but I did lift our hands between us.

Henri peered at them too. "What do you think?"

I took in his shade of tan against mine. Then I met his eyes. "Fits pretty good, I think."

He squeezed my fingers, not saying anything else as we walked out of the clubhouse.

The magic was richer than normal, I thought, as we headed to the golf cart building, and Henri wasted no time pulling out a two-seater with a little bed in the back. He steered us down the main path and away from the clubhouse. After a few minutes, we went in a different direction than I ever had before, the magic in the air getting that much stronger the further we got from the residential area.

Were we going into a more magical part of the forest? The nerves along my spine prickled.

He glanced at me. "Cold?"

I shook my head. "Not too bad. It's the magic here." I'd gotten used to it, for the most part, but now? It was hard not to shiver. Why hadn't we ever gone this direction before? I could hear the river in the distance.

Henri nodded and kept driving, and sometime later, he let go of the accelerator and we rolled to a stop.

I perked up. "What's that sound?" The trees were dense, but it was easy to see a land mass rising up ahead. And I could feel a faint hum of what felt like magic in the distance.

Henri slipped out of the golf cart and came around. "There's a waterfall I want to show you."

"Is this *the* waterfall?"

His face got scowly, but he nodded.

Too soon, I guessed. "I like waterfalls."

"Come on, it isn't too far," he said, gesturing me to follow with a tick of his head.

I did. Henri hiked toward the hill, and I tagged along right behind him, so close I could grab his belt if I had to. The terrain was steep, but the path was clear and wider than a game trail. We hiked up and up a little more, the sound of water falling getting louder as we followed the switchback. Just as I started to get sweaty, the tree line broke.

There it was.

A tall, narrow waterfall, around 100 feet tall.

"It's glowing," I gasped, stunned.

Beside me, Henri smiled.

"Is it bioluminescent?" A faint pinkish purple glow covered the boulders alongside the cascade. I'd seen pictures of shores and lakes covered in the light-producing bacteria before, but those had always been blue.

"It's not. It's the magic here."

That got me to turn toward him and away from the incredible glowing sight. "Really?" I was in awe, suddenly feeling like this might be the closest I ever got to a religious experience. It explained everything. How it smelled so good, and now that I had a chance to notice, it felt like I'd been plugged into a power outlet after taking a hit of some kind of drug. The urge to fall to my knees pressed at some part of my brain, and for once, it was easy to look away from Henri and focus on this.

There were purples! Pinks! Lilacs!

"It's been like this as far back as our records of this land go. The stream never weakens, never runs out. It's fed by that river you met yesterday," Henri said in a steady voice that almost sounded reverent. "This is sacred land for us."

I understood. Shimmering water pooled below it before exiting into a narrow creek. I blew out a low whistle of wonder. Of amazement.

This was what the boys had been looking for.

No wonder.

How could something like this exist? It could have come from a movie set for a different planet. Somewhere beautiful with jellyfish birds that hung from the glowing foliage and purple dragons that crept across massive branches of trees belonging in a jungle . . .

"My ancestors claimed that a large chunk of the meteor landed in this area. See the trees? Do you see how the trunks are twisted? They're the oldest on the property. I'm not sure there's anywhere else on Earth with trees that look like these. We've tested the water, and it's totally uncontaminated. Probably some of the only water in this country that you can drink out of without worrying about bacteria." He paused. "Not that we tell anyone about it."

My lips formed an O. "You can drink it?"

"Sure."

I wanted to try some of that water, dang it. I took a step forward just as he laughed, his hand reaching for the back of my shirt. "Only on a supermoon or a special occasion, tiger. We'll all come out here and do it. It's a ritual."

"Oh. That makes sense." I laughed. Sacred. Right.

Henri tugged me backward until I bumped into him. "I'll make sure you get some when the time is right."

I lifted my face. "Promise?"

"Yeah, I promise," he said with a smile that touched my heart because I'd never seen him use it before on anyone, not even Agnes, which made me think about everything else that had been on my mind.

There was a lot.

I sighed and let my shoulders fall. "Henri . . ."

He ignored me. "Come here, there's a boulder we can sit on," he said, pulling me to the left, a few feet away, where there was indeed a flat-ish rock. He took a seat in the center of it, and I didn't struggle when he tugged me down and onto his thigh.

I reeled back and grinned. "Hi."

"Hi," he replied, his arm slinging low around my back as a support.

I folded my hands and raised my eyebrows. "So, what are we doing?"

"Practice," he explained, setting that warm hand possessively on my thigh. "How does it feel?" As much as I liked Serious Henri, I liked Flirty Henri just as much.

I patted his knee. "I don't really know what to do with myself, but it's pretty comfortable." Leaning into him, I whispered, "Am I really sitting on your lap right now?"

"Yeah." The corners of his mouth twitched, and I took a second to absorb the stubble that covered his jaw and upper lip.

He had such expressive eyes when he didn't have his neutral face on. "You don't need to do anything but sit there and try this out."

I looked down at his legs under me and patted the inside of his thigh. "It has good padding. I could see this being a nice spot to hang out on a regular basis. It has good back support." Planting my palm on the muscle right above his knee, I tested it out. It was rock-hard. "How much do you squat?"

"Not as much as I can."

There was a long, deep howl far, far away, but it sounded like a coyote—unless there was some coyote god that lived on the ranch that I didn't know about, which was definitely possible.

Which reminded me . . .

"Henri . . ." I started, dread making my stomach feel funny.

"Nina . . ." he teased.

I was grateful for my good night vision when I could see his eyes and the color of them so clearly. His face was open, his body language easygoing. *I'm sitting on his lap.*

Dang it, I needed to focus. "I need to tell you something before we talk about anything else."

"What are you worried about?" The hand on my hip gave it a little rub.

I turned a little more toward him and put my palms on him, one on his shoulder, the other on his impressive thigh. I *was* slightly concerned.

More than slightly.

"Hey," Henri murmured, grazing the skin under my chin with his free hand. "Don't. There's nothing for you to be worried about. I know you. I like everything about you, even the smelly stuff."

My face went red. "Huh?" What smelly stuff?

"You've thrown up on my bed more than once—"

I squawked. "What the . . . ? I don't remember that!" I laughed.

"You were five or six," Henri explained, smiling a little.

"The first day I met the kids, they talked about Matti peeing his bed, not anything about vomit," I told him.

His smile grew. "He did pee, and you did throw up, but I don't feel bad making fun of Matti. I never told anyone about what you did," he tried to reassure me.

I squinted. "Why do you even remember that?"

"You know how hard it is to get the smell of stomach acid and Doritos to go away?" he asked in a voice that sounded serious, but his expression gave him away. He had that glimmer in his eyes.

"I'm sorry?"

A hand palmed my lower back as he looked at me. "All I'm saying is that we're past you being nervous around me. You weren't even that way when Duncan was hanging off my tail like a Christmas ornament."

I blinked at him.

He patted my back. "Now tell me what you think we need to talk about that's stressing you out."

He was smart. He had to know. This wouldn't be so much of a shock for him, would it? Searching his rough, handsome face, all I found was sincerity reflected back at me. Affection in the lines at the corners of his mouth. Maybe even more than that.

But a small part of me was aware that this could change everything.

The universal truth was, you couldn't build anything worthwhile—not a friendship, much less a relationship—on secrets and lies.

And I would never do that to Henri.

"First off," I swallowed, "if we had kids, there's a chance they might turn out like me. They might have my magic."

His eyes narrowed, and the way he agreed made it seem like that was a moot comment. "I know."

"You're fine with that?"

"Why wouldn't I be?"

"Because—"

"Cricket." He almost sighed. "If I could pick one person to have your gift—it is a gift, Nina, your face says you don't believe that, but it's true—I would pick you."

I pressed my lips together, and his expression went so tender, I wanted to throw my arms around him.

"You're the kindest and one of the most loving people I've ever met. I knew it minutes after I saw you. That's why you smell like a honey bun. That's how love and kindness come across. Who better to have the power you have than someone who understands the value of life the way you do? It'd be so easy to do with that whatever you wanted, and I can't imagine what your fucking parent has to be like if you got it from them, but you're no angel of death. You're an angel of . . ." Henri's forehead wrinkled.

"Of?" The word came out a little broken. So much hope hung on whatever his answer would be.

Those beautiful eyes roamed my face as he drew a circle over my back with his thumb. After a moment, he nodded. "Love."

There was no stopping me then.

I wrapped my arms around his neck, and I *felt* relief punch through my lungs during the longest exhale of my life.

I'd hoped my whole life that someone would see what was truly inside of me, someone who could see beyond my skin suit and my parents' inheritance. And I had been so lucky so far to find a few people that did. But for a long time, I'd resigned myself to having to live the rest of my life through a filter, without someone I could share everything with, and then one day, the universe gave me the most perfect boy, and that boy gave me a choice that led me here.

To someone who could see *me*, maybe not for who I always was, but who I wanted to be.

And I squeezed that MFer as tight as I could, telling him *thank you* with my whole body.

Thank you for seeing me. Thank you for accepting me. Thank you for being who he was.

Warm arms wrapped around the middle of my back, and the next thing I felt was Henri drawing me into his body like we were two pieces that fit together.

But . . .

"You aren't just letting me borrow money or a car, Fluffy. This would be our whole lives. You'd be stuck with me forever. I know what you promised Matti, but that still doesn't mean you need to do this if you don't want to," I rambled out in dang near one breath, my mouth mostly buried against the crook in his neck.

He hugged me tighter. "I'm not doing you a favor, and you're not doing me one either. And you're damn right this would be our whole lives." His words were muffled into my hair, but I understood. "You think I do things that I don't want to?"

"I think you would be willing to do things that you feel obligated to if they're for the best of your people."

Arms loosening, he leaned back. His expression was clear. His face open.

"See? I'm sure you don't do things that you don't really want to, but there's some gray area there too." I hadn't let go of his neck and still wouldn't. "You're one of the most responsible people I've ever met. Responsible people are the least selfish people there are. That's what you meant earlier, isn't it? About not doing what you wanted to?"

He stayed right where he was too, still watching me that way he did when I thought he might be seeing me through a different scope.

Maybe we hadn't known each other all that long as adults, but I felt like I understood him. The essence of him. And I thought that maybe he'd been Atlas once upon a time, with the weight of the world on those powerful shoulders.

It made me love him a little more.

"And I appreciate that you aren't trying to lie to yourself or me and say, '*No, I don't*,' because we both know it's the truth." I nudged him and smiled. "You're a good man. It's one of my favorite things about you.

"But *this* isn't you having to be decent to people who get on your nerves because you have manners. This is your life. Your future. And I don't want to take that away from you, even if I really like sitting on your lap and kissing you and just spending time with you in general." I braced myself. "And even if I am a little in love with you," I told him honestly.

Those perfect nostrils flared, and Henri leaned in enough to press his forehead to mine. "You miss the part where I said you're mine? Where I told you that you're my priority over every other person here? Or anywhere else? Have you missed me losing my shit every time I've thought that I might lose you?" Those amber eyes bounced around my face for a moment, then two, and then he said in a harsh voice, "Everything you said just now is why I want to do this with you. Why I feel the way I do about you. Because you're responsible enough to acknowledge that, to worry about it. Anybody else wouldn't give a shit about what was best for someone else as long as it worked in their favor, but *you do*." He let go of me with one arm and used that hand to wrap around the nape of my neck. "You're a good person, and I could look at your face all day, and every single part of your body might be straight from a fantasy."

My eyes went wide, but he ignored me.

"No part of being with you would be a hardship or a sacrifice." He slipped his arm around my lower back one more time, his forearm tight to it. "And what you are, or what our children might be, doesn't factor into my decision at all, because that's what this is. My choice. So what if you scare the fuck out of people? You're a protector. Randall and Ani got nothing on you, Cricket." He smiled. "Neither do I. And if we had a child and they had your magic? We would teach them to do the right thing, like your parents taught you."

He nodded slowly, watching me process his words.

"Who would ever expect that the person they need to worry about the most on this ranch looks like a forest princess?"

I opened my mouth, closed it, then laughed, hard. "I can't even tell you how touched I am you think I look like a forest princess, and that you would say it with a straight face. Did someone tell you Pascal called me that?"

He nodded. "He couldn't remember your name at first and kept calling you that."

I laughed again and brushed the side of his neck with my thumb. Maybe I wouldn't take all of Pascal's future kids, maybe just the first one. "Look, I want to make sure, that's all. You're so handsome, you could have already been mated a million times to a million other people."

"Thank you." He sounded so sincere.

"But so could I," I told him, half joking.

That wiped the smile right off his face.

"To very handsome men too, Fluff." I was messing with him now.

His eyes went a little squinty, and I was eating it up with a spoon.

"Listen to me, though. This is serious. Your cousin—or nephew, or whatever Matti is—is my best friend."

The arm on my lower back slid just a little lower. "I know. And you know how our biology works. I wouldn't sign up for this unless you checked every single one of my boxes."

I shivered. He was right. I knew he was right, but . . .

His gaze moved from my face, down my chest, and lower before making a slow, quiet trek back up. "All of them."

Did I want to believe him? More than anything. *Anything*.

I still opened my mouth to insist, but he started talking again.

"I like your smile," he said, balling up his fist between us and raising his pinky finger, which was almost the size of my thumb.

I blinked. "Proceed."

His smile grew a fraction as he lifted his ring finger next. "You have a good heart."

I nodded because I thought I did, have a good heart that was, and that made him smile even more.

His middle finger came up next. "You're funny."

"I am funny," I agreed.

That got him to laugh and bump his forehead to mine briefly before his index finger went up. "You're brave."

"Sometimes I'm a chicken," I butted in. "Just to set realistic expectations. The only reason I handled those bogeymen that well was because I've seen their kind before." I paused. "And I guess their physical appearance didn't really scare me either."

He nodded like he already knew that. "I can deal with our

taxes in the future. I could start practicing how to remove ticks now, if you'd like," Henri said with a straight face.

I leaned back so far, it was only my arms clinging to him and the one he had around my back that kept me from falling right off. "Stop it." Teasing Henri might end up being the death of me.

He winked before raising his thumb. "I like your face. More than any other face I've ever seen." With his forearm, he lifted me back up to sitting, his face so intent. "I just like you, Nina. *I love you*. Everything about you. The way you are with all the kids. How you'd do anything for Duncan. How patient you are with Agnes. Margaret told me all about how nice you were with her, when I know how difficult she can be."

If everything before hadn't been enough to win over whatever leftover reluctance was in my body, what he said next lassoed my heart, my soul, and everything else in. "You're everything I've ever wanted in a mate, and I didn't even know what that was until you bit my leg."

My body didn't know what to do with itself. I wasn't even sure I was able to gape at him. But somehow, some way, after a moment, with my voice weak, I managed to say, "You love me?"

His nod was so slow. "I love you."

Air rushed out of my lungs. "Well, you already know how I feel about you because you pointed it out. And everything you said? I've thought the same things so many times." I clutched his shoulders tighter, the muscles firm beneath my fingers. "But . . . the other thing I need to tell you is that Duncan still hasn't met the people from Alaska who might be like him. If they invite him, and he decides to leave and asks me to go with him . . . I don't think I can say no. And it isn't because I'm not crazy about you, because I am, but because—"

Mount Henri Blackrock crushed me to him. "*I know*. He's your boy. You wouldn't be the person I know you are if you would." Henri tucked my head under his chin, clutching me so tight I wish I could've stayed there forever. "I've already thought about it."

I hoped that was a good thing.

He didn't wait to tell me what conclusion he'd reached, fortunately. "This land is always going to be mine. I'd never give it to anyone else; all this shit with Dom has settled that. But that doesn't mean I couldn't leave. Doesn't mean we couldn't come back some day if it came down to it."

He'd said *we*.

"What the hell are you saying right now?" I muttered into his shirt, overwhelmed and in awe and equal amounts disbelief.

"They can survive without me. They have before," he answered steadily, without a hint of hesitation or grief over the idea he'd just voiced. "As much as I love this land, I don't think I could let it keep me from you."

I pressed my face even deeper into his shirt, inhaling that rain and cedar scent that was all him.

"I'd resent it if you left. If I felt stuck here. It's been frustrating enough wanting to do what I want to do and having that interrupted by things that don't need to be my responsibility anymore."

I didn't want to do it, but I slowly lifted my head and peered into his eyes. "You would leave here? For me and Duncan?"

There was nothing but a fierce kind of determination in his eyes and features. "For you two, yeah." He paused. "But we'd have to invite Agnes." His throat bobbed. "I don't know if you know, but Dom might be gone. Nobody's seen him in a week, not even his uncle."

I had questions about this supposed uncle, but I saved them for later.

"Really?" I asked, feeling so bad.

He lifted his hand. "It's not your fault. It's a good thing for everyone if he doesn't come back." He blinked. "I would've probably ended up having to hurt him if he stayed and ever talked to you the way he did again."

My gazed moved from one of his eyes to the other, love bursting inside of me, and I could barely say, "I can't believe you almost let me go on dates with other people, you ass." I cupped his face in my hands. "I felt sick to my stomach thinking about it."

"You smelled upset every time anyone brought it up, you included," he confirmed.

"*And you knew?*"

The fondest smile I'd ever seen came over his face. "I told you, you're easy to read. I don't open up my senses for just anybody." He held me just a little tighter. "You project emotions easier than anyone I've ever met, and you make a lot of faces, Cricket."

I smacked him on the arm. "You were going to risk me mating someone else?"

"It wasn't a risk if I wasn't going to let it get anywhere near there." He leaned forward again, bringing his forehead to mine, his lips almost skimming mine as he said fiercely, "I would mate you even if the one-year period wasn't a thing, Nina."

"You're sure?" I asked, hope singing in my soul. "I might have more dream visits from my DNA donor, and Franklin would be your uncle-in-law," I warned him.

"Franklin and I will be fine."

"I would want you to be a dad to Duncan."

"I've got no problem with that."

"And again, if we had a child, they might be like me," I reminded him.

"A forest prince or princess would be a gift," he said with a straight face that anchored my entire existence to this moment. "There's a chance they could be like me too."

"Strong and wonderful? What a freaking burden."

He smiled. "They'd inherit this land if that's what they wanted. Any child of ours could. Would you be fine with that?"

"What do you think?" I had to groan as I squeezed his hands right back and said, looking him right in the eyes, "All right then." I pressed my mouth to his before pulling away just enough to say, "You're going to be stuck with me, Fluff, because there's nobody else on this planet I would rather be with than you."

Chapter Twenty-Seven

"I'm sorry, but *what*?" Sienna practically screeched into our video call.

At her side, Matti stared blankly at the screen. That was his stunned face. It took a lot to get to him, but with this, that would be twice in the last few months I'd rendered him speechless.

Who would have known that a magical puppy and me mating his relative would have that effect on him?

I cleared my throat and let my eyes stray to the empty spot on my bed where Duncan usually slept. Instead, tonight, he was passed out in Agnes's room. I'd had to take a picture of him curled up in a ball, snoring away, with Agnes tucked under her comforter, and her newest sleeping nanny, a very nice woman who was Pascal's aunt, reading a book on the twin-sized bed along the wall. She'd waved Henri and me off when we'd snuck inside to see what they'd been up to after finding Franklin passed out in the media room with a kids movie playing in the background, abandoned.

In my head, I moved him to the bottom of my nanny list. Then again, if I'd been alive half as long as he had, I'd be tired too.

We had barely backed out of Agnes's room before a soft "Henri" had us both turning to Franklin peeking around the corner of the hall, awake. We'd split up at that point, with Henri saying he wanted to give Franklin our news, and me wanting to call Matti and Sienna. I didn't think I could wait until tomorrow.

Which was how I found myself in my room after everything that had happened that evening.

Henri and I had kissed a little before wandering around the waterfall, where he'd pointed out up close the majestic and otherworldly trees with their shimmering trunks and three-times-larger-than-normal leaves. He'd tugged one toward my nose, and I'd been amazed at the fact they'd smelled like maple. The whole night had just been . . . a meteor shower in my heart, especially when Henri asked if I'd be willing to get mated sooner rather than later. Then he'd asked if I'd be willing to do it there, at the bottom of the waterfall, where so many of his ancestors had done the same.

All of them, actually.

That might have been the easiest "yes" of my life, other than Duncan.

I was still struggling to accept just how fast things had escalated, but I wasn't complaining. If anything, it felt like a load off. More than that, it just felt *right*.

"You're mating Henri?" It was Matti who stuttered the question out, stunned face still engaged. Not even his mustache had twitched.

I wasn't sure I'd ever gotten him to stutter as an adult before. "Yes," I confirmed.

"When?" Sienna screeched, but at 50 percent power, leaning forward, her face this weird mixture of a dozen different emotions, like her body couldn't pick one to focus on.

"The next full moon. We said soon, as long as neither one of us changes our minds between now and then. My three-month period here is going to be over in about two weeks." It said something to me that I didn't see us changing our minds. I wasn't wishy-washy, and neither was he. Plus, I'd been the one to bring up that last stipulation, and Henri had just about rolled his eyes. He hadn't agreed or disagreed, now that I thought about it. "The sooner the better, if you know what I mean." I winked.

Matti's expression told me that he either wasn't paying attention or he was letting all mentions of his cousin having sex go in one ear and out the other. I'd bet it was the first option.

Sienna, though, formed a triangle with her hands. It was her "thinking face." "Set a date. I can take off work to be there, or I'll call in sick." She fake coughed.

That got Matti to snap out of it. He gave his wife a hurt expression. "You're going to leave me?"

She shrugged, smiling while she did it. "If you can't take time off, yes. My best friend only gets married once."

"We'll be there if I have to call out sick," Matti claimed, like I'd expect anything else. "But Henri? Really?"

I blinked, thinking he had to be joking.

He wasn't.

"It was your idea in the first place!" I reminded him. "Did you start having second thoughts and didn't tell me?"

It was Matti's turn to shrug. "I didn't think you'd listen. He doesn't like being told what to do either." He sat up straight. "You've always been family, but now it's going to be legal." Just as I started to touch my chest in pleasure, he ruined it. "Also, I've seen his dick by accident once, and I don't want to know anything else about it. Deal?"

I was laughing while I agreed, and I remained smiling as we talked for a little while longer before getting off our video call. It seemed like they were both planning on coming to visit for the mating, we just had to look at the calendar. And I needed to get in contact with my parents to give them the news. This whole thing was surreal to even think about, but in a good way.

I'd *known* we felt something for each other. I was still smiling as I turned off the light and snuggled in bed, even as I wondered what Henri had gotten wrapped up with. A small part of me had expected him to spend the night since Duncan was with Agnes, but I managed to fall asleep a lot faster than I probably ever had. It had been a long, emotional couple of days.

And almost instantly, at least it felt like it, a voice spoke into that familiar dream-that-wasn't-a-dream.

Child

Nina

It is I—

I sat up gasping, like a zombie coming back to life in a horror movie, blinking awake a moment before my bedroom door opened and a familiar body barged in.

Henri kneeled on the hardwood floor, his hands finding my upper arms, and I leaned forward into him, right against his warm, bare chest.

"You okay?" he asked, rubbing his hands up and down my triceps.

I slipped my arms around his waist like I had its location memorized. "I'm okay," I whispered as he pulled me out from beneath the covers. He sat on the edge of the bed and set me on his lap, like I wasn't a full-grown adult.

"What happened?" he asked, stroking a hand down my spine as he did.

"It was the same voice. He said my name, and right before I woke up, he started to say something else, but . . ." I already couldn't remember what that had been. Not that it mattered, because it didn't. "What'd you hear?"

"Only 'child.' Franklin told me the other night that he could control it so only those in the clubhouse heard him, if that makes you feel better. I think he ends the dreams when they reach him."

"I didn't know that. We haven't talked about this whole situation enough." I rubbed my hand across his back, from one side of his ribs to the opposite set; his skin was smooth. It made me feel so much better. "This is pissing me off now. Franklin said they're not immortal. He keeps this up, and I'll find him in Alaska, and when he's sleeping, I'll drag him into a lake."

A hand stroked the back of my head as his pecs rose under my cheek. "A river would be better."

I smiled against his chest. "That's a good idea." I hugged him tighter, really eating up the fact he was shirtless. Was this what I had to look forward to every night? I slid my palm a little higher, from shoulder blade to shoulder blade, enjoying the feel of all those grooves and valleys his muscles constructed and the silky-smooth skin over them. "You think it's true? About Franklin making him feel bad? And that that's probably why he's reaching out now?"

"I think it could be. He keeps trying."

A grunt went through my throat. Seemed a little too late to me, and I didn't think I was really the type of person to hold a grudge, unless we were talking about Dominic and Duncan's would-be kidnappers.

And the Jenny Greenteeth.

"We can find him, if you want. After the snow melts next spring, the water levels will be high, and it gets flowing fast with the runoff; it'll take him far from wherever he is. Around here, you'll get some distance. I'm sure the rivers in Alaska are the same if not more powerful." He paused and lowered his voice. "That's what we do to trespassers around here."

Was he being serious? "How many bodies have you put in it to know that?" I laughed.

"A few, but they were alive, and it was to teach a lesson."

"Did it work?"

"They never came back."

"So how do you know they were alive afterward?" I snickered.

He stroked my back, and I felt like a cat on the verge of purring. "I didn't say they were alive afterward, but they were when we put them in."

I laughed even louder. "BS. You probably fished them out a hundred feet down the river."

Henri didn't disagree, but he made a soft puffing sound that had to be a dry chuckle as his hand went up higher than it had before, coming up to the middle of my back. "If he wakes you up again, we'll start figuring out where he is or how to do something about him in the spring."

"You think we can do something about him?" I whispered.

"We can give it our best shot. We'll talk to Franklin, see what he can do. I know a lot of people," he replied, his hand still stroking, still soothing.

I want in. I reached for his shoulder and swept my hand downward to his wrist and back up. "That's a good plan." Leaning back, I pulled his arm between us and drew my thumb down one of the prominent veins on his forearm. "What happened with Franklin?" I asked.

Henri's sigh said it all.

"That crappy, huh?"

"Franklin asked if we reached an agreement. I told him the news. He had a question about a situation we're having with the well."

That didn't sound so bad. "What's wrong with the well?"

"We're going to have to drill for another one sooner than we'd planned," he explained. "While we were talking about that, he got a phone call from Alaska." His eyes met mine, and I was sure he felt my whole body freeze. "They're coming to visit at the end of the month."

That was two weeks from now.

I let out a long, deep breath from my nose, and Henri gave me a look. "Is that why you didn't come upstairs?"

He blinked. "No, I didn't want to ruin the night, but I told Franklin I would give you the news. It's Ani's night off, and there was an intruder that I had to help Randall with. By the time I got back, you were asleep, and I didn't want to wake you."

"You can wake me up whenever you want," I told him, back down to holding his thick wrist. I tried to think about the notice Franklin had given him and decided I really wasn't in the mood to talk about it. Tackling it tomorrow would be soon enough. "I want to come back to the Alaskan people visiting later"—I was going to pretend it wasn't happening until then—"but did everything go okay with the intruder? Who was it?"

His hand kept going up and down my back, and it felt like he'd spread his fingers. "Two leprechauns. Your gnome fan club has been spreading the word about you. I'm going to need to have a talk with them."

"Leprechauns?" I squeaked.

"Mm-hmm," Henri answered, watching me as I stroked his wrist and forearm. "They wanted to meet with the 'fertile one' they've heard about."

"You don't think it was the bogeymen?"

"No. The gnomes work at a mine not too far from here, and they somehow told the leprechauns, who also want to procreate, and they decided to give it a shot, even if they 'got eaten,'" he muttered, not sounding excited about it. "We're going to have to set up a hotline for you. Maybe when Pascal's done being grounded he can be your secretary. He's got good people skills."

I reeled back. "That's crazy, Henri," I told him. "I'm sorry."

He shook his head, his expression fond. "There's nothing for you to apologize for. It's not crazy. Our numbers, as magical beings in general, have gone down a lot in the last century." Soft lips pressed against my forehead. "Told you your magic is a gift."

"But that's not how it works!"

"You tell them that, and they'll do with it what they want. Nothing wrong with some hope." His palm went further up right then, and he wrapped his hand around the nape of my neck. "Or maybe it does work that way and you haven't tried yet. Maybe instead of pinching flames, you blow on them?"

I'd never thought of it like that. Hmm . . . maybe that was something I could ask Franklin about.

Henri shrugged. "It's your decision if you want to do anything with it or not. You don't need to meet anyone you don't want to. You don't have to do anything you don't want to," he emphasized. "If it was up to me, I'd kick everybody out of here that doesn't belong, especially when they're looking for you. Eventually, someone's going to trespass, and I'll need to make an example out of them, but I'm only being forgiving because I understand how bad some of the magical out there want to continue their lines. I can't blame them for their desperation."

"Did you tell the leprechauns to come back?" My most important question was: were they dressed in green? Did they wear little top hats? Sienna was going to scream when I told her about them.

"I told them to come to the gates and they'd get their answer. Otherwise, I'd eat them for dinner."

"I see." I smiled and leaned over to press my cheek to the spot where his shoulder met his neck. "You smell good, Fluff," I murmured.

What had to be his cheek pressed to the side of my head. I could hear him inhaling. The hand on my neck gave it a gentle squeeze. "I think the same about you." The arms around me closed in. "About the best thing ever."

"What's better?" I asked, rubbing the tip of my nose along the tendon of his neck.

"Not better, but I won't complain about a grilled medium rare T-bone," he deadpanned.

I laughed. "Thank you?"

Both of his hands smoothed up and down alongside my spine. "I'm hungry right now."

I slid my own palms over his upper arms. "I never understood that saying about wanting to climb someone like a tree, but I get it now."

His chuckle was soft and puffy. "You can climb me anytime you want."

I leaned back and looked at him. He didn't need to tell me twice. I hadn't been able to stop thinking about how he'd said before I could do whatever I wanted to him.

Hands flat, I stroked over his arms, over bulging trapezius muscles, and then went forward, briefly holding his powerful pectorals, skimming on down over his ribs, the flat plain of his hard stomach, and meeting his eyes as I trailed a line with my thumbs along the band of his sleep pants.

Henri's abs flexed when I did that. There was no six-pack or eight-pack, but instead it was all firm, bulky muscle for me to touch, and that's what I did, holding his rib cage in my palms, dragging my hands up to just beneath his armpits and back down to his waist, grabbing, molding. And it felt so *mine* I didn't want to share.

I met those intense eyes. "How do you feel about premarital sex?"

His eyelids fell over those clear, bright irises, his lips parting just a little.

"Because I'm for it," I told him and paused. "It's been years since my last relationship, for the record."

"I'm for doing anything with you." Before I could mentally prepare, he picked me up and sat me on his thighs, straddling him. "I can count my partners on one hand, and my only relationship was while I was in college."

I tried not to frown at his admission, since I was the one who'd started it, but I was pretty sure I failed. "Is it weird I'm jealous over people I'll hopefully never meet?"

Henri's hands molded around my hips possessively. "No, because I'm jealous as hell, and I don't think I want to know anything about that part of your life." His hands pulled me up higher on his lap. "You'll never have a reason to be jealous over my life before you, Nina. I wouldn't have done that to my future mate."

Right, because most werewolves didn't mess around much.

I knew that well. Matti and Sienna hadn't been virgins when they met, but neither one of them had ever been that casual about sex either. Maybe there had been a one-night stand or two, but that was the extent of it, other than the relationships they'd had. Werewolves were too possessive, and some of them hotheaded, and relationship drama was something everyone tried to avoid.

Henri dragged his nose up my neck, done with that part of our conversation. "The more you smell like me, the better."

This might be the best day of my life, I decided, taking his bottom lip between my teeth and giving it a suck, his grumble so deep I felt it between my legs. "I want you to smell just as much like me as you want me to smell like you," I admitted in return. "Before you leave for work, I'm going to rub my cheek all over you, mark you up real good every morning."

His groan in response was going to be burned into my core memories. "How did you know that's exactly what I was thinking about doing to you every day? Cover you up so there's no doubt you've got a possessive, obsessive mate at home."

A little whimper rose up my chest.

But he wasn't done. "You can mark me up all you want, Nina, any time you want. The more, the better."

"Anybody messes with you, they're messing with me," I groaned, rocking against him, scrambling even closer to him. I buried my face into his neck and bit his trap muscle, earning a savage groan and a buck of his hips I had to cling to, to hold on.

Henri's hands went down to my ass. "I guess we're starting tonight?"

Lowering me onto my back on the bed, his hands slid under my shirt, palms flat on the band of my underwear at my hips.

I arched my back. "Yes, please. Right now would be great."

Those long fingers slipped between my underwear and the tender skin there, and he tugged the plain gray underwear down my legs before dropping them on the floor. I let my thighs fall apart as he kneeled on the mattress, one palm shaping my right inner thigh, his thumb rubbing a circle inches from my center. A deep grumble filled his chest. "How can you be this damn perfect?"

Before I could argue with him, he slipped his forearm under my thighs, spread my legs even wider, and his mouth went straight to sucking between my legs.

I almost levitated off the bed, slapping a hand over my mouth to keep from crying out at the sensation of his tongue dipping low, tasting. Licking. Henri's hands hugged my thighs to his cheeks, his mouth moving to suck my clit.

My hands went to his head, cupping it, crushing him against the middle of my body. "Henri," I choked.

He shook his head right where he was, literally rubbing his stubbled cheek against my seam, his tongue licking up one lower lip, then the other. Sucking one, then giving the other the same attention. "You taste so goddamn good, Nina," he murmured.

Henri sucked and thrust his tongue inside of me until I was coming straight into his mouth, my stomach muscles clenching and unclenching over and over again. One brawny arm hooked under both my thighs, the other going low around my back, picking me up. "I don't trust myself to notice if the kids come up here," he explained, standing up. "When we get our own house, we'll get one with a puppy door we can lock."

Our own house. The sound of that was almost as good as the orgasm he'd just given me. It made all this seem so . . . real. So wonderful.

I nodded and kissed him, feeling the dampness on his cheeks, knowing it was me he was covered in, and I loved it. I brushed my tongue against his, fully aware he was heading toward the bathroom door, opening it and kicking it closed in a smooth motion behind us before locking it. Bathrooms were the only rooms in the clubhouse that didn't have a small doggy door at the bottom.

My butt landed on the counter with the sink, a moment before hungry hands took over. His and mine yanked. I pulled his sleeping pants and underwear down as far as I could and met his eyes just as he wrapped a fist around the erection that I'd worked up and down the other night in my trailer. The head was fat, thick veins lining the length of him. He was in perfect proportion to the rest of his incredible body, and I felt like the luckiest person in the whole world.

His voice was hoarse as he worked his hand up and down. "I don't have a condom."

I shook my head, eyeing the length of him, the girth, the pretty pink and lilac color flushed throughout it. "I don't either." I pressed my forehead to his sternum, wrapping my hand around his, his fingers flexing beneath mine. "I don't take birth control either," I admitted shakily, lifting my gaze to find him looking at me with an expression that turned me on even more. His features didn't say he was disappointed, if anything he liked the sound of it. "But I have this thermometer that tells me when I'm in the clear and when I'm not . . ."

His lips parted, his eyelids dropping even lower over his incredible irises. "You know what you are." His palm squeezed his length tight. "I could still get you pregnant."

I did know what I was, and I hugged him tighter with my legs, urging him closer. "We can wait, if you don't want to risk it. But the idea of your bare cock—"

His growl made my nipples hard.

Under my fingers, he notched the big tip of his penis between my legs and pushed. Henri's broad head made its way inside of me, slowly, inch by inch, seesawing in and out, dipping a little before retreating, filling me and filling me, as he took my mouth. When he was halfway in, he pulled all the way out and pushed back deeper, this shaky, monumental grunt going through his chest and into mine.

His hand went to my hip, under my shirt, palming the bare skin there just as he . . .

He was in, every inch, his pelvis flush to mine, and I was gasping, and he was grunting, low and fierce. Grinding our groins together deep, my clit rubbing against the trunk of him. I wrapped my arms around his neck, clung.

"Once we get married, we can do this all time," he growled against my ear, licking the shell of it. "In the bed, in the shower, on the floor . . ."

"Bent over the sink?"

The sound he made in his throat was barely human as his hips snapped forward and he ground his pelvis against mine. "On my face, on my lap." He pulled out, then thrust deep, so dang deep. He moved his head so his lips were at my other ear. "But I'm coming in this perfect pussy every—"

I grabbed his face and kissed him hard, and he met my kisses, tongue touching tongue, and between our bodies, I shoved my shirt up so I could feel his skin against mine, my nipples rubbing against his chest. His hand came up and gave one a light pinch as his hips worked and he kept pumping away.

I drew back from his mouth as an orgasm had my muscles spasming almost violently around him, my ab muscles flexing so hard, I pressed my lips to his chest to muffle my cry.

"Next time, I'm not pulling out," he let me know, dipping his head, nipping my shoulder with those strong teeth right before he pulled out just as my orgasm eased, and with that plump head to my mound, his hand wrapped around that tremendous width, it took two pumps of his palm for him to come, for him to shoot a thick, white load between my thighs, a loud choke tightening his entire body. Henri shook, his guttural groan low through the bathroom.

His fingers moved between us, massaging the white cream into my thighs, over the shaved area at the center of me. Marking me with him. There was so much of it too.

I rubbed my hand over his arm, watching him work, watching him cover me with his scent, my thighs still twitching. "I like your artwork, Picasso," I whispered.

He looked up, his eyes bright, pupils wide . . . and he smiled. "Looks good, doesn't it?" he asked, drawing his finger up the crease between my middle and my thigh. "Smells even better."

I groaned and tugged him down again, kissing him, massaging my tongue against his as he held me close to his damp, sweaty body.

"I think I pulled a muscle in my stomach," I told him when we pulled away from each other.

His smile was even softer and dreamier that time. "My glutes are spasming right now," he countered.

I snuck my hand around to cup one of his cheeks, and sure enough, it was. I leaned back and smiled. "Want me to massage 'em?"

I did—massage them, that was—in the shower right afterward. Gave them a little bite too.

And when we went to bed after that, I slept deeper than I ever had before.

Just me and Henri.

Chapter Twenty-Eight

The hardest thing in the world to do is pretend you're fine when you're not. And I was not.

I wasn't even *close* to being fine.

When the knock came late afternoon on a Friday a couple weeks later, I'd been on the verge of having a panic attack all morning. Duncan had been aware I was feeling all kinds of ways; he had nudged me more often than usual lately, pounced on my feet in a way he hadn't done since he'd been a tiny baby, and he'd sent me so many messages of love, I had never been so confident in our bond.

But I was still so nervous.

I couldn't help it. I'd been dreading this day since Henri had shared the news with me—Franklin confirming it the next morning. I wanted to be calm and cool and mature. I wanted to be ready to roll with whatever happened with my head held high and joy in my heart. Chances were, and I knew it in my bones, that my boy wouldn't up and decide to leave if these people were like him and he liked them.

He loved me, and he loved the ranch and everyone at it. Some days, I'd swear I could hear him chanting from the nursery *"love, love, love"* alllllll day.

But there was one tiny possibility that I couldn't ignore: that he *might* change his mind. I wouldn't be able to blame him either. It was obvious how much he'd flourished here. How much more could he benefit from feeling even more included? More accepted? I'd been just fine being something different around so many werewolves, but who was I to tell him what would make him the most comfortable?

Every decision I had made, for years, was with him in mind, and I would always do whatever was best for him.

But I still willed my body not to overreact. Nothing had even happened yet. Since when did I get upset over what-ifs?

There was a sigh from the other side of the door, and I knew who it was before the voice even said, "It smells like a bakery up here, Cricket. I'm coming in."

My hands were still pressed flat against my stomach when the door opened and Henri slipped in, closing it immediately behind him.

He'd been in here a lot lately. So much, that his phone charger was plugged in to my outlet, and there was a neatly folded undershirt of his on top of my dresser. *And that had kept me from having a meltdown too.* Knowing he was there. Knowing he supported me in whatever happened next.

But in that moment, the man I was very much crazy over frowned at me. He watched me even closer than I watched him, his hands going to his hips, right over where his flannel shirt met his jeans. "You're not crying, but you smell like a cinnamon roll," he claimed.

I frowned right back at the man I'd spent nearly all my nights with over the last two weeks. He'd been working a lot, but we saw each other when he got home every night, with the exception of three days where he'd worked the graveyard shift because a coworker was sick. When we spent time outside with the kids, we usually ended up back in my room after that, even showering in my bathroom. I had wondered if Duncan would get cautious or weird, but my puppy had his spot on the bed and didn't seem to think twice about the werewolf staying in our room. Lucky, lucky me.

"I feel like I'm going to throw up, Fluff. I don't want to go down there." I made a face. "But I can't cry because I don't want whoever is downstairs to think I'm weak if they see me with puffy eyes, and then they won't trust me to be able to take care of Duncan."

Henri's face softened. "You're not weak," was his first argument. "But you have to meet them. Duncan needs you."

I nodded, knowing dang well my face and body were both giving off every kind of sign possible I was dreading this freaking meeting. I'd purposely avoided thinking about it as much as I could. The Alaskans were coming, and there wasn't anything I could do about it—nothing I wanted to do about it—so it was up to me to deal with it.

Henri came over, stopping right in front of me, so close his shins brushed my knees. His hand clasped my chin between his thumb and index finger, tilting my face up and giving me every inch of his amber gaze. "No one is taking him away from you." He paused. "From us. *No one*."

That didn't help in the way I thought he wanted it to. It was too sweet. "It . . ." It took me a second to try and get my voice steady, ignoring the way I failed and it still broke as I whispered, "It isn't that I'm so scared someone will try and take him away. No one is taking my donut unless they want to meet their ancestors."

His eyes moved from one of mine to the other.

I pressed my lips together and rehearsed the words in my head twice before I got them out. "I'm scared he's going to choose to leave . . . and not ask me to go with him," I whispered. We'd talked about this already, more than once, but I couldn't help but bring it up again.

Maybe if I said it enough, it would get easier.

Or maybe if I said it out loud, it couldn't come true.

His thumb drew a line under my chin. "He won't. If he wants you to go, we'll deal with it, Nina," he promised. "I can get a job anywhere, and you can work from anywhere." He paused and his throat bobbed. "You don't need to work if you don't want to. We haven't talked about it yet, but we should."

"Talk about what?" And had he said I didn't need to work?

"Finances," he explained. I wasn't going to say he was projecting discomfort, but more . . . he sort of looked embarrassed? Was he *sheepish*? "How the property taxes get paid on this land."

That was an instant distraction, and I squinted at him. "I did try to guess one day how much you owe yearly but . . . Why are your ears turning red?"

His ears got even redder when I called them out. It was adorable. So was the expression that came over his face. "I live within my means, of what I make off my job."

"What does that mean exactly?"

His cute ears went even more crimson, turning a color that made me think of Duncan's eyes, and he shook his head very slowly.

"Fluffy Blackrock, *are you rich*?" I whispered.

"It's complicated," was his reply, definitely 100 percent uncomfortable. "I'll tell you everything after we get today over with. Deal?"

I wanted to hear everything now because that sure sounded suspicious. "Am I going to give you a hard time?"

He didn't wait to nod, his features sober, but his eyes . . . there was amusement there in between his ruby red ears. "There's a trust, and I got an inheritance when I turned twenty-one. We'll talk about it later though, yeah?"

"Deal, but it doesn't make a difference to me," I told him with a smile that got me one right back. A nice, soft one.

"I know, Cricket," he agreed.

I poked his forearm. "Were you trying to distract me right now?"

Henri's eyebrows went up that infamous millimeter. "It worked for a couple minutes." His smile eased the tension in my body. "But you need to know, Duncan's not going to choose to leave you. I'd bet every acre of this property, he would live in a nuclear power plant for the rest of his life before he gave you up," he said, looking me dead in the eye the entire time.

I knew he was right, but . . .

"The love you two have for each other is the same I smell in every close family. He isn't going to choose strangers. Duncan thinks you're his, the same way you think he's yours."

It wasn't like I didn't know that, but it was different hearing it from Henri. A little bit of relief eased the worst of my stomachache. Only the worst. I had to press my lips together before I said, "Okay . . . and if they try and take him, you'll gouge out their eyes for us, so I don't need to?"

Another line was drawn over my chin. "No, but I'm glad your sense of humor is back."

I was only partially joking, but I gave him a tight smile and tried to play it off even though I was pretty sure he was well aware I wasn't bloodthirsty under normal circumstances, but when it came to my donut, I'd become a cannibal.

For him too, I figured.

Fortunately, he didn't quit smiling. "Come on. The faster we get it over with, the faster we can move on." He looked at me. "Matti and Sienna get here in a few days, and your parents get here an hour later, and after that, the moon is going to be watching over us under the waterfall, and you're going to be my mate."

That had to be the only thing in the world able to pull me fully out of my panic. To give me hope for the future.

Whatever else happened, I'd have the rest of my life with the most handsome, wonderful man I'd ever met.

He bent his head and brushed his warm lips over mine. "Let's get it over with."

"I will, but I don't want to," I whispered.

The corner of his mouth curled. "I'll be with you both the whole time." He eyed my wrist. "Leave the bracelet. You've got nothing to hide here ever again."

I didn't, did I? With less nerves than ever before, I tugged it off and tossed it onto my bed. That familiar discomfort I'd lived with every time I took it off didn't circle back to me for once.

Before I could ponder that any more, Henri extended his hand, all long, tan fingers and a broad palm. "Good. Come on."

I took it, letting him pull me up to my feet too. He was right. The faster we got this over with, the faster we could move on.

We had plans. Important ones. Some I hadn't been as excited over because I'd been so worried about this.

Henri held my hand as he tugged me out of the room and

down the stairs. I took some deep breaths and made a few promises to the universe if it let this go well. Duncan already had his head sticking out of the door to Agnes's room when we made it to the first floor. He came running over, crashing against my legs before turning and rubbing against Henri's too. He knew what was happening today. I'd taken a sick day, which hadn't turned out to be a total lie, because I was sick, but with freaking nerves.

I stroked him a couple of times, kissed the top of his snout, and smiled. He knew I wasn't all right to start with. There was no point in making it worse by opening my mouth and letting him hear it. I could do this. We had multiple plans set up, depending on how everything went.

We weren't getting split up. No one was leaving anybody.

Henri didn't make a peep, but his thumb rubbed against the meaty part of my hand softly as the three of us headed down the hall toward the meeting room where there were voices coming from.

"Love," Duncan said to me before we got to the doorway.

I stopped right there to crouch and hug him, my heart in my arms. "I love you more than anything, Donut. Everything is going to be fine. I'm nervous about meeting these people. Okay? But I won't let anything happen. I swear on my life."

A much bigger body dropped to the same level as us, and a hand landed on Duncan's back a moment before another one did the same to the middle of mine.

We both looked at him.

And Henri said, in that velvet voice, looking back and forth between the two of us, his hands resting on our backs, "You're both mine, and you don't have anything to be worried about. Understand?"

I blinked, and Duncan's beautiful fluffy tail swayed behind us. His *"yes"* resonating in my head.

The hand on my back slid a couple inches higher between my shoulder blades. His Adam's apple bobbed, and his jaw went tight. "From now on, we go through everything together. All right?"

I nodded, and Duncan . . . Duncan put his paw on Henri's knee.

I'd been holding it together with tape, and all of a sudden, the most intense urge to cry hit right in the back of my eyes, especially when the werewolf royalty smiled softly at not just me but my boy too. "Come on, you two. Everything is going to be fine."

He was right.

Henri had said it—we'd go through everything together from now on.

I kissed Duncan before I stood up and kissed Henri on the cheek too, giving him a smile when I pulled back. *Thank you*, I mouthed.

He dipped his chin at me, his expression grave, like he was ready to go to battle.

We went inside.

In the room were Franklin and Ema, the elder female with the silver-blue hair. They were standing in front of three men, two I had never seen before, and the other one was Ilya, the Alaskan leader who had invited me to their compound. The two strangers though were much older than him. They were both thin, their hair more white than silver, their faces just as stern as Henri's usually was.

I couldn't sense their magic, I realized, and glanced at their wrists to see that they had familiar-ish beaded bracelets on.

Both men were already facing the doorway, their eyes glued to the gangly puppy standing front and center between Henri and me.

The men looked at each other.

"Ah, yes." Franklin waved us over, beaming like a proud dad. Or uncle.

With my chin held high and, hopefully, all the rest of my emotions carefully hidden, I walked over to the group, with Duncan so close he stepped on my ankle a couple of times. I didn't smile, mostly because the strangers didn't either, and I wasn't sure if that was normal or if it was a bad thing. The older men had their brown eyes glued to Duncan, and Ilya was looking back and forth between Henri and me, a smug expression on his face.

I lifted my fingers at him before holding out my hand to one of the older men; the man flinched a little when he seemed to finally notice me. "Hello there," he said, glancing at his companions before taking my hand with an unexpected gentleness. Out of nowhere, he grinned before turning to the leader of the community, every inch of his serious face disappearing like I'd imagined it.

Ilya, the Alaskan leader, shrugged. "Told you."

The older man focused back on me, his grin still in place while he murmured in a surprisingly kind voice, "*You're* the pup's guardian?"

Duncan leaned against my lower leg, sending me a dose of "*love.*"

"Yes?" I replied. He seemed amused. What had Ilya told him? "I'm Nina. Thank you for coming all the way here," I went on, not sure what was going on. When he let go of my hand, I aimed for the other older man and took his too.

He was smirking by that point too.

Did they know who my father was?

I didn't have time to worry about that though. If they knew, they knew. I gestured toward my boy, watching the strangers closely when I did. "This is Duncan," I told them.

Duncan plopped on his butt and aimed those bright red eyes at each man. His tail was straight in the air, attentive and watchful. His nostrils flared as he smelled them better. With all he'd grown, his ears didn't look so massive on his head anymore. I'd looked up pictures of adolescent bloodhounds, and Duncan's body—with the exception of his tail and coloring—was identical to them. Big ol' ears, intelligent eyes, long and lean, and still growing.

No one reacted; no one said a single word.

The two strange men continued inspecting Duncan, and he looked at them right back. His tail had stopped swishing and was standing straight up, motionless. I made myself stay relaxed, kept my breathing even, my hands loose.

I hadn't thought about it until then, but if they were the same as Duncan, could they speak telepathically too?

A silent minute later, one of the older men turned to the other, and they both smiled much bigger than I ever would have imagined from how emotionless their faces had seemed when we'd first walked in.

"He's perfect," a voice I didn't recognize said in my head.

I froze and caught the eye of the first older man who winked at me.

It was Ilya who ordered in that tone that was very close to Henri's Great Wolf one, "Tell them how you found him."

Beside me, Henri grunted. "What did I tell you about demanding anything from mine?"

Not making a smug face was almost impossible.

The other leader sighed before narrowing his eyes in irritation. "Can you please tell them how you found the pup, Nina?" he asked pretty sarcastically.

Fluffy looked at me and nodded an encouragement.

This man would always have my back, and I loved him so much. And so, I exhaled slowly, then I told the strangers the story. All of it.

The men from Alaska didn't say a word until I was done.

There were more looks, followed by an overbearing silence that even Franklin and Ema seemed uncertain over. It was obvious from their body language. We were all being weird.

I rocked on my heels, hoping someone could just say *something*.

I waited and I waited and I—

"Love," Duncan told me.

His entire attention was focused on me. And I smiled so hard I felt it in my chest. *Love you too*, I mouthed to him.

Ilya noticed. "What did he say?"

I tugged my donut's ear gently. "He told me he loved me."

The two older men shared yet another look, and I had to tap into my inner Henri to keep from making a face, because that was getting annoying. Did they find what they were looking for in him? Was he whatever they thought he was?

Couldn't they just tell me?

"Duncan, would you come here?" the winking older man asked, and I appreciated it because I was dang near certain he could've asked him telepathically instead.

If Duncan answered, it was only to him, but a moment later, my boy trotted over. With a lot more agility than I would have expected, both men kneeled to pet him, touching his ears, checking his teeth, even rubbing their fingers over his tail in a way that said they had no fear of his magical fire.

They smiled the entire time, and I didn't imagine the wistfulness when one of them sighed and said, "We've thought for so long that we were the last of our kind."

I swallowed hard at what that implied.

The other one tickled him beneath the chin, and Duncan wagged, earning an even wider grin from the man. "You're a good-looking young man, little brother."

That . . . that didn't mean biologically that was the case . . . but . . . *but could it be?*

"We haven't seen our mother in sixty years," the winking man explained, his attention still on my donut. "We weren't sure . . ."

The question was poised on my tongue, ready. Two of them actually.

"Is he?" Franklin was the one who asked, his voice slightly high.

Was he what?

"Without a doubt." The winking man chuckled with *delight* when Duncan leaned his head into his hand. "He is utterly and completely a hellhound."

My donut was a *hellhound*?

The fact he'd answered just like that . . . *it didn't matter*. It didn't matter because he'd said *hellhound*, and my mouth had dropped open, and a part of me couldn't believe it, but a bigger part of me could. That had been on my list of beings I'd thought were a possibility. But there hadn't been enough information about them to know for sure, and this man had just said *without a doubt*.

Duncan was a *hellhound*.

From the little I had read about them, there were stories in which hellhounds were legends that guarded the underworld. I could have sworn I might have read that in other folklore, they were rumored to be protectors of women. But the one idea I could remember to be the most common myth about hellhounds, was that they were highly feared, epic beings.

The thing was, there wasn't a single scary thing about my boy.

The closest thing to hell he knew was getting a bath.

I couldn't believe it. My Duncan donut was a *hellhound*.

And said hellhound turned to me over his shoulder, and he winked. *"Yes,"* he told me.

I stared at him. "Did you know what you are?" I wanted to think I sounded calm, but there was probably zero chance that was the actual case. I might as well have sucked a helium balloon dry.

Those ridiculously cute eyelashes covered Dunky's ruby eyes, his ears twitching. *"Love"* was the answer he decided to go with.

I laughed in freaking awe. "That's not a yes or a no, Duncan."

The tail that had gotten us into this new stage of our life swayed. *"Yes."*

Yes!

Before I could ask anything else, or celebrate this absolute miracle of a discovery, three different phones went off at the same time, and Ema, Franklin, and Henri pulled theirs out. The three of them frowned at whatever was on the screen. I'd learned that they, along with the ranch's security, all had access to the cameras at the gate, and they were notified when someone was there.

Franklin lifted his head first, his normally sneaky face formed into this super irritated one that he aimed at the Alaskan leader.

Ilya, the firebreather according to Henri, crossed his arms over his chest and raised a dark eyebrow. "Is he at the gate?" he asked Franklin in a flat, unamused tone.

My biological uncle glared. "You brought him with you?" he spat out so out of character that even Ema looked at him strangely.

Beside me, Henri tipped his phone to give me a view of it. On the screen, the camera angle showed a man in maybe his fifties, partially hanging out of a driver side door, jabbing at the intercom keypad over and over again. There was nothing that special about him; he looked like a normal man in a T-shirt, being obnoxious with the way he kept pressing the keypad aggressively, like he didn't understand why it wasn't working.

"Is that who I think it is?" Henri asked from above my head.

Who did . . .

No.

My head snapped up.

"He wasn't invited," Ilya was quick to explain with a sneer. "He was on the same flight and wouldn't say a word about where he was going, like we couldn't piece his plans together."

My uncle let out a curse I was surprised he knew in the first place.

Ilya raised an eyebrow but basically shrugged with his eyes. "There's not much I'm unwilling to do, but I'm not arguing with him. He's gotten more stubborn every year."

I blinked and met my favorite set of amber eyes.

Henri's forehead was furrowed. "I'm getting real sick of people showing up without an invitation," he growled. I pointed at myself, and his expression instantly changed. "Not you, Cricket."

I smiled, then I wiped it off in a way that he'd be proud of. We had business to get to. "Is that your brother?" I straight-up asked Franklin.

The dream god had already stuffed his phone back into the little case at his hip, and based off the energy he was radiating, this was the angriest I'd ever seen him. "It is." His eyes narrowed from behind his glasses. "I didn't invite him, Nina."

I believed him and said that.

"He's seemed real melancholic since your visit, Franklin," one of the hellhound men admitted, the one who didn't wink. "He's constantly pacing. It's quite irritating."

"He overheard me talking to my second about the daughter of a fertility goddess mating with the Great Wolf," Ilya said casually in a way that didn't come across as all that apologetic. Especially when he knew he was my DNA donor. Did he have to stir shit up?

"A truck is pulling in behind his. They're getting out and talking . . . I think it might be Dominic? He's . . . he's punching in the code to open the gate," Ema told us, the only one still paying attention to the camera. "Who is this? Where are Ani and Randall? Why would Dominic allow a stranger in? He knows he doesn't have that authority! Where is security?"

"Ani is in town, and Randall is off along the western fence right now. There's no way he can get back in time." Henri's entire body, all Viking and warrior pedigree, turned to me. His face though, had Murder Henri written all over it. "I'll deal with Dominic, but what do you want to do about our visitor, Nina?"

What did I want to do about it?

"I don't know," I answered honestly, wondering what in the world Dom was thinking letting a total stranger onto the ranch. It was one thing for Fluff to have allowed the bogeymen to come and go, but even I knew how important their hierarchy was around here. And you didn't let a stranger in unless the right person said so. Buttttt I was going to let Henri handle it. Him dealing with that asshole seemed past due to me, honestly.

Plus, I had bigger fish to worry about. A box jellyfish to be specific. "I want to tell him to screw off," I told him, "but at the same time, I don't really want to put in the effort either."

But I thought about what Ilya had mentioned. How he wasn't willing to argue with him. I didn't see the hellhound brothers lining up to do it either, not at their ages. Franklin probably would, but . . .

Maybe it wasn't official yet, but the people here *were* my

people. At least the kids and some of the adults. Since the incident at the river with Shiloh and Pascal, the parents at the nursery had totally changed their behavior. Phoebe and her husband had brought me little things every chance they could, like fresh loaves of bread, jelly that she'd made, and even though I'd only seen him in passing after school before he was herded back to Ema's house with Pascal where they were busy being grounded, I'd been blessed with more thank-you cards from my favorite satyr.

Every one of Pascal's family members had either gifted me something directly or they'd left it in the kitchen. A scarf, a beautiful pendant, a painting of the village, candy . . . The parents of the rest of the kids had started inviting me to their houses, offered to take Duncan. It had only taken risking my life, but it was all right. I didn't mind.

And it was them I thought of in that moment.

If it was up to anyone to deal with an aggravated death god, it was me.

Setting my shoulders, I looked up at Henri. "Let's go with option A. Someone needs to tell him to fuck off."

There were two, maybe three, distinct choking sounds. At least one of them was from one of the adult hellhounds, the second may have been from Ilya, and the third was definitely from my brand-new uncle. Ema slapped him on the back, he was choking so hard.

Henri ignored them and smiled his Teasing Henri smile. "I can do that." Right in front of my eyes, Teasing Henri turned into Great Wolf Henri. "He and I are past due for a conversation too."

I raised my eyebrows at Mr. Protective. "Sure, but not alone. We go together," I clarified.

That smile got slightly bigger, but he nodded.

Duncan, who had been standing with the older men, turned to us, kicked one leg back, then the other, yawning so wide.

Had I just seen a little flash of red in his mouth? It was there and gone so fast, I might have imagined it.

"*Yes,*" my puppy said.

"You're coming too, Dunky?" I asked, not exactly surprised.

"*Yes,*" he confirmed, trotting over, setting a paw on my foot.

Henri glanced back and forth between us and said, "Let's go." Everyone else got a "We'll be back."

Franklin hustled over, fidgeting with his belt. "I have a few words for him as well," he claimed, still looking so aggravated over the situation.

I guess we were all going. I raised my eyebrows at Henri, who seemed just as surprised as I did.

The hellhound men were smiling, even more amused than we were, from the looks of it. But they knew him from their settlement. It was Ema who was frowning in confusion. She didn't know anything about anything, and she wasn't going to find out right then either.

"Take your time," the winking hellhound said as the four of us hustled out of the room, Franklin leading the way, with Henri behind him, then me and Duncan.

We were going to confront my DNA dad—a very old being who had just pitched a fit trying to get into the ranch before one of ours had let him drive on in.

This wasn't where I thought my life would take me, but . . . we were here.

"When I pictured having kids, I always wished for a son I could rely on," Henri said over his shoulder when we were in the hallway.

I glanced at my sidekick, and he looked up at me. I blew him a kiss.

"And when I wanted a partner, I thought I'd want one I could rely on," Fluffy added.

"Seems to me you got both," I told his back.

"Seems to me, I did," he agreed as we made it to the front door. "A strong mate and a strong son who would come with me to face two pains in my ass." Henri made a soft sound. "I wish you could sense how lucky I feel right now."

"Yeah, you are," I cheered him on, my heart almost bursting. He had a point. Here I was with my mate, my boy, and my uncle.

"Just like we're lucky to have you charging ahead with us too. Right, Dunky?"

"*Yes.*"

Ahead of Henri, Franklin glanced over his shoulder, a pleased expression on his face.

I caught the silhouette of Henri's smile as he held the door for us. Shades of black and gray and blue filled the night, shadowing everything in its path. A car door slammed shut in the near distance.

"He's close," Henri murmured beside me. "Still near the gate for some reason."

"Too close," Franklin agreed, a pissy expression back on his features.

Henri's hand took mine as we reached the edge of the parking lot.

That's when he slowed down and stared toward the rows of cars just as I sensed werewolf magic approaching from the same direction he was focused in. Henri didn't look at me as he lifted my hand and pressed his lips to the back of it, murmuring, "Give me one minute to deal with this once and for all."

"We'll wait," I promised as he released my fingers right as a blond man appeared, heading straight and fast in the direction of the clubhouse. Someone was in a rush.

But he knew we were there, and his attention turned to us even as he kept moving, calling out, "Just here to get my shit, I'm not going to talk to your precious princess, Henri." Dom's tone was sarcastic. "I'm only here to—"

Henri moved like a lightning bolt.

He was beside me one moment, and in the next—faster than my eyes could follow—he was slamming up against Dominic's chest, hand reaching for the other man's throat, and Henri Blackrock lifted him up with a single hand so high, so fluidly, his booted feet dangled.

Duncan plopped down between my feet, and I didn't need to see his face to know we were both gaping at the sheer unbelievable strength of the newest member of our family.

I'd known he was strong. Visually, it was obvious. And I'd seen him use a log as a javelin, and Dom had to be somewhere in the two-hundred-pound range, but Henri was holding him up like he was a stuffed animal.

His head was tipped up, Dom was that high off the ground, and Henri let out a snarl louder and more intimidating than anything I could have ever imagined.

Franklin whistled beside me.

"I forgave you for giving up Agnes. I tried to brush off you choosing to fight me over taking control of the ranch. I tried to forget about you trying to take something else that was mine." Fluff's voice was deep. "I might have been able to forgive you for being rude to her and your daughter. I would've eventually gotten over you leaving your responsibilities without a goddamn warning," Henri sneered, lifting him up another inch or two higher as Dom finally started sputtering, like it had taken his body a second to realize what was going on. His fingers went to the ones wrapped around his throat, like he was trying to peel them off.

He gasped.

But Henri wasn't even close to being done as his upper arm flexed, and I would've sworn he was squeezing his throat tighter. "But you just violated the one rule I can't brush off. You put us at harm and let a stranger onto our land—"

"He's . . . Ni . . . Nina . . ." Dom gasped, still trying to pry Henri's fingers off.

"I don't give a shit who he is!" Henri roared. "You know the rules! And you're lucky I have other things to deal with right now or I'd make you regret every bullshit word that's ever come out of your mouth."

"Hen . . . Henri!" the blond gasped even more faintly, slapping now, his eyes watering.

And Franklin, Dunky, and I stood there and watched.

Henri though, shook his hand like my boy shook his stuffed toys in his mouth, and said, "You think *you* could fight *me*? You think you would live afterward?" Henri didn't laugh, but there was something dark in his voice . . .

Something I liked a lot.

But I was too busy watching this and regretting not having popcorn while I did it.

That hand holding up Dom, a six-foot-tall-plus man, went up another inch or two higher. "I *let* you hit me," Henri told him. "That wasn't a sucker punch, you piece of shit. I let you strike me. I let you say every word you wanted to because I've got nothing to fucking prove to you, but that shit is over now. Your time here is done. Every connection to the ranch is severed. We don't exist to you from this moment forward, and you will never think, speak, or write about anyone here ever again, or I will find you."

Dom's face was so red, and his eyes so bulging and shiny, I wasn't sure if it was because of the position he was in or because he was literally being excommunicated right then and there.

Taking his time, and showing off that insane strength again, Henri lowered him to the ground, but he kept his fingers where they were, wrapped around his throat.

I'd swear I saw him squeeze them before the Great Wolf 2.0— Murder Henri lurking in there, strongly—pulled Dominic toward him until their faces were inches apart. "You breathe because I let you breathe," Henri informed him through clenched teeth. "You live because I let you live. Do you understand?"

I didn't know if Dominic did, but my entire reproductive system understood.

Dom sucked in a breath so ragged, his eyes tearing up even more, I almost didn't understand his "Yes." But he repeated himself, the hostility, his arrogance, extinguished. Those blue eyes just like Agnes's didn't even swing around the second Henri's finger must have loosened. Dom looked at Henri, and I meant really looked at him. Like he had ripped a veil off his existence and showed him that everything he'd ever known was a lie.

And I didn't even waste my time following Dom when he took off the way he'd come.

Franklin didn't either, because out of my peripheral vision, we both just stared at Henri.

And then my biological uncle let out the most amused sound

I'd ever heard leave his body, and he jerked so hard, it was like that surprised him too. "Well, I was wondering when you would finally put him in his place. That went on for too long, Henri."

"I was hoping he'd learn," the man I was set to mate soon grumbled, before meeting my eyes and being very unapologetic about everything.

I beamed at him as Franklin huffed. "People like that never learn on their own. I know from experience."

We all turned at the same time as we felt a strong presence make its way closer to where we were.

Where I'd thought Duncan's mom's magic had been enormous, this other one seemed to be on the same level.

It felt both very similar to Franklin's and very different at the same time. There was a smoothness to both of theirs, where a werewolf's was wild, but that was the only major likeness between them. The one coming toward us felt dark and bottomless. The same way an ocean would feel at night, I figured.

If this was what other people sensed around me, I understood now.

"Child," the figure called out as he cut in between a row of cars.

He must have parked in the back.

"Don't you 'child' her, you imbecile," Franklin was the one who snapped, so at odds with his khaki pants and the sweater vest layered over a button-down shirt. "What are you doing here?"

The figure's steps faltered. "Imbecile! I'm here to see my daughter!" the man shouted, stepping right up into using his outdoor voice.

"Now she's your daughter?" my apparent champion, Uncle Franklin over here, shot back without missing a beat.

Henri peeked at me, and we blinked at each other.

This might have been in the top five most surreal moments in my life. Standing in a magical forest with a hellhound, a wolf god, and a god of dreams. My baby, my future mate, and my uncle. And the man who thought he was my father—a death god.

And the two oldest were bickering?

"She has always been my daughter!" the other man exclaimed, honestly sounding insulted. He even sniffed before raising his voice again. "Your resemblance to your mother is uncanny."

He was talking to me now?

Henri must have not liked that much either because I heard him grumble from deep in his chest, but honestly... honestly... I wasn't worked up about this. Not at all. About any of this. It caught me off guard, if anything. Waiting around for the Alaskan people had been gut-wrenching and nerve-racking, and this had nothing on that.

I had no control over other people's actions, but in this case, I didn't have anything to lose.

My life was whole and complete, and this person coming into it wouldn't change anything. Not for the better, and I wouldn't let him for the worse. And neither would the men standing around me, it seemed.

That's why they were here.

Fierce protectiveness rose up inside of me one more time, even stronger than before, reminding me that of all of us here, maybe Franklin might have the most power in his body, but I had this man's magic in me.

There was going to be no bowing tonight. Not thanking the gods that this MFer was here, paying attention to me. There would be no altars or rejoicing.

Maybe I'd give him a tiny bit of credit for coming, but I didn't owe him shit.

"I wouldn't know if I look like her. I never met her either," I told him in a flat, casual voice.

I still couldn't see my DNA dad's face even though he wasn't that far away. The lighting just happened to hit his features in the perfect way to obscure them. His body, on the other hand, was visible.

And he was clenching his hands into fists at his sides. "It was a mutual decision that we allowed others to raise you. You are the only child we conceived together, and the only child either of us had in centuries. You might very well be the last for both of us," the man explained, a weird inflection to his words.

"Because you're a useless old bastard!" Franklin threw out, surprising me again.

My mouth twitched, and I squinted, trying really hard to see more than just his silhouette.

"It was not a decision we took lightly," my biological father tried to argue as he took a few more steps, finally getting into a spot where his features were visible.

I would've walked right by him in public.

He was a handsome-looking man in maybe his fifties, younger than Franklin, I thought. He looked like he should have been an actor with his pale skin, classic bone structure, and deep black hair. But the most striking of all *was* his presence. It was some of the purest magic I had ever felt, like Duncan's mom, my old neighbor, my uncle, and the pink waterfall.

I wondered though, at that moment, why in the world Dominic would have let him into the community when he'd reacted so poorly to me? Had he had a bracelet on before and he'd taken it off? I could wonder about it later.

There were other things to focus on at the moment. Like how his voice wasn't a total shock to my ears. But standing there, looking at the man I had wondered over from time to time throughout my life . . . *I didn't feel anything for him.* Not happiness. Not relief.

I didn't feel any more complete than I had ten minutes ago.

And that acknowledgment gave me a strength of its own.

If anything, it made it real, real easy to draw on my inner brat.

"Have you always been good at making excuses, or is that something new?" I asked.

Franklin's head swiveled toward me.

The man claiming to be my father took another step forward, jabbing his finger . . . at me?

That had gotten under his skin? Mr. Big Bad Death didn't like being told he made up excuses? What a surprise.

"Do you understand who you are disrespecting? I've been

known by many names, been feared by thousands! Civilizations erected altars in my memory! They worshipped at my feet!" He was getting wound up right in front of our eyes, taking another step forward. "I am a god! And *you* are my offspring. *You* owe me your very life."

Henri's body tensed beside mine.

But it was a deep, resonant howl that made me flinch.

Then it made my eyes go wider than they ever had before.

Because it wasn't Henri who made it.

The howl, a different pitch from any other werewolf I'd ever met, pierced through the air, leaden and great, and it *was coming from Duncan.*

My mouth could have hit the floor from shock.

And then my boy almost had me falling to my ass, but I managed just to stumble into Henri instead.

Because there was a flame erupting from my donut's throat as his head arched upward to the sky and he "awoo"ed like he had never "awoo"ed before.

It was as ponderous as the pines around us, as magical as the moon itself, with a depth that seemed so at odds with his size.

I'd never heard a war cry, but for whatever reason that was the first thought that came into my head when I heard it.

And it was so freaking *beautiful*.

"Holy magical shhhhh . . ." I whispered, in pure amazement.

A hand landed on my shoulder, and I heard Henri's whoosh of an exhale at my ear.

As the howl came to an end, my puppy posed there standing, looking so dang majestic, so ethereal, it choked me up.

He was straight out of a millennia-old tale in that moment.

I squeaked.

"Where did that come from, Donut?" I cried before dropping to my knees and stroking from his head down his spine. I forgot all about where we were and who was in front of us and everything that was happening and everything that was going to happen. "That was the most beautiful thing I've ever heard!" No offense to Henri.

"Yes," my donut agreed, his whole focus still out on the man who stood frozen in the middle of his spiel. *"Love."*

"I love you too," I promised, giving him another long pet. "That was incredible!"

He'd had fire coming out of his throat! Nobody said anything about that! I hugged him so tight.

Fire! From his throat!

I lifted my head. "Henri, *did you see that?*"

He was already grinning, his eyes wide and bright, as he nodded. "That was great, Duncan."

He deserved another hug, and I gave it to him.

"This is the child you mentioned, my brother?" my DNA dad decided to ask in a voice that didn't sound so angry anymore. It actually sounded . . . intrigued? "My child bonded with a hellhound? And you didn't think to tell me that's why you were poking around with the brothers?"

I wasn't going to bother acknowledging him calling me his child again, and apparently neither was everyone else.

"I don't need to tell you anything," Franklin replied tersely.

My biological father huffed, and I watched his body language change as I got back to my feet. He seemed to relax? "I see." His huff was a little lighter. "I supposed I would like to hear this story in the future, how you came about giving me a hellhound grandchild."

I wasn't sure if I stumbled into Henri or he stumbled into me.

Hellhound grandchild? Was this man who I had never actually met before already referring to my Dunky as his grandchild? This wasn't a dream. It couldn't be.

But then he ruined it again. "Is this the man I've heard is attempting to taint my bloodline?" he went on, literally digging himself into the world's deepest hole.

Henri and I made eye contact, his lip curled with a snarl.

I didn't need to fight his battles. He'd cemented that by shaking Dom like a rag doll. I bowed and flipped my hand, palm up, to give him the floor. Something told me he wanted it.

And this flirty, funny man hidden beneath layer after layer of responsibility and duty, with the strength of how many men I had no idea, winked at me. But only me. Because when he faced the direction of my father, all that affection was wiped clean and His Fluffy Highness was out. Jaw line rigid, chin high, his glare on point.

He was unbelievable.

"The only person assuming anything here is you," the Great Wolf growled, an absolute menace. "This is my forest, and you're trespassing."

My DNA dad's scoff echoed. "Is that supposed to intimidate me?" my father asked, his tone back to that one that couldn't mean anything good. "She is *my* daughter."

A laugh rumbled out of Henri's chest, and it wasn't an amused one. It was honestly sort of scary. I liked it.

Out of the corner of my eye, I noticed even Franklin turned to him like he was surprised he had that in him. But I guess it was one thing to know you were stronger than a normal werewolf, and another thing to incite a death god. Then again, Henri wasn't just any old wolf.

"Everything you see here is mine. *She* is *mine*." His magic—bright and more intense than ever, like he'd had it hidden within him—carried through the night on swift wings, covering everything in its path with possession. "And I'll remove your bowels and shove them down your throat if you think you have any say in our future," Henri snarled, the muscles of his back flexing visibly through his shirt.

I had to throw my hand over my heart because *I had freaking known it!* He would disembowel someone for me! I knew it, I knew it, I knew it!

I must have made a sound because he glanced over his shoulder.

The expression on my face must have said I was in love with him because his lit up, a smile spreading across his face, which had been so pissed a second ago. His eyebrow went up that millimeter. "You didn't even smile that much when we agreed to mate."

"Violence might be my love language." I still had my hand over my heart. "I knew you would do some shady stuff to protect me. I just knew it, Fluff."

He reached back, and his hand nudged mine.

I took it.

"Always," Henri claimed, his own voice a hoarse promise in the night.

"All the bowels?"

"Slowly and painfully," he promised.

My nose tickled, and a weight hit my calf, and I peeked down to find Duncan leaning against me, though his attention was still aimed at my biological father. The fire in his throat was gone and his tail was normal-looking, by his standards.

Steeling my spine, I gripped Henri's hand tighter and faced my DNA dad with him. He had moved a little closer, and it was really easy to see all of his features now. Good. Now there'd be no mistaking my intent. "This isn't your bloodline, it's mine, and if my future children turn out to be the size of a miniature pony when they're toddlers, you don't have a say in it," I let him know.

For whatever reason, that piqued his attention, and my biological father took two steps forward. "What's your surname?" he demanded.

"Is he talking to me or you?" I whispered to Henri.

"I don't know."

"I know your surname, child!" my DNA dad bellowed. "The werewolf!"

Duncan growled.

"Why does he want to know your last name?" I asked him as I bent to comfort my boy, even though it might be worth seeing magical fire come out of his throat. I still couldn't believe he'd done that. I had to ask the hellhound brothers what was up with that. "It's okay, Donut. He wasn't a good dad; I'm not surprised he isn't a good granddad, yelling like that."

"He isn't good at anything," Franklin chimed in, his attention still on his brother.

"He's asking so he can guess my ancestry," Henri answered me before bellowing, "I'm a Blackrock and a Nyberg."

My biological father narrowed his eyes. "Your mother was—"

"Yes," Henri didn't bother letting him finish his question.

"I see." He blinked again, even slower.

I guess he knew Henri's mom.

Duncan let out a quiet, long "awoo" that had us all looking at him. *"Yes."* His tail wagged, the blue so bright in the night. His eyes like two red coals against his coat. He was beautiful.

The other man stirred. "I have no problem with it, my grandson," my biological father said, taking another step closer, answering a question I hadn't heard.

He kept coming, closer and closer until he was about ten feet away, and Henri side-stepped so that a small part of his body blocked me from my DNA dad. I wrapped my arms around his forearm and rested the side of my head against his triceps, waiting.

"Agnes," Henri called out as a white puppy bounded over, and she came to a stand on the other side of Duncan.

The little white wolf snapped her jaws at my father like the fearless menace—gnomes not counting—she was.

My biological father's expression turn amused before he met my eyes with dark, nearly black eyes. "I was only aware of one child," he noted.

"She's ours too," I claimed, Henri's fingers jerking in mine.

"So many allies, I see. The sasquatch with the anger problem wasn't particularly friendly, either."

Spencer? An ally? Since when?

"I allowed him his disrespect when he met me at my car on the way in, but only to an extent. I made it clear what would happen if he continued, and he went back home. Their kind isn't known for their loyalty. I'm surprised it went as far as it did," my father explained with a frown. *So that was what had made him take so long getting here during the Dom incident.* "Your gnomes even had the nerve to ignore my calls when I asked for them."

My little buddies did what?

"You're upset with me, and I can understand why you might feel that way," my father started to say, and I opened my mouth to tell him that I wasn't sure I'd ever actually been *upset* with him—I hadn't cared enough or thought enough about him or my biological mom to feel most things—but I managed to keep my mouth closed. "You have several reasons to not be thrilled with my presence because of it."

More than several, but I didn't say it out loud either.

"You may very well be my last child, and I would like to make amends for the dishonor I did you by not being a part of your life," he continued with his soliloquy.

I blinked, and I think I might have even heard Henri and Duncan do the same.

"I would like to get to know you and the rest of our family." My DNA dad sounded like he finally finished.

The rest of *our* family?

His eyes darted to Henri and Duncan.

I narrowed mine at him.

His intentions *sounded* nice. But intentions and actions were two totally different things, and I didn't know him. Didn't trust him.

Maybe he felt bad now for his choices. But . . .

The sound of a throat clearing had me turning to my uncle who was still glaring. His voice was very low as he asked, "You have no interest?"

I shrugged. "Honestly . . . not right now."

His answering nod was resolute, and I was pretty sure I saw pleasure flash across his features briefly. What followed was the sharp sound of something heavy hitting the ground like a couple sacks of potatoes from a two-story building. But it wasn't any kind of potato that met the gravel.

It was my DNA dad sprawled on the ground.

"He'll be asleep for some time. Would one of you help me drag him out of the way so he isn't run over? His people can deal with him later," Franklin just about chirped with more glee than I'd heard out of him yet, his hands going to his hips.

Henri squeezed my fingers at the same time as I blinked.

The man who was responsible for the great and terrible magic in me was out cold.

My uncle cleared his throat again. "He's sleeping. I didn't kill him."

I wasn't sure that was ever a sentence I'd imagined hearing, but . . . this was my life now.

And maybe I should've been irritated, but it was pretty freaking awesome.

Chapter Twenty-Nine

I knew it was dumb.

I also knew that there was no reason why we couldn't wait one more day to do this.

There's no rush, Franklin had insisted earlier when I'd stammered my way through our plan.

There was, but there wasn't.

The hellhound brothers had decided on the same day we'd met that they wanted to extend their visit. They'd explained their desire to spend more time with Duncan, who was, in fact, their little brother. Henri confirmed it too, after they'd taken off their bracelets and let the cool wash of their magic fill everyone's senses. Whether they had the same dad or not wasn't something I needed to know badly enough to ask any time soon. But maybe someday.

Their mother, they explained, was a long-lived being, known as the first hellhound in many places, and a fairy hound in others. But unlike Duncan, their mother had raised them until they'd turned fifteen and had left them behind in Alaska, where they'd spent the majority of their lives since. No one knew why she had abandoned Duncan without an explanation, much less what she'd been up to since leaving her children so many years ago, but at some point, I reminded myself that it didn't matter.

It wasn't like I wanted her to come back.

That was a terrible thought, but I wasn't going to apologize for it. Not anymore. I loved him, I called dibs on him, and that was the whole point as to why I needed to get this conversation over with.

Well, needed the hellhound brothers to get this conversation over with. I was just an innocent bystander. A bystander whose whole world hinged on the outcome of it.

Like the moon had been able to tell that these few days were some of the most important in my life, she had been out in her full glory every night since the siblings had arrived. Brilliant and bold, making the magic in the air so much sweeter and stronger. Her light felt like a hug to me.

Or as Pascal had called it, moonshine. The nonalcoholic kind.

A big, furry body appeared between some trees up ahead, and I sat up straight, catching the amber eyes set in a dark, sharp face. A predator. This forest's largest one.

Henri was so quiet when he wanted to be.

The imposing wolf, part Amarok, part Fenrir, stalked over while I sat there in the clearing, his long face dipping low to nose at my cheeks, at my neck, slipping between my hair and my nape, warm and damp.

And even though I hadn't felt like laughing up until then, I did.

It tickled.

The stunning wolf, my official mate as of tomorrow, curled around my body before slowly lowering himself to the ground, his ribs and side pressed against my back so close I could lean into him. I reached for him and slid my fingers into his coat as much as I could, wiry and soft at the same time. That jaw full of sharp, sharp teeth skimmed the top of my head.

With my other hand, I touched the long leg on one side of me as two puppies appeared in the same direction from where he'd come from. One pounced on the other, taking turns chasing each other on their way over. Agnes, the much bigger but still small white wolf, and Duncan, sleeker and with those ridiculous ears I liked draping over my face every chance I had.

"They're going to talk to him right now," I told Wolf Henri, sliding my fingers back and forth through his coat. He was so solid behind me, I could really let myself sink in.

Like I was sure I would always be able to, even when he was in his other form.

I twisted some of the black strands between my fingertips. "I need to know, Fluff. I want to get it over with," I admitted, turning my cheek into his fur. "I like them, and I can tell he does too."

The side of his snout brushed against mine, the sounds of his breathing soothing.

"I'm still struggling to comprehend that they're brothers, because of their age gap, but who am I to talk? Franklin is at least four thousand years old, from the stuff he's mentioned," I rambled to him about the man I'd left in the kitchen, along with my parents and best friends. They had so many questions for him.

Wolf Henri laid the bottom of his jaw back on the top of my head as the sound of the clubhouse's door opening and closing told me who was coming.

"Look at him, Fluff. He doesn't look like he could be a weapon of mass destruction," I murmured, and as if the universe was listening, it tripped him. Duncan's paw caught on something, and he went butt over head, tumbling once before shooting up to his feet again, like nothing had happened.

I grinned even as that familiar low-grade fear filled my stomach.

But whatever happens, we're going to be together.

Between us, we could face anything.

Like my harbinger of death biological parent, who had gotten knocked out by his brother and left to sleep in the yard for hours until Franklin had taken pity and, with help, had loaded him into his car and taken him to a nearby motel. When he got back, my uncle had given me the basics. My DNA dad was going to back off, but he wanted to talk. Eventually. In the future, but in the near future.

He seemed like a stubborn goat with an ego problem, but of course he would be just that.

And I'd agreed. A part of me hoped he would forget and change his mind—it wouldn't be the first time he did—but another very small and petty part of me was glad he had regrets and was forced to live with them now. And that very tiny, itty-bitty part of me hoped he would try and work at it, that he would come to grovel. I had questions.

We'd see.

I wasn't holding my breath.

Plus, I had to survive this first.

Henri made a deep sound in that barrel chest as two men walked across the patchy mountain grass. I was sure the brothers, who told me all about how they'd been called the Huodou when they'd lived briefly in China, could sense my nerves, but I'd decided I wasn't going to hide them. Duncan meant the world to me; I'd never downplay that.

The brothers and I had already discussed our game plan for this. They had shared with me what they would say to Duncan, and I appreciated that they'd been willing to, so we were all on the same page. I couldn't blame them for hoping there was a chance the donut might go back with them. It wouldn't be fair to not present him with every option he had either. Even if that option made me want to curl into a ball.

Duncan and Agnes bounded over right on time, my boy coming straight for us, body-slamming me in his excitement, his head and limbs rubbing over parts of mine. I hugged him and petted him and groaned when he stepped on sensitive places. Then I watched as he climbed over me to pounce on Henri, running up his body in a way that reminded me of a lion cub trying to play with its father.

Henri laid there, nosing Duncan back, letting him use him like a trampoline.

And then I watched as my puppy took a flying leap off before charging toward the adult hellhounds, biting at their pants before running circles around their legs. One of the brothers gave me a subtle nod before they kneeled. There were smiles and pets, and it was easy to see the three of them not only genuinely like each other, but that there was a bond there.

They were telepathic just like Dunky, they had confirmed. He couldn't communicate with them any more clearly than he did with me, but they understood enough. One day, when he was older, that gift would allow him to include more and more people in his conversations, slowly but surely.

My hand strayed back to Henri's leg, the one closest to me, and I held it as he set his head on top of mine again.

We hadn't mentioned Alaska to Agnes, who hadn't warmed up to the men, but she came and sat to the side of Fluff, and the three of us watched as Duncan plopped on his butt and stared up at his much, much older brothers. Listening. Paying attention.

They were probably telling him how happy they were to meet him. To know he existed. To see him doing so well.

Then I imagined that they probably started explaining about how they lived very far from here, and that their place was in some ways a lot like ours.

At some point, they were going to get to the part where they told him that eventually, someday, he would be able to turn into a human boy, and how that fire that came out of his throat would become so much stronger and could be dangerous if he didn't learn how to manage his emotions well. The same went for his tail. They wouldn't tell him yet that when he got to a certain age, his bite would become deadly, but we had at least a decade or two before then, they'd warned me.

And lastly, the brothers would invite their young sibling to come and live with them. They would promise to care for him and teach him . . .

My eyes started watering, dang it, and I lifted my arm to wipe at my face with my forearm before the side of Wolf Henri's cheek lowered and he let me use him as a napkin.

Everything was going to be fine.

We had gone over this a hundred times by this point. It was just fear that made me irrational.

Even if Duncan decided he wanted to go, we'd all leave together. And maybe one day, when he was old enough, he might go off on his own and live his life wherever and however he wanted, like all children did.

I wiped my eyes on Henri again, curling my fingers into his coat, holding on to him, letting him anchor me and ease the worries and the fear of a future I had no control over.

But that was life in general.

My parents had left their parents, and then I'd left mine, and that was the way things were. But it didn't mean anyone forgot. It didn't mean there weren't visits. That anyone was really, truly left behind. That there wasn't love.

You could never forget love.

Love was the one thing that could survive illness and distance, and even time.

My throat was in a knot as the hellhound brothers eventually stopped talking, and the three of them stared at each other, communicating telepathically, I assumed.

My stomach sank when one brother smiled gently, then so did the other. And I watched one of them nod and dab at his face, joy writing itself all over his craggy features. They were really nice men.

And I couldn't look. *I couldn't.* I tipped my head up to the moon, reclined even more into Henri, and I thought that I loved this place, this ranch, and remembered what I'd told myself when we first got here.

The grass would always be green where you took care of it.

I could love anything I watered. A person, a place, a plant, a life.

I could be happy wherever Duncan and Henri were. Even wherever my little bonsai cactus hybrid, Agnes, was. They were what mattered. Not the mountain range, not the magic, not money, or much less people who didn't matter. The sun would shine almost everywhere, and the moon would continue its reign no matter where we ended up.

And I was so busy thinking that I had moved so many times,

once more wouldn't make a difference, that I wasn't ready for the body that slammed into me.

For the *"no, no, no, love, love, love"* that my donut projected at me, each word one dart after another. *"Family, family, family,"* Duncan chose.

Chapter Thirty

Three Years Later

Adding on to my never-ending list of things in my life I would've never expected to encounter, I had one more to pencil in—arguing with a sasquatch about the benefits of using a filter in a showerhead.

"Do whatever you want, Spencer," I said as we walked through the woods, the moon our only source of light. "I'm just telling you what I read."

Beside me, I caught Henri glancing down, his face that smooth mask he usually wore around most of the ranch members, but that gleam in his eye was all Tease Henri. My Henri. The one who got a kick out of me giving a giant, pain-in-the-ass mythical creature a hard time for being stubborn.

"I will do whatever I want," Spencer grumbled back from his spot on my other side, with several feet separating us. He sniffed, his overly long arms swinging at his sides. "I'll consider it."

He'd consider it. I lifted my eyes as subtly as I could and raised my eyebrows at Fluffy, who looked even more amused than he had a moment before. We could laugh about it later, in bed, like we usually did. It was the only place where we both felt comfortable talking about everything and anything that we couldn't around the ranch without the worry of being overheard.

Not that Henri kept his thoughts and opinions to himself—he was an expert at expressing them as politely and politically as he could manage—but sometimes a man had to unload.

And so did I.

And we did it in our soundproof bedroom, where we could complain about the dumb crap members of the ranch did that we couldn't comprehend.

And it was where we could gossip.

In this case, I had a feeling we were going to have a good laugh over pissy freaking Spencer being concerned his hair was flat—his words, not mine. He'd been trying different hair treatments and nothing was working, he claimed. *Conditioner wasn't cutting it anymore.*

While we weren't *friends*, and he still had a chip on his shoulder that could probably block out the sun for a minute or two, the sasquatch and I had eventually come to an understanding—sort of—after the night that he'd said whatever it was that had pissed off my DNA dad enough to threaten him. I'd bought him two more conditioner bars, and Henri and I had gone to deliver them a week later. And that had sparked our . . . frenemies-ship. More friends than enemies, but with his prickly personality, I had a feeling that was as good as anyone was ever going to get with him.

With one exception.

And it was enough that when Spencer sensed something out in the woods that shouldn't be there, he now called Henri to let him know, which was exactly what had happened tonight. I'd tagged along, and the two of us had run into the sasquatch, who wanted to scope out what he'd sensed. It had turned out to be a new donsey of gnomes visiting from northwest Canada.

Word had gotten around that our gnomes had, over the last three years, had *six* baby gnomes—an astronomical amount in such a short period of time, they'd admitted. And they had come to visit to see what their secret was since our donsey—group of gnomes—wouldn't admit anything incriminating through their communication system. Henri had made it real clear to them, years ago, that they needed to stop telling other people about me.

My friends the gnomes had kept their word and kept my secret as much as they could.

But every so often, a whisper got around, and a magical being showed up looking for . . . *me*.

I'd become some people's best friends, and there were others who made sure to stay fifty feet away from me at all times, and I was all right with that.

A warm, familiar hand brushed mine, and I widened my fingers to slip them through Henri's as he bumped me with his elbow. Going out to check on intruders had turned into one of our favorite things to do together—when he wasn't on rotation to be on call, that was. Just last month a basilisk, this reptile-looking creature, had found its way onto the ranch. But the dummy made a very poor choice—he said he didn't like the way I smelled and then threatened me—and Henri had tossed him into a river with more force than usual.

It had been epic.

And the second we'd gotten home and had a minute to ourselves, I'd showed Henri just how much I'd loved his gesture by pushing him against the wall in our room and taking full advantage of our soundproofed walls.

Just thinking about that night had me sighing.

But the hairy giant following along with us at that moment grunted, then suddenly did a sharp left and walked away without a word, like usual.

Like I said, we weren't friends, but we tolerated each other.

And the man I more than tolerated squeezed my hand in his, winking at me when I tipped my head up toward him.

I beamed.

We'd talk about it at home.

"What do you think the elders are going to say about these gnomes?" I asked the adult love of my life.

Henri made a slight face. "Ema will probably pitch a fit that they need to meet them, and then she and Franklin will get into it. It's our gnomes these new ones will need to worry about. These mines around here have been theirs for a couple of centuries." His fingertips toyed with the bare skin at my wrist. "You're probably going to need to talk to them about it."

It wasn't an official title or anything, but I was known as the Gnome Liaison, at least to Henri and my uncle.

I thought it was because they were grateful for their children that they came whenever I called for them. And maybe a little because they appreciated the treats I offered them whenever we met. We didn't see them often, but traces of their existence could be found every once in a while. Just a month ago, the most beautiful amethyst geode had been left on our front porch. A few months before that, a silver bracelet that happened to fit me perfectly had sat on our mat.

They were very generous with me.

And if it came down to a gnome fight, my money was on our gnomes, and so was my loyalty.

"I'll see if I can get their attention tomorrow, as long as they don't get into gang fights tonight," I told him, angling my face up again. Looking at him was one of my favorite things in the whole world. "I was hoping for some one-on-one time with my favorite mate."

A rough thumb stroked the inside of my palm, those amber eyes I knew so well now flaring. "Your only one. The rest are meeting the bottom of the river."

I grinned, and my favorite mate dipped his head down to rub his cheek against my neck and the side of my face, marking me with his scent, like he loved doing. And I loved getting. When his lips skimmed my throat, I shivered.

And not for the first time, I thanked Matti for what he'd done, bringing us here. For giving me the opportunity to know Henri. I loved him, down to my bones and to the magic that lived mostly quietly in my body; I was sure it had to be embedded into my DNA by this point.

My Great Wolf was loving and possessive, protective and obsessive. He believed in me. Trusted in me.

He was the best mate that anyone could have given me . . . if there was someone in charge of that kind of thing—Fate or Love.

I was nuts about him in every way.

It was a fact that I couldn't keep my hands off him. Just that morning, before he'd gone to work, he'd rolled me over onto my hands and knees and done some riding himself that had me gasping into my pillow and clutching our sheets for dear life. Before him, I thought I'd had a pretty normal sex drive, but since we'd become mated, it had hit another level. For both of us, we'd agreed. Maybe it was my fault, or maybe it was just our chemistry. I wasn't sure, and I wasn't going to ask questions either. No one would ever be able to convince me it wasn't a great problem to have.

We weren't the only ones suffering either, it seemed.

Everyone around the ranch had been getting it on, and there had been results from it.

Maggie had been the second victim of my magic, having a little boy that had stunned the crap out of every single one of us. Shiloh had a beautiful baby brother that we both swore was going to be an ogre when the time came. Pascal's parents had a little girl a few months ago who screamed so loud, I was considering getting another job at the ranch when she was old enough to be one of the kids I took care of after school.

In total, there had been twelve births at the ranch in the last few years—another record, Henri had explained.

And now, I peeked at my mate again, taking in the strong line of his jaw, the hard curves of those powerful, thick muscles, and I thought about how much I loved running my hands up and down them. Maybe before we went to bed . . .

Henri suddenly stopped walking, his head swiveling toward me. "What are you thinking about?" he asked, eyebrow already rising.

"You know what."

Those arms, that I loved being in, wrapped around me, drawing me in to a chest I'd set my head on countless times by that point. His voice was rough, and I'd swear he was flexing against me as he murmured, "Cricket . . ."

His ringtone decided right then to explode from his pocket. As always, at the wrong moment. But it was his personal phone, not the ranch cell, and I was the one who slipped my hand into his pocket—squeezing his leg in the process—and pulled it out to hand it to him. He frowned at the screen before showing it to me.

Franklin's name was on it—or as I fondly called him, Uncle Frankie, which he loved and tried to act like he hated, but now even Agnes called him that. Henri referred to him that way, but only in our room when we were cracking up.

Swiping at the screen twice, he held the phone between us, saying, "What's wrong?"

My uncle's voice was clear through the speaker. "Are you . . . almost back?"

I blinked, and then so did Henri. It wasn't every day a being, who had lived so many lifetimes he wasn't sure how old he really was, sounded rattled. "Yes, is there an emergency?"

Even I heard the man who had taken his time getting to know me, who I had taken my time to get to know in return, gulp. "I wouldn't refer to it as an emergency, but the two of you should get back here as soon as you can."

"If there's an issue, tell me now," my bossy Great Wolf responded, taking my hand again as we started walking, faster now, heading straight for our house. "Is it the kids?"

"It's . . ." My uncle cleared his throat. "The children are fine. You'll see when you get here." The line clicked, and I almost laughed at getting hung up on.

"What was that?" I asked, trying to think and only coming up with one solution. "Do you think his brother randomly showed up again?"

His brother. My DNA dad. The man who I didn't have anywhere near the relationship with that I had with Uncle Frankie, but . . . he'd spent the last couple of years trying his best to win us over in his own way, to give him credit.

A death god could be just as annoying and stubborn as you would think since he was used to getting his way.

Henri shook his head. "No, I don't sense him out here." He suddenly frowned, and his nostrils flared on and off, his expression never leaving. "There is something different in the air."

"Does it smell like fire? Because I knew Matti shouldn't have told them that story about us trying to start a campfire and burning our eyebrows off."

The concern cleared for a moment as he chuckled down at me. "It doesn't smell like fire," he assured me, slowing down a moment before he lowered his head. He kissed me soft and sweet, his tongue licking at the seam of my lips, before slanting his mouth and kissing me a little deeper.

I groaned.

He groaned.

He never messed around when he kissed me, that was for sure.

Those comforting arms slid around me one more time and pulled me up against his chest. His cheek rubbed the side of my neck, the breath from his nostrils the best kind of tickle. "We're going to finish that conversation in a little bit."

I smiled and kissed his shoulder, then his throat. He smelled even better now than he had years ago. "You're dang right we will."

The look he gave me said he wasn't going to forget. I wouldn't let him anyway.

We were almost to the house when Henri sniffed again. "I smell Pascal, but it's not recent."

"He was over earlier. He brought me some sunflowers and told me I looked pretty." I smiled. "I think you're going to need to go growl at him."

Henri snickered. "That little fucker."

I batted my eyelashes.

"He hasn't forgotten he owes you his life . . . how many times now? Ten?"

It had to be more than that, but who was keeping track? Maybe everyone other than him. Pascal was a handful—the biggest handful of them all. But he was just as likable as he'd always been, and it made up for all the gray hairs he was responsible for on so many people—mostly his parents and me. Henri would be in fourth place.

He was lucky he was cute.

But not as lucky as I was, I thought again, just looking at Henri.

We had tied our lives together on the first full moon right after my three-month period, under a bright starry sky, right beside the sacred, magical waterfall washed with pink and purple. I'd held Duncan in my arms for the majority of the ceremony that had taken place in front of the elders, my parents, the hellhounds, Matti, Sienna, Agnes, Randall, Ani, and her mate. My parents, the hellhounds, and Sienna had been required to swear an oath never to speak of the waterfall again; something they had all been more than willing to do, fortunately.

That night had been the most beautiful night of my life and the official beginning to something I hadn't even known I'd needed—a bigger family. But that was exactly what had happened. Afterward, Henri, Duncan, and I had approached Agnes and asked if she wanted to live with us. Her initial answer had been a no, but a week later, she'd changed her mind.

Little did she know, we had already set up a room for her.

And that had just been the start of our new family.

Our oldest member was Franklin, followed by our surprise additions as of a year and a half ago—the hellhound brothers, who had come to visit three times before leaving their lives in Alaska behind to move here, closer to their "baby brother." It had taken several discussions among the elders and a lot of pointing out gray areas in the community's guidelines before the brothers had gotten the green light to move, but it had worked out.

All of them spent a ton of time at our house, one of the closest to the clubhouse, which made sense to me considering how much everyone relied on Henri even with him working less hours as a deputy and around the ranch. I helped out as much as I could, tagging along every time I wasn't working or with the kids.

There wasn't a single thing I would have traded the last three years for.

To top it all off, I was going to be an aunt soon! Sienna was pregnant, and Matti was losing his mind. We still saw each other as often as we had before, it just took more work for them to come, or for me to leave for a couple of days to visit them in Chicago.

My precious donut had graduated into being a full-on bear claw, he was so dang big. And that reminded me . . . "Still smell the different thing?" On the ranch, that could mean anything.

Henri didn't look concerned, just baffled. "Yeah, let's see what it is."

I tucked my hand into the back of his pants and let him finish leading us into our house.

Henri came to a sudden stop just as I'd closed the door behind us. "What is that smell?" he asked.

Standing in the living room was Franklin. In his arms was a sleeping seven-month-old, drooling away. Our Nicolas, named after my dad. In a playpen in the corner was a sprawled-out two-year-old clutching a stuffed wolf. Shima, or as most of us called her, Shim-Shim. She was named after the woman who had raised Henri—his older brother's wife, who was also Matti's grandma. They were our two youngest. A perfect blend of both of us with their dark hair and tan skin. They were happy, sweet babies, and we were all crazy about them. Not just Henri and me, but everyone on the ranch.

There was something beautiful about seeing the future, holding it in my arms. I already wondered about what all the kids would do in the future. If Duncan would ever try to look for his biological mom. If Agnes would go to school far away. What Shima and Nicolas would grow up to be.

Mostly though, I wondered if they'd choose to be the protectors of the ranch when they were older, or if they'd want a more managerial role like Henri. Or maybe they would go off and become big city boys and girls like their uncle Matti had done.

The only thing I did know somehow was that whatever happened, the burden of this place wouldn't just weigh down one set of shoulders, like it had for Henri, but hopefully be spread out over several. Because I had a feeling, at the rate we were going, we'd probably end up with another four, on top of the four we already had. Just that morning, I thought I'd seen that ultra possessive glint that brewed in Henri's irises right before we'd gotten pregnant the last two times.

Who knew though? Just wondering over it filled me with an unbelievable sense of joy. The future had never seemed like such a beautiful place.

I loved it here. I loved it with my whole heart. The way it smelled, the way the trees cast different shadows on the community throughout the year. The way the people worked together to keep this place going, just a little nook of safety in the world.

I had told Henri once that something in the air here told me that I was home. That the land tried to whisper in my ear that I belonged, its message mixed in the breezes that swept through. And I thought that the children held me down here with their little hands, tying me even more to this place than I already was.

And Henri had looked me dead in the eye and told me that I was supposed to be here, and everything and everyone around me knew it.

Including the best babysitter on the ranch, Franklin.

My uncle gestured in the direction of the bedrooms down the hall, his face tight. "See for yourself," he warned Henri, his eyes a little wild for him.

That was . . . cryptic.

And as much as I wanted to smell the babies and their brand-newness, I could tell he meant business.

So we did go see, shooting each other confused glances as we leaned over the playpen to smile down at a snoring Shima. We stopped at Agnes's room first. He cracked the door, and I shoved my head underneath his arm to peek in too. My mini wolf had sprouted up too over the years, and her blonde hair was spilled over her pillow as she slept surrounded by anime posters and merchandise.

He closed the door, and I followed him down the hall to the other room, but just as we got to it, it opened on its own, very, very slowly. Which wasn't unheard of. We had tied a rope to the handle so Duncan could get out easily if it closed. He had outgrown the hellhound door he'd had when we'd first moved in. But instead of a sixty-pound, five-year-old pup who came out . . . a little boy stood in the doorway. In underwear and a T-shirt that was a little too big for him because I'd made sure to leave clothes in a dresser on the off chance he might ever need them. I'd guessed on a size when I bought it a year ago.

The boy had black hair so dark it was almost blue, eyes a shade of striking brown. His skin was pale. His body long and lanky.

I had never seen him before, and at the same time, I knew his face as well as I knew Henri's. As well as I knew my own. It was small, and a little elfish . . .

I grabbed Henri's hand in absolute fucking shock.

"Mom?" a croaky voice whispered, like he was trying out words for the first time . . . because he was.

HOLY MAGICAL SHIT.

I might have said it out loud, I might've not.

I barely managed to throw my arms out wide just in time to catch Duncan launching himself at me. The tallest five-year-old I'd ever seen. Those scrawny arms wrapped around my neck, and he hugged me with a strength that was too much for his age.

"Donut," I gasped, hugging him so close, so tight. "What happened?"

He tucked his cheek against my shoulder, smelling every bit like the boy I'd spent the last five years of my life with. My ride or die, still. My sweet, even-tempered boy who had grown to communicate with me telepathically in sentences over the last couple of years. Every once in a while, Henri and Agnes had both mentioned they'd understood a "yes" or a "no" from time to time, but that had been the extent of his abilities with everyone else, other than his brothers.

I couldn't believe it was him.

"I was sleeping," he told me in that crackling, brand-new voice, "and I felt funny. I woke up, and I looked like you," Duncan said, taking his time with every word. "I was coming to get you."

I hugged him and hugged him, and I hugged him even more. He was talking! He was walking!

It wasn't that I had ever given up hope that he'd turn into a two-legged boy—I didn't care if he ever did. I had always just known how much easier his life would be if he did, without that crippling fear of being found out, of being able to live without the possibility of a stranger taking him looming constantly over our heads. This place had been a safe haven, and I'd never worried that anything would happen to him while he was here since everyone was so protective of the kids, but now . . .

I grabbed his cheeks. "Are you okay?"

"Yeah," he answered softly, his eyes sparkling. "I wasn't scared."

Beside us, Henri dropped to a knee, his eyes a little glassy, his smile a little funny. He mouthed *wow*, and I mouthed it right back, reaching out with my arm to clutch him.

And Duncan leaned away from me a little and looked at Henri too.

His smile . . . I would remember his smile forever. Would remember his words, this moment, everything from the way it smelled to the paint on the walls, the same way I would the night of our mating ceremony.

My Duncan Donut looked at Henri and whispered, "Hi, Dad."

I fell back on my butt a moment before Henri scooted in even closer, one of those brawny arms capturing both of us in them. I'd heard his voice so many times by now, I could tell when something minor was bothering him, when he was trying not to laugh . . . but I wasn't expecting the watery chuckle that came before a "Hi, son," that had me sensing Duncan's absolute joy in my own chest.

An explosion of *"love"* I knew better than almost anything.

Henri's hand came up to cup Duncan's head as he leaned toward him, and my boy and my mate touched their foreheads together. His voice was so throaty and thick. "How do you look just like your mom, huh?"

Their bond had grown slowly and organically over time, and

it had become one of the greatest blessings in my life, one of those things I could have only hoped for. And if I'd had dreams, their relationship being what it was now, would have been one of them.

He was a real boy, and I couldn't believe it.

A gasp had us all turning our heads to find Agnes in the hall. Her mouth was open in a way that made me think she'd learned it from me. "Duncan?" she squeaked.

Henri didn't even get a chance to invite his Ladybug over.

Agnes Blackrock, the girl who a year ago would have still hesitated at a pile of hugs, threw herself at us. She was the greatest big sister to her siblings, and by example, Duncan had become the best big brother. It had been natural to them to love Shima and Nicolas, not just a little bit, but so fiercely, it took my breath away every time I saw them together.

They reminded me that love didn't know the word DNA.

And the little girl who had been left by the people who should have been there for her at the start of her life, who didn't trust easily, didn't love easily, didn't believe easily, hugged us just as tight as Henri did.

Epilogue

Once upon a December, in the middle of the most magical forest in North America, three women stood shoulder to shoulder under a brilliant full moon.

Each watched a small home surrounded by towering pines.

Through the smallest of the home's windows, a blonde girl stood in her room, holding a cell phone to her face as she told her friend on the other line, "I need to go. My mom needs me."

Three much bigger windows gave a clear view of a living area. In it was a tall, muscular man with his arm over the shoulders of a dark-haired woman plastered to his side. Her belly round in the way that only someone in her last trimester could be.

Across from them, on the floor, sat three other figures. A slim dark-haired boy and two much older white-haired men, holding Lego pieces up to the fan above their heads. On the couch beside them was a man with salt-and-pepper hair, one leg crossed over the other. A toddler sat on his right, drinking from a sippy cup, watching the group on the floor, and a slightly older child stood on the man's other side, sticking a small finger in his ear.

The shortest of the three women made a soft sound in her throat as she watched the big man stroke his wife's back with a loving hand. "They look happy," she claimed in a wistful tone.

"They smell happy," the tallest added in a monotone voice, though her brown eyes remained glued to the three males on the floor laughing.

The third one huffed. "I don't know why you're doing this to yourselves. They'll never know what you did."

Neither of the two women tore their gazes away from the windows and the people inside, but the shortest woman made a delicate gesture with her body. "They don't need to," she replied, her head held high, her bronze skin burnished under the moonlight. "It's a burden we take on as mothers. To do what's necessary, even at our expense."

Another huff left the third woman's chest as she shook her head, but she wasn't fooling the others.

A mother was always a mother, no matter how old their child got.

And on that Christmas night, the Night, the Moon, and the Hound stood in the trees and watched an ancient uncle, two older brothers, a father and a husband, a mother and a wife, two sons, and two daughters rejoice in the love of the family they had built, never knowing of the audience that stood in the tree line.

Never knowing that it wasn't the universe or Fate that brought them all together, but a series of regrets and a strong sense of atonement that led to this moment in time.

And more than anything else, an incredible amount of love.